THE GOOD OLD
STUFF

ALSO BY GARDNER DOZOIS

ANTHOLOGIES

A Day in the Life
Another World
Best Science Fiction Stories of
    the Year #6–10
The Best of Isaac Asimov's
    Science Fiction Magazine
Time-Travellers from Isaac
    Asimov's Science Fiction
    Magazine
Transcendental Tales from Isaac
    Asimov's Science Fiction
    Magazine
Isaac Asimov's Aliens
Isaac Asimov's Mars
Isaac Asimov's SF Lite
Isaac Asimov's War
Isaac Asimov's Planet Earth
    (with Sheila Williams)
Isaac Asimov's Robots
    (with Sheila Williams)
Isaac Asimov's Cyberdreams
    (with Sheila Williams)
Isaac Asimov's Skin Deep
    (with Sheila Williams)
Isaac Asimov's Ghosts
    (with Sheila Williams)
Isaac Asimov's Vampires
    (with Sheila Williams)
Isaac Asimov's Moons
    (with Sheila Williams)
Isaac Asimov's Christmas
    (with Sheila Williams)
Isaac Asimov's Detectives
    (with Sheila Williams)
The Year's Best Science Fiction,
    #1–15
Future Earths: Under African
    Skies (with Mike Resnick)

Future Earths: Under South
    American Skies (with Mike
    Resnick)
Future Power (with Jack Dann)
Aliens! (with Jack Dann)
Unicorns! (with Jack Dann)
Magicats! (with Jack Dann)
Magicats 2 (with Jack Dann)
Bestiary! (with Jack Dann)
Mermaids! (with Jack Dann)
Sorcerers! (with Jack Dann)
Demons! (with Jack Dann)
Dogtales! (with Jack Dann)
Ripper! (with Susan Casper)
Seaserpents! (with Jack Dann)
Dinosaurs! (with Jack Dann)
Little People! (with Jack Dann)
Dragons! (with Jack Dann)
Horses! (with Jack Dann)
Unicorns 2 (with Jack Dann)
Invaders! (with Jack Dann)
Angels! (with Jack Dann)
Dinosaurs II (with Jack Dann)
Hackers (with Jack Dann)
Timegates (with Jack Dann)
Clones (with Jack Dann)
Modern Classics of Science
    Fiction
Modern Classic Short Novels of
    Science Fiction
Modern Classics of Fantasy
Killing Me Softly
Dying For It
Immortals (with Jack Dann)
Roads Not Taken (with Stanley
    Schmidt)
The Good New Stuff
    (forthcoming)

FICTION

Strangers
The Visible Man (collection)
Nightmare Blue (with George
    Alec Effinger)
The Peacemaker
Geodesic Dreams (collection)

Slow Dancing Through Time
    (with Jack Dann, Michael
    Swanwick, Susan Casper, and
    Jack C. Haldeman II)

NONFICTION

The Fiction of James Tiptree, Jr.

THE GOOD OLD STUFF

STUFF

ADVENTURE SF
IN THE GRAND TRADITION

EDITED BY

GARDNER DOZOIS

ST. MARTIN'S GRIFFIN

NEW YORK

Library of Congress Cataloging-in-Publication Data

The good old stuff/edited by Gardner Dozois.—1st St. Martin's Griffin ed.
    p. cm.
   ISBN 0-312-19275-4
   1. Science fiction, American. I. Dozois, Gardner R.
PS648. S3G66 1998
813' .0876208—dc21   98-23489
                                        CIP

First St. Martin's Griffin Edition: December 1998

10 9 8 7 6 5 4 3 2 1

For Janet Kagan and Bob Walters—
who like the good old stuff.

Contents

I would like to thank the following people for their help and support on this project:

Susan Casper, Janet Kagan, Barry N. Malzberg, Darrell Schweitzer, Virginia Kidd, Vaughne Lee Hansen, Kirby McCauley, Kay McCauley, Ralph M. Vicinanza, Chris Lotts, Richard Curtis, Ginjer Buchanan, Jennifer Uram, Mark McCloud, Eleanor Wood, Ashley D. Grayson, Dan Hooker, Gordon R. Dickson, David W. Wixon, Poul Anderson, Brian W. Aldiss, L. Sprague de Camp, Catharine Crook de Camp and, of course, special thanks to my own editor on this project, Gordon Van Gelder.

Preface

We say, in short, that we grew from the pulps to *Astounding,* and from *Astounding* into our present enlightenment. These are lies. We read the pulps and *ASF* simultaneously and with equal voracity, they were two sides of the one coin, and our special relationship with the pulps was more intriguing, racier, and in some ways more genuine, while our relationship with *Astounding* was respectable. And our present enlightenment, which will no doubt dim in the hindsight of years to come, derives not linearly from *ASF* but from a complex action of the love/hate relationship between the pulps and "modern science fiction" within ourselves.

—Algis Budrys, *The Magazine of Fantasy & Science Fiction,* January 1977

Science fiction can be a window on worlds we'd never otherwise see and people and creatures we'd never otherwise know, it can provide us with insights into the inner workings of our society that are difficult to gain in any other way, grant us perspectives into social mores and human nature itself mostly otherwise unreachable; it can be an invaluable tool with which to take preconceived notions and received wisdom to pieces and reassemble them into something new, it can prepare us for the inevitable and sometimes dismaying changes ahead of us, helping to buffer us against the winds of Future Shock; it can be terrifying and cautionary, it can be chastening and angry, it can be sad and elegiac, it can be wise and profound—but sometimes it's just *fun.*

Sometimes it's "just" pure entertainment. Sometimes it's an *adventure*—the sort of adventure unavailable anywhere else, where new worlds open up before us to be discovered and explored, and monstrous new threats undreamed of on our familiar Earth loom up and confront us at every step.

Fun is a concept not much talked about in our harried, hurried, anxious, serious-minded—if not downright grim—society these days, where everyone is constantly and apprehensively looking over their shoulder for a stock market crash, a nuclear attack, an asteroid impact, Ebola, El Niño, global warming, the destruction of the ozone layer, acid rain, cancer-causing agents in the food, Mad Cow Disease, microwave radiation, desertification, kidnappers from Flying Saucers, insane dictators, sinister government conspiracies, corporate downsizing, and all the other Dooms that daily hang suspended over our heads on the thinnest of threads. Fun, in fact, is often looked at as a shameful indulgence that should not be bothered with when there are More Important things to confront.

But nobody, no matter how intense and dedicated and committed, can be serious *all* the time. Sometimes, you've got to relax and enjoy yourself.

The same is true of science fiction as a genre, no matter how serious-minded and substantial and profound it gets—sometimes the writers turn one out just for fun, a fast-paced, no-holds-barred, flat-out *adventure* story, pure entertainment, with any more serious implications or troubling social issues—and they *do* get raised, even in the most seemingly insubstantial of tales—largely left to be dealt with in the subtext . . . the *fore*ground of such stories being occupied with action, wonder, color, and—another almost outmoded concept—adventure.

These are the kind of stories people are talking about when they say "they don't write 'em like that anymore." Well, yes, they *do*, actually, as I hope to demonstrate in the follow-up anthology to the one you're now holding in your hand, *The Good New Stuff*, due out early next year. For *this* book, though, it seemed worthwhile, in a day when adventure SF—even if it *is* still around—is the least talked-about and critically evaluated of the different types of science fiction, and perhaps the least esteemed, to give you a book of some of the classic SF adventure stories. These stories still hold up *as* adventures, as fresh and exciting and entertaining as anything being written today, but also they're seminal stories that helped to shape the field, and they hold within them the seeds of much later work and of much work yet to come.

As with my other retrospective anthologies, *Modern Classics of Science Fiction, Modern Classic Short Novels of Science Fiction,* and *Modern Classics of Fantasy,* a big part of my motivation for putting this anthology together was to battle the loss of historical memory in the genre, which seems to be accelerating all the time, so that now even stuff published as recently as the early '80s seems to already be out-of-print and forgotten. The shelf life for books is so short now, and things come back into print so rarely once they go *out* of it (and back-issue copies of magazines and second-hand copies of old books are so difficult to find, even in SF speciality bookstores and dealer's rooms at SF conventions), that many younger readers have probably never had a chance to read the stories here, even those stories that were famous in their day, even the Hugo-winners; many younger readers may not have even heard of the *authors* whose work is assembled here, something that I've discovered, to my dismay, in talking to bright and literate young readers who consider themselves hardcore SF fans and yet have never heard of Cordwainer Smith or Alfred Bester or Fritz Leiber or Leigh Brackett or James Schmitz or Murray Leinster or A. E. van Vogt (and even most young readers who *have* heard of them, have never *read* anything by them). This book, and similar books, and the re-issues of classic work that *do* occasionally still appear from publishers such as NESFA Press and Tor and Tachyon Press and White Wolf, are bandages on a gaping wound—but, alas, at the moment, they seem to be the best remedy that can be applied.

I've found, to my surprise, that many people don't seem to *care* whether the old stuff is available or not, or whether they've read it or not. The attitude seems to be that nothing that wasn't in print five years ago is worth bothering with anyway. Who cares whether a bunch of moldy old pulp stories are available to be read?

Unfortunately, to feel that way is to assign huge chunks of the genre's history to the dumpster—and to be ignorant of the past means that you can't even understand (or appreciate) the *present*, let alone have the slightest idea where you're going in the future, or why.

Besides, I don't happen to think that these old stories are moldy—in fact, I think that most readers will get as much or more entertainment value out of this book as they would out of any modern volume. Old wine may not necessarily always be the best—but it's not always vinegar, either.

As usual with these retrospective anthologies, though, once I actually sat down to put it together, I found that there were many more stories that I would have *liked* to use than I had *room* to use. Winnowing-screens were clearly called for.

Ever since the specific *science fiction* adventure story began to precipitate out from the larger and older tradition of the generalized pulp adventure story, the form that slowly emerged as being most specific to science fiction, (differentiating it from the kind of Lost World/Lost Race adventure that went all the way back into the middle of the 19th Century—it was usually different in tone as well from the more solemn, slower-paced, Visit To A Future Society story popular with Hugo Gernsback and other editors, which, especially after Wells, tended toward Utopian polemic and ran to guided tours of the Great Steam Grommet Works) was the *Space* Adventure story.

Although the SF adventure story has always had—and still has—other branches as well, the Space Adventure story or the Space Opera remains to this day probably the most characteristic sort of SF adventure tale. Thus that's the kind of story I've primarily stuck with for this anthology (although I've also included a story that takes place on an Alternate Earth, as well as a story that takes place in a devastated Future Earth after a nuclear holocaust, and I'd like to pretend piously that I did it to be inclusive and to cover all the bases, but really, truth be known, it was just because they were such good stories, and had affected me so powerfully as a kid, that I couldn't resist them). I also decided that, however adventure-driven it was, the story *also* had to qualify as genuine science fiction, by the aesthetic standards and the standards of scientific knowledge of its time; I didn't want the stereo-typical "Bat Durston" stories, where a cowboy story is retold as a science fiction story by the simple expedient of swapping the term "horse" for "spaceship" and "six-gun" for "blaster," and so forth; this requirement also omitted much of the stuff from the *Weird Tales* of the '30s and the *Planet Stories* of the '40s, which were just horror stories or sword & sorcery tales recast as science fiction in a similarly naive one-for-one way. So Planetary Romances, Other World Adventures, Space Adventure, and Space Opera were acceptable only if they were *more* than translated versions of standard boilerplate adventure stories common to other pulp genres, if they had some quality of vision or invention or intent that solidly centered them as adventures germane to *science fiction*, stories that wouldn't be possible—with the same kind of impact, anyway—if translated to other forms.

(Of course these judgment calls are subjective. I believe that I can discern subtle differences in flavor between the Space Adventure, the Space Opera, the Planetary Romance, and the tale of off-Earth Other World adventure—later on, in the next volume, I'll claim to be able to discern differences in flavor between cyberpunk, hard science fiction, radical hard science fiction, and the New Baroque Space Opera as well—just as I can discern differences between Vanilla, French Vanilla, Vanilla Fudge, and Chocolate Chip ice-cream, but the differences in flavor are subtle, hard to articulate, and, in the end, what tastes like Vanilla to me might taste like Chocolate Chip to you.)

Even after making these decisions, though, the potential stories I wanted to use outweighed the room available for them by a factor of three or four. If I'd been editing the multi-dimensional, infinitely expandable ideal edition of this anthology, I'd have gladly put all of them in, and so been able to cover the entire development of the space adventure tale with something like the kind of completeness it deserves, starting all the way back in the Superscience days of the '20s and '30s. Unfortunately, out here in the real world, this volume could only contain a certain finite amount of material, so something else had to go. More winnowing-screens were called for, and I had further decisions to make—some fairly Draconian decisions, at that—as to what historical periods I was going to cover in this book, and which periods I was *not* going to cover.

In order to make these decisions more understandable, we should really pause here for a comprehensive history of the development of the genre space adventure tale, from its beginnings in the Gernsback *Amazing Stories* of the late '20s all the way through to the '90s, but we don't have room for that. Suffice it to say—in a brutally compressed and distorted version of the truth, with no allowance made for dozens of exceptions and contradictions—that by the time the earliest of the stories collected here saw print, after

World War II, science fiction had passed through what is sometimes referred to retroactively as the "Superscience" era of the '20s and '30s, the first great Age of the Space Opera, when writers such as E. E. "Doc" Smith, Ray Cummings, Raymond Z. Gallun, Edmond Hamilton, John W. Campbell, Jack Williamson, Clifford D. Simak, and others greatly widened the stage upon which the science fiction adventure story could be played; before E. E. Smith, for instance, SF writers rarely ventured outside of the solar system for settings for their stories, but by the end of the "Superscience" era, the rest of the Galaxy—and, indeed, the rest of the universe—was their playground. They also increased both the permissible scope for an adventure and the size of the stakes at risk; it was not for nothing that Edmond Hamilton, for instance, was referred to as "World-Wrecker" or "Planet-Buster" Hamilton, and the space fleets of immense mile-long space-dreadnoughts armed with awesome world-shattering super-scientific weapons that have continued to prowl through deep space throughout all of the subsequent history of science fiction (and on out of the print media and onto television and movie screens, and onto computer monitors in the form of space-adventure computer games) were first launched on their paper voyages in the pages of the pulp magazines of the '20s and '30s.

By 1948, though—which is when the earliest story here, A. E. van Vogt's "The Rull," appeared—we'd *also* gone through the Campbellian revolution in science fiction, when the new editor of *Astounding* magazine, John W. Campbell, had, by sheer force of will (aided by the example of radical new writers such as Robert A. Heinlein and Isaac Asimov), changed the consensus definition of what a "good" science fiction story should be like, downplaying and devaluing the more garish and melodramatic lowest-common-denominator pulp stuff in favor of better-written, more thoughtful material that actually made a stab at rigor and scientific possibility, the aim being to produce the "kind of story that could be printed in a magazine of the year two thousand A.D." as a contemporary story of the day, a story with "no gee-whiz," where the author would "just take the technology for granted." (There would be exceptions, of course, and much adventure stuff, including some rather garish Space Opera, continued to appear in *Astounding*—and later, *Analog*, after the magazine changed its name . . . a move that in itself was symbolic of Campbell's desire to move away from pulpishness and toward respectability and unsmiling polemic purpose—throughout Campbell's lifetime; but that was the often-stated goal. And, in spite of Campbell's occasional seduction by fast-paced widescreen adventure stories too juicy to resist—such as Frank Herbert's *Dune*, which, in spite of some canny ideas about the nature of society that were just the sort of thing that Campbell liked, was fundamentally a baroque Space Opera on a scale not seen since the Superscience era—that was the direction in which he consciously tried to steer the magazine.)

One result of the Campbellian revolution—an ironic one, since Campbell himself was one of the most widescreen planet-busters of the "Superscience" era—was to make the Space Adventure tale or the Space Opera somewhat *declassé:* outmoded, outdated, passed-by, no longer the arena where the Cutting Edge work of the day was being done. The very term "Space Opera"—coined in 1941 by Wilson Tucker (on the model of the older, and also negative, terms "Soap Opera" and "Horse Opera") to describe the "hacky, grinding, stinking, outworn, spaceship yarn"—has a derisive edge to it, a disapproving edge that has stuck with the term ever since. Even today, Space Opera has a raffish, slightly disreputable, Not Quite Nice, disapproved-of outlaw tang to it—so that people who *like* Space Opera are often just the faintest bit hang-dog or shamefaced about admitting it, as if they've been caught in a Guilty Pleasure, something we like even though we know it's Bad for us, and probably not Politically Correct, like admitting to binging on potato chips or Chocolate Chip Cookie Dough ice cream, or being caught out ordering a junk-food hamburger for dinner instead of a healthy Chef's salad, or watching *Gunsmoke* reruns instead of *Masterpiece Theater.* (Ironically, it may be this very whiff of Beyond-The-Pale that has attracted new writers, seeking for a chance to run up the pirate flag and be Outlaws, to the form in the '80s and the '90s.)

The effect of the Campbellian revolution was exacerbated in the beginning of the decade of the '50s by the founding of two *new* major SF magazines, *Galaxy* and *The Magazine of Fantasy & Science Fiction*, whose editors would push the accepted model for the science fiction story even further in the direction of psychological and sociological maturity and literary sophistication of style and conceptualization, sometimes further than Campbell himself was willing to go—and would also therefore push it even further away from the familiar pulp adventure tale, which as a result became even more *declassé.*

Another ironic effect of all this, the Campbellian revolution followed by the launching of *Galaxy* and *F&SF*, was that literary standards went up throughout the field, even at magazines such as *Planet Stories* and *Thrilling Wonder Stories* and *Startling Stories*, whose readers now *also* wanted to get a product that was better written line-by-line . . . so that even in the pulp adventure market, a clumsy and poorly written story that would have been accepted without question in 1935 might have more difficulty getting into print in 1955—and the level of craft needed to get an adventure story into one of the mainline magazines such as *Astounding* or *Galaxy* or *F&SF* rose sharply. The literary ante had been upped, permanently, for the entire genre, low-end as well as high-end. (And some of the stuff those "low-end" markets would publish as the SF adventure story struggled to evolve, work by Jack Vance, Ray Bradbury, Charles Harness, Theodore Sturgeon, and others, although not widely accepted at the time, would in retrospect look just as good if not better than much of the more "respectable" fare offered by the mainline magazines.)

This helped me set one parameter for the book. I didn't want a book comprised of dusty museum pieces, literary curiosities so out-of-date in terms of style and aesthetics that they could only be enjoyed through a lens of nostalgia; I wanted a book that contemporary readers could *enjoy*, stories that would be as vivid and entertaining to today's readers as anything else they can find on the bookstore shelves—and that meant that a certain median level of line-by-line craft was essential. The blunt truth is, many of the classic stories of the '20s and '30s, although they contain the seeds of much later work within them, are so poorly written line-by-line (and so dated stylistically even when they aren't clumsy) that they are opaque and impenetrable to many modern readers. So I decided that I would omit coverage here of the "Superscience" era of the '30s (already heavily covered anyway in anthologies such as Isaac Asimov's *Before the Golden Age* and Damon Knight's *Science Fiction of the Thirties*), and concentrate on work published after World War II instead, a period of swift change and forced evolution in the magazine market, when many of the aesthetic lessons of the Campbellian revolution had already been absorbed and applied. Besides, "after World War II" made a neat and symbolically obvious starting point—the science fiction scenes before the war and after the war were radically different, and even some of the authors who had been publishing pre-war, such as Jack Williamson and Clifford D. Simak, would change their styles and approaches radically after the war.

Deciding to start after World War II set one limiting parameter, but that still left almost fifty years to cover until the present day, too much territory to cover adequately in one volume. The book would have to be broken into two volumes, and was, with the upcoming volume to be called *The Good New Stuff*. But the question still remained: where to break it?

The SF adventure story, and particularly those specialized forms known as the Space Adventure and Space Opera, underwent hothouse forced evolution in the '50s and in the early and mid-'60s. In retrospect this time might be seen as the second great Age of the Space Opera, although that fact is often obscured by the attention paid—both then and now—to the work being done outside the compress of the Space Adventure, especially by the *Galaxy* writers. And yet, during those years, writers such as Poul Anderson and Jack Vance and James H. Schmitz were at their most prolific, L. Sprague de Camp was publishing his tales of the Viagens Interplanetarias, Cordwainer Smith was producing the best of his Instrumentality stories,

Brian W. Aldiss was helping to invent the modern science-fantasy form with the outrageous and gorgeously colored adventures (loudly attacked at the time for not being scientifically plausible—as indeed they were *not*, although to protest that is almost to miss the point) of his "Hothouse" series, Robert A. Heinlein was (with mixed success) diluting the Space Adventure story to make it acceptable to the readers of *The Saturday Evening Post*, while, at the same time, with his so-called "juvenile" novels—actually Young Adult novels, by today's classification system—he was addicting whole new generations of readers to that form (as was Andre Norton), Hal Clement was turning out his two best books—both vivid otherworld adventures—*Mission of Gravity* and *Cycle of Fire* . . . and Alfred Bester was raising the stakes for baroque Space Opera in 1956 with *The Stars My Destination* (still one of the most influential SF novels ever written, and a story that was no more typical of H. L. Gold's *Galaxy*, where the emphasis was usually on biting social satire, than Frank Herbert's "Dune" stories were of *Analog*—it's hard to resist a good adventure story!), just as Frank Herbert would raise them again, at least in terms of the complexity of the social background—Bester had more headlong momentum and bravura—in *Dune*.

By the mid-'60s, there would even be a magazine again that specialized—although in a defacto way—in ripsnorting adventure tales (*Thrilling Wonder Stories*, *Planet Stories*, and *Startling Stories* had all disappeared at the end of the '50s, along with more than forty other titles that had appeared during the genre's short-lived '50s Boom), Frederik Pohl's *Worlds of If* magazine. Although designed as a second-string back-up magazine in which to dump stuff that was good but not good *enough* for Pohl's front-line magazine, *Galaxy*—it was "*Galaxy's* remainder outlet," to use Pohl's own blunt phrase—*Worlds of If* always seemed much livelier and looser and more entertaining to me than its somewhat gray older sister, and, somewhat to Pohl's annoyance, it kept winning the Hugo Award for Best Magazine instead of the more "respectable" *Galaxy*. In addition to much memorable work off the mainline of the development of the Space Adventure by Harlan Ellison, Samuel R. Delany, James Tiptree, Jr., Robert Silverberg, Philip K. Dick, R. A. Lafferty, and others, Pohl's *Worlds of If* also published Larry Niven's early "Known Space" stories and Fred Saberhagen's long sequence of "Berserker" stories, and started something of a mini-boom in the even-more-specialized form of the "Interstellar Espionage" story, a form Keith Laumer started out *satirizing* in his "Retief" stories—although later Retief stories more-or-less became the very thing they'd originally been mocking, with perhaps a slight satirical edge maintained—which quickly became one of the most popular series to appear in *If*. They were later joined by similar series—without the satire—by C. C. MacApp and others; some of Saberhagen's "Berserker" stories can also be seen as falling into this category. This form was also popular elsewhere in the SF world of the mid-'60s, with Poul Anderson's "Dominic Flandry" series and Jack Vance's Demon Princes novels only the most prominent examples, and it's tempting to wonder, considering the timing, whether Ian Fleming's James Bond novels, then on the bestseller charts, weren't really the hidden influence here.

A good argument could be made, though, that by the mid-'60s the true home of Space Opera in the United States was not in any of the magazines anyway, but rather at Ace Books, especially the Ace Doubles line, which in addition to returning almost all of Edgar Rice Burroughs's work to print, produced under the editorship of Donald A. Wollheim a long sequence of cheaply priced (affordable even to teenagers! A key point), garish-looking paperback editions of adventure books by Poul Anderson, John Brunner, Andre Norton, Jack Vance, Gordon R. Dickson, Tom Purdom, Kenneth Bulmer, G. C. Edmondson, Keith Laumer, A. Bertram Chandler, Marion Zimmer Bradley, Avram Davidson, and dozens of other authors—including, in the late '60s, innovative Space Opera work by brand-new writers such as Samuel R. Delany and Ursula K. Le Guin.

However, by the late '60s and early '70s, perhaps because of the prominence of the "New Wave" revolution in SF, which concentrated both on introspective, stylistically "experimental" work and work with more immediate sociological and political "relevance" to the tempestuous social scene of the day (critics like Aldiss would call for more stories dealing with the Vietnam War, the "youth movement," the ecology, the sexual revolution, the psychedelic scene, and so forth, while, in England, Michael Moorcock would utter his famous demand for work with "real drugs, real sex, really shocking ideas about society"), perhaps because of scientific proof that the other planets of the solar system were not likely abodes for life of *any* sort, let alone oxygen-breathing humanoid natives that you could have swordfights with and/or fall in love with, perhaps because the now more-widely-understood limitations of Einsteinian relativity had come to make even the less flamboyant idea of far-flung interstellar empires seem improbable at best (there were those, even SF writers, who said that the whole idea of interstellar *flight* itself was wishful nonsense, forget about interstellar empires!), science fiction as a genre was turning away from the Space Adventure tale, which now became even more outmoded and *declassé* than it had been before.

Stalwarts such as Poul Anderson and Jack Vance and Larry Niven continued to soldier on (and there would be one last seminal book published in the '60s, coming out right at the end of the decade, Samuel R. Delany's *Nova*—a book which, although its influence was not immediately apparent, clearly had immense impact on the later Space Opera work of the new writers of the '80s and '90s), but there would be less Space Adventure stuff written in the following ten years or so than in any other comparable period in SF history. The generation of new writers who would come to prominence in the late '60s and early '70s would write almost none of it, for instance. By far the majority of work published during this period was set on Earth, often in the near future. Even the solar system had been largely deserted as a setting for stories, let alone the distant stars.

Not until the late '70s and early '80s would new writers such as John Varley, George R. R. Martin, Bruce Sterling, Michael Swanwick, and others, begin to grow interested in the Space Adventure again. By the '90s, a whole new boom in Baroque Space Opera would be underway, fueled by authors such as Iain M. Banks, Dan Simmons, Paul J. McAuley, Orson Scott Card, Vernor Vinge, Stephen Baxter, Stephen R. Donaldson, Alexander Jablokov, Charles Sheffield, Peter F. Hamilton, and a dozen others, ushering in the third great Age of Space Opera.

But that's clearly territory for *The Good New Stuff*. It became obvious that the natural breaking point for this volume was the beginning of the '70s, with the Space Adventure tale just about to fade into an interregnum . . . and that's where I've ended it. The follow-up volume, *The Good New Stuff*, due out in January of 1999, will take up the story after the interregnum, in the mid-'70s.

It's hard to deny that another of my major reasons for putting this anthology together was a nostalgic one. Just xeroxing the stories from crumbling old magazines and paperback collections, looking at the lurid covers and the garish pulp blurbs, having the cheap ink rub off on my fingers, smelling that curiously unique and instantly identifiable smell of old, brittle, yellowing paper, provided me with a nostalgic rush of such intensity that I was often able to remember where I was and what I was doing when I read the story for the first time thirty or more years before—and actually *reading* the stories again filled me with a much greater rush of images, outlandish settings, bizarre characters, strange creatures, odd concepts, vivid color, wild action.

But reading these stories again—as I had to read them over and over again to prepare this book for publication—I was struck by how well most of them hold up, even by today's standards. There isn't a story here that I wouldn't buy today, if it were somehow crossing my desk for the first time. So I don't think that this book is *merely* an aging reader's nostalgia trip, although it is inarguably *also* that. I think that these stories, like all good stories, are timeless. And I hope that this book—no doubt long out-of-print by then, sitting in a dusty heap in some secondhand book store, perhaps battered and coverless, waiting to be discovered by someone restless or bored enough to dust it off and pick it up—will still be offering its store of entertainment and wonder to new readers fifty years from *now*.

So sit back in a comfortable chair, break out the potato chips and ice cream (or a snifter of fine brandy, if you'd rather), and enjoy. Few—if any—adventure stories ever written in any genre are better than the ones you are about to read, forged in the crucible of a market where stories competed with each other on the basis of how exciting they were, and didn't get bought if they *weren't* exciting.

This is the Good Old Stuff. Have fun.

—Gardner Dozois

THE GOOD OLD
STUFF

A. E. van Vogt

THE RULL

A. E. van Vogt was one of the first genre writers ever to publish an actual science fiction *book,* at a time when science fiction as a commercial publishing category did not yet exist, and almost all SF writers—even later giants such as Robert A. Heinlein—were able to publish novels *only* as serials in science fiction magazines. It's indicative of the prestige and popularity that van Vogt could claim at the time that he was one of the first authors to whom publishers would turn when taking the first tentative steps toward establishing science fiction as a viable publishing category—which makes it all the more ironic that his work is all but forgotten today by most readers in the genre that he helped to shape.

Van Vogt's stories were more complex, ornate, and recomplicated than the work of many of his predecessors from the Superscience days of the '30s—his most famous piece of writing advice is that you should throw a new idea into a story every five hundred words, a theory he seems to have consciously tried to apply in his own work. Van Vogt upped the stakes for Space Opera in the late '40s and early and mid-'50s with work like *The Voyage of the Space Beagle, The Weapon Shops of Isher, The World of Null-A, Slan,* and *The War Against the Rull,* increasing the Imagination Ante you had to come up with in order to sit down at the high-stakes table and play with the Big Boys, much as Alfred Bester and Jack Vance would do toward the end of the '50s, Cordwainer Smith and Frank Herbert would do in the mid-'60s, and Samuel R. Delany would do in the late '60s. Nobody, however, with the possible exception of the Bester of *The Stars My Destination* (who was himself clearly influenced by van Vogt), ever came close to matching van Vogt for headlong, breakneck pacing, or for the electric, crackling, paranoid tension with which he was capable of suffusing his work . . . as should be more than evident in the story that follows, which gives us one of the classic SF situations: a man pitted against an alien in a situation where there is no escape and to lose the struggle is to die, and where *both* adversaries are willing to do whatever it takes in order to *win* . . .

Van Vogt is the author of 65 books, including, in addition to those named above, *The Empire of the Atom, The Wizard of Linn, The Players of Null-A, Null-A Three, The Book of Ptath, The Weapon Makers, The House That Stood Still, Masters of Time, The Universe Makers, Quest for the Future, Computerworld,* and *The Silkie,* among many others. In 1996, he was honored with a long-overdue Grandmaster Nebula Award for Life Achievement. Most of van Vogt's work is long out-of-print and usually unfindable, but by the time you read these words, a reprint of one of his best-known novels, *Slan,* should be available as a trade paperback from Tor, and *The Voyage of the Space Beagle*—a landmark volume that, among other distinctions, was one of the chief inspirations for the original *Star Trek* series and was a seminal influence on the movie *Alien* as well—should be available as part of a three-novel omnibus volume (matched with novels by Poul Anderson and Barry N. Malzberg) from White Wolf Borealis called *Three in Space: White Wolf Rediscovery Trio #2.* We can only hope that more of van Vogt's books will come back into print again in the days ahead. (I myself would particularly like to see *The War Against the Rull*—one of my favorite van Vogt books—and back in print again, although a good historical case could be made for reprinting a half-dozen other van Vogt titles as well.)

1

Trevor Jamieson saw the other space boat out of the corner of his eye. He was sitting in a hollow about a dozen yards from the edge of the precipice, and some score of feet from the doorway of his own lifeboat. He had been intent on his survey book, annotating a comment beside the voice graph, to the effect that Laertes III was so close to the invisible dividing line between Earth-controlled and Rull-controlled space that its prior discovery by man was in itself a major victory in the Rull-human war.

He had written: "The fact that ships based on this planet could strike at several of the most densely populated areas of the galaxy, *Rull* or *human,* gives it an AA priority on all available military equipment. Preliminary defense units should be set up on Mount Monolith, where I am now, within three weeks. . . ."

It was at that point that he saw the other boat, above and somewhat to his left, approaching the tableland. He glanced up at it, and froze where he was, torn between two opposing purposes. His first impulse, to run for the lifeboat, yielded to the realization that the movement would be seen instantly by the electronic reflexes of the other ship. For a moment, then, he had the dim hope that, if he remained quiet enough, neither he nor his ship would be observed.

Even as he sat there, perspiring with indecision, his tensed eyes noted the Rull markings and the rakish design of the other vessel. His vast knowledge of things Rull enabled him to catalogue it instantly as a survey craft.

A *survey* craft. The Rulls had discovered the Laertes sun.

The terrible potentiality was that, behind this small craft, might be fleets of battleships, whereas he was alone. His own lifeboat had been dropped by the *Orion* nearly a parsec away, while the big ship was proceeding at anti-gravity speeds. That was to insure that Rull energy tracers did not record its passage through this area of space. The *Orion* was to head for the nearest base, load up with planetary defense equipment, and then return. She was due in ten days.

Ten days. Jamieson groaned inwardly and drew his legs under him and clenched his hand about the survey book. But still the possibility that his ship, partially hidden under a clump of trees, might escape notice if *he* remained quiet, held him there in the open. His head tilted up, his eyes glared at the alien, and his brain willed it to turn aside. Once more, while he waited, the implications of the disaster that could be here struck deep.

The Rull ship was a hundred yards away now and showed no signs of changing its course. In seconds it would cross the clump of trees, which half hid the lifeboat.

In a spasm of movement, Jamieson launched himself from his chair. With complete abandon, he dived for the open doorway of his machine. As the door clanged behind him, the boat shook as if it had been struck by a giant. Part of the ceiling sagged; the floor heaved under him, and the air grew hot and suffocating. Gasping, Jamieson slid into the control chair and struck the main emergency switch. The rapid-fire blasters huzzaed into automatic firing positions and let go with a hum and a deep-throated *ping*. The refrigerators whined with power; a cold blast of air blew at his body. The relief was so quick that a second passed before Jamieson realized that the atomic engines had failed to respond. And that the lifeboat, which should have already been sliding into the air, was still lying inert in an exposed position.

Tense, he stared into the visiplates. It took a moment to locate the Rull ship. It was at the lower edge of one plate, tumbling slowly out of sight beyond a clump of trees a quarter of a mile away. As he watched, it disappeared; and then the crash of the landing came clear and unmistakable from the sound board in front of him.

The relief that came was weighted with an awful reaction. Jamieson sank into the cushions of the control chair, weak from the narrowness of his escape. The weakness ended abruptly as a thought struck him. There had been a sedateness about the way the enemy ship fell. *The crash hadn't killed the Rulls aboard.* He was alone in a damaged lifeboat on an impassable mountain with one or more of the most remorseless creatures ever spawned. For ten days he must fight in the hope that man would still be able to seize the most valuable planet discovered in half a century.

Jamieson opened the door and went out onto the tableland. He was still trembling with reaction, but it was rapidly growing darker and there was no time to waste. He walked quickly to the top of the nearest hillock a hundred feet away, taking the last few feet on his hands and knees. Cautiously, he peered over the rim. Most of the mountaintop was visible. It was a rough oval some eight hundred yards wide at its narrowest, a wilderness of scraggly brush and upjutting rock, dominated here and there by clumps of trees. There was not a movement to be seen, and not a sign of the Rull ship. Over everything lay an atmosphere of desolation, and the utter silence of an uninhabited wasteland.

The twilight was deeper now that the sun had sunk below the southwest precipice. And the deadly part was that, to the Rulls, with their wider vision and more complete equipment, the darkness would mean nothing. All night long he would have to be on the defensive against beings whose nervous systems outmatched his in every function except, possibly, intelligence. On that level, and that alone, human beings claimed equality. The very comparison made him realize how desperate his situation was. He needed an advantage. If he could get to the Rull wreck and cause them some kind of damage before it got pitch-dark, before they recovered from the shock of the crash, that alone might make the difference between life and death for him.

It was a chance he had to take. Hurriedly, Jamieson backed down the hillock and, climbing to his feet, started along a shallow wash. The ground was rough with stone and projecting edges of rock and the gnarled roots and tangle of hardy growth. Twice he fell, the first time gashing his right hand. It slowed him mentally and physically. He had never before tried to make speed over the pathless wilderness of the tableland. He saw that in ten minutes he had covered a distance of no more than a few hundred yards. He stopped. It was one thing to be bold on the chance of making a vital gain. It was quite another to throw away his life on a reckless gamble. The defeat would not be his alone but man's.

As he stood there he grew aware of how icy cold it had become. A chilling wind from the east had sprung up. By midnight the temperature would be zero. He began to retreat. There were several defenses to rig up before night; and he had better hurry. An hour later, when the moonless darkness lay heavily over the mountain of mountains, Jamieson sat tensely before his visiplates. It was going to be a long night for a man who dared not sleep. Somewhere about the middle of it, Jamieson saw a movement at the remote perimeter of his all-wave vision plate. Finger on blaster control, he waited for the object to come into sharper focus. It never did. The cold dawn found him weary but still alertly watching for an enemy that was acting as cautiously as he himself. He began to wonder if he had actually seen anything.

Jamieson took another antisleep pill and made a more definite examination of the atomic motors. It didn't take long to verify his earlier diagnosis. The basic gravitation pile had been thoroughly frustrated. Until it could be reactivated on the *Orion*, the motors were useless. The conclusive examination braced him. He was committed irrevocably to this deadly battle of the tableland. The idea that had been turning over in his mind during the night took on new meaning. This was the first time in his knowledge that a Rull and a human being had faced each other on a limited field of action, where neither was a prisoner. The great battles in space were ship against ship and fleet against fleet. Survivors either escaped or were picked up by overwhelming forces.

Unless he was bested before he could get organized, here was a priceless opportunity to try some tests on the Rulls—and without delay. Every moment of daylight must be utilized to the uttermost limit.

Jamieson put on his special "defensive" belts and went outside. The dawn was brightening minute by minute; and the vistas that revealed themselves with each increment of light-power held him, even as he tensed his body for the fight ahead. Why, he thought, in sharp, excited wonder, this is happening on the strangest mountain ever known.

Mount Monolith stood on a level plain and reared up precipitously to a height of eight thousand two hundred feet. The most majestic pillar in the known universe, it easily qualified as one of the hundred nature wonders of the galaxy.

He had walked the soil of planets a hundred thousand light-years from Earth, and the decks of great ships that flashed from the eternal night into the blazing brightness of suns red and suns blue, suns yellow and white and orange and violet, suns so wonderful and different that no previous imaginings could match the reality.

Yet, here he stood on a mountain on far Laertes, one man compelled by circumstances to pit his cunning against one or more of the supremely intelligent Rull enemy.

Jamieson shook himself grimly. It was time to launch his attack—and discover the opposition that could be mustered against him. That was Step One, and the important point about it was to insure that it wasn't also Step Last. By the time the Laertes sun peered palely over the horizon that was the northeast cliff's edge, the assault was under way. The automatic defensors, which he had set up the night before, moved slowly from point to point ahead of the mobile blaster. He cautiously saw to it that one of the three defensors also brought up his rear. He augmented that basic protection by crawling from one projecting rock after another. The machines he manipulated from a tiny hand control, which was connected to the visiplates that poked out from his headgear just above his eyes. With tensed eyes, he watched the wavering needles that would indicate movement or that the defensor screens were being subjected to energy opposition.

Nothing happened. As he came within sight of the Rull craft, Jamieson halted, while he seriously pondered the problem of no resistance. He didn't like it. It was possible that all the Rulls aboard had been killed, but he doubted it.

Bleakly he studied the wreck through the telescopic eyes of one of the defensors. It lay in a shallow indentation, its nose buried in a wall of gravel. Its lower plates were collapsed versions of the original. His single energy blast of the day before, completely automatic though it had been, had really dealt a smashing blow to the Rull ship.

The over-all effect was of lifelessness. If it were a trick, then it was a very skillful one. Fortunately, there were tests he could make, not final but evidential and indicative.

The echoless height of the most unique mountain ever discovered hummed with the fire sound of the mobile blaster. The noise grew to a roar as the unit's pile warmed to its task and developed its maximum kilocurie of activity. Under that barrage, the hull of the enemy craft trembled a little and changed color slightly, but that was all. After ten minutes, Jamieson cut the power and sat baffled and indecisive.

The defensive screens of the Rull ship were full on. Had they gone on automatically after his first shot of the evening before? Or had they been put up deliberately to nullify just such an attack as this? He couldn't be sure. That was the trouble; he had no positive knowledge.

The Rull could be lying inside dead. (Odd, how he was beginning to think in terms of one rather than several, but the degree of caution being used by the opposition—if opposition existed—matched his own, and indicated the caution of an individual moving against unknown odds.) It could be wounded and incapable of doing anything against him. It could have spent the night marking up the tableland with nerve control lines—he'd have to make sure he never looked directly at the ground—or it could simply be waiting for the arrival of the greater ship that had dropped it onto the planet.

Jamieson refused to consider that last possibility. That way was death, without qualification of hope. Frowning, he studied the visible damage he had done to the ship. All the hard metals had held together, so far as he could see, but the whole bottom of the ship was dented to a depth that varied from one to four feet. Some radiation must have got in, and the question was, what would it have damaged? He had examined dozens of captured Rull survey craft, and if this one ran to the pattern, then in the front would be the control center, with a sealed-off blaster chamber. In the rear the engine room, two storerooms, one for fuel and equipment, the other for food and—

For food. Jamieson jumped, and then with wide eyes noted how the food section had suffered greater damage than any other part of the ship. Surely,

surely, some radiation must have got into it, poisoning it, ruining it, and instantly putting the Rull, with his swift digestive system, into a deadly position.

Jamieson sighed with the intensity of his hope and prepared to retreat. As he turned away, quite incidentally, accidentally, he glanced at the rock behind which he had shielded himself from possible direct fire. Glanced at it and saw the lines on it. Intricate lines, based on a profound and inhuman study of human neurons. He recognized them for what they were and stiffened in horror. He thought, Where—*where* am I being directed?

That much had been discovered after his return from Mira 23, with his report of how he had been apparently, instantly, hypnotized; the lines impelled movement to somewhere. Here, on this fantastic mountain, it could only be to a cliff. But which one?

With a desperate will, he fought to retain his senses a moment longer. He strove to see the lines again. He saw, briefly, flashingly, five wavering verticals and above them three lines that pointed east with their wavering ends. The pressure built up inside him, but still he fought to keep his thoughts self-motivated. Fought to remember if there were any wide ledges near the top of the east cliff. There were. He recalled them in a final agony of hope. There, he thought, that one, that one. Let me fall on that one. He strained to hold the ledge image he wanted and to repeat, many times, the command that might save his life. His last dreary thought was that here was the answer to his doubts. The Rull *was* alive. Blackness came like a curtain of pure essence of night.

2

From the far galaxy had he come, a cold, remorseless leader of leaders, the *yeli*, Meesh, the Iin of Ria, the high Aaish of Yeel. And other titles, and other positions, and power. Oh, the power that he had, the power of death, the power of life and the power of the Leard ships.

He had come in his great anger to discover what was wrong. Many years before, the command had been given: Expand into the Second Galaxy. Why were they-who-could-not-be-more-perfect so slow in carrying out these instructions? What was the nature of the two-legged creatures whose multitudinous ships, impregnable planetary bases and numerous allies had fought those-who-possessed-Nature's-supreme-nervous-system to an impasse?

"Bring me a live human being!"

The command echoed to the ends of Riatic space. It produced a dull survivor of an Earth cruiser, a sailor of low degree with an I.Q. of ninety-six, and a fear index of two hundred and seven. The creature made vague efforts to kill himself, and squirmed on the laboratory tables, and finally escaped into death when the scientists were still in the beginning of the experiments which *he* had ordered to be performed before his own eyes.

"Surely this is not the enemy."

"Sire, we capture so few that are alive. Just as we have conditioned our own, so do they seem to be conditioned to kill themselves in case of capture."

"The environment is wrong. We must create a situation where the captured does not know himself to be a prisoner. Are there any possibilities?"

"The problem will be investigated."

He had come, as the one who would conduct the experiment, to the sun where a man had been observed seven periods before. The man was in a small craft—as the report put it—"which was precipitated suddenly out of subspace and fell toward this sun. The fact that it used no energy aroused the suspicions of our observing warship, which might otherwise have paid no attention to so small a machine. And so, because an investigation was made immediately, we have a new base possibility, and of course an ideal situation for the experiment."

The report continued: "No landings have been made yet, as you instructed; so far as we know, our presence is not suspected. It may be assumed that there was an earlier human landing on the third planet, for the man quickly made that curious mountaintop his headquarters. It will be ideal for your purposes."

A battle group patrolled the space around the sun. But *he* came down in a small ship, and because he had contempt for his enemy, he had flown in over the mountains, fired his disabling blast at the ship on the ground—and then was struck by a surprisingly potent return blast that sent his machine spinning to a crash. Death almost came in those seconds. But he crawled out of his control chair, shocked but still alive. With thoughtful eyes, he assessed the extent of the disaster that had befallen him. He had issued commands that he would call when he wanted them to return. But he could not call. The radio was shattered beyond repair. He had an uneasy sensation when he discovered that his food was poisoned.

Swiftly, he stiffened to the necessity of the situation. The experiment would go on, with one proviso. When the need for food became imperative, he would kill the man, and so survive until the commanders of the ships grew alarmed and came down to see what had happened.

He spent part of the sunless period exploring the cliff's edge. Then he hovered on the perimeter of the man's defensor energies, studying the lifeboat and pondering the possible actions the other might take against him. Finally, with a tireless patience, he examined the approaches to his own ship. At key points, he drew the lines-that-could-seize-the-minds-of-men. There was satisfaction, shortly after the sun came up, in seeing the enemy "caught" and "compelled." The satisfaction had but one drawback. He could not take the advantage of the situation that he wanted. The difficulty was that the man's blaster had been left focused on his main airlock. It was not emitting energy, but the Rull did not doubt that it would fire automatically if the door opened.

What made the situation serious was that, when he tried the emergency exit, it was jammed. It hadn't been. With the forethought of his kind, he had tested it immediately after the crash. Then, it opened. Now it didn't. The ship, he decided, must have settled while he was out during the sunless period. Actually, the reason for what had happened didn't matter. What counted was that he was locked in just when he wanted to be outside. It was not as if he had definitely decided to destroy the man immediately. If capturing him meant gaining control of his food supply, then it would be unnecessary to give him death. It was important to be able to make the decision, however, while the man was helpless. And the further possibility that the *elled* fall might kill him made the *yeli* grim. He didn't like accidents to disturb his plans.

From the beginning the affair had taken a sinister turn. He had been caught up by forces beyond his control, by elements of space and time which he had always taken into account as being theoretically possible, but he had never considered them as having personal application.

That was for the depths of space where the Leard ships fought to extend the frontiers of the perfect ones. Out there lived alien creatures that had been spawned by Nature before the ultimate nervous system was achieved. All those aliens must die because they were now unnecessary, and because, existing, they might accidentally discover means of upsetting the balance of Yeelian life. In civilized Ria accidents were forbidden.

The Rull drew his mind clear of such weakening thoughts. He decided against trying to open the emergency door. Instead, he turned his blaster against a crack in the hard floor. The frustrators blew their gases across the area where he had worked, and the suction pumps caught the swirling radioactive stuff and drew it into a special chamber. But the lack of an open door as a safety valve made the work dangerous. Many times he paused while the air was cleansed, so that he could come out again from the frustrating chamber to which he retreated whenever the heat made his nerves tingle—a more reliable guide than any instrument that had to be watched.

The sun was past the meridian when the metal plate finally lifted clear and gave him an opening into the gravel and rock underneath. The problem of tunneling out into the open was easy except that it took time and physical effort. Dusty and angry and hungry, the Rull emerged from the hole near the center of the clump of trees beside which his craft had fallen.

His plan to conduct an experiment had lost its attraction. He had obstinate qualities in his nature, but he reasoned that this situation could be reproduced for him on a more civilized level. No need to take risks or to be uncomfortable. He would kill the man and chemically convert him to food until the ships came down to rescue him. With hungry gaze, he searched the ragged, uneven east cliff, peering down at the ledges, crawling swiftly along until he had virtually circumvented the tableland. He found nothing he could be sure about. In one or two places the ground looked lacerated as by the passage of a body, but the most intensive examination failed to establish that anyone had actually been there.

Somberly, the Rull glided toward the man's lifeboat. From a safe distance, he examined it. The defense screens were up, but he couldn't be sure they had been put up before the attack of the morning, or had been raised since then, or had come on automatically at his approach. He couldn't be sure. That was the trouble. Everywhere on the tableland around him was a barrenness, a desolation unlike anything he had ever known. The man could be dead, his smashed body lying at the remote bottom of the mountain. He could be inside the ship badly injured; he had, unfortunately, *had* time to get back to the safety of his craft. Or he could be waiting inside, alert, aggressive, and conscious of his enemy's uncertainty, determined to take full advantage of that uncertainty.

The Rull set up a watching device that would apprise him when the door opened. Then he returned to the tunnel that led into his ship, laboriously crawled through it, and settled himself to wait out the emergency. The hunger in him was an expanding force, hourly taking on a greater urgency. It was time to stop moving around. He would need all his energy for the crisis. The days passed.

Jamieson stirred in an effluvium of pain. At first it seemed all-enveloping, a mist of anguish that bathed him in sweat from head to toe. Gradually, then, it localized in the region of his lower left leg. The pulse of the pain made a rhythm in his nerves. The minutes lengthened into an hour, and then he finally thought, Why, I've got a sprained ankle! There was more to it than that, of course. The pressure that had driven him here oppressed his life force. How long he lay there, partly conscious, was not clear, but when he finally opened his eyes, the sun was still shining on him, though it was almost directly overhead.

He watched it with the mindlessness of a dreamer as it withdrew slowly past the edge of the overhanging precipice. It was not until the shadow of the cliff suddenly plopped across his face that he started to full consciousness with a sudden memory of deadly danger. It took a while for him to shake the remnants of the effect of the nerve lines from his brain. And, even as it was fading, he sized up, to some extent, the difficulties of his position. He saw that he had tumbled over the edge of a cliff to a steep slope.

The angle of descent of the slope was a sharp fifty-five degrees, and what had saved him was that his body had been caught in the tangled growth near the edge of the greater precipice beyond. His foot must have twisted in those roots and been sprained.

As he finally realized the nature of his injuries, Jamieson braced up. He was safe. In spite of having suffered an accidental defeat of major proportions, his intense concentration on this slope, his desperate will to make *this* the place where he must fall, had worked out. He began to climb. It was easy enough on the slope, steep as it was; the ground was rough, rocky and scraggly with brush. It was when he came to the ten-foot overhanging cliff that his ankle proved what an obstacle it could be. Four times he slid back reluctantly; and then, on the fifth try, his fingers, groping, caught an unbreakable root. Triumphantly, he dragged himself to the safety of the tableland.

Now that the sound of his scraping and struggling was gone, only his heavy breathing broke the silence of the emptiness. His anxious eyes studied the uneven terrain. The tableland spread before him with not a sign of a moving figure anywhere. To one side, he could see his lifeboat. Jamieson began to crawl toward it, taking care to stay on rock as much as possible. What had happened to the Rull he did not know. And since, for several days, his ankle would keep him inside his ship, he might as well keep his enemy guessing during that time.

It was getting dark, and he was inside the ship, when a peevish voice said in his ear, "When do we go home? When do I eat again?"

It was the Ploian, with his perennial question about returning to Ploia. Jamieson shrugged aside his momentary feeling of guilt. He had forgotten all about his companion these many hours.

As he "fed" the being, he thought, not for the first time, How could he explain the Rull-human war to this untutored mind? More important, how could he explain his present predicament?

Aloud, he said, "Don't you worry. You stay with me, and I'll see that you get home." That—plus the food—seemed to satisfy the being.

For a time, then, Jamieson considered how he might use the Ploian against the Rull. But the fact was that his principal ability was not needed. There was no point in letting a starving Rull discover that his human opponent had a method of scrambling the electrical system of his ship.

3

Jamieson lay in his bunk thinking. He could hear the beating of his heart. There were the occasional sounds when he dragged himself out of bed. The radio, when he turned it on, was dead—no static, not even the fading in and out of a wave. At this colossal distance, even subspace radio was impossible. He listened on all the more active Rull wave lengths. But the silence was there too. Not that they would be broadcasting if they were in the vicinity. He was cut off here in this tiny ship on an uninhabited planet, with useless motors. He tried not to think of it like that. Here, he told himself, is the opportunity of a lifetime for an experiment. He warmed to the idea as a moth to flame. Live Rulls were hard to get hold of. And here was an ideal situation. *We're prisoners, both of us.* That was the way he tried to picture it. Prisoners of an environment and, therefore, in a curious fashion, prisoners of each other. Only each was free of the conditioned need to kill himself.

There were things a man might discover. The great mysteries—as far as men were concerned—that motivated Rull actions. Why did they want to destroy other races totally? Why did they needlessly sacrifice valuable ships in attacking Earth machines that ventured into their sectors of space when they knew that the intruders would leave in a few weeks anyway?

The potentialities of this fight of man against Rull on a lonely mountain exhilarated Jamieson as he lay on his bunk, scheming, turning the problem over in his mind. There were times during those dog days when he crawled over to the control chair and peered for an hour at a stretch into the visiplates. He saw the tableland and the vista of distance beyond it. He saw the sky of Laertes III, pale orchid in color, silent and lifeless. He saw the prison. Caught here, he thought bleakly. Trevor Jamieson, whose quiet voice in the scientific council chambers of Earth's galactic empire spoke with considerable authority—that Jamieson was here, alone, lying in a bunk, waiting for a leg to heal, so that he might conduct an experiment with a Rull. It seemed incredible. But he grew to believe it as the days passed.

On the third day, he was able to move around sufficiently to handle a few heavy objects. He began work immediately on the light-screen. On the fifth day it was finished. Then the story had to be recorded. That was easy. Each sequence had been so carefully worked out in bed that it flowed from his mind onto the visiwire.

He set it up about two hundred yards from the lifeboat, behind a screening of trees. He tossed a can of food a dozen feet to one side of the screen.

The rest of the day dragged. It was the sixth day since the arrival of the Rull, the fifth since he had sprained his ankle. Came the night.

4

A gliding shadow, undulating under the starlight of Laertes III, the Rull approached the screen the man had set up. How bright it was, shining in the darkness of the tableland, a blob of light in a black universe of uneven ground and dwarf shrubbery. When he was a hundred feet from the light, he sensed the food—and realized that here was a trap. For the Rull, six days without food had meant a stupendous loss of energy, visual blackouts on a dozen color levels, a dimness of life-force that fitted with the shadows, not the sun. That inner world of disjointed nervous systems was like a run-down battery, with a score of organic "instruments" disconnecting one by one as the energy level fell. The *yeli* recognized dimly, but with a savage anxiety, that the keenest edges of that nervous system might never be fully restored. Speed was essential. A few more steps downward, and then the old, old conditioning of mandatory self-inflicted death would apply even to the high Aaish of the Yeel.

The reticulated body grew quiet. The visual centers which were everywhere accepted light on a narrow band from the screen. From beginning to end, he watched the story as it unfolded, and then watched it again, craving repetition with all the ardor of a primitive.

The picture began in deep space with the man's lifeboat being dropped from a launching lock of a battleship. It showed the battleship going to a military base, and there taking on supplies and acquiring a vast fleet of reinforcements, and then starting on the return journey. The scene switched to the lifeboat dropping down on Laertes III, showed everything that had subsequently happened, suggested the situation was dangerous to them both—and pointed out the only safe solution. The final sequence of each showing of the story was of the Rull approaching the can, to the left of the screen, and opening it. The method was shown in detail, as was the visualization of the Rull busily eating the food inside. Each time that sequence drew near, a tenseness came over the Rull, a will to make the story real. But it was not until the seventh showing had run its course that he glided forward, closing the last gap between himself and the can. It was a trap, he knew, perhaps even death—it didn't matter. To live, he had to take the chance. Only by this means, by risking what was in the can, could he hope to remain alive for the necessary time.

How long it would take for the commanders cruising up there in the black of space—how long it would be before they would decide to supersede his command, he didn't know. But they would come. Even if they waited until the enemy ships arrived before they dared to act against his strict orders, they would come. At that point they could come down without fear of suffering from his ire. Until then he would need all the food he could get. Gingerly, he extended a sucker and activated the automatic opener of the can.

It was shortly after four in the morning when Jamieson awakened to the sound of an alarm ringing softly. It was still pitch-dark outside—the Laertes day was twenty-six side-real hours long, and dawn was still three hours away. He did not get up at once. The alarm had been activated by the opening of the can of food. It continued to ring for a full fifteen minutes, which was just about perfect. The alarm was tuned to the electronic pattern emitted by the can, once it was opened, and so long as any food remained in it. The lapse of time involved fitted with the capacity of one of the Rull mouths in absorbing three pounds of treated food. For fifteen minutes, accordingly, a member of the Rull race, man's mortal enemy, had been subjected to a pattern of mental vibrations corresponding to its own thoughts. It was a pattern to which the nervous systems of other Rulls had responded in laboratory experiments. Unfortunately, those others had killed themselves on awakening, and so no definite results had been proved. But it had been established by the ecphoriometer that the unconscious and not the conscious mind was affected. It was the beginning of hypnotic indoctrination and control.

Jamieson lay in bed, smiling quietly to himself. He turned over finally to go back to sleep, and then he realized how excited he was. It was the greatest moment in the history of Rull-human warfare. Surely he wasn't going to let it pass unremarked. He climbed out of bed and poured himself a drink.

The attempt of the Rull to attack him through his unconscious mind had emphasized his own possible actions in that direction. Each race had discovered some of the weaknesses of the other. Rulls used their knowledge to exterminate. Man tried for communication and hoped for association. Both were ruthless, murderous, pitiless in their methods. Outsiders sometimes had difficulty distinguishing one from the other. But the difference in purpose was as great as the difference between black and white, the absence, as compared to the presence, of light. There was only one trouble with the immediate situation. Now that the Rull had food, he might develop a few plans of his own.

Jamieson returned to bed and lay staring into the darkness. He did not underrate the resources of the Rull, but since he had decided to conduct an experiment, no chances must be considered too great. He turned over finally and slept the sleep of a man determined that things were working in his favor.

Morning. Jamieson put on his cold-proof clothes and went out into the chilly dawn. Again he savored the silence and the atmosphere of isolated grandeur. A strong wind was blowing from east, and there was an iciness in it that stung his face. He forgot that. There were things to do on this morning of mornings. He would do them with his usual caution.

Paced by defensors and the mobile blaster, he headed for the metal screen. It stood in open high ground, where it would be visible from a dozen different hiding places, and so far as he could see it was undamaged. He tested the automatic mechanism, and for good measure ran the picture through one showing.

He had already tossed another can of food in the grass near the screen, and he was turning away when he thought, That's odd. The metal framework looks as if it's been polished.

He studied the phenomenon in a de-energizing mirror and saw that the metal had been covered with a clear varnish-like substance. A dreadful sickness came over him as he recognized it. He decided in agony: If the cue is not to fire at all, I won't do it. I'll fire even if the blaster turns on me.

He scraped some of the "varnish" into a receptacle and began his retreat to the lifeboat. He was thinking violently: Where does he get all this stuff? That isn't part of the equipment of a survey craft.

The first suspicion was on him that what was happening was not just an accident. He was pondering the vast implications of that when off to one side he saw the Rull. For the first time, in his many days on the tableland, he saw the Rull.

What's the cue?

Memory of purpose came to the Rull shortly after he had eaten. It was a dim memory at first, but it grew stronger. It was not the only sensation of his returning energy. His visual centers interpreted more light. The starlit tableland grew brighter, not as bright as it could be for him, by a large percentage, but the direction was up instead of down. He felt unutterably fortunate that it was no worse.

He had been gliding along the edge of the precipice. Now he paused to peer down. Even with his partial light vision, the view was breath-taking. There was distance below and distance afar. From a spaceship, the effect of height was minimized. But gazing down that wall of gravel into those depths was a different experience. It emphasized how greatly he had suffered, how completely he had been caught by an accident. And it reminded him of what he had been doing before the hunger. He turned instantly away from the cliff and hurried to where the wreckage of his ship had gathered dust for days—bent and twisted wreckage, half buried in the hard ground of Laertes III. He glided over the dented plates inside to one in which he had the day before sensed a quiver of anti-gravity oscillation—tiny, potent, tremendous minutiae of oscillation, capable of being influenced.

The Rull worked with intensity and purposefulness. The plate was still firmly attached to the frame of the ship. And the first job, the extremely difficult job, was to tear it completely free. The hours passed.

With a tearing sound, the hard plate yielded to the slight rearrangement of its nucleonic structure. The shift was infinitesimal, partly because the directing nervous energy of his body was not at norm and partly because it was calculated to be small. There was such a thing as releasing energy enough to blow up a mountain.

Not, he discovered finally, that there was any danger in this plate. He found that out the moment he crawled onto it. The sensation of power that pulsed from it was so slight that, briefly, he doubted that it would lift from the ground. But it did. The test run lasted seven feet and gave him his measurement of the limited force he had available. Enough for an attack only.

There were no doubts in his mind. The experiment was over. His only purpose must be to kill the man, and the question was, how could he insure that the man did not kill him while he was doing it? The varnish!

He applied it painstakingly, dried it with a drier, and then, picking up the plate again, he carried it on his back to the hiding place he wanted. When he had buried it and himself under the dead leaves of a clump of brush, he grew calmer. He recognized that the veneer of his civilization was off. It shocked him, but he did not regret it. In giving him the food, the two-legged being was obviously doing something to him. Something dangerous. The only answer to the entire problem of the experiment of the tableland was to deal death without delay. He lay tense, ferocious, beyond the power of any vagrant thoughts, waiting for the man to come.

What happened then was as desperate a venture as Jamieson had seen in Service. Normally, he would have handled it expertly. But he was watching intently—for the paralysis to strike him. The paralysis that was of the varnish. And so, it was the unexpected normal act that confused him. The Rull flew out of a clump of trees mounted on the antigravity plate. The surprise of that was so great that it almost succeeded. The plates had been drained of all such energies, according to his tests, the first morning. Yet here was one alive again and light again with the special antigravity lightness which Rull scientists had brought to the peak of perfection.

The action of movement through space toward him was, of course, based on the motion of the planet as it turned on its axis. The speed of the attack, starting as it did from zero, did not come near the eight-hundred-mile-an-hour velocity of the spinning planet, but it was swift enough. The apparition of metal and reticulated Rull body charged at him through the air. And even as he drew his weapon and fired at it, he had a choice to make, a restraint to exercise: *Do not kill!*

That was hard, oh, hard. The necessity imposed a limitation so stern that during the second it took him to adjust, the Rull came to within ten feet of him. What saved him was the pressure of the air on the metal plate. The air tilted it like the wing of a plane becoming air-borne. He fired his irresistible weapon at the bottom of the metal plate, seared it, and deflected it to a crash landing in a clump of bushes twenty feet to his right. Jamieson was deliberately slow in following up his success. When he reached the bushes, the Rull was fifty feet beyond them and disappearing into a clump of trees. He did not pursue it or fire a second time. Instead, he gingerly pulled the Rull antigravity plate out of the brush and examined it.

The question was, how had the Rull degravitized it without the elaborate machinery necessary? And if it were capable of creating such a "parachute" for itself why hadn't it floated down to the forest far below, where food would be available and where it would be safe from its human enemy? One question was answered the moment he lifted the antigravity plate. It was about normal weight, its energy apparently exhausted after traveling less than a hundred feet. It had obviously never been capable of making the mile-and-a-half trip to the forest and plain below.

Jamieson took no chances. He dropped the plate over the nearest precipice and watched it fall into distance. He was back in the lifeboat when he remembered the "varnish." There had been no cue; not yet. He tested the scraping he had brought with him. Chemically, it turned out to be simple resin, used to make varnishes. Atomically, it was stabilized. Electronically, it transformed light into energy on the vibration level of human thought. It was alive all right. But what was the recording? He made a graph of every material and energy level, for comparison purposes. As soon as he had established that it had been altered on the electronic level—which had been obvious but which, still, had to be proved—he recorded the images on a visiwire. The result was a hodgepodge of dreamlike fantasies.

Symbols. He took down his book, *Symbol Interpretations of the Unconscious*, and found the cross-reference: "Inhibitions Mental." On the referred page and line, he read, "Do not kill!"

"Well, I'll be . . ." Jamieson said aloud into the silence of the lifeboat interior. "That's what happened."

He was relieved, and then not so relieved. It had been his personal intention not to kill at this stage. But the Rull hadn't known that. By working such a subtle inhibition, it had dominated the attack even in defeat. That was the trouble. So far he had gotten out of situations but had created no successful ones in retaliation. He had a hope, but that wasn't enough.

He must take no more risks. Even his final experiment must wait until the day the *Orion* was due to arrive. Human beings were just a little too weak in certain directions. Their very life cells had impulses which could be stirred by the cunning and the remorseless. He did not doubt that, in the final issue, the Rull would try to stir him toward self-destruction.

5

On the ninth night, the day before the *Orion* was due, Jamieson refrained from putting out a can of food. The following morning he spent half an hour at the radio trying to contact the battleship. He made a point of broadcasting a detailed account of what had happened so far, and he described what his plans were, including his intention of testing the Rull to see if it had suffered any injury from its period of hunger.

Subspace was totally silent. Not a pulse of vibration answered his call. He finally abandoned the attempt to establish contact and went outside and swiftly set up the instruments he would need for his experiment. The tableland had the air of a deserted wilderness. He tested his equipment, then looked at his watch. It was eleven minutes to noon. Suddenly jittery, he decided not to wait the extra minutes. He walked over, hesitated, and then pressed a button. From a source near the screen, a rhythm on a very high energy level was being broadcast. It was a variation of the rhythm pattern to which the Rull had been subjected for four nights. Slowly Jamieson retreated toward the lifeboat. He wanted to try again to contact the *Orion*. Looking back, he saw the Rull glide into the clearing and head straight for the source of the vibration. As Jamieson paused involuntarily, fascinated, the main alarm system of the lifeboat went off with a roar. The sound echoed with an alien eeriness on the wings of the icy wind that was blowing, and it acted like a cue. His wrist radio snapped on, synchronizing automatically with the powerful radio in the lifeboat.

A voice said urgently, "Trevor Jamieson, this is the *Orion*. We heard your earlier calls but refrained from answering. An entire Rull fleet is cruising in the vicinity of the Laertes sun. In approximately five minutes, an attempt will be made to pick you up. Meanwhile, *drop everything.*"

Jamieson dropped. It was a physical movement, not a mental one. Out of the corner of one eye, even as he heard his own radio, he saw a movement in the sky: two dark blobs that resolved into vast shapes. There was a roar as the Rull super-battleships flashed by overhead. A cyclone followed their passage that nearly tore him from the ground, where he clung desperately to the roots of intertwining brush. At top speed, obviously traveling under gravitonic power, the enemy warships made a sweeping turn and came back toward the tableland. Jamieson expected death momentarily, but the fire flashed past; then the thunder of the released energies rolled toward him, a colossal sound, almost yet not quite submerging his awareness of what had happened. His lifeboat! They had fired at his lifeboat.

He groaned as he pictured it destroyed in one burst of intolerable flame. And then there was no time for thought of anguish.

A third warship came into view, but, as Jamieson strained to make out its contours, it turned and fled.

His wrist radio clicked on. "Cannot help you now. Save yourself. Our four accompanying battleships and attendant squadrons will engage the Rull fleet, and try to draw them toward our larger battle group cruising near the star, Bianca, and then re——"

A flash of fire in the distant sky ended the message. It was a full minute before the cold air of Laertes III echoed to the remote burst of the broadside. The sound died slowly, reluctantly, as if little overtones of it were clinging to each molecule of air. The silence that settled finally was, strangely, not peaceful, but a fateful, quiescent stillness, alive with unmeasurable threat.

Shakily, Jamieson climbed to his feet. It was time to assess the immediate danger that had befallen him. The greater danger he dared not even think about. He headed first for his lifeboat. He didn't have to go all the way. The entire section of the cliff had been sheared away. Of the ship, there was no sign. He had expected it, but the shock of the reality was numbing. He crouched like an animal and stared up into the sky. Not a movement was there, not a sound came out of it, except the sound of the east wind. He was alone in a universe between heaven and earth, a human being poised at the edge of an abyss.

Into his mind, tensely waiting, pierced a sharp understanding. The Rull ships had flown once over the mountain to size up the situation on the tableland and then had tried to destroy him. Equally disturbing and puzzling was the realization that battleships of the latest design were taking risks to defend his opponent on this isolated mountain.

He'd have to hurry. At any moment they might risk one of their destroyers in a rescue landing. As he ran, he felt himself one with the wind. He knew that feeling, that sense of returning primitiveness during moments of excitement. It was like that in battles, and the important thing was to yield one's whole body and soul to it. There was no such thing as fighting efficiently with half your mind or half your body. All was demanded.

He expected falls, and he had them. Each time he got up, almost unaware of the pain, and ran on again. He arrived bleeding, almost oblivious to a dozen cuts. And the sky remained silent.

From the shelter of a line of brush, he peered at the Rull. The captive Rull, *his* Rull to do with as he pleased. To watch, to force, to educate—the fastest education in the history of the world. There wasn't any time for a leisurely exchange of information. From where he lay, he manipulated the controls of the screen.

The Rull had been moving back and forth in front of the screen. Now it speeded up, then slowed, then speeded up again, according to his will.

Nearly a thousand years before, in the twentieth century, the classic and timeless investigation had been made of which this was one end result. A man called Pavlov fed a laboratory dog at regular intervals, to the accompaniment of the ringing of a bell. Soon the dog's digestive system responded as readily to the ringing of the bell without the food as to the food and the bell together. Pavlov himself did not, until late in his life, realize the most important reality behind his conditioning process. But what began on that remote day ended with a science that could brainwash animals and aliens—and men—almost at will. Only the Rulls baffled the master experimenters in the later centuries when it was an exact science. Defeated by the will to death of all the Rull captives, the scientists foresaw the doom of Earth's galactic empire unless some beginning could be made in penetrating the minds of Rulls. It was his desperate bad luck that he had no time for penetrations. There was death here for those who lingered.

But even the bare minimum of what he had to do would take time. Back and forth, back and forth; the rhythm of obedience had to be established. The image of the Rull on the screen was as lifelike as the original. It was three-dimensional, and its movements were like those of an automaton: Basic nerve centers were affected. The Rull could no more help falling into step than it could resist the call of the food impulse. After it had followed that mindless pattern for fifteen minutes, changing pace at his direction, Jamieson started the Rull and its image climbing trees. Up, then down again, half a dozen times. At that point, Jamieson introduced an image of himself.

Tensely, with one eye on the sky and one on the scene before him, he watched the reactions of the Rull. When, after a few minutes, he substituted himself for his image, he was satisfied that this Rull had temporarily lost its normal hate and suicide conditioning when it saw a human being.

Now that he had reached the stage of final control, he hesitated. It was time to make his tests. Could he afford the time? He realized that he had to. This opportunity might not occur again in a hundred years.

When he finished the tests twenty-five minutes later, he was pale with excitement. He thought, This is it. We've got it. He spent ten precious minutes broadcasting his discovery by means of his wrist radio—hoping that the transmitter on his lifeboat had survived its fall down the mountain—and was rebroadcasting the message out through subspace. There was not a single answer to his call, however, during the entire ten minutes.

Aware that he had done what he could, Jamieson headed for the cliff's edge he had selected as a starting point. He looked down and shuddered, then remembered what the *Orion* had said: "An entire Rull fleet cruising..."

Hurry!

He lowered the Rull to the first ledge. A moment later he fastened the harness around his own body and stepped into space. Sedately, with easy strength, the Rull gripped the other end of the rope and lowered him down to the ledge beside it. They continued on down and down. It was hard work although they used a very simple system. A long plastic line spanned the spaces for them. A metal climbing rod held position after position while the rope did its work.

On each ledge, Jamieson burned the rod at a downward slant into solid rock. The rope slid through an arrangement of pulleys in the metal as the Rull and he, in turn, lowered to ledges farther down. The moment they were both safely in the clear of one ledge, Jamieson would explode the rod out of the rock, and it would drop down ready for use again. The day sank toward darkness like a restless man into sleep. Jamieson's whole being filled with the melancholy of the fatigue that dragged at his muscles.

He could see that the Rull was growing more aware of him. It still co-operated, but it watched him with intent eyes each time it swung him down. The conditioned state was ending. The Rull was emerging from its trance. The process should be complete before night.

There was a time, then, when Jamieson despaired of getting down before the shadows fell. He had chosen the western, sunny side for that fantastic descent down a sheer, brown and black cliff like no other in the known worlds of space. He watched the Rull with quick, nervous glances during the moments when they were together on a ledge.

At 4:00 P.M. Jamieson had to pause again for a rest. He walked to the side of the ledge away from the Rull and sank down on a rock. The sky was silent and windless now, a curtain drawn across the black space above, concealing what must already be the greatest Rull-human battle in ten years. It was a tribute to the five Earth battleships that no Rull ship had yet attempted to rescue the Rull on the tableland. Possibly, of course, they didn't want to give away the presence of one of their own kind.

Jamieson gave up the futile speculation. Wearily, he compared the height of the cliff above with the depth that remained below. He estimated they had come two thirds of the distance. He saw that the Rull had turned to face the valley. Jamieson turned and gazed with it. The scene, even from this reduced elevation, was still spectacular. The forest began a quarter of a mile from the bottom of the cliff, and it almost literally had no end. It rolled up over the hills and down into the shallow valleys. It faltered at the edge of a broad river, then billowed out again, and climbed the slopes of mountains that sprawled mistily in distance.

Time to get going again. At twenty-five minutes after six, they reached a ledge a hundred and fifty feet above the uneven plain. The distance strained the capacity of the rope, but the initial operation of lowering the Rull to freedom and safety was achieved without incident. Jamieson gazed down curiously at the creature. What would it do now that it was in the clear?

It merely waited. Jamieson stiffened. He was not taking any such chance as that. He waved imperatively at the Rull and took out his blaster. The Rull backed away, but only into the safety of a group of rocks. Blood-red, the sun was sinking behind the mountains. Darkness moved over the land. Jamieson ate his dinner, and as he was finishing, he saw a movement below. He watched as the Rull glided along close to the foot of the precipice, until it disappeared beyond an outjut of the cliff.

Jamieson waited briefly, then swung out on the rope. The descent strained his strength, but there was solid ground at the bottom. Three quarters of the way down, he cut his finger on a section of the rope that was unexpectedly rough. When he reached the ground, he noticed that his finger was turning an odd gray. In the dimness, it looked strange and unhealthy. As he stared at it, the color drained from his face. He thought in bitter anger. The Rull must have smeared it on the rope on the way down.

A pang went through his body and was followed instantly by a feeling of rigidity. With a gasp, he clutched at his blaster, intending to kill himself. His hand froze in mid-air. He toppled stiffly, unable to break his fall. There was the shock of contact with the hard ground, then unconsciousness.

The will to death is in all life. Every organic cell ecphorizes the inherited engrams of its inorganic origin. The pulse of life is a squamous film superimposed on an underlying matter so intricate in its delicate balancing of different energies that life itself is but a brief, vain straining against that balance. For an instant of eternity a pattern is attempted. It takes many forms, but these are apparent. The real shape is always a time and not a space shape. And that shape is a curve. Up and then down. Up from darkness into the light, then down again into the blackness.

The male salmon sprays his mist of milt onto the eggs of the female. And instantly he is seized with a mortal melancholy. The male bee collapses from the embrace of the queen he has won, back into that inorganic mold from which he climbed for one single moment of ecstasy. In man, the fateful pattern is impressed time and again into numberless ephemeral cells, but only the pattern endures.

The sharp-minded Rull scientists, probing for chemical substances that would shock man's system into its primitive forms, had, long before, found the special secret of man's will to death.

The *yeli*, Meesh, gliding toward Jamieson, did not think of the process.

He had been waiting for the opportunity. It had occurred. Briskly, he removed the man's blaster; then he searched for the key to the lifeboat. Then he carried Jamieson a quarter of a mile around the base of the cliff to where the man's ship had been catapulted by the blast from the Rull warships. Five minutes later the powerful radio inside was broadcasting on Rull wave lengths an imperative command to the Rull fleet.

Dimness. Inside and outside his skin. Jamieson felt himself at the bottom of a well, peering out of night into twilight. As he lay, a pressure of something swelled around him, lifted him higher and higher, and nearer to the mouth of the well. He struggled the last few feet, a distinct mental effort, and looked over the edge. Consciousness.

He was lying on a raised table inside a room which had several large mouselike openings at the floor level, openings that led to other chambers. Doors, he identified, odd-shaped, alien, unhuman. Jamieson cringed with the stunning shock of recognition. He was inside a Rull warship.

He could not decide if the ship were in motion, but he guessed that it was. The Rull would not linger in the vicinity of a planet.

He was able to turn his head, and he saw that nothing material held him. Of such things he knew as much as any Rull, so in an instant he had located the source of gravitonic beams that interlaced across him.

The discovery was of abstract value, he realized bitterly. He began to nerve himself, then, for the kind of death that he could expect. Torture by experiment.

Nerving himself was a simple procedure. It had been discovered that if a man could contemplate every possible type of torture, and what he would do while it was occurring, and became angry rather than afraid, he could maintain himself to the very edge of death with a minimum of pain.

Jamieson was hurriedly cataloguing the types of torture he might receive when a plaintive voice said into his ear, "Let's go home, huh?"

It took a moment to recover; it took seconds to consider that the Ploian was probably invulnerable to energy blasts such as had been dealt his lifeboat by the Rull warship. And at least a minute went by before Jamieson said in a low voice, "I want you to do something for me."

"Of course."

"Go into that box over there and let the energy flow through you."

"Oh, goody. I've been wanting to go in there."

An instant later the electric source of the gravitonic beams was obviously rechanneled. For Jamieson was able to sit up. He moved hastily away from the box and called, "Come out."

It required several calls to attract the Ploian's attention. Then Jamieson asked, "Have you looked this ship over?"

"Yes," the Ploian replied.

"Is there a section through which all the electric energy is channeled?"

"Yes."

Jamieson drew a deep breath. "Go into it and let the energy flow through you. Then come back here."

"Oh, you're so good to me," the Ploian responded.

Jamieson took the precaution of hastily finding a nonmetallic object to stand on. He was barely in a safe position when a hundred thousand volts crackled from every metal plate.

"What now?" said the Ploian two minutes later.

"Look the ship over and see if any Rulls are alive."

Almost instantly, Jamieson was informed that about a hundred Rulls were still alive. From the reports of the Ploian, the survivors were already staying away from contact with metal surfaces. Jamieson accepted the information thoughtfully. Then he described the radio equipment to the Ploian, and finished, "Whenever anyone attempts to use this equipment, you go inside it and let the electricity flow through you—understand?"

The Ploian agreed to do this, and Jamieson added, "Report back to me periodically, but only at times when no one is trying to use the radio. And don't go into the main switchboard without my permission."

"Consider it done," the Ploian said.

Five minutes later the Ploian located Jamieson in the weapon room. "Somebody tried to use the radio just now; but he gave up finally, and went away."

"Fine," said Jamieson. "Keep watch—and listen—and join me as soon as I'm through here."

Jamieson proceeded on the positive assumption that he had one decisive advantage over the Rull survivors: he knew when it was safe to touch metal. They would have to rig up elaborate devices before they could dare move.

In the weapon control room he worked with energy cutting tools, hurriedly but effectively. His purpose: to make certain that the gigantic blasters could not be fired until the weapon control wiring was totally repaired.

That job done, he headed for the nearest lifeboat. The Ploian joined him as he was edging his way through an opening.

"There're some Rulls that way," the Ploian warned. "Better go this way."

They finally entered a Rull lifeboat without mishap. A few minutes later Jamieson launched the small craft, but five days went by before they were picked up.

The high Aaish of Yeell was not on the ship to which Jamieson had been taken as a captive. And so he was not among the dead, and, indeed, did not learn of the escape of the prisoner for some time. When the information was finally brought to him, his staff took it for granted that he would punish the Rull survivors of the wrecked battleship.

Instead, he said thoughtfully, "So that was the enemy? A very powerful being."

He silently considered the week of anguish he had endured. He had recovered almost all of his perceptive powers—so he was able to have a very unusual thought for an individual of his high estate.

He said, using the light-wave communicator, "I believe that this is the first time that a Prime Leader has visited the battlefront. Is this not correct?"

It was correct. A Super-General had come from rear headquarters to the "front lines." Top brass had come out of the sheltered and protected home planet and risked a skin so precious that all of Ria shuddered anxiously when the news was released.

The greatest Rull continued his speculations: "It would seem to me that we have not received the most accurate intelligence about human beings. There appears to have been an attempt to underestimate their abilities, and while I commend the zeal and courage of such attempts, my reaction is that this war is not likely to be successful in any decisive way. It is therefore my conclusion that the Central Council reexamine the motives for the continuation of the battle effort. I do not foresee an immediate disengagement, but it might well be that the fighting could gradually dissipate, as we assume a defensive position in this area of space, and perhaps turn our attention to other galaxies."

Far away, across light-years of space, Jamieson was reporting to an august body, the Galactic Convention:

"I feel that this was a Very Important Person among the Rulls; and, since I had him under complete hypnosis for some time, I think we should have a favorable reaction. I told him that the Rulls were underestimating human beings, and that the war would not be successful, and I suggested that they turn their attention to other galaxies."

Years were to pass before men would finally be certain that the Rull-human war was over. At the moment, the members of the convention were fascinated by the way in which a mind-reading baby ezwal had been used to contact an invisible Ploian; and of how this new ally had been the means of a human being escaping from a Rull battleship with such vital information as Jamieson had brought with him.

It was justification for all the hard years and patient effort that men had devoted to a policy of friendship with alien races. By an overwhelming majority the convention created for Jamieson a special position which would be called: Administrator of Races.

He would return to Carson's Planet as the ultimate alien authority, not only for ezwals, but as it turned out, the wording of his appointment was later interpreted to mean that he was Man's negotiator with the Rull.

While these matters developed, the galactic-wide Rull-human war ended.

James H. Schmitz

THE SECOND NIGHT
OF SUMMER

Although he lacked van Vogt's paranoid tension and ornately Byzantine plots, the late James H. Schmitz was considerably better at *people* than van Vogt was, crafting even his villains as complicated, psychologically complex, and non-stereotypical characters, full of surprising quirks and behaviors that you didn't see in a lot of other Space Adventure stuff. And his universes, although they come with their own share of monsters and sinister menaces, seem as if they would be more pleasant places in which to live than most Space Opera universes, places where you could have a viable, ordinary, and decent life once the plot was through requiring you to battle for existence against some Dread Implacable Monster; Schmitz even has sympathy for the *monsters,* who are often seen in the end not to be monsters at all, but rather creatures with agendas and priorities and points-of-view of their own, from which perspectives their actions are justified and some-times admirable—a tolerant attitude almost unique amidst the Space Adventure tales of the day, most of which were frothingly xenophobic.

Similarly, Schmitz was decades ahead of the curve in his portrayal of female characters—years before the Women's Movement of the '70s would come along to raise the consciousness of SF writers (or attempt to), Schmitz was not only fre-quently using women as the heroines in swashbuckling tales of interplanetary ad-venture—itself almost unheard of at the time—but he was also treating them as the total equal of the male characters, every bit as competent and brave and smart (and ruthless, when needs be), without saddling them with any of the "fe-male weaknesses"—like an inclination to faint or cower under extreme stress, and/or seek protection behind the muscular frame of the Tough Male Hero) that would mar the characterization of women by some writers for years to come. (The Schmitz Woman, for instance, is every bit as tough and competent as the Heinlein Woman—who, to be fair, isn't prone to fainting in a crisis either—but *without* her annoying tendency to think that nothing in the universe is as impor-tant as marrying Her Man and settling down to have as many babies as possible.) In the vivid and suspenseful story that follows, for instance, the hero of the piece is not only a woman, but an *old* woman, named Grandma Wannattel—a choice that most adventure writers wouldn't even make *now,* in 1998, let alone in 1950, which is when Schmitz made it!

The novel *The Witches of Karres* is usually thought of as Schmitz's best work, but I myself am fond of the "Vega" stories—one of which is "The Second Night of Summer"—which were collected in the book *Agent of Vega,* a book that is long out-of-print, alas, but one which—if you can find it—delivers as pure a jolt of Widescreen Space Opera Sense Of Wonder as can be found anywhere. Also atypically among writers of Space Adventure, Schmitz did most of his best work at short lengths, most of it for *Astounding* (and later for *Analog,* after the magazine had changed its name) and for *Galaxy,* including such memorable stories as "Grandpa," "Balanced Ecology," "Lion Loose . . .," "Greenface," "The Searcher," "The Winds of Time," "The Custodians," and dozens of others, plus a large number of stories about the adventures of a PSI-powered teenager, Telzey Amberdon. Schmitz's stories have been collected in *A Nice Day For Screaming and Other Tales of The Hub, A Pride of Monsters,* and, most recently, the posthumous collection *The Best of James H. Schmitz;* the "Telzey Amberdon" stories have been collected in *The Universe Against Her* and *The Telzey Toy.* Schmitz's other books include *The Demon Breed, A Tale of Two Clocks,* and *The Eternal Frontiers.*

Most of Schmitz's work is out-of-print, although copies of *The Witches of Karres* still show up in used bookstores with some frequency. Your best choice of sampling his work would probably be his most recent book, published in 1991, *The Best of James H. Schmitz,* which does contain several of his best stories—you could try ordering it from the publisher, NESFA Press (NESFA PRESS, P.O. Box 809, Framingham, MA 97101-0203; www.nesfa.org), although I have no idea whether they have any left in stock or not; the price *was* $18.95, but you'd better write first and ask for information.

On the night after the day that brought summer officially to the land of Wend, on the planet of Noorhut, the shining lights were seen again in the big hollow at the east end of Grimp's father's farm.

Grimp watched them for more than an hour from his upstairs room. The house was dark, but an occasional murmur of voices floated up to him through the windows below. Everyone in the farmhouse was looking at the lights.

On the other farms around and in the village, which was over a hill and another two miles up the valley, every living soul who could get within view of the hollow was probably doing the same. For a time, the agitated yelling of the Village Guardian's big pank-hound had sounded clearly over the hill, but he had quieted down then very suddenly—or had *been* quieted down, more likely, Grimp suspected. The Guardian was dead-set against anyone making a fuss about the lights—and that included the pank-hound, too.

There was some excuse for the pank-hound's excitement, though. From the window, Grimp could see there were a lot more lights tonight than had turned up in previous years—big, brilliant-blue bubbles, drifting and rising and falling silently all about the hollow. Sometimes one would lift straight up for several hundred feet, or move off over the edge of the hollow for about the same distance, and hang there suspended for a few minutes, before floating back to the others. That was as far as they ever went away from the hollow.

There was, in fact, no need for the Halpa detector-globes to go any farther than that to get the information wanted by those who had sent them out, and who were listening now to the steady flow of brief reports, in some Halpa equivalent of human speech-thought, coming back to them through the globes:

"No signs of hostile activity in the vicinity of the break-through point. No weapons or engines of power within range of detection. The area shows no significant alterations since the last investigation. Sharp curiosity among those who observe us consciously—traces of alarm and suspicion. But no overt hostility."

The reports streamed on without interruption, repeating the same bits of information automatically and incessantly, while the globes floated and dipped soundlessly above and about the hollow.

Grimp continued to watch them, blinking sleepily now and then, until a spreading glow over the edge of the valley announced that Noorhut's Big Moon was coming up slowly, like a Planetary Guardian, to make its own inspection of the lights. The globes began to dim out then, just as they always had done at moonrise in the preceding summers; and even before the top rim of the Big Moon's yellow disk edged over the hills, the hollow was completely dark.

Grimp heard his mother starting up the stairs. He got hurriedly into bed. The show was over for the night and he had a lot of pleasant things to think about before he went to sleep.

Now that the lights had showed up, his good friend Grandma Erisa Wannattel and her patent-medicine trailer were sure to arrive, too. Sometime late tomorrow afternoon, the big draft-trailer would come rolling up the valley road from the city. For that was what Grandma Wannattel had done the past four summers—ever since the lights first started appearing above the hollow for the few nights they were to be seen there each year. And since four years were exactly half of Grimp's whole life, that made Grandma's return a mathematical certainty for him.

Other people, of course, like the Village Guardian, might have a poor opinion of Grandma, but just hanging around her and the trailer and the gigantic, exotic-looking rhinocerine pony that pulled it was, in Grimp's opinion, a lot better even than going to the circus.

And vacations started the day after tomorrow! The whole future just now, in fact, looked like one good thing after another, extending through a vista of summery infinities.

Grimp went to sleep happily.

At about the same hour, though at a distance greater than Grimp's imagination had stretched as yet, eight large ships came individually out of the darkness between the stars that was their sea, and began to move about Noorhut in a carefully timed pattern of orbits. They stayed much too far out to permit any instrument of space-detection to suspect that Noorhut might be their common center of interest.

But that was what it was. Though the men who crewed the eight ships bore the people of Noorhut no ill will, hardly anything could have looked less promising for Noorhut than the cargo they had on board.

Seven of them were armed with a gas which was not often used any more. A highly volatile lethal catalyst, it sank to the solid surface of a world over which it was freed and spread out swiftly there to the point where its presence could no longer be detected by any chemical means. However, its effect of drawing the final breath almost imperceptibly out of all things that were oxygen-breathing was not noticeably reduced by diffusion.

The eighth ship was equipped with a brace of torpedoes, which were normally released some hours after the gas-carriers dispersed their invisible death. They were quite small torpedoes, since the only task remaining for them would be to ignite the surface of the planet that had been treated with the catalyst.

All those things might presently happen to Noorhut. But they would happen only if a specific message was flashed from it to the circling squadron—the message that Noorhut already was lost to a deadly foe who must, at any cost now, be prevented from spreading out from it to other inhabited worlds.

Next afternoon, right after school, as Grimp came expectantly around the bend of the road at the edge of the farm, he found the village policeman sitting there on a rock, gazing tearfully down the road.

"Hello, Runny," said Grimp, disturbed. Considered in the light of gossip he'd overheard in the village that morning, this didn't look so good for Grandma. It just didn't look good.

The policeman blew his nose on a handkerchief he carried tucked into the front of his uniform, wiped his eyes, and gave Grimp an annoyed glance.

"Don't *you* call me Runny, Grimp!" he said, replacing the handkerchief. Like Grimp himself and most of the people on Noorhut, the policeman was brown-skinned and dark-eyed, normally a rather good-looking young fellow. But his eyes were swollen and red-rimmed now; and his nose, which was a bit larger than average, anyway, was also red and swollen and undeniably runny. He had hay-fever bad.

Grimp apologized and sat down thoughtfully on the rock beside the policeman, who was one of his numerous cousins. He was about to mention that he had overheard Vellit using the expression when she and the policeman came through the big Leeth-flower orchard above the farm the other evening—at a much less leisurely rate than was their custom there. But he thought better of it. Vellit was the policeman's girl for most of the year, but she broke their engagement regularly during hay-fever season and called him cousin instead of dearest.

"What are you doing here?" Grimp asked bluntly instead.

"Waiting," said the policeman.

"For what?" said Grimp, with a sinking heart.

"Same individual you are, I guess," the policeman told him, hauling out the handkerchief again. He blew. "This year she's going to go right back where she came from or get pinched."

"Who says so?" scowled Grimp.

"The Guardian, that's who," said the policeman. "That good enough for you?"

"He can't do it!" Grimp said hotly. "It's our farm and she's got all her licenses."

"He's had a whole year to think up a new list she's got to have," the policeman informed him. He fished in the breastpocket of his uniform; pulled out a folded paper and opened it. "He put thirty-four items down here I got to check—she's bound to miss on one of them."

"It's a dirty trick!" said Grimp, rapidly scanning as much as he could see of the list.

"Let's us have more respect for the Village Guardian, Grimp!" the policeman said warningly.

"Uh-huh," muttered Grimp. "Sure . . ." If Runny would just move his big thumb out of the way. But what a list! Trailer; rhinocerine pony (beast, heavy draft, imported); patent medicines; household utensils; fortune-telling; pets; herbs; miracle-healing—

The policeman looked down, saw what Grimp was doing and raised the paper out of his line of vision. "That's an official document," he said, warding Grimp off with one hand and tucking the paper away with the other. "Let's us not get our dirty hands on it."

Grimp was thinking fast. Grandma Wannattel did have framed licenses for some of the items he'd read hanging around inside the trailer, but certainly not thirty-four of them.

"Remember that big skinless werret I caught last season?" he asked.

The policeman gave him a quick glance, looked away again and wiped his eyes thoughtfully. The season on werrets would open the following week and he was as ardent a fisherman as anyone in the village—and last summer Grimp's monster werret had broken a twelve-year record in the valley.

"Some people," Grimp said idly, staring down the valley road to the point where it turned into the woods, "would sneak after a person for days who's caught a big werret, hoping he'd be dumb enough to go back to that pool."

The policeman flushed and dabbed the handkerchief gingerly at his nose.

"Some people would even sit in a haystack and use spyglasses, even when the hay made them sneeze like crazy," continued Grimp quietly.

The policeman's flush deepened. He sneezed.

"But a person isn't that dumb," said Grimp. "Not when he knows there's anyway two werrets there six inches bigger than the one he caught."

"*Six inches?*" the policeman repeated a bit incredulously—eagerly.

"Easy," nodded Grimp. "I had a look at them again last week."

It was the policeman's turn to think. Grimp idly hauled out his slingshot, fished a pebble out of his small-pebble pocket and knocked the head off a flower twenty feet away. He yawned negligently.

"You're pretty good with that slingshot," the policeman remarked. "You must be just about as good as the culprit that used a slingshot to ring the fire-alarm signal on the defense unit bell from the top of the school house last week."

"That'd take a pretty good shot," Grimp admitted.

"And who then," continued the policeman, "dropped pepper in his trail, so the pank-hound near coughed off his head when we started to track him. The Guardian," he added significantly, "would like to have a clue about that culprit, all right."

"Sure, sure," said Grimp, bored. The policeman, the Guardian, and probably even the pank-hound, knew exactly who the culprit was; but they wouldn't be able to prove it in twenty thousand years. Runny just had to realize first that threats weren't going to get him anywhere near a record werret.

Apparently, he had; he was settling back for another bout of thinking. Grimp, interested in what he would produce next, decided just to leave him to it. . . .

Then Grimp jumped up suddenly from the rock.

"There they are!" he yelled, waving the slingshot.

A half-mile down the road, Grandma Wannattel's big, silvery trailer had come swaying out of the woods behind the rhinocerine pony and turned up toward the farm. The pony saw Grimp, lifted its head, which was as long as a tall man, and bawled a thunderous greeting. Grandma Wannattel stood up on the driver's seat and waved a green silk handkerchief.

Grimp started sprinting down the road.

The werrets should turn the trick—but he'd better get Grandma informed, just the same, about recent developments here, before she ran into Runny.

Grandma Wannattel flicked the pony's horny rear with the reins just before they reached the policeman, who was waiting at the side of the road with the Guardian's check-list unfolded in his hand.

The pony broke into a lumbering trot, and the trailer swept past Runny and up around the bend of the road, where it stopped well within the boundaries of the farm. They climbed down and Grandma quickly unhitched the pony. It waddled, grunting, off the road and down into the long, marshy meadow above the hollow. It stood still there, cooling its feet.

Grimp felt a little better. Getting the trailer off community property gave Grandma a technical advantage. Grimp's people had a favorable opinion of her, and they were a sturdy lot who enjoyed telling off the Guardian any time he didn't actually have a law to back up his orders. But on the way to the farm, she had confessed to Grimp that, just as he'd feared, she didn't have anything like thirty-four licenses. And now the policeman was coming up around the bend of the road after them, blowing his nose and frowning.

"Just let me handle him alone," Grandma told Grip out of the corner of her mouth.

He nodded and strolled off into the meadow to pass the time with the pony. She'd had a lot of experience in handling policemen.

"Well, well, young man," he heard her greeting his cousin behind him. "That looks like a bad cold you've got."

The policeman sneezed.

"Wish it were a cold," he said resignedly. "It's hay-fever. Can't do a thing with it. Now I've got a list here—"

"Hay-fever?" said Grandma. "Step up into the trailer a moment. We'll fix that."

"About this list—" began Runny, and stopped. "You think you got something that would fix it?" he asked skeptically. "I've been to I don't know how many doctors and they didn't help any."

"Doctors!" said Grandma. Grimp heard her heels click up the metal steps that led into the back of the trailer. "Come right in, won't take a moment."

"Well—" said Runny doubtfully, but he followed her inside.

Grimp winked at the pony. The first round went to Grandma.

"Hello, pony," he said.

His worries couldn't reduce his appreciation of Grandma's fabulous draft-animal. Partly, of course, it was just that it was such an enormous beast. The long, round barrel of its body rested on short legs with wide, flat feet which were settled deep in the meadow's mud by now. At one end was a spiky tail, and at the other a very big, wedge-shaped head, with a blunt, badly chipped horn set between nose and eyes. From nose to tail and all around, it was covered with thick, rectangular, horny plates, a mottled green-brown in color.

Grimp patted its rocky side affectionately. He loved the pony most for being the ugliest thing that had ever showed up on Noorhut. According to Grandma, she had bought it from a bankrupt circus which had imported it from a planet called Treebel; and Treebel was supposed to be a world full of hot swamps, inexhaustibly explosive volcanoes and sulphurous stenches.

One might have thought that after wandering around melting lava and under rainfalls of glowing ashes for most of its life, the pony would have considered Noorhut pretty tame. But though there wasn't much room for expression around the solid slab of bone supporting the horn, which was the front of its face, Grimp thought it looked thoroughly contented with its feet sunk out of sight in Noorhut's cool mud.

"You're a big fat pig!" he told it fondly.

The pony slobbered out a long, purple tongue and carefully parted his hair.

"Cut it out!" said Grimp. "Ugh!"

The pony snorted, pleased, curled its tongue about a huge clump of weeds, pulled them up and flipped them into its mouth, roots, mud and all. It began to chew.

Grimp glanced at the sun and turned anxiously to study the trailer. If she didn't get rid of Runny soon, they'd be calling him back to the house for supper before he and Grandma got around to having a good talk. And they weren't letting him out of doors these evenings, while the shining lights were here.

He gave the pony a parting whack, returned quietly to the road and sat down out of sight near the back door of the trailer, where he could hear what was going on.

". . . so about the only thing the Guardian could tack on you now," the policeman was saying, "would be a Public Menace charge. If there's any trouble about the lights this year, he's likely to try that. He's not a bad Guardian, you know, but he's got himself talked into thinking you're sort of to blame for the lights showing up here every year."

Grandma chuckled. "Well, I try to get here in time to see them every summer," she admitted. "I can see how that might give him the idea."

"And of course," said the policeman, "we're all trying to keep it quiet about them. If the news got out, we'd be having a lot of people coming here from the city, just to look. No one but the Guardian minds you being here, only you don't want a lot of city people tramping around your farms."

"Of course not," agreed Grandma. "And I certainly haven't told anyone about them myself."

"Last night," the policeman added, "everyone was saying there were twice as many lights this year as last summer. That's what got the Guardian so excited."

Chafing more every minute, Grimp had to listen then to an extended polite argument about how much Runny wanted to pay Grandma for her hay-fever medicines, while she insisted he didn't owe her anything at all. In the end, Grandma lost and the policeman paid up—much too much to take from any friend of Grimp's folks, Grandma protested to the last. And then, finally, that righteous minion of the law came climbing down the trailer steps again, with Grandma following him to the door.

"How do I look, Grimp?" he beamed cheerfully as Grimp stood up.

"Like you ought to wash your face sometime," Grimp said tactlessly, for he was fast losing patience with Runny. But then his eyes widened in surprise.

Under a coating of yellowish grease, Runny's nose seemed to have returned almost to the shape it had out of hay-fever season, and his eyelids were hardly puffed at all! Instead of flaming red, those features, furthermore, now were only a delicate pink in shade. Runny, in short, was almost handsome again.

"Pretty good, eh?" he said. "Just one shot did it. And I've only got to keep the salve on another hour. Isn't that right, Grandma?"

"That's right," smiled Grandma from the door, clinking Runny's money gently out of one hand into the other. "You'll be as good as new then."

"Permanent cure, too," said Runny. He patted Grimp benevolently on the head. "And next week we go werret-fishing, eh, Grimp?" he added greedily.

"I guess so," Grimp said, with a trace of coldness. It was his opinion that Runny could have been satisfied with the hay-fever cure and forgotten about the werrets.

"It's a date!" nodded Runny happily and took his greasy face whistling down the road. Grimp scowled after him, half-minded to reach for the slingshot then and there and let go with a medium stone at the lower rear of the uniform. But probably he'd better not.

"Well, that's that," Grandma said softly.

At that moment, up at the farmhouse, a cow horn went "Whoop-whoop!" across the valley.

"Darn," said Grimp. "I knew it was getting late, with him doing all that talking! Now they're calling me to supper." There were tears of disappointment in his eyes.

"Don't let it fuss you, Grimp," Grandma said consolingly. "Just jump up in here a moment and close your eyes."

Grimp jumped up into the trailer and closed his eyes expectantly.

"Put out your hands," Grandma's voice told him.

He put out his hands, and she pushed them together to form a cup. Then something small and light and furry dropped into them, caught hold of one of Grimp's thumbs, with tiny, cool fingers, and chittered.

Grimp's eyes popped open.

"It's a lortel!" he whispered, overwhelmed.

"It's for you!" Grandma beamed.

Grimp couldn't speak. The lortel looked at him from a tiny, black, human face with large blue eyes set in it, wrapped a long, furry tail twice around his wrist, clung to his thumb with its fingers, and grinned and squeaked.

"It's wonderful!" gasped Grimp. "Can you really teach them to talk?"

"Hello," said the lortel.

"That's all it can say so far," Grandma said. "But if you're patient with it, it'll learn more."

"I'll be patient," Grim promised, dazed. "I saw one at the circus this winter, down the valley at Laggand. They said it could talk, but it never said anything while I was there."

"Hello!" said the lortel.

"Hello!" gulped Grimp.

The cow horn whoop-whooped again.

"I guess you'd better run along to supper, or they might get mad," said Grandma.

"I know," said Grimp. "What does it eat?"

"Bugs and flowers and honey and fruit and eggs, when it's wild. But you just feed it whatever you eat yourself."

"Well, good-by," said Grimp. "And golly—thanks, Grandma."

He jumped out of the trailer. The lortel climbed out of his hand, ran up his arm and sat on his shoulder, wrapping its tail around his neck.

"It knows you already," Grandma said. "It won't run away."

Grimp reached up carefully with his other hand and patted the lortel.

"I'll be back early tomorrow," he said. "No school. . . . They won't let me out after supper as long as those lights keep coming around."

The cow horn whooped for the third time, very loudly. This time it meant business.

"Well, good-by," Grimp repeated hastily. He ran off, the lortel hanging on to his shirt collar and squeaking.

Grandma looked after him and then at the sun, which had just touched the tops of the hills with its lower rim.

"Might as well have some supper myself," she remarked, apparently to no one in particular. "But after that I'll have to run out the go-buggy and create a diversion."

Lying on its armor-plated belly down in the meadow, the pony swung its big head around toward her. Its small yellow eyes blinked questioningly.

"What makes you think a diversion will be required?" Its voice asked into her ear. The ability to produce such ventriloquial effects was one of the talents that made the pony well worth its considerable keep to Grandma.

"Weren't you listening?" she scolded. "That policeman told me the Guardian's planning to march the village's defense unit up to the hollow after supper, and start them shooting at the Halpa detector-globes as soon as they show up."

The pony swore an oath meaningless to anyone who hadn't been raised on the planet Treebel. It stood up, braced itself, and began pulling its feet out of the mud in a succession of loud, sucking noises.

"I haven't had an hour's straight rest since you talked me into tramping around with you eight years ago!" it complained.

"But you've certainly been seeing life, like I promised," Grandma smiled.

The pony slopped in a last, enormous tongueful of wet weeds. "That I have!" it said, with emphasis.

It came chewing up to the road.

"I'll keep a watch on things while you're having your supper," it told her.

As the uniformed twelve-man defense unit marched in good order out of the village, on its way to assume a strategic position around the hollow on Grimp's father's farm, there was a sudden, small explosion not very far off.

The Guardian, who was marching in the lead with a gun over his shoulder and the slavering pank-hound on a leash, stopped short. The unit broke ranks and crowded up behind him.

"What was that?" the Guardian inquired.

Everybody glanced questioningly around the rolling green slopes of the valley, already darkened with evening shadows. The pank-hound sat down before the Guardian, pointed its nose at the even darker shadows in the woods ahead of them and growled.

"Look!" a man said, pointing in the same direction.

A spark of bright green light had appeared on their path, just where it entered the woods. The spark grew rapidly in size, became as big as a human head—then bigger! Smoky green streamers seemed to be pouring out of it. . . .

"I'm going home right now," someone announced at that point, sensibly enough.

"Stand your ground!" the Guardian ordered, conscious of the beginnings of a general withdrawal movement behind him. He was an old soldier. He unslung his gun, cocked it and pointed it. The pank-hound got up on his six feet and bristled.

"Stop!" the Guardian shouted at the green light.

It expanded promptly to the size of a barrel, new streamers shooting out from it and fanning about like hungry tentacles.

He fired.

"*Run!*" everybody yelled then. The pank-hound slammed backward against the Guardian's legs, upsetting him, and streaked off after the retreating unit. The green light had spread outward jerkily into the shape of something like a many-armed, writhing starfish, almost the size of the trees about it. Deep, hooting sounds came out of it as it started drifting down the path toward the Guardian.

He got up on one knee and, in a single drumroll of sound, emptied all thirteen charges remaining in his gun into the middle of the starfish. It hooted more loudly, waved its arms more wildly, and continued to advance.

He stood up quickly then, slung the gun over his shoulder and joined the retreat. By the time the unit reached the first houses of the village, he was well up in the front ranks again. And a few minutes later, he was breathlessly organizing the local defenses, employing the tactics that had shown their worth in the raids of the Laggand Bandits nine years before.

The starfish, however, was making no attempt to follow up the valley people's rout. It was still on the path at the point where the Guardian had seen it last, waving its arms about and hooting menacingly at the silent trees.

"That should do it, I guess," Grandma Wannattel said. "Before the first projection fizzles out, the next one in the chain will start up where they can see it from the village. It ought to be past midnight before anyone starts bothering about the globes again. Particularly since there aren't going to be any globes around tonight—that is, if the Halpa attack-schedule has been correctly estimated."

"I wish we were safely past midnight right now," the rhinocerine pony worriedly informed her. Its dark shape stood a little up the road from the trailer, outlined motionlessly like a ponderous statue against the red evening sky. Its head was up; it looked as if it were listening. Which it was, in its own way—listening for any signs of activity from the hollow.

"No sense getting anxious about it," Grandma remarked. She was perched on a rock at the side of the road, a short distance from the pony, with a small black bag slung over her shoulder. "We'll wait here another hour till it's good and dark and then go down to the hollow. The breakthrough might begin a couple of hours after that."

"It *would* have to be us again!" grumbled the pony. In spite of its size, its temperament was on the nervous side. And while any companion of Zone Agent Wannattel was bound to run regularly into situations that were far from soothing, the pony couldn't recall any previous experience that had looked as extremely unsoothing as the prospects of the night-hours ahead. On far-off Vega's world of Jeltad, in the planning offices of the Department of Galactic Zones, the decision to put Noorhut at stake to win one round in mankind's grim war with the alien and mysterious Halpa might have seemed as distressing as it was unavoidable. But the pony couldn't help feeling that the distress would have become a little more acute if Grandma's distant employers had happened to be standing right here with the two of them while the critical hours approached.

"I'd feel a lot better myself if Headquarters hadn't picked us for this particular operation," Grandma admitted. "Us and Noorhut. . . ."

Because, by what was a rather singular coincidence, considering how things stood there tonight, the valley was also Grandma's home. She had been born, quite some while before, a hundred and eighty miles farther inland, at the foot of the dam of the great river Wend, which had given its name to the land, and nowadays supplied it with almost all its required power.

Erisa Wannattel had done a great deal of traveling since she first became aware of the fact that her varied abilities and adventuresome nature needed a different sort of task to absorb them than could be found on Noorhut, which was progressing placidly up into the final stages of a rounded and balanced planetary civilization. But she still liked to consider the Valley of the Wend as her home and headquarters, to which she returned as often as her work would permit. Her exact understanding of the way people there thought about things and did things also made them easy for her to manipulate; and on occasion that could be very useful.

In most other places, the means she had employed to turn the Guardian and his troop back from the hollow probably would have started a panic or brought armed ships and radiation guns zooming up for the kill within minutes. But the valley people had considered it just another local emergency. The bronze alarm bell in the village had pronounced a state of siege, and cow horns passed the word up to the outlying farms. Within minutes, the farmers were pelting down the roads to the village with their families and guns; and, very soon afterward, everything quieted down again. Guard lines had been set up by then, with the women and children quartered in the central buildings, while the armed men had settled down to watching Grandma's illusion projections—directional video narrow beams—from the discreet distance marked by the village boundaries.

If nothing else happened, the people would just stay there till morning and then start a cautious investigation. After seeing mysterious blue lights dancing harmlessly over Grimp's farm for four summers, this section of Wend was pretty well conditioned to fiery apparitions. But even if they got too adventurous, they couldn't hurt themselves on the projections, which were designed to be nothing but very effective visual displays.

What it all came to was that Grandma had everybody in the neighborhood rounded up and immobilized where she wanted them.

In every other respect, the valley presented an exceptionally peaceful twilight scene to the eye. There was nothing to show that it was the only present point of contact between forces engaged in what was probably a war of intergalactic proportions—a war made wraithlike but doubly deadly by the circumstance that, in over a thousand years, neither side had found out much more about the other than the merciless and devastating finality of its forms of attack. There never had been any actual battles between Mankind and the Halpa, only alternate and very thorough massacres—all of them, from Mankind's point of view, on the wrong side of the fence.

The Halpa alone had the knowledge that enabled them to reach their human adversary. That was the trouble. But, apparently, they could launch their attacks only by a supreme effort, under conditions that existed for periods of less than a score of years, and about three hundred years apart as Mankind measured time.

It was hard to find any good in them, other than the virtue of persistence. Every three hundred years, they punctually utilized that brief period to execute one more thrust, carefully prepared and placed, and carried out with a dreadfully complete abruptness, against some new point of human civilization—and this time the attack was going to come through on Noorhut.

"Something's starting to move around in that hollow!" the pony announced suddenly. "It's not one of their globe-detectors."

"I know," murmured Grandma. "That's the first of the Halpa themselves. They're going to be right on schedule, it seems. But don't get nervous. They can't hurt anything until their transmitter comes through and revives them. We've got to be particularly careful now not to frighten them off. They seem to be even more sensitive to emotional tensions in their immediate surroundings than the globes."

The pony made no reply. It knew what was at stake and why eight big ships were circling Noorhut somewhere beyond space-detection tonight. It knew, too, that the ships would act only if it was discovered that Grandma had failed. But—

The pony shook its head uneasily. The people on Treebel had never become civilized to the point of considering the possibility of taking calculated risks on a planetary scale—not to mention the fact that the lives of the pony and of Grandma were included in the present calculation. In the eight years it had been accompanying her on her travels, it had developed a tremendous respect for Erisa Wannattel's judgment and prowess. But, just the same, frightening the Halpa off, if it still could be done, seemed like a very sound idea right now to the pony.

As a matter of fact, as Grandma well knew, it probably could have been done at this stage by tossing a small firecracker into the hollow. Until they had established their planetary foothold, the Halpa took extreme precautions. They could spot things in the class of radiation weapons a hundred miles away, and either that or any suggestion of local aggressiveness or of long-range observation would check the invasion attempt on Noorhut then and there.

But one of the principal reasons she was here tonight was to see that nothing *did* happen to stop it. For this assault would only be diverted against some other world then, and quite probably against one where the significance of the spying detector-globes wouldn't be understood before it was too late. The best information system in the Galaxy couldn't keep more than an insignificant fraction of its population on the alert for dangers like that—

She bounced suddenly to her feet and, at the same instant, the pony swung away from the hollow toward which it had been staring. They both stood for a moment then, turning their heads about, like baffled hounds trying to fix a scent on the wind.

"It's Grimp!" Grandma exclaimed.

The rhinocerine pony snorted faintly. "Those are his thought images, all right," it agreed. "He seems to feel you need protection. Can you locate him?"

"Not yet," said Grandma anxiously. "Yes, I can. He's coming up through the woods on the other side of the hollow, off to the left. The little devil!" She was hustling back to the trailer. "Come on, I'll have to ride you there. I can't even dare use the go-buggy this late in the day."

The pony crouched beside the trailer while she quickly snapped on its saddle from the top of the back steps. Six metal rings had been welded into the horny plates of its back for this purpose, so it was a simple job. Grandma clambered aloft, hanging onto the saddle's hand-rails.

"Swing wide of the hollow!" she warned. "This could spoil everything. But make all the noise you want. The Halpa don't care about noise as such—it has to have emotional content before they get interested—and the quicker Grimp spots us, the easier it will be to find him."

The pony already was rushing down into the meadow at an amazing rate of speed—it took a lot of very efficient muscle to drive as heavy a body as that through the gluey swamps of Treebel. It swung wide of the hollow and of what it contained, crossed a shallow bog farther down the meadow with a sound like a charging torpedo-boat, and reached the woods.

It had to slow down then, to avoid brushing off Grandma.

"Grimp's down that slope somewhere," Grandma said. "He's heard us."

"They're making a lot of noise!" Grimp's thought reached them suddenly and clearly. He seemed to be talking to someone. "But we're not scared of them, are we?"

"Bang-bang!" another thought-voice came excitedly.

"It's the lortel," Grandma and the pony said together.

"That's the stuff!" Grimp resumed approvingly. "We'll sling-shoot them all if they don't watch out. But we'd better find Grandma soon."

"Grimp!" shouted Grandma. The pony backed her up with a roaring call.

"Hello?" came the lortel's thought.

"Wasn't that the pony?" asked Grimp. "All right—let's go that way."

"Here we come, Grimp!" Grandma shouted as the pony descended the steep side of a ravine with the straightforward technique of a rockslide.

"That's Grandma!" thought Grimp. "Grandma!" he yelled. "Look out! There's monsters all around!"

"What you missed!" yelled Grimp, dancing around the pony as Grandma Wannattel scrambled down from the saddle. "There's monsters all around the village and the Guardian killed one and I slingshot another till he fizzled out and I was coming to find you—"

"Your mother will be worried!" began Grandma as they rushed into each other's arms.

"No," grinned Grimp. "All the kids are supposed to be sleeping in the school house and she won't look there till morning and the schoolteacher said the monsters were all"—he slowed down cautiously—"ho-lucy-nations. But he wouldn't go look when the Guardian said they'd show him one. He stayed right in bed. But the Guardian's all right—he killed one and I slingshot another and the lortel learned a new word. Say 'bang-bang,' lortel!" he invited.

"Hello!" squeaked the lortel.

"Aw," said Grimp disappointedly. "He can say it, though. And I've come to take you to the village so the monsters don't get you. Hello, pony!"

"Bang-bang," said the lortel, distinctly.

"See?" cried Grimp. "He isn't scared at all—he's a real brave lortel! If we see some monsters don't you get scared either, because I've got my slingshot," he said, waving it blood-thirstily, "and two back pockets still full of medium stones. The way to do it is to kill them all!"

"It sounds like a pretty good idea, Grimp," Grandma agreed. "But you're awfully tired now."

"No, I'm not!" Grimp said surprised. His right eye sagged shut and then his left; and he opened them both with an effort and looked at Grandma.

"That's right," he admitted. "I am . . ."

"In fact," said Grandma, "you're asleep!"

"No, I'm n———" objected Grimp. Then he sagged toward the ground, and Grandma caught him.

"In a way I hate to do it," she panted, wrestling him aboard the pony which had lain down and flattened itself as much as it could to make it easier. "He'd probably enjoy it. But we can't take a chance. He's a husky little devil, too," she groaned, giving a final boost, "and those ammunition pockets don't make him any lighter!" She clambered up again herself and noticed that the lortel had transferred itself to her coat collar.

The pony stood up cautiously.

"Now what?" it said.

"Might as well go straight to the hollow," said Grandma, breathing hard. "We'll probably have to wait around there a few hours, but if we're careful it won't do any harm."

"Did you find a good deep pond?" Grandma asked the pony a little later, as it came squishing up softly through the meadow behind her to join her at the edge of the hollow.

"Yes," said the pony. "About a hundred yards back. That should be close enough. How much more waiting do you think we'll have to do?"

Grandma shrugged carefully. She was sitting in the grass with what, by daylight, would have been a good view of the hollow below. Grimp was asleep with his head on her knees; and the lortel, after catching a few bugs in the grass and eating them, had settled down on her shoulder and dozed off too.

"I don't know," she said. "It's still three hours till Big Moonrise, and it's bound to be some time before then. Now you've found a waterhole, we'll just stay here together and wait. The one thing to remember is not to let yourself start getting excited about them."

The pony stood huge and chunky beside her, its forefeet on the edge of the hollow, staring down. Muddy water trickled from its knobby flanks. It had brought the warm mud-smells of a summer pond back with it to hang in a cloud about them.

There was vague, dark, continuous motion at the bottom of the hollow. A barely noticeable stirring in the single big pool of darkness that filled it.

"If I were alone," the pony said, "I'd get out of here! I know when I ought to be scared. But you've taken psychological control of my reactions, haven't you?"

"Yes," said Grandma. "It'll be easier for me, though, if you help along as much as you can. There's really no danger until their transmitter has come through."

"Unless," said the pony, "they've worked out some brand-new tricks in the past few hundred years."

"There's that," Grandma admitted. "But they've never tried changing their tricks on us yet. If it were us doing the attacking, we'd vary our methods each time, as much as we could. But the Halpa don't seem to think just like we do about anything. They wouldn't still be so careful if they didn't realize they were very vulnerable at this point."

"I hope they're right about that!" the pony said briefly.

Its head moved then, following the motion of something that sailed flutteringly out of the depths of the hollow, circled along its far rim, and descended again. The inhabitants of Treebel had a much deeper range of dark-vision than Grandma Wannattel, but she was also aware of that shape.

"They're not much to look at," the pony remarked. "Like a big, dark rag of leather, mostly."

"Their physical structure is believed to be quite simple," Grandma agreed slowly. The pony was tensing up again, and it was best to go on talking to it, about almost anything at all. That always helped, even though the pony knew her much too well by now to be really fooled by such tricks.

"Many very efficient life-forms aren't physically complicated, you know," she went on, letting the sound of her voice ripple steadily into its mind. "Parasitical types, particularly. It's pretty certain, too, that the Halpa have the hive-mind class of intelligence, so what goes for the nerve-systems of most of the ones they send through to us might be nothing much more than secondary reflex-transmitters. . . ."

Grimp stirred in his sleep at that point and grumbled. Grandma looked down at him. "You're sound asleep!" she told him severely, and he was again.

"You've got plans for that boy, haven't you?" the pony said, without shifting its gaze from the hollow.

"I've had my eye on him," Grandma admitted, "and I've already recommended him to Headquarters for observation. But I'm not going to make up my mind about Grimp till next summer, when we've had more time to study him. Meanwhile, we'll see what he picks up naturally from the lortel in the way of telepathic communication and sensory extensions. I think Grimp's the kind we can use."

"He's all right," the pony agreed absently. "A bit murderous, though, like most of you. . . ."

"He'll grow out of it!" Grandma said, a little annoyedly, for the subject of human aggressiveness was one she and the pony argued about frequently. "You can't hurry developments like that along too much. All of Noorhut should grow out of that stage, as a people, in another few hundred years. They're about at the turning-point right now—"

Their heads came up together, then, as something very much like a big, dark rag of leather came fluttering up from the hollow and hung in the dark air above them. The representatives of the opposing powers that were meeting on Noorhut that night took quiet stock of one another for a moment.

The Halpa was about six foot long and two wide, and considerably less than an inch thick. It held its position in the air with a steady, rippling motion, like a bat the size of a man. Then, suddenly, it extended itself with a snap, growing taut as a curved sail.

The pony snorted involuntarily. The apparently featureless shape in the air turned towards it and drifted a few inches closer. When nothing more happened, it turned again and fluttered quietly back down into the hollow.

"Could it tell I was scared?" the pony asked uneasily.

"You reacted just right," Grandma said soothingly. "Startled suspicion at first, and then just curiosity, and then another start when it made that jump. It's about what they'd expect from creatures that would be hanging around the hollow now. We're like cows to them. They can't tell what things are by their looks, like we do—"

But her tone was thoughtful, and she was more shaken than she would have cared to let the pony notice. There had been something indescribably menacing and self-assured in the Halpa's gesture. Almost certainly, it had only been trying to draw a reaction of hostile intelligence from them, probing, perhaps, for the presence of weapons that might be dangerous to its kind.

But there was a chance—a tiny but appalling chance—that the things *had* developed some drastically new form of attack since their last breakthrough, and that they already were in control of the situation. . . .

In which case, neither Grimp nor anyone else on Noorhut would be doing any more growing-up after tomorrow.

Each of the eleven hundred and seventeen planets that had been lost to the Halpa so far still traced a fiery, forbidding orbit through space—torn back from the invaders only at the cost of depriving it, by humanity's own weapons, of the conditions any known form of life could tolerate.

The possibility that this might also be Noorhut's future had loomed as an ugly enormity before her for the past four years. But of the nearly half a hundred worlds which the Halpa were found to be investigating through their detector-globes as possible invasion points for this period, Noorhut finally had been selected by Headquarters as the one where local conditions were most suited to meet them successfully. And that meant in a manner which must include the destruction of their only real invasion weapon, the fabulous and mysterious Halpa transmitter. Capable as they undoubtedly were, they had shown in the past that they were able or willing to employ only one of those instruments for each period of attack. Destroying the transmitter meant therefore that humanity would gain a few more centuries to figure out a way to get back at the Halpa before a new attempt was made.

So on all planets but Noorhut the detector-globes had been encouraged carefully to send back reports of a dangerously alert and well-armed population. On Noorhut, however, they had been soothed along . . . and just as her home-planet had been chosen as the most favorable point of encounter, so was Erisa Wannattel herself selected as the agent most suited to represent humanity's forces under the conditions that existed there.

Grandma sighed gently and reminded herself again that Headquarters was as unlikely to miscalculate the overall probability of success as it was to select the wrong person to achieve it. There was only the tiniest, the most theoretical, of chances that something might go wrong and that she would end her long career with the blundering murder of her own home-world.

But there was that chance.

"There seem to be more down there every minute!" the pony was saying.

Grandma drew a deep breath.

"Must be several thousand by now," she acknowledged. "It's getting near breakthrough time, all right, but those are only the advance forces." She added, "Do you notice anything like a glow of light down there, towards the center?"

The pony stared a moment. "Yes," it said. "But I would have thought that was way under the red for you. Can you see it?"

"No," said Grandma. "I get a kind of feeling, like heat. That's the transmitter beginning to come through. I think we've got them!"

The pony shifted its bulk slowly from side to side.

"Yes," it said resignedly, "or they've got us."

"Don't think about that," Grandma ordered sharply and clamped one more mental lock shut on the foggy, dark terrors that were curling and writhing under her conscious thoughts, threatening to emerge at the last moment and paralyze her actions.

She had opened her black bag and was unhurriedly fitting together something composed of a few pieces of wood and wire, and a rather heavy, stiff spring. . . .

"Just be ready," she added.

"I've been ready for an hour," said the pony, shuffling its feet unhappily.

They did no more talking after that. All the valley had become quiet about them. But slowly the hollow below was filling up with a black, stirring, slithering tide. Bits of it fluttered up now and then like strips of black smoke, hovered a few yards above the mass and settled again.

Suddenly, down in the center of the hollow, there was something else.

The pony had seen it first, Grandma Wannattel realized. It was staring in that direction for almost a minute before she grew able to distinguish something that might have been a group of graceful miniatures spires. Semi-transparent in the darkness, four small domes showed at the corners, with a larger one in the center. The central one was about twenty feet high and very slender.

The whole structure began to solidify swiftly. . . .

The Halpa Transmitter's appearance of crystalline slightness was perhaps the most mind-chilling thing about it. For it brought instantly a jarring sense of what must be black distance beyond all distances, reaching back unimaginably to its place of origin. In that unknown somewhere, a prodigiously talented and determined race of beings had labored for human centuries to prepare and point some stupendous gun . . . and were able then to bridge the vast interval with nothing more substantial than this dark sliver of glass that had come to rest suddenly in the valley of the Wend.

But, of course, the Transmitter was all that was needed; its deadly poison lay in a sluggish, almost inert mass about it. Within minutes from now, it would waken to life, as similar transmitters had wakened on other nights on those lost and burning worlds. And in much less than minutes after that, the Halpa invaders would be hurled by their slender machine to every surface section of Noorhut—no longer inert, but quickened into a ravening, almost indestructible form of vampiric life, dividing and sub-dividing in its incredibly swift cycle of reproduction, fastening to feed anew, growing and dividing again—

Spreading, at that stage, much more swiftly than it could be exterminated by anything but the ultimate weapons!

The pony stirred suddenly, and she felt the wave of panic roll up in it.

"It's the Transmitter, all right," Grandma's thought reached it quickly. "We've had two descriptions of it before. But we can't be sure it's *here* until it begins to charge itself. Then it lights up—first at the edges, and then at the center. Five seconds after the central spire lights up, it will be energized too much to let them pull it back again. At least, they couldn't pull it back after that, the last time they were observed. And then we'd better be ready—"

The pony had been told all that before. But as it listened it was quieting down again.

"And you're going to go on sleeping!" Grandma Wannattel's thought told Grimp next. "No matter what you hear or what happens, you'll sleep on and know nothing at all any more until I wake you up. . . ."

Light surged up suddenly in the Transmitter—first into the four outer spires, and an instant later into the big central one, in a sullen red glow. It lit the hollow with a smoky glare. The pony took two startled steps backwards.

"Five seconds to go!" whispered Grandma's thought. She reached into her black bag again and took out a small plastic ball. It reflected the light from the hollow in dull crimson gleamings. She let it slip down carefully inside the shaftlike frame of the gadget she had put together of wood and wire. It clicked into place there against one end of the compressed spring.

Down below, they lay now in a blanket fifteen feet thick over the wet ground, like big, black, water-sogged leaves swept up in circular piles about the edges of the hollow. The tops and sides of the piles were stirring and shivering and beginning to slide down toward the Transmitter.

". . . five, and go!" Grandma said aloud. She raised the wooden catapult to her shoulder.

The pony shook its blunt-horned head violently from side to side, made a strangled, bawling sound, surged forward and plunged down the steep side of the hollow in a thundering rush.

Grandma aimed carefully and let go.

The blanket of dead-leaf things was lifting into the air ahead of the pony's ground-shaking approach in a weightless, silent swirl of darkness which instantly blotted both the glowing Transmitter and the pony's shape from sight. The pony roared once as the blackness closed over it. A second later, there was a crash like the shattering of a hundred-foot mirror—and at approximately the same moment, Grandma's plastic ball exploded somewhere in the center of the swirling swarm.

Cascading fountains of white fire filled the whole of the hollow. Within the fire, a dense mass of shapes fluttered and writhed frenziedly like burning rags. From down where the fire boiled fiercest rose continued sounds of brittle substances suffering enormous violence. The pony was trampling the ruined Transmitter, making sure of its destruction.

"Better get out of it!" Grandma shouted anxiously. "What's left of that will all melt now anyway!"

She didn't know whether it heard her or not. But a few seconds later, it came pounding up the side of the hollow again. Blazing from nose to rump, it tramped past Grandma, plunged through the meadow behind her, shedding white sheets of fire that exploded the marsh grass in its tracks, and hurled itself headlong into the pond it had selected previously. There was a great splash, accompanied by sharp hissing noises. Pond and pony vanished together under billowing clouds of steam.

"That was pretty hot!" its thought came to Grandma.

She drew a deep breath.

"Hot as anything that ever came out of a volcano!" she affirmed. "If you'd played around in it much longer, you'd have fixed up the village with roasts for a year."

"I'll just stay here for a while, till I've cooled off a bit," said the pony.

Grandma found something strangling her then, and discovered it was the lortel's tail. She unwound it carefully. But the lortel promptly reanchored itself with all four hands in her hair. She decided to leave it there. It seemed badly upset.

Grimp, however, slept on. It was going to take a little maneuvering to get him back into the village undetected before morning, but she would figure that out by and by. A steady flow of cool night-air was being drawn past them into the hollow now and rising out of it again in boiling, vertical columns of invisible heat. At the bottom of the deluxe blaze she'd lit down there, things still seemed to be moving about—but very slowly. The Halpa were tough organisms, all right, though not nearly so tough, when you heated them up with a really good incendiary, as were the natives of Treebel.

She would have to make a final check of the hollow around dawn, of course, when the ground should have cooled off enough to permit it—but her century's phase of the Halpa War did seem to be over. The defensive part of it, at any rate—

Wet, munching sounds from the pond indicated the pony felt comfortable enough by now to take an interest in the parboiled vegetation it found floating around it. Everything had turned out all right.

So she settled down carefully on her back in the long marsh grass without disturbing Grimp's position too much, and just let herself faint for a while.

• • •

By sunrise, Grandma Wannattel's patent-medicine trailer was nine miles from the village and rolling steadily southwards up the valley road through the woods. As usual, she was departing under a cloud.

Grimp and the policeman had showed up early to warn her. The Guardian was making use of the night's various unprecedented disturbances to press through a vote on a Public Menace charge against Grandma in the village; and since everybody still felt rather excited and upset, he had a good chance just now of getting a majority.

Grimp had accompanied her far enough to explain that this state of affairs wasn't going to be permanent. He had it all worked out.

Runny's new immunity to hay-fever had brought him and the pretty Vellit to a fresh understanding overnight; they were going to get married five weeks from now. As a married man, Runny would then be eligible for the post of Village Guardian at the harvest elections—and between Grimp's cousins and Vellit's cousins, Runny's backers would just about control the vote. So when Grandma got around to visiting the valley again next summer, she needn't worry any more about police interference or official disapproval. . . .

Grandma had nodded approvingly. That was about the kind of neighborhood politics she'd begun to play herself at Grimp's age. She was pretty sure by now that Grimp was the one who eventually would become her successor, and the guardian not only of Noorhut and the star-system to which Noorhut belonged, but of a good many other star-systems besides. With careful schooling, he ought to be just about ready for the job by the time she was willing, finally, to retire.

An hour after he had started back to the farm, looking suddenly a little forlorn, the trailer swung off the valley road into a narrow forest path. Here the pony lengthened its stride, and less than five minutes later they entered a curving ravine, at the far end of which lay something that Grimp would have recognized instantly, from his one visit to the nearest port city, as a small spaceship.

A large round lock opened soundlessly in its side as they approached. The pony came to a stop. Grandma got down from the driver's seat and unhitched it. The pony walked into the lock, and the trailer picked its wheels off the ground and floated in after it. Grandma Wannattel walked in last, and the lock closed quietly on her heels.

The ship lay still a moment longer. Then it was suddenly gone. Dead leaves went dancing for a while about the ravine, disturbed by the breeze of its departure.

In a place very far away—so far that neither Grimp nor his parents nor anyone in the village except the schoolteacher had ever heard of it—a set of instruments began signalling for attention. Somebody answered them.

Grandma's voice announced distinctly:

"This is Zone Agent Wannattel's report of the successful conclusion of the Halpa operation on Noorhut—"

High above Noorhut's skies, eight great ships swung instantly out of their watchful orbits about the planet and flashed off again into the blackness of the boundless space that was their sea and their home.

L. Sprague de Camp

THE GALTON WHISTLE

L. Sprague de Camp is a seminal figure, one whose career spans almost the entire development of modern SF and fantasy. Much of the luster of the "Golden Age" of *Astounding* during the late '30s and the '40s is due to the presence in those pages of de Camp, along with his great contemporaries Robert A. Heinlein, Theodore Sturgeon, and A. E. van Vogt. At the same time, for *Astounding*'s sister fantasy magazine, *Unknown,* he helped to create a whole new modern style of fantasy writing—funny, whimsical, and irreverent—of which he is still the most prominent practitioner. (De Camp's stories for *Unknown* are among the best short fantasies ever written, and include such classics as "The Wheels of If," "Nothing in the Rules," "The Hardwood Pile," and—written in collaboration with Fletcher Pratt—the famous "Harold Shea" stories that would later be collected as *The Complete Enchanter*.) In science fiction, he is the author of *Lest Darkness Fall,* in my opinion one of the three or four best Alternate Worlds novels ever written (it was reprinted in 1996, by Baen Books, bound in a package with David Drake's *To Bring the Light*), as well as the at-the-time highly controversial novel (although it now looks rather tame) *Rogue Queen,* and a body of expertly-crafted short fiction such as "Judgment Day," "Divide and Rule," "A Gun for Dinosaur," and "Aristotle and the Gun."

De Camp may be primarily known today as a humorist, perhaps best remembered for the *Unknown* stories and the "Howard Shea" saga, but everything he writes has a strong element of fast-paced adventure to it—just as even the most headlong and swashbuckling of his adventure tales contains a generous portion of wry humor. His greatest contribution to the evolution of the Space Opera is the "Viagens Interplanetarias"—which means "interplanetary tours" in Portuguese, the language of the dominant political and economic power of de Camp's future Earth, Brazil—sequence of stories and novels (sometimes also referred to as the "Krishna" series, after the name of the alien planet on which many of them take place), detailing the intricate and sometimes contentious interrelations that develop between Earthmen and the intelligent native species who inhabit the nearby regions of space. Intelligence is a quality that suffuses every de Camp story, just as surely as does humor—de Camp's Space Opera is just *smarter* than that of most of his contemporaries: you can see that a very shrewd mind is working out the background details and structure of what such an interstellar society would be like, and the consequences that would inevitably result, insisting on logic, rigor, and consistency even within the framework of the Interplanetary Swashbuckler (there's no such thing as Faster Than Light travel in the Viagens universe, for instance—and *that* generates some inevitable and surprising consequences that few other authors writing a Space Adventure tale would have bothered to deal with . . .). The intelligence of the conceptualization that went into the background of the Viagens stories shows up everywhere, not least in de Camp's prediction that Brazil would be the dominant power on Earth by the middle of the 21st Century, the old superpowers having by then exhausted and bankrupted themselves—a prediction considered to be wild and extravagantly unlikely when de Camp made it back in the '50s, but one which seems increasingly credible these days, and one which makes the Viagens stories still look remarkably contemporary, in spite of being almost half a century old. Nor, in spite of all the intellectual rigor that went into them, are they the least bit solemn or slow—instead, they remain among the most colorful and vivid stories of Interplanetary Adventure ever written: as the sly and suspenseful story that follows will amply demonstrate.

The Viagens Interplanetarias stories were assembled in the landmark collection *The Continent Makers and Other Tales of the Viagens* (long out of print, alas, but it can be found in many libraries). The Viagens or "Krishna" novels, some of them recently re-issued, include *The Hand of Zei, The Tower of Zanid, The Queen of Zamba, The Virgin of Zesh, The Prisoner of Zhamanak,* and *The Hostage of Zir.* The single best of these novels, in my opinion, is *The Hand of Zei,* which makes a good entry-point into the series, and which is still often findable in secondhand bookstores. De Camp has continued to produce an occasional "Krishna" novel well into the '90s, the most recent of which are *The Bones of Zora, The Stones of Nomuru,* and *The Swords of Zinjahan,* all written in collaboration with his wife, Catherine Crook de Camp.

De Camp's other books include *The Glory That Was, The Great Fetish,* and *The Reluctant King;* with Fletcher Pratt, in addition to the "Harold Shea" books, *The Carnelian Cube, The Land of Unreason,* and the collection *Tales from Gavagan's Bar;* with Catherine Crook de Camp, in addition to their collaborative "Krishna" novels, *The Incorporated Knight* and *The Pixilated Peeress;* de Camp has also written a number of "Conan" novels in posthumous collaboration with the late Robert E. Howard. He has also written a long sequence of critically-acclaimed historical novels, including *The Bronze God of Rhodes, An Elephant for Aristotle, The Dragon of the Ishtar Gate,* and *The Arrows of Hercules,* as well as a number of nonfiction books on scientific and technical topics, literary biographies such as his painstaking examination of the life of H. P. Lovecraft, *Lovecraft: A Biography,* and *Dark Valley Destiny: The Life of Robert E. Howard,* and critical/biographical studies of fantasy and fantasy writers such as *Literary Swordsmen and Sorcerers.* As editor, his anthologies include *Swords & Sorcery, The Spell of Seven, The Fantastic Swordsmen,* and *Warlocks and Warriors.* His short fiction has been collected in *The Best of L. Sprague de Camp, A Gun for Dinosaur, The Purple Pterodactyls,* and *Rivers in Time.* De Camp has won the Grandmaster Nebula Award, and the Gandalf or Grandmaster of Fantasy Award, as well as the prestigious Life Achievement Award given by the World Fantasy Convention. In 1997, he won a Hugo Award for his autobiography, *Time and Change*. He and his wife live in Texas.

Adrian Frome regained consciousness to the sound of harsh Dzlieri consonants. When he tried to move, he found he was tied to a tree by creepers, and that the Vishnuvan centaurs were cavorting around him, fingering weapons and gloating.

"I think," said one, "that if we skinned him carefully and rolled him in salt . . ."

Another said: "Let us rather open his belly and draw forth his guts little by little. Flaying is too uncertain; Earthmen often die before one is half done."

Frome saw that his fellow-surveyors had indeed gone, leaving nothing but two dead zebras (out of the six they had started out with) and some smashed apparatus. His head ached abominably. Quinlan must have conked him from behind while Hayataka was unconscious, and then packed up and shoved off, taking his wounded chief but leaving Frome.

The Dzlieri yelled at one another until one said: "A pox on your fancy slow deaths! Let us stand off and shoot him, thus ridding ourselves of him and bettering our aim at once. Archers first. What say you?"

The last proposal carried. They spread out as far as the dense vegetation allowed.

The Dzlieri were not literally centaurs in the sense of looking like handsome Greek statues. If you imagine the front half of a gorilla mounted on the body of a tapir you will have a rough idea of their looks. They had large mobile ears, a caricature of a human face covered with red fur, four-fingered hands, and a tufted tail. Still, the fact that they were equipped with two arms and four legs apiece made people who found the native name hard call them centaurs, though the sight of them would have scared Pheidias or Praxiteles out of his wits.

"Ready?" said the archery enthusiast. "Aim low, for his head will make a fine addition to our collection if you spoil it not."

"Wait," said another. "I have a better thought. One of their missionaries told me a Terran legend of a man compelled by his chief to shoot a fruit from the head of his son. Let us therefore . . ."

"No! For then you will surely spoil his head!" And the whole mob was yelling again.

Lord, thought Frome, how they talk! He tested his bonds, finding that someone had done a good job of tying him up. Although badly frightened, he pulled himself together and put on a firm front: "I say, what are you chaps up to?"

They paid him no heed until the William Tell party carried the day and one of them, with a trader's stolen rifle slung over his shoulder, approached with a fruit the size of a small pumpkin.

Frome asked: "Does that gun of yours shoot?"

"Yes," said the Dzlieri. "I have bullets that fit, too!"

Frome doubted this, but said: "Why not make a real sporting event of it? Each of us put a fruit on our heads and the other try to shoot it off?"

The Dzlieri gave the gargling sound that passed for laughter. "So you can shoot us, eh? How stupid think you we are?"

Frome, thinking it more tactful not to say, persisted with the earnestness of desperation: "Really, you know, it'll only make trouble if you kill me, whereas if you let me go . . ."

"Trouble we fear not," roared the fruit-bearer, balancing the fruit on Frome's head. "Think you we should let go such a fine head? Never have we seen an Earthman with yellow hair on head and face."

Frome cursed the coloration that he had always been rather proud of hitherto, and tried to compose more arguments. It was hard to think in the midst of this deafening racket.

The pseudo-pumpkin fell off with a thump. The Dzlieri howled, and he who had placed it came back and belted Frome with a full-armed slap across the face. "That will teach you to move your head!" Then he tied it fast with a creeper that went over the fruit and under Frome's chin.

Three Dzlieri had been told off to loose the first flight.

"Now look here, friends," said Frome, "you know what the Earthmen can do if they—"

T-twunk! The bowstrings snapped; the arrows came on with a sharp whistle. Frome heard a couple hit. The pumpkin jerked, and he became aware of a sharp pain in his left ear. Something sticky dripped onto his bare shoulder.

The Dzlieri shouted. "Etsnoten wins the first round!"

"Was that not clever, to nail his ear to the tree?"

"Line up for the next flight!"

"Hoy!" Hooves drummed and more Dzlieri burst into view. "What is this?" asked one in a crested brass helmet.

They explained, all jabbering at once.

"So," said the helmeted one, whom the others addressed as Mishinatven. (Frome realized that this must be the insurgent chief who had seceded from old Kamatobden's rule. There had been rumors of war . . .) "The other Earthman knocked him witless, bound him, and left him for us, eh? After slaying our fellows there in the brush?" He pointed to the bodies of the two Dzlieri that had fallen to the machine-gun in the earlier skirmish.

Mishinatven then addressed Frome in the Brazilo-Portuguese of the spaceways, but very brokenly: "Who—you? What—name?"

"I speak Dzlieri," said Frome. "I'm Frome, one of the survey-party from Bembom. Your folk attacked us without provocation this morning as we were breaking camp, and wounded our chief."

"Ah. One of those who bounds and measures our country to take it from us?"

"No such thing at all. We only wish . . ."

"No arguments. I think I will take you to God. Perhaps you can add to our store of the magical knowledge of the Earthmen. For instance, what are these?" Mishinatven indicated the rubbish left by Quinlan.

"That is a thing for talking over distances. I fear it's broken beyond repair. And that's a device for telling direction, also broken. That—" (Mishinatven had pointed to the radar-target, an aluminum structure something like a kite and something like a street-sign) "is—uh—a kind of totem-pole we were bringing to set up on Mount Ertma."

"Why? That is my territory."

"So that by looking at it from Bembom with our radar—you know what radar is?"

"Certainly; a magic eye for seeing through fog. Go on."

"So you see, old fellow, by looking at this object with the radar from Bembom we could tell just how far and in what direction Mount Ertma was, and use this information in our maps."

Mishinatven was silent, then said: "This is too complicated for me. We must consider the deaths of my two subjects against the fact that they were head-hunting, which God has forbidden. Only God can settle this question." He turned to the others. "Gather up these things and bring them to Amnairad for salvage." He wrenched out the arrow that had pierced Frome's ear and cut the Earthman's bonds with a short hooked sword like an oversized linoleum-knife. "Clamber to my back and hold on."

Although Frome had ridden zebras over rough country (the Viagens Interplanetarias having found a special strain of Grévy's zebra, the big one with narrow stripes on the rump, best for travel on Vishnu where mechanical transport was impractical) he had never experienced anything like this wild bareback ride. At least he was still alive, and hoped to learn who "God" was. Although Mishinatven had used the term *gimoa-brtsqun*, "supreme spirit," the religion of the Dzlieri was demonology and magic of a low order, without even a centaur-shaped creator-god to head its pantheon. Or, he thought uneasily, by "taking him to God" did they simply mean putting him to death in some formal and complicated manner?

Well, even if the survey was washed up for the time being, perhaps he could learn something about the missing missionary and the trader. He had come out with Hayataka, the chief surveyor, and Pete Quinlan, a new man with little background and less manners. He and Quinlan had gotten on each other's nerves, though Frome had tried to keep things smooth. Hayataka, despite his technical skill and experience, was too mild and patient a little man to keep such an unruly subordinate as Quinlan in line.

First the Dzlieri guide had run off, and Quinlan had begun making homesick noises. Hayataka and Frome, however, had agreed to try for Mount Ertma by travelling on a magnetic bearing, though cross-country travel on this steaming soup kettle of a planet with its dense jungle and almost constant rain was far from pleasant.

They had heard of the vanished Earthfolk yesterday when Quinlan had raised Comandante Silva himself on the radio: ". . . and when you get into the Dzlieri country, look for traces of Sirat Mongkut and Elena Millán. Sirat Mongkut is an entrepreneur dealing mainly in scrap-metals with the Dzlieri, and has not been heard of for a Vishnuvan year. Elena Millán is a Cosmotheist missionary who has not been heard of in six weeks. If they're in trouble, try to help them and get word to us . . ."

After signing off, Quinlan had said: "Ain't that a hell of a thing, now? As if the climate and bugs and natives wasn't enough, it's hunting a couple of fools we are. What was that first name? It don't sound like any Earthly name I ever heard."

Hayataka answered: "Sirat Mongkut. He's a Thai—what you would call a Siamese."

Quinlan laughed loudly. "You mean a pair of twins joined together?"

Then this morning a party of Dzlieri, following the forbidden old custom of hunting heads, had rushed the camp. They had sent a javelin through both Hayataka's calves and mortally wounded the two zebras before Frome had knocked over two and scattered the rest with the light machine-gun.

Quinlan, however, had panicked and run. Frome, trying to be fairminded, couldn't blame the lad too much; he'd panicked on his first trailtrip himself. But when Quinlan had slunk back, Frome, furious, had promised him a damning entry in his fitness report. Then they had bound Hayataka's wounds and let the chief surveyor put himself out with a trancepill while they got ready to retreat to Bembom.

Quinlan must have brooded over his blighted career, slugged Frome, and left him for the Dzlieri, while he hauled his unconscious supervisor back to Bembom.

After a couple of hours of cross-country gallop, the party taking Frome to Amnairad began to use roads. Presently they passed patches of clearings where the Dzlieri raised the pushball-sized lettuce-like plants they ate. Then they entered a "town," which to human eyes looked more like a series of corrals with stables attached. This was Amnairad. Beyond loomed Mount Ertma, its top hidden in the clouds. Frome was surprised to see a half-dozen zebras in one of the enclosures; that meant men.

At the center of this area they approached a group of "buildings"—inclosed structures made of poles with sheets of matting stretched between them. Up to the biggest structure the cavalcade cantered. At the entrance a pair of Dzlieri, imposing in helmets, spears, and shields, blocked the way.

"Tell God we have something for him," said Mishinatven.

One of the guards went into the structure and presently came out again. "Go on in," he said. "Only you and your two officers, Mishinatven. And the Earthman."

As they trotted through the maze of passages, Frome heard the rain on the matting overhead. He noted that the appointments of this odd place seemed more civilized than one would expect of Dzlieri, who, though clever in some ways, seemed too impulsive and quarrelsome to benefit from civilizing influences. They arrived in a room hung with drapes, of native textiles and decorated with groups of crossed Dzlieri weapons: bows, spears and the like.

"Get off," said Mishinatven. "God, this is an Earthman named Frome we found in the woods. Frome, this is God."

Frome watched Mishinatven to see whether to prostrate himself on the pounded-clay floor or what. But as the Dzlieri took the sight of his deity quite casually, Frome turned to the short, burly man with the flat Mongoloid face, wearing a pistol and sitting in an old leather armchair of plainly human make.

Frome nodded, saying: "Delighted to meet you, God old thing. Did your name used to be—uh—Sirat Mongkut before your deification?"

The man smiled faintly, nodded, and turned his attention to the three Dzlieri, who were all trying to tell the story of finding Frome and shouting each other down.

Sirat Mongkut straightened up and drew from his pocket a small object hung round his neck by a cord: a brass tube about the size and shape of a cigarette. He placed one end of this in his mouth and blew into it, his yellow face turning pink with effort. Although Frome heard no sound, the

Dzlieri instantly fell silent. Sirat put the thing back in his pocket, the cord still showing, and said in Portuguese:

"Tell us how you got into that peculiar predicament, Senhor Frome."

Unable to think of any lie that would serve better than simple truth, Frome told Sirat of his quarrel with Quinlan and its sequel.

"Dear, dear," said Sirat. "One would almost think you two were a pair of my Dzlieri. I am aware, however, that such antipathies arise among Earthmen, especially when a few of them are confined to enforced propinquity for a considerable period. What would your procedure be if I released you?"

"Try to beat my way back to Bembom, I suppose. If you could lend me a Grévy and some rations. . . ."

Sirat shook his head, still smiling like a Cheshire-cat. "I fear that is not within the bourne of practicability. But why are you in such a hurry to get back? After the disagreement of which you apprised me, your welcome will hardly be fraternal; your colleague will have reported his narrative in a manner to place you in the worst possible light."

"Well, what then?" said Frome, thinking that the entrepreneur must have swallowed a dictionary in his youth. He guessed that Sirat was determined not to let him go, but on the contrary might want to use him. While Frome had no intention of becoming a renegade, it wouldn't hurt to string him along until he learned what was up.

Sirat asked: "Are you a college-trained engineer?"

Frome nodded. "University of London; Civil Engineering."

"Can you run a machine-shop?"

"I'm not an expert machinist, but I know the elements. Are you hiring me?"

Sirat smiled. "I perceive you usually anticipate me by a couple of steps. That is, roughly, the idea I had in mind. My Dzlieri are sufficiently clever metal-workers but lack the faculty of application; moreover I find it difficult to elucidate the more complicated operations to organisms from the pre-machine era. And finally, Senhor, you arrive at an inopportune time, when I have projects under way news of which I do not desire to have broadcast. Do you comprehend?"

Frome at once guessed Sirat was violating Interplanetary Council Regulation No. 368, Section 4, Sub-section 26, Paragraph 15, which forbade imparting technical information to intelligent but backward and warlike beings like the Dzlieri without special permission. This was something Silva should know about. All he said, though, was:

"I'll see what I can do."

"Good." Sirat rose. "I will patch up your ear and then show you the shop myself. Accompany us, Mishinatven."

The Siamese led the way through the maze of mat-lined passages and out. The "palace" was connected by a breezeway with a smaller group of structures in which somebody was banging on an anvil; somebody was using a file; somebody was pumping the bellows of a simple forge.

In a big room several Dzlieri were working on metal parts with home-made tools, including a crank-operated lathe and boring-mill. In one corner rose a pile of damaged native weapons and tools. As his gaze roamed the room, Frome saw a rack holding dozens of double-barrelled guns.

Sirat handed one to Frome. "Two-centimeter smooth-bores, of the simplest design. My Dzlieri are not yet up to complicated automatic actions, to say nothing of shock-guns and paralyzers and such complex weapons. That is why the guns they expropriate from traders seldom remain long in use. They will not clean guns, nor believe that each gun requires appropriate ammunition. Therefore the guns soon get out of order and they are unable to effect repairs. But considering that we are not yet up to rifling the barrels, and that vision is limited in the jungle, one of these with eight-millimeter buckshot is quite as effective as an advanced gun.

"Now," he continued, "I contemplate making you my shop foreman. You will first undergo a training-course by working in each department in turn for a few days. As for your loyalty—I trust to your excellent judgment not to attempt to depart from these purlieus. You shall start in the scrap-sorting department today, and when you have completed your stint, Mishinatven will escort you to your quarters. As my Dzlieri have not yet evolved a monetary economy, you will be recompensed in copper ingots. Lastly, I trust I shall have the gratification of your companionship for the evening repast tonight?"

The scrap-sorting room was full of piles of junk, both of human and of native origin. Idznamen, the sorter, harangued Frome on such elementary matters as how to tell brass from iron. When Frome impatiently said: "Yes, yes, I know that," Idznamen glowered and went right on. Meanwhile Frome was working up a state of indignation. An easy-going person most of the time, he was particular about his rights, and now was in a fine fury over the detention of him, a civil servant of the mighty Viagens, by some scheming renegade.

During the lecture Frome prowled, turning over pieces of junk. He thought he recognized a motor-armature that had vanished from Bembom recently. Then there was a huge copper kettle with a hole in its bottom. Finally he found the remains of the survey-party's equipment, including the radar-target.

Hours later, tired and dirty, he was dismissed and taken by Mishinatven to a small room in this same building. Here he found a few simple facilities for washing up. He thought he should mow the incipient yellow beard in honor of dining with God, but Mishinatven did not know what a razor was. The Dzlieri hung around, keeping Frome in sight. Evidently Sirat was taking no chances with his new associate.

At the appointed time, Mishinatven led him to the palace and into Sirat's dining-room, which was fixed up with considerable elegance. Besides a couple of Dzlieri guards, two people were there already: Sirat Mongkut and a small dark girl, exquisitely formed but clad in a severely plain Earthly costume—much more clothes than human beings normally wore on this steaming planet.

Sirat said: "My dear, allow me to present Senhor Adrian Frome; Senhor, I have the ineffable pleasure of introducing Senhorita Elena Millán. Will you partake of a drink?" he added, offering a glass of *moikhada*.

"Righto," said Frome, noticing that Sirat already held one but that Miss Millán did not.

"It is contrary to her convictions," said Sirat. "I hope to cure her of such unwarranted extremism, but it consumes time. Now narrate your recent adventures to us again."

Frome obliged.

"What a story!" said Elena Millán. "So that handsome North European coloring of yours was almost your death! You Northerners ought to stick to the cold planets like Ganesha. Not that I believe Junqueiros's silly theory of the superiority of the Mediterranean race."

"He might have a point as far as Vishnu is concerned," said Frome. "I do notice that the climate seems harder on people like Van der Gracht and me than on natives of tropical countries like Mehtalal. But perhaps I'd better dye my hair black to discourage these chaps from trying to collect my head as a souvenir."

"Truly I regret the incident," said Sirat. "But perhaps it is a fortunate misfortune. Is there not an English proverb about ill winds? Now, as you observe, I possess a skilled mechanic and another human being with whom to converse. You have no conception of the *ennui* of seeing nobody but extraterrestrials."

Frome watched them closely. So this was the missing missionary! At least she had a friendly smile and a low sweet voice. Taking the bull by the horns he asked:

"How did Miss Millán get here?"

Elena Millán spoke: "I was travelling with some Dzlieri into Mishinatven's territory, when a monster attacked my party and ate one of them. I should have been eaten, too, had not Mr. Sirat come along and shot the beast. And now . . ."

She looked at Sirat, who said with his usual smile: "And now she finds it difficult to accustom herself to the concept of becoming the foundress of a dynasty."

"What?" said Frome.

"Oh, have I not enlightened you? I am imbued with considerable ambitions—exalted, I think, is the word I want. Nothing that need involve me with Bembom, I trust, but I hope before many years have elapsed to bring a sizable area under my sovereignty. I already rule Mishinatven's people for all practical purposes, and within a few weeks I propose to have annexed old Kamatobden's as well. Then for the tribe of Romeli living beyond Bembom . . ." He referred to the other intelligent species of the planet, six-limbed ape-like beings who quarreled constantly with the Dzlieri.

"You see yourself as a planetary emperor?" said Frome. This should certainly be reported back to his superiors at Bembom without delay!

Sirat made a deprecating motion. "I should not employ so extravagant a term—at least not yet. It is a planet of large land area. But—you comprehend the general idea. Under unified rule I could instill real culture into the Dzlieri and Romeli, which they will never attain on a basis of feuding tribes." He chuckled. "A psychologist once asserted that I had a power-complex because of my short stature. Perhaps he was correct; but is that any pretext for neglecting to put this characteristic to good use?"

"And where does Miss Millán come in?" asked Frome.

"My dear Frome! These primitives can comprehend the dynastic principle, but are much too backward for your recondite democratic ideals, as the failure of attempts to teach the representative government has amply demonstrated. Therefore we must have a dynasty, and I have elected Miss Millán to assist me in founding it."

Elena's manner changed abruptly and visibly. "I never shall," she said coldly. "If I ever marry, it will be because the Cosmos has infused my spiritual self with a Ray of its Divine Love."

Frome choked on his drink, wondering how such a nice girl could talk such tosh.

Sirat smiled. "She will alter her mind. She does not know what is beneficial for her, poor infant."

Elena said: "He walks in the darkness of many lives' accumulated karma, Mr. Frome, and so cannot understand spiritual truths."

Sirat grinned broadly. "Just a benighted old ignoramus. I suppose, my love, you would find our guest more amenable to your spiritual suasion?"

"Judging by the color of his aura, yes." (Frome glanced nervously about.) "If his heart were filled with Cosmic Love, I could set his feet on the Seven-Fold Path to Union with the Infinite."

Frome almost declared he wouldn't stand by and see an Earthwoman put under duress—not while he had his health—but thought better of it. Such an outburst would do more harm than good. Still, Adrian Frome had committed himself mentally to helping Elena, for while he affected a hardboiled attitude towards women, he was secretly a sentimental softhead towards anything remotely like a damsel in distress.

Sirat said: "Let us discuss less rarefied matters. How are affairs proceeding at Bembom, Mr. Frome? The information brought hither by my Dzlieri is often garbled in transit."

After that the meal went agreeably enough. Frome found Sirat Mongkut, despite his extraordinarily pedantic speech, a shrewd fellow with a good deal of charm, though obviously one who let nothing stand in his way. The girl, too, fascinated him. She seemed to be two different people—one, a nice normal girl whom he found altogether attractive; the other, a priestess of the occult who rather frightened him.

When Sirat dismissed his guests, a Dzlieri escorted each of them out of the room. Mishinatven saw to it that Frome was safely in bed (Frome had to move the bed a couple of times to avoid the drip of rain-water through the mat ceiling) before leaving him. As for Adrian Frome, he was too tired to care whether they mounted guard over him or not.

During the ensuing days Frome learned more of the workings of the shop and revived his familiarity with the skills that make a metal-worker. He also got used to being tailed by Mishinatven or some other Dzlieri. He supposed he should be plotting escape, and felt guilty because he had not been able to devise any clever scheme for doing so. Sirat kept his own person guarded, and Frome under constant surveillance.

And assuming Frome could give his guards the slip, what then? Even if the Dzlieri failed to catch him in his flight (as they probably would) or if he were not devoured by one of the carnivores of the jungle, without a compass, he would get hopelessly lost before he had gone one kilometer and presently die of the deficiency-diseases that always struck down Earthmen who tried to live on an exclusively Vishnuvan diet.

Meanwhile he liked the feeling of craftsmanship that came from exercising his hands on the tough metals, and found the other human beings agreeable to know.

One evening Sirat said: "Adrian, I should like you to take tomorrow off to witness some exercises I am planning."

"Glad to," said From. "You coming, Elena?"

She said: "I prefer not to watch preparations for the crime of violence."

Sirat laughed. "She still thinks she can convert the Dzlieri to pacifism.

You might as well instruct a horse to perform on the violin. She tried it on Chief Kamatobden and he thought her simply deranged."

"I shall yet bring enlightenment to these strayed souls," she said firmly.

The exercises took place in a large clearing near Amnairad. Sirat sat on a saddled zebra watching squadrons of Dzlieri maneuver at breakneck speed with high precision: some with native weapons, some with the new shotguns. A troop of lancers would thunder across the field in line abreast; then a square of musketeers would run onto the field, throw themselves down behind stumps and pretend to fire, and then leap up and scatter into the surrounding jungle, to reassemble elsewhere. There was some target practice like trapshooting, but no indiscriminate firing; Sirat kept the ammunition for his new guns locked up and doled it out only for specific actions.

Frome did not think Sirat was in a position to attack Bembom—yet. But he could certainly make a sweep of the nearby Vishnuvan tribes, whose armies were mere yelling mobs by comparison with his. And then . . . Silva *must* be told about this.

Sirat seemed to be controlling the movements in the field, though he neither gestured nor spoke. Frome worked his way close enough to the *renegado* to see that he had the little brass tube in his mouth and was going through the motions of blowing into it. Frome remembered: a Galton whistle, of course! It gave out an ultrasonic blast above the limits of human hearing, and sometimes people back on Earth called their dogs with them. The Dzlieri must have a range of hearing beyond 20,000 cycles per second.

At dinner that night he asked Sirat about this method of signalling.

Sirat answered: "I thought you would so conjecture. I have worked out a system of signals, something like Morse. There is no great advantage in employing the whistle against hostile Dzlieri, since they can perceive it also; but with human beings or Romeli . . . For instance, assume some ill-intentioned Earthman were to assault me in my quarters when my guards were absent? A blast would bring them running without the miscreant's knowing I had called.

"That reminds me," continued the adventurer, "tomorrow I desire you to commence twenty more of these, for my subordinate officers. I have decided to train them in the use of the device as well. And I must request haste, since I apprehend major movements in the near future."

"Moving against Kamatobden, eh?" said Frome.

"You may think so if you wish. Do not look so fearful, Elena; I will take good care of myself. Your warrior shall return."

Maybe, thought Frome, that's what she's scared of.

• • •

Frome looked over the Galton whistle Sirat had left with him. He now ran the whole shop and knew where he could lay hands on a length of copper tubing (probably once the fuel-line of a helicopter) that should do for the duplication of the whistle.

With the help of one of the natives he completed the order by nightfall, plus one whistle the Dzlieri had spoiled. Sirat came over from the palace and said: "Excellent, my dear Adrian. We shall go far together. You must pardon my not inviting you to dine with me tonight, but I am compelled to confer with my officers. Will you and Miss Millán carry on in the regular dining-room in my absence?"

"Surely, Dom Sirat," said Frome. "Glad to."

Sirat wagged a forefinger. "However, let me caution you against exercising your charm too strongly on my protégée. An inexperienced girl like that might find a tall young Englishman glamorous, and the results would indubitably be *most* deplorable for all concerned."

When the time came, he took his place opposite Elena Millán at the table. She said: "Let us speak English, since some of our friends here" (she referred to the ubiquitous Dzlieri guards) "know a little Portuguese, too. Oh, Adrian, I'm so afraid!"

"Of what; Sirat? What's new?"

"He has been hinting that if I didn't fall in with his dynastic plans, he would compel me. You know what that means."

"Yes. And you want me to rescue you?"

"I—I should be most grateful if you could. While we are taught to resign ourselves to such misfortunes, as things earned in earlier incarnations, I don't think I could bear it. I should kill myself."

Frome pondered. "D'you know when he's planning this attack?"

"He leaves the day after tomorrow. Tomorrow night the Dzlieri will celebrate."

That meant a wild orgy, and Sirat might well take the occasion to copy his subjects. On the other hand, the confusion afforded a chance to escape.

"I'll try to cook up a scheme," he told her.

Next day Frome found his assistants even more restless and insubordinate than usual. About noon they walked out for good. "Got to get ready for the party!" they shouted. "To hell with work!"

Mishinatven had vanished, too. Frome sat alone, thinking. After a while he wandered around the shop, handling pieces of material. He noticed the spoilt Galton whistle lying where he had thrown it the day before; the remaining length of copper tubing from which he had made the whistles; the big copper kettle he had never gotten around either to scrapping or to fixing. Slowly an idea took shape.

He went to the forge-room and started the furnace up again. When he had a hot fire, he brazed a big thick patch over the hole in the kettle, on the inside where it would take pressure. He tested the kettle for leakage and found none. Then he sawed a length off the copper tube and made another Galton whistle, using the spoilt one as a model.

In the scrap-sorting room he found a length of plastic which he made into a sealing-ring or gasket to go between the kettle and its lid. He took off the regular handle of the kettle, twisted a length of heavy wire into a shorter bail, and installed it so that it pressed the lid tightly down against the gasket. Finally he made a little conical adapter of sheet-copper and brazed it to the spout of the kettle, and brazed the whistle to the adapter. He then had an air-tight kettle whose spout ended in the whistle.

Then it was time for dinner.

Sirat seemed in a rollicking good humor and drank more moikhada than usual.

"Tomorrow," he said, "tomorrow we cast the die. What was that ancient European general who remarked about casting the die when crossing a river? Napoleon? Anyway, let us drink to tomorrow!" He raised his goblet theatrically. "Will you not weaken, Elena? Regrettable; you do not know what you miss. Come, let us fall upon the provender, lest my cook decamp to the revellers before we finish."

From outside came Dzlieri voices in drunken song, and sounds of a fight. The high shriek of a female Dzlieri tore past the palace, followed by the laughter and hoofbeats of a male in pursuit.

These alarming sounds kept the talk from reaching its usual brilliance. When the meal was over, Sirat said:

"Adrian, you must excuse me; I have a portentous task to accomplish. Please return to your quarters. Not you, Elena; kindly remain where you are."

Frome looked at the two of them, then at the guards, and went. In passing through the breezeway he saw a mob of Dzlieri dancing around a bonfire. The palace proper seemed nearly deserted.

Instead of going to his room he went into the machine-shop. He lit a cresset to see by, took the big copper kettle out to the pump, and half filled it with several liters of water. Then he staggered back into the shop and heaved the kettle up on top of the forge. He clamped the lid on, stirred the coals, and pumped the bellows until he had a roaring fire.

He hunted around the part of the shop devoted to the repair of tools and weapons until he chose a big spear with a three-meter shaft and a broad keen-edged half-meter head. Then he went back to the forge with it.

After a long wait, a faint curl of water-vapor appeared in the air near the spout of the kettle. It grew to a long plume, showing that steam was shooting out fast. Although Frome could hear nothing, he could tell by touching a piece of metal to the spout that the whistle was vibrating at a tremendous frequency.

Remembering that ultrasonics have directional qualities, Frome slashed through the matting with the broad blade of the spear until the forge-room lay open to view in several directions. Then he went back into the palace.

By now he knew the structure well. Towards the center of the maze Sirat had his private suite: a sitting-room, bedroom, and bath. The only way into this suite was through an always-guarded door into the sitting-room.

Frome walked along the hallway that ran beside the suite and around the corner to the door into the sitting-room. He listened, ear to the matting. Although it was hard to hear anything over the racket outside, he thought he caught sounds of struggle within. And from up ahead came Dzlieri voices.

He stole to the bend in the corridor and heard: ". . . surely some demon must have sent this sound to plague us. In truth it makes my head ache to the splitting-point!"

"It is like God's whistle," said the other voice, "save that it comes not from God's chambers, and blows continually. Try stuffing a bit of this into your ears."

The first voice (evidently that of one of the two regular guards) said: "It helps a little; remain you here on guard while I seek the medicine-man."

"That I will, but send another to take your place, for God will take it amiss if he finds but one of us here. And hasten, for the scream drives me to madness!"

Dzlieri hooves departed. Frome grinned in his whiskers. He might take a chance of attacking the remaining guard, but if the fellow's ears were plugged there was a better way. Sirat would have closed off his bedroom from the sitting-room by one of those curtains of slats that did duty for doors.

Frome retraced his steps until he was sure he was opposite the bedroom. Then he thrust his spear into the matting, slashed downward, and pushed through the slit into a bedroom big enough for basketball.

Sirat Mongkut looked up from what he was doing. He had tied Elena's wrists to the posts at the head of the bed, so that she lay supine, and now, despite her struggles, was tying one of her ankles to one of the posts at the foot. Here was a conqueror who liked to find his dynasties in comfort.

"Adrian!" cried Elena.

Sirat's hand flashed to his hip—and came away empty. Frome's biggest gamble had paid off: he assumed that just this once Sirat might have discarded his pistol. Frome had planned, if he found Sirat armed, to throw the spear at him; now he could take the surer way.

He gripped the big spear in both hands, like a bayonetted rifle, and ran towards Sirat. The stocky figure leaped onto the bed and then to the floor on the far side, fumbling for his whistle. Frome sprang onto the bed in pursuit, but tripped on Elena's bound ankle and almost sprawled headlong. By the time he recovered he had staggered nearly the width of the room. Meanwhile Sirat, having avoided Frome's rush, put his whistle to his mouth, and his broad cheeks bulged with blowing.

Frome gathered himself for another charge. Sirat blew and blew, his expression changing from confidence to alarm as nobody came. Frome knew that no Dzlieri in the neighborhood could hear the whistle over the continuous blast of the one attached to the kettle. But Sirat, unable to hear ultrasonics, did not know his signals were jammed.

As Frome started towards him again, Sirat threw a chair. It flew with deadly force; part of it gave Frome's knuckles a nasty rap while another part smote him on the forehead, sending him reeling back. Sirat darted across the room again on his short legs and tore from the wall one of those groups of native weapons he ornamented his palace with.

Down with a clatter came the mass of cutlery: a pair of crossed battle-axes, a gisarme, and a brass buckler. By the time Frome, having recovered from the impact of the chair, came up, Sirat had possessed himself of the buckler and one of the axes. He whirled and brought up the buckler just in time to ward off a lunge of the spear. Then he struck out with his ax and spun himself half around as he met only empty air. Frome, seeing the blow coming, had leaped back.

Sirat followed, striking out again and again. Frome gave ground, afraid to parry for fear of having his spear ruined, then drove Sirat back again by jabs at his head, legs, and exposed arm. They began to circle, the spearpoint now and then clattering against the shield. Frome found that he could hold Sirat off by his longer reach, but could not easily get past the buckler. Round they went, *clank! clank!*

Sirat was slow for a second and Frome drove the spearpoint into his right thigh, just above the knee . . . But the thrust, not centered, inflicted only a flesh-wound and a great rip in Sirat's pants. Sirat leaped forward, whirling his ax, and drove Frome back almost to the wall before the latter stopped him with his thrusts.

They circled again. Then came a moment when Sirat was between Frome and the door to the sitting-room. Quick as a flash Sirat threw his ax at Frome, dropped his shield, turned, and ran for the curtained door, calling "Help!"

Frome dodged the ax, which nevertheless hit him a jarring blow in the shoulder. As he recovered, he saw Sirat halfway to safety, hands out to wrench the curtain aside. He could not possibly catch the Siamese before the latter reached the sitting-room and summoned his delinquent guards to help him.

Frome threw his spear like a javelin. The shaft arced through the air and the point entered Sirat's broad back. In it went. And in, until half its length was out of sight.

Sirat fell forward, face down, clutching at the carpet and gasping. Blood ran from his mouth.

Frome strode over to where the would-be emperor lay and wrenched out the spear. He held it poised, ready to drive home again, until Sirat ceased to move. He was almost sorry . . . But there was no time for Hamlet-like attitudes; he wiped the blade on Sirat's clothes, carried it over to the bed, and sawed through Elena's bonds with the edge. Without waiting for explanations he said:

"If we're quick, we may get away before they find out. That is, if the guards haven't heard the noise in here."

"They will think it was he and I," she replied. "Before he dragged me in here he told them not to come in, no matter what they heard, unless he whistled for them."

"Serves him right. I'm going down-street to get some of his zebras. Where's that bloody gun of his?"

"In that chest," she said, pointing. "He locked it in there, I suppose because he was afraid I'd snatch it and shoot him—as though I could kill any sentient being."

"How do we get into—" Frome began, and stopped as he saw that the chest had a combination lock. "I fear we don't. How about his ammunition-chest in the storeroom?"

"That has a combination lock, too."

"*Tamates!*" growled Frome. "It looks as though we'd have to start out without a gun. While I'm gone, try to collect a sack of tucker from the kitchen, and whatever else looks useful." And out he went through the slit.

Outside the palace, he took care to saunter as if on legitimate business. The Dzlieri, having cast off what few inhibitions they normally possessed, were too far gone in their own amusements to pay him much heed, though one or two roared greetings at him.

Catching the zebras, though, was something else. The animals dodged around the corral, evading with ease his efforts to seize their bridles. Finally he called to a Dzlieri he knew:

"Mzumelitsen, lend a hand, will you? God wants a ride."

"Wait till I finish what I am doing," said the Dzlieri.

Frome waited until Mzumelitsen finished what he was doing and came over to help collect three zebras. Once caught, the animals followed Frome back to the palace tamely enough. He hitched them to the rail in the rear and went into the machine-shop, where he rummaged until he found a machete and a hatchet. He also gathered up the radar-target, which looked still serviceable if slightly battered.

When he got back he found that Elena had acquired a bag of food, a supply of matches, and a few other items. These they loaded on one of the zebras, and the other two they saddled.

When they rode out of Amnairad, the Dzlieri celebration was still in its full raucous swing.

Next day they were beginning to raise the lower slopes of the foothills of Mount Ertma when Frome held up a hand and said: "Listen!"

Through the muffling mass of the Vishnuvan jungle they heard loud Dzlieri voices. Then the sound of bodies moving along the trail came to their ears.

Frome exchanged one look with Elena and they broke into a gallop.

The pursuers must have been coming fast also, for the sounds behind became louder and louder. Frome caught a glimpse of the gleam of metal behind them. Whoops told them the Dzlieri had seen them, too.

Frome said: "You go on; I'll lead them off the trail and lose them."

"I won't! I won't desert you—"

"Do as I say!"

"But—"

"Go on!" he yelled so fiercely that she went. Then he sat waiting until they came into sight, fighting down his own fears, for he had no illusions about being able to "lose" the Dzlieri in their native jungle.

They poured up the trail towards him with triumphant screams. If he only had a gun . . . At least they did not seem to have any, either. They had only a few guns that would shoot (not counting the shotguns, whose shells were still locked up) and would have divided into many small parties to scour the trails leading out from their center.

Frome turned the zebra's head off into the jungle. Thank the gods the growth was thinner here than lower down, where the jungle was practically impassable off the trails.

He kicked his mount into an irregular run and vainly tried to protect his face from the lashing branches. Thorns ripped his skin and a trunk gave his right leg a brutal blow. As the Dzlieri bounded off the trail after him, he guided his beast in a wide semicircle around them to intersect the trail again behind his pursuers.

When he reached the trail, and could keep his eyes open again, he saw that the whole mob was crowding after him and gaining, led by Mishinatven. As the trail bent, Sirat's lieutenant cut across the corner and hurled himself back on the path beside the Earthman. Frome felt for his machete, which had been slapping against his left leg. The Dzlieri thundered at him from the right, holding a javelin up for a stab.

"Trickster! Deicide!" screamed Mishinatven, and thrust. Frome slashed through the shaft. As they galloped side by side, the point grazed Frome's arm and fell to the ground.

Mishinatven swung the rest of the shaft and whacked Frome's shoulders. Frome slashed back; heard the clang of brass as the Dzlieri brought up his buckler. Mishinatven dropped the javelin and snatched out his short sword. Frome parried the first cut and, as Mishinatven recovered, struck at the Dzlieri's sword-hand and felt the blade bite bone. The sword spun away.

Frome caught the edge of the buckler with his left hand, pulled it down, and hacked again and again until the brass was torn from his grip by the fall of his foe.

The others were still coming. Looking back, Frome saw that they halted when they came to their fallen leader.

Frome pulled on his reins. The best defense is a bloody strong attack. If he charged them now . . . He wheeled the zebra and went for them at a run, screeching and whirling his bloody blade.

Before he could reach them, they scattered into the woods with cries of despair. He kept right on through the midst of them and up the long slope until they were far behind and the exhaustion of his mount forced him to slow down.

When he finally caught up with Elena Millán, she looked at him with horror. He wondered why until he realized that with blood all over he must be quite a sight.

They made the last few kilometers on foot, leading their zebras zigzag among the immense boulders that crested the peak and beating the beasts to make them buck-jump up the steep slopes. When they arrived at the top, they tied the beasts to bushes and threw themselves down to rest.

Elena said: "Thank the Cosmos that's over! I could not have gone on much further."

"We're not done yet," said Frome. "When we get our breath we'll have to set up the target."

"Are we safe here?"

"By no means. Those Dzlieri will go back to Amnairad and fetch the whole tribe, then they'll throw a cordon around the mountain to make sure we shan't escape. We can only hope the target brings a rescue in time."

Presently he forced himself to get up and go to work again. In half an hour, with Elena's help, the radar target was up on its pole, safely guyed against the gusts.

Then Adrian Frome flopped down again. Elena said: "You poor creature! You're all over bruises."

"Don't I know it! But it might have been a sight worse."

"Let me at least wash those scratches, lest you get infected."

"That's all right; Vishnuvan germs don't bother Earthfolk. Oh, well, if you insist . . ." His voice trailed off sleepily.

He woke up some hours later to find that Elena had gotten a fire going despite the drizzle and had a meal laid out.

"Blind me, what have we here?" he exclaimed. "I say, you're the sort of trail-mate to have!"

"That is nothing. It's you who are wonderful. And to think I've always been prejudiced against blond men, because in Spanish novels the villain is always pictured as a blond!"

Frome's heart, never so hard as he made it out to be, was full to over-flowing. "Perhaps this isn't the time to say this but—uh—I'm not a very spiritual sort of bloke, but I rather love you, you know."

"I love you too. The Cosmos has sent a love-ray . . ."

"*Oi!*" It was a jarring reminder of that other Elena. "That's enough of that, my girl. Come here."

She came.

When Peter Quinlan got back to Bembom with the convalescing Hay-ataka, Comandante Silva listened eagerly to Quinlan's story until he came to his flight from Mishinatven's territory.

". . . after we started," said Quinlan, "while Hayataka was still out, they attacked again. I got three, but not before they had killed Frome with javelins. After we beat them off I buried—"

"Wait! You say Frome was killed?"

"*Pois sim.*"

"And you came right back here, without going to Ertma?"

"Naturally. What else could I do?"

"Then who set up the radar target on the mountain?"

"*What?*"

"Why yes. We sent up our radars on the ends of the base-line yesterday, and the target showed clearly on the scopes."

"I don't understand," said Quinlan.

"Neither do I, but we'll soon find out. *Amigo,*" he said to the sergeant Martins, "tell the aviation group to get the helicopter ready to fly to Mount Ertma, at once."

When the pilot homed on the radar target, he came out of the clouds to see a kite-like polygonal structure gleaming with a dull gray aluminum fin-ish on top of a pole on the highest peak of Mount Ertma. Beside the pole were two human beings sitting on a rock and three tethered zebras munching the herbage.

The human beings leaped to their feet and waved wildly. The pilot brought his aircraft around, tensely guiding it through gusts that threatened to dash it against the rocks, and let the rope-ladder uncoil through the trap-door. The man leaped this way and that, like a fish jumping for a fly, as the ladder whipped about him. Finally he caught it.

Just then a group of Dzlieri came out of the trees. They pointed and jabbered and ran towards the people whipping out javelins.

The smaller of the two figures was several rungs up the ladder when the larger one, who had just begun his ascent, screamed up over the whirr of the rotor-blades and the roar of the wind:

"Straight up! Quick!"

More Dzlieri appeared—scores of them—and somewhere a rifle barked. The pilot (just as glad it was not he dangling from an aircraft bucking through a turbulent overcast) canted his blades and rose until the clouds closed in below.

The human beings presently popped into the cabin, gasping from their climb. They were a small dark young woman and a tall man with a centimeter of butter-colored beard matted with dried blood. Both were nearly naked save for tattered canvas boots and a rag or two elsewhere, and were splashed with half-dried mud. The pilot recognized Adrian Frome, the surveyor.

"Home, Jayme," said Frome.

Frome, cleaned, shaved and looking his normal self once more except for a notch in his left ear, sat down across the desk from Silva, who said: "I cannot understand why you ask for a transfer to Ganesha now of all times. You're the hero of Bembom. I can get you a permanent P-5 appointment; perhaps even a P-6. Quinlan will be taken to Krishna for trial; Hayataka is retiring on his pension; and I shall be hard up for surveyors. So why must you leave?"

Frome smiled a wry, embarrassed smile. "You'll manage, *chefe*. You still have Van der Gracht and Mehtalal, both good men. But I'm quite determined, and I'll tell you why. When Elena and I got to the top of that mountain we were in a pretty emotional state, and what with one thing and another, and not having seen another human female for weeks, I asked her to marry me and she accepted."

Silva's eyebrows rose. "Indeed! My heartiest congratulations! But what has that to do with—"

"Wait till you hear the rest! At first everything was right as rain. She claimed it was the first time she'd been kissed, and speaking as a man of some experience I suppose it was. However, she soon began telling me *her* ideas. In the first place this was to be a purely spiritual marriage, the purpose of which was to put my feet on the sevenfold path of enlightenment so I could be something better than a mere civil engineer in my next incarnation—a Cosmotheist missionary, for example. Now I ask you!

"Well, at first I thought that was just a crochet I'd get her over in time; after all we don't let our women walk over us the way the Americans do. But then she started preaching Cosmotheism to me. And during the two and a half days we were up there, I'll swear she didn't stop talking five minutes except when she was asleep. The damndest rot you ever heard—rays and cosmic love and vibrations and astral planes and so on. I was never so bored in my life."

"I know," said Silva. He too had suffered.

"So," concluded Frome, "about that time I began wishing I could give her back to Sirat Mongkut. I was even sorry I'd killed the blighter. Although he'd have caused no end of trouble if he'd lived, he was a likeable sort of scoundrel at that. So here I am with one unwanted fiancée, and I just *can't* explain the facts of life to her. She once said as a joke that I'd be better off on Ganesha, and damned if I don't think she was right. Now if you'll just indorse that application . . . Ah, *muito obrigado*, Senhor Augusto! If I hurry I can just catch the ship to Krishna. Cheerio!"

Jack Vance

THE NEW PRIME

Much as SF authors writing today about phenomonology or the nature of reality write inevitably in the shadow of Philip K. Dick, so writers describing distant
worlds and alien societies with strange alien customs write in the shadow of Jack
Vance. No one in the history of the field has brought more intelligence, imagination, or inexhaustible fertility of invention to that theme than Vance, a fertility
which shows no sign of slackening even here at the end of the '90s, with recent
books such as *Night Lamp* being as richly and lushly imaginative as the stuff he
was writing in the '50s; even ostensible potboilers such as his *Planet of Adventure* series are full of vivid and richly portrayed alien societies, and bizarre and
often profoundly disturbing insights into the ways in which human psychology
might be altered by immersion in alien values and cultural systems. No one is better than Vance is at delivering that quintessential "sense of wonder" that is at the
heart of science fiction, and reading him has left me a legacy of evocative images
that will stay with me forever.

Like his colleagues L. Sprague de Camp and Fritz Leiber, Vance has produced
some of the very best work of the last fifty years in several different genres, and
is of immense evolutionary importance to the development both of modern fantasy *and* of modern science fiction. In fantasy, his classic novel *The Dying Earth*—
together with the related "Cugel the Clever" stories, collected in *The Eyes of the
Overworld, Cugel's Saga,* and *Rhialto the Marvellous*—would have enormous impact on future generations of fantasy writers. (It could be argued—and has
been—that these works are actually science fiction—or at least a hybrid form
called "science fantasy"—rather than fantasy, taking place in a future so many
millions of years from now that technology has indeed become indistinguishable
from magic, as per Arthur C. Clarke's famous dictum. These arguments are not
without merit, and are hard to refute—nevertheless, for anyone who has kept an
eye on the fantasy genre over the last few decades, or ever read a slushpile,
Vance's influence on the fantasy field is hard to deny, no matter what hairs tax-
onomists split.) In the same way, his most famous SF novels—*The Dragon Masters, The Last Castle, Big Planet, Emphyrio,* the five-volume "Demon Princes"
series (the best known of which are *The Star King* and *The Killing Machine*), *Blue
World, The Anome, The Languages of Pao,* among many others—have had a
widespread impact on generations of science fiction writers. And his effect on the
specialized form of Space Adventure or Space Opera (as differentiated from science fiction in general) is immense—with the possible exception of Poul Ander-

son, nobody has written more of that sort of work, or written at such a consistently high level of quality, as has Jack Vance.

Born in San Francisco in 1920, Vance served throughout World War II in the U.S. Merchant Navy. Most of the individual stories that would later be melded into his first novel, *The Dying Earth,* were written while Vance was at sea—he was unable to sell them, a problem he would also have with the book itself, the market for fantasy being almost non-existent at the time. *The Dying Earth* was eventually published in an obscure edition in 1950 by a small semi-professional press, went out of print almost immediately, and remained out of print for more than a decade thereafter. Nevertheless, it became an underground cult classic, and its effect on future generations of writers, both in and out of the fantasy genre, is incalculable: for one example out of many, *The Dying Earth* is a major influence on Gene Wolfe's *The Book of the New Sun* (Wolfe has said, for instance, that *The Book of Gold* which is mentioned by Severian is supposed to be *The Dying Earth*).

In SF, especially during the '50s and '60s, Vance was sometimes criticized for not being "rigorous" enough in his writing, for turning out Space Opera rather than "real" science fiction; I suspect this is one of the things that largely kept him out of *Astounding,* the leading market of his day (most of his work for *Astounding* would be rather bland by Vance's standards, only one story there, the later novella "The Miracle Workers," being full-throated Vancian Future Baroque—a somewhat atypical style for *Astounding,* and I can't help but wonder if John W. Campbell took the story mostly because it deals fairly centrally with psionics, a pet Campbellian topic of the time). Instead, he had to sell the bulk of his work to lower-paying "salvage" markets such as *Thrilling Wonder Stories* and *Startling Stories,* the last resort for a story before you relegated it to the trunk. Certainly it's true that there are few hard-science restraints on his fictional settings, where people in tiny personal spaceships zip easily and effortlessly across immense gulfs of space, vast powers and potencies are manipulated, and the universe is full to bursting with both strange alien races *and* curiously mutated variations on the normal human stock (this is one of Vance's major themes, in fact: how plastic and changeable the stuff of human nature is, how what we think of as "humanity" itself can be shaped and molded like wax, under the proper sort of environmental pressures, often with profoundly disturbing results), and there is little in his work that resembles either the broad social satire popular in *Galaxy* magazine at the time under H. L. Gold or the sober speculations about the impact of scientific advancement on current human society that was *Astounding*'s preferred stock-in-trade. The irony is that, in retrospect, the stuff he was writing for those lowly "salvage markets" seems just as significant—if not *more* significant—as most of the stuff that was appearing in the more-respectable magazines, ostensibly at the forefront of the field.

In fact, Vance would do some of his best early work for magazines such as

Thrilling Wonder Stories and *Startling Stories* and the short-lived *Worlds Beyond* in the mid '50s—"The Five Gold Bands," "Abercrombie Station," "The Houses of Izam," "The Kokod Warriors" and the other "Magnus Ridolph" stories, and the magazine version of "Big Planet," among others.

The story that follows, "The New Prime," one of Vance's best from that period, is yet another demonstration of the ease and fertility of his imagination; instead of settling for *one* background for the story, as most writers would have done, Vance—glorying in his strength and inventiveness—gives us *five* instead, each as rich, evocative, and ornate as the others—and each capable, in the hands of an ordinary writer, of having served as the background for an entire novel all by itself. Vance, though, as you will see, is no ordinary writer . . .

By the late '50s and early '60s, Vance was doing some of his best work, and some of the best work of the period, most of it by this time for the new Pohl *Galaxy* and for *F&SF*—"The Men Return," the underrated *The Languages of Pao* (one of only a handful of books even today to deal with semantics as a science; Delany *Babel-17* and Ian Watson's *The Embedding* are two later examples), the wonderful *The Star King* and *The Killing Machine* (two of the best hybrids of SF and the mystery/espionage novel ever written), "Green Magic," *The Blue World*, "The Dragon Master," "The Last Castle," and many others. Throughout the '70s and into the '80s, he would continue to produce a steady stream of memorable work, including the brilliant *Emphyrio, The Anome, Trullion: Alastor 2262*, the "Planet of Adventure" series, *The Face, The Book of Dreams*, and at least a dozen others.

By the '90s, ironically enough, the erosion of the midlist by a changing publishing environment had driven Vance, once the King of the Paperback Shelves, out of mass-market altogether. Although much of Vance's work *is* still in print, it's largely available as expensive hardcovers from small-press specialty publishers such as Underwood-Miller (now known just as Charles F. Miller, after the business partnership split up), who've made something of a pocket industry out of reprinting Vance novels (contact them at Charles F. Miller, 708 Westover Drive, Lancaster, PA 17601, for a listing of Vance titles available); this is an ironic turnaround from the old days, when almost nothing by Vance was available in a hardcover edition, but almost all of his titles were available in paperback—now, it's just the reverse! Recently, Tor has been bringing some of Vance's novels back into print in omnibus trade paperback editions, reprinting his "Demon Princess" series, for instance, in two omnibus volumes, and collecting three of his "Alastor" novels in the omnibus *Alastor*—the recent *Night Lamp* is also available as a trade paperback—and this may be the best and most cost-effective place to sample his work, although some of Vance's old mass-market paperbacks still turn up fairly often in used-book stores.

Vance has won two Hugo Awards, a Nebula Award, two World Fantasy Awards (one the prestigious Life Achievement Award), a Grandmaster Nebula Award for

Life Achievement, and the Edgar Award for best mystery novel. His other books include *The Palace of Love, City of the Chasch, The Dirdir, The Pnume, The Gray Prince, The Brave Free Men, Space Opera, Showboat World, Marune: Alastor 933, Wyst: Alastor 1716, Lyonesse, The Green Pearl, Madouc, Araminta Station, Ecce and Olde Earth,* and *Throy,* among many others. His short fiction has been collected in *Eight Fantasms and Magics, The Best of Jack Vance, Green Magic, Lost Moons, The Complete Magnus Ridolph, The World Between and Other Stories, The Dark Side of the Moon,* and *The Narrow Land.* His most recent books are the novels *Night Lamp* and *Ports of Call.*

Music, carnival lights, the slide of feet on waxed oak, perfume, muffled talk and laughter.

Arthur Caversham of twentieth-century Boston felt air along his skin, and discovered himself to be stark naked.

It was at Janice Paget's coming-out party: three hundred guests in formal evening-wear surrounded him.

For a moment he felt no emotion beyond vague bewilderment. His presence seemed the outcome of logical events, but his memory was fogged and he could find no definite anchor of certainty.

He stood a little apart from the rest of the stag line, facing the red and gold calliope where the orchestra sat. The buffet, the punch bowl, the champagne wagons, tended by clowns, were to his right; to the left, through the open flap of the circus tent, lay the garden, now lit by strings of colored lights, red, green, yellow, blue, and he caught a glimpse of a merry-go-round across the lawn.

Why was he here? He had no recollection, no sense of purpose. . . . The night was warm; the other young men in the full-dress suits must feel rather sticky, he thought. . . . An idea tugged at a corner of his mind. There was a significant aspect of the affair that he was overlooking.

He noticed that the young men nearby had moved away from him. He heard chortles of amusement, astonished exclamations. A girl dancing past saw him over the arm of her escort; she gave a startled squeak, jerked her eyes away, giggling and blushing.

Something was wrong. These young men and women were startled and amazed by his naked skin to the point of embarrassment. The gnaw of urgency came closer to the surface. He must do something. Taboos felt with such intensity might not be violated without unpleasant consequences; such was his understanding. He was lacking garments; these he must obtain.

He looked about him, inspecting the young men who watched him with ribald delight, disgust, or curiosity. To one of these latter he addressed himself.

"Where can I get some clothing?"

The young man shrugged. "Where did you leave yours?"

Two heavyset men in dark blue uniforms entered the tent; Arthur Caversham saw them from the corner of his eye, and his mind worked with desperate intensity.

This young man seemed typical of those around him. What sort of appeal would have meaning for him? Like any other human being, he could be moved to action if the right chord were struck. By what method could he be moved?

Sympathy?

Threats?

The prospect of advantage or profit?

Caversham rejected all of these. By violating the taboo he had forfeited his claim to sympathy. A threat would excite derision, and he had no profit or advantage to offer. The stimulus must be more devious. . . . He reflected that young men customarily banded together in secret societies. In the thousand cultures he had studied this was almost infallibly true. Longhouses, drug-cults, tongs, instruments of sexual initiation—whatever the name, the external aspects were near-identical: painful initiation, secret signs and passwords, uniformity of group conduct, obligation to service. If this young man were a member of such an association, he might react to an appeal to this group-spirit.

Arthur Caversham said, "I've been put in this taboo situation by the brotherhood; in the name of the brotherhood, find me some suitable garments."

The young man stared, taken aback. "Brotherhood? . . . You mean fraternity?" Enlightenment spread over his face. "Is this some kind of hell-week stunt?" He laughed. "If it is, they sure go all the way."

"Yes," said Arthur Caversham. "My fraternity."

The young man said, "This way, then—and hurry, here comes the law. We'll take off under the tent. I'll lend you my topcoat till you make it back to your house."

The two uniformed men, pushing quietly through the dancers, were almost upon them. The young man lifted the flap of the tent, Arthur Caversham ducked under, his friend followed. Together they ran through the many-colored shadows to a little booth painted with gay red and white stripes that was near the entrance to the tent.

"You stay back, out of sight," said the young man. "I'll check out my coat."

"Fine," said Arthur Caversham.

The young man hesitated. "What's your house? Where do you go to school?"

Arthur Caversham desperately searched his mind for an answer. A single fact reached the surface.

"I'm from Boston."

"Boston U? Or MIT? Or Harvard?"

"Harvard."

"Ah." The young man nodded. "I'm Washington and Lee myself. What's your house?"

"I'm not supposed to say."

"Oh," said the young man, puzzled but satisfied. "Well—just a minute. . . ."

Bearwald the Halforn halted, numb with despair and exhaustion. The remnants of his platoon sank to the ground around him, and they stared back to where the rim of the night flickered and glowed with fire. Many villages, many wood-gabled farmhouses had been given the torch, and the Brands from Mount Medallion reveled in human blood.

The pulse of a distant drum touched Bearwald's skin, a deep *thrumm-thrumm-thrumm*, almost inaudible. Much closer he heard a hoarse human cry of fright, then exultant killing-calls, not human. The Brands were tall, black, man-shaped but not men. They had eyes like lamps of red glass, bright white teeth, and tonight they seemed bent on slaughtering all the men of the world.

"Down," hissed Kanaw, his right arm-guard, and Bearwald crouched. Across the flaring sky marched a column of tall Brand warriors, rocking jauntily, without fear.

Bearwald said suddenly, "Men—we are thirteen. Fighting arm to arm with these monsters we are helpless. Tonight their total force is down from the mountain; the hive must be near deserted. What can we lose if we undertake to burn the home-hive of the Brands? Only our lives, and what are these now?"

Kanaw said, "Our lives are nothing; let us be off at once."

"May our vengeance be great," said Broctan the left armguard. "May the home-hive of the Brands be white ashes this coming morn. . . ."

Mount Medallion loomed overhead; the oval hive lay in Pangborn Valley. At the mouth of the valley, Bearwald divided the platoon into two halves, and placed Kanaw in the van of the second. "We move silently twenty yards apart; thus if either party rouses a Brand, the other may attack from the rear and so kill the monster before the vale is roused. Do all understand?"

"We understand."

"Forward then, to the hive."

The valley reeked with an odor like sour leather. From the direction of the hive came a muffled clanging. The ground was soft, covered with runner moss; careful feet made no sound. Crouching low, Bearwald could see the shapes of his men against the sky—here indigo with a violent rim. The angry glare of burning Echevasa lay down the slope to the south.

A sound. Bearwald hissed, and the columns froze. They waited. *Thud-thud-thud-thud* came the steps—then a hoarse cry of rage and alarm.

"Kill, kill the beast!" yelled Bearwald.

The Brand swung his club like a scythe, lifting one man, carrying the body around with the after-swing. Bearwald leapt close, struck with his blade, slicing as he hewed; he felt the tendons part, smelled the hot gush of Brand blood.

The clanging had stopped now, and Brand cries carried across the night.

"Forward," panted Bearwald. "Out with your tinder, strike fire to the hive. Burn, burn, burn. . . ."

Abandoning stealth he ran forward; ahead loomed the dark dome. Immature Brands came surging forth, squeaking and squalling, and with them came the genetrices—twenty-foot monsters crawling on hands and feet, grunting and snapping as they moved.

"Kill!" yelled Bearwald the Halforn. "Kill! Fire, fire, fire!"

He dashed to the hive, crouched, struck spark to tinder, puffed. The rag, soaked with saltpeter, flared; Bearwald fed it straw, thrust it against the hive. The reed-pulp and withe crackled.

He leapt up as a horde of young Brands darted at him. His blade rose and fell; they were cleft, no match for his frenzy. Creeping close came the great Brand genetrices, three of them, swollen of abdomen, exuding an odor vile to his nostrils.

"Out with the fire!" yelled the first. "Fire, out. The Great Mother is tombed within; she lies too fecund to move. . . . Fire, woe, destruction!" And they wailed, "Where are the mighty? Where are our warriors?"

Thrumm-thrumm-thrumm came the sound of skindrums. Up the valley rolled the echo of hoarse Brand voices.

Bearwald stood with his back to the blaze. He darted forward, severed the head of a creeping genetrix, jumped back. . . . Where were his men? "Kanaw!" he called. "Laida! Theyat! Gyorg! Broctan!"

He craned his neck, saw the flicker of fires. "Men! Kill the creeping mothers!" And leaping forward once more, he hacked and hewed, and another genetrix sighed and groaned and rolled flat.

The Brand voices changed to alarm; the triumphant drumming halted; the thud of footsteps came loud.

At Bearwald's back the hive burnt with a pleasant heat. Within came a shrill keening, a cry of vast pain.

In the leaping blaze he saw the charging Brand warriors. Their eyes glared like embers, their teeth shone like white sparks. They came forward, swinging their clubs, and Bearwald gripped his sword, too proud to flee.

After grounding his air sled Ceistan sat a few minutes inspecting the dead city Therlatch: a wall of earthen brick a hundred feet high, a dusty portal, and a few crumbled roofs lifting above the battlements. Behind the city the desert spread across the near, middle, and far distance to the hazy shapes of the Allune Mountains at the horizon, pink in the light of the twin suns Mig and Pag.

Scouting from above he had seen no sign of life, nor had he expected any, after a thousand years of abandonment. Perhaps a few sand-crawlers wallowed in the heat of the accident bazaar. Otherwise the streets would feel his presence with great surprise.

Jumping from the air sled, Ceistan advanced toward the portal. He passed under, stood looking right and left with interest. In the parched air the brick buildings stood almost eternal. The wind smoothed and rounded all harsh angles; the glass had been cracked by the heat of day and chill of night; heaps of sand clogged the passageways.

Three streets led away from the portal and Ceistan could find nothing to choose between them. Each was dusty, narrow, and each twisted out of his line of vision after a hundred yards.

Ceistan rubbed his chin thoughtfully. Somewhere in the city lay a brass-bound coffer, containing the Crown and Shield Parchment. This, according to tradition, set a precedent for the fiefholder's immunity from energy-tax. Glay, who was Ceistan's liege-lord, having cited the parchment as justification for his delinquency, had been challenged to show validity. Now he lay in prison on charge of rebellion, and in the morning he would be nailed to the bottom of an air sled and sent drifting into the west, unless Ceistan returned with the parchment.

After a thousand years, there was small cause for optimism, thought Ceistan. However, the lord Glay was a fair man and he would leave no stone unturned. . . . If it existed, the chest presumably would lie in state, in the town's Legalic, or the Mosque, or in the Hall of Relics, or possibly in the Sumptuar. He would search all of these, allowing two hours per building; the eight hours so used would see the end to the pink daylight.

At random he entered the street in the center and shortly came to a plaza at whose far end rose the Legalic, the Hall of Records and Decisions. At the façade Ceistan paused, for the interior was dim and gloomy. No sound came from the dusty void save the sigh and whisper of the dry wind. He entered.

The great hall was empty. The walls were illuminated with frescoes of red and blue, as bright as if painted yesterday. There were six to each wall, the top half displaying a criminal act and the bottom half the penalty.

Ceistan passed through the hall, into the chambers behind. He found but dust and the smell of dust. Into the crypts he ventured, and these were lit by embrasures. There was much litter and rubble, but no brass coffer.

Up and out into the clean air he went, and strode across the plaza to the Mosque, where he entered under the massive architrave.

The Nunciator's Confirmatory lay wide and bare and clean, for the tessellated floor was swept by a powerful draft. A thousand apertures opened from the low ceiling, each communicating with a cell overhead; thus arranged so that the devout might seek counsel with the Nunciator as he passed below without disturbing their attitudes of supplication. In the center of the pavilion a disk of glass roofed a recess. Below was a coffer and in the coffer rested a brass-bound chest. Ceistan sprang down the steps in high hopes.

But the chest contained jewels—the tiara of the Old Queen, the chest vellopes of the Gonwand Corps, the great ball, half emerald, half ruby, which in the ancient ages was rolled across the plaza to signify the passage of the old year.

Ceistan tumbled them all back in the coffer. Relics on this planet of dead cities had no value, and synthetic gems were infinitely superior in luminosity and water.

Leaving the Mosque, he studied the height of the suns. The zenith was past, the moving balls of pink fire leaned to the west. He hesitated, frowning and blinking at the hot earthen walls, considering that not impossibly both coffer and parchment were fable, like so many others regarding dead Therlatch.

A gust of wind swirled across the plaza and Ceistan choked on a dry throat. He spat, and an acrid taste bit his tongue. An old fountain opened in the wall nearby; he examined it wistfully, but water was not even a memory along these dead streets.

Once again he cleared his throat, spat, turned across the city toward the Hall of Relics.

He entered the great nave, past square pillars built of earthen brick. Pink shafts of light struck down from the cracks and gaps in the roof, and he was like a midge in the vast space. To all sides were niches cased in glass, and each held an object of ancient reverence: the armor in which Plange the Forewarned led the Blue Flags; the coronet of the First Serpent; an array of antique Padang skulls; Princess Thermosteraliam's bridal gown of woven cobweb palladium, as fresh as the day she wore it; the original Tablets of Legality; the great conch throne of an early dynasty; a dozen other objects. But the coffer was not among them.

Ceistan sought for entrance to a possible crypt, but except where the currents of dusty air had channeled grooves in the porphyry, the floor was smooth.

Out once more into the dead streets, and now the suns had passed behind the crumbled roofs, leaving the streets in magenta shadow.

With leaden feet, burning throat, and a sense of defeat, Ceistan turned to the Sumptuar, on the citadel. Up the wide steps, under the verdigris-fronted portico into a lobby painted with vivid frescoes. These depicted the maidens of ancient Therlatch at work, at play, amid sorrow and joy; slim creatures with short, black hair and glowing ivory skin, as graceful as water vanes, as round and delectable as chermoyan plums. Ceistan passed through the lobby with many side-glances, reflecting that these ancient creatures of delight were now the dust he trod under his feet.

He walked down a corridor which made a circuit of the building, and from which the chambers and apartments of the Sumptuar might be entered. The wisps of a wonderful rug crunched under his feet, and the walls displayed moldy tatters, once tapestries of the finest weave. At the entrance to each chamber a fresco pictured the Sumptuar maiden and the sign she served; at each of these chambers Ceistan paused, made a quick investigation, and so passed on to the next. The beams slanting in through the cracks served him as a gauge of time, and they flattened ever more toward the horizontal.

Chamber after chamber after chamber. There were chests in some, altars in others, cases of manifestos, triptychs, and fonts in others. But never the chest he sought.

And ahead was the lobby where he had entered the building. Three more chambers were to be searched, then the light would be gone.

He came to the first of these, and this was hung with a new curtain. Pushing it aside, he found himself looking into an outside court, full in the long light of the twin suns. A fountain of water trickled down across steps of apple-green jade into a garden as soft and fresh and green as any in the north. And rising in alarm from a couch was a maiden, as vivid and delightful as any in the frescoes. She had short, dark hair, a face as pure and delicate as the great white frangipani she wore over her ear.

For an instant Ceistan and the maiden stared eye to eye; then her alarm faded and she smiled shyly.

"Who are you?" Ceistan asked in wonder. "Are you a ghost or do you live here in the dust?"

"I am real," she said. "My home is to the south, at the Palram Oasis, and this is the period of solitude to which all maidens of the race submit when aspiring for Upper Instruction. . . . So without fear may you come beside me, and rest, and drink of fruit wine and be my companion through the lonely night, for this is my last week of solitude and I am weary of my aloneness."

Ceistan took a step forward, then hesitated. "I must fulfill my mission. I seek the brass coffer containing the Crown and Shield Parchment. Do you know of this?"

She shook her head. "It is nowhere in the Sumptuar." She rose to her feet, stretching her ivory arms as a kitten stretches. "Abandon your search, and come let me refresh you."

Ceistan looked at her, looked up at the fading light, looked down the corridor to the two doors yet remaining. "First I must complete my search; I owe duty to my lord Glay, who will be nailed under an air sled and sped west unless I bring him aid."

The maiden said with a pout, "Go then to your dusty chamber; and go with a dry throat. You will find nothing, and if you persist so stubbornly, I will be gone when you return."

"So let it be," said Ceistan.

He turned away, marched down the corridor. The first chamber was bare and dry as a bone. In the second and last, a man's skeleton lay tumbled in a corner; this Ceistan saw in the last rosy light of the twin suns.

There was no brass coffer, no parchment. So Glay must die, and Ceistan's heart hung heavy.

He returned to the chamber where he had found the maiden, but she had departed. The fountain had been stopped, and moisture only filmed the stones.

Ceistan called, "Maiden, where are you? Return; my obligation is at an end. . . ."

There was no response.

Ceistan shrugged, turned to the lobby and so outdoors, to grope his way through the deserted twilight street to the portal and his air sled.

Dobnor Daksat became aware that the big man in the embroidered black cloak was speaking to him.

Orienting himself to his surroundings, which were at once familiar and strange, he also became aware that the man's voice was condescending, supercilious.

"You are competing in a highly advanced classification," he said. "I marvel at your . . . ah, confidence." And he eyed Daksat with a gleaming and speculative eye.

Daksat looked down at the floor, frowned at the sight of his clothes. He wore a long cloak of black-purple velvet, swinging like a bell around his ankles. His trousers were of scarlet corduroy, tight at the waist, thigh, and calf, with a loose puff of green cloth between calf and ankle. The clothes were his own, obviously: they looked wrong and right at once, as did the carved gold knuckle-guards he wore on his hands.

The big man in the dark cloak continued speaking, looking at a point over Daksat's head, as if Daksat were nonexistent.

"Clauktaba has won Imagist honors over the years. Bel-Washab was the Korsi Victor last month; Tol Morabait is an acknowledged master of the technique. And then there is Ghisel Ghang of West Ind, who knows no peer in the creation of fire-stars, and Pulakt Havjorska, the Champion of the Island Realm. So it becomes a matter of skepticism whether you, new, inexperienced, without a fund of images, can do more than embarrass us all with your mental poverty."

Daksat's brain was yet wrestling with his bewilderment, and he could feel no strong resentment at the big man's evident contempt. He said, "Just what is all this? I'm not sure that I understand my position."

The man in the black cloak inspected him quizzically. "So, now you commence to experience trepidation? Justly, I assure you." He sighed, waved his hands. "Well, well—young men will be impetuous, and perhaps you have formed images you considered not discreditable. In any event, the public eye will ignore you for the glories of Clauktaba's geometrics and Ghisel Ghang's star-bursts. Indeed, I counsel you, keep your images small, drab, and confined; you will so avoid the faults of bombast and discord. . . . Now, it is time to go to your Imagicon. This way, then. Remember, grays, browns, lavenders, perhaps a few tones of ocher and rust; then the spectators will understand that you compete for the schooling alone, and do not actively challenge the masters. This way then. . . ."

He opened a door and led Dobnor Daksat up a stair and so out into the night.

They stood in a great stadium, facing six great screens forty feet high. Behind them in the dark sat tier upon tier of spectators—thousands and thousands, and their sounds came as a soft crush. Daksat turned to see them, but all their faces and their individualities had melted into the entity as a whole.

"Here," said the big man, "this is your apparatus. Seat yourself and I will adjust the ceretemps."

Daksat suffered himself to be placed in a heavy chair, so soft and deep that he felt himself to be floating. Adjustments were made at his head and neck and the bridge of his nose. He felt a sharp prick, a pressure, a throb, and then a soothing warmth. From the distance, a voice called out over the crowd:

"Two minutes to gray mist! Two minutes to gray mist! Attend, Imagists, two minutes to gray mist!"

The big man stooped over him. "Can you see well?"

Daksat raised himself a trifle. "Yes . . . all is clear."

"Very well. At 'gray mist,' this little filament will glow. When it dies, then it is your screen, and you must imagine your best."

The far voice said, "One minute to gray mist! The order is Pulakt Havjorska, Tol Morabait, Ghisel Ghang, Dobnor Daksat, Clauktaba, and Bel-Washab. There are no handicaps; all colors and shapes are permitted. Relax then, ready your lobes, and now—gray mist!"

The light glowed on the panel of Daksat's chair, and he saw five of the six screens light to a pleasant pearl-gray, swirling a trifle as if agitated, excited. Only the screen before him remained dull. The big man, who stood behind him, reached down, prodded. "Gray mist, Daksat; are you deaf and blind?"

Daksat thought gray mist, and instantly his screen sprang to life, displaying a cloud of silver-gray, clean and clear.

"Humph," he heard the big man snort. "Somewhat dull and without interest—but I suppose good enough. . . . See how Cluktaba's rings with hints of passion already, quivers with emotion."

And Daksat, noting the screen to his right, saw this to be true. The gray, without actually displaying color, flowed and filmed as if suppressing a vast flood of light.

Now, to the far left, on Pulakt Havjorska's screen, color glowed. It was a gambit image, modest and restrained—a green jewel dripping a rain of blue and silver drops which struck a black ground and disappeared in little orange explosions.

Then Tol Morabait's screen glowed: a black and white checkerboard with certain of the squares flashing suddenly green, red, blue, and yellow— warm, searching colors, pure as shafts from a rainbow. The image disappeared in a flush mingled of rose and blue.

Ghisel Ghang wrought a circle of yellow which quivered, brought forth a green halo, which in turn bulged giving rise to a larger band of brilliant black and white. In the center formed a complex kaleidoscopic pattern. The pattern suddenly vanished in a brilliant flash of light; on the screen for an instant or two appeared the identical pattern in a complete new suit of colors. A ripple of sound from the spectators greeted this *tour de force*.

The light on Daksat's panel died. Behind him he felt a prod. "Now."

Daksat eyed the screen and his mind was blank of ideas. He ground his teeth. Anything. Anything. A picture . . . he imagined a view across the meadowlands beside the River Melramy.

"Hm," said the big man behind him. "Pleasant. A pleasant fantasy, and rather original."

Puzzled, Daksat examined the picture on the screen. So far as he could distinguish, it was an uninspired reproduction of a scene he knew well. Fantasy? Was that what was expected? Very well, he'd produce fantasy. He imagined the meadows glowing, molten, white-hot. The vegetation, the old cairns slumped into a viscous seethe. The surface smoothed, became a mirror which reflected the Copper Crags.

Behind him the big man grunted. "A little heavy-handed, that last, and thereby you destroyed the charming effect of those unearthly colors and shapes. . . ."

Daksat slumped back in his chair, frowning, eager for his turn to come again.

Meanwhile Clauktaba created a dainty white blossom with purple stamens on a green stalk. The petals wilted, the stamens discharged a cloud of swirling yellow pollen.

Then Bel-Washab, at the end of the line, painted his screen a luminous underwater green. It rippled, bulged, and a black irregular blot marred the surface. From the center of the blot seeped a trickle of hot gold that quickly meshed and veined the black blot.

Such was the first passage.

There was a pause of several seconds. "Now," breathed the voice behind Daksat, "now the competition begins."

On Pulakt Havjorska's screen appeared an angry sea of color: waves of red, green, blue, an ugly mottling. Dramatically, a yellow shape appeared at the lower right, vanquished the chaos. It spread over the screen, the center went lime-green. A black shape appeared split, bowed softly and easily to both sides. Then turning, the two shapes wandered into the background, twisting, bending with supple grace. Far down a perspective they merged, darted forward like a lance, spread out into a series of lances, formed a slanting pattern of slim black bars.

"Superb!" hissed the big man. "The timing, so just, so exact!"

Tol Morabait replied with a fuscous brown field threaded with crimson lines and blots. Vertical green hatching formed at the left, strode across the screen to the right. The brown field pressed forward, bulged through the green bars, pressed hard, broke, and segments flitted forward to leave the screen. On the black background behind the green hatching, which now faded, lay a human brain, pink, pulsing. The brain sprouted six insectlike legs, scuttled crabwise back into the distance.

Ghisel Ghang brought forth one of his fire-bursts—a small pellet of bright blue exploding in all directions, the tips working and writhing through wonderful patterns in the five colors, blue, violet, white, purple, and light green.

Dobnor Daksat, rigid as a bar, sat with hands clenched and teeth grinding into teeth. Now! Was not his brain as excellent as those of the far lands? Now!

On the screen appeared a tree, conventionalized in greens and blues, and each leaf was a tongue of fire. From these fire wisps of smoke arose on high to form a cloud which worked and swirled, then emptied a cone of rain about the tree. The flames vanished and in their places appeared starshaped white flowers. From the cloud came a bolt of lightning, shattering the tree to agonized fragments of glass. Another bolt into the brittle heap and the screen exploded in a great gout of white, orange, and black.

The voice of the big man said doubtfully, "On the whole, well done, but mind my warning, and create more modest images, since—"

"Silence!" said Dobnor Daksat in a harsh voice.

So the competition went, round after round of spectacles, some sweet as canmel honey, others as violent as the storms that circle the poles. Color strove with color, patterns evolved and changed, sometimes in glorious cadence, sometimes in the bitter discord necessary to the strength of the image.

And Daksat built dream after dream, while his tension vanished, and he forgot all save the racing pictures in his mind and on the screen, and his images became as complex and subtle as those of the masters.

"One more passage," said the big man behind Daksat, and now the imagists brought forth the master-dreams: Pulakt Havjorska, the growth and decay of a beautiful city; Tol Morabait, a quiet composition of green and white interrupted by a marching army of insects who left a dirty wake, and who were joined in battle by men in painted leather armor and tall hats, armed with short swords and flails. The insects were destroyed and chased off the screen; the dead warriors became bones and faded to twinkling blue dust. Ghisel Ghang created three fire-bursts simultaneously, each different, a gorgeous display.

Daksat imagined a smooth pebble, magnified it to a block of marble, chipped it away to create the head of a beautiful maiden. For a moment she stared forth and varying emotions crossed her face—joy at her sudden existence, pensive thought, and at last fright. Her eyes turned milky opaque blue, the face changed to a laughing sardonic mask, black-cheeked with a fleering mouth. The head tilted, the mouth spat into the air. The head flattened into a black background, the drops of spittle shone like fire, became stars, constellations, and one of these expanded, became a planet with configurations dear to Daksat's heart. The planet hurtled off into darkness, the constellations faded. Dobnor Daksat relaxed. His last image. He sighed, exhausted.

The big man in the black cloak removed the harness in brittle silence. At last he asked, "The planet you imagined in that last screening, was that a creation or a remembrance of actuality? It was none of our system here, and it rang with the clarity of truth."

Dobnor Daksat stared at him, puzzled, and the words faltered in his throat. "But it is—home! This world! Was it not this world?"

The big man looked at him strangely, shrugged, turned away. "In a moment now the winner of the contest will be made known and the jeweled brevet awarded."

The day was gusty and overcast, the galley was low and black, manned by the oarsmen of Belaclaw. Ergan stood on the poop, staring across the two miles of bitter sea to the coast of Racland, where he knew the sharp-faced Racs stood watching from the headlands.

A gout of water erupted a few hundred yards astern.

Ergan spoke to the helmsman. "Their guns have better range than we bargained for. Better stand offshore another mile and we'll take our chances with the current."

Even as he spoke, there came a great whistle and he glimpsed a black pointed projectile slanting down at him. It struck the waist of the galley, exploded. Timber, bodies, metal flew everywhere, and the galley laid its broken back into the water, doubled up and sank.

Ergan, jumping clear, discarded his sword, casque, and greaves almost as he hit the chill gray water. Gasping from the shock, he swam in circles, bobbing up and down in the chop; then, finding a length of timber, he clung to it for support.

From the shores of Racland a longboat put forth and approached, bow churning white foam as it rose and fell across the waves. Ergan turned loose the timber and swam as rapidly as possible from the wreck. Better drowning than capture; there would be more mercy from the famine-fish that swarmed the waters than from the pitiless Racs.

So he swam, but the current took him to the shore, and at last, struggling feebly, he was cast upon a pebbly beach.

Here he was discovered by a gang of Rac youths and marched to a nearby command post. He was tied and flung into a cart and so conveyed to the city Korsapan.

In a gray room he was seated facing an intelligence officer of the Rac secret police, a man with the gray skin of a toad, a moist gray mouth, eager, searching eyes.

"You are Ergan," said the officer. "Emissary to the Bargee of Salomdek. What was your mission?"

Ergan stared back eye to eye, hoping that a happy and convincing response would find his lips. None came, and the truth would incite an immediate invasion of both Belaclaw and Salomdek by the tall, thin-headed Rac soldiers, who wore black uniforms and black boots.

Ergan said nothing. The officer leaned forward. "I ask you once more; then you will be taken to the room below." He said "Room Below" as if the words were capitalized, and he said it with soft relish.

Ergan, in a cold sweat, for he knew of the Rac torturers, said, "I am not Ergan; my name is Ervard; I am an honest trader in pearls."

"This is untrue," said the Rac. "Your aide was captured, and under the compression pump he blurted up your name with his lungs."

"I am Ervard," said Ergan, his bowels quaking.

The Rac signaled. "Take him to the Room Below."

A man's body, which has developed nerves as outposts against danger, seems especially intended for pain, and cooperates wonderfully with the craft of the torturer. These characteristics of the body had been studied by the Rac specialists, and other capabilities of the human nervous system had been blundered upon by accident. It had been found that certain programs of pressure, heat, strain, friction, torque, surge, jerk, sonic and visual shock, vermin, stench, and vileness created cumulative effects, whereas a single method, used to excess, lost its stimulation thereby.

All this lore and cleverness was lavished upon Ergan's citadel of nerves, and they inflicted upon him the entire gamut of pain: the sharp twinges, the dull, lasting joint-aches which groaned by night, the fiery flashes, the assaults of filth and lechery, together with shocks of occasional tenderness when he would be allowed to glimpse the world he had left.

Then back to the Room Below.

But always: "I am Ervard the trader." And always he tried to goad his mind over the tissue barrier to death, but always the mind hesitated at the last toppling step, and Ergan lived.

The Racs tortured by routine, so that the expectation, the approach of the hour, brought as much torment as the act itself. And then the heavy, unhurried steps outside the cell, the feeble thrashing around to evade, the harsh laughs when they cornered him and carried him forth, and the harsh laughs when three hours later they threw him sobbing and whimpering back to the pile of straw that was his bed.

"I am Ervard," he said, and trained his mind to believe that this was the truth, so that never would they catch him unaware. "I am Ervard! I am Ervard, I trade in pearls!"

He tried to strangle himself on straw, but a slave watched always, and this was not permitted.

He attempted to die by self-suffocation, and would have been glad to succeed, but always as he sank into blessed numbness, so did his mind relax and his motor nerves take up the mindless business of breathing once more.

He ate nothing, but this meant little to the Racs, as they injected him full of tonics, sustaining drugs, and stimulants, so that he might always be keyed to the height of his awareness.

"I am Ervard," said Ergan, and the Racs gritted their teeth angrily. The case was now a challenge; he defied their ingenuity, and they puzzled long and carefully upon refinements and delicacies, new shapes to the iron tools, new types of jerk ropes, new directions for the strains and pressures. Even when it was no longer important whether he was Ergan or Ervard, since war now raged, he was kept and maintained as a problem, an ideal case; so he was guarded and cosseted with even more than usual care, and the Rac torturers mulled over their techniques, making changes here, improvements there.

Then one day the Belaclaw galleys landed and the feather-crested soldiers fought past the walls of Korsapan.

The Racs surveyed Ergan with regret. "Now we must go, and still you will not submit to us."

"I am Ervard," croaked that which lay on the table. "Ervard the trader."

A splintering crash sounded overhead.

"We must go," said the Racs. "Your people have stormed the city. If you tell the truth, you may live. If you lie, we kill you. So there is your choice. Your life for the truth."

"The truth?" muttered Ergan. "It is a trick—" And then he caught the victory chant of the Belaclaw soldiery. "The truth? Why not? . . . Very well." And he said, "I am Ervard," for now he believed this to be the truth.

Galactic Prime was a lean man with reddish-brown hair, sparse across a fine arch of skull. His face, undistinguished otherwise, was given power by great dark eyes flickering with a light like fire behind smoke. Physically, he had passed the peak of his youth; his arms and legs were thin and loose-jointed; his head inclined forward as if weighted by the intricate machinery of his brain.

Arising from the couch, smiling faintly, he looked across the arcade to the eleven Elders. They sat at a table of polished wood, backs to a wall festooned with vines. They were grave men, slow in their motions, and their faces were lined with wisdom and insight. By the ordained system, Prime was the executive of the universe, the Elders the deliberative body, invested with certain restrictive powers.

"Well?"

The Chief Elder without haste raised his eyes from the computer. "You are the first to arise from the couch."

Prime turned a glance up the arcade, still smiling faintly. The others lay variously: some with arms clenched, rigid as bars; others huddled in fetal postures. One had slumped from the couch half to the floor; his eyes were open, staring at remoteness.

Prime returned his gaze to the Chief Elder, who watched him with detached curiosity. "Has the optimum been established?"

The Chief Elder consulted the computer. "Twenty-six thirty-seven is the optimum score."

Prime waited, but the Chief Elder said no more. Prime stepped to the alabaster balustrade beyond the couches. He leaned forward, looked out across the vista—miles and miles of sunny haze, with a twinkling sea in the distance. A breeze blew past his face, ruffling the scant russet strands of his hair. He took a deep breath, flexed his fingers and hands, for the memory of the Rac torturers was still heavy on his mind. After a moment he swung around, leaned back, resting his elbows upon the balustrade. He glanced once more down the line of couches; there were still no signs of vitality from the candidates.

"Twenty-six thirty-seven," he muttered. "I venture to estimate my own score at twenty-five ninety. In the last episode I recall an incomplete retention of personality."

"Twenty-five seventy-four," said the Chief Elder. "The computer judged Bearwald the Halforn's final defiance of the Brand warriors unprofitable."

Prime considered. "The point is well made. Obstinacy serves no purpose unless it advances a predetermined end. It is a flaw I must seek to temper." He looked along the line of Elders, from face to face. "You make no enunciations, you are curiously mute."

He waited; the Chief Elder made no response.

"May I inquire the high score?"

"Twenty-five seventy-four."

Prime nodded. "Mine."

"Yours is the high score," said the Chief Elder.

Prime's smile disappeared: a puzzled line appeared across his brow. "In spite of this, you are still reluctant to confirm my second span of authority; there are still doubts among you."

"Doubts and misgivings," replied the Chief Elder.

Prime's mouth pulled in at the corners, although his brows were still raised in polite inquiry. "Your attitude puzzles me. My record is one of selfless service. My intelligence is phenomenal, and in this final test, which I designed to dispel your last doubts, I attained the highest score. I have proved my social intuition and flexibility, my leadership, devotion to duty, imagination, and resolution. In every commensurable aspect, I fulfill best the qualifications for the office I hold."

The Chief Elder looked up and down the line of his fellows. There were none who wished to speak. The Chief Elder squared himself in his chair, sat back.

"Our attitude is difficult to represent. Everything is as you say. Your intelligence is beyond dispute, your character is exemplary, you have served your term with honor and devotion. You have earned our respect, admiration, and gratitude. We realize also that you seek this second term from praise-worthy motives: you regard yourself as the man best able to coordinate the complex business of the galaxy."

Prime nodded grimly. "But you think otherwise."

"Our position is perhaps not quite so blunt."

"Precisely what is your position?" Prime gestured along the couches. "Look at these men. They are the finest of the galaxy. One man is dead. That one stirring on the third couch has lost his mind; he is a lunatic. The others are sorely shaken. And never forget that this test has been expressly designed to measure the qualities essential to the Galactic Prime."

"This test has been of great interest to us," said the Chief Elder mildly. "It has considerably affected our thinking."

Prime hesitated, plumbing the unspoken overtones of the words. He came forward, seated himself across from the line of Elders. With a narrow glance he searched the faces of the eleven men, tapped once, twice, three times with his fingertips on the polished wood, leaned back in the chair.

"As I have pointed out, the test has gauged each candidate for the exact qualities essential to the optimum conduct of office, in this fashion: Earth of the twentieth century is a planet of intricate conventions; on Earth the candidate, as Arthur Caversham, is required to use his social intuition—a quality highly important in this galaxy of two billion suns. On Belotsi, Bearwald the Halforn is tested for courage and the ability to conduct positive action. At the dead city Therlatch on Praesepe Three, the candidate, as Ceistan, is rated for devotion to duty, and as Dobnor Daksat at the Imagicon on Staff, his creative conceptions are rated against the most fertile imaginations alive. Finally as Ergan, on Chankozar, his will, persistence, and ultimate fiber are explored to their extreme limits.

"Each candidate is placed in the identical set of circumstances by a trick of temporal, dimensional, and cerebroneural meshing, which is rather complicated for the present discussion. Sufficient that each candidate is objectively rated by his achievements, and that the results are commensurable."

He paused, looked shrewdly along the line of grave faces. "I must emphasize that although I myself designed and arranged the test, I thereby gained no advantage. The mnemonic synapses are entirely disengaged from incident to incident, and only the candidate's basic personality acts. All were tested under precisely the same conditions. In my opinion the scores registered by the computer indicate an objective and reliable index of the candidate's ability for the highly responsible office of Galactic Executive."

The Chief Elder said, "The scores are indeed significant."

"Then—you approve my candidacy?"

The Chief Elder smiled. "Not so fast. Admittedly you are intelligent, admittedly you have accomplished much during your term as Prime. But much remains to be done."

"Do you suggest that another man would have achieved more?"

The Chief Elder shrugged. "I have no conceivable way of knowing. I point out your achievements, such as the Glenart civilization, the Dawn Time on Masilis, the reign of King Karal on Aevir, the suppression of the Arkid Revolt. There are many such examples. But there are also shortcomings: the totalitarian governments on Earth, the savagery on Belotsi and Chankozar, so pointedly emphasized in your test. Then there is the decadence of the planets in the Eleven Hundred Ninth Cluster, the rise of the priest-kings on Fiir, and much else."

Prime clenched his mouth and the fires behind his eyes burnt more brightly.

The Chief Elder continued. "One of the most remarkable phenomena of the galaxy is the tendency of humanity to absorb and manifest the personality of the Prime. There seems to be a tremendous resonance which vibrates from the brain of the Prime through the minds of man from Center to the outer fringes. It is a matter which should be studied, analyzed, and subjected to control. The effect is as if every thought of the Prime is magnified a billion-fold, as if every mood sets the tone for a thousand civilizations, every facet of his personality reflects in the ethics of a thousand cultures."

Prime said tonelessly, "I have remarked this phenomenon and have thought much on it. Prime's commands are promulgated in such a way as to exert subtle rather than overt influence; perhaps here is the background of the matter. In any event, the fact of this influence is even more reason to select for the office a man of demonstrated virtue."

"Well put," said the Chief Elder. "Your character is indeed beyond reproach. However, we of the Elders are concerned by the rising tide of authoritarianism among the planets of the galaxy. We suspect that this principle of resonance is at work. You are a man of intense and indomitable will, and we feel that your influence has unwittingly prompted an irruption of autarchies."

Prime was silent a moment. He looked down the line of couches where the other candidates were recovering awareness. They were men of various races: a pale Northkin of Palast, a stocky red Hawolo, a gray-haired gray-eyed Islander from the Sea Planet—each the outstanding man of the planet of his birth. Those who had returned to consciousness sat quietly, collecting their wits, or lay back on the couch, trying to expunge the test from their minds. There had been a toll taken: one lay dead, another bereft of his wits crouched whimpering beside his couch.

The Chief Elder said, "The objectionable aspects of your character are perhaps best exemplified by the test itself."

Prime opened his mouth; the Chief Elder held up his hand. "Let me speak; I will try to deal fairly with you. When I am done, you may say your say.

"I repeat that your basic direction is displayed by the details of the test that you devised. The qualities you measured were those which you considered the most important: that is, those ideals by which you guide your own life. This arrangement I am sure was completely unconscious, and hence completely revealing. You conceive the essential characteristics of the Prime to be social intuition, aggressiveness, loyalty, imagination, and dogged persistence. As a man of strong character you seek to exemplify these ideals in your own conduct; therefore it is not at all surprising that in this test, designed by you, with a scoring system calibrated by you, your score should be highest.

"Let me clarify the idea by an analogy. If the Eagle were conducting a test to determine the King of Beasts, he would rate all the candidates on their ability to fly; necessarily he would win. In this fashion the Mole would consider ability to dig important; by his system of testing *he* would inevitably emerge King of Beasts."

Prime laughed sharply, ran a hand through his sparse red-brown locks. "I am neither Eagle nor Mole."

The Chief Elder shook his head. "No. You are zealous, dutiful, imaginative, indefatigable—so you have demonstrated, as much by specifying tests for these characteristics as by scoring high in these same tests. But conversely, by the very absence of other tests you demonstrate deficiencies in your character."

"And these are?"

"Sympathy. Compassion. Kindness." The Chief Elder settled back in his chair. "Strange. Your predecessor two times removed was rich in these qualities. During his term, the great humanitarian systems based on the idea of human brotherhood sprang up across the universe. Another example of resonance—but I digress."

Prime said with a sardonic twitch of his mouth, "May I ask this: have you selected the next Galactic Prime?"

The Chief Elder nodded. "A definite choice has been made."

"What was his score in the test?"

"By your scoring system—seventeen eighty. He did poorly as Arthur Caversham; he tried to explain the advantages of nudity to the policeman. He lacked the ability to concoct an instant subterfuge; he has little of your quick craft. As Arthur Caversham he found himself naked. He is sincere and straightforward, hence tried to expound the positive motivations for his state, rather than discover the means to evade the penalties."

"Tell me more about this man," said Prime shortly.

"As Bearwald the Halforn, he led his band to the hive of the Brands on Mount Medallion, but instead of burning the hive, he called forth to the queen, begging her to end the useless slaughter. She reached out from the doorway, drew him within and killed him. He failed—but the computer still rated him highly on his forthright approach.

"At Therlatch, his conduct was as irreproachable as yours, and at the Imagicon his performance was adequate. Yours approached the brilliance of the Master Imagists, which is high achievement indeed.

"The Rac tortures are the most trying element of the test. You knew well you could resist limitless pain; therefore you ordained that all other candidates must likewise possess this attribute. The new Prime is sadly deficient here. He is sensitive, and the idea of one man intentionally inflicting pain upon another sickens him. I may add that none of the candidates achieved a perfect count in the last episode. Two others equaled your score—"

Prime evinced interest. "Which are they?"

The Chief Elder pointed them out—a tall hard-muscled man with rock-hewn face standing by the alabaster balustrade gazing moodily out across the sunny distance, and a man of middle age who sat with his legs folded under him, watching a point three feet before him with an expression of imperturbable placidity.

"One is utterly obstinate and hard," said the Chief Elder. "He refused to say a single word. The other assumes an outer objectivity when unpleasantness overtakes him. Others among the candidates fared not so well; therapy will be necessary in almost all cases."

Their eyes went to the witless creature with vacant eyes who padded up and down the aisle, humming and muttering quietly to himself.

"The tests were by no means valueless," said the Chief Elder. "We learned a great deal. By your system of scoring, the competition rated you most high. By other standards which we Elders postulated, your place was lower."

With a tight mouth, Prime inquired, "Who is this paragon of altruism, kindliness, sympathy, and generosity?"

The lunatic wandered close, fell on his hands and knees, crawled whimpering to the wall. He pressed his face to the cool stone, stared blankly up at Prime. His mouth hung loose, his chin was wet, his eyes rolled apparently free of each other.

The Chief Elder smiled in great compassion; he stroked the mad creature's head. "This is he. Here is the man we select."

The old Galactic Prime sat silent, mouth compressed, eyes burning like far volcanoes.

At his feet the new Prime, Lord of Two Billion Suns, found a dead leaf, put it into his mouth and began to chew.

THAT SHARE OF GLORY

The late C. M. Kornbluth first started selling stories as a teenage prodigy in 1940, making his first sale to *Super Science Stories,* and wrote vast amounts of pulp fiction under many different pseudonyms in the years before World War II, most of it unknown today. Only after the war, in the booming SF scene of the early '50s, did Kornbluth begin to attract some serious attention. As a writer, C. M. Kornbluth first came to widespread prominence with a series of novels written in collaboration with Frederik Pohl, including *The Space Merchants* (one of the most famous SF novels of the '50s), *Gladiator-at-Law* (a book that comes to seem less and less like a satire every time you turn on your television set), *Search the Sky,* and *Wolfbane* (perhaps the best of the Pohl/Kornbluth novels, and decades ahead of its time in its depiction of humans forced to function as plug-in component parts in an organic alien computer); he also produced two fairly routine novels in collaboration with Judith Merril as "Cyril Judd," *Outpost Mars* and *Gunner Cade,* that were moderately well-received at the time but largely forgotten today, as well as two long-forgotten mainstream novels in collaboration with Pohl. As a solo writer—in addition to several mainstream novels under different pseudonyms—he produced three interesting but largely unsuccessful novels (*Not This August,* a Cold War saga about the military conquest of the United States by the USSR, *The Syndic,* a caustic but ultimately somewhat lightweight *Galaxy*-style satire of a future America run by gangsters, and, the weakest of the lot, *Take-off,* a then-theoretical novel about the conquest of space), but they had little impact on the SF world of the day.

What *did* have a powerful impact on the SF world, though, was Kornbluth's short fiction. Kornbluth was a master of the short story, working with a sophistication, maturity, elegance, and grace rarely seen in the genre, then or now. He was one of those key authors—one also thinks of Damon Knight, Theodore Sturgeon, Alfred Bester, Algis Budrys, and a few others—who were busy in the '50s redefining what you could do with the instrument known as the science fiction short story, and greatly expanding its range. In the years before his tragically early death in 1958 (on his way in to Manhattan for a meeting in which he was going to be offered the editorship of *The Magazine of Fantasy & Science Fiction,* by the way; now *there's* an interesting basis for an Alternate Worlds scenario! One wonders what stories he would have bought, and what effect his editorship would have had on the evolution of SF . . .), Kornbluth created some of the best short work of the '50s, including the classic "The Little Black Bag," "The Marching

Morons," "Shark Ship," "Two Dooms," "The Mindworm," "Gomez," "The Last Man Left in the Bar," "The Advent on Channel Twelve," "Ms. Found in a Chinese Fortune Cookie," "With These Hands," and dozens of others . . .

. . . Including the hugely entertaining story that follows, a somewhat atypical story for Kornbluth—for the fact is that, except for this one famous story (and one or two other exceptions, such as the much weaker "The Slave"), Kornbluth rarely wrote straightforward adventure stories, under the Kornbluth byline anyway, especially Space Adventure stories of the swashbuckling, hard-nosed, rapacious, fast-paced sort that follows, where sharp-eyed cool-headed entrepreneurs haggle and brawl and wheel-and-deal their way across the Universe, out-thinking their adversaries and out-*tricking* them when backed into a corner. "That Share of Glory," in fact, is such a perfect *Astounding* story, so much the Platonic Ideal of what a story for John Campbell's *Astounding* of that period should be like, that I can't help but wonder if Kornbluth's tongue wasn't in his cheek when he wrote it, or if he wasn't deliberately (with the cool-eyed calculation of the characters in the story) writing stuff that he knew would "push Campbell's buttons," a popular game among writers of the day. Even if one or both of those things are true, though, it hardly matters—Kornbluth may have told his friends or even himself that that's what he was doing, but there's too much conviction in his voice here, and he does too good a job, for me to believe that he didn't like the stuff himself, whatever he may have claimed that he'd *rather* drink instead. For all of the cynical, jaded facade that he was famous for projecting, nobody but a True Believer at heart, one who somewhere, down deep, still thrilled to the dream of venturing out among the wonders and terrors of deep space, out to the unknown stars, could possibly have written the adventure that follows . . .

Kornbluth won no major awards during his lifetime, but "The Meeting," a story of his completed from a partial draft by Pohl years after his death, won a Hugo Award in 1972. Kornbluth's solo short work was collected in *The Explorers, A Mile Beyond the Moon, The Marching Morons, Thirteen O'Clock and Other Zero Hours,* and *The Best of C. M. Kornbluth.* Pohl and Kornbluth's collaborative short work has been collected in *The Wonder Effect, Critical Mass, Before the Universe,* and *Our Best.* Until recently, I would have said that everything by Kornbluth was long out of print, but, fortunately, NESFA Press published a massive retrospective Kornbluth collection in 1996, *His Share of Glory: The Complete Short Fiction of C. M. Kornbluth* (NESFA Press, P.O. Box 809, Framingham, MA 07101-0203, www.nesfa.org $27.00), a collection which, true to its name, assembles almost everything Kornbluth ever wrote under his own name, and one which belongs in every serious SF reader's library.

Young Alen, one of a thousand in the huge refectory, ate absent-mindedly as the reader droned into the perfect silence of the hall. Today's lesson happened to be a word list of the Thetis VIII planet's seagoing folk.

"*Tlon*—a ship," droned the reader.

"*Rtlo*—some ships, number unknown."

"*Long*—some ships, number known, always modified by cardinal."

"*Ongr*—a ship in a collection of ships, always modified by ordinal."

"*Ngrt*—first ship in a collection of ships; an exception to *ongr.*"

A lay brother tiptoed to Alen's side. "The Rector summons you," he whispered.

Alen had no time for panic, though that was the usual reaction to a summons from the Rector to a novice. He slipped from the refectory, stepped onto the northbound corridor and stepped off at his cell, a minute later and a quarter mile farther on. Hastily, but meticulously, he changed from his drab habit to the heraldic robes in the cubicle with its simple stool, washstand, desk, and paperweight or two. Alen, a levelheaded young fellow, was not aware that he had broken any section of the Order's complicated Rule, but he was aware that he could have done so without knowing it. It might, he thought, be the last time he would see the cell.

He cast a glance which he hoped would not be the final one over it; a glance which lingered a little fondly on the reel rack where were stowed: *Nicholson on Martian Verbs*, *The New Oxford Venusian Dictionary*, the ponderous six-reeler *Deutsche-Ganymedische Konversasionslexikon* published long ago and far away in Leipzig. The later works were there, too: *The Tongues of the Galaxy—an Essay in Classification*, *A Concise Grammar of Cephean*, *The Self-Pronouncing Vegan II Dictionary*—scores of them, and, of course, the worn reel of old Machiavelli's *The Prince*.

Enough of that! Alen combed out his small, neat beard and stepped onto the southbound corridor. He transferred to an eastbound at the next intersection and minutes later was before the Rector's lay secretary.

"You better review your Lyran irregulars," said the secretary disrespectfully. "There's a trader in there who's looking for a cheap herald on a swindling trip to Lyra VI." Thus unceremoniously did Alen learn that he was not to be ejected from the Order but that he was to be elevated to Journeyman. But as a herald should, he betrayed no sign of his immense relief. He did, however, take the secretary's advice and sensibly reviewed his Lyran.

While he was in the midst of a declension which applied only to inanimate objects, the voice of the Rector—and what a mellow voice it was!—floated through the secretary's intercom.

"Admit the novice, Alen," said the Master Herald.

A final settling of his robes and the youth walked into the Rector's huge office, with the seal of the Order blazing in diamonds above his desk. There was a stranger present; presumably the trader—a blackbearded fellow whose rugged frame didn't carry his Vegan cloak with ease.

Said the Rector: "Novice, this is to be the crown of your toil if you are acceptable to—?" He courteously turned to the trader, who shrugged irritably.

"It's all one to me," growled the blackbeard. "Somebody cheap, somebody who knows the cant of the thievish Lyran gem peddlers, above all, somebody *at once*. Overhead is devouring my flesh day by day as the ship waits at the field. And when we are spaceborne, my imbecile crew will doubtless waste liter after priceless liter of my fuel. And when we land the swindling Lyrans will without doubt make my ruin complete by tricking me even out of the minute profit I hope to realize. Good Master Herald, let me have the infant cheap and I'll bid you good day."

The Rector's shaggy eyebrows drew down in a frown. "Trader," he said sonorously, "our mission of galactic utilitarian culture is not concerned with your margin of profit. I ask you to test this youth and, if you find him able, to take him as your Herald on your voyage. He will serve you well, for he has been taught that commerce and words, its medium, are the unifying bonds which will one day unite the cosmos into a single humankind. Do not conceive that the College and Order of Heralds is a mere aid to you in your commercial adventure."

"Very well," growled the trader. He addressed Alen in broken Lyran: "Boy, how you make up Vegan stones of three fires so Lyran women like, come buy, buy again?"

Alen smoothly replied: "The Vegan triple-fire gem finds most favor on Lyra and especially among its women when set in a wide glass anklet if large, and when arranged in the Lyran 'lucky five' pattern in a glass thumb ring if small." He was glad, very glad, he had come across—and as a matter of course memorized, in the relentless fashion of the Order—a novel which touched briefly on the Lyran jewel trade.

The trader glowered and switched to Cephean—apparently his native tongue. "That was well-enough said, Herald. Now tell me whether you've got guts to man a squirt in case we're intercepted by the thieving so-called Customs collectors of Eyolf's Realm between here and Lyra?"

Alen knew the Rector's eyes were on him. "The noble mission of our Order," he said, "forbids me to use any weapon but the truth in furthering cosmic utilitarian civilization. No, master trader, I shall not man one of your weapons."

The trader shrugged. "So I must take what I get. Good Master Herald, make me a price."

The Rector said casually: "I regard this chiefly as a training mission for our novice; the fee will be nominal. Let us say twenty-five per cent of your net as of blastoff from Lyra, to be audited by Journeyman-Herald Alen."

The trader's howl of rage echoed in the dome of the huge room. "It's not fair!" he roared. "Who but you thievish villains with your Order and your catch-'em-young and your years of training can learn the tongues of the galaxy? What chance has a decent merchant busy with profit and loss got to learn the cant of every race between Sirius and the Coalsack? It's not fair! It's not fair and I'll say so until my dying breath!"

"Die outside if you find our terms unacceptable," said the Rector. "The Order does not haggle."

"Well I know it," sighed the trader brokenly. "I should have stuck to my own system and my good father's pump-flange factory. But no! I had to pick up a bargain in gems on Vega! Enough of this—bring me your contract and I'll sign it."

The Rector's shaggy eyebrows went up. "There is no contract," he said. "A mutual trust between Herald and trader is the cornerstone upon which cosmos-wide amity and understanding will be built."

"At twenty-five per cent for an unlicked pup," muttered blackbeard to himself in Cephean.

None of his instructors had played Polonius as Alen, with the seal of the Journeyman-Herald on his brow, packed for blastoff and vacated his cell. He supposed they knew that twenty years of training either had done their work or had not.

The trader taking Alen to the field where his ship waited was less wise. "The secret of successful negotiation," he weightily told his Herald, "is to yield willingly. This may strike you as a paradox, but it is the veritable key to my success in maintaining the profits of my good father's pump-flange trade. The secret is to yield with rueful admiration of your opponent—but *only in unimportant details*. Put up a little battle about delivery date or about terms of credit and then let him have his way. But you never give way a hair's breadth on your asking price unless—"

Alen let him drivel on as they drove through the outer works of the College. He was glad the car was open. For the first time he was being accorded the doffed hat that is the due of Heralds from their inferiors in the Order, and the grave nod of salutation from equals. Five-year-old postulants seeing his brow seal tugged off their headgear with comical celerity; fellow novices, equals a few hours before, uncovered as though he were the Rector himself.

The ceremonial began to reach the trader. When, with a final salutation, a lay warder let them through the great gate of the curtain wall, he said with some irritation, "They appear to hold you in high regard, boy."

"I am better addressed as Herald," said Alen composedly.

"A plague descend on the College and Order! Do you think I don't know my manners? Of course, I call a Herald 'Herald,' but we're going to be cooped up together and you'll be working for me. What'll happen to ship's discipline if I have to kowtow to you?"

"There will be no problem," said Alen.

Blackbeard grunted and trod fiercely on the accelerator.

"That's my ship," he said at length. "*Starsong*. Vegan registry—it may help passing through Eyolf's Realm, though it cost me overmuch in bribes. A crew of eight, lazy, good-for-nothing wastrels—Agh! Can I believe my eyes?" The car jammed to a halt before the looming ship, and blackbeard was up the ladder and through the port in a second. Settling his robes, Alen followed.

He found the trader fiercely denouncing his chief engineer for using space drive to heat the ship; he had seen the faint haze of a minimum exhaust from the stern tubes.

"For that, dolt," screamed blackbeard, "we have a thing known as electricity. Have you by chance ever heard of it? Are you aware that a chief engineer's responsibility is the efficient and *economical* operation of his ship's drive mechanism?"

The chief, a cowed-looking Cephean, saw Alen with relief and swept off his battered cap. The Herald nodded gravely and the trader broke off in irritation. "We need none of that bowing and scraping for the rest of the voyage," he declared.

"Of course not, sir," said the chief. "O'course not. I was just welcoming the Herald aboard. Welcome aboard, Herald. I'm Chief Elwon, Herald. And I'm glad to have a Herald with us." A covert glance at the trader. "*I've* voyaged with Heralds and without, and I don't mind saying I feel safer indeed with you aboard."

"May I be taken to my quarters?" asked Alen.

"Your—" began the trader, stupefied.

The chief broke in, "I'll fix you a cabin, Herald. We've got some bulkheads I can rig aft for a snug little space, not roomy, but the best a little ship like this can afford."

The trader collapsed into a bucket seat as the chief bustled aft and Alen followed.

"Herald," the chief said with some embarrassment after he had collared two crewmen and set them to work, "you'll have to excuse our good master trader. He's new to the interstar lanes and he doesn't exactly know the jets yet. Between us we'll get him squared away."

Alen inspected the cubicle run up for him—a satisfactory enclosure affording him the decent privacy he rated. He dismissed the chief and the crewmen with a nod and settled himself on the cot.

Beneath the iron composure in which he had been trained, he felt scared and alone. Not even old Machiavelli seemed to offer comfort or council: "There is nothing more difficult to take in hand, more perilous to conduct, or more uncertain in its success, than to take the lead in the introduction of a new order of things," said Chapter Six.

But what said Chapter Twenty-Six? "Where the willingness is great, the difficulties cannot be great."

Starsong was not a happy ship. Blackbeard's nagging stinginess hung over the crew like a thundercloud, but Alen professed not to notice. He walked regularly fore and aft for two hours a day greeting the crew members in their various native tongues and then wrapping himself in the reserve the Order demanded—though he longed to salute them man-to-man, eat with them, gossip about their native planets, the past misdeeds that had brought them to their berths aboard the miserly *Starsong*, their hopes for the future. The Rule of the College and Order of Heralds decreed otherwise. He accepted the uncoverings of the crew with a nod and tried to be pleased because they stood in growing awe of him that ranged from Chief Elwon's lively appreciation of a Herald's skill to Wiper Jukkl's superstitious reverence. Jukkl was a low-browed specimen from a planet of the decadent Sirius system. He outdid the normal slovenliness of an all-male crew on a freighter—a slovenliness in which Alen could not share. Many of his waking hours were spent in his locked cubicle burnishing his metal and cleaning and pressing his robes. A Herald was never supposed to suggest by his appearance that he shared mortal frailties.

Blackbeard himself yielded a little, to the point of touching his cap sullenly. This probably was not so much awe at Alen's studied manner as respect for the incisive, lightning-fast job of auditing the Herald did on the books of the trading venture—absurdly complicated books with scores of accounts to record a simple matter of buying gems cheap on Vega and chartering a ship in the hope of selling them dearly on Lyra. The complicated books and overlapping accounts did tell the story, but they made it very easy for an auditor to erroneously read a number of costs as far higher than they actually were. Alen did not fall into the trap.

On the fifth day after blastoff, Chief Elwon rapped, respectfully but urgently, on the door of Alen's cubicle.

"If you please, Herald," he urged, "could you come to the bridge?"

Alen's heart bounded in his chest, but he gravely said, "My meditation must not be interrupted. I shall join you on the bridge in ten minutes."

And for ten minutes he methodically polished a murky link in the massive gold chain that fastened his boat-cloak—the "meditation." He donned the cloak before stepping out; the summons sounded like a full-dress affair in the offing.

The trader was stamping and fuming. Chief Elwon was riffling through his spec book unhappily. Astrogator Hufner was at the plot computer running up trajectories and knocking them down again. A quick glance showed Alen that they were all high-speed trajectories in the evasive-action class.

"Herald," said the trader grimly, "we have broken somebody's detector bubble." He jerked his thumb at a red-lit signal. "I expect we'll be overhauled shortly. Are you ready to earn your twenty-five per cent of the net?"

Alen overlooked the crudity. "Are you rigged for color video, merchant?" he asked.

"We are."

"Then I am ready to do what I can for my client."

He took the communicator's seat, stealing a glance in the still-blank screen. The reflection of his face was reassuring, though he wished he had thought to comb his small beard.

Another light flashed on, and Hufner quit the operator to study the detector board. "Big, powerful, and getting closer," he said tersely. "Scanning for us with directionals now. Putting out plenty of energy—"

The loudspeaker of the ship-to-ship audio came to life.

"What ship are you?" it demanded in Vegan. "We are a Customs cruiser of the Realm of Eyolf. What ship are you?"

"Have the crew man the squirts," said the trader softly to the chief.

Elwon looked at Alen, who shook his head. "Sorry, sir," said the engineer apologetically. "The Herald—"

"We are the freighter *Starsong*, Vegan registry," said Alen into the audio mike as the trader choked. "We are carrying Vegan gems to Lyra."

"They're on us," said the astrogator despairingly, reading his instruments. The ship-to-ship video flashed on, showing an arrogant, square-jawed face topped by a battered naval cap.

"Lyra indeed? We have plans of our own for Lyra. You will heave to—" began the officer in the screen, before he noted Alen. "My pardon, Herald," he said sardonically. "Herald, will you please request the ship's master to heave to for boarding and search? We wish to assess and collect Customs duties. You are aware, of course, that your vessel is passing through the Realm."

The man's accented Vegan reeked of Algol IV. Alen switched to that obscure language to say, "We were not aware of that. Are you aware that there is a reciprocal trade treaty in effect between the Vegan system and the

Realm which specifies that freight in Vegan bottoms is dutiable only when consigned to ports in the Realm?"

"You speak Algolian, do you? You Heralds have not been underrated, but don't plan to lie your way out of this. Yes, I am aware of some such agreement as you mentioned. We shall board you, as I said, and assess and collect duty in kind. If, regrettably, there has been any mistake, you are of course free to apply to the Realm for reimbursement. Now, heave to!"

"I have no intentions of lying. I speak the solemn truth when I say that we shall fight to the last man any attempt of yours to board and loot us."

Alen's mind was racing furiously through the catalog of planetary folkways the Rule had decreed that he master. Algol IV—some ancestor worship; veneration of mother; hand-to-hand combat with knives; complimentary greeting, "May you never strike down a weaker foe"; folk-hero Gaarek unjustly accused of slaying a cripple and exiled but it was an enemy's plot—

A disconcerted shadow was crossing the face of the officer as Alen improvised: "You will, of course, kill us all. But before this happens I shall have messaged back to the College and Order of Heralds the facts in the case, with a particular request that your family be informed. Your name, I think, will be remembered as long as Gaarek's—though not in the same way, of course; the Algolian whose hundred-man battle cruiser wiped out a virtually unarmed freighter with a crew of eight."

The officer's face was dark with rage. "You devil!" he snarled. "Leave my family out of this! I'll come aboard and fight you man-to-man if you have the stomach for it!"

Alen shook his head regretfully. "The Rule of my Order forbids recourse to violence," he said. "Our only permissible weapon is the truth."

"We're coming aboard," said the officer grimly. "I'll order my men not to harm your people. We'll just be collecting customs. If your people shoot first, my men will be under orders to do nothing more than disable them."

Alen smiled and uttered a sentence or two in Algolian.

The officer's jaw dropped and he croaked, after a pause, "I'll cut you to ribbons. You can't say that about my mother, you—" and he spewed back some of the words Alen had spoken.

"Calm yourself," said the Herald gravely. "I apologize for my disgusting and unheraldic remarks. But I wished to prove a point. You would have killed me if you could; I touched off a reaction which had been planted in you by your culture. I will be able to do the same with the men of yours who come aboard. For every race of man there is the intolerable insult that must be avenged in blood.

"Send your men aboard under orders not to kill if you wish; I shall goad them into a killing rage. We shall be massacred, yours will be the blame and you will be disgraced and disowned by your entire planet." Alen hoped desperately that the naval crews of the Realm were, as reputed, a barbarous and undisciplined lot—

Evidently they were, and the proud Algolian dared not risk it. In his native language he spat again, "You devil!" and switched back into Vegan. "Freighter *Starsong,*" he said bleakly, "I find that my space fix was in error and that you are not in Realm territory. You may proceed."

The astrogator said from the detector board, incredulously, "He's disengaging. He's off us. He's accelerating. Herald, *what* did you say to him?"

But the reaction from blackbeard was more gratifying. Speechless, the trader took off his cap. Alen acknowledged the salute with a grave nod before he started back to his cubicle. It was just as well, he reflected, that the trader didn't know his life and his ship had been unconditionally pledged in a finish fight against a hundred-man battle cruiser.

Lyra's principal spaceport was pocked and broken, but they made a fair-enough landing. Alen, in full heraldic robes, descended from *Starsong* to greet a handful of port officials.

"Any metals aboard?" demanded one of them.

"None for sale," said the Herald. "We have Vegan gems, chiefly triple-fire." He knew that the dull little planet was short of metals and, having made a virtue of necessity, was somehow prejudiced against their import.

"Have your crew transfer the cargo to the Customs shed," said the port official studying *Starsong*'s papers. "And all of you wait there."

All of them—except Alen—lugged numbered sacks and boxes of gems to the low brick building designated. The trader was allowed to pocket a handful for samples before the shed was sealed—a complicated business. A brick was mortared over the simple ironwood latch that closed the ironwood door, a pat of clay was slapped over the brick, and the port seal stamped in it. A mechanic with what looked like a pottery blowtorch fed by powdered coal played a flame on the clay seal until it glowed orange-red and that was that.

"Herald," said the port official, "tell the merchant to sign here and make his fingerprints."

Alen studied the document; it was a simple identification form. Blackbeard signed with the reed pen provided and fingerprinted the document. After two weeks in space he scarcely needed to ink his fingers first.

"Now tell him that we'll release the gems on his written fingerprinted order to whatever Lyran citizens he sells to. And explain that this round-about system is necessary to avoid metal smuggling. Please remove *all* metal from your clothes and stow it on your ship. Then we will seal that, too, and put it under guard until you are ready to take off. We regret that we will have to search you before we turn you loose, but we can't afford to have our economy disrupted by irresponsible introduction of metals." Alen had not realized it was that bad.

After the thorough search that extended to the confiscation of forgotten watches and pins, the port officials changed a sheaf of the trader's uranium-backed Vegan currency into Lyran legal tender based on man-hours. Black-beard made a partial payment to the crew, told them to have a good liberty and check in at the port at sunset the next day for probable takeoff.

Alen and the trader were driven to town in an unlikely vehicle whose power plant was a pottery turbine. The driver, when they were safely out on the open road, furtively asked whether they had any metal they wanted to discard.

The trader asked sharply in his broken Lyran: "What you do you get metal? Where sell, how use?"

The driver, following a universal tendency, raised his voice and lapsed into broken Lyran himself to tell the strangers: "Black market science men pay much, much for little bit metal. Study, use build. Politicians make law no metal, what I care politicians? But you no tell, gentlemen?"

"We won't tell," said Alen. "But we have no metal for you."

The driver shrugged.

"Herald," said the trader, "what do you make of it?"

"I didn't know it was a political issue. We concern ourselves with the basic patterns of a people's behavior, not the day-to-day expressions of the patterns. The planet's got no heavy metals, which means there were no metals available to the primitive Lyrans. The lighter metals don't occur in native form or in easily split compounds. They proceeded along the ceramic line instead of the metallic line and appear to have done quite well for themselves up to a point. No electricity, of course, no aviation and no space flight."

"And," said the trader, "naturally the people who make these buggies and that blowtorch we saw are scared witless that metals will be imported and put them out of business. So naturally they have laws passed prohibiting it."

"Naturally," said the Herald, looking sharply at the trader. But black-beard was back in character a moment later. "An outrage," he growled. "Trying to tell a man what he can and can't import when he sees a decent chance to make a bit of profit."

The driver dropped them at a boardinghouse. It was half-timbered construction, which appeared to be swankier than the more common brick. The floors were plate glass, roughened for traction. Alen got them a double room with a view.

"What's that thing?" demanded the trader, inspecting the view.

The thing was a structure looming above the slate and tile roofs of the town—a round brick tower for its first twenty-five meters and then wood for another fifteen. As they studied it, it pricked up a pair of ears at the top and began to flop them wildly.

"Semaphore," said Alen.

A minute later blackbeard piteously demanded from the bathroom, "*How do you make water come out of the tap? I touched it all over but nothing happened.*"

"You have to turn it," said Alen, demonstrating. "And that thing—you pull it sharply down, hold it, and then release."

"Barbarous," muttered the trader. "Barbarous."

An elderly maid came in to show them how to string their hammocks and ask if they happened to have a bit of metal to give her for a souvenir. They sent her away and, rather than face the public dining room, made a meal from their own stores and turned in for the night.

It's going well, though Alen drowsily; going very well indeed.

He awoke abruptly, but made no move. It was dark in the double room, and there were stealthy, furtive little noises nearby. A hundred thoughts flashed through his head of Lyran treachery and double-dealing. He lifted his eyelids a trifle and saw a figure silhouetted against the faint light of the big window. If a burglar, he was a clumsy one.

There was a stirring from the other hammock, the trader's. With a subdued roar that sounded like "Thieving villains!" blackbeard launched himself from the hammock at the intruder. But his feet tangled in the hammock cords and he belly-flopped on the floor.

The burglar, if it was one, didn't dash smoothly and efficiently for the door. He straightened himself against the window and said resignedly, "You need not fear. I will make no resistance."

Alen rolled from the hammock and helped the trader to his feet. "He said he doesn't want to fight," he told the trader.

Blackbeard seized the intruder and shook him like a rat. "So the rogue is a coward too!" he boomed. "Give us a light, Herald."

Alen uncovered the slow-match, blew it to a flame, squeakily pumped up a pressure torch until a jet of pulverized coal sprayed from its nozzle and ignited it. A dozen strokes more and there was enough heat feeding back from the jet to maintain the pressure cycle.

Through all of this the trader was demanding in his broken Lyran, "What make here, thief? What reason thief us room?"

The Herald brought the hissing pressure lamp to the window. The intruder's face was not the unhealthy, neurotic face of a criminal. Its thin lines told of discipline and thought.

"What did you want here?" asked Alen.

"Metal," said the intruder simply. "I thought you might have a bit of iron."

It was the first time a specific metal had been named by any Lyran. He used, of course, the Vegan word for iron.

"You are particular," remarked the Herald. "Why iron?"

"I have heard that it possesses certain properties—perhaps you can tell me before you turn me over to the police. Is it true, as we hear, that a mass of iron whose crystals have been aligned by a sharp blow will strongly attract another piece of iron with a force related to the distance between them?"

"It is true," said the Herald, studying the man's face. It was lit with excitement. Deliberately Alen added, "This alignment is more easily and uniformly ejected by placing the mass of iron in an electric field—that is, a space surrounding the passage of an electron stream through a conductor." Many of the words he used had to be Vegan; there were no Lyran words for "electric," "electron," or "conductor."

The intruder's face fell. "I have tried to master the concept you refer to," he admitted. "But it is beyond me. I have questioned other interstar voyagers and they have touched on it; but I cannot grasp it— But thank you, sir; you have been very courteous. I will trouble you no further while you summon the watch."

"You give up too easily," said Alen. "For a scientist, much too easily. If we turn you over to the watch, there will be hearings and testimony and whatnot. Our time is limited here on your planet; I doubt that we can spare any for your legal processes."

The trader let go of the intruder's shoulder and grumbled, "Why you no ask we have iron, I tell you no. Search, search, take all metal away. We no police you. I sorry hurted you arms. Here for you." Blackbeard brought out a palmful of his sample gems and picked out a large triple-fire stone. "You not be angry me," he said, putting it in the Lyran's hand.

"I can't—" said the scientist.

Blackbeard closed his fingers over the stone and growled, "I give, you take. Maybe buy iron with, eh?"

"That's so," said the Lyran. "Thank you both, gentlemen. Thank you—"

"You go," said the trader. "You go, we sleep again."

The scientist bowed with dignity and left their room.

"Gods of space," swore the trader. "To think that Jukkl, the *Starsong*'s wiper, knows more about electricity and magnetism than a brainy fellow like that."

"And they are the key to physics," mused Alen. "A scientist here is dead-ended forever, because their materials are all insulators! Glass, clay, glaze, wood."

"Funny, all right," yawned blackbeard. "Did you see me collar him once I got on my feet? Sharp, eh? Good night, Herald." He gruntingly hauled himself into the hammock again, leaving Alen to turn off the hissing light and cover the slow-match with its perforated lid.

They had roast fowl of some sort or other for breakfast in the public dining room. Alen was required by his Rule to refuse the red wine that went with it. The trader gulped it approvingly. "A sensible, though backward people," he said. "And now if you'll inquire of the management where the thievish jewel buyers congregate, we can get on with our business and perhaps be off by dawn tomorrow."

"So quickly?" asked Alen, almost forgetting himself enough to show surprise.

"My charter on *Starsong*, good Herald—thirty days to go, but what might not go wrong in space? And then there would be penalties to mulct me of whatever minute profit I may realize."

Alen learned that Gromeg's Tavern was the gem mart and they took another of the turbine-engined cabs through the brick-paved streets.

Gromeg's was a dismal, small-windowed brick barn with heavyset men lounging about, an open kitchen at one end and tables at the other. A score of smaller, sharp-faced men were at the tables, sipping wine and chatting.

"I am Journeyman-Herald Alen," announced Alen clearly, "with Vegan gems to dispose of."

There was a silence of elaborate unconcern, and then one of the dealers spat and grunted, "Vegan gems. A drug on the market. Take them away, Herald."

"Come, master trader," said Alen in the Lyran tongue. "The gem dealers of Lyra do not want your wares." He started for the door.

One of the dealers called languidly, "Well, wait a moment. I have nothing better to do; since you've come all this way, I'll have a look at your stuff."

"You honor us," said Alen. He and blackbeard sat at the man's table. The trader took out a palmful of samples, counted them meaningfully, and laid them on the boards.

"Well," said the gem dealer, "I don't know whether to be amused or insulted. I am Garthkint, the gem dealer—not a retailer of *beads*. However, I have no hard feelings. A drink for your frowning friend, Herald? I know you gentry don't indulge." The drink was already on the table, brought by one of the hulking guards.

Alen passed Garthkint's own mug of wine to the trader, explaining politely: "In my master trader's native Cepheus it is considered honorable for the guest to sip the drink his host laid down and none other. A charming custom, is it not?"

"Charming, though unsanitary," muttered the gem dealer—and he did not touch the drink he had ordered for blackbeard.

"I can't understand a word either of you is saying—too flowery. Was this little rat trying to drug me?" demanded the trader in Cephean.

"No," said Alen. "Just trying to get you drunk." To Garthkint in Lyran, he explained, "The good trader was saying that he wishes to leave at once. I was agreeing with him."

"Well," said Garthkint, "perhaps I can take a couple of your gauds. For some youngster who wishes a cheap ring."

"He's getting to it," Alen told the trader.

"High time," grunted blackbeard.

"The trader asks me to inform you," said Alen, switching back to Lyran, "that he is unable to sell in lots smaller than five hundred gems."

"A compact language, Cephean," said Garthkint, narrowing his eyes.

"Is it not?" Alen blandly agreed.

The gem dealer's forefinger rolled an especially fine three-fire stone from the little pool of gems on the table. "I suppose," he said grudgingly, "that this is what I must call the best of the lot. What, I am curious to know, is the price you would set for five hundred equal in quality and size to this poor thing?"

"This," said Alen, "is the good trader's first venture to your delightful planet. He wishes to be remembered and welcomed all of the many times he anticipates returning. Because of this he has set an absurdly low price, counting good will as more important than a prosperous voyage. Two thousand Lyran credits."

"Absurd," snorted Garthkint. "I cannot do business with you. Either you are insanely rapacious or you have been pitifully misguided as to the value of your wares. I am well known for my charity; I will assume that the latter is the case. I trust you will not be too downcast when I tell you that five hundred of these muddy, undersized out-of-round objects are worth no more than two hundred credits."

"If you are serious," said Alen with marked amazement, "we would not dream of imposing on you. At the figure you mention, we might as well not sell at all but return with our wares to Cepheus and give these gems to children in the streets for marbles. Good gem trader, excuse us for taking up so much of your time and many thanks for your warm hospitality in the matter of the wine." He switched to Cephean and said: "We're dickering now. Two thousand and two hundred. Get up; we're going to start to walk out."

"What if he lets us go?" grumbled blackbeard, but he did heave himself to his feet and turn to the door as Alen rose.

"My trader echoes my regrets," the Herald said in Lyran. "Farewell."

"Well, stay a moment," said Garthkint. "I am well known for my soft heart toward strangers. A charitable man might go as high as five hundred and absorb the inevitable loss. If you should return some day with a passable lot of *real* gems, it would be worth my while for you to remember who treated you with such benevolence and give me fair choice."

"Noble Lyran," said Alen, apparently almost overcome. "I shall not easily forget your combination of acumen and charity. It is a lesson to traders. It is a lesson to me. I shall *not* insist on two thousand. I shall cut the throat of my trader's venture by reducing his price to eighteen hundred credits, though I wonder how I shall dare tell him of it."

"What's going on now?" demanded blackbeard.

"Five hundred and eighteen hundred," said Alen. "We can sit down again."

"Up, down—up, down," muttered the trader.

They sat, and Alen said in Lyran: "My trader unexpectedly endorses the reduction. He says, 'Better to lose some than all'—an old proverb in the Cephean tongue. And he forbids any further reduction."

"Come, now," wheedled the gem dealer. "Let us be men of the world about this. One must give a little and take a little. Everybody knows he can't have his own way forever. I shall offer a good, round eight hundred credits and we'll close on it, eh? Pilquis, fetch us a pen and ink!" One of the burly guards was right there with an inkpot and a reed pen. Garthkint had a Customs form out of his tunic and was busily filling it in to specify the size, number, and fire of gems to be released to him.

"What's it now?" asked blackbeard.

"Eight hundred."

"Take it!"

"Garthkint," said Alen regretfully, "you heard the firmness and decision in my trader's voice? What can I do? I am only speaking for him. He is a hard man but perhaps I can talk him around later. I offer you the gems at a ruinous fifteen hundred credits."

"Split the difference," said Garthkint resignedly.

"Done at eleven-fifty," said Alen.

That blackbeard understood. "Well done!" he boomed at Alen and took a swig at Garthkint's wine cup. "Have him fill in 'Sack eighteen' on his paper. It's five hundred of that grade."

The gem dealer counted out twenty-three fifty-credit notes and blackbeard signed and fingerprinted the release.

"Now," said Garthkint, "you will please remain here while I take a trip to the spaceport for my property." Three or four of the guards were suddenly quite close.

"You will find," said Alen dryly, "that our standard of commercial morality is no lower than yours."

The dealer smiled politely and left.

"Who will be the next?" asked Alen of the room at large.

"I'll look at your gems," said another dealer, sitting at the table.

With the ice breaking down, the transactions went quicker. Alen had disposed of a dozen lots by the time their first buyer returned.

"It's all right," he said. "We've been tricked before, but your gems are as represented. I congratulate you, Herald, on driving a hard, fair bargain."

"That means," said Alen regretfully, "that I should have asked for more." The guards were once more lounging in corners and no longer seemed so menacing.

They had a midday meal and continued to dispose of their wares. At sunset Alen held a final auction to clean up the odd lots that remained over and was urged to stay to dinner.

The trader, counting a huge wad of the Lyran manpower-based notes, shook his head. "We should be off before dawn, Herald," he told Alen. "Time is money, time is money."

"They are very insistent."

"And I am very stubborn. Thank them and let us be on our way before anything else is done to increase my overhead."

Something did turn up—a city watchman with a bloody nose and split lip.

He demanded of the Herald, "Are you responsible for the Cephean maniac known as Elwon?"

Garthkint glided up to mutter in Alen's ear, "Beware how you answer!"

Alen needed no warning. His grounding included Lyran legal concepts—and on the backward little planet touched with many relics of feudalism, "responsible" covered much territory.

"What has Chief Elwon done?" he parried.

"As you see," the watchman glumly replied, pointing to his wounds. "And the same to three others before we got him out of the wrecked wine shop and into the castle. Are you responsible for him?"

"Let me speak with my trader for a moment. Will you have some wine meantime?" He signaled and one of the guards brought a mug.

"Don't mind if I do. I can use it," sighed the watchman.

"We are in trouble," said Alen to blackbeard. "Chief Elwon is in the castle—prison—for drunk and disorderly conduct. You as his master are considered responsible for his conduct under Lyran law. You must pay his fines or serve his penalties. Or you can disown him, which is considered dishonorable but sometimes necessary. For paying his fine or serving his time you have a prior lien on his services, without pay—but of course that's unenforceable off Lyra."

Blackbeard was sweating a little. "Find out from the policeman how long all this is likely to take. I don't want to leave Elwon here and I do want us to get off as soon as possible. Keep him occupied, now, while I go about some business."

The trader retreated to a corner of the darkening barnlike tavern, beckoning Garthkint and a guard with him as Alen returned to the watchman.

"Good keeper of the peace," he said, "will you have another?"

He would.

"My trader wishes to know what penalties are likely to be levied against the unfortunate Chief Elwon."

"Going to leave him in the lurch, eh?" asked the watchman a little belligerently. "A fine master you have!"

One of the dealers at the table indignantly corroborated him. "If you foreigners aren't prepared to live up to your obligations, why did you come here in the first place? What happens to business if a master can send his man to steal and cheat and then say, 'Don't blame *me*—it was *his* doing!' "

Alen patiently explained, "On other planets, good Lyrans, the tie of master and man is not so strong that a man would obey if he were ordered to go and steal or cheat."

They shook their heads and muttered. It was unheard of.

"Good watchman," pressed the Herald, "my trader does not *want* to disown Chief Elwon. Can you tell me what recompense would be necessary—and how long it would take to manage the business?"

The watchman started on a third cup which Alen had unostentatiously signaled for. "It's hard to say," he told the Herald weightily. "For my damages, I would demand a hundred credits at least. The three other members of the watch battered by your lunatic could ask no less. The wine shop suffered easily five hundred credits' damage. The owner of it was beaten, but that doesn't matter, of course."

"No imprisonment?"

"Oh, a flogging, of course." Alen started before he recalled that the "flogging" was a few half-hearted symbolic strokes on the covered shoulders with a light cane. "But no imprisonment. His Honor, Judge Krarl, does not sit on the night bench. Judge Krarl is a newfangled reformer, stranger. He professes to believe that mulcting is unjust—that it makes it easy for the rich to commit crime and go scot-free."

"But doesn't it?" asked Alen, drawn off course in spite of himself. There was pitying laughter around him.

"Look you," a dealer explained kindly. "The good watchman suffers battery, the mad Cephean or his master is mulcted for damages, the watchman is repaid for his injuries. What kind of justice is it to the watchman if the mad Cephean is locked away in a cell, unfined?"

The watchman nodded approvingly. "Well said," he told the dealer. "Luckily we have on the night bench a justice of the old school, His Honor, Judge Treel. Stern, but fair. You should hear him! 'Fifty credits! A hundred credits and the lash! Robbed a ship, eh? Two thousand credits!' " He returned to his own voice and said with awe, "For a murder, he never assesses less than *ten thousand credits!*"

And if the murderer couldn't pay, Alen knew, he became a "public charge," "responsible to the state"—that is, a slave. If he could pay, of course, he was turned loose.

"And His Honor, Judge Treel," he pressed, "is sitting tonight? Can we possibly appear before him, pay the fines, and be off?"

"To be sure, stranger. I'd be a fool if I waited until morning, wouldn't I?" The wine had loosened his tongue a little too far and he evidently realized it. "Enough of this," he said. "Does your master honorably accept responsibility of the Cephean? If so, come along with me, the two of you, and we'll get this over with."

"Thanks, good watchman. We are coming."

He went to blackbeard, now alone in his corner, and said, "It's all right. We can pay off—about a thousand credits—and be on our way."

The trader muttered darkly, "Lyran jurisdiction or not, it's coming out of Elwon's pay. The bloody fool!"

They rattled through the darkening streets of the town in one of the turbine-powered wagons, the watchman sitting up front with the driver and the trader and the Herald behind.

"Something's burning," said Alen to the trader, sniffing the air.

"This stinking buggy—" began blackbeard. "Oops," he said, interrupting himself and slapping at his cloak.

"Let me, trader," said Alen. He turned back the cloak, licked his thumb, and rubbed out a crawling ring of sparks spreading across a few centimeters of the cloak's silk lining. And he looked fixedly at what had started the little fire. It was an improperly covered slow-match protruding from a holstered device that was unquestionably a hand weapon.

"I bought it from one of their guards while you were parleying with the policeman," explained blackbeard embarrassedly. "I had a time making him understand. That Garthkint fellow helped." He fiddled with the perforated cover of the slow-match, screwing it on more firmly.

"A pitiful excuse for a weapon," he went on, carefully arranging his cloak over it. "The trigger isn't a trigger and the thumb safety isn't a safety. You pump the trigger a few times to build up pressure, and a little air squirts out to blow the match to life. Then you uncover the match and pull back the cocking piece. This levers a dart into the barrel. *Then* you push the thumb safety which puffs coal dust into the firing chamber and also swivels down the slow-match onto a touch-hole. *Poof,* and away goes the dart if you didn't forget any of the steps or do them in the wrong order. Luckily, I also got a knife."

He patted the nape of his neck and said, "That's where they carry 'em here. A little sheath between the shoulder blades—wonderful for a fast draw-and-throw, though it exposes you a little more than I like when you reach. The knife's black glass. Splendid edge and good balance.

"And the thieving Lyrans knew they had me where it hurt. Seven thousand, five hundred credits for the knife and gun—if you can call it that—and the holsters. By rights I should dock Elwon for them, the bloody fool. Still, it's better to buy his way out and leave no hard feelings behind us, eh, Herald?"

"Incomparably better," said Alen. "And I am amazed that you even entertain the idea of an armed jail-delivery. What if Chief Elwon had to serve a few days in a prison? Would that be worse than forever barring yourself from the planet and blackening the names of all traders with Lyra? Trader, do not hope to put down the credits that your weapons cost you as a legitimate expense of the voyage. I will not allow it when I audit your books. It was a piece of folly on which you spent personal funds, as far as the College and Order of Heralds is concerned."

"Look here," protested blackbeard. "You're supposed to be spreading utilitarian civilization, aren't you? What's utilitarian about leaving one of my crewmen here?"

Alen ignored the childish argument and wrapped himself in angry silence. As to civilization, he wondered darkly whether such a trading voyage and his part in it were relevant at all. Were the slanders true? Was the College and Order simply a collection of dupes headed by cynical oldsters greedy for luxury and power?

Such thoughts hadn't crossed his mind in a long time. He'd been too busy to entertain them, cramming his head with languages, folkways, mores, customs, underlying patterns of culture, of hundreds of galactic peoples— and for what? So that this fellow could make a profit and the College and Order take a quarter of that profit. If civilization was to come to Lyra, it would have to come in the form of metal. If the Lyrans didn't want metal, *make* them take it.

What did Machiavelli say? "The chief foundations of all states are good laws and good arms; and as there cannot be good laws where the state is not well-armed, it follows that where they are well-armed, they have good laws." It was odd that the teachers had slurred over such a seminal idea, emphasizing instead the spiritual integrity of the weaponless College and Order—or was it?

The disenchantment he felt creeping over him was terrifying.

"The castle," said the watchman over his shoulder, and their wagon stopped with a rattle before a large but unimpressive brick structure of five stories.

"You wait," the trader told the driver after they got out. He handed him two of his fifty-credit bills. "You wait, you get many, many more money. You understand, wait?"

"I wait plenty much," shouted the driver delightedly. "I wait all night, all day. You wonderful master. You great, great master, I wait—"

"All right," growled the trader, shutting him off. "You wait."

The watchman took them through an entrance hall lit by hissing pressure lamps and casually guarded by a few liveried men with truncheons. He threw open the door of a medium-sized, well-lit room with a score of people in it, looked in, and uttered a despairing groan.

A personage on a chair that looked like a throne said sharply, "Are those the star travelers? Well, don't just stand there. Bring them in!"

"Yes, Your Honor, Judge Krarl," said the watchman unhappily.

"It's the wrong judge!" Alen hissed at the trader. "This one gives out jail sentences!"

"Do what you can," said blackbeard grimly.

The watchman guided them to the personage in the chair and indicated a couple of low stools, bowed to the chair, and retired to stand at the back of the room.

"Your Honor," said Alen, "I am Journeyman-Herald Alen, Herald for the trading voyage—"

"Speak when you're spoken to," said the judge sharply. "Sir, with the usual insolence of wealth you have chosen to keep us waiting. I do not take this personally; it might have happened to Judge Treel, whom—to your evident dismay—I am replacing because of a sudden illness, or to any other member of the bench. But as an insult to our justice, we cannot overlook it. Sir, consider yourself reprimanded. Take your seats. Watchman, bring in the Cephean."

"Sit down," Alen murmured to the trader. "This is going to be bad."

A watchman brought in Chief Elwon, bleary-eyed, tousled, and sporting a few bruises. He gave Alen and the trader a shamefaced grin as his guard sat him on a stool beside them. The trader glared back.

Judge Krarl mumbled perfunctorily: "Let battle be joined among the several parties in this dispute let no man question our impartial awarding of the victory speak now if you yield instead to our judgment. *Well?* Speak up, you watchmen!"

The watchman who had brought the Herald and the trader started and said from the back of the room, "I yield instead to Your Honor's judgment."

Three other watchmen and a battered citizen, the wine-shop keeper, mumbled in turn, "I yield instead to Your Honor's judgment."

"Herald, speak for the accused," snapped the judge.

Well, thought Alen, I can try. "Your Honor," he said, "Chief Elwon's master does not yield to Your Honor's judgment. He is ready to battle the other parties in the dispute or their masters."

"What insolence is this?" screamed the judge, leaping from his throne. "The barbarous customs of other worlds do not prevail in this court! Who spoke of battle—" He shut his mouth with a snap, evidently abruptly realizing that *he* had spoken of battle, in an archaic phrase that harked back to the origins of justice on the planet. The judge sat down again and told Alen, more calmly, "You have mistaken a mere formality. The offer was not made in earnest." Obviously, he didn't like the sound of that himself, but he proceeded, "Now say 'I yield instead to Your Honor's judgment,' and we can get on with it. For your information, trial by combat has not been practiced for many generations on our enlightened planet."

Alen said politely, "Your Honor, I am a stranger to many of the ways of Lyra, but our excellent College and Order of Heralds instructed me well in the underlying principles of your law. I recall that one of your most revered legal maxims declares: 'The highest crime against man is murder; the highest crime against man's society is breach of promise.'"

Purpling, the judge snarled, "Are you presuming to bandy law with me, you slippery-tongued foreigner? Are you presuming to accuse me of the high crime of breaking my promise? For your information, a promise consists of an offer to do, or refrain from doing, a thing in return for a consideration. There must be the five elements of promiser, promisee, offer, substance, and consideration."

"If you will forgive a foreigner," said Alen, suddenly feeling the ground again under his feet, "I maintain that you offered the parties in the dispute your services in awarding the victory."

"An empty argument," snorted the judge. "Just as an offer with substance from somebody to nobody for a consideration is no promise, or an offer without substance from somebody to somebody for a consideration is no promise, so my offer was no promise, for there was no consideration involved."

"Your Honor, must the consideration be from the promisee to the promiser?"

"Of course not. A third party may provide the consideration."

"Then I respectfully maintain that your offer was a promise, since a third party, the government, provided you with the considerations of salary and position in return for offering your services to the disputants."

"Watchmen, clear the room of disinterested persons," said the judge hoarsely. While it was being done, Alen swiftly filled in the trader and Chief Elwon. Blackbeard grinned at the mention of a five-against-one battle royal, and the engineer looked alarmed.

When the doors closed leaving the nine of them in privacy, the judge said bitterly, "Herald, where did you learn such devilish tricks?"

Alen told him: "My College and Order instructed me well. A similar situation existed on a planet called England during an age known as the Victorious. Trial by combat had long been obsolete, there as here, but had never been declared so—there as here. A litigant won a hopeless lawsuit by publishing a challenge to his opponent and appearing at the appointed place in full armor. His opponent ignored the challenge and so lost the suit by default. The English dictator, one Disraeli, hastily summoned his parliament to abolish trial by combat."

"And so," mused the judge, "I find myself accused in my own chamber of high crime if I do not permit you five to slash away at each other and decide who won."

The wine-shop keeper began to blubber that he was a peaceable man and didn't intend to be carved up by that blackbearded, bloodthirsty star traveler. All he wanted was his money.

"Silence!" snapped the judge. "Of course there will be no combat. Will you, shopkeeper, and you, watchmen, withdraw if you receive satisfactory financial settlements?"

They would.

"Herald, you may dicker with them."

The four watchmen stood fast by their demand for a hundred credits apiece, and got it. The terrified shopkeeper regained his balance and demanded a thousand. Alen explained that his black-bearded master from a rude and impetuous world might be unable to restrain his rage when he, Alen, interpreted the demand and, ignoring the consequences, might beat him, the shopkeeper, to a pulp. The asking price plunged to a reasonable five hundred, which was paid over. The shopkeeper got the judge's permission to leave and backed out, bowing.

"You see, trader," Alen told blackbeard, "that it was needless to buy weapons when the spoken word—"

"And now," said the judge with a sneer, "we are easily out of *that* dilemma. Watchmen, arrest the three star travelers and take them to the cages."

"Your Honor!" cried Alen, outraged.

"Money won't get you out of *this* one. I charge you with treason."

"The charge is obsolete—" began the Herald hotly, but he broke off as he realized the vindictive strategy.

"Yes, it is. And one of its obsolete provisions is that treason charges must be tried by the parliament at a regular session, which isn't due for two hundred days. You'll be freed and I may be reprimanded, but by my head, for two hundred days you'll regret that you made a fool of *me*. Take them away."

"A trumped-up charge against us. Prison for two hundred days," said Alen swiftly to the trader as the watchmen closed in.

"Why buy weapons?" mocked the blackbeard, showing his teeth. His left arm whipped up and down, there was a black streak through the air—and the judge was pinned to his throne with a black glass knife through his throat and the sneer of triumph still on his lips.

The trader, before the knife struck, had the clumsy pistol out, with the cover off the glowing match and the cocking piece back. He must have pumped and cocked it under his cloak, thought Alen numbly as he told the watchmen, without prompting, "Get back against the wall and turn around." They did. They wanted to live, and the grinning blackbeard who had made meat of the judge with a flick of the arm was a terrifying figure.

"Well done, Alen," said the trader. "Take their clubs, Elwon. Two for you, two for the Herald. Alen, don't argue! I had to kill the judge before he raised an alarm—nothing but death will silence his breed. You may have to kill too before we're out of this. Take the clubs." He passed the clumsy pistol to Chief Elwon and said, "Keep it on their backs. The thing that looks like a thumb safety is a trigger. Put a dart through the first one who tries to make a break. Alen, tell the fellow on the end to turn around and come to me slowly."

Alen did. Blackbeard swiftly stripped him, tore and knotted his clothes into ropes and bound and gagged him. The others got the same treatment in less than ten minutes.

The trader holstered the gun and rolled the watchmen out of the line of sight from the door of the chamber. He recovered his knife and wiped it on the judge's shirt. Alen had to help him prop the body behind the throne's high back.

"Hide those clubs," blackbeard said. "Straight faces. Here we go."

They went out, single file, opening the door only enough to pass. Alen, last in line, told one of the liveried guards nearby, "His honor, Judge Krarl, does not wish to be disturbed."

"That's news?" asked the tipstaff sardonically. He put his hand on the Herald's arm. "Only yesterday he gimme a blast when I brought him a mug of water he asked me for himself. An outrageous interruption, he called me, and he asked for the water himself. What do you think of that?"

"Terrible," said Alen hastily. He broke away and caught up with the trader and the engineer at the entrance hall. Idlers and loungers were staring at them as they headed for the waiting wagon.

"I wait!" the driver told them loudly. "I wait long, much. You pay more, more?"

"We pay more," said the trader. "You start."

The driver brought out a smoldering piece of punk, lit a pressure torch, lifted the barn-door section of the wagon's floor to expose the pottery turbine and preheated it with the torch. He pumped squeakily for minutes, spinning a flywheel with his other hand, before the rotor began to turn on its own. Down went the hatch, up onto the seats went the passengers.

"The spaceport," said Alen. With a slate-pencil screech the driver engaged his planetary gear and they were off.

Through it all, blackbeard had ignored frantic muttered questions from Chief Elwon, who had wanted nothing to do with murder, especially of a judge. "You sit up there," growled the trader, "and every so often you look around and see if we're being followed. Don't alarm the driver. And if we get to the spaceport and blast off without any trouble, keep your story to yourself." He settled down in the back seat with Alen and maintained a gloomy silence. The young Herald was too much in awe of this stranger, so suddenly competent in assorted forms of violence, to question him.

They did get to the spaceport without trouble, and found the crew in the Customs shed, emptied of the gems by dealers with releases. They had built a fire for warmth.

"We wish to leave immediately," said the trader to the port officer. "Can you change my Lyran currency?"

The officer began to sputter apologetically that it was late and the vault was sealed for the night—

"That's all right. We'll change it on Vega. It'll get back to you. Call off your guards and unseal our ship."

They followed the port officer to *Starsong*'s dim bulk out on the field. The officer cracked the seal on her with his club in the light of a flaring pressure lamp held by one of the guards.

Alen was sweating hard through it all. As they started across the field he had seen what looked like two closely spaced green stars low on the horizon toward town suddenly each jerk up and toward each other in minute arcs. The semaphore!

The signal officer in the port administration building would be watching too—but nobody on the field, preoccupied with the routine of departure, seemed to have noticed.

The lights flipped this way and that. Alen didn't know the code and bitterly regretted the lack. After some twenty signals the lights flipped to the "rest" position again as the port officer was droning out a set of takeoff regulations: bearing, height above settled areas, permissible atomic fuels while in atmosphere—Alen saw somebody start across the field toward them from the administration building. The guards were leaning on their long, competent looking weapons.

Alen inconspicuously detached himself from the group around *Starsong* and headed across the dark field to meet the approaching figure. Nearing it, he called out a low greeting in Lyran, using the noncom-to-officer military form.

"Sergeant," said the signal officer quietly, "go and draw off the men a few meters from the star travelers. Tell them the ship mustn't leave, that they're to cover the foreigners, and shoot if—"

Alen stood dazedly over the limp body of the signal officer. And then he quickly hid the bludgeon again and strolled back to the ship, wondering whether he'd cracked the Lyran's skull.

The port was open by then and the crew filing in. He was last. "Close it fast," he told the trader. "I had to—"

"I saw you," grunted blackbeard. "A semaphore message?" He was working as he spoke, and the metal port closed.

"Astrogator and engineer, take over," he told them.

"All hands to their bunks," ordered Astrogator Hufner. "Blast off immediate."

Alen took to his cubicle and strapped himself in. Blastoff deafened him, rattled his bones, and made him thoroughly sick as usual. After what seemed like several wretched hours, they were definitely space-borne under smooth acceleration, and his nausea subsided.

Blackbeard knocked, came in, and unbuckled him.

"Ready to audit the books of the voyage?" asked the trader.

"No," said Alen feebly.

"It can wait," said the trader. "The books are the least important part, anyway. We have headed off a frightful war."

"War? We have?"

"War between Eyolf's Realm and Vega. It is the common gossip of chancelleries and trade missions that both governments have cast longing eyes on Lyrane, that they have plans to penetrate its economy by supplying metals to the planet without metals—by force, if need be. Alen, we have removed the pretext by which Eyolf's Realm and Vega would have attempted to snap up Lyrane and inevitably have come into conflict. Lyra is getting its metal now, and without imperialist entanglements."

"I saw none," the Herald said blankly.

"You wondered why I was in such haste to get off Lyra, and why I wouldn't leave Elwon there. It is because our Vegan gems were most unusual gems. I am not a technical man, but I understand they are actual gems which were treated to produce a certain effect at just about this time."

Blackbeard glanced at his wrist chronometer and said dreamily, "Lyra is getting metal. Wherever there is one of our gems, pottery is decomposing into its constituent aluminum, silicon, and oxygen. Flukes and glazes are decomposing into calcium, zinc, barium, potassium, chromium, *and iron*. Buildings are crumbling, pants are dropping as ceramic belt-buckles disintegrate—"

"It means chaos!" protested Alen.

"It means civilization and peace. An ugly clash was in the making." Blackbeard paused and added deliberately, "Where neither their property nor their honor is touched, most men live content."

"*The Prince*, Chapter Nineteen. You are—"

"There was another important purpose to the voyage," said the trader, grinning. "You will be interested in this." He handed Alen a document which, unfolded, had the seal of the College and Order at its head.

Alen read in a daze, "Examiner Nineteen to the Rector—final clearance of Novice—"

He lingered pridefully over the paragraph that described how he had "with coolness and great resource" foxed the battle cruiser of the Realm, "adapting himself readily in a delicate situation requiring not only physical courage but swift recall, evaluation, and application of a minor planetary culture."

Not so pridefully he read, ". . . inclined toward pomposity of manner somewhat ludicrous in one of his years, though not unsuccessful in dominating the crew by his bearing—"

And, ". . . highly profitable disposal of our gems; a feat of no mean importance since the College and Order must, after all, maintain itself."

And, ". . . cleared the final and crucial hurdle with some mental turmoil if I am any judge, but did clear it. After some twenty years of indoctrination in unrealistic nonviolence, the youth was confronted with a situation where nothing but violence would serve, correctly evaluated this, and applied violence in the form of a truncheon to the head of a Lyran signal officer, thereby demonstrating an ability to learn and common sense as precious as it is rare."

And, finally, simply, "Recommended for training."

"Training?" gasped Alen. "You mean there's more?"

"Not for most, boy. Not for most. The bulk of us are what we seem to be: oily, gun-shy, indispensable adjuncts to trade who feather our nest with percentages. We need those percentages and we need gun-shy Heralds."

Alen recited slowly, "Among other evils which being unarmed brings you, it causes you to be despised."

"Chapter Fourteen," said blackbeard mechanically. "We leave such clues lying by their bedsides for twenty years, and they never notice them. For the few of us who do—more training."

"Will I learn to throw a knife like you?" asked Alen, repelled and fascinated at once by the idea.

"On your own time, if you wish. Mostly it's ethics and morals so you'll be able to weigh the values of such things as knife-throwing."

"Ethics! Morals!"

"We started as missionaries, you know."

"Everybody knows that. Buth the Great Utilitarian Reform—"

"Some of us," said blackbeard dryly, "think it was neither great, utilitarian, nor a reform."

It was a staggering idea. "But we're spreading utilitarian civilization!" protested Alen. "Or if we're not, what's the sense of it all?"

Blackbeard told him, "We have our different motives. One is a sincere utilitarian; another is a gamber—happy when he's in danger and his pulses are pounding. Another is proud and likes to trick people. More than a few conceive themselves as servants of mankind. I'll let you rest for a bit now." He rose.

"But you?" asked Alen hesitantly.

"Me? You will find me in Chapter Twenty-Six," grinned blackbeard. "And perhaps you'll find someone else." He closed the door behind him.

Alen ran through the chapter in his mind, puzzled, until—that was it.

It had a strange and inevitable familiarity to it as if he had always known that he would be saying it aloud, welcomingly, in this cramped cubicle aboard a battered starship:

"God is not willing to do everything, and thus take away our free will and that share of glory which belongs to us."

Leigh Brackett

THE LAST DAYS OF SHANDAKOR

For some unknown reason—they don't grow up with a "boy's adventure" tradition of Young Adult literature to inspire them, perhaps? They're more thoughtful and/or emotionally mature than the men are? Market forces (i.e., male editors) discourage them from writing it? Sunspot cycles?—straightforward adventure SF, especially the space adventure tale—and *especially* Space Opera—has been largely a male domain. There were exceptions then (C. L. Moore, Katherine MacLean, Andre Norton) and there are exceptions now (C. J. Cherryh, Eleanor Arnason, Janet Kagan, Lois McMaster Bujold), but it remains more true than not; certainly male would be the way to bet if you were uncertain of the gender of a particular Space Opera writer. Even today, when some of the Biggest Names in mainline science fiction are women, there are far more men writing that specialized sub-variety known as Space Opera than there are women—and the situation was even more lopsided in the '40s and '50s.

One of the most obvious "exceptions" to the rule was the late Leigh Brackett. Even in the male-dominated world of the adventure pulps of the '40s and '50s, testosterone-drenched venues such as *Planet Stories, Thrilling Wonder Stories,* and *Startling Stories,* where it was taken for granted that the reading audience was primarily composed of equally testosterone-drenched teenage boys, and even in an era where women were expected to stay safely in the kitchen and away from the typewriter keys, nobody could doubt that Leigh Bracket had earned the right to sit at the high-stakes table with The Men. In fact, her stuff was more popular with the readers than the work of most of her male compatriots, and ultimately more influential than almost anything else that appeared in those adventure pulps, with the possible exception of the work of Ray Bradbury and Jack Vance. There is little doubt that she was the Queen of the Planetary Romance during this period, especially as, by the mid-'40s, C. L. Moore—her major competitor for the title, whose work for magazines such as *Weird Tales* in the '30s had always had one foot in the horror genre anyway—had moved away from the adventure pulps and into more respectable mainline science fiction work for *Astounding* (except for the occasional collaboration with her husband Henry Kuttner, where her contribution was often hidden by the work appearing under his solo byline).

Brackett sold her first story in 1940, and by the late '40s and 'early '50s had become one of the mainstays of magazines such as *Planet Stories, Startling Sto-*

ries, *Astonishing Stories,* and *Thrilling Wonder Stories,* particularly *Planet Stories,* where much of her best work appeared. Although her best novel by a considerable margin is the mature, thoughtful *The Long Tomorrow,* one of the best SF novels of any sort of the '50s, that was an atypical work for her. More typical of her output, and more popular, were her series of stories about the savage, swashbuckling, half-feral Eric John Stark—a sort of Conan of the Spaceways, with a touch of Tarzan of Mercury thrown in—that appeared in the magazines and were later expanded into books such as *The Secret of Sinharat* and *People of the Talisman.* Other novels in a similar richly romantic vein included *The Sword of Rhiannon* and *The Nemesis from Terra.* She also wrote more standard interstellar Space Operas, including *The Starmen of Llyrdis, The Big Jump,* and *Alpha Centauri—or Die!,* which are competent, but lack the extravagant color and lush romanticism of her sword-and-planet work.

Brackett's autumnal vision of a decadent, dying Mars, the abode of Lost Cities and attenuated, hypercivilized Elder Races on the brink of extinction, is one of the three most influential conceptualizations of the Red Planet in science fiction, ranking only behind Edgar Rice Burroughs's Barsoom and the Mars of Ray Bradbury's *The Martian Chronicles.* (Burroughs's Mars strongly influenced both Brackett and Bradbury, but although their visions of Mars are clearly similar—close cousins at least, if not blood brothers—it's an open question how much influence was swapped between Brackett and Bradbury, or who influenced *whom*—they were close working colleagues, critiquing each others stories, as early as 1941, and their Martian stories were published roughly contemporaneously, often in the same magazines.) It's hard to sort out whether later influences on the Martian story are coming from Burroughs, Brackett, or Bradbury, and any such judgments must remain subjective to some degree, but I think I can see the influence of Brackett's Mars in particular on Roger Zelazny's famous story "A Rose for Ecclesiastes," and perhaps even on Robert A. Heinlein's Mars in *Red Planet* and *Stranger in a Strange Land.* Her influence on Ursula K. Le Guin is clear, as well as on writers of the '70s such as John Varley and George R. R. Martin and Elizabeth A. Lynn, and has probably continued on down to the '90s in the work of later writers such as Eleanor Arnason (although, with writers of newer generations, you have to take into consideration the possibility that that influence is filtered *through* Le Guin's work, which had an immense impact, rather than directly derived).

Brackett's vision of Mars was never expressed in any clearer or more concentrated form than in the intense, brooding, melancholy story that follows, in which a well-meaning Earthman inadvertently ushers in the last days of an immensely ancient civilization . . .

By the mid 1950s, Brackett had drifted away from science fiction and into crime novels, which subsequently led to her writing scripts for television and for movies such as *Rio Bravo, El Dorado, Hatari!, Rio Lobo,* and *The Long Goodbye.* (Legend has it that after reading her novel *No Good From a Corpse,* Howard Hawks told an assistant to "get me that guy Brackett" to work with William Faulkner on her first major film, the 1946 classic *The Big Sleep*). In the mid-1970s, she briefly returned to science fiction with an attempt to revive her old series hero, Eric John Stark, in the novels *The Ginger Star, The Hounds of Skaith,* and *The Reavers of Skaith,* but by then space probes had determined that none of the planets in the solar system were likely abodes for life, and she felt constrained to abandon the Mars, Venus, and Mercury that had been the settings for her earlier stories and set Stark's new adventures on the planets of distant stars instead. Somehow it was just not the same; the innocent exuberance of her earlier work was gone, and the series faltered and died after three volumes. At about the same time, she edited an anthology of stories drawn from *Planet Stories* magazine, *The Best of Planet Stories No. 1,* which, as the name implies, was supposed to be the first in a series of similar anthologies, but that series died as well, never reaching a second volume. Her last work with any significant impact on science fiction was the screenplay for the immensely successful movie *The Empire Strikes Back,* for which she received in 1980 a posthumous Hugo, her only major award. Her many short stories, which is where she did most of her best work (with the significant exception of *The Long Tomorrow*) have been assembled in the collections *The Coming of the Terrans, The Halfling and Other Stories,* and, most recently (1977), *The Best of Leigh Brackett.* Almost all of Brackett's work is out-of-print.

1

He came alone into the wineshop, wrapped in a dark red cloak, with the cowl drawn over his head. He stood for a moment by the doorway and one of the slim dark predatory women who live in those places went to him, with a silvery chiming from the little bells that were almost all she wore.

I saw her smile up at him. And then, suddenly, the smile became fixed and something happened to her eyes. She was no longer looking at the cloaked man but through him. In the oddest fashion—it was as though he had become invisible.

She went by him. Whether she passed some word along or not I couldn't tell but an empty space widened around the stranger. And no one looked at him. They did not avoid looking at him. They simply refused to see him.

He began to walk slowly across the crowded room. He was very tall and he moved with a fluid, powerful grace that was beautiful to watch. People drifted out of his way, not seeming to, but doing it. The air was thick with nameless smells, shrill with the laughter of women.

Two tall barbarians, far gone in wine, were carrying on some intertribal feud and the yelling crowd had made room for them to fight. There was a silver pipe and a drum and a double-banked harp making old wild music. Lithe brown bodies leaped and whirled through the laughter and the shouting and the smoke.

The stranger walked through all this, alone, untouched, unseen. He passed close to where I sat. Perhaps because I, of all the people in that place, not only saw him but stared at him, he gave me a glance of black eyes from under the shadow of his cowl—eyes like blown coals, bright with suffering and rage.

I caught only a glimpse of his muffled face. The merest glimpse—but that was enough. *Why did he have to show his face to me in that wineshop in Barrakesh?*

He passed on. There was no space in the shadowy corner where he went but space was made, a circle of it, a moat between the stranger and the crowd. He sat down. I saw him lay a coin on the outer edge of the table. Presently a serving wench came up, picked up the coin and set down a cup of wine. But it was as if she waited on an empty table.

I turned to Kardak, my head drover, a Shunni with massive shoulders and uncut hair braided in an intricate tribal knot. "What's all that about?" I asked.

Kardak shrugged. "Who knows?" He started to rise. "Come, JonRoss. It is time we got back to the Serai."

"We're not leaving for hours yet. And don't lie to me, I've been on Mars a long time. What is that man? Where does he come from?"

Barrakesh is the gateway between north and south. Long ago, when there were oceans in equatorial and southern Mars, when Valkis and Jekkara were proud seats of empire and not thieves' dens, here on the edge of the northern Drylands the great caravans had come and gone to Barrakesh for a thousand thousand years. It is a place of strangers.

In the time-eaten streets of rock you see tall Keshi hillmen, nomads from the high plains of Upper Shun, lean dark men from the south who barter away the loot of forgotten tombs and temples, cosmopolitan sophisticates up from Kahora and the trade cities, where there are spaceports and all the appurtenances of modern civilization.

The red-cloaked stranger was none of these.

A glimpse of a face—I am a planetary anthropologist. I was supposed to be charting Martian ethnology and I was doing it on a fellowship grant I had wangled from a Terran university too ignorant to know that the vastness of Martian history makes such a project hopeless.

I was in Barrakesh, gathering an outfit preparatory to a year's study of the tribes of Upper Shun. And suddenly there had passed close by me a man with golden skin and un-Martian black eyes and a facial structure that belonged to no race I knew. I have seen the carven faces of fauns that were a little like it.

Kardak said again, "It is time to go, JonRoss!"

I looked at the stranger, drinking his wine in silence and alone. "Very well, *I'll* ask him."

Kardak sighed. "Earthmen," he said, "are not given much to wisdom." He turned and left me.

I crossed the room and stood beside the stranger. In the old courteous High Martian they speak in all the Low-Canal towns I asked permission to sit.

Those raging, suffering eyes met mine. There was hatred in them, and scorn, and shame. "What breed of human are you?"

"I am an Earthman."

He said the name over as though he had heard it before and was trying to remember. "Earthman. Then it is as the winds have said, blowing across the desert—that Mars is dead and men from other worlds defile her dust." He looked out over the wineshop and all the people who would not admit his presence. "Change," he whispered. "Death and change and the passing away of things."

The muscles of his face drew tight. He drank and I could see now that he had been drinking for a long time, for days, perhaps for weeks. There was a quiet madness on him.

"Why do the people shun you?"

"Only a man of Earth would need to ask," he said and made a sound of laughter, very dry and bitter.

I was thinking, *A new race, an unknown race!* I was thinking of the fame that sometimes comes to men who discover a new thing, and of a Chair I might sit in at the University if I added one bright unheard-of piece of the shadowy mosaic of Martian history. I had had my share of wine and a bit more. That Chair looked a mile high and made of gold.

The stranger said softly, "I go from place to place in this wallow of Barrakesh and everywhere it is the same. I have ceased to be." His white teeth glittered for an instant in the shadow of the cowl. "They were wiser than I, my people. When Shandakor is dead, we are dead also, whether our bodies live or not."

"Shandakor?" I said. It had a sound of distant bells.

"How should an Earthman know? Yes, Shandakor! Ask of the men of Kesh and the men of Shun! Ask the kings of Mekh, who are half around the world! Ask of all the men of Mars—they have not forgotten Shandakor! But they will not tell you. It is a bitter shame to them, the memory and the name."

He stared out across the turbulent throng that filled the room and flowed over to the noisy street outside. "And I am here among them—lost."

"Shandakor is dead?"

"Dying. There were three of us who did not want to die. We came south across the desert—one turned back, one perished in the sand, I am here in Barrakesh." The metal of the wine-cup bent between his hands.

I said, "And you regret your coming."

"I should have stayed and died with Shandakor. I know that now. But I cannot go back."

"Why not?" I was thinking how the name John Ross would look, inscribed in golden letters on the scroll of the discoverers.

"The desert is wide, Earthman. Too wide for one alone."

And I said, "I have a caravan. I am going north tonight."

A light came into his eyes, so strange and deadly that I was afraid. "No," he whispered. "*No!*"

I sat in silence, looking out across the crowd that had forgotten me as well, because I sat with the stranger. *A new race, an unknown city. And I was drunk.*

After a long while the stranger asked me, "What does an Earthman want in Shandakor?"

I told him. He laughed. "You study men," he said and laughed again, so that the red cloak rippled.

"If you want to go back I'll take you. If you don't, tell me where the city lies and I'll find it. Your race, your city, should have their place in history."

He said nothing but the wine had made me very shrewd and I could guess at what was going on in the stranger's mind. I got up.

"Consider it," I told him. "You can find me at the serai by the northern gate until the lesser moon is up. Then I'll be gone."

"Wait." His fingers fastened on my wrist. They hurt. I looked into his face and I did not like what I saw there. But, as Kardak had mentioned, I was not given much to wisdom.

The stranger said, "Your men will not go beyond the Wells of Karthedon."

"Then we'll go without them."

A long long silence. Then he said, "So be it."

I knew what he was thinking as plainly as though he had spoken the words. He was thinking that I was only an Earthman and that he would kill me when we came in sight of Shandakor.

2

The caravan tracks branch off at the Wells of Karthedon. One goes westward into Shun and one goes north through the passes of Outer Kesh. But there is a third one, more ancient than the others. It goes toward the east and it is never used. The deep rock wells are dry and the stone-built shelters have vanished under the rolling dunes. It is not until the track begins to climb the mountains that there are even memories.

Kardak refused politely to go beyond the Wells. He would wait for me, he said, a certain length of time, and if I came back we would go on into Shun. If I didn't—well, his full pay was left in charge of the local headman. He would collect it and go home. He had not liked having the stranger with us. He had doubled his price.

In all that long march up from Barrakesh I had not been able to get a word out of Kardak or the men concerning Shandakor. The stranger had not spoken either. He had told me his name—Corin—and nothing more. Cloaked and cowled he rode alone and brooded. His private devils were still with him and he had a new one now—impatience. He would have ridden us all to death if I had let him.

So Corin and I went east alone from Karthedon, with two led animals and all the water we could carry. And now I could not hold him back.

"There is no time to stop," he said. "The days are running out. There is no time!"

When we reached the mountains we had only three animals left and when we crossed the first ridge we were afoot and leading the one remaining beast which carried the dwindling water skins.

We were following a road now. Partly hewn and partly worn it led up and over the mountains, those naked leaning mountains that were full of silence and peopled only with the shapes of red rock that the wind had carved.

"Armies used to come this way," said Corin. "Kings and caravans and beggars and human slaves, singers and dancing girls and the embassies of princes. This was the road to Shandakor."

And we went along it at a madman's pace.

The beast fell in a slide of rock and broke its neck and we carried the last water skin between us. It was not a heavy burden. It grew lighter and then was almost gone.

One afternoon, long before sunset, Corin said abruptly, "We will stop here."

The road went steeply up before us. There was nothing to be seen or heard. Corin sat down in the drifted dust. I crouched down too, a little distance from him. I watched him. His face was hidden and he did not speak.

The shadows thickened in that deep and narrow way. Overhead the strip of sky flared saffron and then red—and then the bright cruel stars came out. The wind worked at its cutting and polishing of stone, muttering to itself, an old and senile wind full of dissatisfaction and complaint. There was the dry faint click of falling pebbles.

The gun felt cold in my hand, covered with my cloak. I did not want to use it. But I did not want to die here on this silent pathway of vanished armies and caravans and kings.

A shaft of greenish moonlight crept down between the walls. Corin stood up.

"Twice now I have followed lies. Here I am met at last by truth."

I said, "I don't understand you."

"I thought I could escape the destruction. That was a lie. Then I thought I could return to share it. That too was a lie. Now I see the truth. Shandakor is dying. I fled from that dying, which is the end of the city and the end of my race. The shame of flight is on me and I can never go back."

"What will you do?"

"I will die here."

"And I?"

"Did you think," asked Corin softly, "that I would bring an alien creature in to watch the end of Shandakor?"

I moved first. I didn't know what weapons he might have, hidden under that dark red cloak. I threw myself over on the dusty rock. Something went past my head with a hiss and a rattle and a flame of light and then I cut the legs from under him and he fell down forward and I got on top of him, very fast.

He had vitality. I had to hit his head twice against the rock before I could take out of his hands the vicious little instrument of metal rods. I threw it far away. I could not feel any other weapons on him except a knife and I took that, too. Then I got up.

I said, "I will carry you to Shandakor."

He lay still, draped in the tumbled folds of his cloak. His breath made a harsh sighing in his throat. "So be it." And then he asked for water.

I went to where the skin lay and picked it up, thinking that there was perhaps a cupful left. I didn't hear him move. What he did was done very silently with a sharp-edged ornament. I brought him the water and it was already over. I tried to lift him up. His eyes looked at me with a curiously brilliant look. Then he whispered three words, in a language I didn't know, and died. I let him down again.

His blood had poured out across the dust. And even in the moonlight I could see that it was not the color of human blood.

I crouched there for a long while, overcome with a strange sickness. Then I reached out and pushed that red cowl back to bare his head. It was a beautiful head. I had never seen it. If I had, I would not have gone alone with Corin into the mountains. I would have understood many things if I had seen it and not for fame nor money would I have gone to Shandakor.

His skull was narrow and arched and the shaping of the bones was very fine. On that skull was a covering of short curling fibers that had an almost metallic luster in the moonlight, silvery and bright. They stirred under my hand, soft silken wires responding of themselves to an alien touch. And even as I took my hand away the luster faded from them and the texture changed.

When I touched them again they did not stir. Corin's ears were pointed and there were silvery tufts on the tips of them. On them and on his forearms and his breast were the faint, faint memories of scales, a powdering of shining dust across the golden skin. I looked at his teeth and they were not human either.

I knew now why Corin had laughed when I told him that I studied men.

It was very still. I could hear the falling of pebbles and the little stones that rolled all lonely down the cliffs and the shift and whisper of dust in the settling cracks. The Wells of Karthedon were far away. Too far by several lifetimes for one man on foot with a cup of water.

I looked at the road that went steep and narrow on ahead. I looked at Corin. The wind was cold and the shaft of moonlight was growing thin. I did not want to stay alone in the dark with Corin.

I rose and went on along the road that led to Shandakor.

It was a long climb but not a long way. The road came out between two pinnacles of rock. Below that gateway, far below in the light of the little low moons that pass so swiftly over Mars, there was a mountain valley.

Once around that valley there were great peaks crowned with snow and crags of black and crimson where the flying lizards nested, the hawk-lizards with the red eyes. Below the crags there were forests, purple and green and gold, and a black tarn deep on the valley floor. But when I saw it it was dead. The peaks had fallen away and the forests were gone and the tarn was only a pit in the naked rock.

In the midst of that desolation stood a fortress city.

There were lights in it, soft lights of many colors. The outer walls stood up, black and massive, a barrier against the creeping dust, and within them was an island of life. The high towers were not ruined. The lights burned among them and there was movement in the streets.

A living city—and Corin had said that Shandakor was almost dead.

A rich and living city. I did not understand. But I knew one thing. Those who moved along the distant streets of Shandakor were not human.

I stood shivering in that windy pass. The bright towers of the city beckoned and there was something unnatural about all lightlife in the deathly valley. And then I thought that human or not the people of Shandakor might sell me water and a beast to carry it and I could get away out of these mountains, back to the Wells.

The road broadened, winding down the slope. I walked in the middle of it, not expecting anything. And suddenly two men came out of nowhere and barred the way.

I yelled. I jumped backward with my heart pounding and the sweat pouring off me. I saw their broadswords glitter in the moonlight. And they laughed.

They were human. One was a tall red barbarian from Mekh, which lay to the east half around Mars. The other was a leaner browner man from Taarak, which was farther still. I was scared and angry and astonished and I asked a foolish question.

"What are you doing *here?*"

"We wait," said the man of Taarak. He made a circle with his arm to take in all the darkling slopes around the valley. "From Kesh and Shun, from all the countries of the Norlands and the Marches men have come, to wait. And you?"

"I'm lost," I said. "I'm an Earthman and I have no quarrel with anyone." I was still shaking but now it was with relief. I would not have to go to Shandakor. If there was a barbarian army gathered here it must have supplies and I could deal with them.

I told them what I needed. "I can pay for them, pay well."

They looked at each other.

"Very well. Come and you can bargain with the chief."

They fell in on either side of me. We walked three paces and then I was on my face in the dirt and they were all over me like two great wildcats. When they were finished they had everything I owned except the few articles of clothing for which they had no use. I got up again, wiping the blood from my mouth.

"For an outlander," said the man of Mekh, "you fight well." He chinked my money-bag up and down in his palm, feeling the weight of it, and then he handed me the leather bottle that hung at his side. "Drink," he told me. "That much I can't deny you. But our water must be carried a long way across these mountains and we have none to waste on Earthmen."

I was not proud. I emptied his bottle for him. And the man of Taarak said, smiling, "Go on to Shandakor. Perhaps they will give you water."

"But you've taken all my money!"

"They are rich in Shandakor. They don't need money. Go ask them for water."

They stood there, laughing at some secret joke of their own, and I did not like the sound of it. I could have killed them both and danced on their bodies but they had left me nothing but my bare hands to fight with. So presently I turned and went on and left them grinning in the dark behind me.

The road led down and out across the plain. I could feel eyes watching me, the eyes of the sentinels on the rounding slopes, piercing the dim moonlight. The walls of the city began to rise higher and higher. They hid everything but the top of one tall tower that had a queer squat globe on top of it. Rods of crystal projected from the globe. It revolved slowly and the rods sparkled with a sort of white fire that was just on the edge of seeing.

A causeway lifted toward the Western Gate. I mounted it, going very slowly, not wanting to go at all. And now I could see that the gate was open. *Open*—and this was a city under siege!

I stood still for some time, trying to puzzle out what meaning this might have—an army that did not attack and a city with open gates. I could not find a meaning. There were soldiers on the walls but they were lounging at their ease under the bright banners. Beyond the gate many people moved about but they were intent on their own affairs. I could not hear their voices.

I crept closer, closer still. Nothing happened. The sentries did not challenge me and no one spoke.

You know how necessity can force a man against his judgment and against his will?

I entered Shandakor.

3

There was an open space beyond the gate, a square large enough to hold an army. Around its edges were the stalls of merchants. Their canopies were of rich woven stuffs and the wares they sold were such things as have not been seen on Mars for more centuries than men can remember.

There were fruits and rare furs, the long-lost dyes that never fade, furnishings carved from vanished woods. There were spices and wines and exquisite cloths. In one place a merchant from the far south offered a ceremonial rug woven from the long bright hair of virgins. And it was new.

These merchants were all human. The nationalities of some of them I knew. Others I could guess at from traditional accounts. Some were utterly unknown.

Of the throngs that moved about among the stalls, quite a number were human also. There were merchant princes come to barter and there were companies of slaves on their way to the auction block. But the others . . .

I stayed where I was, pressed into a shadowy corner by the gate, and the chill that was on me was not all from the night wind.

The golden-skinned silver-crested lords of Shandakor I knew well enough from Corin. I say lords because that is how they bore themselves, walking proudly in their own place, attended by human slaves. And the humans who were not slaves made way for them and were most deferential as though they knew that they were greatly favored to be allowed inside the city at all. The women of Shandakor were very beautiful, slim golden sprites with their bright eyes and pointed ears.

And there were others. Slender creatures with great wings, some who were lithe and furred, some who were hairless and ugly and moved with a sinuous gliding, some so strangely shaped and colored that I could not even guess at their possible evolution.

The lost races of Mars. The ancient races, of whose pride and power nothing was left but the half-forgotten tales of old men in the farthest corners of the planet. Even I, who had made the anthropological history of Mars my business, had never heard of them except as the distorted shapes of legend, as satyrs and giants used to be known on Earth.

Yet here they were in gorgeous trappings, served by naked humans whose fetters were made of precious metals. And before them too the merchants drew aside and bowed.

The lights burned, many-colored—not the torches and cressets of the Mars I knew but cool radiances that fell from crystal globes. The walls of the buildings that rose around the market-place were faced with rare veined marbles and the fluted towers that crowned them were inlaid with turquoise and cinnabar, with amber and jade and the wonderful corals of the southern oceans.

The splendid robes and the naked bodies moved in a swirling pattern about the square. There was buying and selling and I could see the mouths of the people open and shut. The mouths of the women laughed. But in all that crowded place there was no sound. No voice, no scuff of sandal, no chink of mail. There was only silence, the utter stillness of deserted places.

I began to understand why there was no need to shut the gates. No superstitious barbarian would venture himself into a city peopled by living phantoms.

And I—I was civilized. I was, in my non-mechanical way, a scientist. And had I not been trapped by my need for water and supplies I would have run away right out of the valley. But I had no place to run to and so I stayed and sweated and gagged on the acrid taste of fear.

What were these creatures that made no sound? Ghosts—images—dreams? The human and the non-human, the ancient, the proud, the lost and forgotten who were so insanely present—did they have some subtle form of life I knew nothing about? Could they see me as I saw them? Did they have thought and volition of their own?

It was the solidity of them, the intense and perfectly prosaic business in which they were engaged. Ghosts do not barter. They do not hang jeweled necklets upon their women nor argue about the price of a studded harness.

The solidity and the silence—that was the worst of it. If there had been one small living sound . . .

A dying city, Corin had said. *The days are running out.* What if they had run out? What if I were here in this massive pile of stone with all its count-less rooms and streets and galleries and hidden ways, alone with the lights and the soundless phantoms?

Pure terror is a nasty thing. I had it then.

I began to move, very cautiously, along the wall. I wanted to get away from that market-place. One of the hairless gliding non-humans was bar-tering for a female slave. The girl was shrieking. I could see every drawn muscle in her face, the spasmodic working of her throat. Not the faintest sound came out.

I found a street that paralleled the wall. I went along it, catching glimpses of people—human people—inside the lighted buildings. Now and then men passed me and I hid from them. There was still no sound. I was care-ful how I set my feet. Somehow I had the idea that if I made a noise some-thing terrible would happen.

A group of merchants came toward me. I stepped back into an archway and suddenly from behind me there came three spangled women of the serais. I was caught.

I did not want those silent laughing women to touch me. I leaped back toward the street and the merchants paused, turning their heads. I thought that they had seen me. I hesitated and the women came on. Their painted eyes shone and their red lips glistened. The ornaments on their bodies flashed. They walked straight into me.

I made noise then, all I had in my lungs. And the women passed through me. They spoke to the merchants and the merchants laughed. They went off together down the street. They hadn't seen me. They hadn't heard me. And when I got in their way I was no more than a shadow. They passed through me.

I sat down on the stones of the street and tried to think. I sat for a long time. Men and women walked through me as through the empty air. I sought to remember any sudden pain, as of an arrow in the back that might have killed me between two seconds, so that I hadn't known about it. It seemed more likely that I should be the ghost than the other way around.

I couldn't remember. My body felt solid to my hands as did the stones I sat on. They were cold and finally the cold got me up and sent me on again. There was no reason to hide any more. I walked down the middle of the street and I got used to not turning aside.

I came to another wall, running at right angles back into the city. I fol-lowed that and it curved around gradually until I found myself back at the market-place, at the inner end of it. There was a gateway, with the main part of the city beyond it, and the wall continued. The non-humans passed back and forth through the gate but no human did except the slaves. I realized then that all this section was a ghetto for the humans who came to Shandakor with the caravans.

I remembered how Corin had felt about me. And I wondered—granted that I were still alive and that some of the people of Shandakor were still on the same plane as myself—how they would feel about me if I trespassed in their city.

There was a fountain in the market-place. The water sprang up sparkling in the colored light and filled a wide basin of carved stone. Men and women were drinking from it. I went to the fountain but when I put my hands in it all I felt was a dry basin filled with dust. I lifted my hands and let the dust trickle from them. I could see it clearly. But I saw the water too. A child leaned over and splashed it and it wetted the garments of the people. They struck the child and he cried and there was no sound.

I went on through the gate that was forbidden to the human race.

The avenues were wide. There were trees and flowers, wide parks and garden villas, great buildings as graceful as they were tall. A wise proud city, ancient in culture but not decayed, as beautiful as Athens but rich and strange, with a touch of the alien in every line of it. Can you think what it was like to walk in that city, among the silent throngs that were not human— to see the glory of it, that was not human either?

The towers of jade and cinnabar, the golden minarets, the lights and the colored silks, the enjoyment and the strength. And the people of Shandakor! No matter how far their souls have gone they will never forgive me.

How long I wandered I don't know. I had almost lost my fear in wonder at what I saw. And then, all at once in that deathly stillness, I heard a sound—the quick, soft scuffing of sandaled feet.

4

I stopped where I was, in the middle of a plaza. The tall silver-crested ones drank wine under canopies of dusky blooms and in the center a score of winged girls as lovely as swans danced a slow strange measure that was more like flight than dancing. I looked all around. There were many people. How could you tell which one had made a noise?

Silence.

I turned and ran across the marble paving. I ran hard and then suddenly I stopped again, listening. *Scuff-scuff*—no more than a whisper, very light and swift. I spun around but it was gone. The soundless people walked and the dancers wove and shifted, spreading their white wings.

Someone was watching me. Some one of those indifferent shadows was not a shadow.

I went on. Wide streets led off from the plaza. I took one of them. I tried the trick of shifting pace and two or three times I caught the echo of other steps than mine. Once I knew it was deliberate. Whoever followed me slipped silently among the noiseless crowd, blending with them, protected by them, only making a show of footsteps now and then to goad me.

I spoke to that mocking presence. I talked to it and listened to my own voice ringing hollow from the walls. The groups of people ebbed and flowed around me and there was no answer.

I tried making sudden leaps here and there among the passersby with my arms outspread. But all I caught was empty air. I wanted a place to hide and there was none.

The street was long. I went its length and the someone followed me. There were many buildings, all lighted and populous and deathly still. I thought of trying to hide in the buildings but I could not bear to be closed in between walls with those people who were not people.

I came into a great circle, where a number of avenues met around the very tall tower I had seen with the revolving globe on top of it. I hesitated, not knowing which way to go. Someone was sobbing and I realized that it was myself, laboring to breathe. Sweat ran into the corners of my mouth and it was cold, and bitter.

A pebble dropped at my feet with a brittle *click*.

I bolted out across the square. Four or five times, without reason, like a rabbit caught in the open, I changed course and fetched up with my back against an ornamental pillar. From somewhere there came a sound of laughter.

I began to yell. I don't know what I said. Finally I stopped and there was only the silence and the passing throngs, who did not see nor hear me. And now it seemed to me that the silence was full of whispers just below the threshold of hearing.

A second pebble clattered off the pillar above my head. Another stung my body. I sprang away from the pillar. There was laughter and I ran.

There were infinities of streets, all glowing with color. There were many faces, strange faces, and robes blown out on a night wind, litters with scarlet curtains and beautiful cars like chariots drawn by beasts. They flowed past me like smoke, without sound, without substance, and the laughter pursued me, and I ran.

Four men of Shandakor came toward me. I plunged through them *but their bodies opposed mine, their hands caught me and I could see their eyes, their black shining eyes, looking at me. . . .*

I struggled briefly and then it was suddenly very dark.

The darkness caught me up and took me somewhere. Voices talked far away. One of them was a light young shiny sort of voice. It matched the laughter that had haunted me down the streets. I hated it.

I hated it so much that I fought to get free of the black river that was carrying me. There was a vertiginous whirling of light and sound and stubborn shadow and then things steadied down and I was ashamed of myself for having passed out.

I was in a room. It was fairly large, very beautiful, very old, the first place I had seen in Shandakor that showed real age—Martian age, that runs back before history had begun on Earth. The floor, of some magnificent somber stone the color of a moonless night, and the pale slim pillars that upheld the arching roof all showed the hollowings and smoothnesses of centuries. The wall paintings had dimmed and softened and the rugs that burned in pools of color on that dusky floor were worn as thin as silk.

There were men and women in that room, the alien folk of Shandakor. But these breathed and spoke and were alive. One of them, a girl-child with slender thighs and little pointed breasts, leaned against a pillar close beside me. Her black eyes watched me, full of dancing lights. When she saw that I was awake again she smiled and flicked a pebble at my feet.

I got up. I wanted to get that golden body between my hands and make it scream. And she said in High Martian, "Are you a human? I have never seen one before close to."

A man in a dark robe said, "Be still, Duani." He came and stood before me. He did not seem to be armed but others were and I remembered Corin's little weapon. I got hold of myself and did none of the things I wanted to do.

"What are you doing here?" asked the man in the dark robe.

I told him about myself and Corin, omitting only the fight that he and I had had before he died, and I told him how the hillmen had robbed me.

"They sent me here," I finished, "to ask for water."

Someone made a harsh humorless sound. The man before me said, "They were in a jesting mood."

"Surely you can spare some water and a beast!"

"Our beasts were slaughtered long ago. And as for water . . ." He paused, then asked bitterly, "Don't you understand? We are dying here of thirst!"

I looked at him and at the she-imp called Duani and the others. "You don't show any signs of it," I said.

"You saw how the human tribes have gathered like wolves upon the hills. What do you think they wait for? A year ago they found and cut the buried aqueduct that brought water into Shandakor from the polar cap. All they needed then was patience. And their time is very near. The store we had in the cisterns is almost gone."

A certain anger at their submissiveness made me say, "Why do you stay here and die like mice bottled up in a jar? You could have fought your way out. I've seen your weapons."

"Our weapons are old and we are very few. And suppose that some of us did survive—tell me again, Earthman, how did Corin fare in the world of men?" He shook his head. "Once we were great and Shandakor was mighty. The human tribes of half a world paid tribute to us. We are only the last poor shadow of our race but we will not beg from men!"

"Besides," said Duani softly, "where else could we live but in Shandakor?"

"What about the others?" I asked. "The silent ones."

"They are the past," said the dark-robed man and his voice rang like a distant flare of trumpets.

Still I did not understand. I did not understand at all. But before I could ask more questions a man came up and said, "Rhul, he will have to die."

The tufted tips of Duani's ears quivered and her crest of silver curls came almost erect.

"No, Rhul!" she cried. "At least not right away."

There was a clamor from the others, chiefly in a rapid angular speech that must have predated all the syllables of men. And the one who had spoken before to Rhul repeated, "He will have to die! He has no place here. And we can't spare water."

"I'll share mine with him," said Duani, "for a while."

I didn't want any favors from her and said so. "I came here after supplies. You haven't any, so I'll go away again. It's as simple as that." I couldn't buy from the barbarians, but I might make shift to steal.

Rhul shook his head. "I'm afraid not. We are only a handful. For years our single defense has been the living ghosts of our past who walk the streets, the shadows who man the walls. The barbarians believe in enchantments. If you were to enter Shandakor and leave it again alive the barbarians would know that the enchantment cannot kill. They would not wait any longer."

Angrily, because I was afraid, I said, "I can't see what difference that would make. You're going to die in a short while anyway."

"But in our own way, Earthman, and in our own time. Perhaps, being human, you can't understand that. It is a question of pride. The oldest race of Mars will end well, as it began."

He turned away with a small nod of the head that said *kill him*—as easily as that. And I saw the ugly little weapons rise.

5

There was a split second then that seemed like a year. I thought of many things but none of them were any good. It was a devil of a place to die without even a human hand to help me under. And then Duani flung her arms around me.

"You're all so full of dying and big thoughts!" she yelled at them. "And you're all paired off or so old you can't do anything but think! What about *me?* I don't have anyone to talk to and I'm sick of wandering alone, thinking how I'm going to die! Let me have him just for a little while? I told you I'd share my water."

On Earth a child might talk that way about a stray dog. And it is written in an old Book that a live dog is better than a dead lion. I hoped they would let her keep me.

They did. Rhul looked at Duani with a sort of weary compassion and lifted his hand. "Wait," he said to the men with the weapons. "I have thought how this human may be useful to us. We have so little time left now that it is a pity to waste any of it, yet much of it must be used up in tending the machine. He could do that labor—and a man can keep alive on very little water."

The others thought that over. Some of them dissented violently, not so much on the grounds of water as that it was unthinkable that a human should intrude on the last days of Shandakor. Corin had said the same thing. But Rhul was an old man. The tufts of his pointed ears were colorless as glass and his face was graven deep with years and wisdom had distilled in him its bitter brew.

"A human of our own world, yes. But this man is of Earth and the men of Earth will come to be the new rulers of Mars as we were the old. And Mars will love them no better than she did us because they are as alien as we. So it is not unfitting that he should see us out."

They had to be content with that. I think they were already so close to the end that they did not really care. By ones and twos they left as though already they had wasted too much time away from the wonders that there were in the streets outside. Some of the men still held the weapons on me and others went and brought precious chains such as the human slaves had worn—shackles, so that I should not escape. They put them on me and Duani laughed.

"Come," said Rhul, "and I will show you the machine."

He led me from the room and up a winding stair. There were tall embrasures and looking through them I discovered that we were in the base of the very high tower with the globe. They must have carried me back to it after Duani had chased me with her laughter and her pebbles. I looked out over the glowing streets, so full of splendor and of silence, and asked Rhul why there were no ghosts inside the tower.

"You have seen the globe with the crystal rods?"

"Yes."

"We are under the shadow of its core. There had to be some retreat for us into reality. Otherwise we would lose the meaning of the dream."

The winding stair went up and up. The chain between my ankles clattered musically. Several times I tripped on it and fell.

"Never mind," Duani said. "You'll grow used to it."

We came at last into a circular room high in the tower. And I stopped and stared.

Most of the space in that room was occupied by web of metal girders that supported a great gleaming shaft. The shaft disappeared upward through the roof. It was not tall but very massive, revolving slowly and quietly. There were traps, presumably for access to the offset shaft and the cogs that turned it. A ladder led to a trap in the roof.

All the visible metal was sound with only a little surface corrosion. What the alloy was I don't know and when I asked Rhul he only smiled rather sadly. "Knowledge is found," he said, "only to be lost again. Even we of Shandakor forget."

Every bit of that enormous structure had been shaped and polished and fitted into place by hand. Nearly all the Martian peoples work in metal. They seem to have a genius for it and while they are not and apparently never have been mechanical, as some of our races are on Earth, they find many uses for metal that we have never thought of.

But this before me was certainly the high point of the metalworkers' craft. When I saw what was down below, the beautifully simple power plant and the rotary drive set-up with fewer moving parts than I would have thought possible, I was even more respectful. "How old is it?" I asked and again Rhul shook his head.

"Several thousand years ago there is a record of the yearly Hosting of the Shadows and it was not the first." He motioned me to follow him up the ladder, bidding Duani sternly to remain where she was. She came anyway.

There was a railed platform open to the universe and directly above it swung the mighty globe with its crystal rods that gleamed so strangely. Shandakor lay beneath us, a tapestry of many colors, bright and still, and out along the dark sides of the valley the tribesmen waited for the light to die.

"When there is no one left to tend the machine it will stop in time and then the men who have hated us so long will take what they want of Shandakor. Only fear has kept them out this long. The riches of half a world flowed through these streets and much of it remained."

He looked up at the globe. "Yes," he said, "we had knowledge. More, I think, than any other race of Mars."

"But you wouldn't share it with the humans."

Rhul smiled. "Would you give little children weapons to destroy you? We gave men better ploughshares and brighter ornaments and if they invented a machine we did not take it from them. But we did not tempt and burden them with knowledge that was not their own. They were content to make war with sword and spear and so they had more pleasure and less killing and the world was not torn apart."

"And you—how did you make war?"

"We defended our city. The human tribes had nothing that we coveted, so there was no reason to fight them except in self-defense. When we did we won." He paused. "The other non-human races were more stupid or less fortunate. They perished long ago."

He turned again to his explanations of the machine. "It draws its power directly from the sun. Some of the solar energy is converted and stored within the globe to serve as the light-source. Some is sent down to turn the shaft."

"What if it should stop," Duani said, "while we're still alive?" She shivered, looking out over the beautiful streets.

"It won't—not if the Earthman wishes to live."

"What would I have to gain by stopping it?" I demanded.

"Nothing. And that," said Rhul, "is why I trust you. As long as the globe turns you are safe from the barbarians. After we are gone you will have the pick of the loot of Shandakor."

How I was going to get away with it afterward he did not tell me.

He motioned me down the ladder again but I asked him, "What *is* the globe, Rhul? How does it make the—the Shadows?"

He frowned. "I can only tell you what has become, I'm afraid, mere traditional knowledge. Our wise men studied deeply into the properties of light. They learned that light has a definite effect upon solid matter and they believed, because of that effect, that stone and metal and crystalline things retain a 'memory' of all that they have 'seen.' Why this should be I do not know."

I didn't try to explain to him the quantum theory and the photoelectric effect nor the various experiments of Einstein and Millikan and the men who followed them. I didn't know them well enough myself and the old High Martian is deficient in such terminology.

I only said, "The wise men of my world also know that the impact of light tears away tiny particles from the substance it strikes."

I was beginning to get a glimmering of the truth. Light-patterns "cut" in the electrons of metal and stone—sound-patterns cut in unlikely looking mediums of plastic, each needing only the proper "needle" to recreate the recorded melody or the recorded picture.

"They constructed the globe," said Rhul. "I do not know how many generations that required nor how many failures they must have had. But they found at last the invisible light that makes the stones give up their memories."

In other words they had found their needle. What wave-length or combination of wave-lengths in the electromagnetic spectrum flowed out from those crystal rods, there was no way for me to know. But where they probed the walls and the paving blocks of Shandakor they scanned the hidden patterns that were buried in them and brought them forth again in form and color—as the electron needle brings forth whole symphonies from a little ridged disc.

How they had achieved sequence and selectivity was another matter. Rhul said something about the "memories" having different lengths. Perhaps he meant depth of penetration. The stones of Shandakor were ages old and the outer surfaces would have worn away. The earliest impressions would be gone altogether or at least have become fragmentary and extremely shallow.

Perhaps the scanning beams could differentiate between the overlapping layers of impressions by that fraction of a micron difference in depth. Photons only penetrate so far into any given substance but if that substance is constantly growing less in thickness the photons would have the effect of going deeper. I imagine the globe was accurate in centuries or numbers of centuries, not in years.

However it was, the Shadows of a golden past walked the streets of Shandakor and the last men of the race waited quietly for death, remembering their glory.

Rhul took me below again and showed me what my tasks would be, chiefly involving a queer sort of lubricant and a careful watch over the power leads. I would have to spend most of my time there but not all of it. During the free periods, Duani might take me where she would.

The old man went away. Duani leaned herself against a girder and studied me with intense interest. "How are you called?" she asked.

"John Ross."

"JonRoss," she repeated and smiled. She began to walk around me, touching my hair, inspecting my arms and chest, taking a child's delight in discovering all the differences there were between herself and what we call a human. And that was the beginning of my captivity.

6

There were days and nights, scant food and scanter water. There was Duani. And there was Shandakor. I lost my fear. And whether I lived to occupy the Chair or not, this was something to have seen.

Duani was my guide. I was tender of my duties because my neck depended on them but there was time to wander in the streets, to watch the crowded pageant that was not and sense the stillness and the desolation that were so cruelly real.

I began to get the feel of what this alien culture had been like and how it had dominated half a world without the need of conquest.

In a Hall of Government, built of white marble and decorated with wall friezes of austere magnificence, I watched the careful choosing and the crowning of a king. I saw the places of learning. I saw the young men trained for war as fully as they were instructed in the arts of peace. I saw the pleasure gardens, the theaters, the forums, the sporting fields—and I saw the places of work, where the men and women of Shandakor coaxed beauty from their looms and forges to trade for the things they wanted from the human world.

The human slaves were brought by their own kind to be sold, and they seemed to be well treated, as one treats a useful animal in which one has invested money. They had their work to do but it was only a small part of the work of the city.

The things that could be had nowhere else on Mars—the tools, the textiles, the fine work in metal and precious stones, the glass and porcelain— were fashioned by the people of Shandakor and they were proud of their skill. Their scientific knowledge they kept entirely to themselves, except what concerned agriculture or medicine or better ways of building drains and houses.

They were the lawgivers, the teachers. And the humans took all they would give and hated them for it. How long it had taken these people to attain such a degree of civilization Duani could not tell me. Neither could old Rhul.

"It is certain that we lived in communities, had a form of civil government, a system of numbers and written speech, before the human tribes. There are traditions of an earlier race than ours, from whom we learned these things. Whether or not this is true I do not know."

In its prime Shandakor had been a vast and flourishing city with countless thousands of inhabitants. Yet I could see no signs of poverty or crime. I couldn't even find a prison.

"Murder was punishable by death," said Rhul, "but it was most infrequent. Theft was for slaves. We did not stoop to it." He watched my face, smiling a little acid smile. "That startles you—a great city without suffering or crime or places of punishment."

I had to admit that it did. "Elder race or not, how did you manage to do it? I'm a student of cultures, both here and on my own world. I know all the usual patterns of development and I've read all the theories about them— but Shandakor doesn't fit any of them."

Rhul's smile deepened. "You are human," he said. "Do you wish the truth?"

"Of course."

"Then I will tell you. We developed the faculty of reason."

For a moment I thought he was joking. "Come," I said, "man is a reasoning being—on Earth the only reasoning being."

"I do not know of Earth," he answered courteously. "But on Mars man has always said, 'I reason, I am above the beasts because I reason.' And he has been very proud of himself because he could reason. It is the mark of his humanity. Being convinced that reason operates automatically within him he orders his life and his government upon emotion and superstition.

"He hates and fears and believes, not with reason but because he is told to by other men or by tradition. He does one thing and says another and his reason teaches him no difference between fact and falsehood. His bloodiest wars are fought for the merest whim—and that is why we did not give him weapons. His greatest follies appear to him the highest wisdom, his basest betrayals become noble acts—and that is why we could not teach him justice. We learned to reason. Man only learned to talk."

I understood then why the human tribes had hated the men of Shandakor. I said angrily, "Perhaps that is so on Mars. But only reasoning minds can develop great technologies and we humans of Earth have outstripped yours a million times. All right, you know or knew some things we haven't learned yet, in optics and some branches of electronics and perhaps in metallurgy. But . . ."

I went on to tell him all the things we had that Shandakor did not. "You never went beyond the beast of burden and the simple wheel. We achieved flight long ago. We have conquered space and the planets. We'll go on to conquer the stars!"

Rhul nodded. "Perhaps we were wrong. We remained here and conquered ourselves." He looked out toward the slopes where the barbarian army waited and he sighed. "In the end it is all the same."

Days and nights and Duani, bringing me food, sharing her water, asking questions, taking me through the city. The only thing she would not show me was something they called the Place of Sleep. "I shall be there soon enough," she said and shivered.

"How long?" I asked. It was an ugly thing to say.

"We are not told. Rhul watches the level in the cisterns and when it's time . . ." She made a gesture with her hands. "Let us go up on the wall."

We went up among the ghostly soldiery and the phantom banners. Outside there were darkness and death and the coming of death. Inside there were light and beauty, the last proud blaze of Shandakor under the shadow of its doom. There was an eerie magic in it that had begun to tell on me. I watched Duani. She leaned against the parapet, looking outward. The wind ruffled her silver crest, pressed her garments close against her body. Her eyes were full of moonlight and I could not read them. Then I saw that there were tears.

I put my arm around her shoulders. She was only a child, an alien child, not of my race or breed . . .

"JonRoss."

"Yes?"

"There are so many things I will never know."

It was the first time I had touched her. Those curious curls stirred under my fingers, warm and alive. The tips of her pointed ears were soft as a kitten's.

"Duani."

"What?"

"I don't know . . ."

I kissed her. She drew back and gave me a startled look from those black brilliant eyes and suddenly I stopped thinking that she was a child and I forgot that she was not human and—I didn't care.

"Duani, listen. You don't have to go to the Place of Sleep."

She looked at me, her cloak spread out upon the night wind, her hands against my chest.

"There's a whole world out there to live in. And if you aren't happy there I'll take you to my world, to Earth. There isn't any reason why you have to die!"

Still she looked at me and did not speak. In the streets below the silent throngs went by and the towers glowed with many colors. Duani's gaze moved slowly to the darkness beyond the wall, to the barren valley and the hostile rocks.

"No."

"Why not? Because of Rhul, because of all this talk of pride and race?"

"Because of truth. Corin learned it."

I didn't want to think about Corin. "He was alone. You're not. You'd never be alone."

She brought her hands up and laid them on my cheeks very gently. "That green star, that is your world. Suppose it were to vanish and you were the last of all the men of Earth. Suppose you lived with me in Shandakor forever—would you not be alone?"

"It wouldn't matter if I had you."

She shook her head. "It would matter. And our two races are as far apart as the stars. We would have nothing to share between us."

Remembering what Rhul had told me I flared up and said some angry things. She let me say them and then she smiled. "It is none of that,

JonRoss." She turned to look out over the city. "This is my place and no other. When it is gone I must be gone too."

Quite suddenly I hated Shandakor.

I didn't sleep much after that. Every time Duani left me I was afraid she might never come back. Rhul would tell me nothing and I didn't dare to question him too much. The hours rushed by like seconds and Duani was happy and I was not. My shackles had magnetic locks. I couldn't break them and I couldn't cut the chains.

One evening Duani came to me with something in her face and in the way she moved that told me the truth long before I could make her put it into words. She clung to me, not wanting to talk, but at last she said, "Today there was a casting of lots and the first hundred have gone to the Place of Sleep."

"It is the beginning, then."

She nodded. "Every day there will be another hundred until all are gone."

I couldn't stand it any longer. I thrust her away and stood up. "You know where the 'keys' are. Get these chains off me!"

She shook her head. "Let us not quarrel now, JonRoss. Come. I want to walk in the city."

We had quarreled more than once, and fiercely. She would not leave Shandakor and I couldn't take her out by force as long as I was chained. And I was not to be released until everyone but Rhul had entered the Place of Sleep and the last page of that long history had been written.

I walked with her among the dancers and the slaves and the bright-cloaked princes. There were no temples in Shandakor. If they worshipped anything it was beauty and to that their whole city was a shrine. Duani's eyes were rapt and there was a remoteness on her now.

I held her hand and looked at the towers of turquoise and cinnabar, the pavings of rose quartz and marble, the walls of pink and white and deep red coral, and to me they were hideous. The ghostly crowds, the mockery of life, the phantom splendors of the past were hideous, a drug, a snare.

"The faculty of reason!" I thought and saw no reason in any of it.

I looked up to where the great globe turned and turned against the sky, keeping these mockeries alive. "Have you ever seen the city as it is—without the Shadows?"

"No. I think only Rhul, who is the oldest, remembers it that way. I think it must have been very lonely. Even then there were less than three thousand of us left."

It must indeed have been lonely. They must have wanted the Shadows as much to people the empty streets as to fend off the enemies who believed in magic.

I kept looking at the globe. We walked for a long time. And then I said, "I must go back to the tower."

She smiled at me very tenderly. "Soon you will be free of the tower—and of these." She touched the chains. "No, don't be sad, JonRoss. You will remember me and Shandakor as one remembers a dream." She held up her face, that was so lovely and so unlike the meaty faces of human women, and her eyes were full of somber lights. I kissed her and then I caught her up in my arms and carried her back to the tower.

In that room, where the great shaft turned, I told her, "I have to tend the things below. Go up onto the platform, Duani, where you can see all Shandakor. I'll be with you soon."

I don't know whether she had some hint of what was in my mind or whether it was only the imminence of parting that made her look at me as she did. I thought she was going to speak but she did not, climbing the ladder obediently. I watched her slender golden body vanish upward. Then I went into the chamber below.

There was a heavy metal bar there that was part of a manual control for regulating the rate of turn. I took it off its pin. Then I closed the simple switches on the power plant. I tore out all the leads and smashed the connections with the bar. I did what damage I could to the cogs and the offset shaft. I worked very fast. Then I went up into the main chamber again. The great shaft was still turning but slowly, ever more slowly.

There was a cry from above me and I saw Duani. I sprang up the ladder, thrusting her back onto the platform. The globe moved heavily of its own momentum. Soon it would stop but the white fires still flickered in the crystal rods. I climbed up onto the railing, clinging to a strut. The chains on my wrists and ankles made it hard but I could reach. Duani tried to pull me down. I think she was screaming. I hung on and smashed the crystal rods with the bar, as many as I could.

There was no more motion, no more light. I got down on the platform again and dropped the bar. Duani had forgotten me. She was looking at the city.

The lights of many colors that had burned there were burning still but they were old and dim, cold embers without radiance. The towers of jade and turquoise rose up against the little moons and they were broken and cracked with time and there was no glory in them. They were desolate and very sad. The night lay clotted around their feet. The streets, the plazas and the market-squares were empty, their marble paving blank and bare. The soldiers had gone from the walls of Shandakor, with their banners and their bright mail, and there was no longer any movement anywhere within the gates.

Duani let out one small voiceless cry. And as though in answer to it, suddenly from the darkness of the valley and the slopes beyond there rose a thin fierce howling as of wolves.

"Why?" she whispered. "*Why?*" She turned to me. Her face was pitiful. I caught her to me.

"I couldn't let you die! Not for dreams and visions, nothing. Look, Duani. Look at Shandakor." I wanted to force her to understand. "Shandakor is broken and ugly and forlorn. It is a dead city—but you're alive. There are many cities but only one life for you."

Still she looked at me and it was hard to meet her eyes. She said, "We knew all that, JonRoss."

"Duani, you're a child, you've only a child's way of thought. Forget the past and think of tomorrow. We can get through the barbarians. Corin did. And after that . . ."

"And after that you would still be human—and I would not."

From below us in the dim and empty streets there came a sound of lamentation. I tried to hold her but she slipped out from between my hands. "And I am glad that you are human," she whispered. "You will never understand what you have done."

And she was gone before I could stop her, down into the tower.

I went after her. Down the endless winding stairs with my chains clattering between my feet, out into the streets, the dark and broken and deserted streets of Shandakor. I called her name and her golden body went before me, fleet and slender, distant and more distant. The chains dragged upon my feet and the night took her away from me.

I stopped. The whelming silence rushed smoothly over me and I was bitterly afraid of this dark dead Shandakor that I did not know. I called again to Duani and then I began to search for her in the shattered shadowed streets. I know now how long it must have been before I found her.

For when I found her, she was with the others. The last people of Shandakor, the men and the women, the women first, were walking silently in a long line toward a low flat-roofed building that I knew without telling was the Place of Sleep.

They were going to die and there was no pride in their faces now. There was a sickness in them, a sickness and a hurt in their eyes as they moved heavily forward, not looking, not wanting to look at the sordid ancient streets that I had stripped of glory.

"*Duani!*" I called, and ran forward but she did not turn in her place in the line. And I saw that she was weeping.

Rhul turned toward me, and his look had a weary contempt that was bitterer than a curse. "Of what use, after all, to kill you now?"

"But I did this thing! *I* did it!"

"You are only human."

The long line shuffled on and Duani's little feet were closer to that final doorway. Rhul looked upward at the sky. "There is still time before the sunrise. The women at least will be spared the indignity of spears."

"Let me go with her!"

I tried to follow her, to take my place in line. And the weapon in Rhul's hand moved and there was the pain and I lay as Corin had lain while they went silently on into the Place of Sleep.

The barbarians found me when they came, still half doubtful, into the city after dawn. I think they were afraid of me. I think they feared me as a wizard who had somehow destroyed all the folk of Shandakor.

For they broke my chains and healed my wounds and later they even gave me out of the loot of Shandakor the only thing I wanted—a bit of porcelain, shaped like the head of a young girl.

I sit in the Chair that I craved at the University and my name is written on the roll of the discoverers. I am eminent, I am respectable—I, who murdered the glory of a race.

Why didn't I go after Duani into the Place of Sleep? I could have crawled! I could have dragged myself across those stones. And I wish to God I had. I wish that I had died with Shandakor!

EXPLORATION TEAM

"Murray Leinster" was one of the writing names used by the late William Fitzgerald Jenkins, who also wrote as "Will F. Jenkins" and employed another half-dozen pseudonyms. Although he wrote copiously in many other fields, turning out millions of words of pulp stories, little of it other than the science fiction work he produced as Murray Leinster is known today—and, in fact, little outside of his SF work gained much attention even *during* his lifetime. As Murray Leinster, though, Jenkins had a profound and lasting effect on the development of modern science fiction.

"Leinster" sold his first SF story to *Argosy* in 1919, had work published in Hugo Gernsback's *Amazing* during the '20s, and went on to be one of the mainstays of John W. Campbell's "Golden Age" *Astounding* in the '40s and '50s, where most of his best work appeared. Most of Leinster's novels are heavily dated and long forgotten—one of the few figures of the day who made his reputation almost entirely on his short fiction, he was somehow never able to make much of an impact with his novels, which were widely regarded as inferior to his short work even during his working lifetime—but the best of his short stories remain fresh and powerful today. In his short work, Leinster more or less invented several sub-genres still active today: for instance, he is credited with writing one of the first Alternate History stories, "Sideways In Time," and one of the earliest First Contact stories, the famous "First Contact," and both stories still hold up as among the best treatments of their subjects. Also among his most famous stories is the taut, suspenseful, and scary tale that follows, "Exploration Team," which won Leinster his only Hugo Award in 1956, and which is practically the model of how to write an intricate and intelligent adventure set on an alien world, a story which has been an influence on—if not indeed the inspiration for—countless other stories and novels, as well as television shows and movies, over the years. Nobody before Leinster had ever written the tale of Terran explorers battling a hostile alien planet any better than he wrote it here—and, you know what? Forty years later, nobody has done it any better *yet.*

Leinster's best novel is probably *The Wailing Asteroid,* above-average among Leinster novels for imagination and evocativeness, with some quirky detail work that holds up fairly well. His other novels include *The Pirates of Zan, The Forgotten Planet, The Greks Bring Gifts,* and *The War with the Gizmos.* "Exploration Team" was collected, with other Survey Team stories, as *Colonial Survey,* one of his best collections. His "Med Service" series—not as successful as his Survey

Team stories, but still of interest—was collected in *S.O.S. from Three Worlds* and *Doctor to the Stars;* there were also two Med Service novels, *The Mutant Weapon* and *This World Is Taboo.* Other Leinster collections include *Monsters and Such* and *The Best of Murray Leinster.*

Almost all of Leinster's books are long out-of-print, and almost impossible to find; you probably have the best chance of finding *The Best of Murray Leinster,* published in 1978, in a used-book store, but even that's rather unlikely these days. Fortunately, NESFA Press has just brought out a big retrospective anthology of his work, *First Contacts: The Essential Murray Leinster* (NESFA Press, P.O. Box 809, Framingham, MA 07101-0203, $27), which features most of his best stories. Buy it while you still can, since much of this work is unfindable anywhere else.

A multi-talented man, Will Jenkins, the person behind the Murray Leinster mask, was a successful inventor as well as an author, having created, among other things, a front-projection method for filming backgrounds still used in the film industry today, where it is known as the "Leinster Projector." During World War II, he also came up with an ingenious method for disguising the wake left by submarine periscopes that probably saved the lives of thousands of submarine sailors over the course of the war. He died in 1975.

I

The nearer moon went by overhead. It was jagged and irregular in shape, and was probably a captured asteroid. Huyghens had seen it often enough, so he did not go out of his quarters to watch it hurtle across the sky with seemingly the speed of an atmosphere-flier, occulting the stars as it went. Instead, he sweated over paper work, which should have been odd because he was technically a felon and all his labors on Loren Two felonious. It was odd, too, for a man to do paper work in a room with steel shutters and a huge bald eagle—untethered—dozing on a three-inch perch set in the wall. But paper work was not Huyghens' real task. His only assistant had tangled with a night-walker and the furtive Kodius Company ships had taken him away to where Kodius Company ships came from. Huyghens had to do two men's work in loneliness. To his knowledge, he was the only man in this solar system.

Below him, there were snufflings. Sitka Pete got up heavily and padded to his water pan. He lapped the refrigerated water and sneezed violently. Sourdough Charley waked and complained in a rumbling growl. There were divers other rumblings and mutterings below. Huyghens called reassuringly, "Easy there!" and went on with his work. He finished a climate report, and fed figures to a computer, and while it hummed over them he entered the inventory totals in the station log, showing what supplies remained. Then he began to write up the log proper.

"*Sitka Pete,*" he wrote, "*has apparently solved the problem of killing individual sphexes. He has learned that it doesn't do to hug them and that his claws can't penetrate their hide—not the top hide, anyhow. Today Semper notified us that a pack of sphexes had found the scent-trail to the station. Sitka hid downwind until they arrived. Then he charged from the rear and brought his paws together on both sides of a sphex's head in a terrific pair of slaps. It must have been like two twelve-inch shells arriving from opposite directions at the same time. It must have scrambled the sphex's brains as if they were eggs. It dropped dead. He killed two more with such mighty pairs of wallops. Sourdough Charley watched, grunting, and when the sphexes turned on Sitka, he charged in his turn. I, of course, couldn't shoot too close to him, so he might have fared badly but that Faro Nell came pouring out of the bear quarters to help. The diversion enabled Sitka Pete to resume the use of his new technic, towering on his hind legs and swinging his paws in the new and grisly fashion. The fight ended promptly. Semper flew and screamed above the scrap, but as usual did not join in. Note: Nugget, the cub, tried to mix in but his mother cuffed him out of the way. Sourdough and Sitka ignored him as usual. Kodius Champion's genes are sound!*"

The noises of the night went on outside. There were notes like organ tones—song lizards. There were the tittering giggling cries of night-walkers—not to be tittered back at. There were sounds like tack hammers, and doors closing, and from every direction came noises like hiccups in various keys. These were made by the improbable small creatures which on Loren Two took the place of insects.

Huyghens wrote out:

"*Sitka seemed ruffled when the fight was over. He painstakingly used his trick on every dead or wounded sphex, except those he'd killed with it, lifting up their heads for his pile-driver-like blows from two directions at once, as if to show Sourdough how it was done. There was much grunting as they hauled the carcasses to the incinerator. It almost seemed—*"

The arrival bell clanged, and Huyghens jerked up his head to stare at it. Semper, the eagle, opened icy eyes. He blinked.

Noises. There was a long, deep, contented snore from below. Something shrieked, out in the jungle. Hiccups. Clatterings, and organ notes—

The bell clanged again. It was a notice that a ship aloft somewhere had picked up the beacon beam—which only Kodius Company ships should know about—and was communicating for a landing. But there shouldn't be any ships in this solar system just now! This was the only habitable planet of the sun, and it had been officially declared uninhabitable by reason of inimical animal life. Which meant sphexes. Therefore no colony was permitted, and the Kodius Company broke the law. And there were few graver crimes than unauthorized occupation of a new planet.

The bell clanged a third time. Huyghens swore. His hand went out to cut off the beacon—but that would be useless. Radar would have fixed it and tied it in with physical features like the nearby sea and the Sere Plateau. The ship could find the place, anyhow, and descend by daylight.

"The devil!" said Huyghens. But he waited yet again for the bell to ring. A Kodius Company ship would double-ring to reassure him. But there shouldn't be a Kodius Company ship for months.

The bell clanged singly. The space phone dial flickered and a voice came out of it, tinny from stratospheric distortion:

"*Calling ground! Calling ground! Crete Line ship* Odysseus *calling ground on Loren Two. Landing one passenger by boat. Put on your field lights.*"

Huyghens' mouth dropped open. A Kodius Company ship would be welcome. A Colonial Survey ship would be extremely unwelcome, because it would destroy the colony and Sitka and Sourdough and Faro Nell and Nugget—and Semper—and carry Huyghens off to be tried for unauthorized colonization and all that it implied.

But a commercial ship, landing one passenger by boat— There was simply no circumstances under which that would happen. Not to an unknown, illegal colony. Not to a furtive station!

Huyghens flicked on the landing-field lights. He saw the glare in the field outside. Then he stood up and prepared to take the measures required by discovery. He packed the paper work he'd been doing into the disposal safe. He gathered up all personal documents and tossed them in. Every record, every bit of evidence that the Kodius Company maintained this station went into the safe. He slammed the door. He touched his finger to the disposal button, which would destroy the contents and melt down even the ashes past their possible use for evidence in court.

Then he hesitated. If it were a Survey ship, the button had to be pressed and he must resign himself to a long term in prison. But a Crete Line ship—if the space phone told the truth—was not threatening. It was simply unbelievable.

He shook his head. He got into travel garb and armed himself. He went down into the bear quarters, turning on lights as he went. There were startled snufflings and Sitka Pete reared himself very absurdly to a sitting position to blink at him. Sourdough Charley lay on his back with his legs in the air. He'd found it cooler, sleeping that way. He rolled over with a thump. He made snorting sounds which somehow sounded cordial. Faro Nell padded to the door of her separate apartment—assigned her so that Nugget would not be underfoot to irritate the big males.

Huyghens, as the human population of Loren Two, faced the work force, fighting force, and—with Nugget—four-fifths of the terrestrial nonhuman population of the planet. They were mutated Kodiak bears, descendants of the Kodius Champion for whom the Kodius Company was named. Sitka Pete was a good twenty-two hundred pounds of lumbering, intelligent carnivore. Sourdough Charley would weigh within a hundred pounds of that figure. Faro Nell was eighteen hundred pounds of female charm—and ferocity. Then Nugget poked his muzzle around his mother's furry rump to see what was toward, and he was six hundred pounds of ursine infancy. The animals looked at Huyghens expectantly. If he'd had Semper riding on his shoulder, they'd have known what was expected of them.

"Let's go," said Huyghens. "It's dark outside, but somebody's coming. And it may be bad!"

He unfastened the outer door of the bear quarters. Sitka Pete went charging clumsily through it. A forthright charge was the best way to develop any situation—if one was an oversized male Kodiak bear. Sourdough went lumbering after him. There was nothing hostile immediately outside. Sitka stood up on his hind legs—he reared up a solid twelve feet—and sniffed the air. Sourdough methodically lumbered to one side and then the other, sniffing in his turn. Nell came out, nine-tenths of a ton of daintiness, and rumbled admonitorily at Nugget, who trailed her closely. Huyghens stood in the doorway, his night-sighted gun ready. He felt uncomfortable at sending the bears ahead into a Loren Two jungle at night. But they were qualified to scent danger, and he was not.

The illumination of the jungle in a wide path toward the landing field made for weirdness in the look of things. There were arching giant ferns and columnar trees which grew above them, and the extraordinary lanceolate underbrush of the jungle. The flood lamps, set level with the ground, lighted everything from below. The foliage, then, was brightly lit against the black night-sky—brightly lit enough to dim-out the stars. There were astonishing contrasts of light and shadow everywhere.

"On ahead!" commanded Huyghens, waving. "Hup!"

He swung the bear-quarters door shut. He moved toward the landing field through the lane of lighted forest. The two giant male Kodiaks lumbered ahead. Sitka Pete dropped to all fours and prowled. Sourdough Charley followed closely, swinging from side to side. Huyghens came alertly behind the two of them, and Faro Nell brought up the rear with Nugget following her closely.

It was an excellent military formation for progress through dangerous jungle. Sourdough and Sitka were advance-guard and point, respectively, while Faro Nell guarded the rear. With Nugget to look after, she was especially alert against attack from behind. Huyghens was, of course, the striking force. His gun fired explosive bullets which would discourage even sphexes, and his night-sight—a cone of light which went on when he took up the trigger-slack—told exactly where they would strike. It was not a sportsmanlike weapon, but the creatures of Loren Two were not sportsmanlike antagonists. The night-walkers, for example— But night-walkers feared light. They attacked only in a species of hysteria if it were too bright.

Huyghens moved toward the glare at the landing field. His mental state was savage. The Kodius Company station on Loren Two was completely illegal. It happened to be necessary, from one point of view, but it was still illegal. The tinny voice on the space phone was not convincing, in ignoring that illegality. But if a ship landed, Huyghens could get back to the station before men could follow, and he'd have the disposal safe turned on in time to protect those who'd sent him here.

But he heard the faraway and high harsh roar of a landing-boat rocket—not a ship's bellowing tubes—as he made his way through the unreal-seeming brush. The roar grew louder as he pushed on, the three big Kodiaks padding here and there, sniffing thoughtfully, making a perfect defensive-offensive formation for the particular conditions of this planet.

He reached the edge of the landing field, and it was blindingly bright, with the customary divergent beams slanting skyward so a ship could check its instrument landing by sight. Landing fields like this had been standard, once upon a time. Nowadays all developed planets had landing grids—monstrous structures which drew upon ionospheres for power and lifted and drew down star ships with remarkable gentleness and unlimited force. This sort of landing field would be found where a survey-team was at work, or where some strictly temporary investigation of ecology or bacteriology was under way, or where a newly authorized colony had not yet been able to build its landing grid. Of course it was unthinkable that anybody would attempt a settlement in defiance of the law!

Already, as Huyghens reached the edge of the scorched open space, the night-creatures had rushed to the light like moths on Earth. The air was misty with crazily gyrating, tiny flying things. They were innumerable and of every possible form and size, from the white midges of the night and multi-winged flying worms to those revoltingly naked-looking larger creatures which might have passed for plucked flying monkeys if they had not been carnivorous and worse. The flying things soared and whirred and danced and spun insanely in the glare. They made peculiarly plaintive humming noises. They almost formed a lamp-lit ceiling over the cleared space.

They did hide the stars. Staring upward, Huyghens could just barely make out the blue-white flame of the space-boat's rocket through the fog of wings and bodies.

The rocket-flame grew steadily in size. Once, apparently, it tilted to adjust the boat's descending course. It went back to normal. A speck of incandescence at first, it grew until it was like a great star, and then a more-than-brilliant moon, and then it was a pitiless glaring eye. Huyghens averted his gaze from it. Sitka Pete sat lumpily—more than a ton of him—and blinked wisely at the dark jungle away from the light. Sourdough ignored the deepening, increasing rocket roar. He sniffed the air delicately. Faro Nell held Nugget firmly under one huge paw and licked his head as if tidying him up to be seen by company. Nugget wriggled.

The roar became that of ten thousand thunders. A warm breeze blow outward from the landing-field. The rocket boat hurled downward, and its flame touched the mist of flying things, and they shriveled and burned and were hot. Then there were churning clouds of dust everywhere, and the center of the field blazed terribly—and something slid down a shaft of fire, and squeezed it flat, and sat on it—and the flame went out. The rocket boat sat there, resting on its tail fins, pointing toward the stars from which it came.

There was a terrible silence after the tumult. Then, very faintly, the noises of the night came again. There were sounds like those of organ pipes, and very faint and apologetic noises like hiccups. All these sounds increased, and suddenly Huyghens could hear quite normally. Then a side-port opened with a quaint sort of clattering, and something unfolded from where it had been inset into the hull of the space boat, and there was a metal passageway across the flame-heated space on which the boat stood.

A man came out of the port. He reached back in and shook hands very formally. He climbed down the ladder rungs to the walkway. He marched above the steaming baked area, carrying a traveling bag. He reached the end of the walk and stepped gingerly to the ground. He moved hastily to the edge of the clearing. He waved to the space boat. There were ports. Perhaps someone returned the gesture. The walkway folded briskly back up to the hull and vanished in it. A flame exploded into being under the tail fins. There were fresh clouds of monstrous, choking dust and a brightness like that of a sun. There was noise past the possibility of endurance. Then the light rose swiftly through the dust cloud, and sprang higher and climbed more swiftly still. When Huyghens' ears again permitted him to hear anything, there was only a diminishing mutter in the heavens and a small bright speck of light ascending to the sky and swinging eastward as it rose to intercept the ship which had let it descend.

The night noises of the jungle went on. Life on Loren Two did not need to heed the doings of men. But there was a spot of incandescence in the day-bright clearing, and a short, brisk man looked puzzledly about him with a traveling bag in his hand.

Huyghens advanced toward him as the incandescence dimmed. Sour-dough and Sitka preceded him. Faro Nell trailed faithfully, keeping a ma-ternal eye on her offspring. The man in the clearing stared at the parade they made. It would be upsetting, even after preparation, to land at night on a strange planet, and to have the ship's boat and all links with the rest of the cosmos depart, and then to find one's self approached—it might seem stalked—by two colossal male Kodiak bears, with a third bear and cub be-hind them. A single human figure in such company might seem irrelevant.

The new arrival gazed blankly. He moved, startled. Then Huyghens called:

"Hello, there! Don't worry about the bears! They're friends!"

Sitka reached the newcomer. He went warily downwind from him and sniffed. The smell was satisfactory. Man-smell. Sitka sat down with the solid impact of more than a ton of bear-meat landing on packed dirt. He re-garded the man amiably. Sourdough said *"Whoosh!"* and went on to sample the air beyond the clearing. Huyghens approached. The newcomer wore the uniform of the Colonial Survey. That was bad. It bore the insignia of a senior officer. Worse.

"Hah!" said the just-landed man. "Where are the robots? What in all the nineteen hells are these creatures? Why did you shift your station? I'm Roane, here to make a progress report on your colony."

Huyghens said:

"What colony?"

"Loren Two Robot Installation—" Then Roane said indignantly, "Don't tell me that that idiot skipper dropped me at the wrong place! This is Loren Two, isn't it? And this is the landing field. But where are your robots? You should have the beginning of a grid up! What the devil's happened here and what are these beasts?"

Huyghens grimaced.

"This," he said politely, "is an illegal, unlicensed settlement. I'm a crim-inal. These beasts are my confederates. If you don't want to associate with criminals you needn't, of course, but I doubt if you'll live till morning un-less you accept my hospitality while I think over what to do about your landing. In reason, I ought to shoot you."

Faro Nell came to a halt behind Huyghens, which was her proper post in all out-door movement. Nugget, however, saw a new human. Nugget was a cub, and, therefore, friendly. He ambled forward ingratiatingly. He was four feet high at the shoulders, on all fours. He wriggled bashfully as he approached Roane. He sneezed, because he was embarrassed.

His mother overtook him swiftly and cuffed him to one side. He wailed. The wail of a six-hundred-pound Kodiak bear-cub is a remarkable sound. Roane gave ground a pace.

"I think," he said carefully, "that we'd better talk things over. But if this is an illegal colony, of course you're under arrest and anything you say will be used against you."

Huyghens grimaced again.

"Right," he said. "But now if you'll walk close to me, we'll head back to the station. I'd have Sourdough carry your bag—he likes to carry things— but he may need his teeth. We've half a mile to travel." He turned to the animals. "Let's go!" he said commandingly. "Back to the station! Hup!"

Grunting, Sitka Pete arose and took up his duties as advanced point of a combat team. Sourdough trailed, swinging widely to one side and another. Huyghens and Roane moved together. Faro Nell and Nugget brought up the rear. Which, of course, was the only relatively safe way for anybody to travel on Loren Two, in the jungle, a good half mile from one's fortresslike residence.

But there was only one incident on the way back. It was a night-walker, made hysterical by the lane of light. It poured through the underbrush, uttering cries like maniacal laughter.

Sourdough brought it down, a good ten yards from Huyghens. When it was all over, Nugget bristled up to the dead creature, uttering cub-growls. He feigned to attack it.

His mother whacked him soundly.

II

There were comfortable, settling-down noises below. The bears grunted and rumbled, but ultimately were still. The glare from the landing field was gone. The lighted lane through the jungle was dark again. Huyghens ushered the man from the space boat up into his living quarters. There was a rustling stir, and Semper took his head from under his wing. He stared coldly at the two humans. He spread monstrous, seven-foot wings and fluttered them. He opened his beak and closed it with a snap.

"That's Semper," said Huyghens. "Semper Tyrannis. He's the rest of the terrestrial population here. Not being a fly-by-night sort of creature, he didn't come out to welcome you."

Roane blinked at the huge bird, perched on a three-inch-thick perch set in the wall.

"An eagle?" he demanded. "Kodiak bears—mutated ones you say, but still bears—and now an eagle? You've a very nice fighting unit in the bears."

"They're pack animals, too," said Huyghens. "They can carry some hundreds of pounds without losing too much combat efficiency. And there's no problem of supply. They live off the jungle. Not sphexes, though. Nothing will eat a sphex, even if it can kill one."

He brought out glasses and a bottle. He indicated a chair. Roane put down his traveling bag. He took a glass.

"I'm curious," he observed. "Why Semper Tyrannis? I can understand Sitka Pete and Sourdough Charley as names. The home of their ancestors makes them fitting. But why Semper?"

"He was bred for hawking," said Huyghens. "You sic a dog on something. You sic Semper Tyrannis. He's too big to ride on a hawking glove, so the shoulders of my coats are padded to let him ride there. He's a flying scout. I've trained him to notify us of sphexes, and in flight he carries a tiny television camera. He's useful, but he hasn't the brains of the bears."

Roane sat down and sipped at his glass.

"Interesting . . . very interesting! But this is an illegal settlement. I'm a Colonial Survey officer. My job is reporting on progress according to plan, but nevertheless I have to arrest you. Didn't you say something about shooting me?"

Huyghens said doggedly:

"I'm trying to think of a way out. Add up all the penalties for illegal colonization and I'd be in a very bad fix if you got away and reported this setup. Shooting you would be logical."

"I see that," said Roane reasonably. "But since the point has come up—I have a blaster trained on you from my pocket."

Huyghens shrugged.

"It's rather likely that my human confederates will be back here before your friends. You'd be in a very tight fix if my friends came back and found you more or less sitting on my corpse."

Roane nodded.

"That's true, too. Also it's probable that your fellow terrestrials wouldn't co-operate with me as they have with you. You seem to have the whip hand, even with my blaster trained on you. On the other hand, you could have killed me quite easily after the boat left, when I'd first landed. I'd have been quite unsuspicious. So you may not really intend to murder me."

Huyghens shrugged again.

"So," said Roane, "since the secret of getting along with people is that of postponing quarrels—suppose we postpone the question of who kills whom? Frankly, I'm going to send you to prison if I can. Unlawful colonization is very bad business. But I suppose you feel that you have to do something permanent about me. In your place I probably should, too. Shall we declare a truce?"

Huyghens indicated indifference. Roane said vexedly:

"Then I do! I have to! So—"

He pulled his hand out of his pocket and put a pocket blaster on the table. He leaned back, defiantly.

"Keep it," said Huyghens. "Loren Two isn't a place where you live long unarmed." He turned to a cupboard. "Hungry?"

"I could eat," admitted Roane.

Huyghens pulled out two mealpacks from the cupboard and inserted them in the readier below. He set out plates.

"Now—what happened to the official, licensed, authorized colony here?" asked Roane briskly. "License issued eighteen months ago. There was a landing of colonists with a drone fleet of equipment and supplies. There've been four ship-contacts since. There should be several thousand robots being industrious under adequate human supervision. There should be a hundred-mile-square clearing, planted with food plants for later human arrivals. There should be a landing grid at least half-finished. Obviously there should be a space beacon to guide ships to a landing. There isn't. There's no clearing visible from space. That Crete Line ship has been in orbit for three days, trying to find a place to drop me. Her skipper was fuming. Your beacon is the only one on the planet, and we found it by accident. What happened?"

Huyghens served the food. He said dryly:

"There could be a hundred colonies on this planet without any one knowing of any other. I can only guess about your robots, but I suspect they ran into sphexes."

Roane paused, with his fork in his hand.

"I read up on this planet, since I was to report on its colony. A sphex is part of the inimical animal life here. Cold-blooded belligerent carnivore, not a lizard but a genus all its own. Hunts in packs. Seven to eight hundred pounds, when adult. Lethally dangerous and simply too numerous to fight. They're why no license was ever granted to human colonists. Only robots could work here, because they're machines. What animal attacks machines?"

Huyghens said:

"What machine attacks animals? The sphexes wouldn't bother robots, of course, but would robots bother the sphexes?"

Roane chewed and swallowed.

"Hold it! I'll agree that you can't make a hunting-robot. A machine can discriminate, but it can't decide. That's why there's no danger of a robot revolt. They can't decide to do something for which they have no instructions. But this colony was planned with full knowledge of what robots can and can't do. As ground was cleared, it was enclosed in an electric fence which no sphex could touch without frying."

Huyghens thoughtfully cut his food. After a moment:

"The landing was in the wintertime," he observed. "It must have been, because the colony survived a while. And at a guess, the last ship-landing was before thaw. The years are eighteen months long here, you know."

Roane admitted:

"It was in winter that the landing was made. And the last ship-landing was before spring. The idea was to get mines in operation for material, and to have ground cleared and enclosed in sphex-proof fence before the sphexes came back from the tropics. They winter there, I understand."

"Did you ever see a sphex?" Huyghens asked. Then added, "No, of course not. But if you took a spitting cobra and crossed it with a wildcat, painted it tan-and-blue and then gave it hydrophobia and homicidal mania at once—why you might have one sphex. But not the race of sphexes. They can climb trees, by the way. A fence wouldn't stop them."

"An electrified fence," said Roane. "Nothing could climb that!"

"No one animal," Huyghens told him. "But sphexes are a race. The smell of one dead sphex brings others running with blood in their eyes. Leave a dead sphex alone for six hours and you've got them around by the dozen. Two days and there are hundreds. Longer, and you've got thousands of them! They gather to caterwaul over their dead pal and hunt for whoever or whatever killed him."

He returned to his meal. A moment later he said:

"No need to wonder what happened to your colony. During the winter the robots burned out a clearing and put up an electrified fence according to the book. Come spring, the sphexes came back. They're curious, among their other madnesses. A sphex would try to climb the fence just to see what was behind it. He'd be electrocuted. His carcass would bring others, raging because a sphex was dead. Some of them would try to climb the fence—and die. And their corpses would bring others. Presently the fence would break down from the bodies hanging on it, or a bridge of dead beasts' carcasses would be built across it—and from as far downwind as the scent carried there'd be loping, raging, scent-crazed sphexes racing to the spot. They'd pour into the clearing through or over the fence, squalling and screeching for something to kill. I think they'd find it."

Roane ceased to eat. He looked sick.

"There were . . . pictures of sphexes in the data I read. I suppose that would account for . . . everything."

He tried to lift his fork. He put it down again.

"I can't eat," he said abruptly.

Huyghens made no comment. He finished his own meal, scowling. He rose and put the plates into the top of the cleaner. There was a whirring. He took them out of the bottom and put them away.

"Let me see those reports, eh?" he asked dourly. "I'd like to see what sort of a set-up they had—those robots."

Roane hesitated and then opened his traveling bag. There was a microviewer and reels of films. One entire reel was labeled "Specifications for Construction, Colonial Survey," which would contain detailed plans and all requirements of material and workmanship for everything from desks, office, administrative personnel, for use of, to landing grids, heavy-gravity planets, lift-capacity one hundred thousand Earth-tons. But Huyghens found another. He inserted it and spun the control swiftly here and there, pausing only briefly at index frames until he came to the section he wanted. He began to study the information with growing impatience.

"Robots, robots, robots!" he snapped. "Why don't they leave them where they belong—in cities to do the dirty work, and on airless planets where nothing unexpected ever happens! Robots don't belong in new colonies! Your colonists depended on them for defense! Dammit, let a man work with robots long enough and he thinks all nature is as limited as they are! This is a plan to set up a controlled environment! On Loren Two! Controlled environment—" He swore, luridly. "Complacent, idiotic, deskbound half-wits!"

"Robots are all right," said Roane. "We couldn't run civilization without them."

"But you can't tame a wilderness with 'em!" snapped Huyghens. "You had a dozen men landed, with fifty assembled robots to start with. There were parts for fifteen hundred more—and I'll bet anything I've got that the ship-contacts landed more still."

"They did," admitted Roane.

"I despise 'em," growled Huyghens. "I feel about 'em the way the old Greeks and Romans felt about slaves. They're for menial work—the sort of work a man will perform for himself, but that he won't do for another man for pay. Degrading work!"

"Quite aristocratic!" said Roane with a touch of irony. "I take it that robots clean out the bear quarters downstairs."

"No!" snapped Huyghens. "I do! They're my friends! They fight for me! They can't understand the necessity and no robot would do the job right!"

He growled, again. The noises of the night went on outside. Organ tones and hiccupings and the sound of tack hammers and slamming doors. Somewhere there was a singularly exact replica of the discordant squeaking of a rusty pump.

"I'm looking," said Huyghens at the micro-viewer, "for the record of their mining operations. An open-pit operation wouldn't mean a thing. But if they had driven a tunnel, and somebody was there supervising the robots when the colony was wiped out, there's an off-chance he survived a while."

Roane regarded him with suddenly intent eyes.

"And—"

"Dammit," snapped Huyghens, "if so I'll go see! He'd . . . they'd have no chance at all, otherwise. Not that the chance is good in any case!"

Roane raised his eyebrows.

"I'm a Colonial Survey officer," he said. "I've told you I'll send you to prison if I can. You've risked the lives of millions of people, maintaining non-quarantined communication with an unlicensed planet. If you did rescue somebody from the ruins of the robot colony, does it occur to you that they'd be witnesses to your unauthorized presence here?"

Huyghens spun the viewer again. He stopped. He switched back and forth and found what he wanted. He muttered in satisfaction: "They did run a tunnel!" Aloud he said, "I'll worry about witnesses when I have to."

He pushed aside another cupboard door. Inside it were the odds and ends a man makes use of to repair the things about his house that he never notices until they go wrong. There was an assortment of wires, transistors, bolts, and similar stray items that a man living alone will need. When to his knowledge he's the only inhabitant of a solar system, he especially needs such things.

"What now?" asked Roane mildly.

"I'm going to try to find out if there's anybody left alive over there. I'd have checked before if I'd known the colony existed. I can't prove they're all dead, but I may prove that somebody's still alive. It's barely two weeks' journey away from here! Odd that two colonies picked spots so near!"

He absorbedly picked over the oddments he'd selected. Roane said vexedly:

"Confound it! How can you check whether somebody's alive some hundreds of miles away—when you didn't know he existed half an hour ago?"

Huyghens threw a switch and took down a wall panel, exposing electronic apparatus and circuits behind. He busied himself with it.

"Ever think about hunting for a castaway?" he asked over his shoulder. "There's a planet with some tens of millions of square miles on it. You know there's a ship down. You've no idea where. You assume the survivors have power—no civilized man will be without power very long, so long as he can smelt metals!—but making a space beacon calls for high-precision measurements and workmanship. It's not to be improvised. So what will your ship-wrecked civilized man do, to guide a rescue ship to the one or two square miles he occupies among some tens of millions on the planet?"

Roane fretted visibly.

"What?"

"He's had to go primitive, to begin with," Roane explained. "He cooks his meat over a fire, and so on. He has to make a strictly primitive signal. It's all he can do without gauges and micrometers and very special tools. But he can fill all the planet's atmosphere with a signal that searchers for him can't miss. You see?"

Roane thought irritably. He shook his head.

"He'll make," said Huyghens, "a spark transmitter. He'll fix its output at the shortest frequency he can contrive—it'll be somewhere in the five-to-fifty-meter wave-band, but it will tune very broad—and it will be a plainly human signal. He'll start it broadcasting. Some of those frequencies will go all around the planet under the ionosphere. Any ship that comes in under the radio roof will pick up his signal, get a fix on it, move and get another fix, and then go straight to where the castaway is waiting placidly in a hand-braided hammock, sipping whatever sort of drink he's improvised out of the local vegetation."

Roane said grudgingly:

"Now that you mention it, of course—"

"My space phone picks up microwaves," said Huyghens, "I'm shifting a few elements to make it listen for longer stuff. It won't be efficient, but it will pick up a distress signal if one's in the air. I don't expect it, though."

He worked. Roane sat still a long time, watching him. Down below, a rhythmic sort of sound arose. It was Sourdough Charley, snoring. He lay on his back with his legs in the air. He'd discovered that he slept cooler that way. Sitka Peter grunted in his sleep. He was dreaming. In the general room of the station Semper, the eagle, blinked his eyes rapidly and then tucked his head under a gigantic wing and went to sleep. The noises of the Loren Two jungle came through the steel-shuttered windows. The nearer moon—which had passed overhead not long before the ringing of the arrival bell—again came soaring over the eastern horizon. It sped across the sky at the apparent speed of an atmosphere-flier. Overhead, it could be seen to be a jagged irregular mass of rock or metal, plunging blindly about the great planet forever.

Inside the station, Roane said angrily:

"See here, Huyghens! You've reason to kill me. Apparently you don't intend to. You've excellent reason to leave that robot colony strictly alone. But you're preparing to help, if there's anybody alive to need it. And yet you're a criminal—and I mean a criminal! There've been some ghastly bacteria exported from planets like Loren Two! There've been plenty of lives lost in consequence, and you're risking more! Why do you do it? Why do you do something that could produce monstrous results to other beings?"

Huyghens grunted.

"You're only assuming there are no sanitary and quarantine precautions taken in my communications. As a matter of fact, there are. They're taken, all right! As for the rest, you wouldn't understand."

"I don't understand," snapped Roane, "but that's no proof I can't! Why are you a criminal?"

Huyghens painstakingly used a screwdriver inside the wall panel. He delicately lifted out a small electronic assembly. He carefully began to fit in a spaghettied new assembly with larger units.

"I'm cutting my amplification here to hell-and-gone," he observed, "but I think it'll do. I'm doing what I'm doing," he added calmly, "I'm being a criminal because it seems to me befitting what I think I am. Everybody acts according to his own real notion of himself. You're a conscientious citizen, and a loyal official, and a well-adjusted personality. You consider yourself an intelligent rational animal. But you don't act that way! You're reminding me of my need to shoot you or something similar, which a merely rational animal would try to make me forget. You happen, Roane, to be a man. So am I. But I'm aware of it. Therefore, I deliberately do things a merely rational animal wouldn't, because they're my notion of what a man who's more than a rational animal should do."

He very carefully tightened one small screw after another. Roane said annoyedly:

"Oh. Religion."

"Self-respect," corrected Huyghens. "I don't like robots. They're too much like rational animals. A robot will do whatever it can that its supervisor requires it to do. A merely rational animal will do whatever it can that circumstances require it to do. I wouldn't like a robot unless it had some idea of what was befitting it and would spit in my eye if I tried to make it do something else. The bears downstairs, now— They're no robots! They are loyal and honorable beasts, but they'd turn and tear me to bits if I tried to make them do something against their nature. Faro Nell would fight me and all creation together, if I tried to harm Nugget. It would be unintelligent and unreasonable and irrational. She'd lose out and get killed. But I like her that way! And I'll fight you and all creation when you make me try to do something against my nature. I'll be stupid and unreasonable and irrational about it." Then he grinned over his shoulder. "So will you. Only you don't realize it."

He turned back to his task. After a moment he fitted a manual-control knob over a shaft in his haywire assembly.

"What did somebody try to make you do?" asked Roane shrewdly. "What was demanded of you that turned you into a criminal? What are you in revolt against?"

Huyghens threw a switch. He began to turn the knob which controlled the knob of his makeshift-modified receiver.

"Why," he said amusedly, "when I was young the people around me tried to make me into a conscientious citizen and a loyal employee and a well-adjusted personality. They tried to make me into a highly intelligent rational animal and nothing more. The difference between us, Roane, is that I found it out. naturally, I rev—"

He stopped short. Faint, crackling, crisp frying sounds came from the speaker of the space phone now modified to receive what once were called short waves.

Huyghens listened. He cocked his head intently. He turned the knob very, very slowly. Then Roane made an arrested gesture, to call attention to something in the sibilant sound. Huyghens nodded. He turned the knob again, with infinitesimal increments.

Out of the background noise came a patterned mutter. As Huyghens shifted the tuning, it grew louder. It reached a volume where it was unmistakable. It was a sequence of sounds like discordant buzzing. There were three half-second buzzings with half-second pauses between. A two-second pause. Three full-second buzzings with half-second pauses between. Another two-second pause and three half-second buzzings, again. Then silence for five seconds. Then the pattern repeated.

"The devil!" said Huyghens. "That's a human signal! Mechanically made, too! In fact, it used to be a standard distress-call. It was termed an S O S, though I've no idea what that meant. Anyhow, somebody must have read old-fashioned novels, some time, to know about it. And so someone is still alive over at your licensed, but now smashed-up, robot colony. And they're asking for help. I'd say they're likely to need it."

He looked at Roane.

"The intelligent thing to do is sit back and wait for a ship—either of my friends or yours. A ship can help survivors or castaways much better than we can. A ship can even find them more easily. But maybe time is important to the poor devils! So I'm going to take the bears and see if I can reach them. You can wait here, if you like. What say? Travel on Loren Two isn't a picnic! I'll be fighting nearly every foot of the way. There's plenty of 'inimical animal life' here!"

Roane snapped angrily:

"Don't be a fool! Of course I'm coming! What do you take me for? And two of us should have four times the chance of one!"

Huyghens grinned.

"Not quite. You forget Sitka Pete and Sourdough Charley and Faro Nell. There'll be five of us if you come, instead of four. And, of course, Nugget has to come—and he'll be no help—but Semper may make up for him. You won't quadruple our chances, Roane, but I'll be glad to have you if you want to be stupid and unreasonable and not at all rational—and come along."

III

There was a jagged spur of stone looming precipitously over a river-valley. A thousand feet below, a broad stream ran westward to the sea. Twenty miles to the east, a wall of mountains rose sheer against the sky. Its peaks seemed to blend to a remarkable evenness of height. There was rolling, tumbled ground between for as far as the eye could see.

A speck in the sky came swiftly downward. Great pinions spread, and flapped, and icy eyes surveyed the rocky space. With more great flappings, Semper the eagle came to ground. He folded his huge wings and turned his head jerkily, his eyes unblinking. A tiny harness held a miniature camera against his chest. He strutted over the bare stone to the highest point. He stood there, a lonely and arrogant figure in the vastness.

There came crashings and rustlings, and then snuffling sounds. Sitka Pete came lumbering out into the clear space. He wore a harness too, and a pack. The harness was complex, because it had not only to hold a pack in normal travel, but, when he stood on his hind legs, it must not hamper the use of his forepaws in combat.

He went cagily all over the open area. He peered over the edge of the spur's farthest tip. He prowled to the other side and looked down. He scouted carefully. Once he moved close to Semper and the eagle opened his great curved beak and uttered an indignant noise. Sitka paid no attention.

He relaxed, satisfied. He sat down untidily, his hind legs sprawling. He wore an air approaching benevolence as he surveyed the landscape about and below him.

More snufflings and crashings. Sourdough Charley came into view with Huyghens and Roane behind him. Sourdough carried a pack, too. Then there was a squealing and Nugget scurried up from the rear, impelled by a whack from his mother. Faro Nell appeared, with the carcass of a staglike animal lashed to her harness.

"I picked this place from a space photo," said Huyghens, "to make a directional fix from. I'll get set up."

He swung his pack from his shoulders to the ground. He extracted an obviously self-constructed device which he set on the ground. It had a whip aerial, which he extended. Then he plugged in a considerable length of flexible wire and unfolded a tiny, improvised directional aerial with an even tinier booster at its base. Roane slipped his pack from his shoulders and watched. Huyghens slipped headphones over his ears. He looked up and said sharply:

"Watch the bears, Roane. The wind's blowing up the way we came. Anything that trails us—sphexes, for example—will send its scent on before. The bears will tell us."

He busied himself with the instruments he'd brought. He heard the hissing, frying, background noise which could be anything at all except a human signal. He reached out and swung the small aerial around. Rasping, buzzing tones came in, faintly and then loudly. This receiver, though, had been made for this particular wave band. It was much more efficient than the modified space phone had been. It picked up three short buzzes, three long ones, and three short ones again. Three dots, three dashes, and three dots. Over and over again. S O S. S O S. S O S.

Huyghens took a reading and moved the directional aerial a carefully measured distance. He took another reading. He shifted it yet again and again, carefully marking and measuring each spot and taking notes of the instrument readings. When he finished, he had checked the direction of the signal not only by loudness but by phase—he had as accurate a fix as could possibly be had with portable apparatus.

Sourdough growled softly. Sitka Pete whiffed the air and arose from his sitting position. Faro Nell whacked Nugget, sending him whimpering to the farthest corner of the flea place. She stood bristling, facing down-hill the way they'd come.

"Damn!" said Huyghens.

He got up and waved his arm at Semper, who had turned his head at the stirrings. Semper squawked in a most un-eaglelike fashion and dived off the spur and was immediately fighting the down-draught beyond it. As Huyghens reached his weapon, the eagle came back overhead. He went magnificently past, a hundred feet high, careening and flapping in the tricky currents. He screamed, abruptly, and circled and screamed again. Huyghens swung a tiny vision plate from its strap to where he could look into it. He saw, of course, what the little camera on Semper's chest could see—reeling, swaying terrain as Semper saw it, though without his breadth of field. There were moving objects to be seen through the shifting trees. Their coloring was unmistakable.

"Sphexes," said Huyghens dourly. "Eight of them. Don't look for them to follow our track, Roane. They run parallel to a trail on either side. That way they attack in breadth and all at once when they catch up. And listen! The bears can handle anything they tangle with! It's our job to pick off the loose ones! And aim for the body! The bullets explode."

He threw off the safety of his weapon. Faro Nell, uttering thunderous growls, went padding to a place between Sitka Pete and Sourdough. Sitka glanced at her and made a whuffing noise, as if derisive of her blood-curdling sounds. Sourdough grunted in a somehow solid fashion. He and Sitka moved farther away from Nell to either side. They would cover a wider front.

There was no other sign of life than the shrillings of the incredibly tiny creatures which on this planet were birds, and Faro Nell's deep-bass, raging growls, and then the click of Roane's safety going off as he got ready to use the weapon Huyghens had given him.

Semper screamed again, flapping low above the treetops, following parti-colored, monstrous shapes beneath.

Eight blue-and-tan fiends came racing out of the underbrush. They had spiny fringes, and horns, and glaring eyes, and they looked as if they had come straight out of hell. On the instant of their appearance they leaped, emitting squalling, spitting squeals that were like the cries of fighting tom-cats ten thousand times magnified. Huyghens' rifle cracked, and its sound was wiped out in the louder detonation of its bullet in sphexian flesh. A tan-and-blue monster tumbled over, shrieking. Faro Nell charged, the very im-personation of white-hot fury. Roane fired, and his bullet exploded against a tree. Sitka Pete brought his massive forepaws in a clapping, monstrous ear-boxing motion. A sphex died.

Then Roane fired again. Sourdough Charley whuffed. He fell forward upon a spitting bi-colored fiend, rolled him over, and raked with his hind claws. The belly-hide of the sphex was tenderer than the rest. The creature rolled away, snapping at its own wounds. Another sphex found itself shaken loose from the tumult about Sitka Pete. It whirled to leap on him from be-hind—and Huyghens fired very coldly—and two plunged upon Faro Nell and Roane blasted one and Faro Nell disposed of the other in truly awesome fury. Then Sitka Pete heaved himself erect—seeming to drip sphexes—and Sourdough waddled over and pulled one off and killed it and went back for another. And both rifles cracked together and there was suddenly nothing left to fight.

The bears prowled from one to another of the corpses. Sitka Pete rumbled and lifted up a limp head. Crash! Then another. He went over the lot, whether or not they showed signs of life. When he had finished, they were wholly still.

Semper came flapping down out of the sky. He had screamed and fluttered overhead as the fight went on. Now he landed with a rush. Huyghens went soothingly from one bear to another, calming them with his voice. It took longest to calm Faro Nell, licking Nugget with impassioned solicitude and growling horribly as she licked.

"Come along, now," said Huyghens, when Sitka showed signs of intending to sit down again. "Heave these carcasses over a cliff. Come along! Sitka! Sourdough! Hup!"

He guided them as the two big males somewhat fastidiously lifted up the nightmarish creatures they and the guns together had killed, and carried them to the edge of the spur of stone. They let the dead beasts go bouncing and sliding down into the valley.

"That," said Huyghens, "is so their little pals will gather round them and caterwaul their woe where there's no trail of ours to give them ideas. If we'd been near a river, I'd have dumped them in to float downriver and gather mourners wherever they stranded. Around the station I incinerate them. If I had to leave them, I'd make tracks away. About fifty miles upwind would be a good idea."

He opened the pack Sourdough carried and extracted giant sized swabs and some gallons of antiseptic. He tended the three Kodiaks in turn, swabbing not only the cuts and scratches they'd received, but deeply soaking their fur where there could be suspicion of spilled sphex blood.

"This antiseptic deodorizes, too," he told Roane. "Or we'd be trailed by any sphex who passed to leeward of us. When we start off, I'll swab the bears' paws for the same reason."

Roane was very quiet. He'd missed his first shot with a bullet-firing weapon—a beam hasn't the stopping-power of an explosive bullet—but he'd seemed to grow savagely angry with himself. The last few seconds of the fight, he'd fired very deliberately and every bullet hit. Now he said bitterly:

"If you're instructing me so I can carry on should you be killed, I doubt that it's worth while!"

Huyghens felt in his pack and unfolded the enlargements he'd made of the space photos of this part of the planet. He carefully oriented the map with distant landmarks. He drew a painstakingly accurate line across the photo.

"The S O S signal comes from somewhere close to the robot colony," he reported. "I think a little to the south of it. Probably from a mine they'd opened up, on the far side—of course—of the Sere Plateau. See how I've marked this map? Two fixes, one from the station and one from here. I came away off-course to get a fix here so we'd have two position-lines to the transmitter. The signal could have come from the other side of the planet. But it doesn't."

"The odds would be astronomical against other castaways," protested Roane.

"No-o-o-o," said Huyghens. "Ships have been coming here. To the robot-colony. One could have crashed. And I have friends, too."

He repacked his apparatus and gestured to the bears. He led them beyond the scene of combat and very carefully swabbed off their paws, so they could not possibly leave a trail of sphex-blood scent behind them. He waved Semper, the eagle, aloft.

"Let's go," he told the Kodiaks. "Yonder! Hup!"

The party headed downhill and into the jungle again. Now it was Sourdough's turn to take the lead, and Sitka Pete prowled more widely behind him. Faro Nell trailed the men, with Nugget. She kept an extremely sharp eye upon the cub. He was a baby, still. He only weighed six hundred pounds. And of course she watched against danger from the rear.

Overhead, Semper fluttered and flew in giant circles and spirals, never going very far away. Huyghens referred constantly to the screen which showed what the air-borne camera saw. The image tilted and circled and banked and swayed. It was by no means the best air-reconnaissance that could be imagined. But it was the best that would work. Presently Huyghens said:

"We swing to the right, here. The going's bad straight ahead, and it looks like a pack of sphexes has killed and is feeding."

Roane was upset. He was dissatisfied with himself. So he said:

"It's against reason for carnivores to be as thick as you say! There has to be a certain amount of other animal life for every meat-eating beast! Too many of them would eat all the game and starve!"

"They're gone all winter," explained Huyghens, "which around here isn't as severe as you might think. And a good many animals seem to breed just after the sphexes go south. Also, the sphexes aren't around all the warm weather. There's a sort of peak, and then for a matter of weeks you won't see a one of them, and suddenly the jungle swarms with them again. Then, presently, they head south. Apparently they're migratory in some fashion, but nobody knows." He said dryly: "There haven't been many naturalists around on this planet. The animal life is inimical."

Roane fretted. He was a senior officer in the Colonial Survey, and he was accustomed to arrival at a partly or completely-finished colonial set-up, and to pass upon the completion or non-completion of the planned installation as designed. Now he was in an intolerably hostile environment, depending upon an illegal colonist for his life, engaged upon a demoralizingly indefinite enterprise—because the mechanical spark-signal could be working long after its constructors were dead—and his ideas about a number of matters were shaken. He was alive, for example, because of three giant Kodiak bears and a bald eagle. He and Huyghens could have been surrounded by ten thousand robots, and they'd have been killed. Sphexes and robots would have ignored each other, and sphexes would have made straight for the men, who'd have had less than four seconds in which to discover for themselves that they were attacked, prepare to defend themselves, and kill eight sphexes.

Roane's convictions as a civilized man were shaken. Robots were marvelous contrivances for doing the expected: accomplishing the planned; coping with the predicted. But they also had defects. Robots could only follow instructions—if this thing happens, do this, if that thing happens do that. But before something else, neither this nor that, robots were helpless. So a robot civilization worked only in an environment where nothing unanticipated ever turned up, and human supervisors never demanded anything unexpected. Roane was appalled. He'd never encountered the truly unpredictable before in all his life and career.

He found Nugget, the cub, ambling uneasily in his wake. The cub flattened his ears miserably when Roane glanced at him. It occurred to the man that Nugget was receiving a lot of disciplinary thumpings from Faro Nell. He was knocked about physically, pretty much as Roane was being knocked about psychologically. His lack of information and unfitness for independent survival in this environment was being hammered into him.

"Hi, Nugget," said Roane ruefully. "I feel just about the way you do!"

Nugget brightened visibly. He frisked. He tended to gambol. He looked very hopefully up into Roane's face—and he stood four feet high at the shoulder and would overtop Roane if he stood erect.

Roane reached out and patted Nugget's head. It was the first time in all his life that he'd ever petted an animal.

He heard a snuffling sound behind him. Skin crawled at the back of his neck. He whirled.

Faro Nell regarded him—eighteen hundred pounds of she-bear only ten feet away and looking into his eyes. For one panicky instant Roane went cold all over. Then he realized that Faro Nell's eyes were not burning. She was not snarling. She did not emit those blood-curdling sounds which the bare prospect of danger to Nugget had produced up on the rocky spur. She looked at him blandly. In fact, after a moment she swung off on some independent investigation of a matter that had aroused her curiosity.

The traveling party went on, Nugget frisking beside Roane and tending to bump into him out of pure cub-clumsiness. Now and again he looked adoringly at Roane, in the instant and overwhelming affection of the very young.

Roane trudged on. Presently he glanced behind again. Faro Nell was now ranging more widely. She was well satisfied to have Nugget in the immediate care of a man. From time to time he got on her nerves.

A little while later, Roane called ahead.

"Huyghens! Look here! I've been appointed nursemaid to Nugget!"

Huyghens looked back.

"Oh, slap him a few times and he'll go back to his mother."

"The devil I will!" said Roane querulously. "I like it!"

The traveling party went on.

When night fell, they camped. There could be no fire, of course, because all the minute night-things about would come eagerly to dance in the glow. But there could not be darkness, equally, because night-walkers hunted in the dark. So Huyghens set out the barrier lamps which made a wall of twilight about their halting place, and the staglike creature Faro Nell had carried became their evening meal. Then they slept—at least the men did—and the bears dozed and snorted and waked and dozed again. But Semper sat immobile with his head under his wing on a tree limb. And presently there was a glorious cool hush and all the world glowed in morning light diffused through the jungle by a newly risen sun. And they arose, and traveled again.

This day they stopped stock-still for two hours while sphexes puzzled over the trail the bears had left. Huyghens discoursed calmly on the need for an anti-scent, to be used on the boots of men and the paws of bears, which would make the following of their trails unpopular with sphexes. And Roane seized upon the idea and absorbedly suggested that a sphex-repellent odor might be worked out, which would make a human revolting to a sphex. If that were done—why—humans could go freely about unmolested.

"Like stink-bugs," said Huyghens, sardonically. "A very intelligent idea! Very rational! You can feel proud!"

And suddenly Roane, very obscurely, was not proud of the idea at all.

They camped again. On the third night they were at the base of that remarkable formation, the Sere Plateau, which from a distance looked like a mountain-range but was actually a desert tableland. And it was not reasonable for a desert to be raised high, while lowlands had rain, but on the fourth morning they found out why. They saw, far, far away, a truly monstrous mountain-mass at the end of the long-way expanse of the plateau. It was like the prow of a ship. It lay, so Huyghens observed, directly in line with the prevailing winds, and divided them as a ship's prow divides the waters. The moisture-bearing air-currents flowed beside the plateau, not over it, and its interior was pure sere desert in the unscreened sunshine of high altitudes.

• • •

It took them a full day to get halfway up the slope. And here, twice as they climbed, Semper flew screaming over aggregations of sphexes to one side of them or the other. These were much larger groups than Huyghens had ever seen before—fifty to a hundred monstrosities together, where a dozen was a large hunting-pack elsewhere. He looked in the screen which showed him what Semper saw, four to five miles away. The sphexes padded uphill toward the Sere Plateau in a long line. Fifty—sixty—seventy tan-and-azure beasts out of hell.

"I'd hate to have that bunch jump us," he said candidly to Roane. "I don't think we'd stand a chance."

"Here's where a robot tank would be useful," Roane observed.

"Anything armored," conceded Huyghens. "One man in an armored station like mine would be safe. But if he killed a sphex he'd be besieged. He'd have to stay holed up, breathing the smell of dead sphex, until the odor had gone away. And he mustn't kill any others or he'd be besieged until winter came."

Roane did not suggest the advantages of robots in other directions. At that moment, for example, they were working their way up a slope which averaged fifty degrees. The bears climbed without effort despite their burdens. For the men it was infinite toil. Semper, the eagle, manifested impatience with bears and men alike, who crawled so slowly up an incline over which he soared.

He went ahead up the mountainside and teetered in the air-currents at the plateau's edge. Huyghens looked in the visionplate by which he reported.

"How the devil," panted Roane—they had stopped for a breather, and the bears waited patiently for them—"do you train bears like these? I can understand Semper."

"I don't train them," said Huyghens, staring into the plate. "They're mutations. In heredity the sex-linkage of physical characteristics is standard stuff. But there's been some sound work done on the gene-linkage of psychological factors. There was need, on my home planet, for an animal who could fight like a fiend, live off the land, carry a pack and get along with men at least as well as dogs do. In the old days they'd have tried to breed the desired physical properties into an animal who already had the personality they wanted. Something like a giant dog, say. But back home they went at it the other way about. They picked the wanted physical characteristics and bred for the personality—the psychology. The job got done over a century ago—a Kodiak bear named Kodius Champion was the first real success. He had everything that was wanted. These bears are his descendants."

"They look normal," commented Roane.

"They are!" said Huyghens warmly. "Just as normal as an honest dog!

They're not trained, like Semper. They train themselves!" He looked back into the plate in his hands, which showed the ground five and six and seven thousand feet higher. "Semper, now, is a trained bird without too much brains. He's educated—a glorified hawk. But the bears want to get along with men. They're emotionally dependent on us! Like dogs. Semper's a servant, but they're companions and friends. He's trained, but they're loyal. He's conditioned. They love us. He'd abandon me if he ever realized he could—he thinks he can only eat what men feed him. But the bears wouldn't want to. They like us. I admit that I like them. Maybe because they like me."

Roane said deliberately:

"Aren't you a trifle loose-tongued, Huyghens? I'm a Colonial Survey officer. I have to arrest you sooner or later. You've told me something that will locate and convict the people who set you up here. It shouldn't be hard to find where bears were bred for psychological mutations, and where a bear named Kodius Champion left descendants! I can find out where you came from now, Huyghens!"

Huyghens looked up from the plate with its tiny swaying television image, relayed from where Semper floated impatiently in mid-air.

"No harm done," he said amiably. "I'm a criminal there, too. It's officially on record that I kidnapped these bears and escaped with them. Which, on my home planet, is about as heinous a crime as a man can commit. It's worse than horse-theft back on Earth in the old days. The kin and cousins of my bears are highly thought of. I'm quite a criminal, back home."

Roane stared.

"Did you steal them?" he demanded.

"Confidentially," said Huyghens, "no. But prove it!" Then he said: "Take a look in this plate. See what Semper can see up at the plateau's edge."

Roane squinted aloft, where the eagle flew in great sweeps and dashes. Somehow, by the experience of the past few days, Roane knew that Semper was screaming fiercely as he flew. He made a dart toward the plateau's border.

Roane looked at the transmitter picture. It was only four inches by six, but it was perfectly without grain and in accurate color. It moved and turned as the camera-bearing eagle swooped and circled. For an instant the screen showed the steeply sloping mountainside, and off at one edge the party of men and bears could be seen as dots. Then it swept away and showed the top of the plateau.

There were sphexes. A pack of two hundred trotted toward the desert interior. They moved at leisure, in the open. The viewing camera reeled, and there were more. As Roane watched and as the bird flew higher, he could see still other sphexes moving up over the edge of the plateau from a small erosion-defile here and another one there. The Sere Plateau was alive with the hellish creatures. It was inconceivable that there should be game enough for them to live on. They were visible as herds of cattle would be visible on grazing planets.

It was simply impossible.

"Migrating," observed Huyghens. "I said they did. They're headed somewhere. Do you know, I doubt that it would be healthy for us to try to cross the plateau through such a swarm of sphexes?"

Roane swore, in abrupt change of mood.

"But the signal's still coming through! Somebody's alive over at the robot colony! Must we wait till the migration's over?"

"We don't know," Huyghens pointed out, "that they'll stay alive. They may need help badly. We have to get to them. But at the same time—"

He glanced at Sourdough Charley and Sitka Pete, clinging patiently to the mountainside while the men rested and talked. Sitka had managed to find a place to sit down, though one massive paw anchored him in his place.

Huyghens waved his arm, pointing in a new direction.

"Let's go!" he called briskly. "Let's go! Yonder! Hup!"

IV

They followed the slopes of the Sere Plateau, neither ascending to its level top—where sphexes congregated—nor descending into the foothills where sphexes assembled. They moved along hillsides and mountain-flanks which sloped anywhere from thirty to sixty degrees, and they did not cover much distance. They practically forgot what it was to walk on level ground. Semper, the eagle, hovered overhead during the daytime, not far away. He descended at nightfall for his food from the pack of one of the bears.

"The bears aren't doing too well for food," said Huyghens dryly. "A ton of bear needs a lot to eat. But they're loyal to us. Semper hasn't any loyalty. He's too stupid. But he's been conditioned to think that he can only eat what men feed him. The bears know better, but they stick to us regardless. I rather like these bears."

It was the most self-evident of understatements. This was at an encampment on the top of a massive boulder which projected from a mountainous stony wall. This was six days from the start of their journey. There was barely room on the boulder for all the party. And Faro Nell fussily insisted that Nugget should be in the safest part, which meant near the mountain-flank. She would have crowded the men outward, but Nugget whimpered for Roane. Wherefore, when Roane moved to comfort him, Faro Nell contentedly drew back and snorted at Sitka and Sourdough and they made room for her near the edge.

It was a hungry camp. They had come upon tiny rills upon occasion, flowing down the mountain side. Here the bears had drunk deeply and the men had filled canteens. But this was the third night, and there had been no game at all. Huyghens made no move to bring out food for Roane or himself. Roane made no comment. He was beginning to participate in the relationship between bears and men, which was not the slavery of the bears but something more. It was two-way. He felt it.

"It would seem," he said fretfully, "that since the sphexes don't seem to hunt on their way uphill, that there should be some game. They ignore everything as they file uphill."

This was true enough. The normal fighting formation of sphexes was line abreast, which automatically surrounded anything which offered to flee and outflanked anything which offered fight. But here they ascended the mountain in long lines, one after the other, following apparently long-established trails. The wind blew along the slopes and carried scent only sidewise. But the sphexes were not diverted from their chosen paths. The long processions of hideous blue-and-tawny creatures—it was hard to think of them as natural beasts, male and female and laying eggs like reptiles on other planets—simply climbed.

"There've been other thousands of beasts before them," said Huyghens. "They must have been crowding this way for days or even weeks. We've seen tens of thousands in Semper's camera. They must be uncountable, altogether. The first-comers ate all the game there was, and the last-comers have something else on whatever they use for minds."

Roane protested: "But so many carnivores in one place is impossible! I know they are here, but they can't be!"

"They're cold-blooded," Huyghens pointed out. "They don't burn food to sustain body-temperature. After all, lots of creatures go for long periods without eating. Even bears hibernate. But this isn't hibernation—or estivation, either."

He was setting up the radiation-wave receiver in the darkness. There was no point in attempting a fix here. The transmitter was on the other side of the Sere Plateau, which inexplicably swarmed with the most ferocious and deadly of all the creatures of Loren Two. The men and bears would commit suicide by crossing here.

But Huyghens turned on the receiver. There came the whispering, scratchy sound of background-noise. Then the signal. Three dogs, three dashes, three dots. Three dots, three dashes, three dots. It went on and on and on. Huyghens turned it off. Roane said:

"Shouldn't we have answered that signal before we left the station? To encourage them?"

"I doubt they have a receiver," said Huyghens. "They won't expect an answer for months, anyhow. They'd hardly listen all the time, and if they're living in a mine-tunnel and trying to sneak out for food to stretch their supplies—why, they'll be too busy to try to make complicated recorders or relays."

Roane was silent for a moment or two.

"We've got to get food for the bears," he said presently. "Nugget's weaned, and he's hungry."

"We will," Huyghens promised. "I may be wrong, but it seems to me that the number of sphexes climbing the mountain is less than yesterday and the day before. We may have just about crossed the path of their migration. They're thinning out. When we're past their trail, we'll have to look out for night-walkers and the like again. But I think they wiped out all animal life on their migration-route."

He was not quite right. He was waked in darkness by the sound of slappings and the grunting of bears. Feather-light puffs of breeze beat upon his face. He struck his belt-lamp sharply and the world was hidden by a whitish film which snatched itself away. Something flapped. Then he saw the stars and the emptiness on the edge of which they camped. Then big white things flapped toward him.

Sitka Pete whuffed mightily and swatted. Faro Nell grunted and swung. She caught something in her claws. She crunched. The light went off as Huyghens realized. Then he said:

"Don't shoot, Roane!" He listened, and heard the sounds of feeding in the dark. It ended. "Watch this!" said Huyghens.

The belt-light came on again. Something strangely-shaped and pallid like human skin reeled and flapped crazily toward him. Something else. Four. Five—ten—twenty—more . . .

A huge hairy paw reached up into the light-beam and snatched a flying thing out of it. Another great paw. Huyghens shifted the light and the three great Kodiaks were on their hind legs, swatting at creatures which flittered insanely, unable to resist the fascination of the glaring lamp. Because of their wild gyrations it was impossible to see them in detail, but they were those unpleasant night-creatures which looked like plucked flying monkeys but were actually something quite different.

The bears did not snarl or snap. They swatted, with a remarkable air of businesslike competence and purpose. Small mounds of broken things built up about their feet.

Suddenly there were no more. Huyghens snapped off the light. The bears crunched and fed busily in the darkness.

"Those things are carnivores *and* blood-suckers, Roane," said Huyghens calmly. "They drain their victims of blood like vampire bats—they've some trick of not waking them—and when they're dead the whole tribe eats. But bears have thick furs, and they wake when they're touched. And they're omnivorous—they'll eat anything but sphexes, and like it. You might say that those night-creatures came to lunch. But they stayed. They are it—for the bears, who are living off the country as usual."

Roane uttered a sudden exclamation. He made a tiny light, and blood flowed down his hand. Huyghens passed over his pocket kit of antiseptic and bandages. Roane stanched the bleeding and bound up his hand. Then he realized that Nugget chewed on something. When he turned the light, Nugget swallowed convulsively. It appeared that he had caught and devoured the creature which had drawn blood from Roane. But Roane had lost none to speak of, at that.

In the morning they started along the sloping scarp of the plateau once more. During the morning, Roane said painfully:

"Robots wouldn't have handled those vampire-things, Huyghens."

"Oh, they could be built to watch for them," said Huyghens, tolerantly. "But you'd have to swat for yourself. I prefer the bears.'

He led the way on. Here their jungle-formation could not apply. On a steep slope the bears ambled comfortably, the tough pads of their feet holding fast on the slanting rock, but the men struggled painfully. Twice Huyghens halted to examine the ground about the mountains' bases through binoculars. He looked encouraged as they went on. The monstrous peak which was like the bow of a ship at the end of the Sere Plateau was visibly nearer. Toward midday, indeed, it looked high above the horizon, no more than fifteen miles away. And at midday Huyghens called a final halt.

"No more congregations of sphexes down below," he said cheerfully, "and we haven't seen a climbing line of them in miles." The crossing of a sphex-trail meant simply waiting until one party had passed, and then crossing before another came in view. "I've a hunch we've crossed their migration-route. Let's see what Semper tells us!"

He waved the eagle aloft. And Semper, like all creatures other than men, normally functioned only for the satisfaction of his appetite, and then tended to loaf or sleep. He had ridden the last few miles perched on Sitka Pete's pack. Now he soared upward and Huyghens watched in the small vision-plate.

Semper went soaring—and the image on the plate swayed and turned and turned—and in minutes was above the plateau's edge. And here there was some vegetation and the ground rolled somewhat, and there were even patches of brush. But as Semper towered higher still, the inner desert appeared. But nearby it was clear of beasts. Only once, when the eagle banked sharply and the camera looked along the long dimension of the plateau, did Huyghens see any sign of the blue-and-tan beasts. There he saw what looked like masses amounting to herds. But, of course, carnivores do not gather in herds.

"We go straight up," said Huyghens in satisfaction. "We cross the plateau here—and we can edge downwind a bit, even. I think we'll find something interesting on our way to your robot colony."

He waved to the bears to go ahead uphill.

They reached the top hours later—barely before sunset. And they saw game. Not much, but game at the grassy, brushy border of the desert. Huyghens brought down a shaggy ruminant which surely would not live on a desert. When night fell there was an abrupt chill in the air. It was much colder than night-temperatures on the slopes. The air was thin. Roane thought confusedly and presently guessed at the cause. In the lee of the prow-mountain the air was calm. There were no clouds. The ground radiated its heat to empty space. It could be bitterly cold in the nighttime, here.

"And hot by day," Huyghens agreed when he mentioned it. "The sunshine's terrifically hot where the air is thin, but on most mountains there's wind. By day, here, the ground will tend to heat up like the surface of a planet without atmosphere. It may be a hundred and forty or fifty degrees on the sand at midday. But it should be cold at night."

It was. Before midnight Huyghens built a fire. There could be no danger of night-walkers where the temperature dropped to freezing.

In the morning the men were stiff with cold, but the bears snorted and moved about briskly. They seemed to revel in the morning chill. Sitka and Sourdough Charley, in fact, became festive and engaged in a mock fight, whacking each other with blows that were only feigned, but would have crushed in the skull of any man. Nugget sneezed with excitement as he watched them. Faro Nell regarded them with female disapproval.

They went on. Semper seemed sluggish. After a single brief flight he descended and rode on Sitka's pack, as on the previous day. He perched there, surveying the landscape as it changed from semi-arid to pure desert in their progress. His air was arrogant. But he would not fly. Soaring birds do not like to fly when there are no winds to make currents of which to take advantage. On the way, Huyghens painstakingly pointed out to Roane exactly where they were on the enlarged photograph taken from space, and the exact spot from which the distress-signal seemed to come.

"You're doing it in case something happens to you," said Roane. "I admit it's sense, but—what could I do to help those survivors even if I got to them, without you?"

"What you've learned about sphexes would help," said Huyghens. "The bears would help. And we left a note back at my station. Whoever grounds at the landing field back there—and the beacon's working again—will find instructions to come to the place we're trying to reach."

Roane plodded alongside him. The narrow non-desert border of the Sere Plateau was behind them, now. They marched across powdery desert sand.

"See here," said Roane. "I want to know something! You tell me you're listed as a bear-thief on your home planet. You tell me it's a lie—to protect your friends from prosecution by the Colonial Survey. You're on your own, risking your life every minute of every day. You took a risk in not shooting me. Now you're risking more in going to help men who'd have to be witnesses that you were a criminal. What are you doing it for?"

Huyghens grinned.

"Because I don't like robots. I don't like the fact that they're subduing men—making men subordinate to them."

"Go on," insisted Sourdough. "I don't see why disliking robots should make you a criminal. Nor men subordinating themselves to robots, either!"

"But they are," said Huyghens mildly. "I'm a crank, of course. But—I live like a man on this planet. I go where I please and do what I please. My helpers, the bears, are my friends. If the robot colony had been a success, would the humans in it have lived like men? Hardly! They'd have to live the way the robots let them! They'd have to stay inside a fence the robots built. They'd have to eat foods that robots could raise, and no others. Why—a man couldn't move his bed near a window, because if he did the house-tending robots couldn't work! Robots would serve them—the way the robots determined—but all they'd get out of it would be jobs servicing the robots!"

Roane shook his head.

"As long as men want robot service, they have to take the service that robots can give. If you don't want those services—"

"I want to decide what I want," said Huyghens, again mildly, "instead of being limited to choose among what I'm offered. On my home planet we halfway tamed it with dogs and guns. Then we developed the bears, and we finished the job with them. Now there's population-pressure and the room for bears and dogs—and men—is dwindling. More and more people are being deprived of the power of decision, and being allowed only the power of choice among the things robots allow. The more we depend on robots, the more limited those choices become. We don't want our children to limit themselves to wanting what robots can provide! We don't want them shriveling to where they abandon everything robots can't give—or won't! We want them to be men—and women. Not damned automatons who live *by* pushing robot-controls so they can live *to* push robot-controls. If that's not subordination to robots—"

"It's an emotional argument," protested Roane. "Not everybody feels that way."

"But I feel that way," said Huyghens. "And so do a lot of others. This is a big galaxy and it's apt to contain some surprises. The one sure thing about a robot and a man who depends on them is that they can't handle the unexpected. There's going to come a time when we need men who can. So on my home planet, some of us asked for Loren Two, to colonize. It was refused—too dangerous. But men can colonize anywhere if they're men. So I came here to study the planet. Especially the sphexes. Eventually, we expected to ask for a license again, with proof that we could handle even those beasts. I'm already doing it in a mild way. But the Survey licensed a robot colony—and where is it?"

Roane made a sour face.

"You picked the wrong way to go about it, Huyghens. It was illegal. It is. It was the pioneer spirit, which is admirable enough, but wrongly directed. After all, it was pioneers who left Earth for the stars. But—"

Sourdough raised up on his hind legs and sniffed the air. Huyghens swung his rifle around to be handy. Roane slipped off the safety-catch of his own. Nothing happened.

"In a way," said Roane vexedly, "you're talking about liberty and freedom, which most people think is politics. You say it can be more. In principle, I'll concede it. But the way you put it, it sounds like a freak religion."

"It's self-respect," corrected Huyghens.

"You may be—"

Faro Nell growled. She bumped Nugget with her nose, to drive him closer to Roane. She snorted at him. She trotted swiftly to where Sitka and Sourdough faced toward the broader, sphex-filled expanse of the Sere Plateau. She took up her position between them.

Huyghens gazed sharply beyond them and then all about.

"This could be bad!" he said softly. "But luckily there's no wind. Here's a sort of hill. Come along, Roane!"

He ran ahead, Roane following and Nugget plumping heavily with him. They reached the raised place—actually a mere hillock no more than five or six feet above the surrounding sand, with a distorted cactuslike growth protruding from the ground. Huyghens stared again. He used his binoculars.

"One sphex," he said curtly. "Just one! And it's out of all reason for a sphex to be alone! But it's not rational for them to gather in hundreds of thousands, either!" He wetted his finger and held it up. "No wind at all."

He used the binoculars again.

"It doesn't know we're here," he added. "It's moving away. Not another one in sight—" He hesitated, biting his lips. "Look here, Roane! I'd like to kill that one lone sphex and find out something. There's a fifty per cent chance I could find out something really important. But—I might have to run. If I'm right—" Then he said grimly, "It'll have to be done quickly. I'm going to ride Faro Nell—for speed. I doubt Sitka or Sourdough would stay behind. But Nugget can't run fast enough. Will you stay here with him?"

Roane drew in his breath. Then he said calmly:

"You know what you're doing. Of course."

"Keep your eyes open. If you see anything, even at a distance, shoot and we'll be back—fast! Don't wait until something's close enough to hit. Shoot the instant you see anything—if you do!"

Roane nodded. He found it peculiarly difficult to speak again. Huyghens went over to the embattled bears. He climbed up on Faro Nell's back, holding fast by her shaggy fur.

"Let's go!" he snapped. "That way! Hup!"

The three Kodiaks plunged away at a dead run, Huyghens lurching and swaying on Faro Nell's back. The sudden rush dislodged Semper from his perch. He flapped wildly and got aloft. Then he followed effortlessly, flying low.

It happened very quickly. A Kodiak bear can travel as fast as a race horse on occasion. These three plunged arrow-straight for a spot perhaps half a mile distant, where a blue-and-tawny shape whirled to face them. There was the crash of Huyghens' weapon from where he rode on Faro Nell's back— the explosion of the weapon and the bullet was one sound. The somehow unnatural spiky monster leaped and died.

Huyghens jumped down from Faro Nell. He became feverishly busy at something on the ground—where the parti-colored sphex had fallen. Semper banked and whirled and came down to the ground. He watched, with his head on one side.

Roane stared, from a distance. Huyghens was doing something to the dead sphex. The two male bears prowled about. Faro Nell regarded Huyghens with intense curiosity. Back at the hillock, Nugget whimpered a little. Roane patted him roughly. Nugget whimpered more loudly. In the distance, Huyghens straightened up and took three steps toward Faro Nell. He mounted. Sitka turned his head back toward Roane. He seemed to see or sniff something dubious. He reared upward. He made a noise, apparently, because Sourdough ambled to his side. The two great beasts began to trot back. Semper flapped wildly and—lacking wind—lurched crazily in the air. He landed on Huyghens' shoulder and his talons clung there.

Then Nugget howled hysterically and tried to swarm up Roane, as a cub tries to swarm up the nearest tree in time of danger. Roane collapsed, and the cub upon him—and there was a flash of stinking scaly hide, while the air was filled with the snarling, spitting squeals of a sphex in full leap. The beast had overjumped, aiming at Roane and the cub while both were upright and arriving when they had fallen. It went tumbling.

Roane heard nothing but the fiendish squalling, but in the distance Sitka and Sourdough were coming at rocketship speed. Faro Nell let out a roar and fairly split the air. And then there was a furry cub streaking toward her, bawling, while Roane rolled to his feet and snatched up his gun. He raged through pure instinct. The sphex crouched to pursue the cub and Roane swung his weapon as a club. He was literally too close to shoot—and perhaps the sphex had only seen the fleeing bear-cub. But he swung furiously.

And the sphex whirled. Roane was toppled from his feet. An eight-hundred-pound monstrosity straight out of hell—half wildcat and half spitting cobra with hydrophobia and homicidal mania added—such a monstrosity is not to be withstood when in whirling its body strikes one in the chest.

That was when Sitka arrived, bellowing. He stood on his hind legs, emitting roars like thunder, challenging the sphex to battle. He waddled forward. Huyghens arrived, but he could not shoot with Roane in the sphere of an explosive bullet's destructiveness. Faro Nell raged and snarled, torn between the urge to be sure that Nugget was unharmed, and the frenzied fury of a mother whose offspring has been endangered.

Mounted on Faro Nell, with Semper clinging idiotically to his shoulder, Huyghens watched helplessly as the sphex spat and squalled at Sitka, having only to reach out one claw to let out Roane's life.

V

They got away from there, though Sitka seemed to want to lift the limp carcass of his victim in his teeth and dash it repeatedly to the ground. He seemed doubly raging because a man—with whom all Kodius Champion's descendants had an emotional relationship—had been mishandled. But Roane was not grievously hurt. He bounced and swore as the bears raced for the horizon. Huyghens had flung him up on Sourdough's pack and snapped for him to hold on. He bumped and chattered furiously:

"Dammit, Huyghens! This isn't right! Sitka got some deep scratches! That horror's claws may be poisonous!"

But Huyghens snapped, "Hup! Hup!" to the bears, and they continued their race against time. They went on for a good two miles, when Nugget wailed despairingly of his exhaustion and Faro Nell halted firmly to nuzzle him.

"This may be good enough," said Huyghens. "Considering that there's no wind and the big mass of beasts is down the plateau and there were only those two around here. Maybe they're too busy to hold a wake, even! Anyhow—"

He slid to the ground and extracted the antiseptic and swabs.

"Sitka first," snapped Roane. "I'm all right!"

Huyghens swabbed the big bear's wounds. They were trivial, because Sitka Pete was an experienced sphex-fighter. Then Roane grudgingly let the curiously-smelling stuff—it reeked of ozone—be applied to the slashes on his chest. He held his breath as it stung. Then he said dourly:

"It was my fault, Huyghens. I watched you instead of the landscape. I couldn't imagine what you were doing."

"I was doing a quick dissection," Huyghens told him. "By luck, that first sphex was a female, as I hoped. And she was just about to lay her eggs. Ugh! And now I know why the sphexes migrate, and where, and how it is that they don't need game up here."

He slapped a quick bandage on Roane. He led the way eastward, still putting distance between the dead sphexes and his party. It was a crisp walk, only, but Semper flapped indignantly overhead, angry that he was not permitted to ride again.

"I'd dissected them before," said Huyghens. "Not enough's been known about them. Some things needed to be found out if men were ever to be able to live here."

"With bears?" asked Roane ironically.

"Oh, yes," said Huyghens. "But the point is that sphexes come to the desert here to breed—to mate and lay their eggs for the sun to hatch. It's a particular place. Seals return to a special place to mate—and the males at least don't eat for weeks on end. Salmon return to their native streams to spawn. They don't eat, and they die afterward. And eels—I'm using Earth examples, Roane—travel some thousands of miles to the Sargasso to mate and die. Unfortunately, sphexes don't appear to die, but it's clear that they have an ancestral breeding place and that they come here to the Sere Plateau to deposit their eggs!"

Roane plodded onward. He was angry: angry with himself because he hadn't taken elementary precautions; because he'd felt too safe, as a man in a robot-served civilization forms the habit of doing; because he hadn't used his brain when Nugget whimpered, in even a bear-cub's awareness that danger was near.

"And now," Huyghens added, "I need some equipment that the robot colony had. With it, I think we can make a start toward making this a planet that men can live like men on!"

Roane blinked.

"What's that?"

"Equipment," said Huyghens impatiently. "It'll be at the robot colony.

Robots were useless because they wouldn't pay attention to sphexes. They'd still be. But take out the robot controls and the machines will do! They shouldn't be ruined by a few months' exposure to weather!"

Roane marched on and on. Presently he said:

"I never thought you'd want anything that came from that colony, Huyghens!"

"Why not?" demanded Huyghens impatiently. "When men make machines do what they want, that's all right. Even robots—when they're where they belong. But men will have to handle flame-casters in the job I want them for. There have to be some, because there was a hundred-mile clearing to be burned off. And Earth-sterilizers—intended to kill the seeds of any plants that robots couldn't handle. We'll come back up here, Roane, and at the least we'll destroy the spawn of these infernal beasts! If we can't do more than that—just doing that every year will wipe out the race in time. There are probably other hordes than this, with other breeding places. But we'll find them, too. We'll make this planet into a place where men from my world can come—and still be men!"

Roane said sardonically:

"It was sphexes that beat the robots. Are you sure you aren't planning to make this world safe for robots?"

Huyghens laughed shortly.

"You've only seen one night-walker," he said. "And how about those things on the mountain-slope—which would have drained you of blood and then feasted? Would you care to wander about this planet with only a robot bodyguard, Roane? Hardly! Men can't live on this planet with only robots to help them—and stop them from being fully men! You'll see!"

They found the colony after only ten days more of travel and after many sphexes and more than a few staglike creatures and shaggy ruminants had fallen to their weapons and the bears. But first they found the survivors of the colony.

There were three of them, hard-bitten and bearded and deeply embittered. When the electrified fence went down, two of them were away at a mine-tunnel, installing a new control-panel for the robots who worked in it. The third was in charge of the mining operation. They were alarmed by the stopping of communication with the colony and went back in a tank-truck to find out what had happened, and only the fact that they were unarmed saved them. They found sphexes prowling and caterwauling about the fallen colony, in numbers they still did not wholly believe. And the sphexes smelled men inside the armored vehicle, but couldn't break in. In turn, the men couldn't kill them, or they'd have been trailed to the mine and besieged there for as long as they could kill an occasional monster.

The survivors stopped all mining—of course—and tried to use remote-controlled robots for revenge and to get supplies for them. Their mining-robots were not designed for either task. And they had no weapons. They improvised miniature throwers of burning rocket-fuel, and they sent occasional prowling sphexes away screaming with scorched hides. But this was useful only because it did not kill the beasts. And it cost fuel. In the end they barricaded themselves and used the fuel only to keep a spark-signal going against the day when another ship came to seek the colony. They stayed in the mine as in a prison, on short rations, waiting without real hope. For diversion they could only contemplate the mining-robots they could not spare fuel to run and which could not do anything but mine.

When Huyghens and Roane reached them, they wept. They hated robots and all things robotic only a little less than they hated sphexes. But Huyghens explained, and armed them with weapons from the packs of the bears, and they marched to the dead colony with the male Kodiaks as point and advance-guard, and with Faro Nell bringing up the rear. They killed sixteen sphexes on the way. In the now overgrown clearing there were four more. In the shelters of the colony they found only foulness and the fragments of what had been men. But there was some food—not much, because the sphexes clawed at anything that smelled of men, and had ruined the plastic packets of radiation-sterilized food. But there were some supplies in metal containers which were not destroyed.

And there was fuel, which men could dispense when they got to the control-panels of the equipment. There were robots everywhere, bright and shining and ready for operation, but immobile, with plants growing up around and over them.

They ignored those robots. But lustfully they fueled tracked flame-casters—adapting them to human rather than robot operation—and the giant soil-sterilizer which had been built to destroy vegetation that robots could not be made to weed out or cultivate. And they headed back for the Sere Plateau, burning-eyed and filled with hate.

But Nugget became a badly spoiled bear-cub, because the freed men approved passionately of anything that would even grow up to kill sphexes. They petted him to excess, when they camped.

And they reached the plateau by a sphex-trail to the top. And Semper scouted for sphexes, and the giant Kodiaks disturbed them and the sphexes came squalling and spitting to destroy them—and while Roane and Huyghens fired steadily, the great machines swept up with their special weapons. The Earth-sterilizer, it was found, was deadly against animal life as well as seeds, when its diathermic beam was raised and aimed. But it had to be handled by a man. No robot could decide just when it was to be used, and against what target.

Presently the bears were not needed, because the scorched corpses of sphexes drew live ones from all parts of the plateau even in the absence of noticeable breezes. The official business of the sphexes was presumably finished, but they came to caterwaul and seek vengeance—which they did not find. Presently the survivors of the robot colony drove machines—as men needed to do, here—in great circles around the hugest heap of slaughtered fiends, destroying new arrivals as they came. It was such a killing as men had never before made on any planet, but there would not be many left of the sphex-horde which had bred in this particular patch of desert. There might be other hordes elsewhere, and other breeding places, but the normal territory of this mass of monsters would see few of them this year.

Or next year, either. Because the soil-sterilizer would go over the dug-up sand where the sphex-spawn lay hidden for the sun to hatch. And the sun would never hatch them.

But Huyghens and Roane, by that time, were camped on the edge of the plateau with the Kodiaks. They were technically upwind from the scene of slaughter—and somehow it seemed more befitting for the men of the robot colony to conduct it. After all, it was those men whose companions had been killed.

There came an evening when Huyghens amiably cuffed Nugget away from where he sniffed too urgently at a stag-steak cooking on the campfire. Nugget ambled dolefully behind the protecting form of Roane and sniveled.

"Huyghens," said Roane painfully, "we've got to come to a settlement of our affairs. I'm a Colonial Survey officer. You're an illegal colonist. It's my duty to arrest you."

Huyghens regarded him with interest.

"Will you offer me lenience if I tell on my confederates," he asked mildly, "or may I plead that I can't be forced to testify against myself?"

Roane said vexedly:

"It's irritating! I've been an honest man all my life, but—I don't believe in robots as I did, except in their place. And their place isn't here. Not as the robot colony was planned, anyhow. The sphexes are nearly wiped out, but they won't be extinct and robots can't handle them. Bears and men will have to live here or—the people who do will have to spend their lives behind sphex-proof fences, accepting only what robots can give them. And there's much too much on this planet for people to miss it! To live in a robot-managed controlled environment on a planet like Loren Two wouldn't . . . it wouldn't be self-respecting!"

"You wouldn't be getting religious, would you?" asked Huyghens dryly. "That was your term for self-respect before."

Semper, the eagle, squawked indignantly as Sitka Pete almost stepped on him, approaching the fire. Sitka Pete sniffed, and Huyghens spoke to him sharply, and he sat down with a thump. He remained sitting in an untidy lump, looking at the steak and drooling.

"You don't let me finish!" protested Roane querulously. "I'm a Colonial Survey officer, and it's my job to pass on the work that's done on a planet before any but the first-landed colonists may come there to live. And of course to see that specifications are followed. Now—the robot colony I was sent to survey was practically destroyed. As designed, it wouldn't work. It couldn't survive."

Huyghens grunted. Night was falling. He turned the meat over the fire.

"Now, in emergencies," said Roane carefully, "colonists have the right to call on any passing ship for aid. Naturally! So— I've always been an honest man before, Huyghens—my report will be that the colony as designed was impractical, and that it was overwhelmed and destroyed except for three survivors who holed up and signaled for help. They did, you know!"

"Go on," grunted Huyghens.

"So," said Roane querulously, "it just happened—just happened, mind you—that a ship with you and Sitka and Sourdough and Faro Nell on board—and Nugget and Semper, too, of course—picked up the distress-call. So you landed to help the colonists. And you did. That's the story. Therefore it isn't illegal for you to be here. It was only illegal for you to be here when you were needed. But we'll pretend you weren't."

Huyghens glanced over his shoulder in the deepening night. He said calmly:

"I wouldn't believe that if I told it myself. Do you think the Survey will?"

"They're not fools," said Roane tartly. "Of course they won't! But when my report says that because of this unlikely series of events it is practical to colonize the planet, whereas before it wasn't—and when my report proves that a robot colony alone is stark nonsense, but that with bears and men from your world added, so many thousand colonists can be received per year— And when that much is true, anyhow—"

Huyghens seemed to shake a little as a dark silhouette against the flames. A little way off, Sourdough sniffed the air hopefully. With a bright light like the fire, presently naked-looking flying things might appear to be slapped down out of the air. They were succulent—to a bear.

"My reports carry weight," insisted Roane. "The deal will be offered, anyhow! The robot colony organizers will have to agree or they'll have to fold up. It's true! And your people can hold them up for nearly what terms they choose."

Huyghens' shaking became understandable. It was laughter.

"You're a lousy liar, Roane," he said, chuckling. "Isn't it unintelligent and unreasonable and irrational to throw away a lifetime of honesty just to get me out of a jam? You're not acting like a rational animal, Roane. But I thought you wouldn't, when it came to the point."

Roane squirmed.

"That's the only solution I can think of. But it'll work."

"I accept it," said Huyghens, grinning. "With thanks. If only because it means another few generations of men living like men on a planet that is going to take a lot of taming. And—if you want to know—because it keeps Sourdough and Sitka and Nell and Nugget from being killed because I brought them here illegally."

Something pressed hard against Roane. Nugget, the cub, pushed urgently against him in his desire to get closer to the fragrantly cooking meat. He edged forward. Roane toppled from where he squatted on the ground. He sprawled. Nugget sniffed luxuriously.

"Slap him," said Huyghens. "He'll move back."

"I won't!" said Roane indignantly from where he lay. "I won't do it! He's my friend!"

Poul Anderson

THE SKY PEOPLE

Poul Anderson has been one of the stalwarts of adventure SF writing for more than fifty years now, and has probably written more of it, at a level of quality that's not only consistent but extremely high, than any other writer—in fact, if any writer of the post–World War II generation deserves the title Father Of Modern Space Opera, it would have to be Anderson; only Jack Vance has produced a body of work extensive and memorable enough to rival his claim on that title. And, like Vance, Anderson is still producing first-rate work well into the '90s, work which holds up admirably in terms of imagination and scope in head-to-head competition with the work of any of the Young Turks on the current scene; his 1995 story "Genesis," for instance, is a Modern Space Opera as complex, inventive, and sci-entifically up-to-date as anything being turned out by writers younger than him by decades (many of whom weren't even born when he started writing), and could validly have been included in the follow-up anthology to *this* anthology, *The Good New Stuff.*

Anderson had trained to be a scientist, taking a degree in physics from the University of Minnesota, but the writing life proved to be more seductive, and he never did get around to working in his original field of choice. Instead, the sales mounted steadily, until by the late '50s and early '60s he may have been one of the most prolific writers in the genre, and by the mid '60s was also on his way to becoming one of the most honored and respected writers in the genre as well. At one point during this period (in addition to non-related work, and lesser series such as the "Hoka" stories he was writing in collaboration with Gordon R. Dick-son), Anderson was running three of the most popular and prestigious series in science fiction *all at the same time:* the "Technic History" series detailing the ex-ploits of the wily trader Nicholas van Rijn (which includes novels such as *The Man Who Counts, The Trouble Twisters, Satan's World, Mirkheim, The People of the Wind,* and collections such as *Trader to the Stars* and *The Earth Book of Storm-gate*); the extremely popular series relating the adventures of interstellar secret agent Dominic Flandry, probably the most successful attempt to cross SF with the spy thriller, next to Jack Vance's "Demon Princes" novels (the Flandry series in-cludes novels such as *A Circus of Hells, The Rebel Worlds, The Day of Their Re-turn, Flandry of Terra, A Knight of Ghosts and Shadows, A Stone in Heaven,* and *The Game of Empire,* and collections such as *Agent of the Terran Empire*); and, my own personal favorite, a series that took us along on assignment with the agents of the Time Patrol (including the collections *The Guardians of Time, Time Patrolman, The Shield of Time,* and *The Time Patrol*).

It's hard to convey a sense of how astonishing this was, especially in the somewhat more limited compress of the science fiction world of the day. It's as if you should find out that the most popular and high-selling series on the B. Dalton's bestseller list, Isaac Asimov's *Robot* novels, say, and Orson Scott Card's *Ender* series, and Anne McCaffery's *Dragonrider* books, were actually all being written by the *same person.*

The effect was staggering—and when you add to it the impact of the best of Anderson's non-series novels, work such as *Brain Wave, Three Hearts and Three Lions, The Night Face, The Enemy Stars,* and *The High Crusade,* all of which was being published in *addition* to the series books, it becomes clear that Anderson dominated the late '50s and the pre-New Wave '60s in a way that only Robert A. Heinlein, Isaac Asimov, and Arthur C. Clarke could rival. And, like them, he remained an active and dominant figure right through the '70s and '80s as well, and is still turning up on bestseller lists almost to the end of the decade of the '90s.

Almost any of the best stories from any of Anderson's major series would have been an appropriate choice for this anthology; one of his "Time Patrol" stories was an early favorite in the running, and there were exploits of Dominic Flandry or Nicholas van Rijn that would have served equally as well, as would some of his non-series work. I kept coming back to the big, vivid, and powerful novella that follows, though—an evocative story full of color and action that, in spite of all the swordplay and swashbuckling, also examines a subtle point with a good deal of profundity: just what *is* civilization, anyway? And are you sure you'll recognize it when you *see* it . . . ?

In the course of his 51-year career, Poul Anderson has published over a hundred books (in several different fields, as Anderson has written historical novels, fantasies, and mysteries, in addition to SF), sold hundreds of short pieces to every conceivable market, and won seven Hugo Awards, three Nebula Awards, and the Tolkein Memorial Award. In 1998 he was presented with the Grandmaster Nebula Award for life achievement. His other books include *Tau Zero, Orion Shall Rise, The Broken Sword, The Boat of a Million Years,* and *Harvest of Stars.* His short work has been collected in *The Queen of Air and Darkness and Other Stories, Guardians of Time, The Earth Book of Stormgate, Fantasy, The Unicorn Trade* (with Karen Anderson), *Past Times, Time Patrolman,* and *Explorations.* His most recent books are the novels *The Stars Are Also Fire* and *The Fleet of Stars.* Anderson lives in Orinda, California, with his wife and fellow writer, Karen.

The rover fleet got there just before sunrise. From its height, five thousand feet, the land was bluish gray, smoked with mists. Irrigation canals caught the first light as if they were full of mercury. Westward the ocean gleamed, its far edge dissolved into purple and a few stars.

Loklann sunna Holber leaned over the gallery rail of his flagship and pointed a telescope at the city. It sprang to view as a huddle of walls, flat roofs, and square watchtowers. The cathedral spires were tinted rose by a hidden sun. No barrage balloons were aloft. It must be true what rumor said, that the Perio had abandoned its outlying provinces to their fate. So the portable wealth of Meyco would have flowed into S' Antón, for safe-keeping—which meant that the place was well worth a raid. Loklann grinned.

Robra sunna Stam, the *Buffalo*'s mate, spoke. "Best we come down to about two thousand," he suggested. "To make sure the men aren't blown sideways, to the wrong side of the town walls."

"Aye." The skipper nodded his helmeted head. "Two thousand, so be it."

Their voices seemed oddly loud up here, where only the wind and a creak of rigging had broken silence. The sky around the rovers was dusky immensity, tinged red gold in the east. Dew lay on the gallery deck. But when the long wooden horns blew signals, it was somehow not an interruption, nor was the distant shouting of orders from other vessels, thud of crew feet, clatter of windlasses and hand-operated compressor pumps. To a Sky Man, those sounds belonged in the upper air.

Five great craft spiraled smoothly downward. The first sunrays flashed off gilt figureheads, bold on sharp gondola prows, and rioted along the extravagant designs painted on gas bags. Sails and rudders were unbelievably white across the last western darkness.

"Hullo, there," said Loklann. He had been studying the harbor through his telescope. "Something new. What could it be?"

He offered the tube to Robra, who held it to his remaining eye. Within the glass circle lay a stone dock and warehouses, centuries old, from the days of the Perio's greatness. Less than a fourth of their capacity was used now. The normal clutter of wretched little fishing craft, a single coasting schooner . . . and yes, by Oktai the Stormbringer, a monster thing, bigger than a whale, seven masts that were impossibly tall!

"I don't know." The mate lowered the telescope. "A foreigner? But where from? Nowhere in this continent—"

"I never saw any arrangement like that," said Loklann. "Square sails on the topmasts, fore-and-aft below." He stroked his short beard. It burned like spun copper in the morning light; he was one of the fair-haired blue-eyed men, rare even among the Sky People and unheard of elsewhere. "Of course," he said, "we're no experts on water craft. We only see them in passing." A not unamiable contempt rode his words: sailors made good slaves, at least, but naturally the only fit vehicle for a fighting man was a rover abroad and a horse at home.

"Probably a trader," he decided. "We'll capture it if possible."

He turned his attention to more urgent problems. He had no map of S' Antón, had never even seen it before. This was the farthest south any Sky People had yet gone plundering, and almost as far as any had ever visited; in bygone days aircraft were still too primitive and the Perio too strong. Thus Loklann must scan the city from far above, through drifting white vapors, and make his plan on the spot. Nor could it be very complicated, for he had only signal flags and a barrel-chested hollerer with a megaphone to pass orders to the other vessels.

"That big plaza in front of the temple," he murmured. "Our contingent will land there. Let the *Stormcloud* men tackle that big building east of it . . . see . . . it looks like a chief's dwelling. Over there, along the north wall, typical barracks and parade ground—*Coyote* can deal with the soldiers. Let the *Witch of Heaven* men land on the docks, seize the seaward gun emplacements and that strange vessel, then join the attack on the garrison. *Fire Elk*'s crew should land inside the east city gate and send a detachment to the south gate, to bottle in the civilian population. Having occupied the plaza, I'll send reinforcements wherever they're needed. All clear?"

He snapped down his goggles. Some of the big men crowding about him wore chain armor, but he preferred a cuirass of hardened leather, Mong style; it was nearly as strong and a lot lighter. He was armed with a pistol, but had more faith in his battle ax. An archer could shoot almost as fast as a gun, as accurately—and firearms were getting fabulously expensive to operate as sulfur sources dwindled.

He felt a tightness which was like being a little boy again, opening presents on Midwinter Morning. Oktai knew what treasures he would find, of gold, cloth, tools, slaves, of battle and high deeds and eternal fame. Possibly death. Someday he was sure to die in combat; he had sacrificed so much to his josses, they wouldn't grudge him war-death and a chance to be reborn as a Sky Man.

"Let's go!" he said.

He sprang up on a gallery rail and over. For a moment the world pinwheeled; now the city was on top and now again his *Buffalo* streaked past. Then he pulled the ripcord and his harness slammed him to steadiness. Around him, air bloomed with scarlet parachutes. He gauged the wind and tugged a line, guiding himself down.

II

Don Miwel Carabán, calde of S' Antón d' Inio, arranged a lavish feast for his Maurai guests. It was not only that this was a historic occasion, which might even mark a turning point in the long decline. (Don Miwel, being that rare combination, a practical man who could read, knew that the withdrawal of period troops to Brasil twenty years ago was not a "temporary adjustment." They would never come back. The outer provinces were on their own.) But the strangers must be convinced that they had found a nation rich, strong, and basically civilized, that it was worthwhile visiting the Meycan coasts to trade, ultimately to make alliance against the northern savages.

The banquet lasted till nearly midnight. Though some of the old irrigation canals had choked up and never been repaired, so that cactus and rattlesnake housed in abandoned pueblos, Meyco Province was still fertile. The slant-eyed Mong horsemen from Tekkas had killed off innumerable peons when they raided five years back; wooden pitchforks and obsidian hoes were small use against saber and arrow. It would be another decade before population had returned to normal and the periodic famines resumed. Thus Don Miwel offered many courses, beef, spiced ham, olives, fruits, wines, nuts, coffee, which last the Sea People were unfamiliar with and didn't much care for, et cetera. Entertainment followed—music, jugglers, a fencing exhibition by some of the young nobles.

At this point the surgeon of the *Dolphin*, who was rather drunk, offered to show an Island dance. Muscular beneath tattoos, his brown form went through a series of contortions which pursed the lips of the dignified Dons. Miwel himself remarked, "It reminds me somewhat of our peons' fertility rites," with a strained courtesy that suggested to Captain Ruori Rangi Lohannaso that peons had an altogether different and not very nice culture.

The surgeon threw back his queue and grinned. "Now let's bring the ship's wahines ashore to give them a real hula," he said in Maurai-Ingliss.

"No," answered Ruori. "I fear we may have shocked them already. The proverb goes, 'When in the Solomon Islands, darken your skin.' "

"I don't think they know how to have any fun," complained the doctor.

"We don't yet know what the taboos are," warned Ruori. "Let us be as grave, then, as these spike-bearded men, and not laugh or make love until we are back on shipboard among our wahines."

"But it's stupid! Shark-toothed Nan eat me if I'm going to—"

"Your ancestors are ashamed," said Ruori. It was about as sharp a rebuke as you could give a man whom you didn't intend to fight. He softened his tone to take out the worst sting, but the doctor had to shut up. Which he did, mumbling an apology and retiring with his blushes to a dark corner beneath faded murals.

Ruori turned back to his host. "I beg your pardon, S'ñor," he said, using the local tongue. "My men's command of Spañol is even less than my own."

"Of course." Don Miwel's lean black-clad form made a stiff little bow. It brought his sword up, ludicrously, like a tail. Ruori heard a smothered snort of laughter from among his officers. And yet, thought the captain, were long trousers and ruffled shirt any worse than sarong, sandals, and clan tattoos? Different customs, no more. You had to sail the Maurai Federation, from Awaii to his own N'Zealann and west to Mlaya, before you appreciated how big this planet was and how much of it a mystery.

"You speak our language most excellently, S'ñor," said Doñita Tresa Carabán. She smiled. "Perhaps better than we, since you studied texts centuries old before embarking, and the Spañol has changed greatly since."

Ruori smiled back. Don Miwel's daughter was worth it. The rich black dress caressed a figure as good as any in the world; and, while the Sea People paid less attention to a woman's face, he saw that hers was proud and well formed, her father's eagle beak softened to a curve, luminous eyes and hair the color of midnight oceans. It was too bad these Meycans—the nobles, at least—thought a girl should be reserved solely for the husband they eventually picked for her. He would have liked her to swap her pearls and silver for a lei and go out in a ship's canoe, just the two of them, to watch the sunrise and make love.

However—

"In such company," he murmured, "I am stimulated to learn the modern language as fast as possible."

She refrained from coquetting with her fan, a local habit the Sea People found alternately hilarious and irritating. But her lashes fluttered. They were very long, and her eyes, he saw, were gold-flecked green. "You are learning cab'llero manners just as fast, S'ñor," she said.

"Do not call our language 'modern,' I pray you," interrupted a scholarly-looking man in a long robe. Ruori recognized Bispo Don Carlos Ermosillo, a high priest of that Esu Carito who seemed cognate with the Maurai Lesu Haristi. "Not modern, but corrupt. I too have studied ancient books, printed before the War of Judgment. Our ancestors spoke the true Spañol. Our version of it is as distorted as our present-day society." He sighed. "But what can one expect, when even among the well born, not one in ten can write his own name?"

"There was more literacy in the high days of the Perio," said Don Miwel. "You should have visited us a hundred years ago, S'ñor Captain, and seen what our race was capable of."

"Yet what was the Perio itself but a successor state?" asked the Bispo bitterly. "It unified a large area, gave law and order for a while, but what did it create that was new? Its course was the same sorry tale as a thousand kingdoms before, and therefore the same judgment has fallen on it."

Doñita Tresa crossed herself. Even Ruori, who held a degree in engineering as well as navigation, was shocked. "Not atomics?" he exclaimed.

"What? Oh. The old weapons, which destroyed the old world. No, of course not." Don Carlos shook his head. "But in our more limited way, we have been as stupid and sinful as the legendary forefathers, and the results have been parallel. You may call it human greed or el Dío's punishment as you will; I think the two mean much the same thing."

Ruori looked closely at the priest. "I should like to speak with you further, S'ñor," he said, hoping it was the right title. "Men who know history, rather than myth, are rare these days."

"By all means," said Don Carlos. "I should be honored."

Doñita Tresa shifted on light, impatient feet. "It is customary to dance," she said.

Her father laughed. "Ah, yes. The young ladies have been getting quite impatient, I am sure. Time enough to resume formal discussions tomorrow, S'ñor Captain. Now let the music begin."

He signalled. The orchestra struck up. Some instruments were quite like those of the Maurai, others wholly unfamiliar. The scale itself was different. . . . They had something like it in Stralia, but—a hand fell on Ruori's arm. He looked down at Tresa. "Since you do not ask me to dance," she said, "may I be so immodest as to ask you?"

"What does 'immodest' mean?" he inquired.

She blushed and tried to explain, without success. Ruori decided it was another local concept which the Sea People lacked. By that time the Meycan girls and their cavaliers were out on the ballroom floor. He studied them for a moment. "The motions are unknown to me," he said, "but I think I could soon learn."

She slipped into his arms. It was a pleasant contact, even though nothing would come of it. "You do very well," she said after a minute. "Are all your folk so graceful?"

Only later did he realize that was a compliment for which he should have thanked her; being an Islander, he took it at face value as a question and replied, "Most of us spend a great deal of time on the water. A sense of balance and rhythm must be developed or one is likely to fall into the sea."

She wrinkled her nose. "Oh, stop," she laughed. "You're as solemn as S' Osé in the cathedral."

Ruori grinned back. He was a tall young man, brown as all his race but with the gray eyes which many bore in memory of Ingliss ancestors. Being a N'Zealanner, he was not tattooed as lavishly as some Federation men. On the other hand, he had woven a whalebone filigree into his queue, his sarong was the finest batik, and he had added thereto a fringed shirt. His knife, without which a Maurai felt obscenely helpless, was in contrast: old, shabby until you saw the blade, a tool.

"I must see this god, S' Osé," he said. "Will you show me? Or no. I would not have eyes for a mere statue."

"How long will you stay?" she asked.

"As long as we can. We are supposed to explore the whole Meycan coast. Hitherto the only Maurai contact with the Merikan continent has been one voyage from Awaii to Calforni. They found desert and a few savages. We have heard from Okkaidan traders that there are forests still farther north, where yellow and white men strive against each other. But what lies south of Calforni was unknown to us until this expedition was sent out. Perhaps you can tell us what to expect in Su-Merika."

"Little enough by now," she sighed, "even in Brasil."

"Ah, but lovely roses bloom in Meyco."

Her humor returned. "And flattering words in N'Zealann," she chuckled.

"Far from it. We are notoriously straightforward. Except, of course, when yarning about voyages we have made."

"What yarns will you tell about this one?"

"Not many, lest all the young men of the Federation come crowding here. But I will take you aboard my ship, Doñita, and show you to the compass. Thereafter it will always point toward S' Antón d' Inio. You will be, so to speak, my compass rose."

Somewhat to his surprise, she understood, and laughed. She led him across the floor, supple between his hands.

Thereafter, as the night wore on, they danced together as much as decency allowed, or a bit more, and various foolishness which concerned no one else passed between them. Toward sunrise the orchestra was dismissed and the guests, hiding yawns behind well-bred hands, began to take their departure.

"How dreary to stand and receive farewells," whispered Tresa. "Let them think I went to bed already." She took Ruori's hand and slipped behind a column and thence out onto a balcony. An aged serving woman, stationed to act as duenna for couples that wandered thither, had wrapped up in her mantle against the cold and fallen asleep. Otherwise the two were alone among jasmines. Mists floated around the palace and blurred the city; far off rang the *"Todos buen"* of pikemen tramping the outer walls. Westward the balcony faced darkness, where the last stars glittered. The seven tall topmasts of the Maurai *Dolphin* caught the earliest sun and glowed.

Tresa shivered and stood close to Ruori. They did not speak for a while.

"Remember us," she said at last, very low. "When you are back with your own happier people, do not forget us here."

"How could I?" he answered, no longer in jest.

"You have so much more than we," she said wistfully. "You have told me how your ships can sail unbelievably fast, almost into the wind. How your fishers always fill their nets, how your whale ranchers keep herds that darken the water, how you even farm the ocean for food and fiber and . . ." She fingered the shimmering material of his shirt. "You told me this was made by craft out of fishbones. You told me that every family has its own spacious house and every member of it, almost, his own boat . . . that even small children on the loneliest island can read, and have printed books . . . that you have none of the sicknesses which destroy us . . . that no one hungers and all are free—oh, do not forget us, you on whom el Dío has smiled!"

She stopped, then, embarrassed. He could see how her head lifted and nostrils dilated, as if resenting him. After all, he thought, she came from a breed which for centuries had given, not received, charity.

Therefore he chose his words with care. "It has been less our virtue than our good fortune, Doñita. We suffered less than most in the War of Judgment, and our being chiefly Islanders prevented our population from outrunning the sea's rich ability to feed us. So we—no, we did not retain any lost ancestral arts. There are none. But we did re-create an ancient attitude, a way of thinking, which has made the difference—science."

She crossed herself. "The atom!" she breathed, drawing from him.

"No, no, Doñita," he protested. "So many nations we have discovered lately believe science was the cause of the old world's ruin. Or else they think it was a collection of cut-and-dried formulas for making tall buildings or talking at a distance. But neither is true. The scientific method is only a means of learning. It is a . . . a perpetual starting afresh. And that is why you people here in Meyco can help us as much as we can help you, why we have sought you out and will come knocking hopefully at your doors again in the future."

She frowned, though something began to glow within her. "I do not understand," she said.

He cast about for an example. At last he pointed to a series of small holes in the balcony rail. "What used to be here?" he asked.

"Why . . . I do not know. It has always been like that."

"I think I can tell you. I have seen similar things elsewhere. It was a wrought-iron grille. But it was pulled out a long time ago and made into weapons or tools. No?"

"Quite likely," she admitted. "Iron and copper have grown very scarce. We have to send caravans across the whole land, to Támico ruins, in great peril from bandits and barbarians, to fetch our metal. Time was when there were iron rails within a kilometer of this place. Don Carlos has told me."

He nodded. "Just so. The ancients exhausted the world. They mined the ores, burned the oil and coal, eroded the land, until nothing was left. I exaggerate, of course. There are still deposits. But not enough. The old civilization used up the capital, so to speak. Now sufficient forest and soil have come back that the world could try to reconstruct machine culture—except that there aren't enough minerals and fuels. For centuries men had been forced to tear up the antique artifacts, if they were to have any metal at all. By and large, the knowledge of the ancients hasn't been lost; it has simply become unusable, because we are so much poorer than they."

He leaned forward, earnestly. "But knowledge and discovery do not depend on wealth," he said. "Perhaps because we did not have much metal to cannibalize in the Islands, we turned elsewhere. The scientific method is just as applicable to wind and sun and living matter as it was to oil, iron, or uranium. By studying genetics we learned how to create seaweeds, plankton, fish that would serve our purposes. Scientific forest management gives us adequate timber, organic-synthesis bases, some fuel. The sun pours down energy which we know how to concentrate and use. Wood, ceramics, even stone can replace metal for most purposes. The wind, through such principles as the airfoil or the Venturi law or the Hilsch tube, supplies force, heat, refrigeration; the tides can be harnessed. Even in its present early stage, paramathematical psychology helps control population, as well as— no, I am talking like an engineer now, falling into my own language. I apologize."

"What I wanted to say was that if we can only have the help of other people, such as yourselves, on a worldwide scale, we can match our ancestors, or surpass them . . . not in their ways, which were often shortsighted and wasteful, but in achievements uniquely ours. . . ."

His voice trailed off. She wasn't listening. She stared over his head, into the air, and horror stood on her face.

Then trumpets howled on battlements, and the cathedral bells crashed to life.

"What the nine devils!" Ruori turned on his heel and looked up. The zenith had become quite blue. Lazily over S' Antón floated five orca shapes. The new sun glared off a jagged heraldry painted along their flanks. He estimated dizzily that each of them must be three hundred feet long.

Blood-colored things petaled out below them and drifted down upon the city.

"The Sky People!" said a small broken croak behind him. "Sant'sima Marí, pray for us now!"

III

Loklann hit flagstones, rolled over, and bounced to his feet. Beside him a carved horseman presided over fountain waters. For an instant he admired the stone, almost alive; they had nothing like that in Canyon, Zona, Corado, any of the mountain kingdoms. And the temple facing this plaza was white skywardness.

The square had been busy, farmers and handicrafters setting up their booths for a market day. Most of them scattered in noisy panic. But one big man roared, snatched a stone hammer, and dashed in his rags to meet Loklann. He was covering the flight of a young woman, probably his wife, who held a baby in her arms. Through the shapeless sack dress Loklann saw that her figure wasn't bad. She would fetch a price when the Mong slave dealer next visited Canyon. So could her husband, but there wasn't time now, still encumbered with a chute. Loklann whipped out his pistol and fired. The man fell to his knees, gaped at the blood seeping between fingers clutched to his belly, and collapsed. Loklann flung off his harness. His boots thudded after the woman. She shrieked when fingers closed on her arm and tried to wriggle free, but the brat hampered her. Loklann shoved her toward the temple. Robra was already on its steps.

"Post a guard!" yelled the skipper. "We may as well keep prisoners in here, till we're ready to plunder it."

An old man in priest's robes tottered to the door. He held up one of the cross-shaped Meycan josses, as if to bar the way. Robra brained him with an ax blow, kicked the body off the stairs, and urged the woman inside.

It sleeted armed men. Loklann winded his oxhorn bugle, rallying them. A counterattack could be expected any minute. . . . Yes, now.

A troop of Meycan cavalry clanged into view. They were young, proud-looking men in baggy pants, leather breastplate and plumed helmet, blowing cloak, fire-hardened wooden lances but steel sabres —very much like the yellow nomads of Tekkas, whom they had fought for centuries. But so had the Sky People. Loklann pounded to the head of his line, where his standard bearer had raised the Lightning Flag. Half the *Buffalo's* crew fitted together sections of pike tipped with edged ceramic, grounded the butts, and waited. The charge crested upon them. Their pikes slanted down. Some horses spitted themselves, others reared back screaming. The pikemen jabbed at their riders. The second paratroop line stepped in, ax and sword and hamstringing knife. For a few minutes murder boiled. The Meycans broke. They did not flee, but they retreated in confusion. And then the Canyon bows began to snap.

Presently only dead and hurt cluttered the square. Loklann moved briskly among the latter. Those who weren't too badly wounded were hustled into the temple. Might as well collect all possible slaves and cull them later.

From afar he heard a dull boom. "Cannon," said Robra, joining him. "At the army barracks."

"Well, let the artillery have its fun, till our boys get in among 'em," said Loklann sardonically.

"Sure, sure." Robra looked nervous. "I wish they'd let us hear from them, though. Just standing around here isn't good."

"It won't be long," predicted Loklann.

Nor was it. A runner with a broken arm staggered to him. "*Stormcloud*," he gasped. "The big building you sent us against . . . full of swordsmen. . . . They repulsed us at the door—"

"Huh! I thought it was only the king's house," said Loklann. He laughed. "Well, maybe the king was giving a party. Come on, then, I'll go see for myself. Robra, take over here." His finger swept out thirty men to accompany him. They jogged down streets empty and silent except for their bootfalls and weapon-jingle. The housefolk must be huddled terrified behind those blank walls. So much the easier to corral them later, when the fighting was done and the looting began.

A roar broke loose. Loklann led a dash around a last corner. Opposite him he saw the palace, an old building, red-tiled roof and mellow walls and many glass windows. The *Stormcloud* men were fighting at the main door. Their dead and wounded from the last attack lay thick.

Loklann took in the situation at a glance. "It wouldn't occur to those lardheads to send a detachment through some side entrance, would it?" he groaned. "Jonak, take fifteen of our boys and batter in a lesser door and hit the rear of that line. The rest of you help me keep it busy meanwhile."

He raised his red-spattered ax. "A Canyon!" he yelled. "A Canyon!" His followers bellowed behind him and they ran to battle.

The last charge had reeled away bloody and breathless. Half a dozen Meycans stood in the wide doorway. They were nobles: grim men with goatees and waxed mustaches, in formal black, red cloaks wrapped as shields on their left arms and long slim swords in their right hands. Behind them stood others, ready to take the place of the fallen.

"A Canyon!" shouted Loklann as he rushed.

"*Quel Dío wela!*" cried a tall grizzled Don. A gold chain of office hung around his neck. His blade snaked forth.

Loklann flung up his ax and parried. The Don was fast, riposting with a lunge that ended on the raider's breast. But hardened six-ply leather turned the point. Loklann's men crowded on either side, reckless of thrusts, and hewed. He struck the enemy sword; it spun from the owner's grasp. "*Ah, no, Don Miwel!*" cried a young person beside the calde. The older man snarled, threw out his hands, and somehow clamped them on Loklann's ax. He yanked it away with a troll's strength. Loklann stared into eyes that said death. Don Miwel raised the ax. Loklann drew his pistol and fired point blank.

As Don Miwel toppled, Loklann caught him, pulled off the gold chain, and threw it around his own neck. Straightening, he met a savage thrust. It glanced off his helmet. He got his ax back, planted his feet firmly, and smote.

The defending line buckled.

Clamor lifted behind Loklann. He turned and saw weapons gleam beyond his own men's shoulders. With a curse he realized—there had been more people in the palace than these holding the main door. The rest had sallied out the rear and were now on his back!

A point pierced his thigh. He felt no more than a sting, but rage flapped black before his eyes. "Be reborn as the swine you are!" he roared. Half unaware, he thundered loose, cleared a space for himself, lurched aside and oversaw the battle.

The newcomers were mostly palace guards, judging from their gaily striped uniforms, pikes, and machetes. But they had allies, a dozen men such as Loklann had never seen or heard of. Those had the brown skin and black hair of Injuns, but their faces were more like a white man's; intricate blue designs covered their bodies, which were clad only in wraparounds and flower wreaths. They wielded knives and clubs with wicked skill.

Loklann tore his trouser leg open to look at his wound. It wasn't much. More serious was the beating his men were taking. He saw Mork sunna Brenn rush, sword uplifted, at one of the dark strangers, a big man who had added a rich-looking blouse to his skirt. Mork had killed four men at home for certain, in lawful fights, and nobody knew how many abroad. The dark man waited, a knife between his teeth, hands hanging loose. As the blade came down, the dark man simply wasn't there. Grinning around his knife, he chopped at the sword wrist with the edge of a hand. Loklann distinctly heard bones crack. Mork yelled. The foreigner hit him in the Adam's apple. Mork went to his knees, spat blood, caved in, and was still. Another Sky Man charged, ax aloft. The stranger again evaded the weapon, caught the moving body on his hip, and helped it along. The Sky Man hit the pavement with his head and moved no more.

Now Loklann saw that the newcomers were a ring around others who did not fight. Women. By Oktai and man-eating Ulagu, these bastards were leading out all the women in the palace! And the fighting against them had broken up; surly raiders stood back nursing their wounds.

Loklann ran forward. "A Canyon! A Canyon!" he shouted.

"Ruori Rangi Lohannaso," said the big stranger politely. He rapped a string of orders. His party began to move away.

"Hit them, you scum!" bawled Loklann. His men rallied and straggled after. Rearguard pikes prodded them back. Loklann led a rush to the front of the hollow square.

The big man saw him coming. Gray eyes focused on the calde's chain and became full winter. "So you killed Don Miwel," said Ruori in Spañol. Loklann understood him, having learned the tongue from prisoners and concubines during many raids further north. "You lousy son of a skua."

Loklann's pistol rose. Ruori's hand blurred. Suddenly the knife stood in the Sky Man's right biceps. He dropped his gun. "I'll want that back!" shouted Ruori. Then, to his followers: "Come, to the ship."

Loklann stared at blood rivering down his arm. He heard a clatter as the refugees broke through the weary Canyon line. Jonak's party appeared in the main door—which was now empty, its surviving defenders having left with Ruori.

A man approached Loklann, who still regarded his arm. "Shall we go after 'em, Skipper?" he said, almost timidly. "Jonak can lead us after 'em."

"No," said Loklann.

"But they must be escorting a hundred women. A lot of young women too."

Loklann shook himself, like a dog coming out of a deep cold stream. "No. I want to find the medic and get this wound stitched. Then we'll have a lot else to do. We can settle with those outlanders later, if the chance comes. Man, we've a city to sack!"

IV

There were dead men scattered on the wharves, some burned. They looked oddly small beneath the warehouses, like rag dolls tossed away by a weeping child. Cannon fumes lingered to bite nostrils.

Atel Hamid Seraio, the mate, who had been left aboard the *Dolphin* with the enlisted crew, led a band to meet Ruori. His salute was in the Island manner, so casual that even at this moment several of the Meycans looked shocked. "We were about to come for you, Captain," he said.

Ruori looked toward that forest which was the *Dolphin*'s rig. "What happened here?" he asked.

"A band of those devils landed near the battery. They took the emplacements while we were still wondering what it was all about. Part of them went off toward that racket in the north quarter, I believe where the army lives. But the rest of the gang attacked us. Well, with our gunwale ten feet above the dock, and us trained to repel pirates, they didn't have much luck. I gave them a dose of flame."

Ruori winced from the blackened corpses. Doubtless they had deserved it, but he didn't like the idea of pumping flaming blubber oil across live men.

"Too bad they didn't try from the seaward side," added Atel with a sigh. "We've got such a lovely harpoon catapult. I used one like it years ago off Hinja, when a Sinese buccaneer came too close. His junk sounded like a whale."

"Men aren't whales!" snapped Ruori.

"All right, Captain, all right, all right." Atel backed away from his violence, a little frightened. "No ill-speaking meant."

Ruori recollected himself and folded his hands. "I spoke in needless anger," he said formally. "I laugh at myself."

"It's nothing, Captain. As I was saying, we beat them off and they finally withdrew. I imagine they'll bring back reinforcements. What shall we do?"

"That's what I don't know," said Ruori in a bleak tone. He turned to the Meycans, who stood with stricken, uncomprehending faces. "Your pardon is prayed, Dons and Doñitas," he said in Spañol. "He was only relating to me what had happened."

"Don't apologize!" Tresa Carabán spoke, stepping out ahead of the men. Some of them looked a bit offended, but they were too tired and stunned to reprove her forwardness, and to Ruori it was only natural that a woman act as freely as a man. "You saved our lives, Captain. More than our lives."

He wondered what was worse than death, then nodded. Slavery, of course—ropes and whips and a lifetime's unfree toil in a strange land. His eyes dwelt upon her, the long hair disheveled past smooth shoulders, gown ripped, weariness and a streak of tears across her face. He wondered if she knew her father was dead. She held herself straight and regarded him with an odd defiance.

"We are uncertain what to do," he said awkwardly. "We are only fifty men. Can we help your city?"

A young nobleman, swaying on his feet, replied: "No. The city is done. You can take these ladies to safety, that is all."

Tresa protested: "You are not surrendering already, S'ñor Dónoju!"

"No, Doñita," the young man breathed. "But I hope I can be shriven before returning to fight, for I am a dead man."

"Come aboard," said Ruori curtly.

He led the way up the gangplank. Liliu, one of the ship's five wahines, ran to meet him. She threw arms about his neck and cried, "I feared you were slain!"

"Not yet." Ruori disengaged her as gently as possible. He noticed Tresa standing stiff, glaring at them both. Puzzlement came—did these curious Meycans expect a crew to embark on a voyage of months without taking a few girls along? Then he decided that the wahines' clothing, being much like his men's, was against local mores. To Nan with their silly prejudices. But it hurt that Tresa drew away from him.

The other Meycans stared about them. Not all had toured the ship when she first arrived. They looked in bewilderment at lines and spars, down fathoms of deck to the harpoon catapult, capstans, bowsprit, and back at the sailors. The Maurai grinned encouragingly. Thus far most of them looked on this as a lark. Men who skindove after sharks, for fun, or who sailed outrigger canoes alone across a thousand ocean miles to pay a visit, were not put out by a fight.

But they had not talked with grave Don Miwel and merry Don Wan and gentle Bispo Ermosillo, and then seen those people dead on a dance floor, thought Ruori in bitterness.

The Meycan women huddled together, ladies and servants, to weep among each other. The palace guards formed a solid rank around them. The nobles, and Tresa, followed Ruori up on the poop deck.

"Now," he said, "let us talk. Who are these bandits?"

"The Sky People," whispered Tresa.

"I can see that." Ruori cocked an eye on the aircraft patrolling overhead. They had the sinister beauty of as many barracuda. Here and there columns of smoke reached toward them. "But who are they? Where from?"

"They are Nor-Merikans," she answered in a dry little voice, as if afraid to give it color. "From the wild highlands around the Corado River, the Grand Canyon it has cut for itself—mountaineers. There is a story that they were driven from the eastern plains by Mong invaders, a long time ago; but as they grew strong in the hills and deserts, they defeated some Mong tribes and became friendly with others. For a hundred years they have harried our northern borders. This is the first time they have ventured so far south. We never expected them—I suppose their spies learned most of our soldiers are along the Río Gran, chasing a rebel force. They sailed southwesterly, above our land—" She shivered.

The young Dónoju spat. "They are heathen dogs! They know nothing but to rob and burn and kill!" He sagged. "What have we done that they are loosed on us?"

Ruori rubbed his chin thoughtfully. "They can't be quite such savages," he murmured. "Those blimps are better than anything my own Federation has tried to make. The fabric . . . some tricky synthetic? It must be, or it wouldn't contain hydrogen any length of time. Surely they don't use helium! But for hydrogen production on that scale, you need industry. A good empirical chemistry, at least. They might even electrolyze it . . . good Lesu!"

He realized he had been talking to himself in his home language. "I beg your pardon," he said. "I was wondering what we might do. This ship carried no flying vessels."

Again he looked upward. Atel handed him his binoculars. He focused on the nearest blimp. The huge gas bag and the gondola beneath—itself as big as many a Maurai ship—formed an aerodynamically clean unit. The gondola seemed to be light, woven cane about a wooden frame, but strong. Three-fourths of the way up from its keel a sort of gallery ran clear around, on which the crew might walk and work. At intervals along the rail stood muscle-powered machines. Some must be for hauling, but others suggested catapults. Evidently the blimps of various chiefs fought each other occasionally, in the northern kingdoms. That might be worth knowing. The Federation's political psychologists were skilled at the divide-and-rule game. But for now . . .

The motive power was extraordinarily interesting. Near the gondola bows two lateral spars reached out for some fifty feet, one above the other. They supported two pivoted frames on either side, to which square sails were bent. A similar pair of spars pierced the after hull: eight sails in all. Shark-fin control surfaces were braced to the gas bag. A couple of small retractable windwheels, vaned and pivoted, jutted beneath the gondola, evidently serving the purpose of a false keel. Sails and rudders were trimmed by lines running through block and tackle to windlasses on the gallery. By altering their set, it should be possible to steer at least several points to windward. And, yes, the air moved in different directions at different levels. A blimp could descend by pumping out cells in its gas bag, compressing the hydrogen into storage tanks; it could rise by reinflating or by dropping ballast (though the latter trick would be reserved for home stretches, when leakage had depleted the gas supply). Between sails, rudders, and its ability to find a reasonably favoring wind, such a blimp could go roving across several thousand miles, with a payload of several tons. Oh, a lovely craft!

Ruori lowered his glasses. "Hasn't the Perio built any air vessels, to fight back?" he asked.

"No," mumbled one of the Meycans. "All we ever had was balloons. We don't know how to make a fabric which will hold the lifting-gas long enough, or how to control the flight. . . ." His voice trailed off.

"And being a nonscientific culture, you never thought of doing systematic research to learn those tricks," said Ruori.

Tresa, who had been staring at her city, whirled about upon him. "It's easy for you!" she screamed. "You haven't stood off Mong in the north and Raucanians in the south for century after century. You haven't had to spend twenty years and ten thousand lives making canals and aqueducts, so a few less people would starve. You aren't burdened with a peon majority who can only work, who cannot look after themselves because they have never been taught how because their existence is too much of a burden for our land to afford it. It's easy for you to float about with your shirtless doxies and poke fun at us! What would you have done, S'ñor Almighty Captain?"

"Be still," reproved young Dónoju. "He saved our lives."

"So far!" she said, through teeth and tears. One small dancing shoe stamped the deck.

For a bemused moment, irrelevantly, Ruori wondered what a doxie was. It sounded uncomplimentary. Could she mean the wahines? But was there a more honorable way for a woman to earn a good dowry than by hazarding her life, side by side with the men of her people, on a mission of discovery and civilization? What did Tresa expect to tell her grandchildren about on rainy nights?

Then he wondered further why she should disturb him. He had noticed it before, in some of the Meycans, an almost terrifying intensity between man and wife, as if a spouse were somehow more than a respected friend and partner. But what other relationship was possible? A psychological specialist might know; Ruori was lost.

He shook an angry head, to clear it, and said aloud: "This is no time for inurbanity." He had to use a Spañol word with not quite the same connotation. "We must decide. Are you certain we have no hope of repelling the pirates?"

"Not unless S' Antón himself passes a miracle," said Dónoju in a dead voice.

Then, snapping erect: "There is only a single thing you can do for us, S'ñor. If you will leave now, with the women—there are high-born ladies among them, who must not be sold into captivity and disgrace. Bear them south to Port Wanawato, where the calde will look after their welfare."

"I do not like to run off," said Ruori, looking at the men fallen on the wharf.

"S'ñor, these are *ladies!* In el Dío's name, have mercy on them!"

Ruori studied the taut, bearded faces. He did owe them a great deal of hospitality, and he could see no other way he might ever repay it. "If you wish," he said slowly. "What of yourselves?"

The young noble bowed as if to a king. "Our thanks and prayers will go with you, my lord Captain. We men, of course, will now return to battle." He stood up and barked in a parade-ground voice: "Atten-tion! Form ranks!"

A few swift kisses passed on the main deck, and then the men of Meyco had crossed the gangplank and tramped into their city.

Ruori beat a fist on the taffrail. "If we had some way," he mumbled. "If I could do something." Almost hopefully: "Do you think the bandits might attack us?"

"Only if you remain here," said Tresa. Her eyes were chips of green ice. "Would to Marí you had not pledged yourself to sail!"

"If they come after us at sea—"

"I do not think they will. You carry a hundred women and a few trade goods. The Sky People will have their pick of ten thousand women, as many men, and our city's treasures. Why should they take the trouble to pursue you?"

"Aye . . . aye. . . ."

"Go," she said. "You dare not linger."

Her coldness was like a blow. "What do you mean?" he asked. "Do you think the Maurai are cowards?"

She hesitated. Then, in reluctant honesty: "No."

"Well, why do you scoff at me?"

"Oh, go away!" She knelt by the rail, bowed head in arms, and surrendered to herself.

Ruori left her and gave his orders. Men scrambled into the rigging. Furled canvas broke loose and cracked in a young wind. Beyond the jetty, the ocean glittered blue, with small whitecaps; gulls skimmed across heaven. Ruori saw only the glimpses he had had before, as he led the retreat from the palace.

A weaponless man, his head split open. A girl, hardly twelve years old, who screamed as two raiders carried her into an alley. An aged man fleeing in terror, zigzagging, while four archers took potshots at him and howled laughter when he fell transfixed and dragged himself along on his hands. A woman sitting dumb in the street, her dress torn, next to a baby whose brains had been dashed out. A little statue in a niche, a holy image, a faded bunch of violets at its feet, beheaded by a casual war-hammer. A house that burned, and shrieks from within.

Suddenly the aircraft overhead were not beautiful.

To reach up and pull them out of the sky!

Ruori stopped dead. The crew surged around him. He heard a short-haul chantey, deep voices vigorous from always having been free and well fed, but it echoed in a far corner of his brain.

"Casting off," sang the mate.

"Not yet! Not yet! Wait!"

Ruori ran toward the poop, up the ladder and past the steersman to Doñita Tresa. She had risen again, to stand with bent head past which the hair swept to hide her countenance.

"Tresa," panted Ruori. "Tresa, I've an idea. I think—there may be a chance—perhaps we can fight back after all."

She raised her eyes. Her fingers closed on his arm till he felt the nails draw blood.

Words tumbled from him. "It will depend . . . on luring them . . . to us. At least a couple of their vessels . . . must follow us . . . to sea. I think then—I'm not sure of the details, but it may be . . . we can fight . . . even drive them off—"

Still she stared at him. He felt a hesitation. "Of course," he said, "we may lose the fight. And we do have the women aboard."

"If you lose," she asked, so low he could scarcely hear it, "will we die or be captured?"

"I think we will die."

"That is well." She nodded. "Yes. Fight, then."

"There is one thing I am unsure of. How to make them pursue us." He paused. "If someone were to let himself . . . be captured by them—and told them we were carrying off a great treasure—would they believe that?"

"They might well." Life had come back to her tones, even eagerness. "Let us say, the calde's hoard. None ever existed, but the robbers would believe my father's cellars were stuffed with gold."

"Then someone must go to them." Ruori turned his back to her, twisted his fingers together and slogged toward a conclusion he did not want to reach. "But it could not be just anyone. They would club a man in among the other slaves, would they not? I mean, would they listen to him at all?"

"Probably not. Very few of them know Spañol. By the time a man who babbled of treasure was understood, they might be halfway home." Tresa scowled. "What shall we do?"

Ruori saw the answer, but could not get it past his throat.

"I am sorry," he mumbled. "My idea was not so good after all. Let us be gone."

The girl forced her way between him and the rail to stand in front of him, touching as if they danced again. Her voice was altogether steady. "You know a way."

"I do not."

"I have come to know you well, in one night. You are a poor liar. Tell me."

He looked away. Somehow, he got out: "A woman—not any woman, but a very beautiful one—would she not soon be taken to their chief?"

Tresa stood aside. The color drained from her cheeks.

"Yes," she said at last. "I think so."

"But then again," said Ruori wretchedly, "she might be killed. They do much wanton killing, those men. I cannot let anyone who was given into my protection risk death."

"You heathen fool," she said through tight lips. "Do you think the chance of being killed matters to me?"

"What else could happen?" he asked, surprised. And then: "Oh, yes, of course, the woman would be a slave if we lost the battle afterward. Though I should imagine, if she is beautiful, she would not be badly treated."

"And is that all you—" Tresa stopped. He had never known it was possible for a smile to show pure hurt. "Of course. I should have realized. Your people have your own ways of thinking."

"What do you mean?" he fumbled.

A moment more she stood with clenched fists. Then, half to herself: "They killed my father; yes, I saw him dead in the doorway. They would leave my city a ruin peopled by corpses."

Her head lifted. "I will go," she said.

"You?" He grabbed her shoulders. "No, surely not you! One of the others—"

"Should I send anybody else? I am the calde's daughter."

She pulled herself free of him and hurried across the deck, down the ladder toward the gangway. Her gaze was turned from the ship. A few words drifted back. "Afterward, if there is an afterward, there is always the convent."

He did not understand. He stood on the poop, staring after her and abominating himself until she was lost to sight. Then he said, "Cast off," and the ship stood out to sea.

V

The Meycans fought doggedly, street by street and house by house, but in a couple of hours their surviving soldiers had been driven into the northeast corner of S' Antón. They themselves hardly knew that, but a Sky chief had a view from above; a rover was now tethered to the cathedral, with a rope ladder for men to go up and down, and the companion vessel, skeleton crewed, brought their news to it.

"Good enough," said Loklann. "We'll keep them boxed in with a quarter of our force. I don't think they'll sally. Meanwhile the rest of us can get things organized. Let's not give these creatures too much time to hide themselves and their silver. In the afternoon, when we're rested, we can land parachuters behind the city troops, drive them out into our lines and destroy them."

He ordered the *Buffalo* grounded, that he might load the most precious loot at once. The men, by and large, were too rough—good lads, but apt to damage a robe or a cup or a jeweled cross in their haste; and sometimes those Meycan things were too beautiful even to give away, let alone sell.

The flagship descended as far as possible. It still hung at a thousand feet, for hand pumps and aluminum-alloy tanks did not allow much hydrogen compression. In colder, denser air it would have been suspended even higher. But ropes snaked from it to a quickly assembled ground crew. At home there were ratcheted capstans outside every lodge, enabling as few as four women to bring down a rover. One hated the emergency procedure of bleeding gas, for the Keepers could barely meet demand, in spite of a new sunpower unit added to their hydroelectric station, and charged accordingly. (Or so the Keepers said, but perhaps they were merely taking advantage of being inviolable, beyond any kings, to jack up prices. Some chiefs, including Loklann, had begun to experiment with hydrogen production for themselves, but it was a slow thing to puzzle out an art that even the Keepers only half understood.)

Here, strong men replaced machinery. The *Buffalo* was soon pegged down in the cathedral plaza, which it almost filled. Loklann inspected each rope himself. His wounded leg ached, but not too badly to walk on. More annoying was his right arm, which hurt worse from stitches than from the original cut. The medic had warned him to go easy with it. That meant fighting left-handed, for the story should never be told that Loklann sunna Holber stayed out of combat. However, he would only be half himself.

He touched the knife which had spiked him. At least he'd gotten a fine steel blade for his pains. And . . . hadn't the owner said they would meet again, to settle who kept it? There were omens in such words. It could be a pleasure to reincarnate that Ruori.

"Skipper. Skipper, sir."

Loklann glanced about. Yuw Red-Ax and Allan sunna Rickar, men of his lodge, had hailed him. They grasped the arms of a young woman in black velvet and silver. The beweaponed crowd, moiling about, was focusing on her; raw whoops lifted over the babble.

"What is it?" said Loklann brusquely. He had much to do.

"This wench, sir. A looker, isn't she? We found her down near the waterfront."

"Well, shove her into the temple with the rest till—oh." Loklann rocked back on his heels, narrowing his eyes to meet a steady green glare. She was certainly a looker.

"She kept hollering the same words over and over: '*Shef, rey, ombro gran.*' I finally wondered if it didn't mean 'chief,' " said Yuw, "and then when she yelled 'khan' I was pretty sure she wanted to see you. So we didn't use her ourselves," he finished virtuously.

"*Aba tu Español?*" said the girl.

Loklann grinned. "Yes," he replied in the same language, his words heavily accented but sufficient. "Well enough to know you are calling me 'thou.' " Her pleasantly formed mouth drew into a thin line. "Which means you think I am your inferior—or your god, or your beloved."

She flushed, threw back her head (sunlight ran along crow's-wing hair) and answered: "You might tell these oafs to release me."

Loklann said the order in Angliz. Yuw and Aalan let go. The marks of their fingers were bruised into her arms. Loklann stroked his beard. "Did you want to see me?" he asked.

"If you are the leader, yes," she said. "I am the calde's daughter, Doñita Tresa Carabán." Briefly, her voice wavered. "That is my father's chain of office you are wearing. I came back on behalf of his people, to ask for terms."

"What?" Loklann blinked. Someone in the warrior crowd laughed.

It must not be in her to beg mercy, he thought; her tone remained brittle. "Considering your sure losses if you fight to a finish, and the chance of provoking a counterattack on your homeland, will you not accept a money ransom and a safe-conduct, releasing your captive and ceasing your destruction?"

"By Oktai," murmured Loklann. "Only a woman could imagine we—" He stopped. "Did you say you came back?"

She nodded. "On the people's behalf. I know I have no legal authority to make terms, but in practice—"

"Forget that!" he rapped. "Where did you come back from?"

She faltered. "That has nothing to do with—"

There were too many eyes around. Loklann bawled orders to start systematic plundering. He turned to the girl. "Come aboard the airship," he said. "I want to discuss this further."

Her eyes closed, for just a moment, and her lips moved. Then she looked at him—he thought of a cougar he had once trapped—and she said in a flat voice: "Yes. I do have more arguments."

"Any woman does," he laughed, "but you better than most."

"Not that!" she flared. "I meant—no. Marí, pray for me." As he pushed a way through his men, she followed him.

They went past furled sails, to a ladder let down from the gallery. A hatch stood open to the lower hull, showing storage space and leather fetters for slaves. A few guards were posted on the gallery deck. They leaned on their weapons, sweating from beneath helmets, swapping jokes; when Loklann led the girl by, they yelled good-humored envy.

He opened a door. "Have you ever seen one of our vessels?" he asked. The upper gondola contained a long room, bare except for bunk frames on which sleeping bags were laid. Beyond, a series of partitions defined cabinets, a sort of galley, and at last, in the very bow, a room for maps, tables, navigation instruments, speaking tubes. Its walls slanted so far outward that the glazed windows would give a spacious view when the ship was aloft. On a shelf, beneath racked weapons, sat a small idol, tusked and four-armed. A pallet was rolled on the floor.

"The bridge," said Loklann. "Also the captain's cabin."

He gestured at one of four wicker chairs, lashed into place. "Be seated, Doñita. Would you like something to drink?"

She sat down but did not reply. Her fists were clenched on her lap. Loklann poured himself a slug of whiskey and tossed off half at a gulp. "Ahhh! Later we will get some of your own wine for you. It is a shame you have no art of distilling here."

Desperate eyes lifted to him, where he stood over her. "S'ñor," she said, "I beg of you, in Carito's name—well, in your mother's, then—spare my people."

"My mother would laugh herself ill to hear that," he said. Leaning forward: "See here, let us not spill words. You were escaping, but you came back. Where were you escaping to?"

"I—does that matter?"

Good, he thought, she was starting to crack. He hammered: "It does. I know you were at the palace this dawn. I know you fled with the dark foreigners. I know their ship departed an hour ago. You must have been on it, but left again. True?"

"Yes." She began to tremble.

He sipped molten fire and asked reasonably: "Now, tell me, Doñita, what you have to bargain with. You cannot have expected we would give up the best part of our booty and a great many valuable slaves for a mere safe-conduct. All the Sky kingdoms would disown us. Come now, you must have more to offer, if you hope to buy us off."

"No . . . not really—"

His hand exploded against her cheek. Her head jerked from the blow. She huddled back, touching the red mark, as he growled: "I have no time for games. Tell me! Tell me this instant what thought drove you back here from safety, or down in the hold you go. You'd fetch a good price when the traders next visit Canyon. Many homes are waiting for you: a woods runner's cabin in Orgon, a Mong khan's yurt in Tekkas, a brothel as far east as Chai Ka-Go. Tell me now, truly, what you know, and you will be spared that much."

She looked downward and said raggedly: "The foreign ship is loaded with the calde's gold. My father had long wanted to remove his personal treasure to a safer place than this, but dared not risk a wagon train across country. There are still many outlaws between here and Fortlez d' S' Ernán; that much loot would tempt the military escort itself to turn bandit. Captain Lohannaso agreed to carry the gold by sea to Port Wanawato, which is near Fortlez. He could be trusted because his government is anxious for trade with us; he came here officially. The treasure had already been loaded. Of course, when your raid came, the ship also took those women who had been at the palace. But can you not spare them? You'll find more loot in the foreign ship than your whole fleet can lift."

"By Oktai!" whispered Loklann.

He turned from her, paced, finally stopped and stared out the window. He could almost hear the gears turn in his head. It made sense. The palace had been disappointing. Oh, yes, a lot of damask and silverware and what not, but nothing like the cathedral. Either the calde was less rich than powerful, or he concealed his hoard. Loklann had planned to torture a few servants and find out which. Now he realized there was a third possibility.

Better interrogate some prisoners anyway, to make sure—no, no time. Given a favoring wind, that ship could outrun any rover without working up a sweat. It might already be too late to overhaul. But if not—h'm. Assault would be no cinch. That lean, pitching hull was a small target for paratroopers, and with rigging in the way . . . Wait. Bold men could always find a road. How about grappling to the upper works? If the strain tore the rigging loose, so much the better: a weighted rope would then give a clear slideway to the deck. If the hooks held, though, a storming party could nevertheless go along the lines, into the topmasts. Doubtless the sailors were agile too, but had they ever reefed a rover sail in a Merikan thunderstorm, a mile above the earth?

He could improvise as the battle developed. At the very least, it would be fun to try. And at most, he might be reborn a world conqueror, for such an exploit in this life.

He laughed aloud, joyously. "We'll do it!"

Tresa rose. "You will spare the city?" she whispered hoarsely.

"I never promised any such thing," said Loklann. "Of course, the ship's cargo will crowd out most of the stuff and people we might take otherwise. Unless, hm, unless we decide to sail the ship to Calforni, loaded, and meet it there with more rovers. Yes, why not?"

"You oathbreaker," she said, with a hellful of scorn.

"I only promised not to sell you," said Loklann. His gaze went up and down here. "And I won't."

He took a stride forward and gathered her to him. She fought, cursing; once she managed to draw Ruori's knife from his belt; but his cuirass stopped the blade.

Finally he rose. She wept at his feet, her breast marked red by her father's chain. He said more quietly, "No, I will not sell you, Tresa. I will keep you."

VI

"Blimp ho-o-o!"

The lookout's cry hung lonesome for a minute between wind and broad waters. Down under the mainmast, it seethed with crewmen running to their posts.

Ruori squinted eastward. The land was a streak under cumulus clouds, mountainous and blue-shadowed. It took him a while to find the enemy, in all that sky. At last the sun struck them. He lifted his binoculars. Two painted killer whales lazed his way, slanting down from a mile altitude.

He sighed. "Only two," he said.

"That may be more than plenty for us," said Atel Hamid. Sweat studded his forehead.

Ruori gave his mate a sharp look. "You're not afraid of them, are you? I daresay that's been one of their biggest assets, superstition."

"Oh, no, Captain. I know the principle of buoyancy as well as you do. But those people are tough. And they're not trying to storm us from a dock this time; they're in their element."

"So are we." Ruori clapped the other man's back. "Take over. Tanaroa knows what's going to happen, but use your own judgment if I'm spitted."

"I wish you'd let me go," protested Atel. "I don't like being safe here. It's what can happen aloft that worries me."

"You won't be too safe for your liking." Ruori forced a grin. "And somebody has to steer this tub home to hand in those lovely reports to the Geoethnic Research Endeavor."

He swung down the ladder to the main deck and hurried to the mainmast shrouds. His crew yelled around him, weapons gleamed. The two big box kites quivered, taut canvas, lashed to a bollard and waiting. Ruori wished there had been time to make more.

Even as it was, though, he had delayed longer than seemed wise, first heading far out to sea and then tacking slowly back, to make the enemy search for him while he prepared. (Or planned, for that matter. When he dismissed Tresa, his ideas had been little more than a conviction that he could fight.) Assuming they were lured after him at all, he had risked their losing patience and going back to the land. For an hour, now, he had dawdled under mainsail, genoa, and a couple of flying jibs, hoping the Sky People were lubbers enough not to find that suspiciously little canvas for this good weather.

But here they were, and here was an end to worry and remorse on a certain girl's behalf. Such emotions were rare in an Islander; and to find himself focusing them thus on a single person, out of earth's millions, had been horrible. Ruori swarmed up the ratlines, as if he fled something.

The blimps were still high, passing overhead on an upper-level breeze. Down here was almost a straight south wind. The aircraft, unable to steer really close-hauled, would descend when they were sea-level upwind of him. Regardless, estimated a cold part of Ruori, the *Dolphin* could avoid their clumsy rush.

But the *Dolphin* wasn't going to.

The rigging was now knotted with armed sailors. Ruori pulled himself onto the mainmast crosstrees and sat down, casually swinging his legs. The ship heeled over in a flaw and he hung above greenish-blue, white-streaked immensity. He balanced, scarcely noticing, and asked Hiti: "Are you set?"

"Aye." The big harpooner, his body a writhe of tattoos and muscles, nodded a shaven head. Lashed to the fid where he squatted was the ship's catapult, cocked and loaded with one of the huge irons that could kill a sperm whale at a blow. A couple more lay alongside in their rack. Hiti's two mates and four deckhands poised behind him, holding the smaller harpoons—mere six-foot shafts—that were launched from a boat by hand. The lines of all trailed down the mast to the bows.

"Aye, let 'em come now." Hiti grinned over his whole round face. "Nan eat the world, but this'll be something to make a dance about when we come home!"

"If we do," said Ruori. He touched the boat ax thrust into his loincloth. Like a curtain, the blinding day seemed to veil a picture from home, where combers broke white under the moon, longfires flared on a beach and dancers were merry, and palm trees cast shadows for couples who stole away. He wondered how a Meycan calde's daughter might like it . . . if her throat had not been cut.

"There's a sadness on you, Captain," said Hiti.

"Men are going to die," said Ruori.

"What of it?" Small kindly eyes studied him. "They'll die willing, if they must, for the sake of the song that'll be made. You've another trouble than death."

"Let me be!"

The harpooner looked hurt, but withdrew into silence. Wind streamed and the ocean glittered.

The aircraft steered close. They would approach one on each side. Ruori unslung the megaphone at his shoulder. Atel Hamid held the *Dolphin* steady on a broad reach.

Now Ruori could see a grinning god at the prow of the starboard airship. It would pass just above the topmasts, a little to windward. . . . Arrows went impulsively toward it from the yardarms, without effect, but no one was excited enough to waste a rifle cartridge. Hiti swiveled his catapult. "Wait," said Ruori. "We'd better see what they do."

Helmeted heads appeared over the blimp's gallery rail. A man stepped up—another, another, at intervals; they whirled triple-clawed iron grapnels and let go. Rutor saw one strike the foremast, rebound, hit a jib. . . . The line to the blimp tautened and sang but did not break; it was of leather. . . . The jib ripped, canvas thundered, struck a sailor in the belly and knocked him from his yard. . . . The man recovered to straighten out and hit the water in a clean dive. Lesu grant he lived. . . . The grapnel bumped along, caught the gaff of the fore-and-aft mainsail, wood groaned. . . . The ship trembled as line after line snapped tight.

She leaned far over, dragged by leverage. Her sails banged. No danger of capsizing—yet—but a mast could be pulled loose. And now, over the gallery rail and seizing a rope between hands and knees, the pirates came. Whooping like boys, they slid down to the grapnels and clutched after any rigging that came to hand.

One of them sprang monkeylike onto the mainmast gaff, below the crosstrees. A harpooner's mate cursed, hurled his weapon, and skewered the invader. "Belay that!" roared Hiti. "We need those irons!"

Ruori scanned the situation. The leeward blimp was still maneuvering in around its mate, which was being blown to port. He put the megaphone to his mouth and a solar-battery amplifier cried for him: "Hear this! Hear this! Burn that second enemy now, before he grapples! Cut the lines to the first one and repel all boarders!"

"Shall I fire?" called Hiti. "I'll never have a better target."

"Aye."

The harpooner triggered his catapult. It unwound with a thunder noise. Barbed steel smote the engaged gondola low in a side, tore through, and ended on the far side of interior planking.

"Wind 'er up!" bawled Hiti. His own gorilla hands were already on a crank lever. Somehow two men found space to help him.

Ruori slipped down the futtock shrouds and jumped to the gaff. Another pirate had landed there and a third was just arriving, two more aslide behind him. The man on the spar balanced barefooted, as good as any sailor, and drew a sword. Ruori dropped as the blade whistled, caught a mainsail grommet one-handed, and hung there, striking with his boat ax at the grapnel line. The pirate crouched and stabbed at him. Ruori thought of Tresa, smashed his hatchet into the man's face, and flipped him off, down to the deck. He cut again. The leather was tough, but his blade was keen. The line parted and whipped away. The gaff swung free, almost yanking Ruori's fingers loose. The second Sky Man toppled, hit a cabin below and spattered. The men on the line slid to its end. One of them could not stop; the sea took him. The other was smashed against the masthead as he pendulumed.

Ruori pulled himself back astride the gaff and sat there awhile, heaving air into lungs that burned. The fight ramped around him, on shrouds and spars and down on the decks. The second blimp edged closer.

Astern, raised by the speed of a ship moving into the wind, a box kite lifted. Atel sang a command and the helmsman put the rudder over. Even with the drag on her, the *Dolphin* responded well; a profound science of fluid mechanics had gone into her design. Being soaked in whale oil, the kite clung to the gas bag for a time—long enough for "messengers" of burning paper to whirl up its string. It burst into flame.

The blimp sheered off, the kite fell away, its small gunpowder load exploded harmlessly. Atel swore and gave further orders. The *Dolphin* tacked. The second kite, already aloft and afire, hit target. It detonated.

Hydrogen gushed out. Sudden flames wreathed the blimp. They seemed pale in the sun-dazzle. Smoke began to rise, as the plastic between gas cells disintegrated. The aircraft descended like a slow meteorite to the water.

Its companion vessel had no reasonable choice but to cast loose unsevered grapnels, abandoning the still outnumbered boarding party. The captain could not know that the *Dolphin* had only possessed two kites. A few vengeful catapult bolts spat from it. Then it was free, rapidly falling astern. The Maurai ship rocked toward an even keel.

The enemy might retreat or he might plan some fresh attack. Ruori did not intend that it should be either. He megaphoned: "Put about! Face that scum-gut!" and led a rush down the shrouds to a deck where combat still went on.

For Hiti's gang had put three primary harpoons and half a dozen lesser ones into the gondola.

Their lines trailed in tightening catenaries from the blimp to the capstan in the bows. No fear now of undue strain. The *Dolphin*, like any Maurai craft, was meant to live off the sea as she traveled. She had dragged right whales alongside; a blimp was nothing in comparison. What counted was speed, before the pirates realized what was happening and found ways to cut loose.

"*Tohiha, hioha, itoki, itoki!*" The old canoe chant rang forth as men tramped about the capstan. Ruori hit the deck, saw a Canyon man fighting a sailor, sword against club, and brained the fellow from behind as he would any other vermin. (Then he wondered, dimly shocked, what made him think thus about a human being.) The battle was rapidly concluded; the Sky Men faced hopeless odds. But half a dozen Federation people were badly hurt. Ruori had the few surviving pirates tossed into a lazarct, his own casualties taken below to anesthetics and antibiotics and cooing Doñitas. Then, quickly, he prepared his crew for the next phase.

The blimp had been drawn almost to the bowsprit. It was canted over so far that its catapults were useless. Pirates lined the gallery deck, howled and shook their weapons. They outnumbered the *Dolphin* crew by a factor of three or four. Ruori recognized one among them—the tall yellow-haired man who had fought him outside the palace; it was a somehow eerie feeling.

"Shall we burn them?" asked Atel.

Ruori grimaced. "I suppose we have to," he said. "Try not to ignite the vessel itself. You know we want it."

A walking beam moved up and down, driven by husky Islanders. Flame spurted from a ceramic nozzle. The smoke and stench and screams that followed, and the things to be seen when Ruori ordered cease fire, made the hardest veteran of corsair patrol look a bit ill. The Maurai were an unsentimental folk, but they did not like to inflict pain.

"Hose," rasped Ruori. The streams of water that followed were like some kind of blessing. Wicker that had begun to burn hissed into charred quiescence.

The ship's grapnels were flung. A couple of cabin boys darted past grown men to be first along the lines. They met no resistance on the gallery. The uninjured majority of pirates stood in a numb fashion, their armament at their feet, the fight kicked out of them. Jacob's ladders followed the boys; the *Dolphin* crew swarmed aboard the blimp and started collecting prisoners.

A few Sky Men lurched from behind a door, weapons aloft. Ruori saw the tall fair man among them. The man drew Ruori's dagger, left-handed, and ran toward him. His right arm seemed nearly useless. "A Canyon, a Canyon!" he called, the ghost of a war cry.

Ruori sidestepped the charge and put out a foot. The blond man tripped. As he fell, the hammer of Ruori's ax clopped down, catching him on the neck. He crashed, tried to rise, shuddered, and lay twitching.

"I want my knife back." Ruori squatted, undid the robber's tooled leather belt, and began to hogtie him.

Dazed blue eyes looked up with a sort of pleading. "Are you not going to kill me?" mumbled the other in Spañol.

"Haristi, no," said Ruori, surprised. "Why should I?"

He sprang erect. The last resistance had ended; the blimp was his. He opened the forward door, thinking the equivalent of a ship's bridge must lie beyond it.

Then for a while he did not move at all, nor did he hear anything but the wind and his own blood.

It was Tresa who finally came to him. Her hands were held out before her, like a blind person's, and her eyes looked through him. "You are here," she said, flat and empty voiced.

"Doñita," stammered Ruori. He caught her hands. "Doñita, had I known you were aboard, I would never have . . . have risked—"

"Why did you not burn and sink us, like that other vessel?" she asked. "Why must this return to the city?"

She wrenched free of him and stumbled out onto the deck. It was steeply tilted, and bucked beneath her. She fell, picked herself up, walked with barefoot care to the rail and stared out across the ocean. Her hair and torn dress fluttered in the wind.

VII

There was a great deal of technique to handling an airship. Ruori could feel that the thirty men he had put aboard this craft were sailing it as awkwardly as possible. An experienced Sky Man would know what sort of thermal and downdrafts to expect, just from a glance at land or water below; he could estimate the level at which a desired breeze was blowing, and rise or fall smoothly; he could even beat to windward, though that would be a slow process much plagued by drift.

Nevertheless, an hour's study showed the basic principles. Ruori went back to the bridge and gave orders in the speaking tube. Presently the land came nearer. A glance below showed the *Dolphin*, with a cargo of war captives, following on shortened sail. He and his fellow aeronauts would have to take a lot of banter about their celestial snail's pace. Ruori did not smile at the thought or plan his replies, as he would have done yesterday. Tresa sat so still behind him.

"Do you know the name of this craft, Doñita?" he asked, to break the silence.

"He called it *Buffalo,*" she said, remote and uninterested.

"What's that?"

"A sort of wild cattle."

"I gather, then, he talked to you while cruising in search of me. Did he say anything else of interest?"

"He spoke of his people. He boasted of the things they have which we don't . . . engines, powers, alloys . . . as if that made them any less a pack of filthy savages."

At least she was showing some spirit. He had been afraid she had started willing her heart to stop; but he remembered he had seen no evidence of that common Maurai practice here in Meyco.

"Did he abuse you badly?" he asked, not looking at her.

"You would not consider it abuse," she said violently. "Now leave me alone, for mercy's sake!" He heard her go from him, through the door to the after sections.

Well, he thought, after all, her father was killed. That would grieve anyone, anywhere in the world, but her perhaps more than him. For a Meycan child was raised solely by its parents; it did not spend half its time eating or sleeping or playing with any casual relative, like most Island young. So the immediate kin would have more psychological significance here. At least, this was the only explanation Ruori could think of for the sudden darkness within Tresa.

The city hove into view. He saw the remaining enemy vessels gleam above. Three against one . . . yes, today would become a legend among the

Sea People, if he succeeded. Ruori knew he should have felt the same reckless pleasure as a man did surfbathing, or shark fighting, or sailing in a typhoon, any breakneck sport where success meant glory and girls. He could hear his men chant, beat war-drum rhythms out with hands and stamping feet. But his own heart was Antarctic.

The nearest hostile craft approached. Ruori tried to meet it in a professional way. He had attired his prize crew in captured Sky outfits. A superficial glance would take them for legitimate Canyonites, depleted after a hard fight for the captured Maurai ship at their heels.

As the northerners steered close in the leisurely airship fashion, Ruori picked up his speaking tube. "Steady as she goes. Fire when we pass abeam."

"Aye, aye," said Hiti.

A minute later the captain heard the harpoon catapult rumble. Through a port he saw the missile strike the enemy gondola amidships. "Pay out line," he said. "We want to hold her for the kite, but not get burned ourselves."

"Aye, I've played swordfish before now." Laughter bubbled in Hiti's tones.

The foe sheered, frantic. A few bolts leaped from its catapults; one struck home, but a single punctured gas cell made slight difference. "Put about!" cried Ruori. No sense in presenting his beam to a broadside. Both craft began to drift downwind, sails flapping. "Hard alee!" The *Buffalo* became a drogue, holding its victim to a crawl. And here came the kite prepared on the way back. This time it included fish hooks. It caught and held fairly on the Canyonite bag. "Cast off!" yelled Ruori. Fire whirled along the kite string. In minutes it had enveloped the enemy. A few parachutes were blown out to sea.

"Two to go," said Ruori, without any of his men's shouted triumph.

The invaders were no fools. Their remaining blimps turned back over the city, not wishing to expose themselves to more flame from the water. One descended, dropped hawsers, and was rapidly hauled to the plaza. Through his binoculars, Ruori saw armed men swarm aboard it. The other, doubtless with a mere patrol crew, maneuvered toward the approaching *Buffalo*.

"I think that fellow wants to engage us," warned Hiti. "Meanwhile number two down yonder will take on a couple of hundred soldiers, then lay alongside us and board."

"I know," said Ruori. "Let's oblige them."

He steered as if to close with the sparsely manned patroller. It did not avoid him, as he had feared it might; but then, there was a compulsive bravery in the Sky culture. Instead, it maneuvered to grapple as quickly as possible. That would give its companion a chance to load warriors and rise. It came very near.

Now to throw a scare in them, Ruori decided. "Fire arrows," he said. Out on deck, hardwood pistons were shoved into little cylinders, igniting tinder at the bottom; thus oil-soaked shafts were kindled. As the enemy came in range, red comets began to streak from the *Buffalo* archers.

Had his scheme not worked, Ruori would have turned off. He didn't want to sacrifice more men in hand-to-hand fighting; instead, he would have tried seriously to burn the hostile airship from afar, though his strategy needed it. But the morale effect of the previous disaster was very much present. As blazing arrows thunked into their gondola, a battle tactic so two-edged that no northern crew was even equipped for it, the Canyonites panicked and went over the side. Perhaps, as they parachuted down, a few noticed that no shafts had been aimed at their gas bag.

"Grab fast!" sang Ruori. "Douse any fires!"

Grapnels thumbed home. The blimps rocked to a relative halt. Men leaped to the adjacent gallery; bucketsful of water splashed.

"Stand by," said Ruori. "Half our boys on the prize. Break out the lifelines and make them fast."

He put down the tube. A door squeaked behind him. He turned, as Tresa reentered the bridge. She was still pale, but she had combed her hair, and her head was high.

"Another!" she said with a note near joy. "Only one of them left!"

"But it will be full of their men." Ruori scowled. "I wish now I had not accepted your refusal to go aboard the *Dolphin*. I wasn't thinking clearly. This is too hazardous."

"Do you think I care for that?" she said. "I am a Carabán."

"But I care," he said.

The haughtiness dropped from her; she touched his hand, fleetingly, and color rose in her cheeks. "Forgive me. You have done so much for us. There is no way we can ever thank you."

"Yes, there is," said Ruori.

"Name it."

"Do not stop your heart just because it has been wounded."

She looked at him with a kind of sunrise in her eyes.

His boatswain appeared at the outer door. "All set, Captain. We're holding steady at a thousand feet, a man standing by every valve these two crates have got."

"Each has been assigned a particular escape line?"

"Aye." The boatswain departed.

"You'll need one too. Come." Ruori took Tresa by the hand and led her onto the gallery. They saw sky around them, a breeze touched their faces and the deck underfoot moved like a live thing. He indicated many light cords from the *Dolphin's* store, bowlined to the rail. "We aren't going to risk parachuting with untrained men," he said. "But you've no experience in skinning down one of these. I'll make you a harness which will hold you safely. Ease yourself down hand over hand. When you reach the ground, cut loose." His knife slashed some pieces of rope and he knotted them together with a seaman's skill. When he fitted the harness on her, she grew tense under his fingers.

"But I am your friend," he murmured.

She eased. She even smiled, shakenly. He gave her his knife and went back inboard.

And now the last pirate vessel stood up from the earth. It moved near; Ruori's two craft made no attempt to flee. He saw sunlight flash on edged metal. He knew they had witnessed the end of their companion craft and would not be daunted by the same technique. Rather, they would close in, even while their ship burned about them. If nothing else, they could kindle him in turn and then parachute to safety. He did not send arrows.

When only a few fathoms separated him from the enemy, he cried: "Let go the valves!"

Gas whoofed from both bags. The linked blimps dropped.

"Fire!" shouted Ruori. Hiti aimed his catapult and sent a harpoon with anchor cable through the bottom of the attacker. "Burn and abandon!"

Men on deck touched off oil which other men splashed from jars. Flames sprang high.

With the weight of two nearly deflated vessels dragging it from below, the Canyon ship began to fall. At five hundred feet the tossed lifelines draped across flat rooftops and trailed in the streets. Ruori went over the side. He scorched his palms going down.

He was not much too quick. The harpooned blimp released compressed hydrogen and rose to a thousand feet with its burden, seeking sky room. Presumably no one had yet seen that the burden was on fire. In no case would they find it easy to shake or cut loose from one of Hiti's irons.

Ruori stared upward. Fanned by the wind, the blaze was smokeless, a small fierce sun. He had not counted on his fire taking the enemy by total surprise. He had assumed they would parachute to earth, where the Meycans could attack. Almost, he wanted to warn them.

Then flame reached the remaining hydrogen in the collapsed gas bags. He heard a sort of giant gasp. The topmost vessel became a flying pyre. The wind bore it out over the city walls. A few antlike figures managed to spring free. The parachute of one was burning.

"Sant'sima Marí," whispered a voice, and Tresa crept into Ruori's arms and hid her face.

VIII

After dark, candles were lit throughout the palace. They could not blank the ugliness of stripped walls and smoke-blackened ceilings. The guardsmen who lined the throne room were tattered and weary. Nor did S' Antón itself rejoice, yet. There were too many dead.

Ruori sat throned on the calde's dais, Tresa at his right and Páwolo Dónoju on his left. Until a new set of officials could be chosen, these must take authority. The Don sat rigid, not allowing his bandaged head to droop; but now and then his lids grew too heavy to hold up. Tresa watched enormous-eyed from beneath the hood of a cloak wrapping her. Ruori sprawled at ease, a little more happy now that the fighting was over.

It had been a grim business, even after the heartened city troops had sallied and driven the surviving enemy before them. Too many Sky Men fought till they were killed. The hundreds of prisoners, mostly from the first Maurai success, would prove a dangerous booty; no one was sure what to do with them.

"But at least their host is done for," said Dónoju.

Ruori shook his head. "No, S'ñor. I am sorry, but you have no end in sight. Up north are thousands of such aircraft, and a strong hungry people. They will come again."

"We will meet them, Captain. The next time we shall be prepared. A larger garrison, barrage balloons, fire kites, cannons that shoot upward, perhaps a flying navy of our own . . . we can learn what to do."

Tresa stirred. Her tone bore life again, though a life which hated. "In the end, we will carry the war to them. Not one will remain in all the Corado highlands."

"No," said Ruori. "That must not be."

Her head jerked about; she stared at him from the shadow of her hood. Finally she said, "True, we are bidden to love our enemies, but you cannot mean the Sky People. They are not human!"

Ruori spoke to a page. "Send for the chief prisoner."

"To hear our judgment on him?" asked Dónoju. "That should be done formally, in public."

"Only to talk with us," said Ruori.

"I do not understand you," said Tresa. Her words faltered, unable to carry the intended scorn. "After everything you have done, suddenly there is no manhood in you."

He wondered why it should hurt for her to say that. He would not have cared if she had been anyone else.

Loklann entered between two guards. His hands were tied behind him and dried blood was on his face, but he walked like a conqueror under the pikes. When he reached the dais, he stood, legs braced apart, and grinned at Tresa.

"Well," he said, "so you find these others less satisfactory and want me back."

She jumped to her feet and screamed: "Kill him!"

"No!" cried Ruori.

The guardsmen hesitated, machetes half drawn. Ruori stood up and caught the girl's wrists. She struggled, spitting like a cat. "Don't kill him, then," she agreed at last, so thickly it was hard to understand. "Not now. Make it slow. Strangle him, burn him alive, toss him on your spears—"

Ruori held fast till she stood quietly.

When he let go, she sat down and wept.

Páwolo Dónoju said in a voice like steel: "I believe I understand. A fit punishment must certainly be devised."

Loklann spat on the floor. "Of course," he said. "When you have a man bound, you can play any number of dirty little games with him."

"Be still," said Ruori. "You are not helping your own cause. Or mine."

He sat down, crossed his legs, laced fingers around a knee, and gazed before him, into the darkness at the hall's end. "I know you have suffered from this man's work," he said carefully. "You can expect to suffer more from his kinfolk in the future. They are a young race, heedless as children, even as your ancestors and mine were once young. Do you think the Perio was established without hurt and harm? Or, if I remember your history rightly, that the Spañol people were welcomed here by the Inios? That the Ingliss did not come to N'Zealann with slaughter, and that the Maurai were not formerly cannibals? In an age of heroes, the hero must have an opponent.

"Your real weapon against the Sky People is not an army, sent to lose itself in unmapped mountains. . . . Your priests, merchants, artists, craftsmen, manners, fashions, learning—there is the means to bring them to you on their knees, if you will use it."

Loklann started. "You devil," he whispered. "Do you actually think to convert us to . . . a woman's faith and a city's cage?" He shook back his tawny mane and roared till the walls rung. "No!"

"It will take a century or two," said Ruori.

Don Páwolo smiled in his young scanty beard. "A refined revenge, S'ñor Captain," he admitted.

"Too refined!" Tresa lifted her face from her hands, gulped after air, held up claw-crooked fingers and brought them down as if into Loklann's eyes. "Even if it could be done," she snarled, "even if they did have souls, what do we want with them, or their children or grandchildren . . . they who murdered our babies today? Before almighty Dío—I am the last Carabán and

I will have my following to speak for me in Meyco—there will never be anything for them but extermination. We can do it, I swear. Many Tekkans would help, for plunder. I shall yet live to see your home burning, you swine, and your sons hunted with dogs."

She turned frantically toward Ruori. "How else can our land be safe? We are ringed in by enemies. We have no choice but to destroy them, or they will destroy us. And we are the last Merikan civilization."

She sat back and shuddered. Ruori reached over to take her hand. It felt cold. For an instant, unconsciously, she returned the pressure, then jerked away.

He sighed in his weariness.

"I must disagree," he said. "I am sorry. I realize how you feel."

"You do not," she said through clamped jaws. "You cannot."

"But after all," he said, forcing dryness, "I am not just a man with human desires. I represent my government. I must return to tell them what is here, and I can predict their response.

"They will help you stand off attack. That is not an aid you can refuse, is it? The men who will be responsible for Meyco are not going to decline our offer of alliance merely to preserve a precarious independence of action, whatever a few extremists may argue for. And our terms will be most reasonable. We will want little more from you than a policy working toward conciliation and close relations with the Sky People, as soon as they have tired of battering themselves against our united defense."

"What?" said Loklann. Otherwise the chamber was very still. Eyes gleamed white from the shadows of helmets, toward Ruori.

"We will begin with you," said the Maurai. "At the proper time, you and your fellows will be escorted home. Your ransom will be that your nation allow a diplomatic and trade mission to enter."

"No," said Tresa, as if speech hurt her throat. "Not him. Send back the others if you must, but not him— to boast of what he did today."

Loklann grinned again, looking straight at her. "I will," he said.

Anger flicked in Ruori, but he held his mouth shut.

"I do not understand," hesitated Don Páwolo. "Why do you favor these animals?"

"Because they are more civilized than you," said Ruori.

"What?" The noble sprang to his feet, snatching for his sword. Stiffly, he sat down again. His tone froze over. "Explain yourself, S'ñor."

Ruori could not see Tresa's face, in the private night of her hood, but he felt her drawing farther from him than a star. "They have developed aircraft," he said, slumping back in his chair, worn out and with no sense of victory; *O great creating Tanaroa, grant me sleep this night!*

"But—"

"That was done from the ground up," explained Ruori, "not as a mere copy of ancient techniques. Beginning as refugees, the Sky People created an agriculture which can send warriors by the thousands from what was desert, yet plainly does not require peon hordes. On interrogation I have learned that they have sunpower and hydroelectric power, a synthetic chemistry of sorts, a well-developed navigation with the mathematics which that implies, gunpowder, metallurgics, aerodynamics. . . . Yes, I daresay it's a lopsided culture, a thin layer of learning above a largely illiterate mass. But even the mass must respect technology, or it would never have been supported to get as far as it has.

"In short," he sighed, wondering if he could make her comprehend, "the Sky People are a scientific race—the only one besides ourselves which we Maurai have yet discovered. And that makes them too precious to lose.

"You have better manners here, more humane laws, higher art, broader vision, every traditional virtue. But you are not scientific. You use rote knowledge handed down from the ancients. Because there is no more fossil fuel, you depend on muscle power; inevitably, then, you have a peon class, and always will. Because the iron and copper mines are exhausted, you tear down old ruins. In your land I have seen no research on wind power, sun power, the energy reserves of the living cell—not to mention the theoretical possibility of hydrogen fusion without a uranium primer. You irrigate the desert at a thousand times the effort it would take to farm the sea, yet have never even tried to improve your fishing techniques. You have not exploited the aluminum which is still abundant in ordinary clays, not sought to make it into strong alloys; no, your farmers use tools of wood and volcanic glass.

"Oh, you are neither ignorant nor superstitious. What you lack is merely the means of gaining new knowledge. You are a fine people; the world is the sweeter for you; I love you as much as I loathe this devil before us. But ultimately, my friends, if left to yourselves, you will slide gracefully back to the Stone Age."

A measure of strength returned. He raised his voice till it filled the hall. "The way of the Sky People is the rough way outward, to the stars. In that respect—and it overrides all others—they are more akin to us Maurai than you are. We cannot let our kin die."

He sat then, in silence, under Loklann's smirk and Dónoju's stare. A guardsman shifted on his feet, with a faint squeak of leather harness.

Tresa said at last, very low in the shadows: "That is your final word, S'ñor?"

"Yes," said Ruori. He turned to her. As she leaned forward, the hood fell back a little, so that candlelight touched her. And the sight of green eyes and parted lips gave him back his victory.

He smiled. "I do not expect you will understand at once. May I discuss it with you again, often? When you have seen the Islands, as I hope you will—"

"You *foreigner!*" she screamed.

Her hand cracked on his cheek. She rose and ran down the dais steps and out of the hall.

Gordon R. Dickson

THE MAN IN THE MAILBAG

Gordon R. Dickson is probably best known for his ambitious "Childe Cycle"—more commonly referred to as the "Dorsai" series—which largely focuses on the history of a race of interstellar mercenary soldiers (the Dorsai) as they work their destiny out against a complex Future History of warring planets and philosophies. But in his forty-eight-year career, Dickson's written just about every kind of science fiction that it's possible to write, from broad slapstick social comedies to broodingly introspective psychological studies, as well as a fair amount of fantasy. The "Childe Cycle" consists of the controversial *Soldier, Ask Not* (considered by many to be an "answer" to Robert A. Heinlein's *Starship Troopers*), *No Room For Man, The Far Call, The Tactics of Mistake, Dorsai!, The Spirit of Dorsai, Young Bleys,* and, most recently, *The Final Encyclopedia* and *The Chantry Guild;* the Dorsai short stories have been collected in *Lost Dorsai.* He won a Hugo Award in 1965 for the short novel version of "Soldier, Ask Not," a Nebula Award in 1966 for "Call Him Lord," and another two Hugo Awards in 1981 for "Lost Dorsai" and "The Cloak and the Staff." His other books include *Arcturus Landing, The Alien Way, Sleepwalker's World, The Last Master, Hour of the Horde, Way of the Pilgrim, Wolf and Iron, Timestorm, Wolfling, The Pritcher Mass, The Space Swimmers,* and a series of fantasy novels that include *The Dragon and the George, The Dragon Knight,* and *The Dragon on the Border.* His most recent novel is *The Dragon and the Djinn.* Dickson's many short stories have been assembled in the collections *In Iron Years, The Book of Gordon R. Dickson, None But Man, Love Not Human, Beginnings, Ends, Invaders!, Mindspan, The Earth Lords, Foreward!, The Man From Earth, Steel Brother,* and others. His long series of comic "Hoka" stories, written with Poul Anderson, have been assembled in the collections *Hoka!* and *Earthman's Burden;* there is also a "Hoka" novel, *Star Prince Charlie.* The story that follows, "The Man in the Mailbag," was later expanded into the novel *Special Delivery,* which was followed by a sequel, *Spacepaw.*

Although they frequently contain a strong element of physical action, Dickson's stories are usually thoughtful and thought-provoking as well, sometimes even somber, revolving around the changes in philosophies and ethics and social codes necessary to ensure humanity's survival in the complex and rapidly evolving social environments we'll have to deal with in the future.

Sometimes, though (the series of "Hoka" stories he wrote in collaboration with Poul Anderson also come to mind), he writes one just for the *fun* of it. And few stories then or now have been as purely entertaining as the fast and funny tale that follows (although, come to think of it, all that speculation about social codes and the most effective way to adapt your behavior in order to manipulate the society you're dealing with is still *there,* afterall, just played in a slightly different key), dealing with the misadventures of a hapless Earthman who must somehow find a way to cope with the huge, boisterous, furry, cantankerous Dilbians, even if he has to literally *kill* himself trying—an outcome which, alas, looks all too *likely. . . .*

The Right Honorable Joshua Guy, Ambassador Plenipotentiary to Dilbia, was smoking tobacco in a pipe. The fumes from it made John Tardy cough and strangle—or, at least, so it seemed.

"Sir?" wheezed John Tardy.

"Sorry," said Joshua, knocking the pipe out in an ashtray where the coals continued to smolder only slightly less villainously than before. "Thought you heard me the first time. I said that naturally as soon as we knew you were being assigned to the job, we let out word that you were deeply attached to the girl."

"To—" John gulped air. Both men were talking Dilbian, to exercise the command of the language John had had hypnoed into him on his way here from the Belt Stars, and the Dilbian nickname for the missing Earthian female sociologist came from his lips automatically—"this Greasy Face?"

"Miss Ty Lamorc," nodded Joshua, smoothly slipping into Basic and then out again. "Greasy Face, if you prefer. By the by, you mustn't go taking all these Dilbian names at face value. The two old gentlemen you're going to meet—Daddy Shaking Knees and Two Answers—aren't what they might sound like. Daddy Shaking Knees got his name from holding up one end of a timber one day in an emergency—after about forty-five minutes, someone noticed his knees beginning to tremble. And Two Answers is a tribute to the Dilbian who can come up with more than one answer to a problem."

About to ask Joshua about his own Dilbian nickname of Little Bite, John Tardy shifted to safe ground. "What about this Schlaff fellow who—"

"Heiner Schlaff," interrupted Joshua Guy, frowning, "made a mistake. You'd think anyone would know better than to lose his head when a Dilbian picks him up. After the first time one picked up Heinie, he wasn't able to step out onto the street without some Dilbian lifting him up to hear him yell for help. The Squeaking Squirt, they called him—very bad for Earth-Dilbian relations." He looked severely at John. "I don't expect anything like that from you." The ambassador's eye seemed to weigh John's chunky body and red hair.

"No, no," said John hastily.

"Decathlon winner in the Olympics four years back, weren't you?"

"Yes," said John. "But what I really want is to get on an exploration team to one of the new planets. I'm a fully qualified biochemist and—"

"I read your file. Well," Joshua Guy said, "do a good job here and who knows?" He glanced out the window beside him at the sprawling log buildings of the local Dilbian town of Humrog, framed against the native conifers and the mountain peaks beyond. "But it's your physical condition that'll count. You understand *why* you have to go it alone, don't you?"

"They told me back on Earth. But if you can add anything—"

"Headquarters never understands the fine points of these situations," said Joshua, almost cheerfully. "To put it tersely—we want to make friends with these Dilbians. They're the race nearest to ours in intelligence that we've run across so far. They'd make fine partners. Unfortunately we don't seem to be able to impress them very much."

"Size?" asked John Tardy.

"Well, yes—size is probably the biggest stumbling block. The fact that we're about lap-dog proportions in relation to them. But it shows up even more sharply in a cultural dissimilarity. They don't give a hang for our mechanical gimmicks and they're all for personal honor and a healthy outdoors life." He looked at John. "You'll say, of course, why not a show of force?"

"I should think—" began John.

"But we don't want to fight them—we want to make friends with them. Let me give you an Earth-type analogy. For centuries, humans have been able to more or less tame most of the smaller wild animals. The large ones, however, being unused to knuckling under to anyone—"

Beep! signaled the annunciator on Joshua's desk.

"Ah, they're here now." Joshua Guy rose. "We'll go into the reception room. Now remember that Boy-Is-She-Built is old Shaking Knees' daughter. It was the fact that the Streamside Terror wanted her that caused all this ruckus and ended up with the Terror's kidnapping Ty Lamorc."

He led the way through the door into the next room. John Tardy followed, his head, in spite of the hypno training, still spinning a little with the odd Dilbian names—in particular Boy-Is-She-Built, the Basic translation of which was only a pale shadow of its Dilbian original. While not by any means a shy person, John rather hesitated to look a father in the eye and refer to the female child of his old age as—further reflections were cut short as he entered the room.

"Ah, there, Little Bite!" boomed the larger of the two black-furred monsters awaiting them. The one who spoke stood well over two and a half meters in height—at least eight feet tall. "This the new one? Two Answers and I came right over to meet him. Kind of bright-colored on top, isn't he?"

John Tardy blinked. But Joshua Guy answered equably enough.

"Some of us have that color hair back home," he said. "This is John Tardy—John, meet Shaking Knees. And the quiet one is Two Answers."

"*Quiet!*" roared the other Dilbian, bursting into gargantuan roars of laughter. "Me *quiet!* That's good!" He bellowed his merriment.

John stared. In spite of the hypno training, he could not help comparing these two to a couple of very large bears who had stood up on their hind legs and gone on a diet. They were leaner than bears—though leanness is relative when you weigh upward of a thousand pounds—and longer-legged. Their noses were more pug, their lower jaws more humanlike than ursinoid in the way of chin. But their complete coat of thick black hair and their bearishness of language and actions made the comparison almost inevitable—though in fact their true biological resemblance was closer to the humans themselves.

"Haven't laughed like that since old Souse Nose fell in the beer vat!" snorted Two Answers, gradually getting himself under control. "All right, Bright Top, what've you got to say for yourself? Think you can take the Streamside Terror with one hand tied behind your back?"

"I'm here," said John Tardy, "to bring back—er—Greasy Face, and—"

"Streamside won't just hand her over. Will he, Knees?" Two Answers jogged his companion with a massively humorous elbow.

"Not that boy!" Shaking Knees shook his head. "Little Bite, I ought never have let you talk me out of a son-in-law like that. Tough? Rough? Tricky? My little girl'd do all right with a buck like that."

"I merely," demurred Joshua, "suggested you make them wait a bit. Boy-Is-She-Built is still rather young—"

"And, boy, is she built!" said Shaking Knees in a tone of fond, fatherly pride. "Still, it's hard to see how she could do much better." He peered suddenly at Joshua. "You wouldn't have something hidden between your paws on this?"

Joshua Guy spread his hands in a wounded manner. "Would I risk one of my own people? Maybe two? All to start something that would make the Terror mad enough to steal Greasy to pay me back?"

"Guess not," admitted Shaking Knees. "But you Shorties are shrewd little characters." His words rang with honest admiration.

"Thanks. The same to you," said Joshua. "Now about the Terror—"

"He headed west through the Cold Mountains," replied Two Answers. "He was spotted yesterday a half-day's hike north, pointed toward Sour Ford and the Hollows. He probably nighted at Brittle Rock Inn there."

"Good," said Joshua. "We'll have to find a guide for my friend here."

"Guide? Ho!" chortled Shaking Knees. "Wait'll you see what *we* got for you." He shouldered past Two Answers, opened the door and bellowed, "Bluffer! Come on in!"

There was a moment's pause, and then a Dilbian even leaner and taller than Shaking Knees shoved his way into the room, which, with this new Dilbian addition, became decidedly crowded.

"There you are," said Shaking Knees, waving a prideful paw. "What more could you want? Walk all day, climb all night, and start out fresh next morning after breakfast. Little Bite, meet the Hill Bluffer!"

"That's me!" boomed the newcomer, rattling the walls. "Anything on two feet walk away from me? Not over solid ground or living rock! When I look at a hill, it knows it's beat, and it lays out flat for my trampling feet!"

"Very good," said Joshua dryly. "But I don't know about my friend here keeping up if you can travel like that."

"Keep up? Hah!" guffawed Shaking Knees. "No, no, Little Bite—don't you recognize the Bluffer here? He's the postman. We're going to mail this half-pint friend of yours to the Terror. Only way. Cost you five kilos of nails."

"Nobody stops the mail," put in the Hill Bluffer.

"Hmm," said Joshua. He glanced at John Tardy. "Not a bad suggestion. The only thing is how you plan to carry him—"

"Who? Him?" boomed the Bluffer, focusing on John. "Why, I'll handle him like he was a week-old pup. I'll wrap him in some real soft straw and tuck him in the bottom of my mailbag and—"

"Hold it," interrupted Joshua. "That's just what I was afraid of. If you're going to carry him, you'll have to do it humanely."

"I won't wear it!" the Hill Bluffer was still roaring, two hours later. The cause of his upset, a system of straps and pads arranged into a rough saddlebag that would ride between his shoulders and bear John, lay on the crushed rock of Humrog's main street. A few Dilbian bystanders had gathered to watch and their bass-voiced comments were not of the sort to bring the Hill Bluffer to a more reasonable frame of mind.

"Listen, you tad!" Shaking Knees was beginning to get a little hot under the neck-fur himself. "This is your mother's uncle's first cousin speaking. You want me to speak to the great-grandfathers of your clan—"

"Arright—arright—arright!" snarled the Hill Bluffer. "Buckle me up in the obscenity thing!"

"That's better!" growled Shaking Knees, simmering down as John Tardy and Joshua Guy went to work to put the saddle on. "Not that I blame you, but—"

"Don't feel so bad at that," said the Hill Bluffer sulkily, wriggling his shoulders under the straps in experimental fashion.

"You'll find it," grunted Joshua, tugging on a strap, "easier to carry than your regular bag."

"That's not the point," groused the Hill Bluffer. "A postman's got dignity. He just don't wear—" He exploded suddenly at a snickering onlooker. *"What's so funny, you? Want to make something out of it? Just say the—"*

"I'll take care of him!" roared Shaking Knees, rolling forward. "What's wrong with you, Split Nose?"

The Dilbian addressed as Split Nose swallowed his grin rather hastily as the Humrog village chief took a hand in the conversation.

"Just passing by," he growled defensively, backing out of the crowd.

"Well, just pass on, friend, pass on!" boomed Shaking Knees. He was rewarded by a hearty laugh from the crowd, and Split Nose rolled off down the street with every indication his hairy ears were burning.

John had taken advantage of this little by-play to mount into the saddlebag. The Hill Bluffer grunted in surprise and looked back at him.

"You're light enough," he said. "How is it? All right back there?"

"Feels fine," said John, unsuspecting.

"Then so long, everybody!" boomed the Hill Bluffer, and, without further warning, barreled off down the main street in the direction of the North Trail, the Cold Mountains and the elusive but dangerous Streamside Terror.

Had it not been for the hypno training, John Tardy would not have been able to recognize this fast and unexpected start for the Dilbian trick it was. He realized instantly, however, that the Hill Bluffer, having lost his enthusiasm for the job at first sight of the harness which was to carry John, was attempting a little strategy to get out of it. Outright refusal to carry John was out of the question, but if John should object to the unceremoniousness of his departure, the Bluffer would be perfectly justified—by Dilbian standards—if he threw up his hands and refused to deliver a piece of mail that insisted on imposing conditions on him. John shut his mouth and hung on.

All the same, it was awkward. John had intended to work out a plan of action with Joshua Guy before he left. Well, there was always the wristphone. He would call Joshua at the first convenient opportunity.

Meanwhile, it was developing that the Hill Bluffer had not exaggerated his ability to cover ground. One moment they were on the main street of Humrog, and the next upon a mountain trail, green pinelike branches whipping by as John Tardy plunged and swayed to the Hill Bluffer's motion like a man on the back of an elephant. It was no time for abstract thought. John clung to the straps before him, meditating rather bitterly on that natural talent of his for athletics which had got him into this, when by all rights he should be on an exploration team on one of the frontier planets right now. He was perfectly qualified, but just because of that decathlon win . . .

He continued to nurse his grievances for something better than an hour, when he was suddenly interrupted by the Hill Bluffer's grunting and slowing down. Peering forward over the postman's shoulder, John discovered another Dilbian who had just stepped out of the woods before them. The newcomer was on the shaggy side. He carried an enormous triangular-headed axe and had some native herbivore roughly the size and shape of a musk-ox slung casually over one shoulder.

"Hello, woodsman," said the Hill Bluffer, halting.

"Hello, postman." The other displayed a gap-toothed array of fangs in a grin. "Got some mail for me?"

"You!" the Hill Bluffer snorted.

"Not so funny. I could get mail," growled the other. He peered around at John. "So that's the Half Pint Posted."

"Oh?" said the Hill Bluffer. "Who told you?"

"The Cobbly Queen, that's who!" retorted the other, curling the right side of his upper lip in the native equivalent of a wink. John Tardy, recalling the Cobblies were the Dilbian equivalent of fairies, brownies, or what-have-you, peered at the woodsman to see if he was serious. John decided he wasn't. Which still left the problem of how he had recognized John.

Remembering the best Dilbian manners were made of sheer brass, John Tardy horned in on the conversation.

"Who're you?" he demanded of the woodsman.

"So it talks, does it?" The woodsman grinned. "They call me Tree Weeper, Half Pint. Because I chop them down, you see."

"Who told you about me?"

"Oh, that'd be telling," grinned Tree Weeper. "Say, you know why they call him the Streamside Terror, Half Pint? It's on account of he likes to fight alongside a stream, pull the other feller in and drown him."

"I know," said John shortly.

"Do you now?" said the other. "Well, it ought to be something to watch. Good going to you, Half Pint, and you too, postman. Me for home."

He turned away into the brush alongside the trail and it swallowed him up. The Hill Bluffer took up his route again without a word.

"Friend of yours?" inquired John, when it became apparent the Hill Bluffer was not going to comment on the meeting.

"Friend?" the Hill Bluffer snorted angrily. "*I'm* a public official!"

"I just thought—" said John. "He seemed to know things."

"That hill hopper! Somebody ahead of us told him!" growled the Bluffer. But he fell unaccountably silent after that and said no more for the next three hours, until—the two of them having left Humrog a couple of hours past noon—they pulled up in the waning sunlight before the roadside inn at Brittle Rock, where they would spend the night.

The first thing John Tardy did, after working some life back into his legs, was to stroll off to the limits of the narrow, rocky ledge on which the inn stood—Brittle Rock was hardly more than a wide spot in the narrow mountain gorge up which their road ran—and put in a call to Joshua Guy with the phone on his wrist. As soon as Joshua got on the beam, John relievedly explained the reason behind his call. It did not go over, apparently, very well.

"Instructions?" floated the faintly astonished voice of the ambassador out of the receiver. "What instructions?"

"The ones you were going to give me. Before I took off so suddenly—"

"But there's absolutely nothing I can tell you," interrupted Joshua. "You've had your hypno training. It's up to you. Find the Terror and get the girl back. You'll have to figure out your own means, my dear fellow."

"But—" John stopped, staring helpless at the phone.

"Well, good luck, then. Call me tomorrow. Call me anytime."

"Thanks," said John.

"Not at all. Luck. Good-by."

"Good-by."

John Tardy clicked off the phone and walked somberly back to the inn. Inside its big front door, he found a wide common room filled with tables and benches. The Hill Bluffer, to the amusement of a host of other travelers, was arguing with a female Dilbian wearing an apron.

"How the unmentionable should I know what to feed him?" the Hill Bluffer was bellowing. "Give him some meat, some beer—anything!"

"But you haven't had the children dragging in pets like I have. Feed one the wrong thing and it dies. And then they cry their little hearts—"

"Talking about me?" John Tardy broke in.

"Oh!" gasped the female, glancing down and retreating half a step. "It talks!"

"Didn't I say he did?" demanded the Bluffer. "Half Pint, what kind of stuff do you eat?"

John fingered the four-inch tubes of food concentrate at his waist. Dilbian food would not poison him, though he could expect little nourishment from it, and a fair chance of an allergic reaction from certain fruits and vegetables. Bulk was all he needed to supplement the concentrates.

"Just give me a little beer," he said.

The room buzzed approval. This little critter, they seemed to feel, could not be too alien if he liked to drink. The female brought him a wastebasket-sized wooden mug that had no handles and smelled like the most decayed of back-lot breweries. John took a cautious sip and held the bitter, sour, flat-tasting liquid in his mouth for an indecisive moment.

He swallowed manfully. The assembled company gave vent to rough-voiced approval, then abruptly turned their attention elsewhere. Looking around, he saw that the Hill Bluffer had gone off somewhere. John climbed up on a nearby bench and got to work on his food concentrates.

After finishing these, he continued to sit where he was for the better part of an hour, but the Hill Bluffer did not return. Struck by a sudden thought, John Tardy climbed down and went back toward the kitchen of the inn. Pushing his way through a hide curtain, he found himself in it—a long room with a stone fire-trough down the center, carcasses hanging from overhead beams, and a dozen or so Dilbians of both sexes equally immersed in argument and the preparation of food and drink. Among them was the female who had brought John the beer.

He stepped into her path as she headed for the front room with a double handful of full mugs.

"Eeeeek!" she exclaimed, or the Dilbian equivalent, stopping so hastily she spilled some of the beer. "There's a good little Shorty," she said in a quavering, coaxing tone. "Good Shorty. Go back now."

"Was the Terror really here last night?" John asked.

"He stopped to pick up some meat and beer, but I didn't see him," she said. "I've no time for hill-and-alley brawlers. Now shoo!"

John Tardy shooed.

As he was heading back to his bench, however, he felt himself scooped up from behind. Looking back over his shoulder, he saw he was being carried by a large male Dilbian with a pouch hanging from one shoulder. This individual carried him to a table where three other Dilbians sat and dropped him on it. John Tardy instinctively got to his feet.

"There he be," said the one who had picked him up. "A genuine Shorty."

"Give him some beer," suggested one with a scar on his face, who was seated at the table.

They did. John prudently drank some.

"Don't hold much," commented one of the others at the table, examining the mug John had set down after what had been actually a very healthy draft for a human. "I wonder if he—"

"Couldn't. Not at that size," replied the one with the pouch. "He's chasing that female Shorty, though. You reckon—?"

Scarface regretted that they did not have the Shorty female there at the moment. Her presence, in his opinion, would have provided the opportunity for interesting and educative experimentation.

"Go to hell!" said John in Basic. He then made the most forceful translation he could manage in Dilbian.

"Tough character!" said the pouched one, and they all laughed. "Better not get tough with me, though."

He made a few humorous swipes at John's red head that would have split it on contact. They laughed again.

"I wonder," said Scarface, "can he do tricks?"

"Sure," John answered promptly. He left his still-ful mug of beer. "Watch. I take a firm grip, rock back, and—" He spun suddenly on one heel, sloshing a wave of beer into their staring faces. Then he was off the table and dodging among Dilbian and table legs toward the front entrance. The rest of the guests, roaring with laughter, made no attempt to halt him. He ducked into the outer darkness.

Fumbling in the gloom, he made his way around the side of the inn and dropped down on a broken keg he found there. He was just making up his mind to stay there until the Hill Bluffer came and found him, when the back kitchen door opened and closed very softly, off to his left.

He slipped off the keg into deeper shadow. He had caught just a glimpse out of the corner of his eye, but he had received the impression of a Dilbian female in the doorway. There was no sound now.

He began to creep backward. Dilbia's one moon was not showing over these latitudes at this season of the year, and the starlight gave only a faint illumination. He stumbled suddenly over the edge of an unseen slope and froze, remembering the cliff edge overhanging the gorge below.

A faint reek of the Dilbian odor came to his nostrils—and a sound of sniffing. Dilbians were no better than human when it came to a sense of smell, but each had a perceptible odor to the nostrils of the other—an odor partly dependent on diet, partly on a differing physiological makeup. The odor John Tardy smelled was part-pine, part-musk.

The sniffing ceased. John held his breath, waiting for it to start again. The pressure built up in his chest, and finally he was forced to exhale. He turned his head slowly from side to side.

Silence.

Only the inner creak of his tense neck muscles turning. There! Was that something? John began to creep back along the edge beside him.

There was a sudden rush, a rearing up of some huge dark shape in the darkness before him. He dodged, felt himself slipping on the edge, and something smashed like a falling wall against the side of his head, and he went whirling down and away into star-shot darkness.

He opened his eyes to bright sunlight.

The sun, just above the mountain peaks, was shining right in his eyes. He blinked and started to roll over, out of its glare, into—

—And grabbed in a sudden cold sweat for the stubby trunk of a dwarf tree growing right out of the cliffside.

For a second then, he hung there, sweating and looking down. He lay on a narrow ledge and the gorge was deep below. How deep, he did not stop to figure. It was deep enough.

He twisted around and looked up the distance of a couple of meters to the ledge on which the inn was built. It was not far. He could climb it. After a little while, with his heart in his throat, John Tardy did.

When he came back around the front of the inn, in the morning sunlight, it was to find the Bluffer orating at a sort of open-air meeting, with the four who had harried John standing hangdog between two axemen and before an elderly Dilbian judgelike on a bench.

"—the mail!" the Hill Bluffer was roaring. "The mail is sacred! Anyone daring to lay fist upon the mail in transit—"

John, tottering forward, put an end to the trial in progress.

Later on, after washing his slight scalp-wound and having taken on some more food concentrates and flat beer for breakfast, John Tardy climbed back up on the Bluffer's back and they were under way once more. Their route today led from Brittle Rock through the mountains to Sour Ford and the Hollows. The Hollows, John had learned, was clan-country for the Terror, and their hope was to catch him before he reached it. The trail now led across swinging rope suspension bridges and along narrow cuts in the rock—all of which the Hill Bluffer took not only with the ease of one well accustomed to them, but with the abstraction of one lost in deep thought.

"Hey!" said John, at last.

"Huh? What?" grunted the Hill Bluffer, coming to suddenly.

"Tell me something," said John, reaching out for anything to keep his carrier awake. "How'd the ambassador get the name Little Bite?"

"You don't know that?" exclaimed the Hill Bluffer. "I thought you Shorties all knew. Well, it was old Hammertoes down at Humrog."

The Bluffer chuckled. "Got drunk and all worked up about Shorties. 'Gimme the good old days,' he said, and went down to just make an example of Little Bite—Shorty One, we called him then. He pushes the door open far as it'll go, but Little Bite's got it fixed to only open part way. So there's Hammertoes, with only one arm through the door, feeling around and hollering, 'All right, Shorty! You can't get away! I'll get you—' when Little Bite picks up something sharp and cuts him a couple times across the knuckles. Old Hammertoes yells bloody murder and yanks his hand back. Slam goes the door."

The Hill Bluffer chortled to himself. "Then old Hammertoes comes back uptown, sucking his knuckles. 'What happened?' says everybody. 'Nothing,' says Hammertoes. 'Something must've happened—look at your hand,' everybody says. 'I tell you nothing happened!' yells Hammertoes.

'He wouldn't let me in where I could grab hold of him, so I come away. And as for my hand, that's got nothing to do with it. He didn't hurt my hand hardly at all. He just give it a little bite!' "

The Hill Bluffer's laughter rolled like thunder between the mountain walls. "Old Hammertoes never did live that down. Every time since, whenever he goes to give somebody a hard time, they all tell him, 'Look out, Hammertoes, or I'm liable to give you a little bite!' "

John Tardy found himself laughing. Possibly it was the time and place of the telling, possibly the story, but he could see the situation in his mind's eye and it was funny.

"You know," said the Bluffer over one furry shoulder when John stopped laughing, "you're not bad for a Shorty." He fell silent, appeared to wrestle with himself for a moment, then came to a stop and sat down in a convenient wide spot on the trail.

"Get off," he said. "Come around where I can talk to you."

John complied. He found himself facing the seated Dilbian, their heads about on a level. Behind the large, black-furred skull, a few white clouds floated in the high blue sky.

"You know," the Bluffer said, "the Streamside Terror's mug's been spilled."

"Spilled?" echoed John—then remembered this as a Dilbian phrase expressing loss of honor. "By me? He's never even seen me."

"By Little Bite," the Bluffer said. "But Little Bite's a Guest in Humrog and the North Country. The Terror couldn't call him to account personally for speaking against Shaking Knees giving the Terror Boy-Is-She-Built. He had to do something, though, so he took Greasy Face."

"Oh," said John.

"So you got to fight the Terror if you want Greasy back."

"*Fight?*" John blurted.

"Man's got his pride," said the Bluffer. "That's why I can't figure you out. I mean you aren't bad for a Shorty. You got guts—like with those drunks last night. But you fighting the Terror—I mean *hell!*" said the Bluffer, in deeply moved tones.

Silently, John Tardy found himself in full agreement with the postman.

"So what're you going to do when you meet Streamside?"

"Well," said John, rather inadequately, "I don't exactly know—"

"Well," growled the Bluffer in his turn, "not my problem. Get on." John went around behind his furry back. "Oh, by the way, know who it was tried to pitch you over the cliff?"

"Who?" asked John.

"The Cobbly Queen—Boy-Is-She-Built!" translated the Bluffer as John looked blank. "She heard about you and got ahead of us somehow . . ."

The Bluffer's voice trailed off into a mutter. "If they're thinking of monkeying with the mail . . ."

John paid no attention. He had his own fish to fry, and very fishy indeed they smelled just at the moment. Swaying on top of the enormous back as they took off again, he found himself scowling over the situation. Headquarters had said nothing about his being expected to fight some monstrous free-style scrapper of an alien race—a sort of gargantuan Billy the Kid with a number of kills to his credit. Joshua Guy had not mentioned it. Just what was going on here, anyway?

Abruptly casting aside the security regulation that recommended a "discreet" use of the instrument, John lifted the wrist that bore his wrist-phone to his lips.

"Josh—" he began, and suddenly checked. A fine trickle of sweat ran coldly down his spine.

The phone was gone.

He had the rest of the morning to ponder this new development in the situation, and a good portion of the afternoon. He might have continued indefinitely if it had not been for a sudden interruption in their journey.

They had crossed a number of spidery suspension bridges during the course of the day, and now they had come to another one, somewhat longer than any met so far. If this had been the only difference, John might have been left to his thoughts. But this bridge was different.

Somebody had fixed it so they couldn't get across.

It happened that their end of the bridge had its anchors sunk in a rock face a little back and some seven or eight meters above their heads. All that had been done, simply enough, was to tighten the two main support cables at the far end. The sag of the span had straightened out, lifting the near end up above them, out of reach.

The Hill Bluffer bellowed obscenely across the gap. There was no response from the windlass on the far side, or the small hut beyond.

"What's happened?" John Tardy asked.

"I don't know," said the Bluffer, suddenly thoughtful. "It isn't supposed to be rucked up except at night, to keep people from sneaking over and not paying toll."

He reached as high as he could, but his fingertips fell far short.

"Lift me up," suggested John.

They tried it, but even upheld by the ankles, at the full stretch of the Bluffer's arms, John was rewarded only by a throat-squeezing view of the Knobby River below.

"It'll take five days to go around by Slide Pass," growled the Bluffer, putting John down.

John went over to examine the rock face. What he discovered about it did not make him happy, though perhaps it should have. It was climbable. Heart tucked in throat, he began to go up it.

"Hey! Where're you going?" bellowed the Hill Bluffer.

John did not answer. He needed his breath; anyway, his destination was obvious. The climb up the rock was not bad for someone who had had some mountain experience, but a reaction set in when he wrapped his arms around the rough six-inch cable. He inched his way upward and got on top, both arms and both legs wrapped around the cable, and began a worm-creep toward the bridge end, floating on nothingness at a rather remarkable distance—seen from this angle—ahead of him.

It occurred to him, after he had slowly covered about a third of the cable-distance in this fashion, that a real hero in a place like this should stand up and tightrope-walk to the bridge proper. This, in addition to impressing the Bluffer, would shorten the suspense considerably. John Tardy concluded he must be a conservative and went on crawling.

Eventually he reached the bridge, crawled out on it and lay panting for a while, then got up and crossed the gorge. At the far end, he knocked loose the lock on the windlass with a heavy rock, and the bridge banged down into position, raising a cloud of dust.

Through this same cloud of dust, the Hill Bluffer was shortly to be seen advancing with a look of grim purpose. He stalked past John and entered the hut—from which subsequently erupted thunderous crashes, thuds and roars.

John Tardy looked about for a place of safety. He had never seen two Dilbians fight, but it was only too apparent now what was going on inside.

He was still looking around, however, when the sound ceased abruptly and the Hill Bluffer emerged, dabbing at a torn ear.

"Old slaver-tongue," he growled. "*She* got at him."

"Who?" asked John.

"Boy-Is-She-Built. Well, mount up, Half Pint. Oh, by the way, that was pretty good."

"Good? What was?"

"Climbing across the bridge that way. Took guts. Well, let's go."

John climbed back up into his saddlebag and thought heavily.

"You didn't kill him?" he asked, as they started out once more.

"Who? Old Winch Rope? Just knocked a little sense into him. Hell, there's got to be somebody to work the bridge. Hang on now. It's all downhill from here and it'll be twilight before we hit the ford."

It was indeed twilight before they reached their stopping place at Sour Ford. John Tardy, who had been dozing, awoke with a jerk and sat up in his saddle, blinking.

In the fading light, they stood in a large, grassy clearing semicircled by forest. Directly before them was a long low log building, and behind it a smooth-flowing river with its farther shore shrouded in tree shadow and the approaching dusk.

"Get down," said the Bluffer.

Stiffly, John Tardy descended, stamped about to restore his circulation, and followed the Bluffer's huge bulk through the hide-curtain of the doorway to the building's oil-lamp lit interior.

John discovered a large room like that at the Brittle Rock Inn—but one that was cleaner, airier, and filled with travelers a good deal less noisy and drunken. Gazing around for the explanation behind this difference, John caught sight of a truly enormous Dilbian, grizzled with age and heavy with fat, seated like a patriarch in a huge chair behind a table at the room's far end.

John and the Bluffer found a table and set about eating. But as soon as they were through, the postman led John up to the patriarch.

"One Man," said the Bluffer in a respectful voice, "this here's the Half Pint Posted."

John Tardy blinked. Up close, One Man had turned out to be even more awe-inspiring than he had seemed from a distance. He overflowed the carved chair he sat in, and the graying fur on top of his head all but brushed against a polished staff of hardwood laid crosswise on pegs driven into the wall two meters above the floor. His massive forearms and great pawlike hands were laid out on the table before him like swollen clubs of bone and muscle. But his face was almost Biblically serene.

"Sit down," he rumbled in a voice so deep it sounded like a great drum sounding far off somewhere in a woods. "I've wanted to see a Shorty. You're my Guest, Half Pint, for as long as you wish. Anyone tell you about me?"

"I'm sorry—" began John.

"Never mind." The enormous head nodded mildly. "They call me One Man, Half Pint, because I once held blood feud all by myself—being an orphan—with a whole clan. And won." He looked calmly at John. "What you might call an impossible undertaking."

"Some of them caught him on a trail once," put in the Hill Bluffer. "He killed all three."

"That was possible," murmured One Man. His eyes were still on John. "Tell me, Half Pint, what are you Shorties doing here, anyhow?"

"Well—" John blinked. "I'm looking for Greasy Face—"

"I mean the entire lot of you," One Man said. "There must be some plan behind it. Nobody asked you all here, you know."

"Well—" said John again, rather lamely, and proceeded to try an explanation. It did not seem to go over very well, a technological civilization being hard to picture with the Dilbian vocabulary.

One Man nodded when John Tardy was through. "I see. If that's the case, what makes you think we ought to like you Shorties?"

"Ought to?" said John, jolted into a reactive answer, for he did not have red hair for nothing. "You don't ought to! It's up to you."

One Man nodded. "Pass me my stick," he said.

One of the Dilbians standing around took down the staff from its pegs and passed it to him. He laid it on the table before him—a young post ten centimeters in thickness—grasping it with fists held over two meters apart.

"No one's ever been able to do this but me," he said.

Without lifting his fists from contact with the table, he rotated them to the outside. The staff sprang upward in the center like a bow, and snapped.

"Souvenir for you," said One Man, handing the pieces to John. "Good night."

He closed his eyes and sat as if dozing. The Bluffer tapped John on a shoulder and led him away, off to their sleeping quarters.

Once in the inn dormitory, however, John found himself totally unable to sleep. He had passed from utter bone-weariness into a sort of feverish wide-awakedness, through which the little episode with One Man buzzed and circled like a persistently annoying fly.

What had been the point of all that talk and wood-breaking?

Suddenly and quietly, John sat up. Beside him, on his heap of soft branches, the Bluffer slept without stirring, as did the rest of the dormitory inhabitants. A single lamp burned high above, hanging from the rooftree. By its light, John got out and examined the broken pieces of wood. There was a little node or knot visible just at the point of breakage. A small thing, but—

John frowned. He seemed surrounded by mysteries. The more he thought of it, the more certain he was that One Man had been attempting to convey some message to him. What was it? For that matter, what was going on between humans and Dilbians, and what had his mission to rescue Greasy Face to do with the business of persuading the recalcitrant Dilbians into a partnership? If that was indeed the aim, as Joshua Guy had said.

John swung out of the pile of boughs and to his feet. One Man, he decided, owed him a few more—and plainer—answers.

He went softly down the length of the dormitory and through the door into the common room of the inn.

There were few Dilbians about—they went early to bed. And One Man was also nowhere to be seen. He had not come into the dormitory, John knew. So either he had separate quarters, or else he had stepped outside for some reason . . .

John Tardy crossed the room and slipped out through the inn entrance.

He paused to accustom his eyes to the darkness and moved off from the building to get away from the window light. Slowly the night took shape around him, the wide face of the river running silver-dark in the faint light of the stars, and the clearing pooled in gloom.

He circled cautiously around the inn to its back. Unlike Brittle Rock, the backyard here was clear of rubbish, sloping gradually to the river. It was given over to smaller huts and outbuildings. Among these the darkness was more profound and he felt his way cautiously.

Groping about in this fashion, quietly, but with some small, unavoidable noise, he saw a thin blade of yellow light. It cut through the parting of two leather curtains in the window of a hut close by him. He stepped eagerly toward it, about to peer through the crack, when, from deep wall shadow, a hand reached out and took his arm.

"Do you *want* to get yourself killed?" hissed a voice.

And, of course, it was human. And, of course, it spoke in Basic.

Whoever had hold of him drew him deeper into the shadow and away from the building where they stood. They came to another hut whose door stood ajar on an interior blackness, and John was led into this darkness. The hand let go of his arm. The door closed softly. There was a scratch, a sputter, and an animal-oil lamp burst into light within the place.

John squinted against the sudden illumination. When he could see again, he found himself looking into the face of one of the best-looking young women he had ever seen.

She was a good fifteen centimeters shorter than he, but at first glance looked taller by reason of her slim outline in the tailored coveralls she wore. To John Tardy, after two days of Dilbians, she looked tiny—fragile. Her chestnut hair swept back in two wide wings on each side of her head. Her eyes were green above sharply marked cheekbones that gave her face a sculptured look. Her nose was thin, her lips firm rather than full, and her small chin was determined.

John blinked. "Who—?"

"I'm Ty Lamorc," she whispered fiercely. "Keep your voice down!"

"Ty Lamorc? *You?*"

"Yes, yes!" she said impatiently. "Now—"

"Are y-you sure?" stammered John. "I mean—"

"Who were you expecting to run into way out here in—oh, I see!" She glared at him. "It's that Greasy Face name the Dilbians gave me. You were expecting some horror."

"Certainly not," said John stoutly.

"Well, for your information, they just happened to see me putting on makeup one day. That's where the name came from."

"Well, naturally. I didn't think it was because—"

"I'll bet! Anyway, never mind that now. The point is, what are *you* doing out here? Do you *want* to get knocked on the head?"

"Who'd knock—" John Tardy stiffened. "The Terror's here!"

"No, no!" She sounded annoyed. "Boy-Is-She-Built is."

"Oh." John frowned. "You know, I still don't get it—her angle on all this, I mean."

"She loves him, of course," said Ty Lamorc. "Actually, they make an ideal couple, by Dilbian standards. Now let's get you back to the inn before she catches you. She won't follow you in there. You're a Guest."

"Now wait—" John took a deep breath. "This is silly. I came out here to find you. I've found you. Let's head back right now. Not to Humrog—"

"You don't," interrupted Ty with feeling, "understand a blasted thing about these people, Half Pint—I mean, Tardy."

"John."

"John, you don't understand the situation. The Streamside Terror left me here with Boy-Is-She-Built because I was slowing him down. That Hill Bluffer of yours is too fast for him, and he wanted to be sure to be in his own clan-country before you caught up with him, in case there would be—" her voice faltered a little—"repercussions to what happens when you meet. It's all a matter of honor, and that's the point. *You're a piece of mail, John.* Don't you understand? The Hill Bluffer's honor is involved, too."

"Oh," said John. He was silent for a while. "You mean he'd insist on delivering me?"

"What do you think?"

"I see." John was silent again. "Well, to blazes with it," he said at last. "Maybe we can make it across a bridge and cut the ropes and get away from it all. We can't leave you here."

Ty Lamorc did not reply at once. When she did, it was with a pat on his arm.

"You're nice," she said softly. "I'll remember that. Now get back to the inn." And then she had blown out the lamp and he could hear her go.

Next morning, One Man was still nowhere to be seen. Nor, in the half hour that elapsed before they got going, did John Tardy catch any glimpse of Ty, or a female Dilbian who might be Boy-Is-She-Built. He mounted into the Hill Bluffer's mailbag with his mind still engrossed by the happenings of the night before, and it continued to be engrossed as they began their third day of journey.

They were descending now into a country of lower altitudes, though they were still in hill country. The ground was more gently hollowed and crested, and several new varieties of trees appeared.

But John had no time to consider this. He rode through the cool hours of the morning and into noon's heat still trying to find a common solution to the riddles that occupied his mind—about One Man, about the abduction of Ty Lamorc, and about his own peculiar lack of briefing.

"Tell me," said John finally to the Hill Bluffer, "is it a fact no other Dilbian could break that stick of One Man's that same way?"

"Nobody ever can," replied the Bluffer, as they rounded a small hill and plunged through a thin belt of trees. "Nobody ever will."

"Well, you know," said John, "back where I come from, we have a trick with something called a phone directory—"

He stopped. For the Hill Bluffer himself had stopped, with a jolt that almost pitched John from the mailbag. John sat up, looked around the Dilbian's head—and stared.

They had passed through the woods. They had emerged into a small valley in which a cluster of buildings stood in the brown color of their peeled and weathered logs, haphazardly about a stream that ran the valley's length. Beyond these houses there was a sort of natural amphitheater made by a curved indentation of the far rock wall of the valley. Past this the path went when it emerged from between the buildings and plunged into the trees again.

However, none of this claimed John's attention after the first second. He blinked, instead, at a living wall of five large Dilbians with axes.

"Who do you think you're stopping?" bellowed the Hill Bluffer.

"Clan Hollows' in full meeting," responded the central axeman. "The Great-Grandfathers want to see you both. You come with us."

The axemen formed around the Bluffer and John. They led off down and through the village and beyond to the amphitheater that was swarming with Dilbians of all ages. Several hundred of them were there, and more accumulating, below a ledge of rock where six ancient Dilbians sat.

"This is the mail!" stormed the Hill Bluffer as soon as they were close. "Listen, you Clan Hollows—"

"Be quiet, postman!" snapped the old Dilbian at the extreme right of the line as it faced John and the Bluffer. "Your honor will be guarded. Call the meeting."

"Great-Grandfathers of Clan Hollows, sitting in judgment upon a point of honor!" chanted a young Dilbian standing just below the ledge. He repeated the cry six times.

There was a stir in the crowd. Looking around, John saw Ty Lamorc. With her was a plump young female that was most likely Boy-Is-She-Built. Boy-Is-She-Built was currently engaged in herding Ty to the foot of the ledge. She accomplished this and immediately began talking.

"I'm Boy-Is-She-Built," she announced.

"We know you," said the Great-Grandfather on the right end.

"I'm speaking here for the Streamside Terror, who's waiting over at

Glenn Hollow for the Shorty known as the Half Pint Posted. That Shorty over there. His mug has been spilled—the Terror's, I mean. This Shorty belongs to him—the male over there, I mean. Not that this female Shorty here with me doesn't belong to him, too. He took her fair and square, and it serves those Shorties right. After all, nobody has more honor than the Terror—"

"That's enough," said the judge. "We will decide—"

"I should think you wouldn't even have to call a meeting over it. After all, it's perfectly plain—"

"I said *that's enough!* Be quiet, female!" roared the end judge.

"Well?" interjected one of the other judges testily. "We've heard the arguments. The Shorties are both here. What's left to say?"

"Can I speak?" boomed a new voice, and the crowd parted to let One Man come up before the ledge of rock. The Great-Grandfathers thawed visibly as only great men can in the company of their peers.

"One Man is always welcome to speak," piped an ancient who had not spoken before, and whose voice, with age, had risen almost to the pitch of a human baritone.

"Thank you," said One Man. He raised his head and his voice rose with it, carrying easily out over the assembled Dilbians. "Just think this over. That's what I've got to say. Think deep about it—because it may be Clan Hollows' decision here is going to be binding on just about everybody—us and Shorties alike."

He waved to the judges and went back into the crowd.

"Thanks, One Man," said the right-end judge. "Now, having heard from everybody important who had something to say, here's our opinion. This is a matter concerning the honor of the Streamside Terror—"

"How about me?" roared the Hill Bluffer. "The mail must—"

"Hold your jaw about the mail!" snapped the right-end judge. "As I was saying, Terror's mug was spilled by the Guest in Humrog. Quite properly, the Terror then spilled the mug of the Guest by stealing off one of the Guest's household. This by itself is a dispute between individuals not touching Clan Hollows. But now here comes along a Shorty who wants to fight Terror for the stolen Shorty. And the question is, can Clan Hollows honorably allow the Terror to do so?"

He paused for a moment, as if to let the point sink in on the crowd.

"For us to do this in honor," he continued, "the combat mentioned must be a matter of honor. And this point arises—is honor possible between a man and a Shorty? We Great-Grandfathers have sat up a full night finding an answer, and to do so we have had to ask ourselves, 'What *is* a Shorty?' That is, is it the same thing as us, a being capable of having honor and suffering its loss?"

He paused again. The crowd muttered its interest.

"A knotty question," said the spokesman, with a touch of complacency in his voice. "But your Great-Grandfathers have settled it."

The crowd murmured this time in admiration.

"What makes honor?" demanded the spokesman rhetorically. "Honor is a matter of rights—rights violated and rights protected. Have the Shorties among us had any rights? Guest-rights, only. Failing Guest-rights, can one imagine a Shorty defending and maintaining its rights in our world?"

A chortle broke out in the crowd and spread through its listening ranks at the picture conjured up.

"Silence!" snapped another of the judges. "This is *not* a house-raising."

The crowd went silent.

"Your display of bad manners," said the right-end judge severely, "has pointed up the same conclusion we came to—by orderly process of discussion. It is ridiculous to suppose a Shorty existing as an honor-bound equal in our world. Accordingly, the rules of honor are not binding. Both Shorties here will be returned unharmed to the Guest in Humrog. The Terror has lost no honor. The matter is closed."

He stood up. So did the other five Great-Grandfathers.

"This meeting," he said, "is ended."

"Not yet it isn't!" bellowed the Hill Bluffer.

He plunged forward to the edge of the rock bench, hauling John Tardy along by the slack in John's jacket.

"What do you all know about Shorties?" he demanded. "I've seen this one in action. When a bunch of drunks at Brittle Rock tried to make him do tricks like a performing animal, he fooled them all and got away. How's that for defending his honor? On our way here, the Knobby Gorge Bridge was cranked up out of our reach. He risked his neck climbing up to get it down again, so's not to be slowed in getting his paws on the Terror. How's that for a willingness to defend his rights? I say this Shorty here's as good as some of us any day. Maybe he isn't any bigger'n a two-year-old baby," roared the Hill Bluffer, "but I'm here today to tell you he's all guts!"

He spun on John. "How about it, Shorty? You want Greasy Face handed back to you like scraps from a plate—"

John's long cogitations at last paid off. These and something just witnessed in the Clan Meeting had thrown the switch he had been hunting for.

"Show me that skulking Terror!" he shouted.

The words had barely passed his lips when he felt himself snatched up. The free air whistled past his face. The Hill Bluffer had grabbed him in two huge hands and was now running toward the far woods with him, like a football player with a ball. A roar of voices followed them; looking back, John saw the whole of Clan Hollows in pursuit.

John blinked. He was being jolted along at something like fifty kilometers an hour, and the crowd was coming along behind at the same rate. Or were they? For a long second, John hesitated, then allowed himself to recognize the inescapable fact. All praise to the postman—the Bluffer was outrunning them!

John felt the thrill of competition in his own soul. He and the Hill Bluffer might be worlds apart biologically, but, by heaven, when it came to real competition . . .

Abruptly, the shadow of the further forest closed about them. The Hill Bluffer ran on dropped needles from the conifers, easing to a lope. John Tardy climbed over his shoulder into the mailbag and hung on.

The forest muffled the roar of pursuit. They descended one side of a small hollow and, coming up the other, the Bluffer dropped to his usual ground-eating walk. On the next downslope, he ran again. And so he continued, alternating his pace as the ground shifted.

"How far to the Terror?" asked John.

"Glen Hollow," puffed the Hill Bluffer. He gave the answer in Dilbian units that worked out to just under eight kilometers.

About ten minutes later, they broke through a small fringe of trees to emerge over the lip of a small cuplike valley containing a meadow split by a stream which, in the meadow's center, spread into a pool. The pool was a good fifty meters across and showed the sort of color that indicates a fair depth. By the poolside, a male Dilbian was just looking up at the sound of their approach..

John leaned forward and said quietly to the Hill Bluffer, "Put me down by the deepest part of the water." Reaching to his waist, he loosened the buckle of the belt threaded through the loops on his pants.

The Hill Bluffer grunted and continued his descent. At the water's margin, some dozen meters from the waiting Dilbian, he stopped.

"Hello, postman," said the Dilbian

"Hello, Terror," answered the Bluffer. "Mail."

The Terror looked curiously past the Bluffer's head at John.

"So that's the Half Pint Posted, is it?" he said. "They let you come?"

"No, we just came," said the Bluffer.

While the Terror stared at John Tardy, John had been examining the Terror. The other Dilbian did not, at first glance, seem to live up to his reputation. He was big, but nowhere near the height of the Hill Bluffer, nor the awe-inspiring massiveness of One Man. John noted, however, with an eye which had judged physical capabilities among his own race, the unusually heavy boning of the other's body, the short, full neck, and, more revealing than any of these, the particularly *poised* balance exhibited by the Terror's thick body.

John Tardy threw one quick glance at the water alongside and slid down from the Bluffer's back. The Bluffer moved off and, with no attempt at the amenities, the Streamside Terror charged.

John turned and dived deep into the pool.

He expected the Terror to follow him immediately, reasoning the other was too much the professional fighter to take chances, even with a Shorty. And, indeed, the water-shock of the big body plunging in after John made him imagine the Terror's great clawed hands all but scratching at his heels. John stroked desperately for depth and distance. He did have a strategy of battle, but it all depended on time and elbow room. He changed direction underwater, angled up to the surface, and, flinging the water from his eyes with a jerk of his head, looked around him.

The Terror, looking the other way, had just broken water four meters off.

John dived again and proceeded to get rid of boots, pants and jacket. He came up again practically under the nose of the Terror and was forced to dive once more. But this time, as he went down, he trailed from one fist the belt he had taken from his trousers, waving in the water like a dark stem of weed.

Coming up the third time at a fairly safe distance, John discovered the Terror had spotted him and was coming after him. John grinned to himself and dove, as if to hide again. But under the water he changed direction and swam directly at his opponent. He saw the heavy legs and arms churning toward him overhead. They moved massively but relatively slowly through the water, and in this he saw the final proof he needed. He had guessed that, effective as the Terror might be against other Dilbians, in the water his very size made him slow and clumsy in comparison to a human—in possibly all but straightaway swimming.

Now John let his opponent pass him overhead. Then, as it went by, he grabbed the foot. And pulled.

The Terror instinctively checked and dived. John, flung surfaceward, let go and dived—this time behind and above the Dilbian. He saw the great back, the churning arms, and then, as the Terror turned once more toward the surface, John closed in, passing the belt around the thick neck and twisting its leather length tight.

At this the Terror, choking, should have headed toward the surface, giving John a chance to breathe. The Dilbian did, John got his breath—and there the battle departed from John's plan entirely.

John had simply failed to give his imagination full rein. He had, in spite of himself, been thinking of the Dilbian in human terms—as a very big man, a man with vast but not inconceivable strength. It is not inconceivable to strangle a giant man with a belt. But how conceivable is it to strangle a grizzly?

John was all but out of reach, stretched at arm's-length by his grip on the belt, trailing like a lamprey attached to a lake trout. But now and then the Terror's huge hand, beating back at him through the water, brushed against him. Only brushed—but each impact slammed John about like a chip in the water. His head rang. The water roared about him. His shoulder numbed to a blow and his ribs gave to another.

His senses began to fog; and he tightened his grip on the belt—for it was, in the end, kill or be killed. If he did not do for the Terror, there was no doubt the Terror would . . . do for . . . him . . .

Choking and gasping, he found his hands no longer on the belt, but clawing at the grassy edge of the pond. Hands were helping him. He pulled himself up on the slippery margin. His knees found solid ground. He coughed water and was suddenly, ungracefully sick. Then he blacked out.

He came around after an indeterminate time to find his head in someone's lap. He blinked upward and a blur of color slowly turned into the face of Ty Lamorc, very white and taut—and crying.

"What?" he croaked.

"Oh, shut up!" she said. She was wiping his damp face with a rag of cloth that was nearly as wet as he was.

"No—" he managed. "I mean—what're *you* doing here?" He tried to sit up.

"Lie down!"

"I'm all right—I think." He struggled into sitting position. The whole area of Glen Hollow, he saw, was aswarm with Dilbians. A short way off, a knot of them were gathered on the pool-bank around something.

"What—?" he began.

"The Terror, Half Pint," said a familiar voice, and he looked up at the looming figure of the Hill Bluffer, mountainous from this angle. "He's still out. It's your fight, all right." He went off, and they could hear him informing the other group down the bank that the Shorty was up and talking.

John Tardy looked at Ty.

"What happened?" he asked.

"They had to pull him out. You made it to shore by yourself." She found a handkerchief somewhere, wiped her eyes and blew her nose vigorously. "You were wonderful."

"*Wonderful?*" said John, still too groggy for subtlety. "I was out of my head to even think of it!" He felt his ribs gingerly. "I better get back to Humrog and have an X-ray of this side."

"Oh, are your ribs broken?"

"Maybe just bruised. Wow!" said John, coming on an especially tender spot.

"Oh!" wept Ty. "You might have been killed! And it's all my fault!"

"Your fault?" said John. He spotted the massive figure of One Man break-ing away from the group around the fallen Terror and hissed quickly at her. "Hurry. Help me up." She assisted him clumsily to his feet. "Tell me, did they find anything around the Terror's neck when they pulled him out?"

She stared at him and wiped her eyes. "Why, no. What should they find around his neck?"

"Nothing," whispered John. "Well!" he said as One Man rolled up to a halt before them. "What do *you* think of the situation?"

"I think, Half Pint," said One Man, "that it's all very interesting. Very in-teresting indeed. I think you Shorties may be getting a few takers now on this business of going off into the sky and learning things."

"You do, eh? How about you, for one?"

"No-o," said One Man slowly. "No, I don't think me. I'm a little too old to jump at new things that quick. Some of the young ones'll be ready, though. The Terror, for one, possibly. He's quite a bright lad, you know. Of course, now that you've done the preliminary spadework, I may put in a good word for you people here and there."

"Mighty nice of you—*now*," said John, a little bitterly.

"Nothing wins like a winner, Half Pint," rumbled One Man. "You Shorties should have known that. Matter of fact, I'm surprised it took you so long to show some common sense. You just don't come in and sit down at a man's table and expect him to take your word for it that you're one of the family. As I said to you once before, who asked you Shorties to come here, anyway, in the first place? And what made you think we had to like you? What if, when you were a lad, some new kid moved into your village? He was half your size, but he had a whole lot of shiny new playthings you didn't have, and he came up and tapped you on the shoulder and said, 'C'mon, from now on we'll play *my* sort of game!' How'd you think *you'd* have felt?"

He eyed John shrewdly out of his hairy face.

"I see," said John, after a moment. "Then why'd you help me?"

"Me? Help you? I was as neutral as they come. What're you talking about?"

"We've got something back home called a phone directory—a book like those manuals Little Bite has down at Humrog. It's about this thick—" he measured with thumb and forefinger. "And for one of us Shorties, you'd say it was a physical impossibility to pick it up and tear it in two. But some of us can do it." He eyed One Man. "Of course, there's a trick to it."

"Well, now," said One Man judiciously, "I can believe it. Directories, thick sticks, or first-class hill-and-alley scrappers—there's a trick to handle almost any of them. Not that I'd ever favor a Shorty over any of us in the long run—don't get that idea." He looked around them. The Streamside

Terror was being helped out of the Glen and most of the crowd was already gone. "We'll have to get together for a chat one of these days, Half Pint. Well, see you in the near future, Shorties."

John Tardy wiped a damp nose with the back of his hand and stared after One Man. Then he turned to Ty Lamorc.

"Now," he said, "what'd you mean—it was all your fault?"

"It was," she said miserably. "It was all my idea. Earth knew we weren't getting through to the Dilbians, so they sent me out. And I—" she gulped— "I recommended they send out a man who conformed as nearly as possible to the Dilbian psychological profile and we'd get him mixed up in a Dilbian emotional situation—to convince them we weren't the utter little aliens we seemed to be. They've got a very unusual culture here. They really have. I never thought Boy-Is-She-Built would catch up with you and nearly kill you and take your wrist-phone away. You were supposed to be able to stay in contact with Joshua Guy so he could always rescue you from the other end."

"I see. And why," queried John, very slowly and patiently, "did you decide not to let *me* in on what was going on?"

"Because," she wailed, "I thought it would be better for you to react like the Dilbians in a natural, extroverted, uncerebral way!"

"I see," said John again. They were still standing beside the pool. He picked her up—she was quite light and slender—and threw her in. There was a shriek and a satisfying splash. John turned and walked off.

After half a dozen steps, he slowed down, turned and went back. She was clinging to the bank.

"Here," he said gruffly, extending his hand.

"Thag you," she said humbly, with her nose full of water, as he hauled her out.

Cordwainer Smith

MOTHER HITTON'S LITTUL KITTONS

The late Cordwainer Smith—in "real" life Dr. Paul M. A. Linebarger, scholar, statesman, and author of the definitive text (still taught from today) on the art of psychological warfare—was a writer of enormous talents who, from 1948 until his untimely death in 1966, produced a double-handful of some of the best short fiction this genre has ever seen—"Alpha Ralpha Boulevard," "A Planet Named Shayol," "On the Storm Planet," "The Ballad of Lost C'Mell," "The Dead Lady of Clown Town," "The Game of Rat and Dragon," "Drunkboat," "The Lady Who Sailed *The Soul,*" "Under Old Earth," "Scanners Live in Vain"—as well as a large number of lesser, but still fascinating, stories, all twisted and blended and woven into an interrelated tapestry of incredible lushness and intricacy. Smith created a baroque cosmology unrivaled even today for its scope and complexity: a millennia-spanning Future History, logically outlandish and elegantly strange, set against a vivid, richly-colored, mythically-intense universe where animals assume the shape of men, vast planoform ships whisper through multidimensional space, immense sick sheep are the most valuable objects in the universe, immortality can be bought, and the mysterious Lords of the Instrumentality rule a hunted Earth too old for history . . .

It is a cosmology that looks as evocative and bizarre today in the 1990s as it did in the 1960s—certainly for sheer sweep and daring of conceptualization, in its vision of how different and *strange* the future will be, it rivals any contemporary vision conjured up by Young Turks such as Bruce Sterling and Greg Bear, and I suspect that it is timeless. It certainly upped the ante for complexity for the Space Adventure, much as A. E. van Vogt had done in the early '50s: after Smith's exotic landscapes and societies and people, the Space Opera scenarios of most other writers seemed flat, dull, and routine by comparison.

Here Smith takes us along on a thief's desperate quest to steal eternal life, with all the money in the world for forfeit, and only the childish-sounding "littul kittons" to bar the way . . .

Cordwainer Smith's books include the novel *Norstrilia* and the collections *Space Lords*—one of the landmark collections of the genre—*The Best of Cordwainer Smith, Quest of the Three Worlds, Stardreamer, You Will Never Be the Same,* and *The Instrumentality of Mankind.* As Felix C. Forrest, he wrote two mainstream novels, *Ria* and *Carola,* and as Carmichael Smith he wrote the thriller *Atomsk.*

His most recent book is the posthumous collection *The Rediscovery of Man: The Complete Short Science Fiction of Cordwainer Smith* (NESFA Press, P.O. Box 809, Framingham, MA 07101-0203, www.nesfa.org, $24.95), a huge book which collects almost all of his short fiction, and which will certainly stand as one of the very best collections of the decade—and a book which belongs in every complete science fiction collection.

Poor communications deter theft;
good communications promote theft;
perfect communications stop theft.

—VAN BRAAM

1

The moon spun. The woman watched. Twenty-one facets had been polished at the moon's equator. Her function was to arm it. She was Mother Hitton, the weapons mistress of Old North Australia.

She was a ruddy-faced, cheerful blonde of indeterminate age. Her eyes were blue, her bosom heavy, her arms strong. She looked like a mother, but the only child she had ever had died many generations ago. Now she acted as mother to a planet, not to a person; the Norstrilians slept well because they knew she was watching. The weapons slept their long, sick sleep.

This night she glanced for the two-hundredth time at the warning bank. The bank was quiet. No danger lights shone. Yet she felt an enemy out somewhere in the universe—an enemy waiting to strike at her and her world, to snatch at the immeasurable wealth of the Norstrilians—and she snorted with impatience. *Come along, little man,* she thought. *Come along, little man, and die. Don't keep me waiting.*

She smiled when she recognized the absurdity of her own thought.

She waited for him.

And he did not know it.

He, the robber, was relaxed enough. He was Benjacomin Bozart, and was highly trained in the arts of relaxation.

No one at Sunvale, here on Ttiollé, could suspect that he was a senior warden of the Guild of Thieves, reared under the light of the starry-violet star. No one could smell the odor of Viola Siderea upon him. "Viola Siderea," the Lady Ru had said, "was once the most beautiful of worlds and it is now the most rotten. Its people were once models for mankind, and now they are thieves, liars and killers. You can smell their souls in the open day." The Lady Ru had died a long time ago. She was much respected, but she was wrong. The robber did not smell to others at all. He knew it. He was no more "wrong" than a shark approaching a school of cod. Life's nature is to live, and he had been nurtured to live as he had to live—by seeking prey.

How else could he live? Viola Siderea had gone bankrupt a long time ago, when the photonic sails had disappeared from space and the planoforming ships began to whisper their way between the stars. His ancestors had been left to die on an off-trail planet. They refused to die. Their ecology shifted and they became predators upon man, adapted by time and genetics to their deadly tasks. And he, the robber, was champion of all his people—the best of their best.

He was Benjacomin Bozart.

He had sworn to rob Old North Australia or to die in the attempt, and he had no intention of dying.

The beach at Sunvale was warm and lovely. Ttiollé was a free and casual transit planet. His weapons were luck and himself: he planned to play both well.

The Norstrilians could kill.

So could he.

At this moment, in this place, he was a happy tourist at a lovely beach. Elsewhere, elsewhen, he could become a ferret among conies, a hawk among doves.

Benjacomin Bozart, thief and warden. He did not know that someone was waiting for him. Someone who did not know his name was prepared to waken death, just for him. He was still serene.

Mother Hitton was not serene. She sensed him dimly but could not yet spot him.

One of her weapons snored. She turned it over.

A thousand stars away, Benjacomin Bozart smiled as he walked toward the beach.

2

Benjacomin felt like a tourist. His tanned face was tranquil. His proud, hooded eyes were calm. His handsome mouth, even without its charming smile, kept a suggestion of pleasantness at its corners. He looked attractive without seeming odd in the least. He looked much younger than he actually was. He walked with springy, happy steps along the beach of Sunvale.

The waves rolled in, white-crested, like the breakers of Mother Earth. The Sunvale people were proud of the way their world resembled Manhome itself. Few of them had ever seen Manhome, but they had all heard a bit of history and most of them had a passing anxiety when they thought of the ancient government still wielding political power across the depth of space. They did not like the old Instrumentality of Earth, but they respected and feared it. The waves might remind them of the pretty side of Earth; they did not want to remember the not-so-pretty side.

This man was like the pretty side of old Earth. They could not sense the power within him. The Sunvale people smiled absently at him as he walked past them along the shoreline.

The atmosphere was quiet and everything around him serene. He turned his face to the sun. He closed his eyes. He let the warm sunlight beat through his eyelids, illuminating him with its comfort and its reassuring touch.

Benjacomin dreamed of the greatest theft that any man had ever planned. He dreamed of stealing a huge load of the wealth from the richest world that mankind had ever built. He thought of what would happen when he would finally bring riches back to the planet of Viola Siderea where he had been reared. Benjacomin turned his face away from the sun and languidly looked over the other people on the beach.

There were no Norstrilians in sight yet. They were easy enough to recognize. Big people with red complexions; superb athletes and yet, in their own way, innocent, young and very tough. He had trained for this theft for two hundred years, his life prolonged for the purpose by the Guild of Thieves on Viola Siderea. He himself embodied the dreams of his own planet, a poor planet once a crossroads of commerce, now sunken to being a minor outpost for spoliation and pilferage.

He saw a Norstrilian woman come out from the hotel and go down to the beach. He waited, and he looked, and he dreamed. He had a question to ask and no adult Australian would answer it.

"Funny," thought he, "that I call them 'Australians' even now. That's the old, old Earth name for them—rich, brave, tough people. Fighting children standing on half the world . . . and now they are the tyrants of all mankind. They hold the wealth. They have the santaclara, and other people live or die depending upon the commerce they have with the Norstrilians. But I won't. And my people won't. We're men who are wolves to man."

Benjacomin waited gracefully. Tanned by the light of many suns, he looked forty though he was two hundred. He dressed casually, by the standards of a vacationer. He might have been an intercultural salesman, a senior gambler, an assistant starport manager. He might even have been a detective working along the commerce lanes. He wasn't. He was a thief. And he was so good a thief that people turned to him and put their property in his hands because he was reassuring, calm, gray-eyed, blond-haired. Benjacomin waited. The woman glanced at him, a quick glance full of open suspicion.

What she saw must have calmed her. She went on past. She called back over the dune, "Come on, Johnny, we can swim out here." A little boy, who looked eight or ten years old, came over the dune top, running toward his mother.

Benjacomin tensed like a cobra. His eyes became sharp, his eyelids narrowed.

This was the prey. Not too young, not too old. If the victim had been too young he wouldn't know the answer; if the victim were too old it was no use taking him on. Norstrilians were famed in combat; adults were mentally and physically too strong to warrant attack.

Benjacomin knew that every thief who had approached the planet of the Norstrilians—who had tried to raid the dream world of Old North Australia—had gotten out of contact with his people and had died. There was no word of any of them.

And yet he knew that hundreds of thousands of Norstrilians must know *the* secret. They now and then made jokes about it. He had heard these jokes when he was a young man, and now he was more than an old man without once coming near the answer. Life was expensive. He was well into his third lifetime and the lifetimes had been purchased honestly by his people. Good thieves all of them, paying out hard-stolen money to obtain the medicine to let their greatest thief remain living. Benjacomin didn't like violence. But when violence prepared the way to the greatest theft of all time, he was willing to use it.

The woman looked at him again. The mask of evil which had flashed across his face faded into benignity; he calmed. She caught him in that moment of relaxation. She liked him.

She smiled and, with that awkward hesitation so characteristic of the Norstrilians, she said, "Could you mind my boy a bit while I go in the water? I think we've seen each other here at the hotel."

"I don't mind," said he. "I'd be glad to. Come here, son."

Johnny walked across the sunlight dunes to his own death. He came within reach of his mother's enemy.

But the mother had already turned.

The trained hand of Benjacomin Bozart reached out. He seized the child by the shoulder. He turned the boy toward him, forcing him down. Before the child could cry out, Benjacomin had the needle into him with the truth drug.

All Johnny reacted to was pain, and then a hammerblow inside his own skull as the powerful drug took force.

Benjacomin looked out over the water. The mother was swimming. She seemed to be looking back at them. She was obviously unworried. To her, the child seemed to be looking at something the stranger was showing him in a relaxed, easy way.

"Now, sonny," said Benjacomin, "tell me, what's the outside defense?" The boy didn't answer.

"What is the outer defense, sonny? What is the outer defense?" repeated Benjacomin. The boy still didn't answer.

Something close to horror ran over the skin of Benjacomin Bozart as he realized that he had gambled his safety on this planet, gambled the plans themselves for a chance to break the secret of the Norstrilians.

He had been stopped by simple, easy devices. The child had already been conditioned against attack. Any attempt to force knowledge out of the child brought on a conditioned reflex of total muteness. The boy was literally unable to talk.

Sunlight gleaming on her wet hair, the mother turned around and called back, "Are you all right, Johnny?"

Benjacomin waved to her instead. "I'm showing him my pictures, ma'am. He likes 'em. Take your time." The mother hesitated and then turned back to the water and swam slowly away.

Johnny, taken by the drug, sat lightly, like an invalid, on Benjacomin's lap.

Benjacomin said, "Johnny, you're going to die now and you will hurt terribly if you don't tell me what I want to know." The boy struggled weakly against his grasp. Benjacomin repeated. "I'm going to hurt you if you don't tell me what I want to know. What are the outer defenses? What are the outer defenses?"

The child struggled and Benjacomin realized that the boy was putting up a fight to comply with the orders, not a fight to get away. He let the child slip through his hands and the boy put out a finger and began writing on the wet sand. The letters stood out.

A man's shadow loomed behind them.

Benjacomin, alert, ready to spin, kill or run, slipped to the ground beside the child and said, "That's a jolly puzzle. That is a good one. Show me some more." He smiled up at the passing adult. The man was a stranger. The stranger gave him a very curious glance which became casual when he saw the pleasant face of Benjacomin, so tenderly and so agreeably playing with the child.

The fingers were still making the letters in the sand.

There stood the riddle in letters: MOTHER HITTON'S LITTUL KITTONS.

The woman was coming back from the sea, the mother with questions. Benjacomin stroked the sleeve of his coat and brought out his second needle, a shallow poison which it would take days or weeks of laboratory work to detect. He thrust it directly into the boy's brain, slipping the needle up behind the skin at the edge of the hairline. The hair shadowed the tiny prick. The incredibly hard needle slipped under the edge of the skull. The child was dead.

Murder was accomplished. Benjacomin casually erased the secret from the sand. The woman came nearer. He called to her, his voice full of pleasant concern, "Ma'am, you'd better come here, I think your son has fainted from the heat."

He gave the mother the body of her son. Her face changed to alarm. She looked frightened and alert. She didn't know how to meet this.

For a dreadful moment she looked into his eyes.

Two hundred years of training took effect . . . She saw nothing. The murderer did not shine with murder. The hawk was hidden beneath the dove. The heart was masked by the trained face.

Benjacomin relaxed in professional assurance. He had been prepared to kill her too, although he was not sure that he could kill an adult, female Norstrilian. Very helpfully said he, "You stay here with him. I'll run to the hotel and get help. I'll hurry."

He turned and ran. A beach attendant saw him and ran toward him. "The child's sick," he shouted. He came to the mother in time to see blunt, puzzled tragedy on her face and with it, something more than tragedy: doubt.

"He's not sick," said she. "He's dead."

"He can't be." Benjacomin looked attentive. He felt attentive. He forced the sympathy to pour out of his posture, out of all the little muscles of his face. "He can't be. I was talking to him just a minute ago. We were doing little puzzles in the sand."

The mother spoke with a hollow, broken voice that sounded as though it would never find the right chords for human speech again, but would go on forever with the ill-attuned flats of unexpected grief. "He's dead," she said. "You saw him die and I guess I saw him die, too. I can't tell what's happened. The child was full of santaclara. He had a thousand years to live but now he's dead. What's your name?"

Benjacomin said, "Eldon. Eldon the salesman, ma'am. I live here lots of times."

3

"Mother Hitton's littul kittons. Mother Hitton's littul kittons."

The silly phrase ran in his mind. Who was Mother Hitton? Who was she the mother of? What were *kittons*? Were they a misspelling for "kittens?" Little cats? Or were they something else?

Had he killed a fool to get a fool's answer?

How many more days did he have to stay there with the doubtful, staggered woman? How many days did he have to watch and wait? He wanted to get back to Viola Siderea; to take the secret, bad as it was, for his people to study. Who was Mother Hitton?

He forced himself out of his room and went downstairs.

The pleasant monotony of a big hotel was such that the other guests looked interestedly at him. He was the man who had watched while the child died on the beach.

Some lobby-living scandalmongers that stayed there had made up fantastic stories that he had killed the child. Others attacked the stories, saying they knew perfectly well who Eldon was. He was Eldon the salesman. It was ridiculous.

People hadn't changed much, even though the ships with the Go-captains sitting at their hearts whispered between the stars, even though people shuffled between worlds—when they had the money to pay their passage back and forth—like leaves falling in soft, playful winds. Benjacomin faced a tragic dilemma. He knew very well that any attempt to decode the answer would run directly into the protective devices set up by the Norstrilians.

Old North Australia was immensely wealthy. It was known the length and breadth of all the stars that they had hired mercenaries, defensive spies, hidden agents and alerting devices.

Even Manhome—Mother Earth herself, whom no money could buy—was bribed by the drug of life. An ounce of the santaclara drug, reduced, crystallized and called "stroon," could give forty to sixty years of life. Stroon entered the rest of the Earth by ounces and pounds, but it was refined back on North Australia by the ton. With treasure like this, the Norstrilians owned an unimaginable world whose resources overreached all conceivable limits of money. They could buy anything. They could pay with other peoples' lives.

For hundreds of years they had given secret funds to buying foreigners' services to safeguard their own security.

Benjacomin stood there in the lobby: "Mother Hitton's littul kittons."

He had all the wisdom and wealth of a thousand worlds stuck in his mind but he didn't dare ask anywhere as to what it meant.

Suddenly he brightened.

He looked like a man who had thought of a good game to play, a pleasant diversion to be welcomed, a companion to be remembered, a new food to be tasted. He had had a very happy thought.

There was one source that wouldn't talk. The library. He could at least check the obvious, simple things, and find out what there was already in the realm of public knowledge concerning the secret he had taken from the dying boy.

His own safety had not been wasted, Johnny's life had not been thrown away, if he could find any one of the four words as a key. *Mother* or *Hitton* or *Littul*, in its special meaning, or *Kitton*. He might yet break through to the loot of Norstrilia.

He swung jubilantly, turning on the ball of his right foot. He moved lightly and pleasantly toward the billiard room, beyond which lay the library. He went in.

This was a very expensive hotel and very old-fashioned. It even had books made out of paper, with genuine bindings. Benjacomin crossed the room. He saw that they had the *Galactic Encyclopedia* in two hundred volumes. He took down the volume headed "Hi-Hi." He opened it from the rear, looking for the name "Hitton" and there it was. "Hitton, Benjamin— pioneer of old North Australia. Said to be originator of part of the defense system. Lived A.D. 10719–17213." That was all. Benjacomin moved among the books. The word "kittons" in that peculiar spelling did not occur anywhere, neither in the encyclopedia nor in any other list maintained by the library. He walked out and upstairs, back to his room.

"Littul" had not appeared at all. It was probably the boy's own childish mistake.

He took a chance. The mother, half blind with bewilderment and worry, sat in a stiff-backed chair on the edge of the porch. The other women talked to her. They knew her husband was coming. Benjacomin went up to her and tried to pay his respects. She didn't see him.

"I'm leaving now, ma'am. I'm going on to the next planet, but I'll be back in two or three subjective weeks. And if you need me for urgent questions, I'll leave my addresses with the police here."

Benjacomin left the weeping mother.

Benjacomin left the quiet hotel. He obtained a priority passage.

The easy-going Sunvale Police made no resistance to his demand for a sudden departure visa. After all, he had an identity, he had his own funds, and it was not the custom of Sunvale to contradict its guests. Benjacomin went on the ship and as he moved toward the cabin in which he could rest for a few hours, a man stepped up beside him. A youngish man, hair parted in the middle, short of stature, gray of eyes.

This man was the local agent of the Norstrilian secret police.

Benjacomin, trained thief that he was, did not recognize the policeman. It never occurred to him that the library itself had been attuned and that the word "kittons" in the peculiar Norstrilian spelling was itself an alert. Looking for that spelling had set off a minor alarm. He had touched the trip-wire.

The stranger nodded. Benjacomin nodded back. "I'm a traveling man, waiting over between assignments. I haven't been doing very well. How are you making out?"

"Doesn't matter to me. I don't earn money; I'm a technician. Liverant is the name."

Benjacomin sized him up. The man was a technician all right. They shook hands perfunctorily. Liverant said, "I'll join you in the bar a little later. I think I'll rest a bit first."

They both lay down then and said very little while the momentary flash of planoform went through the ship. The flash passed. From books and lessons they knew that the ship was leaping forward in two dimensions while, somehow or other, the fury of space itself was fed into the computers—and that these in turn were managed by the Go-captain who controlled the ship.

They knew these things but they could not feel them. All they felt was the sting of a slight pain.

The sedative was in the air itself, sprayed in the ventilating system. They both expected to become a little drunk.

The thief Benjacomin Bozart was trained to resist intoxication and bewilderment. Any sign whatever that a telepath had tried to read his mind would have been met with fierce animal resistance, implanted in his unconscious during early years of training. Bozart was not trained against deception by a technician; it never occurred to the Thieves' Guild back on Viola Siderea that it would be necessary for their own people to resist deceivers. Liverant had already been in touch with Norstrilia—Norstrilia whose money reached across the stars, Norstrilia who had alerted a hundred thousand worlds against the mere thought of trespass.

Liverant began to chatter. "I wish I could go further than this trip. I wish that I could go to Olympia. You can buy anything in Olympia."

"I've heard of it," said Bozart. "It's sort of a funny trading planet with not much chance for businessmen, isn't it?"

Liverant laughed and his laughter was merry and genuine. "Trading? They don't trade. They swap. They take all the stolen loot of a thousand worlds and sell it over again and they change and they paint it and they mark it. That's their business there. The people are blind. It's a strange world, and all you have to do is to go in there and you can have anything you want. Man," said Liverant, "what I could do in a year in that place! Everybody is blind except me and a couple of tourists. And there's all the wealth that everybody thought he's mislaid, half the wrecked ships, the forgotten colonies (they've all been cleaned out) and bang! it all goes to Olympia."

Olympia wasn't really that good and Liverant didn't know why it was his business to guide the killer there. All he knew was that he had a duty and the duty was to direct the trespasser.

Many years before either man was born the code word had been planted in directories, in books, in packing cases and invoices: *Kittons* misspelled. This was the cover name for the outer moon of Norstrilian defense. The use of the cover name brought a raging alert ready into action, with systemic nerves as hot and quick as incandescent tungsten wire.

By the time that they were ready to go to the bar and have refreshments, Benjacomin had half forgotten that it was his new acquaintance who had suggested Olympia rather than another place. He had to go to Viola Siderea to get the credits to make the flight to take the wealth, to win the world of Olympia.

4

At home on his native planet Bozart was a subject of a gentle but very sincere celebration.

The elders of the Guild of Thieves welcomed him. They congratulated him. "Who else could have done what you've done, boy? You've made the opening move in a brand new game of chess. There has never been a gambit like this before. We have a name; we have an animal. We'll try it right here." The Thieves' Council turned to their own encyclopedia. They turned through the name "Hitton" and then found the reference "kitton." None of them knew that a false lead had been planted there—by an agent in their world.

The agent, in his turn, had been seduced years before, debauched in the middle of his career, forced into temporary honesty, blackmailed and sent home. In all the years that he had waited for a dreaded countersign—a countersign which he himself never knew to be an extension of Norstrilian intelligence—he never dreamed that he could pay his debt to the outside world so simply. All they had done was to send him one page to add to the encyclopedia. He added it and then went home, weak with exhaustion. The years of fear and waiting were almost too much for the thief. He drank heavily for fear that he might otherwise kill himself. Meanwhile, the pages remained in order, including the new one, slightly altered for his colleagues. The encyclopedia indicated the change like any normal revision, though the whole entry was new and falsified:

Beneath this passage one revision ready. Dated 24th year of second issue. The reported "Kittons" of Norstrilia are nothing more than the use of organic means to induce the disease in Earth-mutated sheep which produces a virus in its turn, refinable as the santaclara drug. The term "Kittons" enjoyed a temporary vogue as a reference term both to the disease and to the destructibility of the disease in the event of external attack. This is believed to have been connected with the career of Benjamin Hitton, one of the original pioneers of Norstrilia.

The Council of Thieves read it and the Chairman of the Council said, "I've got your papers ready. You can go try them now. Where do you want to go? Through Neuhamburg?"

"No," said Benjacomin. "I thought I'd try Olympia."

"Olympia's all right," said the chairman. "Go easy. There's only one chance in a thousand you'll fail. But if you do, we might have to pay for it."

He smiled wryly and handed Benjacomin a blank mortgage against all the labor and all the property of Viola Siderea.

The Chairman laughed with a sort of snort. "It'd be pretty rough on us if you had to borrow enough on the trading planet to force us to become honest—and then lost out anyhow."

"No fear," said Benjacomin. "I can cover that."

There are some worlds where all dreams die, but square-clouded Olympia is not one of them. The eyes of men and women are bright on Olympia, for they see nothing.

"Brightness was the color of pain," said Nachtigall, "when we could see. If thine eye offend thee, pluck thyself out, for the fault lies not in the eye but in the soul."

Such talk was common in Olympia, where the settlers went blind a long time ago and now think themselves superior to sighted people. Radar wires tickle their living brains; they can perceive radiation as well as can an animal-type man with little aquariums hung in the middle of his face. Their pictures are sharp, and they demand sharpness. Their buildings soar at impossible angles. Their blind children sing songs as the tailored climate proceeds according to the numbers, geometrical as a kaleidoscope.

There went the man, Bozart himself. Among the blind his dreams soared, and he paid money for information which no living person had ever seen.

Sharp-clouded and aqua-skied, Olympia swam past him like another man's dream. He did not mean to tarry there, because he had a rendezvous with death in the sticky, sparky space around Norstrilia.

Once in Olympia, Benjacomin went about his arrangements for the attack on Old North Australia. On his second day on the planet he had been very lucky. He met a man named Lavender and he was sure he had heard the name before. Not a member of his own Guild of Thieves, but a daring rascal with a bad reputation among the stars.

It was no wonder that he had found Lavender. His pillow had told him Lavender's story fifteen times during his sleep in the past week. And, whenever he dreamed, he dreamed dreams which had been planted in his mind by the Norstrilian counterintelligence. They had beaten him in getting to Olympia first and they were prepared to let him have only that which he deserved. The Norstrilian Police were not cruel, but they were out to defend their world. And they were also out to avenge the murder of a child.

The last interview which Benjacomin had with Lavender in striking a bargain before Lavender agreed was a dramatic one.

Lavender refused to move forward.

"I'm not going to jump off anywhere. I'm not going to raid anything. I'm not going to steal anything. I've been rough, of course I have. But I don't get myself killed and that's what you're bloody well asking for."

"Think of what we'll have. The wealth. I tell you, there's more money here than anything else anybody's ever tried."

Lavender laughed. "You think I haven't heard that before? You're a crook and I'm a crook. I don't do anything that's speculation. I want my hard cash down. I'm a fighting man and you're a thief and I'm not going to ask you what you're up to . . . but I want my money first."

"I haven't got it," said Benjacomin.

Lavender stood up.

"Then you shouldn't have talked to me. Because it's going to cost you money to keep me quiet whether you hire me or not."

The bargaining process started.

Lavender looked ugly indeed. He was a soft, ordinary man who had gone to a lot of trouble to become evil. Sin is a lot of work. The sheer effort it requires often shows in the human face.

Bozart stared him down, smiling easily, not even contemptuously.

"Cover me while I get something from my pocket," said Bozart.

Lavender did not even acknowledge the comment. He did not show a weapon. His left thumb moved slowly across the outer edge of his hand. Benjacomin recognized the sign, but did not flinch.

"See," he said. "A planetary credit."

Lavender laughed. "I've heard that, too."

"Take it," said Bozart.

The adventurer took the laminated card. His eyes widened. "It's real," he breathed. "It is real." He looked up, incalculably more friendly. "I never even saw one of these before. What are your terms?"

Meanwhile the bright, vivid Olympians walked back and forth past them, their clothing all white and black in dramatic contrast. Unbelievable geometric designs shone on their cloaks and their hats. The two bargainers ignored the natives. They concentrated on their own negotiations.

Benjacomin felt fairly safe. He placed a pledge of one year's service of the entire planet of Viola Siderea in exchange for the full and unqualified services of Captain Lavender, once of the Imperial Marines Internal Space Patrol. He handed over the mortgage. The year's guarantee was written in. Even on Olympia there were accounting machines which relayed the bargain back to Earth itself, making the mortgage a valid and binding commitment against the whole planet of thieves.

"This," thought Lavender, "was the first step of revenge." After the killer had disappeared his people would have to pay with sheer honesty. Lavender looked at Banjacomin with a clinical sort of concern.

Benjacomin mistook his look for friendliness and Benjacomin smiled his slow, charming, easy smile. Momentarily happy, he reached out his right hand to give Lavender a brotherly solemnification of the bargain. The men shook hands, and Bozart never knew with what he shook hands.

5

"Gray lay the land oh. Gray grass from sky to sky. Not near the weir, dear. Not a mountain, low or high—only hills and gray gray. Watch the dappled, dimpled twinkles blooming on the star bar.

"That is Norstrilia.

"All the muddy gubbery is gone—all the work and the waiting and the pain.

"Beige-brown sheep lie on blue-gray grass while the clouds rush past, low overhead, like iron pipes ceilinging the world.

"Take your pick of sick sheep, man, it's the sick that pays. Sneeze me a planet, man, or cough me up a spot of immortality. If it's barmy there, where the noddies and the trolls like you live, it's too right here.

"That's the book, boy.

"If you haven't seen Norstrilia, you haven't seen it. If you did see it, you wouldn't believe it.

"Charts call it Old North Australia."

Here in the heart of the world was the farm which guarded the world. This was the Hitton place.

Towers surrounded it, and wires hung between the towers, some of them drooping crazily and some gleaming with the sheen not shown by any other metal made by men from Earth. Within the towers there was open land. And within the open land there were twelve thousand hectares of concrete. Radar reached down to within millimeter smoothness of the surface of the concrete and the other radar threw patterns back and forth, down through molecular thinness. The farm went on. In its center there was a group of buildings. That was where Katherine Hitton worked on the task which her family had accepted for the defense of her world.

No germ came in, no germ went out. All the food came in by space transmitter. Within this, there lived animals. The animals depended on her alone. Were she to die suddenly, by mischance or as a result of an attack by one of the animals, the authorities of her world had complete facsimiles of herself with which to train new animal tenders under hypnosis.

This was a place where the gray wind leapt forward released from the hills, where it raced across the gray concrete, where it blew past the radar towers. The polished, faceted, captive moon always hung due overhead. The wind hit the buildings, themselves gray, with the impact of a blow, before it raced over the open concrete beyond and whistled away into the hills.

Outside the buildings, the valley had not needed much camouflage. It looked like the rest of Norstrilia. The concrete itself was tinted very slightly to give the impression of poor, starved, natural soil. This was the farm, and this the woman. Together they were the outer defense of the richest world mankind had ever built.

Katherine Hitton looked out the window and thought to herself, "Forty-two days before I go to market and it's a welcome day that I get there and hear the jig of a music.

Oh, to walk on market day,
And see my people proud and gay!

She breathed deeply of the air. She loved the gray hills—though in her youth she had seen many other worlds. And then she turned back into the building to the animals and the duties which awaited her. She was the only Mother Hitton and these were her littul kittons.

She moved among them. She and her father had bred them from Earth mink, from the fiercest, smallest, craziest little minks that had ever been shipped out from Manhome. Out of these minks they had made their lives to keep away other predators who might bother the sheep on whom the stroon grew. But these minks were born mad.

Generations of them had been bred psychotic to the bone. They lived only to die and they died so that they could stay alive. These were the kittons of Norstrilia. Animals in whom fear, rage, hunger and sex were utterly intermixed; who could eat themselves or each other; who could eat their young, or people, or anything organic; animals who screamed with murder-lust when they felt love; animals born to loathe themselves with a fierce and livid hate and who survived only because their waking moments were spent on couches, strapped tight, claw by claw, so that they could not hurt each other or themselves. Mother Hitton let them waken only a few moments in each lifetime. They bred and killed. She wakened them only two at a time.

All that afternoon she moved from cage to cage. The sleeping animals slept well. The nourishment ran into their blood streams; they lived sometimes for years without awaking. She bred them when the males were only partly awakened and the females aroused only enough to accept her veterinary treatments. She herself had to pluck the young away from their mothers as the sleeping mothers begot them. Then she nourished the young through a few happy weeks of kittonhood, until their adult natures began to take, their eyes ran red with madness and heat and their emotions sounded in the sharp, hideous, little cries they uttered through the building; and the twisting of their neat, furry faces, the rolling of their crazy, bright eyes and the tightening of their sharp, sharp claws.

She woke none of them this time. Instead, she tightened them in their straps. She removed the nutrients. She gave them delayed stimulus medicine which would, when they were awakened, bring them suddenly full waking with no lulled stupor first.

Finally, she gave herself a heavy sedative, leaned back in a chair and waited for the call which would come.

When the shock came and the call came through, she would have to do what she had done thousands of times before.

She would ring an intolerable noise through the whole laboratory.

Hundreds of the mutated minks would awaken. In awakening, they would plunge into life with hunger, with hate, with rage and with sex; plunge against their straps; strive to kill each other, their young, themselves, her. They would fight everything and everywhere, and do everything they could to keep going.

She knew this.

In the middle of the room there was a tuner. The tuner was a direct, emphatic relay, capable of picking up the simpler range of telepathic communications. Into this tuner went the concentrated emotions of Mother Hitton's littul kittons.

The rage, the hate, the hunger, the sex were all carried far beyond the limits of the tolerable, and then all were thereupon amplified. And then the waveband on which this telepathic control went out was amplified, right there beyond the studio, on the high towers that swept the mountain ridge, up and beyond the valley in which the laboratory lay. And Mother Hitton's moon, spinning geometrically, bounced the relay into a hollow englobement.

From the faceted moon, it went to the satellites—sixteen of them, apparently part of the weather control system. These blanketed not only space, but nearby subspace. The Nostrilians had thought of everything.

The short shocks of an alert came from Mother Hitton's transmitter bank.

A call came. Her thumb went numb.

The noise shrieked.

The mink awakened.

Immediately, the room was full of chattering, scraping, hissing, growling and howling.

Under the sound of the animal voices, there was the other sound: a scratchy, snapping sound like hail falling on a frozen lake. It was the individual claws of hundreds of mink trying to tear their way through metal panels.

Mother Hitton heard a gurgle. One of the minks had succeeded in tearing its paw loose and had obviously started to work on its own throat. She recognized the tearing fur, the ripping of veins.

She listened for the cessation of that individual voice, but she couldn't be sure. The others were making too much noise. One mink less.

Where she sat, she was partly shielded from the telepathic relay, but not altogether. She herself, old as she was, felt queer wild dreams go through her. She thrilled with hate as she thought of beings suffering out beyond her—suffering terribly, since they were not masked by the built-in defenses of the Norstrilian communications system.

She felt the wild throb of long-forgotten lust.

She hungered for things she had not known she remembered. She went through the spasms of fear that the hundreds of animals expressed.

Underneath this, her sane mind kept asking, "How much longer can I take it? How much longer must I take it? Lord God, be good to your people here on this world! Be good to poor old me."

The green light went on.

She pressed a button on the other side of her chair. The gas hissed in. As she passed into unconsciousness, she knew that her kittons passed into instant unconsciousness too.

She would waken before they did and then her duties would begin: checking the living ones, taking out the one that had clawed out its own throat, taking out those who had died of heart attacks, re-arranging them, dressing their wounds, treating them alive and asleep—asleep and happy—breeding, living in their sleep—until the next call should come to waken them for the defense of the treasures which blessed and cursed her native world.

6

Everything had gone exactly right. Lavender had found an illegal planoform ship. This was no inconsequential accomplishment, since planoform ships were very strictly licensed and obtaining an illegal one was a chore on which a planet full of crooks could easily have worked a lifetime.

Lavender had been lavished with money—Benjacomin's money.

The honest wealth of the thieves' planet had gone in and had paid the falsifications and great debts, imaginary transactions that were fed to the computers for ships and cargoes and passengers that would be almost untraceably commingled in the commerce of ten thousand worlds.

"Let him pay for it," said Lavender, to one of his confederates, an apparent criminal who was also a Norstrilian agent. "This is paying good money for bad. You better spend a lot of it."

Just before Benjacomin took off Lavender sent on an additional message.

He sent it directly through the Go-captain, who usually did not carry messages. The Go-captain was a relay commander of the Norstrilian fleet, but he had been carefully ordered not to look like it.

The message concerned the planform license—another twenty-odd tablets of stroon which could mortgage Viola Siderea for hundreds upon hundreds of years. The captain said: "I don't have to send that through. The answer is yes."

Benjacomin came into the control room. This was contrary to regulations, but he had hired the ship to violate regulations.

The captain looked at him sharply. "You're a passenger, get out."

Benjacomin said: "You have my little yacht on board. I am the only man here outside of your people."

"Get out. There's a fine if you're caught here."

"It does not matter," Benjacomin said. "I'll pay it."

"You will, will you?" said the Captain. "You would not be paying twenty tablets of stroon. That's ridiculous. Nobody could get that much stroon."

Benjacomin laughed, thinking of the thousands of tablets he would soon have. All he had to do was to leave the planform ship behind, strike once, go past the kittons and come back.

His power and his wealth came from the fact that he knew he could now reach it. The mortgage of twenty tablets of stroon against this planet was a low price to pay if it would pay off at thousands to one. The Captain replied: "It's not worth it, it just is not worth risking twenty tablets for your being here. But I can tell you how to get inside the Norstrilian communications net if that is worth twenty-seven tablets."

Benjacomin went tense.

For a moment he thought he might die. All this work, all this training— the dead boy on the beach, the gamble with the credit, and now this unsuspected antagonist!

He decided to face it out. "What do you know?" said Benjacomin.

"Nothing," said the Captain.

"You said 'Norstrilia.'"

"That I did," said the Captain.

"If you said Norstrilia, you must have guessed it. Who told you?"

"Where else would a man go if you look for infinite riches? If you get away with it. Twenty tablets is nothing to a man like you."

"It's two hundred years' worth of work from three hundred thousand people," said Benjacomin grimly.

"When you get away with it, you will have more than twenty tablets, and so will your people."

And Benjacomin thought of the thousands and thousands of tablets. "Yes, that I know."

"If you don't get away with it, you've got the card."

"That's right. All right. Get me inside the net. I'll pay the twenty-seven tablets."

"Give me the card."

Benjacomin refused. He was a trained thief, and he was alert to thievery. Then he thought again. This was the crisis of his life. He had to gamble a little on somebody.

He had to wager the card. "I'll mark it and then I'll give it back to you." Such was his excitement that Benjacomin did not notice that the card went into a duplicator, that the transaction was recorded, that the message went back to Olympic Center, that the loss and the mortgage against the planet of Viola Siderea should be credited to certain commercial agencies in Earth for three hundred years to come.

Benjacomin got the card back. He felt like an honest thief.

If he did die, the card would be lost and his people would not have to pay. If he won, he could pay that little bit out of his own pocket.

Benjacomin sat down. The Go-captain signalled to his pinlighters. The ship lurched.

For half a subjective hour they moved, the Captain wearing a helmet of space upon his head, sensing and grasping and guessing his way, stepping stone to stepping stone, right back to his home. He had to fumble the passage, or else Benjacomin might guess that he was in the hands of double agents.

But the captain was well trained. Just as well trained as Benjacomin.

Agents and thieves, they rode together.

They planoformed inside the communications net. Benjacomin shook hands with them. "You are allowed to materialize as soon as I call."

"Good luck, Sir," said the Captain.

"Good luck to me," said Benjacomin.

He climbed into his space yacht. For less than a second in real space, the gray expanse of Norstrilia loomed up. The ship which looked like a simple warehouse disappeared into planoform, and the yacht was on its own.

The yacht dropped.

As it dropped, Benjacomin had a hideous moment of confusion and terror.

He never knew the woman down below but she sensed him plainly as he received the wrath of the much-amplified kittons. His conscious mind quivered under the blow. With a prolongation of subjective experience which made one or two seconds seem like months of hurt drunken bewilderment, Benjacomin Bozart swept beneath the tide of his own personality. The moon relay threw minkish minds against him. The synapses of his brain reformed to conjure up might-have-beens, terrible things that never happened to any man. Then his knowing mind whited out in an overload of stress.

His subcortical personality lived on a little longer.

His body fought for several minutes. Mad with lust and hunger, the body arched in the pilot's seat, the mouth bit deep into his own arm. Driven by lust, the left hand tore at his face, ripping out his left eyeball. He screeched with animal lust as he tried to devour himself . . . not entirely without success.

The overwhelming telepathic message of Mother Hitton's littul kittons ground into his brain.

The mutated minks were fully awake.

The relay satellites had poisoned all the space around him with the craziness to which the minks were bred.

Bozart's body did not live long. After a few minutes, the arteries were open, the head slumped forward and the yacht was dropping helplessly toward the warehouses which it had meant to raid. Norstrilian police picked it up.

The police themselves were ill. All of them were ill. All of them were white-faced. Some of them had vomited. They had gone through the edge of the mink defense. They had passed through the telepathic band at its thinnest and weakest point. This was enough to hurt them badly.

They did not want to know.

They wanted to forget.

One of the younger policemen looked at the body and said, "What on earth could do that to a man?"

"He picked the wrong job," said the police captain.

The young policeman said: "What's the wrong job?"

"The wrong job is trying to rob us, boy. We are defended, and we don't want to know how."

The young policeman, humiliated and on the verge of anger, looked almost as if he would defy his superior, while keeping his eyes away from the body of Benjacomin Bozart.

The older man said: "It's all right. He did not take long to die and this is the man who killed the boy Johnny, not very long ago."

"Oh, him? So soon?"

"We brought him." The old police officer nodded. "We let him find his death. That's how we live. Tough, isn't it?"

The ventilators whispered softly, gently. The animals slept again. A jet of air poured down on Mother Hitton. The telepathic relay was still on. She could feel herself, the sheds, the faceted moon, the little satellites. Of the robber there was no sign.

She stumbled to her feet. Her raiment was moist with perspiration. She needed a shower and fresh clothes . . .

Back at Manhome, the Commercial Credit Circuit called shrilly for human attention. A junior subchief of the Instrumentality walked over to the machine and held out his hand.

The machine dropped a card neatly into his fingers.

He looked at the card.

"Debit Viola Siderea—credit Earth Contingency—subcredit Norstrilian account—four hundred million man megayears."

Though all alone, he whistled to himself in the empty room. "We'll all be dead, stroon or no stroon, before they finish paying that!" He went off to tell his friends the odd news.

The machine, not getting its card back, made another one.

Brian W. Aldiss

A KIND OF ARTISTRY

In many ways, Brian W. Aldiss was the *enfant terrible* of the late '50s, exploding into the science fiction world and shaking it up with the ferocious verve and pyrotechnic verbal brilliance of stories like "Poor Little Warrior," "Outside," "The New Father Christmas," "Who Can Replace a Man?", "A Kind of Artistry," and "Old Hundredth," and with the somber beauty and unsettling poetic vision—in the main, of a world where Mankind signally has *not* triumphantly conquered the universe, as the Campbellian dogma of the time insisted that he would—of his classic novels *Starship* and *The Long Afternoon of Earth* (*Non-Stop* and *Hothouse* respectively, in Britain). All this made him one of the most controversial writers of the day . . . and, some years later, he'd be one of the most controversial figures of the New Wave era as well, shaking up the SF world of the mid-'60s in an even more dramatic and drastic fashion with the ferociously Joycean "acid-head war" stories that would be melded into *Barefoot in the Head,* with the irreverent *Cryptozoic!,* and with his surrealistic anti-novel *Report on Probability A.*

But Aldiss has never been willing to work any one patch of ground for very long. By 1976, he had worked his way through two controversial British mainstream bestsellers—*The Hand-Reared Boy* and *A Soldier Erect*—and the strange transmuted Gothic of *Frankenstein Unbound,* and gone on to produce a lyrical masterpiece of science-fantasy, *The Malacia Tapestry,* one of his best books, and certainly one of the best novels of the '70s. Ahead, in the decade of the '80s, was the monumental accomplishment of his *Helliconia* trilogy—*Helliconia Spring, Helliconia Summer,* and *Helliconia Winter*—and by the end of that decade only the grumpiest of reactionary critics could deny that Aldiss was one of the true giants of the field, a figure of artistic complexity and amazing vigor, as much on the Cutting Edge in the '90s as he had been in the '50s.

Although his restless, ambitious work, always evolving and looking for new horizons to pioneer, has often taken him far from the purview of the standard SF adventure tale, Aldiss has clearly retained a deep fondness for Space Opera of the most primordial, planet-busting, swashbuckling sort. As an editor, he has produced some of the key retrospective anthologies of the form, including *Space Opera, Space Odysseys, Evil Earths, All About Venus,* and the two-volume *Galactic Empires.* As a writer, although it's a bit off the mainline of development for Space Opera, Aldiss's monumental *The Long Afternoon of Earth* remains one of the classic visions of the distant future of Earth, and certainly is a foundation-stone of the subgenre of science-fantasy, which is at least cousin-germane to

Space Opera, and sometimes close enough that any perceivable differences between the two are almost subliminal. (Few SF writers have ever had the imagination, poetic skills, and visionary scope to write convincingly about the *really* far future—once you have mentioned Olaf Stapledon, Clark Ashton Smith, Jack Vance, Gene Wolfe, Cordwainer Smith, Michael Moorcock, and M. John Harrison, you have almost exhausted the roster of authors who have handled the theme with any kind of evocativeness or complexity—but Aldiss has almost made a specialty of it, also handling the theme with grace and a wealth of poetic imagination in stories like "Old Hundredth," "The Worm That Flies," and "Full Sun," as well as the novels of the "Helliconia" trilogy, and handling a related theme with similar excellence in *The Malacia Tapestry* as well.)

Oddly, though, one of his most lasting impacts on the space adventure tale was with the elegant and evocative little story that follows, which was not only cited by Roger Zelazny as a direct inspiration for his own story "The Doors of His Face, the Lamps of His Mouth," but whose influence was still showing up decades later in works such as Michael Bishop's "The White Otters of Childhood" and Michael Swanwick's *Stations of the Tide,* and no doubt in many other places where it hasn't yet been detected . . .

Brian W. Aldiss has been publishing science fiction for nearly forty years, and has more than two dozen books to his credit *The Long Afternoon of Earth* won a Hugo Award in 1962. "The Saliva Tree" won a Nebula Award in 1965, and Aldiss's novel *Starship* won the Prix Jules Verne in 1977. He took another Hugo Award in 1987 for his critical study of science fiction, *Trillion Year Spree,* written with David Wingrove. His other books include *An Island Called Moreau, Graybeard, Enemies of the System, A Rude Awakening, Life in the West, Forgotten Life, Remembrance Day,* and *Dracula Unbound,* and a memoir, *Bury My Heart at W. H. Smith's.* His short fiction has been collected in *Space, Time, and Nathaniel, Who Can Replace a Man?, New Arrivals, Old Encounters, Galaxies Like Grains of Sand, Seasons in Flight,* and *A Tupolev Too Far.* His many anthologies include *The Penguin Science Fiction Omnibus,* and, with Harry Harrison, *Decade: The 1940s, Decade: The 1950s,* and *Decade: The 1960s.* His latest books include the novel *Somewhere East of Life,* and a collection *Common Clay: 20-Odd Stories.* Due out shortly is his memoir, *In the Twinkling of an Eye.*

I

A giant rising from the fjord, from the grey arm of sea in the fjord, could have peered over the crown of its sheer cliffs and discovered Endehaaven there on the edge, sprawling at the very start of the island.

Derek Flamifew Ende saw much of this sprawl from his high window; indeed, a growing ill-ease, apprehensions of a quarrel, forced him to see everything with particular clarity, just as a landscape takes on an intense actinic visibility before a thunderstorm. Although he was warmseeing with his face, yet his eye vision wandered over the estate.

All was bleakly neat at Endehaaven—as I should know, for its neatness is my care. The gardens are made to support evergreens and shrubs that never flower; this is My Lady's whim, that likes a sobriety to match the furrowed brow of the coastline. The building, gaunt Endehaaven itself, is tall and lank and severe; earlier ages would have found its structure impossible: for its thousand built-in paragravity units ensure the support of masonry the mass of which is largely an illusion.

Between the building and the fjord, where the garden contrived itself into a parade, stood My Lady's laboratory, and My Lady's pets—and, indeed, My Lady herself at this time, her long hands busy with the minicoypu and the agoutinis. I stood with her, attending the animals' cages or passing her instruments or stirring the tanks, doing always what she asked. And the eyes of Derek Ende looked down on us; no, they looked down on her only.

Derek Flamifew Ende stood with his face over the receptor bowl, reading the message from Star One. It played lightly over his countenance and over the boscises of his forehead. Though he stared down across that achingly familiar stage of his life outside, he still warmsaw the communication clearly. When it was finished, he negated the receptor, pressed his face to it, and flexed his message back.

"I will do as you message, Star One. I will go at once to Festi XV in the Veil Nebula and enter liason with the being you call the Cliff. If possible I will also obey your order to take some of its substance to Pyrylyn. Thank you for your greetings; I return them in good faith. Good-bye."

He straightened and massaged his face: warmlooking over great light distances was always tiring, as if the sensitive muscles of the countenance knew that they delivered up their tiny electrostatic charges to parsecs of vacuum, and were appalled. Slowly his boscises also relaxed, as slowly he gathered together his gear. It would be a long flight to the Veil, and the task that had been set him would daunt the stoutest heart on Earth; yet it was for another reason he lingered: before he could be away, he had to say a farewell to his Mistress.

Dilating the door, he stepped out into the corridor, walked along it with a steady tread—feet covering mosaics of a pattern learnt long ago in his childhood—and walked into the paragravity shaft. Moments later, he was leaving the main hall, approaching My Lady as she stood gaunt, with her rodents scuttling at beast level before her and Vatna Jokull's heights rising behind her, gray with the impurities of distance.

"Go indoors and fetch me the box of name rings, Hols," she said to me; so I passed him, My Lord, as he went to her. He noticed me no more than he noticed any of the other parthenos.

When I returned, she had not turned towards him, though he was speaking urgently to her.

"You know I have my duty to perform, Mistress," I heard him saying. "Nobody else but a normal-born Earthborn can be entrusted with this sort of task."

"This sort of task! The galaxy is loaded inexhaustibly with such tasks! You can excuse yourself forever with such excursions."

He said to her remote back, pleadingly: "You can't talk of them like that. You know of the nature of the Cliff—I told you all about it. You know this isn't an excursion: it requires all the courage I have. And you know that only Earthborns, for some reason, have such courage . . . Don't you, Mistress?"

Although I had come up to them, threading my subservient way between cage and tank, they noticed me not enough even to lower their voices. My Lady stood gazing at the grey heights inland, her countenance as formidable as they; one boscis twitched as she said, "You think you are so big and brave, don't you?"

Knowing the power of sympathetic magic, she never spoke his name when she was angry; it was as if she wished him to disappear.

"It isn't that," he said humbly. "Please be reasonable, Mistress; you know I must go; a man cannot be forever at home. Don't be angry."

She turned to him at last.

Her face was high and stern; it did not receive. Yet she had a beauty of some dreadful kind I cannot describe, if weariness and knowledge can together knead beauty. Her eyes were as grey and distant as the frieze of snow-covered volcano behind her, O My Lady! She was a century older than Derek: though the difference showed not in her skin—which would stay fresh yet a thousand years—but in her authority.

"I'm not angry. I'm only hurt. You know how you have the power to hurt me."

"Mistress—," he said, taking a step toward her.

"Don't touch me," she said. "Go if you must, but don't make a mockery of it by touching me."

He took her elbow. She held one of the minicoypus quiet in the crook of her arm—animals were always docile at her touch—and strained it closer.

"I don't mean to hurt you, Mistress. You know we owe allegiance to Star One; I must work for them, or how else do we hold this estate? Let me go for once with an affectionate parting."

"Affection! You go off and leave me alone with a handful of parthenos and you talk of affection! Don't pretend you don't rejoice to get away from me. You're tired of me, aren't you?"

Wearily he said, as if nothing else would come, "It's not that . . ."

"You see! You don't even attempt to sound sincere. Why don't you go? It doesn't matter what happens to me."

"Oh, if you cold only hear your own self-pity."

Now she had a tear on the icy slope of one cheek. Turning, she flashed it for his inspection.

"Who else should pity me? You don't, or you wouldn't go away from me as you do. Suppose you got killed by this Cliff, what will happen to me?"

"I shall be back, Mistress," he said. "Never fear."

"It's easy to say. Why don't you have the courage to admit that you're only too glad to leave me?"

"Because I'm not going to be provoked into a quarrel."

"Pah, you sound like a child again. You won't answer, will you? Instead you're going to run away, evading your responsibilities."

"I'm not running away!"

"Of course you are, whatever you pretend. You're just immature."

"I'm not, I'm not! And I'm not running away! It takes real courage to do what I'm going to do."

"You think so well of yourself!"

He turned away then, petulantly, without dignity. He began to head towards the landing platform. He began to run.

"Derek!" she called.

He did not answer.

She took the squatting minicoypu by the scruff of its neck. Angrily she flung it into the nearby tank of water. It turned into a fish and swam down into the depths.

II

Derek journeyed toward the Veil Nebula in his fast lightpusher. Lonely it sailed, a great fin shaped like an archer's bow, barnacled all over with the photon cells that sucked its motive power from the dense and dusty emptiness of space. Midway along the trailing edge was the blister in which Derek lay, senseless over most of his voyage.

He woke in the therapeutic bed, called to another resurrection day that was no day, with gentle machine hands easing the stiffness from his muscles.

Soup gurgled in a retort, bubbling up towards a nipple only two inches from his mouth. He drank. He slept again, tired from his long inactivity.

When he woke again, he climbed slowly from the bed and exercised for fifteen minutes. Then he moved forward to the controls. My friend Jon was there.

"How is everything?" Derek asked.

"Everything is in order, My Lord," Jon replied. "We are swinging into the orbit of Festi XV now." He gave the coordinates and retired to eat. Jon's job was the loneliest any partheno could have. We are hatched according to strictly controlled formulae, without the inbred organisations of DNA that assure true Earthborns of their amazing longevity; five more long hauls and Jon will be old and worn out, fit only for the transmuter.

Derek sat at the controls. Did he see, superimposed on the face of Festi, the face he loved and feared? I think he did. I think there were no swirling clouds for him that could erase the clouding of her brow.

Whatever he saw, he settled the lightpusher into a fast low orbit about the desolate planet. The sun Festi was little more than a blazing point some eight hundred million miles away. Like the riding light of a ship it bobbed above a turbulent sea of cloud as they went in.

For a long while, Derek sat with his face in a receptor bowl, checking ground heats far below. Since he was dealing with temperatures approaching absolute zero, this was not simple; yet when the Cliff moved into a position directly below, there was no mistaking its bulk; it stood out as clearly on his senses as if outlined on a radar screen.

"There she goes!" Derek exclaimed.

Jon had come forward again. He fed the time coordinates into the lightpusher's brain, waited, and read off the time when the Cliff would be below them again.

Nodding, Derek began to prepare to jump. Without haste, he assumed his special suit, checking each item as he took it up, opening the paragravs until he floated, then closing them again, clicking down every snap-fastener until he was entirely encased.

"395 seconds to next zenith, My Lord," Jon said.

"You know all about collecting me?"

"Yes, sir."

"I shall not activate the radio beacon till I'm back in orbit."

"I fully understand, sir."

"Right. I'll be moving."

A little animated prison, he walked ponderously into the air lock.

Three minutes before they were next above the Cliff, Derek opened the outer door and dived into the sea of cloud. A brief blast of his suit jets set him free from the lightpusher's orbit. Cloud engulfed him like death as he fell.

The twenty surly planets that swung round Festi held only an infinitesimal fraction of the mysteries of the galaxy. Every globe in the universe huddled its own secret purpose to itself. On some of those globes, as on Earth, the purpose manifested itself in a type of being that could shape itself, burst into the space lanes, and rough-hew its aims in a civilized extraplanetary environment. On others, the purpose remained aloof and dark; only Earthborns, weaving their obscure patterns of will and compulsion, challenged those alien beings, to wrest from them new knowledge that might be added to the pool of the old.

All knowledge has its influence. Over the millennia since interstellar flight had become practicable, mankind was insensibly moulded by its own findings; together with its lost innocence, its genetic stability went out of the galactic window. As man fell like rain over other planets, so his strain lost its original hereditary design: each center of civilization bred new ways of thought, of feeling, of shape—of life. Only on old Earth itself did man still somewhat resemble the men of prestellar days.

That was why it was an Earthborn who dived head-first to meet an entity called the Cliff.

The Cliff had destroyed each of the few spaceships or lightpushers that had landed on its desolate globe. After long study of the being from safe orbits, the wise men of Star One evolved the theory that it destroyed any considerable source of power, as a man will swat a buzzing fly. Derek Ende, going along with no powering but his suit motors, would be safe—or so the theory went.

Riding down on the paragravs, he sank more and more slowly into planetary night. The last of the cloud was whipped from about his shoulders and a high wind thrummed and whistled round the supporters of his suit. Beneath him, the ground loomed. So as not to be blown across it, he speeded his rate of fall; next moment he sprawled full length on Festi XV. For a while he lay there, resting and letting his suit cool.

The darkness was not complete. Though almost no solar light touched this continent, green flares grew from the earth, illuminating its barren contours. Wishing to accustom his eyes to the gloom, he did not switch on his head, shoulder, stomach, or hand lights.

Something like a stream of fire flowed to his left. Because its radiance was poor and guttering, it confused itself with its own shadows, so that the smoke it gave off, distorted into bars by the bulk of the 4G planet, appeared to roll along its course like burning tumbleweed. Further off were larger sources of fire, impure ethane and methane most probably, burning with a sound that came like frying steak to Derek's ears, and spouting upwards with an energy that licked the lowering cloud race with blue light. At another point, blazing on an eminence, a geyser of flame wrapped itself in a thickly swirling mantle of brown smoke, a pall that spread upwards as slowly as porridge. Elsewhere, a pillar of white fire burnt without motion or smoke; it stood to the right of where Derek lay, like a floodlit sword in its perfection.

He nodded approval to himself. His drop had been successfully placed. This was the Region of Fire, where the Cliff lived.

To lie there was content enough, to gaze on a scene never closely viewed by man fulfillment enough—until he realised that a wide segment of landscape offered not the slightest glimmer of illumination. He looked into it with a keen warmsight, and found it was the Cliff.

The immense bulk of the thing blotted out all lights from the ground and rose to eclipse the cloud over its crest.

At the mere sight of it, Derek's primary and secondary hearts began to beat out a hastening pulse of awe. Stretched flat on the ground, his paragravs keeping him level to 1G, he peered ahead at it; he swallowed to clear his choked throat; his eyes strained through the mosaic of dull light in an effort to define the Cliff.

One thing was sure: it was large! He cursed that although photosistors allowed him to use his warmsight on objects beyond the suit he wore, this sense was distorted by the eternal firework display. Then in a moment of good seeing he had an accurate fix: the Cliff was three quarters of a mile away! From first observations, he had thought it to be no more than a hundred yards distant.

Now he knew how large it was. It was enormous!

Momentarily he gloated. The only sort of tasks worth being set were impossible ones. Star One's astrophysicists held the notion that the Cliff was in some sense aware, so they required Derek to take them a pound of its flesh. How do you carve a being the size of a small moon?

All the time he lay there, the wind jarred along the veins and supporters of his suit. Gradually, it occurred to Derek that the vibration he felt from this constant motion was changed. It carried a new note and a new strength. He looked about, placed his gloved hand outstretched on the ground.

The wind was no longer vibrating. It was the earth that shook, Festi itself that trembled. The Cliff was moving!

When he looked back up at it with both his senses, he saw which way it headed. Jarring steadily, it bore down on him.

"If it has intelligence, then it will reason—if it has detected me—that I am too small to offer it harm. So it will offer me none and I have nothing to fear," Derek told himself. The logic did not reassure him.

An absorbent pseudopod, activated by a simple humidity gland in the brow of his helmet, slid across his forehead and removed the sweat that formed there.

Visibility fluttered like a rag in a cellar. The slow forward surge of the

Cliff was still something Derek sensed rather than saw. Now the rolling mattresses of cloud blotted the thing's crest, as it in its turn eclipsed the fountains of fire. To the jar of its approach even the marrow of Derek's bones raised a response.

Something else also responded.

The legs of Derek's suit began to move. The arms moved. The body wriggled.

Puzzled, Derek stiffened his legs. Irresistibly, the knees of the suit hinged, forcing his own to do likewise. And not only his knees: his arms too, stiffly though he braced them on the ground before him, were made to bend to the whim of the suit. He could not keep still without breaking bones.

Thoroughly alarmed he lay there, flexing contortedly to keep rhythm with his suit, performing the gestures of an idiot.

As if it had suddenly learnt to crawl, the suit began to move forward. It shuffled forward over the ground; Derek inside went willy-nilly with it.

One ironic thought struck him. Not only was the mountain coming to Mohammed; Mohammed was perforce going to the mountain . . .

III

Nothing he could do checked his progress; he was no longer master of his movements; his will was useless. With the realisation rode a sense of relief. His Mistress could hardly blame him for anything that happened now.

Through the darkness he went on hands and knees, blundering in the direction of the on-coming Cliff, prisoner in an animated prison.

The only constructive thought that came to him was that his suit had somehow become subject to the Cliff. How, he did not know or try to guess. He crawled. He was almost relaxed now, letting his limbs move limply with the suit movements.

Smoke furled him about. The vibrations ceased, telling him that the Cliff was stationary again. Raising his head, he could see nothing but smoke—produced perhaps by the Cliff's mass as it scraped over the ground. When the blur parted, he glimpsed only darkness. The thing was directly ahead!

He blundered on. Abruptly he began to climb, still involuntarily aping the movements of his suit.

Beneath him was a doughy substance, tough yet yielding. The suit worked its way heavily upwards at an angle of something like sixty-five degrees; the stiffeners creaked, the paragravs throbbed. He was ascending the Cliff.

By this time there was no doubt in Derek's mind that the thing possessed what might be termed volition, if not consciousness. It possessed too a power no man could claim: it could impart that volition to an inanimate object like his suit. Helpless inside it, he carried his considerations a stage further. This power to impart volition seemed to have a limited range: otherwise the Cliff would surely not have bothered to move its gigantic mass at all, but would have forced the suit to traverse all the distance between them. If this reasoning were sound, then the lightpusher was safe from capture in orbit.

The movement of his arms distracted him. His suit was tunneling. Giving it no aid, he lay and let his hands make swimming motions. If it was going to bore into the Cliff, then he could only conclude he was about to be digested: yet he stilled his impulse to struggle, knowing that struggle was fruitless.

Thrusting against the doughy stuff, the suit burrowed into it and made a sibilant little world of movement and friction which stopped directly it stopped, leaving Derek embedded in the most solid kind of isolation.

To ward off growing claustrophobia, he attempted to switch on his headlight; his suit arms remained so stiff he could not bend them enough to reach the toggle. All he could do was lie there helplessly in his shell and stare into the featureless darkness of the Cliff.

But the darkness was not entirely featureless. His ears detected a constant *slither* along the outside surfaces of his suit. His warmsight discerned a meaningless pattern beyond his helmet. Though he focussed his boscises, he could make no sense of the pattern; it had neither symmetry nor meaning for him . . .

Yet for his body it seemed to have some meaning. Derek felt his limbs tremble, was aware of pulses and phantom impressions within himself that he had not known before. The realisation percolated through to him that he was in touch with powers of which he had no cognisance—and, conversely, that something was in touch with him that had no cognisance of his powers.

An immense heaviness overcame him. The forces of life laboured within him. He sensed more vividly than before the vast bulk of the Cliff. Thought it was dwarfed by the mass of Festi XV, it was as large as a good-sized asteroid . . . He could picture an asteroid, formed from a jetting explosion of gas on the face of Festi the sun. Half-solid, half-molten, it swung about its parent on an eccentric orbit. Cooling under an interplay of pressures, its interior crystallised into a unique form. So, with its surface semi-plastic, it existed for many millions of years, gradually accumulating an electrostatic charge that poised . . . and waited . . . and brewed the life acids about its crystalline heart.

Festi was a stable system, but once in every so many thousands of millions of years, the giant first, second, and third planets achieved perihelion with the sun and with each other simultaneously. This happened coincidentally with the asteroid's nearest approach; it was wrenched from its orbit and all but grazed the three lined-up planets. Vast electrical and gravitational forces were unleashed. The asteroid glowed: and woke to consciousness. Life was not born on it: it was born to life, born in one cataclysmic clash!

Before it had more than mutely swallowed the sad-sharp-sweet sensation of consciousness, it was in trouble. Plunging away from the sun on its new course, it found itself snared in the gravitational pull of the 4G planet, Festi XV. It knew no shaping force but gravity; gravity was to it all that oxygen was to cellular life on Earth; yet it had no wish to exchange its flight for captivity; yet it was too puny to resist. For the first time, the asteroid recognised that its consciousness had a use, in that it could to some extent control its environment outside itself. Rather than risk being broken up in Festi's orbit, it sped inwards, and by retarding its own fall performed its first act of volition, an act that brought it down shaken but entire on the planet's surface.

For an immeasurable period, the asteroid—but now it was the Cliff—lay in the shallow crater formed by its impact, speculating without thought. It knew nothing except the inorganic scene about it, and could visualise nothing else, but that scene it knew well. Gradually it came to some kind of terms with the scene. Formed by gravity, it used gravity as thoughtlessly as a man uses breath; it began to move other things, and it began to move itself.

That it should be other than alone in the universe had never occurred to the Cliff. Now it knew there was other life, it accepted the fact. The other life was not as it was; that it accepted. The other life had its own requirements; that it accepted. Of questions, of doubt, it did not know. It had a need; so did the other life; they should both be accommodated, for accommodation was the adjustment to pressure, and that response it comprehended.

Derek Ende's suit began to move again under external volition. Carefully it worked its way backwards. It was ejected from the Cliff. It lay still.

Derek himself lay still. He was barely conscious.

In a half daze, he was piecing together what had happened.

The Cliff had communicated with him; if he ever doubted that, the evidence of it lay clutched in the crook of his left arm.

"Yet it did not—yet it could not communicate with me!" he murmured. But it had communicated: he was still faint with the burden of it.

The Cliff had nothing like a brain. It had not "recognised" Derek's brain. Instead, it had communicated with the only part of him it could recognise; it had communicated direct to his cell organisation, and in particular probably to those cytoplasmic structures, the mitochondria, the power sources of the cell. His brain had been by-passed, his own cells had taken in the information offered.

He recognised his feeling of weakness. The Cliff had drained him of power. Even that could not drain his feeling of triumph. For the Cliff had taken information even as it gave it. The Cliff had learnt that other life existed in other parts of the universe.

Without hesitation, without debate, it had given a fragment of itself to be taken to those other parts of the universe. Derek's mission was completed.

In the Cliff's gesture, Derek read one of the deepest urges of living things: the urge to make an impression on another living thing. Smiling wryly, he pulled himself to his feet.

He was alone in the Region of Fire. The occasional mournful flame still confronted its surrounding dark, but the Cliff had disappeared; he had lain on the threshold of consciousness longer than he thought. He looked at his chronometer, to find it was high time he moved towards his rendezvous with the lightpusher. Stepping up his suit heating to combat the cold that began to seep through his bones, he revved up the paragrav unit and rose. The noisome clouds came down and engulfed him; Festi was lost to view. Soon he had risen beyond cloud or atmosphere.

Under Jon's direction, the space craft homed onto Derek's radio beacon. After a few tricky minutes, they matched velocities and Derek climbed aboard.

"Are you all right?" the partheno asked, as his master staggered into a flight seat.

"Fine—just weak. I'll tell you all about it as I do a report on spool for Pyrylyn. They're going to be pleased with us."

He produced a yellowy grey blob of matter that had expanded to the size of a large turkey and held it out to Jon.

"Don't touch this with your bare hands. Put it in one of the low-temperature lockers under 4Gs. It's a little souvenir from Festi XV."

IV

The Eyebright in Pynnati, one of Pyrylyn's capital cities, was where you went to enjoy yourself on the most lavish scale possible. This was where Derek Ende's hosts took him, with Jon in self-effacing attendance.

They lay in a nest of couches which slowly revolved, giving them a full view of other dance and couch parties. The room itself moved. Its walls were transparent; through them could be seen an ever-changing view as the room slid up and down and about the great metal framework of the Eyebright. First they were on the outside of the structure, with the bright night lights of Pynnati winking up at them as if intimately involved in their delight. Then they slipped inwards in the slow evagination of the building, to be surrounded by other pleasure rooms, their revelers clearly visible as they moved grandly up or down or along.

Uneasily, Derek lay on his couch. A vision of his Mistress's face was before him; he could imagine how she would treat all this harmless festivity: with cool contempt. His own pleasure was consequently reduced to ashes.

"I suppose you'll be moving back to Earth as soon as possible?"

"Eh?" Derek grunted.

"I said, I supposed you would soon be going home again." The speaker was Belix Ix Sappose, Chief Administrator of High Gee Research at Star One; as Derek's host of the evening, he lay next to him.

"I'm sorry, Belix, yes—I shall have to head back back for home soon."

"No 'have to' about it. You have discovered an entirely new life form; we can now attempt communication with the Festi XV entity, with goodness knows what extension of knowledge. The government can easily show its gratitude by awarding you any sort of post here you care to name: I am not without influence in that respect, as you are aware. I don't imagine that Earth in its senescent stage has much to offer a man of your calibre."

Derek thought of what it had to offer. He was bound to it. These decadent people did not understand how anything could be binding.

"Well, what do you say, Ende? I'm not speaking idly." Belix Ix Sappose tapped his antler system impatiently.

"Er . . . Oh, they will discover a great deal from the Cliff. That doesn't concern me. My part of the work is over. I'm just a field worker, not an intellectual."

"You don't reply to my suggestion."

He looked at Belix with only slight vexation. Belix was an unglaat, one of a species that had done as much as any to bring about the peaceful concourse of the galaxy. His backbone branched into an elaborate antler system, from which six sloe-dark eyes surveyed Derek with unblinking irritation. Other members of the party, including Jupkey, Belix's female, were also looking at him.

"I must get back to Earth soon," Derek said. What had Belix said? Offered some sort of post? Restlessly he shifted on his couch, under pressure as always when surrounded by people he knew none too well.

"You are bored, Mr. Ende."

"No, not at all. My apologies, Belix. I'm overcome as always by the luxury of Eyebright. I was watching the nude dancers."

"I fear you are bored."

"Not at all, I assure you."

"May I get you a woman?"

"No, thank you."

"A boy, perhaps?"

"No, thank you."

"Have you ever tried the flowering asexuals from the Cphids?"

"Not at present, thank you."

"Then perhaps you will excuse us if Jupkey and I remove our clothes and join the dance," Belix said stiffly.

As they moved out onto the dance floor to greet the strepent trumpets, Derek heard Jupkey say something of which he caught only the words "arrogant Earthborn." His eyes met Jon's; he saw that the partheno had overheard also.

In an instinctive dismissive gesture of his left hand, Derek revealed his mortification. He rose and began to pace round the room. Often he shouldered his way through a knot of naked dancers, ignoring their complaints.

At one of the doors, a staircase was floating by. He stepped onto it to escape from the crowds.

Four young women were passing down the stairs. They were gaily dressed, with sonant-stones pulsing on their costumes. In their faces youth kept its lantern, lighting them as they laughed and chattered. Derek stopped and beheld the girls. One of them he recognised. Instinctively he called her name: "Eva!"

She had already seen him. Waving her companions on, she came back to him, dancing up the intervening steps.

"So the brave Earthborn climbs once more the golden stairs of Pynnati! Well, Derek Ende, your eyes are as dark as ever, and your brow as high!"

As he looked at her, the strepent trumpets were in tune for him for the first time that evening, and his delight rose up in his throat.

"Eva! . . . And your eyes as bright as ever . . . And you have no man with you."

"The powers of coincidence work on your behalf." She laughed—yes, he remembered that sound!—and then said more seriously, "I heard you were here with Belix Sappose and his female; so I was making the grandly foolish gesture of coming to see you. You remember how devoted I am to foolish gestures."

"So foolish?"

"Probably. You have less change in you, Derek Ende, than the core of Pyrylyn. To suppose otherwise is foolish, to know how unalterable you are and still to see you doubly foolish."

He took her hand, beginning to lead her up the staircase; the rooms moving by them on either side were blurs to his eyes.

"Must you still bring up that old charge, Eva?"

"It lies between us; I do not have to touch it. I fear your unchangeability because I am a butterfly against your grey castle."

"You are beautiful, Eva, so beautiful!—And may a butterfly not rest unharmed on a castle wall?" He fitted into her allusive way of speech with difficulty.

"Walls! I cannot bear your walls, Derek! Am I a bulldozer that I should want to come up against walls? To be either inside or outside them is to be a prisoner."

"Let us not quarrel until we have found some point of agreement," he said. "Here are the stars. Can't we agree about them?"

"If we are both indifferent to them," she said, looking out and impudently winding his arm about her. The staircase had reached the zenith of its travels and moved slowly sideways along the upper edge of Eyebright. They stood on the top step with night flashing their images back at them from the glass.

Eva Coll-Kennerley was a human, but not of Earthborn stock. She was a velure, born on the y-cluster worlds of the dense Third Arm of the galaxy, and her skin was richly covered with the brown fur of her kind. Her mercurial talents were employed in the same research department that enjoyed Belix Sappose's more sober ones; Derek had met her there on an earlier visit to Pyrylyn. Their love had been an affair of swords.

He looked at her now and touched her and could say not one word for himself. When she flashed a liquid eye at him, he essayed an awkward smile.

"Because I am oriented like a compass towards strong men, my lavish offer to you still holds good. Is it not bait enough?"

"I don't think of you as a trap, Eva."

"Then for how many more centuries are you going to refrigerate your nature on Earth? You still remain faithful, if I recall your euphemism for slavery, to your Mistress, to her cold lips and locked heart?"

"I have no choice!"

"Ah yes, my debate on that motion was defeated: and more than once. Is she still pursuing her researches into the transmutability of species?"

"Oh yes, indeed. The mediaeval idea that one species can turn into another was foolish in the Middle Ages; now, with the gradual accumulation of cosmic radiation in planetary bodies, it is correct to a certain definable extent. She is endeavouring to show that cellular bondage can be—"

"Yes, yes, and this serious talk is an eyesore in Eyebright! You are locked away, Derek, doing your sterile deeds of heroism and never entering the real world. If you imagine you can live with her much longer and then come to me, you are mistaken. Your walls grow higher about your ears every century, till I cannot, cannot—oh, it's the wrong metaphor!—cannot scale you!"

Even in his pain, the texture of her fur was joy to his warm-sight. Helplessly he shook his head in an effort to shake her clattering words away.

"Look at you being big and brave and silent even now! You're so arrogant," she said—and then, without perceptible change of tone, "because I still love the bit of you inside the castle, I'll make once more my monstrous and petty offer to you."

"No, please, Eva!—"

"But yes! Forget this tedious bondage of Earth, forget this ghastly matriarchy, live here with me. I don't want you forever. You know I am a eudemonist and judge by standards of pleasure—our liaison need be only for a century or two. In that time, I will deny you nothing your senses may require."

"Eva!"

"After that, our demands will be satisfied. You may then go back to the Lady Mother of Endehaaven for all I care."

"Eva, you know how I spurn this belief, this eudemonism."

"Forget your creed! I'm asking you nothing difficult. Who are you to haggle? Am I fish, to be bought by the kilo, this bit selected, this rejected?"

He was silent.

"*You* don't really need me," he said at last. "You have everything already: beauty, wit, sense, warmth, feeling, balance, comfort. *She* has nothing. She is shallow, haunted, cold—oh, she needs me, Eva . . ."

"You are apologising for yourself, not her."

She had already turned with the supple movement of a velure and was running down the staircase. Lighted chambers drifted up about them like bubbles.

His laboured attempt to explain his heart turned to exasperation. He ran down after her, grasping her arm.

"Listen to me, will you, damn you!"

"Nobody in Pyrylyn would listen to such masochistic nonsense as yours! You are an arrogant fool, Derek, and I am a weak-willed one. Now release me!"

As the next room came up, she jumped through its entrance and disappeared into the crowd.

V

Not all the drifting chambers of Eyebright were lighted. Some pleasures come more delightfully with the dark, and these pleasures were coaxed and cosseted into fruition in shrouded halls where illumination cast only the gentlest ripple on the ceiling and the gloom was sensuous with ylang-ylang and other perfumes. Here Derek found a place to weep.

Sections of his life slid before him as if impelled by the same mechanisms that moved Eyebright. Always, one presence was there.

Angrily he related to himself how he always laboured to satisfy her—yes, in every sphere laboured to satisfy her! And how when that satisfaction was accorded him it came as though riven from her, as a spring sometimes trickles down the split face of a rock. Undeniably there was satisfaction for him in drinking from that cool source—but no, where was the satisfaction when pleasure depended on such extreme disciplining and subduing of himself?

Mistress, I love and hate your needs!

And the discipline had been such . . . so long, also . . . that now when he might enjoy himself far from her, he could scarcely strike a trickle from his own rock. He had walked here before, in this city where the hedonists and eudemonists reigned, walked among the scents of pleasure, walked among the ioblepharous women, the beautiful guests and celebrated beauties, with My Lady away in him, feeling that she showed even on his countenance. People spoke to him: somehow he replied. They manifested gaiety: he tried to do so. They opened to him: he attempted a response. All the time, he hoped they would understand that his arrogance masked only shyness—or did he hope that it was his shyness which masked arrogance? He did not know.

Who could presume to know? The one quality holds much of the other. Both refuse to come forward and share.

He roused from his meditation knowing that Eva Coll-Kennerley was again somewhere near. She had not left the building, then! She was seeking him out!

Derek half-rose from his position in a shrouded alcove. He was baffled to think how she could have traced him here. On entering Eyebright, visitors were given sonant-stones, by which they could be traced from room to room; but judging that nobody would wish to trace him, Derek had switched his stone off even before leaving Belix Sappose's party.

He heard Eva's voice, its unmistakable overtones not near, not far . . .

"You find the most impenetrable bushels to hide your light under . . ."

He caught no more. She had sunk down among tapestries with someone else. She was not after him at all! Waves of relief and regret rolled over him . . . and when he paid attention again, she was speaking his name.

With shame on him, like a wolf creeping towards a camp fire, he crouched forward to listen. At once his warmsight told him to whom Eva spoke. He recognised the pattern of the antlers; Belix was there, with Jupkey sprawled beside him on some elaborate kind of bed.

". . . useless to try again. Derek is too far entombed within himself," Eva said.

"Entombed rather within his conditioning," Belix said. "We found the same. It's conditioning, my dear."

"However he became entombed, I still admire him enough to want to

understand him." Eva's voice was a note or two astray from its usual controlled timbre.

"Look at it scientifically," Belix said, with the weighty inflections of a man
about to produce truth out of a hat. "Earth is the last bastion of a bankrupt
culture. The Earthborns number less than a couple of millions now. They
disdain social graces and occasions. They are served by parthenogenically
bred slaves, all of which are built on the same controlled genetic formula.
They are inbred. In consequence, they have become practically a species
apart. You can see it all in friend Ende. As I say, he's entombed in his conditioning. A tragedy, Eva, but you must face up to it."

"You're probably right, you pontifical old pop," Jupkey said lazily. "Who
but an Earthborn would do what Derek did on Festi?"

"No, no!" Eva said. "Derek's ruled by a woman, not by conditioning.
He's—"

"In Ende's case they are one and the same thing, my dear, believe me.
Consider Earth's social organisation. The partheno slaves have replaced all
but a comparative handful of true Earthborns. That handful has parcelled
out Earth into great estates which it holds by a sinister matriarchalism."

"Yes, I know, but Derek—"

"Derek is caught in the system. The Earthborns had fallen into a mating pattern for which there is no precedent. The sons of a family marry their
mothers, not only to perpetuate their line but because the productive Earthborn female is scarce now that Earth itself is senescent. This is what the
Endes have done; this is what Derek Ende has done. His 'mistress' is both
mother and wife to him. Given the factor of longevity as well—well, naturally you ensure an excessive emotional rigidity that almost nothing can
break. Not even you, my sweet-coated Eva!"

"He was on the point of breaking tonight!"

"I doubt it," Belix said. "Ende may want to get away from his claustrophobic home, but the same forces that drive him off will eventually lure him
back."

"I tell you he was on the point of breaking—only I broke first."

"Well, as Teer Ruche said to me many centuries ago, only a pleasure-
hater knows how to shape a pleasure-hater. I would say you were lucky he
did not break; you would only have had a baby on your hands."

Her answering laugh did not ring true.

"My Lady of Endehaaven, then, must be the one to do it. I will never try
again—though he seems under too much stress to stand for long. Oh, it's
really immoral! He deserves better!"

"A moral judgement from you, Eva!" Jupkey exclaimed amusedly to the
fragrant gloom.

"My advice to you, Eva, is to forget all about the poor fellow. Apart from anything else, he is barely articulate—which would not suit you for a season."

The unseen listener could bear no more. A sudden rage—as much against himself for hearing as against them for speaking—burst over him, freeing him to act. Straightening up, he seized the arm of the couch on which Belix and Jupkey nestled, wildly supposing he could tip them onto the floor.

Too late, his warmsight warned him of the real nature of the couch. Instead of tipping, it swivelled, sending a wave of liquid over him. The two unglaats were lying in a warm bath scented with ylang-ylang and other essences.

Jupkey squealed in anger and fright. Kicking out, she caught Derek on the shin with a hoof; he slipped in the oily liquid and fell. Belix, unaided by warmsight, jumped out of the bath, entangled himself with Derek's legs, and also fell.

Eva was shouting for lights. Other occupants of the hall cried back that darkness must prevail at all costs.

Picking himself up—leaving only his dignity behind—Derek ran for the exit, abandoning the confusion to sort itself out as it would.

Burningly, disgustedly, he made his way dripping from Eyebright. The hastening footsteps of Jon followed him like an echo all the way to the space field.

Soon he would be back at Endehaaven. Though he would always be a failure in his dealings with other humans, there at least he knew every inch of his bleak allotted territory.

Envoi

Had there been a spell over all Endehaaven, it could have been no quieter when My Lord Derek Ende arrived home."

I informed My Lady of the moment when his lightpusher arrived and rode at orbit. In the receptor bowl I watched him and Jon come home, cutting north west across the emaciated wilds of Europe, across Denmark, over the Shetlands, the Faroes, the sea, alighting by the very edge of the island, by the fjord with its silent waters.

All the while the wind lay low as if under some stunning malediction, and none of our tall trees stirred.

"Where is my Mistress, Hols?" Derek asked me, as I went to greet him and assist him out of his suit.

"She asked me to tell you that she is confined to her chambers and cannot see you, My Lord."

He looked me in the eyes as he did so rarely.

"Is she ill?"

"No."

Without waiting to remove his suit, he hurried on into the building.

Over the next two days, he was about but little, preferring to remain in his room. Once he wandered among the experimental tanks and cages. I saw him net a fish and toss it into the air, watching it while it struggled into new form and flew away until it was lost in a jumbled background of cumulus; but it was plain he was less interested in the riddles of stress and transmutation than in the symbolism of the carp's flight.

Mostly he sat compiling the spools on which he imposed the tale of his life. All one wall was covered with files full of these spools: the arrested drumbeats of past centuries. From the later spools I have secretly compiled this record; for all his unspoken self-pity, he never knew the sickness of merely observing.

We parthenos will never understand the luxuries of a divided mind. Surely suffering as much as happiness is a kind of artistry?

On the day that he received a summons from Star One to go upon another quest for them, Derek met My Lady in the Blue Corridor.

"It is good to see you about again, Mistress," he said, kissing her cheek.

She stroked his hair. On her nervous hand she wore one ring with an amber stone; her gown was of olive and umber.

"I was very upset to have you go away from me. The Earth is dying, Derek, and I fear its loneliness. You have left me alone too much. However, I have recovered myself and am glad to see you back."

"You know I am glad to see you. Smile for me and come outside for some fresh air. The sun is shining."

"It's so long since it shone. Do you remember how once it always shone? I can't bear to quarrel any more. Take my arm and be kind to me."

"Mistress, I always wish to be kind to you. And I have all sorts of things to discuss with you. You'll want to hear what I have been doing, and—"

"You won't leave me any more?"

He felt her hand tighten on his arm. She spoke very loudly.

"That was one of the things I wished to discuss—later," he said. "First let me tell you about the wonderful life form with which I made contact on Festi."

As they left the corridor and descended the paragravity shaft, My Lady said wearily, "I suppose that's a polite way of telling me that you are bored here."

He clutched her hands as they floated down. Then he released them and clutched her face instead.

"Understand this, Mistress mine, I love you and want to serve you. You are in my blood; wherever I go I never can forget you. My dearest wish is to make you happy—this you must know. But equally you must know that I have needs of my own."

Grumpily she said, withdrawing her face, "Oh, I know that all right. And I know those needs will always come first with you. Whatever you say or pretend, you don't care a rap about me. You make that all too clear."

She moved ahead of him, shaking off the hand he put on her arm. He had a vision of himself running down a golden staircase and stretching out that same detaining hand to another girl. The indignity of having to repeat oneself, century after century.

"You're lying! You're faking! You're being cruel!" he said.

Gleaming, she turned.

"Am I? Then answer me this—aren't you already planning to leave Endehaaven and me soon?"

He smote his forehead.

He said inarticulately, "Look, you must try to stop this recrimination. Yes, yes, it's true I am thinking . . . But I have to—I reproach myself. I could be kinder. But you shut yourself away when I come back, you don't welcome me—"

"Trust you to find excuses rather than face up to your own nature," she said contemptuously, walking briskly into the garden. Amber and olive and umber, and sable of hair, she walked down the path, her outlines sharp in the winter air; in the perspectives of his mind she did not dwindle.

For some minutes he stood in the threshold, immobilized by antagonistic emotions.

Finally he pushed himself out into the sunlight.

She was in her favourite spot by the fjord, feeding an old badger from her hand. Only her increased attention to the badger suggested that she heard him approach.

His boscises twitched as he said, "If you will forgive a cliché, I apologise."

"I don't mind what you do."

Walking backwards and forwards behind her, he said, "When I was away, I heard some people talking. On Pyrylyn this was. They were discussing the mores of our matrimonial system."

"It's no business of theirs."

"Perhaps not. But what they said suggested a new line of thought to me."

She put the old badger back in his cage without comment.

"Are you listening, Mistress?"

"Do go on."

"Try to listen sympathetically. Consider all the history of galactic exploration—or even before that, consider the explorers of Earth in the pre-space age, men like Shackleton and so on. They were brave men, of course, but wouldn't it be strange if most of them only ventured where they did because the struggle at home was too much for them?"

He stopped. She had turned to him; the half-smile was whipped off his face by her look of fury.

"And you're trying to tell me that that's how you see yourself—a martyr? Derek, how you must hate me! Not only do you go away, you secretly blame me because you go away. It doesn't matter that I tell you a thousand times I want you here—no, it's all my fault! I drive you away! That's what you tell your charming friends on Pyrylyn, isn't it? Oh, how you must hate me!"

Savagely he grasped her wrists. She screamed to me for aid and struggled. I came near but halted, playing my usual impotent part. He swore at her, bellowed for her to be silent, whereupon she cried the louder, shaking furiously in his arms.

He struck her across the face.

At once she was quiet. Her eyes closed: almost, it would seem, in ecstasy. Standing there, she had the pose of a woman offering herself.

"Go on, hit me! You want to hit me!" she whispered.

With the words, with the look of her, he too was altered. As if realising for the first time her true nature, he dropped his fists and stepped back, staring at her sick-mouthed. His heel met no resistance. He twisted suddenly, spread out his arms as if to fly, and fell over the cliff edge.

Her scream pursued him down.

Even as his body hit the water of the fjord, it began to change. A flurry of foam marked some sort of painful struggle beneath the surface. Then a seal plunged into view, dived below the next wave, and swam towards open sea over which already a freshening breeze blew.

GUNPOWDER GOD

A former detective for the Pennsylvania Railroad, the late H. Beam Piper made his first sale in 1947, to *Astounding,* and soon became a robust player in the booming SF scene of the '50s. In the years to come, he would become a mainstay of *Astounding,* with which magazine he was strongly associated, and where much of his best work (such as the classic story "Omnilingual") appeared, but he also sold widely to other magazines of the day such as *Amazing, Future, Weird Tales,* and *Fantastic Universe.* By the late '50s, as the market for SF novels rapidly expanded, he was primarily writing novels, some of them fix-ups assembled from his magazine work, some of them original.

Piper's work was solidly in the adventure tradition of the day—although usually more in the tradition of *Astounding,* where adventure was always mated with serious social/political speculation, than in the more flamboyant, swashbuckling, sword-and-planet interplanetary Romance tradition of *Planet Stories* or *Thrilling Wonder Stories,* or with the planet-busting Superscience Space Opera of the '30s—with only one or two of his later works, produced toward the end of his life, straying into somewhat different territory. His two major series were the "Terro-Human" stories—which explore the rise and fall of interstellar empires and politics in a complex future history scenario rather reminiscent of Asimov's "Foundation" future history, although different in tone, closer to what we would today call "libertarian" in outlook and philosophy, more concerned with politics, economics, and military campaigns, than was Asimov's; perhaps closer in tone to Poul Anderson's contemporaneous "Technic History" cycle—and the more colorful and freewheeling "Paratime Police" stories; both series have been continued after Piper's death by other writers, although not with the conviction that Piper himself brought to them.

Most of Piper's Terro-Human novels, such as *Space Viking, Four-Day Planet,* and *The Cosmic Computer,* are competent but rather routine Space Opera, as were his first two novels, written with John R. McGuire, *Crisis in 2140* and *A Planet for Texans* (the last later reissued as *Lonestar Planet*). Although technically also in the "Terro-Human" sequence, Piper later moved away from straightforward Space Opera and into more thoughtful territory, and broke some intriguing new ground, with his two best novels, *Little Fuzzy* and *Fuzzy Sapiens* (later reissued in an omnibus collection as *The Fuzzy Papers,* and followed much later by a long-lost and posthumously published third "Fuzzy" novel, *Fuzzies and Other People*), which revolve around intelligently argued courtroom battles (as well as the usual

Astounding-style behind-the-scenes political intrigues and Dirty Tricks) waged to prove that the native Fuzzies inhabiting a Terran-colonized planet are intelligent, sentient beings, and deserve the same legal rights as humans, including protection from exploitation and the destruction of their habitats and lifeways by a rapacious mining corporation. This was fairly radical stuff in 1962, when science fiction was much more likely to take the side of the calvary or of the intrepid white settlers than of the Indians lurking in ambush over the hill, or of the Kiplingesque colonial administrators rather than that of the downtrodden native sepoys they rule, and has even more relevance today than it had then, making the Fuzzy novels surprisingly germane and up-to-date in sensibility. (If the Fuzzies seem familiar to you the first time you encounter them, it may be because they are very probably [at least one of] the inspirations for a race of little, fuzzy, cute—but warlike—tribal people in a famous blockbuster SF movie of the 1980s; but if there *was* influence, keep in mind that the movie got them from Piper, not the other way around.)

The Fuzzy novels are substantial enough to make me wonder what kind of books Piper would have written in the '70s and '80s, if he had lived to produce them. Unfortunately, he did not—in 1964, despondent over mounting debts and what he considered the failure of his writing career, he picked up a gun (ironic, since he was an enthusiastic gun collector) and shot and killed himself, just as Alice Sheldon would do—driven by different devils—a little more than twenty years later. A final, bitter irony is that there was a big revival of interest in Piper's work in the late '70s and early '80s, with all of his books coming back into print and proving successful enough with readers that new books in both the Fuzzy and the broader Terro-Human series were commissioned to be written by other authors—but by then Piper was long dead, and received no benefit from the Phoenix-like rebirth of a career that he'd thought was over back in 1964.

Little Fuzzy may be Piper's best book, but his most *entertaining* book by far, and my own personal favorite, is the Alternate History novel *Lord Kalvin of Otherwhen,* assembled from the story that follows, "Gunpowder God," plus two sequels, from the pages of *Astounding,* and published in 1965, after Piper's death. Again, Piper was ahead of the curve here, publishing an Alternate History novel long before Alternate History novels became the rage, as they are in today's publishing scene—and although *Lord Kalvin of Otherwhen* was not the first Alternate History novel (being proceeded by de Camp's *Lest Darkness Fall,* and Ward Moore's *Bring the Jubilee,* among others), it remains one of the best of them, and can be seen to have had an influence on the work of future writers such as R. Garcia y Robertson and G. David Nordley, and particularly on the Alternate History work of Harry Turtledove. I think it holds up well in comparison to the other novels being published today in the Alternate History mini-boom, and, if re-issued, would probably prove to be as popular with today's readers—publishers take note!

"Gunpowder God," the story that follows, is the first and most self-contained of the Lord Kalvin stories, and as an inventive, action-packed, and relentlessly fast-paced adventure tale grounded in a thorough knowledge of history and the potential social consequences of isolated technological breakthroughs, is just as fresh and effective as anything being written today, more than thirty years later.

Piper never saw a short-story collection published in his lifetime, but his short work was posthumously assembled in the early '80s in the collections *Paratime, Foundation, Empire,* and *The Worlds of H. Beam Piper.* His other works include the omnibus volume *Four-Day Planet/Lonestar Planet,* and a mystery novel, *Murder in the Gun Room.* I think most of Piper's work is again out-of-print here in the late '90s, but the books re-issued during the revival of interest in his work in the '80s, mostly from Ace and Baen, may still be findable in used-book stores and SF convention huckster rooms.

Tortha Karf, Chief of Paratime Police, told himself to stop fretting. Only two hundred odd days till Year-End Day, and then, precisely at midnight, he would rise from this chair and Verkan Vall would sit down in it, and after that he would be free to raise grapes and lemons and wage guerrilla war against the rabbits on the island of Sicily, which he owned on one uninhabited Fifth Level time-line. He wondered how long it would take Vall to become as tired of the chief's seat as he was now.

Vall was tired of it already, in anticipation. He'd never wanted to be chief; prestige and authority meant little to him, and freedom much. It was a job somebody had to do, though, and it was the job for which he had been trained, so Vall would take it, and do it, he suspected, better than he himself had done. The job, policing a near-infinity of different worlds, each one of which was this same planet, Earth, would be safe in the hands of Verkan Vall.

Twelve thousand years ago, facing extinction on an exhausted planet, the First Level race had discovered the existence of a second, lateral dimension of time, and a means of physical transposition to and from the worlds of alternate probability parallel to their own. So the conveyers had gone out by stealth, to bring back wealth in abundance to First Level Home Time-Line, a little from here, a little from there, never enough to be missed.

It all had to be policed. Some Paratimers were unscrupulous in dealing with outtime peoples—he'd have retired five years ago, but for the discovery of a huge paratemporal slave trade, only recently smashed. More often, by somebody's bad luck or indiscretion, the Paratime Secret would be endangered, and that had to be preserved at any cost. Not merely the technique of paratemporal transposition, that went without comment, but the very existence of a race possessing it. If for no other reason, and there were many others, it would be utterly immoral to make any outtime people live with the knowledge that there were among them aliens indistinguishable from themselves, watching and exploiting. So there was the Paratime Police.

Second Level; it had been civilized almost as long as the First, but there had been long Dark-Age interludes. Except for paratemporal transposition, it almost equaled First. Third Level civilization was more recent, but still of respectable antiquity. Fourth Level had started late and advanced slowly; some Fourth Level genius was inventing agriculture when the coal-burning steam engine was obsolescent on the Third. And Fifth Level—on a few time-lines, subhuman brutes, fireless and speechless, were using stones to crack nuts and each other's head; on most of it nothing even humanoid had evolved.

Fourth Level was the big one. The others had devolved from low-probability genetic accidents; Fourth had been the maximum probability. It was divided into many sectors and subsectors, on most of which civilization had first appeared in the Nile and Tigris-Euphrates valleys, and, later, on the Indus and the Yangtze. Europo-American Sector; they might have to pull out of that entirely, that would be Chief Verkan's decision. Too many thermonuclear weapons and too many competing national sovereignties, always a disaster-fraught combination. That had happened all over Third Level within Home Time-Line experience. Alexandrian-Roman, off to a fine start with the pooling of Greek theory and Roman engineering ability, and then, a thousand years ago, two half-forgotten religions had been rummaged out of the dustbin and their respective proselytes had begun massacring each other. They were still at it, with pikes and matchlocks, having lost the ability to make anything better. Europo-American would come to that, if its competing politico-economic sectarians kept on. Sino-Hindic, that wasn't a civilization, was a bad case of cultural paralysis. Indo-Turanian, about where Europo-American had been a thousand years ago.

And Aryan-Oriental; the Aryan migration of three thousand years ago, instead of moving west and south as on most sectors, had rolled east into China.

And Aryan-Transpacific, there was one to watch. An off-shoot of Aryan-Oriental; the conquerors of Japan had sailed north and east along the Kuriles and Aleutians, and then spread south and east over North America, bringing with them horses and cattle and iron-working skills, exterminating the Amerinds, splitting into diverse peoples and cultures. There was a civilization along the Pacific coast, and nomads on the plains herding bison and cross-breeding them with Asian cattle, another civilization in the Mississippi Valley, and one around the Great Lakes. And a new one, only four centuries old, on the Atlantic seaboard and back in the Appalachians.

The technological level was about that of Europe in the Middle Ages, a few subsectors slightly higher. But they were going forward. Things, he thought, were about ripe to happen on Aryan-Transpacific.

Well, let Chief Verkan watch that.

She tried to close her mind to the voices around her, and stared at the map between the two candlesticks on the table. There was Tarr-Hostigos overlooking the gap, just a tiny fleck of gold on the parchment, but she could see it all in her mind, the walls, the outer bailey, the citadel and the keep, the watchtower pointing a blunt finger skyward. Below, the little Darro glinted, flowing north to join the Listra and, with it, the broad Athan to the north and east. The town of Hostigos, white walls and slate roofs and busy streets; the checkerboard of fields and forests.

A voice, louder and harsher than the others, brought her back to reality. "He'll do nothing? What in Dralm's name is a Great King for but to keep the peace?"

She looked along the table, from one to another of them. The speaker for the peasants, at the foot, uncomfortable in his feast-day clothes and ill at ease seated among his betters, the speakers for the artisans and the merchants and the townsfolk, the lesser family members, the sworn landholders. Chartiphon, the captain-in-chief, his blond beard streaked with gray like the gray lead-splashes on his gilded breastplate, his long sword on the table in front of him. Old Xentos, the cowl of his priestly robe thrown back from his snowy head, his blue eyes troubled. And her father, Prince Ptosphes of Hostigos, beside whom she sat at the table-head, his mouth tight between pointed mustache and pointed beard. How long it had been since she had seen a smile on her father's lips!

Xentos passed a hand negatively in front of his face.

"The Great King, Kaiphranos, said that it was every prince's duty to guard his own realm; that it was for Prince Ptosphes to keep raiders out of Hostigos."

"Well, great Dralm, didn't you tell him it wasn't just bandits?" the other voice bullyragged. "They're Nostori soldiers; it's war! Gormoth of Nostor means to take all Hostigos, as his grandfather took Sevenhills Valley after the traitor we don't name sold him Tarr-Dombra!"

That was a part of the map her eyes had shunned, the bowl valley to the east, where Dombra Gap split the mountains. It was from thence the Nostori raiders came.

"And what hope have we from Styphon's House?" her father asked. He knew the answer; he wanted them all to hear it at first hand.

"Chartiphon spoke with them," Xentos said. "The priests of Styphon hold no speech with priests of other gods."

"The archpriest wouldn't talk to me," Chartiphon said. "Only one of the upper priests. He took our offerings and said that he would pray to Styphon for us. When I asked for fireseed, he would give us none."

"None at all?" somebody cried. "Then we are under the ban!"

Her father rapped with the pommel of his poignard.

"You've heard the worst, now," he said. "What's in your minds to do? You first, Phosg."

The peasant leader rose awkwardly, cleared his throat.

"Lord, my cottage is as dear to me as this fine castle is to you," he said. "I'll fight for mine as you would for yours."

There was a quick mutter of approval along the table. The others spoke in their turns, a few tried to make speeches. Chartiphon said only: "Fight. What else?"

"Submission to evil is the worst of all sins," Xentos said. "I am a priest of Dralm, and Dralm is a god of peace, but I say, fight with Dralm's blessing."

"Rylla?" her father asked.

"Better die in armor than live in chains," she said. "When the time comes, I will be in armor with the rest of you."

Her father nodded. "I expect no less from any of you." He rose, and all with him. "I thank you all. At sunset, we dine together; until then, servants will attend you. Now, if you please, leave me with my daughter. Xentos, you and Chartiphon stay."

There was a scrape of chairs, a shuffle of feet going out, a murmur of voices in the hall before the door closed. Chartiphon had begun to fill his stubby pipe.

"Sarrask of Sask won't aid us, of course," her father said.

"Sarrask of Sask's a fool," Chartiphon said shortly. "He should know that when Gormoth's conquered Hostigos, his turn will come next."

"He knows it," Xentos said calmly. "He'll try to strike before Gormoth does. But even if he wanted to, he'd not aid us. Not even King Kaiphranos dares aid those whom the priests of Styphon would destroy."

"They want that land in Wolf Valley, for a temple farm," she said slowly. "I know that would be bad, but—"

"Too late," Xentos told her. "Styphon's House is determined upon our destruction, as a warning to others." He turned to her father. "And it was on my advice, Lord, that you refused them."

"I'd have refused against your advice. I swore long ago that Styphon's House should never come into Hostigos while I lived, and by Dralm neither shall they! They come into a princedom, they build a temple, they make a temple farm, and make slaves of the peasants on it. They tax the prince, and force him to tax the people till nobody has anything left. Look at that temple farm in Sevenhills Valley."

"Yes, you'd hardly believe it," Chartiphon said. "They make the peasants on the farms around cart in their manure, till they have none left for their own fields. Dralm only knows what they do with it." He puffed at his pipe. "I wonder why they want Wolf Valley."

"There's something there that makes the water of those springs taste and smell badly," she considered.

"Sulfur," Xentos said. "But why do they want sulfur?"

Corporal Calvin Morrison, Pennsylvania State Police, crouched in the brush at the edge of the old field and looked across the brook at the farmhouse two hundred yards away, scabrous with peeling yellow paint and festooned by a sagging porchroof. A few white chickens pecked disinterestedly in the littered barnyard; there was no other sign of life, but he knew that there was a man inside. A man with a rifle, who would use it; he had murdered once, broken jail, would murder again.

He looked at his watch; the minute hand was squarely on the nine. Jack French and Steve Kovac would be starting down from the road above where they had left the car. He rose, unsnapping the retaining-strap of his holster.

"I'm starting. Watch that middle upstairs window."

"I'm watching," a voice behind assured him. A rifle action clattered softly as a cartridge went into the chamber. "Luck."

He started forward across the weed-grown field. He was scared, as scared as he'd been the first time, back in '52 in Korea, but there was nothing to do about that. He just told his legs to keep moving, knowing that in a few moments he wouldn't have time to be scared. He was almost to the little brook, his hand close to the butt of his Colt, when it happened.

There was a blinding flash, followed by a moment's darkness. He thought he'd been shot; by pure reflex, the .38-special was in his hand. Then, all around him, a flickering iridescence of many colors glowed, in a perfect hemisphere thirty feet across and fifteen high, and in front of him was an oval desk or cabinet, with an instrument panel over it, and a swivel chair from which a man was turning and rising. Young, well-built; wore loose green trousers and black ankle boots and a pale green shirt; a shoulder holster under his left arm, a weapon in his hand.

He was sure it was a weapon, though it looked more like an electric soldering iron, with two slender metal rods instead of a barrel, joined at the front in a blue ceramic knob. It was probably something that made his own Official Police look like a kid's cap pistol, and it was coming up fast to line on him.

He fired, holding the trigger back to keep the hammer down on the fired chamber, and threw himself down, hearing something fall with a crash, landing on his left hand and his left hip and rolling, until the nacreous dome was gone from around him and he bumped hard against something. For a moment, he lay still, then rose to his feet, letting out the trigger of the Colt.

What he'd bumped into was a tree. That wasn't right, there'd been no trees around, nothing but brush. And this tree, and the others, were huge, great columns rising to support a green roof through which only stray gleams of sunlight leaked. Hemlocks, must have been growing here while Columbus was conning Isabella into hocking her jewelry. Come to think of it, there was a stand of trees like this in Alan Seeger Forest. Maybe that was where he was.

He wondered how he was going to explain this.

"While approaching the house," he began aloud and in a formal tone, "I was intercepted by a flying saucer, the operator of which threatened me with a ray pistol. I defended myself with my revolver, firing one round—"

No. That wouldn't do, at all.

He swung out the cylinder of his Colt, ejecting the fired round and replacing it. Then he looked around, and started in the direction of where the farmhouse ought to be, coming to the little brook and jumping across.

Verkan Vall watched the landscape flicker outside the almost invisible shimmer of the transportation field. The mountains stayed the same, but from one time-line to another there was a good deal of randomness about which tree grew where. Occasionally there were glimpses of open country and buildings and installations, the Fifth Level bases his people had established. The red light overhead winked off and on, and each time it went off, a buzzer sounded. The dome of the conveyer became a solid iridescence, and then a cold, inert metal mesh. The red light came on and stayed on. He was picking up the sigma-ray needler from the desk in front of him and holstering it when the door slid open and a lieutenant of Paratime Police looked in.

"Hello, Chief's Assistant. Any trouble?"

In theory, the Ghaldron-Hesthor transposition field was impenetrable from the outside, but in practice, especially when two conveyers going in opposite paratemporal directions interpenetrated, it would go weak, and outside objects, sometimes alive and hostile, would intrude. That was why Paratimers kept weapons at hand, and why conveyers were checked immediately on emergence; it was also why some Paratimers didn't make it home.

"Not this trip. My rocket ready?"

"Yes, sir. Be a little delay about an aircar for the rocketport." The lieutenant stepped inside, followed by a patrolman, who began taking the transportation record tape and the photo-film record out of the cabinet. "They'll call you when it's in."

He and the lieutenant strolled outside into the noise and color of the conveyer-head rotunda. He got out his cigarette case and offered it; the lieutenant flicked his lighter. They had only taken a few first puffs when another conveyer quietly materialized in a vacant space nearby. A couple of Paracops strolled over as the door opened, drawing their needlers. One peeped inside, then holstered his weapon and snatched a radio phone from his belt; the other entered cautiously. Throwing away his cigarette, he strode toward the newly arrived conveyer, the lieutenant following.

The chair was overturned; a Paracop, his tunic off and his collar open, lay on the floor, a needler a few inches from his outstretched hand. His shirt, pale green, was dark with blood. The lieutenant, without touching him, looked at him.

"Still alive," he said. "Bullet, or sword-thrust?"

"Bullet; I can smell nitro powder." Then he saw the hat lying on the floor, and stepped around the fallen man. Two men were coming in with an antigrav stretcher; they and the patrolmen got the wounded man onto it. "Look at this, lieutenant."

The lieutenant glanced at the hat. It was gray felt, wide-brimmed, the crown peaked with four indentations.

"Fourth Level," he said. "Europo-American."

He picked it up, glancing inside. The sweatband was lettered in gold, JOHN B. STETSON COMPANY. PHILADELPHIA, PA., and, hand-inked, *Cpl. Calvin Morrison, Penna. State Police*, and a number.

"I know that outfit," the lieutenant said. "Good men, every bit as good as ours."

"One was a split second better than one of ours." He got out his cigarette case. "Lieutenant, this is going to be a real baddie. This pickup's going to be missed, and the people who'll miss him will be one of the ten best constabulary organizations in the world on their time-line. They won't be put off with the sort of lame-brained explanations that usually get by on Europo-American. They'll want factual proof and physical evidence. And we'll have to find where he came out. A man who can beat a Paracop to the draw won't sink into obscurity on any time-line. He's going to kick up a fuss that'll have to be smoothed over."

"I hope he doesn't come out on a next-door time-line and turn up at a duplicate of his own police post, where a duplicate of himself is on duty.

With identical fingerprints," the lieutenant said. "That would kick up a small fuss."

"Wouldn't it?" He went to the cabinet and took out the synchronized transposition record and photo film. "Have that rocket held; I'll want it after a while. But I'm going over these myself. I'm going to make this operation my own personal baby."

Calvin Morrison dangled black-booted legs over the edge of the low cliff and wished, again, that he hadn't lost his hat. He knew exactly where he was, he was on the little cliff, not more than a big outcrop, above the road where they'd left the car, but there was no road under it now, nor ever had been. And there was a hemlock four feet at the butt growing right where the farmhouse ought to be, and no trace of the stone foundations of it or the barn. But the really permanent features, the Bald Eagles to the north and Nittany Mountain to the south, were exactly as they should be.

That flash and momentary darkness could have been subjective; put that in the unproven column. He was sure the strangely beautiful dome of shimmering light had been real, and so had the oval desk and the instrument panel and the man with the odd weapon. And there was certainly nothing subjective about all this virgin forest where farmlands ought to be.

He didn't for an instant consider questioning either his senses or his sanity; neither did he indulge in dirty language like "incredible," or "impossible." Extraordinary; now there was a good word. He was quite sure that something extraordinary had happened to him. It seemed to break into two parts: (One), the dome of pearly light and what had happened inside it, and, (Two), emerging into this same-but-different place.

What was wrong with both was anachronism, and the anachronisms were mutually contradictory. None of (One) belonged in 1964 or, he suspected, for many centuries to come. None of (Two) belonged in 1964, either, or at any time within two centuries in the past. His pipe had gone out; for a while he forgot to relight it, while tossing those two facts back and forth. Then he got out his lighter and thumbed it, and then buttoned it back in his pocket.

In spite—no, because—of his clergyman father's insistence that he study for and enter the Presbyterian ministry, he was an agnostic. Agnosticism, to him, was refusal either to accept or reject without factual proof. A good philosophy for a cop, by the way. Well, he wasn't going to reject the possibility of time machines; not after having been shanghaied out of his own time in one. Whenever he was, it wasn't the Twentieth Century, and he was never going to get back to it. He made up his mind on that once and for all.

Climbing down from the low cliff, he went to the little brook, and followed it to where it joined a larger stream, just as he knew it would. A bluejay made a fuss at his approach. Two deer ran in front of him. A small black bear regarded him with suspicion and hastened away. Now, if he could find some Indians who wouldn't throw tomahawks first and ask questions afterward . . .

A road dipped to cross the stream. For a moment, he accepted that, then caught his breath. A real, wheel-rutted road! And brown horse-droppings in it; they were the most beautiful things he had seen since he came into this here-and-now. They meant that he hadn't beaten Columbus here, after all. He'd have trouble giving a plausible account of himself, but at least he could do it in English. Maybe he was even in time to get into the Civil War. He waded through the ford and started west along the road, toward where Bellefonte ought to be.

The sun went down in front of him. By now, the big hemlocks were gone, lumbered off, and there was a respectable second growth, mostly hardwoods. Finally, in the dusk, he smelled turned earth beside the road. It was full dark before he saw a light ahead.

The house was only a dim shape, the light came from narrow horizontal windows near the roof. Behind, he thought he could make out stables and, by his nose, pigpens. Two dogs ran into the road and began whauff-whauffing in front of him. "Hello, in there!" he called. Through the open windows he heard voices, a man's, a woman's, another man's. He called again. A bar scraped, and the door swung in. A woman, heavy-bodied, in a dark dress, stood aside for him to enter.

It was all one big room, lighted by one candle on a table and one on the mantel and by the fire on the hearth. Double-deck bunks along one wall, table spread with a meal. There were three men and another woman beside the one who had admitted him, and from the corner of his eye he could see children peering around a door that seemed to open into a shed annex. One of the men, big and blond-bearded, stood with his back to the fire, with something that looked like a short gun in his hands. No it wasn't, either; it was a crossbow, bent and quarrel in place.

The other men were younger, the crossbowman's sons for a guess; they were bearded, too, though one's beard was only a fuzz. They all wore short-sleeved jerkins of leather and cross-gartered hose. One of the younger men had a halberd and the other an axe. The older woman spoke in a whisper to the younger; she went through the door, pushing the children ahead of her.

He lifted his hands pacifically as he entered. "I'm a friend," he said. "I'm going to Bellefonte; how far is it?"

The man with the crossbow said something. The man with the halberd said something. The woman replied. The youth with the axe said something, and they all laughed.

"My name's Calvin Morrison. Corporal, Pennsylvania State Police."
Hell, they wouldn't know the State Police from the Swiss Marines. "Am I
on the road to Bellefonte?"

More back-and-forth. They weren't talking Pennsylvania Dutch, he was
sure of that. Maybe Polish; no, he'd heard enough of that to recognize, if
he couldn't understand, it. He looked around, while they argued, and saw,
in the far corner left of the fireplace, three images on a shelf. He meant to
get a closer look at them. Roman Catholics used images, so did Greek
Catholics, and he could tell the difference.

The man with the crossbow laid his weapon down, but kept it bent and
loaded, and spoke slowly and distinctly. It was no language he had ever
heard before. He replied just as distinctly in English. They all looked at one
another, passing their hands in front of their faces in bafflement. Finally, by
signs, they invited him to sit down and eat, and the children, six of them,
trooped in.

The meal was roast ham, potatoes and succotash. The eating tools were
knives and a few horn spoons; the men used their sheath knives. He took
out his jackknife, a big switchblade he'd taken off an arrest he'd made. It
caused a sensation, and he had to demonstrate it several times. There was
also elderberry wine, strong but not particularly good. Then they left the
table for the women to clear, and the men filled pipes from a tobacco jar
on the mantel, offering it to him. He filled his pipe and lighted it, as they
did theirs, with a twig at the fire. Stepping back, he got a look at the images.

The central figure was an elderly man in a white robe, with a blue eight-
pointed star on the breast. He was flanked, on one side, by a seated female figure, exaggeratedly pregnant, crowned with a grain, and holding a cornstalk,
and, on the other, by a masculine figure in a male shirt, with a spiked mace.
The only really unusual thing about him was that he had the head of a wolf.
Father-god, fertility-goddess, war-god; no, this gang weren't Catholics,
Greek, Roman or any other kind. He bowed to the central figure, touching
his forehead, and repeated the gesture to the other two. There was a grati-
fied murmur behind him; anybody could see he wasn't any heathen. Then he
sat down on a chest against the wall.

They hadn't re-barred the door. The children had been chased back into
the shed after the meal. Nobody was talking, everybody was listening. Now
that he remembered, there had been a vacant place at the table. They'd sent
one of the youngsters off with a message. As soon as he finished his pipe, he
pocketed it, and unobtrusively unsnapped the strap of his holster. It might
have been half an hour before he heard galloping hoofs down the road. He
affected not to hear; so did everybody else. The older man moved over to

where he had put down his crossbow; his elder son got the halberd and a rag as though to polish the blade. The horses clattered to a stop outside, accoutrements jingled. The dogs set up a frantic barking. He slipped the .38 out and cocked it.

The youngest man went to the door. Before he could touch it, it flew open in his face, knocking him backward, and a man—bearded face under a high-combed helmet, steel breastplate, black and orange scarf—burst in, swinging a long sword. Everybody in the room shouted in alarm; this wasn't what they'd been expecting, at all. There was another helmeted head behind the first man, and the muzzle of a short musket. Outside, a shot boomed and one of the dogs howled.

He rose from the chest and shot the man with the sword. Half-cocking with the double action and thumbing the hammer the rest of the way, he shot the man with the musket. The musket went off into the ceiling. A man behind caught a crossbow quarrel through the forehead and pitched forward on top of the other two, dropping a long pistol unfired.

Shifting the Colt to his left hand, he caught up the sword the first man had dropped. It was lighter than it looked, and beautifully balanced. He tramped over the bodies in the doorway, to be confronted by another swordsman outside. For a few moments they cut and parried, and then he drove his point into his opponent's unarmored face and tugged his blade free. The man in front of him went down. The boy who had been knocked down had gotten hold of the dropped pistol and fired it, hitting a man who was holding a clump of horses in the road. The older son dashed out with his halberd, chopping a man down. The father had gotten hold of the musket and ammunition, and was ramming a charge into it.

Driving the point of the sword into the ground, he holstered the .38-special; as one of the loose horses dashed past, he caught the reins and stopped it, vaulting into the saddle. Then, stooping, he retrieved his sword, thankful that even in a motorized age the State Police insisted on teaching their men to ride. The fight was over, at least here. Six attackers were down, presumably dead. The other two were galloping away. Five loose horses milled about, and the two young men were trying to catch them. The older man, priming the pan of the gun, came outside, looking around.

This had only been a sideshow fight, though. The main event was half a mile down the road, where he could hear shots, yells, and screams, and where a sudden orange glare mounted into the night. He was wondering just what he'd cut himself into when the fugitives began streaming up the road. He had no trouble identifying them as such; he'd seen enough of that in Korea. Another fire was blazing up beside the first one.

Some of them had weapons, spears and axes, a few bows, and he saw one big musket. His bearded host shouted at them, and they stopped.

"What's going on, down there?" he demanded loudly.

Babble answered him. One or two tried to push past; he hit at them with his flat, cursing them luridly. The words meant nothing, but the tone did. That had worked for him in Korea, too. They all stopped, in a clump; a few cheered. Many were women and children, and not all the men were armed. Call it twenty effectives. The bodies in the road were quickly stripped of weapons; out of the corner of his eye he saw the two women of the house passing things out the door. Four of the riderless horses had been caught and mounted. More fugitives came up, saw what was going on, and joined.

"All right!" he bawled. "You guys want to live forever?" He swung his sword to include all of them, then stabbed down the road with it. "Let's go!"

A cheer went up, and as he started his horse the whole mob poured after him, shouting. They met more fugitives, who stopped, saw that a counter-attack had been organized, if that were the word for it, and joined. The fire-light was brighter, half a dozen houses must be burning now, but the shooting had stopped. Nobody left to shoot at, he supposed.

Then, when they were halfway to the burning village, there was a blast of forty or fifty shots in less than ten seconds, and more yelling, much of it in alarm. More shots, and then mounted men began streaming up the road; this was a rout. Everybody with guns or bows let fly at them. A horse went down, and another had its saddle emptied. Considering how many shots it had taken for one casualty in Korea, that wasn't bad. He stood up in his stir-rups, which were an inch or so too short for him as it was, and yelled, *Chaaarge!*—like Teddy, in "Arsenic and Old Lace."

A man coming in the opposite direction aimed a cut at his bare head. He parried and thrust, his point glanced from a breastplate, and before he could recover the other's horse had carried him past and among the spears and pitchforks behind. Then he was trading thrusts for cuts with another rider, wondering if none of these imbeciles ever heard that a sword had a point. By this time, the road for a hundred yards ahead, and the open field on the left, was a swirl of horsemen, chopping and firing at each other.

He got his point in under his opponent's armpit, almost had the sword wrenched from his hand, and then saw another rider coming at him, unar-mored and wearing a wide hat and a cloak, aiming a pistol almost as long as the arm that held it. He urged his horse forward, swinging back for a cut at the weapon, and knew that he wouldn't make it. *O.K., Cal; your luck's run out.* There was an upflash from the pan of the pistol, a belch of flame from the muzzle, and something sledged him in the chest.

He hung onto consciousness long enough to kick his feet free of the stirrups. In that last moment, he was aware that the rider who had shot him had been a young girl.

Vekan Vall put the lighter down on the desk and took the cigarette from his mouth. Tortha Karf leaned back in the chair in which he, himself, would be sitting all too soon.

"We had one piece of luck, right at the start. The time-line is one we've already penetrated. One of our people, in a newspaper office in Philadelphia, that's the nearest large city, reported the disappearance. The press associations have it already, there's nothing we can do about that."

"Well, just what did happen, on the pickup time-line?"

"This Corporal Morrison and three other State Policemen were closing in on a house in which a wanted criminal was hiding. Morrison and another man were in front; the other two were coming in from behind. Morrison started forward, his companion covering for him with a rifle. This other man is the nearest to a witness there is, and he was watching the front of the house and was only marginally aware of Morrison. He heard the other two officers pounding on the back door and demanding admittance, and then the man they were after burst out the front door with a rifle in his hands. Morrison's companion shouted at him to halt; the criminal raised his rifle, and the State Police officer shot him, killing him instantly.

"Then, he says, he realized that Morrison was nowhere in sight. He called to him, without answer. The man they were after was dead, he wouldn't run off, so all three of them hunted for Morrison for almost half an hour. Then they took the body in to the county seat and had to go through a lot of formalities, and it was evening before they were back at their substation. A local reporter happened to be there at the time. He got the story, including the disappearance of Morrison, phoned it to his paper, and the press associations got it from there. Now the State Police refuse to discuss, and are even trying to deny, the disappearance."

"They believe their man lost his nerve, bolted, and is now ashamed to come back," Tortha Karf said. "Naturally they wouldn't want anything like that getting out. Are you going to use that line?"

He nodded. "The hat he lost in the conveyer. It will be planted about a mile from the scene, along a stream. Then one of our people will catch a local, preferably a boy of twelve or so, give him a hypno-injection, and instruct him to find the hat and take it to the State Police. The reporter responsible for the original news break will be notified by anonymous phone call. Later, there will be the usual spate of rumors of Morrison having been seen in all sorts of unlikely places."

"How about his family?"

"We're in luck there, too. Unmarried, parents both dead, only a few relatives with whom he didn't maintain contact."

"That's good. How about the exit?"

"We have that approximated; Aryan-Transpacific. We're not quite sure even of the sector, because the transposition field was weak for several thousand parayears and we can't determine the instant he broke out of the conveyer. It'll be thirty or forty days before we have it pinpointed. We have one positive indication to look for at the scene."

The chief nodded. "The empty cartridge?"

"Yes. He used a revolver, they don't eject automatically. As soon as he was out and no longer immediately threatened, he would open his revolver, remove the empty, and replace it. I'm as sure of that as though I saw him do it. We may not be able to find it, but if we do, it'll be positive proof."

He woke, in bed under soft covers, and for a moment lay with his eyes closed. There was a clicking sound near him, and from a distance an anvil rang, and there was shouting. Then he opened his eyes. He was in a fairly large room, paneled walls and a painted ceiling; two windows on one side, both open, and nothing but blue sky visible through them. A woman, stout and gray-haired, sat under one, knitting. His boots stood beside a chest across the room, and on its top were piled his clothes and his belt and revolver. A long unsheathed sword with a swept handguard and a copper pommel leaned against the wall by the boots. His body was stiff and sore, and his upper torso was swathed in bandages.

The woman looked up quickly as he stirred, then put down her knitting and rose, going to a table and pouring water for him. Pitcher and cup were silver, elaborately chased. He took the cup, drank, and handed it back, thanking her. She replaced it on the table and went out.

He wasn't a prisoner, the presence of the sword and revolver proved that. This was the crowd that had surprised the raiders at the village. That whole business had been a piece of luck for him. He ran a hand over his chin and estimated about three days' growth of stubble. His fingernails had grown enough since last trimmed to confirm that. He'd have a nasty hole in his chest, and possibly a broken rib.

The woman returned, accompanied by a man in a cowled blue robe with an eight-pointed white star on his breast. Reversed colors from the image at the peasant's farm; a priest, doubling as doctor. The man laid a hand on his brow, felt his pulse, and spoke in a cheerfully optimistic tone; the bedside manner seemed to be a universal constant. With the woman's help, he changed the bandages and smeared the wound with ointment. The woman took out the old bandages and returned with a steaming bowl. It was turkey broth, with finely minced meat in it. While he was finishing it, two more visitors entered.

One was robed like the doctor, his cowl thrown back. He had white hair, and a good face, gentle and pleasant. His companion was a girl with blond hair cut in what would be a page-boy bob in the Twentieth Century; she had blue eyes and red lips and an impudent tilty little nose dusted with golden freckles. She wore a jerkin of something like brown suede, stitched with gold thread, a yellow under-tunic with long sleeves and a high neck, knit hose and thigh-length boots. There was a gold chain around her neck, and a gold-hilted dagger on her belt. He began to laugh when he saw her; they'd met before.

"You shot me!" he accused, then aimed an imaginary pistol, said, "Bang!" and pointed to his chest.

She said something to the older priest, he replied, and she said something to him, pantomiming shame and sorrow, covering her face with one hand and winking at him over it. When he laughed, she laughed with him. Perfectly natural mistake, she hadn't known which side he was on. The two priests held a lengthy colloquy, and the younger brought him about four ounces of something in a tumbler. It tasted alcoholic and medicinally bitter. They told him, by signs, to go to sleep, and went out, all but the gray-haired woman, who went back to her chair and her knitting. He dozed off.

Late in the afternoon he woke briefly. Outside, somebody was drilling troops. Tramping feet, a voice counting cadence, long-drawn preparatory commands, sharp commands, of execution, clattering equipment. That was another universal constant. He smiled; he wasn't going to have much trouble finding a job, here-and-now, whenever now was.

It wasn't the past. Penn's Colony had never been like this. It was more like Sixteenth Century Europe, but no Sixteenth Century cavalryman, who was as incompetent a swordsman as that gang he'd been fighting, would have lived to wear out his first pair of issue boots. And two years in college and a lot of independent reading had given him at least a nodding acquaintance with most of the gods of his own history, and none, back to Egypt and Sumeria, had been like that trio on the peasant's shrine shelf.

So it was the future. A far future, maybe a thousand years later than 1964, A.D.; a world devastated by atomic wars, blasted back to the Stone Age, and then bootstrap-lifted to something like the end of the Middle Ages. That wasn't important, though. Now was when he was, and now was when he was stuck.

Make the best of it, Cal. You're a soldier; you just got re-assigned, that's all.

He went back to sleep.

• • •

The next morning, after breakfast, he sign-talked the woman watching over him to bring him his tunic, and got out his pipe and tobacco and lighter from the pockets. She brought him a stool to set beside the bed to put things on. The badge on the tunic breast was twisted and lead-splotched; that was why he was still alive.

The old priest and the girl were in, an hour later. This time, she was wearing a red and gray knit frock that could have gone into Bergdorf Goodman's window with a $200 price-tag any day, but the dagger she wore with it wasn't exactly Fifth Avenue. They greeted him, then pulled chairs up beside the bed and got to business.

First they taught him words for "You," and "Me," and "He," and "She," and names. The girl was Rylla. The old priest was Xentos. The younger priest, who came in to see his patient, was Mytron. Calvin Morrison puzzled them; evidently they didn't have surnames here-and-now. They settled for calling him Kalvan. They had several shingle-sized boards of white pine, and sticks of charcoal, to draw pictures. Rylla smoked a pipe, with a small stone bowl and a cane stem, which she carried on her belt along with her dagger. His lighter intrigued her, and she showed him her own. It was a tinderbox, the flint held down by a spring against a semicircular striker which was pushed by hand and returned for another push by a spring. With a spring to drive the striker instead of returning it, it would have done for a gunlock. By noon, they were able to tell him that he was their friend, and he was able to tell Rylla he didn't blame her for shooting him in the skirmish on the road.

They were back in the afternoon, accompanied by a gentleman with a gray mustache and imperial, wearing a garment like a fur-collared bathrobe, with a sword-belt over it. He had a large gold chain around his neck. His name was Ptosphes, and after much pantomime and picture-writing it emerged that he was Rylla's father, that he was Prince of this place, and that this place was Hostigos. Rylla's mother was dead. The raiders with whom he had fought had come from a place called Nostor, to the north and east, ruled by a Prince Gormoth. Gormoth was not well thought of in Hostigos.

The next day, he was up in a chair, and they began giving him solid food, and wine. The wine was excellent; so was the tobacco they gave him. He decided he was going to like it, here-and-now. Rylla was in at least twice a day, sometimes alone, sometimes with Xentos, and sometimes with a big man with a graying beard, Chartiphon, who seemed to be Ptosphes' top soldier. He always wore a sword, and often an ornate but battered steel back-and-breast. Sometimes he visited alone, and occasionally accompanied by a younger officer, a cavalryman named Harmakros. Harmakros had been in the skirmish at the raided village, but Rylla had been in command.

"The gods," he explained, "did not give Prince Ptosphes a son. A Prince should have a son, to rule after him, so the Princess Rylla must be a son to him."

The gods, he thought, ought to be persuaded to furnish Ptosphes with a son-in-law, named Calvin Morrison, no, Kalvan. He made up his mind to give the gods a hand on that.

Chartiphon showed him a map, elaborately illuminated on parchment. Hostigos appeared to be all of Centre and Union counties, a snip of Clinton south and west of where Lock Haven ought to be, and southeastern Lycoming, east of the West Branch, which was the Athan, and south of the Bald Eagles, the Mountains of Hostigos. Nostor was the West Branch Valley from above Lock Haven to the forks of the river, and it obtruded south into Hostigos through Ante's Gap, Dombra Gap, to take in Nippenose, Sevenhills Valley. To the west, all of Blair County, and parts of Huntington and Bedford, was the Princedom of Sask, ruled by Prince Sarrask. Sarrask was no friend; Gormoth was an open enemy.

On a bigger map, he saw that all Pennsylvania and Maryland, Delaware and the southern half of New Jersey, was the Great Kingdom of Hos-Harphax, ruled from Harphax City at the mouth of the Susquehanna by King Kaiphranos. Ptosphes, Gormoth, Sarrask and a dozen other princes were his nominal subjects. Judging from what he had seen on the night of his advent here-and-now, Kaiphranos' authority would be maintained for about one day's infantry march around his capital and ignored elsewhere.

He had a suspicion that Hostigos was in a bad squeeze, between Nostor and Sask. Something was bugging these people. Too often, while laughing with him—she was teaching him to read and write, now, and that was fun—Rylla would remember something she wanted to forget, and then her laughter would be strained. Chartiphon was always preoccupied; occasionally he'd forget, for a moment, what he was talking about. And he never saw Ptosphes smile.

Xentos showed him a map of the world. The world, it seemed, was not round, but flat like a pancake. Hudson's Bay was in the exact center, North America was shaped rather like India, Florida ran almost due east and Cuba north and south. The West Indies were a few random spots to show that the mapmaker had heard about them from somebody. Asia was attached to North America, but it was still blank. An illimitable ocean stretched around the perimeter. Europe, Africa and South America simply weren't. Xentos wanted him to show the country from which he had come. He put his finger down on central Pennsylvania's approximate location. Xentos thought he misunderstood.

"No, Kalvan. This is your home now, and we want you to stay with us, but where is the country you came from?"

"Here," he insisted. "But at another time, a thousand years from now. I had an enemy, an evil sorcerer. Another sorcerer, who was my friend, put a protection on me that I might not be slain by sorcery, so my enemy twisted time around me and hurled me far into the past, before my first known ancestor had been born, and now here I am and here I must stay."

Xentos' hand made a quick circle around the white star on his breast, and he muttered rapidly. Another universal constant.

"What a terrible fate!"

"Yes. I do not like to speak of it, but it was right that you should know. You may tell Prince Ptosphes and Princess Rylla and Chartiphon, but beg them not to speak of it to me. I must forget my old life and make a new one in this time. You may tell the others merely that I come from a far country. From here." He indicated the approximate location of Korea. "I was there, once, fighting in a great war."

"Ah; I knew you had been a warrior." Xentos hesitated, then asked: "Do you know sorcery?"

"No. My father was a priest, as you are, and wished me to become a priest also, and our priest hated sorcery. But I knew that I would never be a good priest, so when this war came, I left my studies and went to fight. Afterward, I was a warrior in my own country, to keep the peace."

Xentos nodded. "If one cannot be a good priest, one should not be a priest at all, and to be a good warrior is almost as good. Tell me, what gods did your people worship?"

"Oh, we had many gods. There was Conformity, and Authority, and Opinion. And there was Status, whose symbols were many and who rode in the great chariot Cadillac, which was almost a god itself. And there was Atombomb, the dread Destroyer, who would someday end the world. For myself, I worshiped none of them. Tell me about your gods, Xentos."

Then he filled his pipe and lit it with the tinderbox he had learned to use in place of his now fuelless Zippo. He didn't need to talk any more; Xentos was telling him about his own god, Dralm, and about Yirtta the All-Mother, and wolf-headed Galzar the god of battle, and Tranth the lame craftsman—funny how often craftsman-gods were lame—and about all the others.

"And Styphon," he added grudgingly. "Styphon is an evil god, and evil men serve him, and are given great wealth and power."

After that, he noticed a subtle change in manner toward him. He caught Rylla looking at him in wondering pity. Chartiphon merely clasped his hand and said, "You'll like it here with us, Kalvan." Prince Ptosphes hemmed and hawed, and said: "Xentos tells me there are things you don't want to talk about, Kalvan. Nobody will mention them to you, ever. We're all happy to have you with us. Stay, and make this your home."

The others treated him with profound respect. They'd been told that he was a prince from a distant land, driven from his throne by treason. They gave him clothes, more than he had ever owned before, and weapons. Rylla gave him a pair of her own pistols, one of which had wounded him in the skirmish. They were two feet long, but lighter than his .38 Colt, the barrels almost paper-thin at the muzzles. They had locks operating on the same principle as the tinderboxes, and Rylla's name was inlaid in gold on the butts. They gave him another, larger room, and a body servant.

As soon as he was able to walk unaided, he went outside to watch the troops being drilled. They had no uniforms except scarves or sashes of Ptosphes' colors, red and blue. The infantry wore leather or canvas jacks sewn with metal plates, and helmets not unlike the one he'd worn in Korea. Some had pikes, some halberds, and some hunting spears, and many had scythe blades with the tangs straightened out, on eight-foot shafts. Foot movements were simple and uncomplicated; the squad was unknown, and they maneuvered by platoons of forty or fifty.

A few of the firearms were huge fifteen-pound muskets, aimed and fired from rests. Most were lighter, arquebuses, calivers, and a miscellany of hunting guns. There would be two or three musketeers and a dozen caliv-ermen or arquebusiers to each spear-and-scythe platoon. There were also archers and crossbowmen. The cavalry were good; they wore cuirasses and high-combed helmets, and were armed with swords and pistols and either lances or short musketoons. The artillery was laughable; wrought-iron six- to twelve-pounders, hand-welded tubes strengthened with shrunk-on bands, without trunnions. They were mounted on four-wheel carts. He made up his mind to do something about that.

He also noticed that while the archers and crossbowmen practiced constantly, not a single practice shot was fired with any firearm.

He took his broadsword to the castle bladesmith and wanted it ground down into a rapier. The bladesmith thought he was crazy. He called in a cav-alry lieutenant and demonstrated with a pair of wooden practice swords. Immediately, the lieutenant wanted a rapier, too. The blacksmith promised to make both of them real rapiers. By the next evening, his own was finished.

"You have enemies on both sides, Nostor and Sask, and that's not good," he said one evening as he and Ptosphes and Rylla and Xentos and Chartiphon sat over a flagon of wine in the Prince's study. "You've made me one of you. Now tell me what I can do to help."

"Well, Kalvan," Ptosphes said, "you could better tell us that. You know many things we don't. The thrusting sword"—he glanced down admiringly at his own new rapier—"and what you told Chartiphon about mounting cannon. What else can you give us to help fight our enemies?"

"Well, I can't teach you to make weapons like that six-shooter of mine, or ammunition for it." He tried, as simply as possible, to explain about machine industry and mass production; they only stared in uncomprehending wonder. "I can show you things you don't know but can do with the tools you have. For instance, we cut spiral grooves in the bores of our guns to make the bullets spin. Grooved guns will shoot harder, farther and straighter than smoothbores. I can show your gunsmiths how to do that with guns you already have. And there's another thing." He mentioned never having seen any practice firing. "You have very little powder, fireseed, you call it. Is that it?"

"We haven't enough in Hostigos to fire all the cannon of this castle once," Chartiphon said. "And we can't get any. The priests of Styphon will give us none, and they send cart after cart of it to Nostor."

"You mean, you get fireseed from the priests of Styphon? Can't you get it from anybody else, or make your own?"

They all looked at him, amazed that he didn't know any better.

"Only Styphon's House can make fireseed, and that by Styphon's aid," Xentos said. "That was what I meant when I said that Styphon gives his servants great wealth, and power even over the Great Kings."

He gave Styphon's House the grudging respect any good cop gives a really smart crook. Styphon's House had a real racket. No wonder this country was a snakepit of warring princes and barons. Styphon's House wanted it that way; it kept them in the powder business. He set down his goblet and laughed.

"You think nobody can make fireseed but Styphon's House?" he demanded. "Why, in my time, even the children could do that." Well, children who got as far as high school chemistry; he'd almost gotten expelled, once. "I can make fireseed, right here on this table!"

Ptosphes threw back his head and laughed. Just a trifle hysterically, but it was the first time he'd ever heard the Prince laugh. Chartiphon banged a fist on the table and shouted, "Ha, Gormoth! Now see how soon your head goes up over your own gate!" And no War Crimes foolishness about it, either. Rylla flung her arms around him. "Kalvan! You really and truly can?"

"But it is only by the power of Styphon . . ." Xentos began.

"Styphon's a big fake; his priests are a pack of impudent swindlers. You want to see me make fireseed? Get Mytron in here; he has everything I need in his dispensary. I want sulfur, he has that, and saltpeter, he has that." Mytron gives sulfur mixed with honey for colds; saltpeter was supposed to cool the blood. "And charcoal, and a couple of brass mortars and pestles, and a flour-screen, and balance-scales."

"Go on, man; hurry!" Ptosphes cried. "Bring him anything he wants."

• • •

Xentos went out. He asked for a pistol, and Ptosphes brought one from a closet behind him. He opened the pan and dumped out the priming on a sheet of parchment, touching it off with a lighted splinter. It scorched the parchment, which it shouldn't have, and left too much black residue. Styphon wasn't a very honest powdermaker; he cheapened his product with too much charcoal and not enough saltpeter. Xentos returned, accompanied by Mytron; the two priests carried jars, and a bucket of charcoal, and the other things. Xentos seemed dazed; Mytron was scared and trying not to show it.

He put Mytron to work grinding charcoal in one mortar and Xentos to grinding saltpeter in the other. The sulfur was already pulverized. Screening each, he mixed them in a dry goblet, saltpeter .75, charcoal .15, sulfur .10; he had to think a little to remember that.

"But it's just dust," Chartiphon objected.

"Yes. The mixture has to be moistened, worked into a dough, pressed into cakes and dried, and then ground and sieved. We can't do all that now, but this will flash. Look."

He primed the pistol with a pinch of it, aimed at a half burned log in the fireplace, and squeezed. The pistol roared and kicked. Ptosphes didn't believe in reduced charges, that was for sure. Outside, somebody shouted, feet pounded, and the door flew open. A guard with a halberd looked in.

"The Lord Kalvan is showing us something with a pistol," Ptosphes said. "There may be more shots; nobody is to worry."

"All right," he said, when the guard closed the door. "Now we see how it fires." He poured in about forty grains, wadded it with a bit of rag, and primed it, handing it to Rylla. "You fire. This is a great moment in the history of Hostigos. I hope."

She pushed down the striker, aimed into the fireplace and squeezed. The report wasn't quite as loud, but it did fire. They tried it with a bullet, which went into the log half an inch. He laid the pistol on the table. The room was full of smoke, and they were all coughing, but nobody cared. Chartiphon went to the door and bawled into the hall for more wine.

"But you said no prayers," Mytron faltered. "You just made fireseed. Just like cooking soup."

"That's right. And soon everybody will make fireseed."

And when that day comes, the priests of Styphon will be out on the sidewalk beating a drum for pennies. Chartiphon wanted to know how soon they would be able to march on Nostor.

"It will take more fireseed than Kalvan can make here on this table," Ptosphes told him. "We will need saltpeter, and charcoal, and sulfur. We will have to teach people how to get these things, and grind and mix them. We will need things we don't have, and tools to make them. And nobody knows all this but Kalvan, and there is only one of him."

Well, glory be, Ptosphes had gotten something from the lecture on production, if nobody else had.

"Mytron knows a few things, I think. Where did you get the sulfur and the saltpeter?" he asked the doctor-priest.

Mytron had downed his first goblet of wine at one gulp. He had taken three to the second; now he was working his way down the third and coming out of shock nicely. It was about as he thought. The saltpeter was found in crude lumps under manure piles and refined; the sulfur was gotten by evaporating water from the sulfur springs in Sugar Valley, Wolf Valley here-and-now. For some reason, mention of this threw both Ptosphes and Chartiphon into a fury. He knew how to extract both, on a quart-jar scale. He was a trifle bewildered when told how much would be needed for military purposes.

"But this'll take time," Chartiphon objected. "And as soon as Gormoth hears about it, he'll attack, before we can get any made."

"Don't let him hear about it. Clamp down the security." He had to explain that. "Cavalry patrols, on all the roads and trails out of Hostigos; let anybody in, but don't let anybody out. And here's another thing. I'll have to give orders, and people won't like them. Will I be obeyed?"

"By anybody who wants to keep his head on his shoulders," Ptosphes said. "You speak with my voice."

"And with mine, Lord Kalvan!" Chartiphon was on his feet, extending his sword for him to touch the hilt. "I am at your orders; you command here."

They gave him a room inside the main gateway of the citadel, across from the guardroom, a big flagstone-floored place with the indefinable but unmistakable flavor of a police court. The walls were white plaster, he could write and draw diagrams on them with charcoal. Paper was unknown, here-and-now. He decided to do something about that, after the war. It was a wonder these people had gotten as far as they had without it. Rylla attached herself to him as adjutant. He gathered in Mytron and the chief priest of Tranth, all the master-artisans in Tarr-Hostigos and some from Hostigo Town, a couple of Chartiphon's officers, and some soldiers to carry messages.

Charcoal was going to be easy, there was plenty of that. For sulfur evaporation he'd need big pans, and sheet iron, larger than a breastplate or a cooking pan—all unavailable. There were bog-iron mines over in Bald Eagle, Listra Valley, and ironworks, but no rolling mill. They'd have to beat sheet iron out by hand in two-foot squares and weld them together like a patch quilt. Saltpeter could be accumulated from all over. Manure piles, at least one to a farm, were the best source, and stables, cellars, underground drains. He set up a saltpeter commission, headed by one of Chartiphon's officers, with authority to go anywhere and enter anything, to hang any subordinate who abused that authority out of hand, and to deal just as summarily with anybody who tried to obstruct.

Mobile units, oxcarts loaded with caldrons, tubs, tools and the like, to go from farm to farm. Peasant women to be collected and taught to leach nitrated soil and purify nitrates.

Grinding mills; there was plenty of water power, and the water wheel was known, here-and-now. Gristmills could be converted. Special grinding equipment, designing of. Sifting screens, cloth. Mixing machines, big casks with counter-rotating paddle wheels inside. Presses to squeeze dough into cakes. Mills to grind caked powder; he spent considerable thought on a set of regulations to prevent anything from striking a spark around them, with bloodthirsty enforcement threats.

During the morning, he ground up the cake he'd made the night before, running it through a couple of sieves to FFFg fineness. A hundred-grain charge in one of the big eight-bore muskets drove the two-ounce ball an inch deeper into a log than an equal charge of Styphon's Best, and fouled the bore much less.

By noon, he was almost sure that most of his War Production Board understood most of what he'd told them. In the afternoon, there was a meeting in the outer bailey of as many of the people who would be working on the Fireseed Project as could be collected. There was an invocation of Dralm by Xentos. Ptosphes spoke, bearing down heavily on the fact that the Lord Kalvan had full authority and would be backed to the limit, by the headsman if necessary. Chartiphon made a speech, picturing the howling wilderness they were going to make of Nostor. He made a speech, himself, emphasizing that the there was nothing whatever of a supernatural nature about fireseed. The meeting then broke up into small groups, everybody having his own job explained to him. He was kept running back and forth from one to another to explain to the explainers.

In the evening, they had a feast. By that time, he and Rylla had gotten a rough table of organization charcoaled onto the wall in his headquarters.

Of the next four days, he spent eighteen hours of each in that room, talking to five or six hundred people. The artisans, who had a guild organization, objected to peasants invading their crafts. The masters complained that the apprentices and young journeymen were becoming intractable, which meant that they had started thinking for themselves. The peasants objected to having their dunghills forked down and the ground under them dug up, and to being put to unaccustomed work. The landlords objected to having the peasants taken from the fields, and predicted that the year's crop would be lost.

"Don't worry about that," he told them. "If we win, we'll eat Gormoth's crops. If we lose, we'll all be too dead to eat."

And the Iron Curtain went down. Itinerant pack traders and wagoners began to collect in Hostigos Town, trapped for the duration. Sooner or later, Gormoth and Sarrask would start wondering why nobody was leaving Hostigos, and send spies in through the woods to find out. Organize some counterespionage; get a few spies of his own into both princedoms.

By the fifth day, the sulfur-evaporation plant was operating, and saltpeter production had started, only a few pounds of each, but that would increase rapidly. He put Mytron in charge of the office, and went out to supervise mill construction. It was at this time that he began wearing armor, at least six and often eight hours a day—helmet over a padded coif, with a band of fine-linked mail around his throat and under his chin, steel back-and-breast over a quilted arming-doublet with mail sleeves, mail under the arms, and a mail skirt to below his hips, and double leather hose with mail between. The whole panoply weighed close to forty pounds, and his life was going to depend on accustoming himself to it.

Verkan Vall watched Tortha Karf spin the empty cartridge on the top of his desk. It was a very valuable empty cartridge; it had cost over ten thousand man-hours of crawling on hands and knees and pawing among dead hemlock needles, not counting transposition time.

"A marvel you found it, Vall. Aryan-Transpacific?"

"Oh, yes. We were sure of that from the first. Styphon's House subsector." He gave the numerical designation of the exact time-line.

"Styphon's House. That's that gunpowder theocracy, isn't it?"

That was it. At one time, Styphon had been a minor god of healing. Still was, on most of Aryan-Transpacific. But, three hundred years ago, on one time-line, a priest of Styphon, trying to concoct a new remedy for something, had mixed a batch of saltpeter, charcoal and sulfur—fortunately for him, a small batch—and put it on the fire. For fifty years, the mixture had been a temple miracle, and then its propellant properties were discovered, and Styphon had gone out of medical practice and into the munitions business. The powder had been improved by priestly researchers; weapons to use it were designed. Now no king or prince without gunpowder stood a chance against one with it. No matter who sat on any throne, Styphon's House was his master, because Styphon's House could throw him off it at will.

"I wonder if this Morrison knows how to make gunpowder," Tortha Karf said.

"I'll find that out. I'm going out there myself."

"You don't have to, you know. You have hundreds of men who could do that."

He shook his head obstinately. "After Year-End Day, I'm going to be chained to that chair of yours. But until then, I'm going to work outtime as much as I can." He leaned over to the map-screen and twiddled the selector until he had the Great Kingdom of Hos-Harphax. "I'm going in about here," he said. "I'll be a pack trader, they go anywhere without question. I'll have a saddle horse and three pack horses, with loads of appropriate merchandise. That's in the adjoining princedom of Sask. I'll travel slowly, to let word travel ahead of me. I may even hear something about this Morrison before I enter Hostigos."

"What'll you do when you find him?"

He shrugged. "That will depend on what he's doing, and particularly how he's accounting for himself. I don't want to, the man's a police officer like ourselves, but I'm afraid I'm going to have to kill him. He knows too much."

"What does he know, Vall?"

"First, he's seen the inside of a conveyer. He knows that it was something completely alien to his own culture and technology. Then, he knows that he was shifted in time, because he wasn't shifted to another place, and he will recognize that the conveyer was the means affecting that shift. From that, he will deduce a race of time-travelers.

"Now, he knows enough of the history of his own time-line to know that he wasn't shifted into the past. And he will also know he wasn't shifted into the future. That's all limestone country, where he was picked up and dropped, and on his own time-line it's been quarried extensively for the past fifty or more years. Traces of those operations would remain for tens of thousands of years, and he will find none of them. So what does that leave?"

"A lateral shift, and people who travel laterally in time," the chief said. "Why, that's the Paratime Secret itself."

There would be a feast at Tarr-Hostigos that evening. All morning cattle and pigs, lowing and squealing, had been driven in and slaughtered. Woodcutters' axes thudded for the roasting pits, casks of wine came up from the cellars. He wished the fireseed mills were as busy as the castle kitchens and bakeries. A whole day's production shot to hell. He said as much to Rylla.

"But, Kalvan, they're all so happy." She was pretty excited about it, herself. "And they've worked so hard."

He had to grant that, and maybe the morale gain would offset a day's work lost. And they had a full hundredweight of fireseed, fifty percent better than Styphon's Best, and half of it made in the last two days.

"It's been so long since anybody had anything to be happy about. When we had feasts, everybody would get drunk as soon as they could, to keep from thinking about what was coming. And now, maybe it won't come at all."

And now, they were all drunk on a hundred pounds of black powder. Five thousand arquebus rounds at the most. They'd have to do better than twenty-five pounds a day; have to get it up to a hundred. Mixing, caking and grinding was the bottleneck, that meant still more mill machinery, and there weren't enough men able to build it. It would mean stopping work on the rifling machinery, and on the carriages and limbers for the light four-pounders the ironworks were turning out.

It would take a year to build the sort of army he wanted, and Gormoth or Nostor would attack in two months at most.

He brought that up, that afternoon, at General Staff meeting. Like rifling and trunnions on cannon and teaching swordsmen to use the point, that was new for here-and-now. You just hauled a lot of peasants together and armed them, that was Organization. You picked a march-route, that was Strategy. You lined up your men somehow and shot or hit anybody in front of you, that was Tactics. And Intelligence was something mounted scouts, if any, brought in at the last moment from a mile ahead. It cheered him to recall that that would be Gormoth's idea of the Art of War. Why, with ten thousand men Gustavus Adolphus or the Duke of Parma or Gonzalo de Córdoba could have gone through all five of these Great Kingdoms like a dose of croton oil.

Ptosphes and Rylla were present *ex officio* as Prince and Heiress-Apparent. The Lord Kalvan was Commander-in-Chief. Chartiphon was Field Marshal and Chief of Operations. Harmakros was G-2, an elderly infantry captain was drillmaster, paymaster, quartermaster, inspector-general and head of the draft board. A civilian merchant, who wasn't losing any money on it, was in charge of supply and procurement. Xentos, who was Ptosphes' chancellor as well as chief ecclesiastic, attended to political matters, and also fifth-column activities, another of Lord Kalvan's marvelous new ideas, mainly because he was in touch with the priests of Dralm in Nostor and Sask, all of whom hated Styphon's House beyond expression.

The first blaze of optimism had died down, he was glad to observe. Chartiphon was grumbling:

"We have three thousand at most; Gormoth has ten thousand, six thousand mercenaries and four thousand of his own people. Making our own fireseed gives us a chance, which we didn't have before, but that's all."

"Two thousand of his own people," somebody said. "He won't take the peasants out of the fields."

"Then he'll attack earlier," Ptosphes said. "While our peasants are getting the harvest in."

He looked at the map painted on one of the walls. Gormoth could invade up the Listra Valley, but that would only give him half of Hostigos—less than that. The whole line of the Mountains of Hostigos was held at every gap except one. Dombra Gap, guarded by Tarr-Dombra, lost by treachery three quarters of a century ago, and Sevenhills Valley behind it.

"We'll have to take Tarr-Dombra and clean Sevenhills Valley out," he said.

Everybody stared at him. It was Chartiphon who first found his voice.

"Man! You never saw Tarr-Dombra, or you wouldn't talk like that. It's smaller than Tarr-Hostigos, but it's even stronger."

"That's right," the retread captain who was G-1 and part of G-4 supported him.

"Do the Nostori think it can't be taken, too?" he asked. "Then it can be. Prince, have you plans of the castle?"

"Oh, yes. On a big scroll, in one of my coffers. It was my grandfather's, and we always hoped . . ."

"I'll want to see them. Later will do. Do you know of any changes made on it since?"

Not on the outside, at least. He asked about the garrison; five hundred, Harmakros thought. A hundred regular infantry of Gormoth's, and four hundred cavalry for patrolling around the perimeter of Sevenhills Valley. They were mercenaries, and they were the ones who had been raiding into Hostigos.

"Then stop killing raiders who can be taken alive. Prisoners can be made to talk." The Geneva Convention was something else unknown here-and-now. He turned to Xentos. "Is there a priest of Dralm in Sevenhills Valley? Can you get in touch with him, and will be help us? Explain that this is a war against Styphon's House."

"He knows that, and he will help, as he can. But he can't get into Tarr-Dombra. There is a priest of Galzar there for the mercenaries, and a priest of Styphon for the lord of the castle. Among the Nostori, Dralm is but a god for the peasants."

That rankled. Yes, the priests of Dralm would help.

"All right. But he can talk to people who can get in, can't he? And he can send messages, and organize an espionage apparatus among his peasants. I want to know everything that can be found out, no matter how trivial. Particularly, I want to know the guard-routine at the castle, and how it's supplied. And I want it observed all the time; Harmakros, you find men to do that. I take it we can't storm the place, or you'd have done that long ago. Then we'll have to surprise it."

Verkan the pack trader went up the road, his horse plodding unhurriedly and the pack horses on the lead-line trailing behind. He was hot and sticky under his steel back-and-breast, and sweat ran down his cheeks from under his helmet into his new beard, but nobody ever saw an unarmed pack trader, so he had to endure it. They were local-made, from an adjoining near-identical time-line, and so were his clothes, his sword, the carbine in the saddle sheath, his horse gear, and the loads of merchandise, all except a metal coffer on top of one pack load.

Reaching the brow of the hill, he started down the other side, and as he did he saw a stir in front of a thatched and whitewashed farm cottage. Men mounting horses; glints of armor, and red-and-blue Hostigi colors. Another cavalry post, the third he'd passed since crossing the border from Sask. The other two had ignored him, but this crowd meant to stop him. Two had lances, the third a musketoon, and the fourth, who seemed to be in command, had his holsters open and his right hand on his horse's neck.

He reined in his horse; the pack horses came to a well-trained stop.

"Good cheer, soldiers," he greeted.

"Good cheer, trader," the man with his hand close to his pistol-butt replied. "From Sask?"

"Sask last. From Ulthor, this trip; Grefftscharr by birth." Ulthor was the lake port to the northwest; Grefftscharr was the kingdom around the Great Lakes. "I'm for Agrys City."

One of the troopers laughed. The sergeant asked: "Have you any fire-seed?"

"About twenty charges." He touched the flask on his belt. "I tried to get some in Sask, but when the priests of Styphon heard that I was coming through Hostigos they'd give me none."

"I know; we're under the ban, here." It did not seem to distress him greatly. "But I'm afraid you'll not see Agrys soon. We're on the edge of war with Nostor, and the Lord Kalvan wants no tales carried, so he's ordered that no one may leave Hostigos."

He cursed; that was expected of him.

"I'd feel ill-used, too, in your place," the sergeant sympathized, "but when princes and lords order, commonfolk obey. It won't be so bad, though. You can get good prices in Hostigos Town or at Tarr-Hostigos, and then, if you know a skilled trade, you can find work at good wages. Or you might take the colors. You're well armed and horsed; the Lord Kalvan welcomes all such."

"The Lord Kalvan? I thought Ptosphes was Prince of Hostigos."

"Why, so he is, Dralm guard him, but the Lord Kalvan, Dralm guard him, too, is the war leader. It's said he's a prince himself, from a far land. It's also said that he's a sorcerer, but that I doubt."

Ah, yes; the stranger prince from afar. And among these people, Corporal Calvin Morrison—he willed himself no longer to think of the man as anything but the Lord Kalvan—would be suspected of sorcery. He chatted pleasantly with the sergeant and the troopers, asking about inns, about prices being paid for things, all the questions a wandering trader would ask, then bade them good luck and rode on. He passed other farms along the road. At most of them, work was going on; men were forking down dunghills and digging under them, fires burned, and caldrons steamed over them. He added that to the cheerfulness with which the sergeant and his men had accepted the ban of Styphon's House.

Styphon, it seemed, had acquired a competitor.

Hostigos Town spread around a low hill and a great spring as large as a small lake, facing the mountains which, on the Europo-American Sector, had been quarried into sheer cliffs. The Lord Kalvan wouldn't fail to notice that. Above the gap stood a strong castle; that would be Tarr-Hostigos, *tarr* meant castle, or stronghold. The streets were crowded with carts and wagons; the artisans' quarter was noisy with the work of smiths and joiners. He found the Sign of the Red Halberd, the inn the sergeant had commended to him. He put up his horses and safe-stowed the packs, all but his personal luggage, his carbine, and the metal coffer. A servant carried the former; he took the coffer over one shoulder and followed to the room he had been given.

When he was alone, he set the coffer down. It was an almost featureless block of bronze, without visible lock or hinges, only two bright steel ovals on the top. Pressing his thumbs to these, he heard a slight click as the photoelectric lock inside responded to his thumbprint patterns. The lid opened. Inside were four globes of gleaming coppery mesh, a few small instruments with dials and knobs, and a little sigma-ray needler, a ladies' model, small enough to be covered by his hand, but as deadly as the big one he usually carried. It was silent, and it killed without trace that any autopsy would reveal.

There was also an antigrav unit, attached to the bottom of the coffer; it was on, the tiny pilot light glowed red. When he switched it off, the floor boards under the coffer creaked. Lined with collapsed metal, it now weighed over half a ton. He pushed down the lid, which only his thumbprints could open, and heard the lock click.

The common room downstairs was crowded and noisy. He found a vacant place at one of the long tables and sat down. Across from him, a man with a bald head and a small straggling beard grinned at him.

"New fish in the net?" he asked. "Welcome. Where from?"

"Ulthor, with three horse loads. My name's Verkan."

"Mine's Skranga." The bald man was from Agrys City.

"They took them all, fifty of them. Paid me less than I asked, but more than I thought they would, so I guess I got a fair price. I had four Trygathi herders, they're all in the cavalry, now. I'm working in the fireseed mill."

"The what?" He was incredulous. "You mean these people make their own fireseed? But nobody but the priests of Styphon can do that."

Skranga laughed. "That's what I thought, when I came here, but anybody can do it. No more trick than boiling soap. See, they get saltpeter from under dunghills, and . . ."

He detailed the process, step by step. The man facing him joined the conversation; he even understood, dimly, the theory. The charcoal was what burned, the sulfur was the kindling, and the saltpeter made the air to blow up the fire and blow the bullet out of the gun. And there was no secrecy about it, at least inside Hostigos. Except for keeping the news out of Nostor until he had enough fireseed for a war, the Lord Kalvan simply didn't care.

"I bless Dralm for bringing me into this," the horse trader said. "When people can leave here, I'm going some place and start making fireseed myself. Why, I'll be rich in a few years, and so can you."

He finished his meal, said he had to return to work, and left. A cavalry officer who had been sitting a few places down the table picked up his cup and flagon and took the vacant seat.

"You just came in?" he asked. "From Nostor?"

"No, from Sask." The answer seemed to disappoint the cavalryman; he went into the Ulthor-Grefftscharr story again. "How long will I be kept from going on?"

"Till we fight the Nostori and beat them. What do the Saski think we're doing here?"

"Waiting to have your throats cut. They don't know anything about your making fireseed."

The officer laughed. "Ha! Some of them'll get theirs cut, if Prince Sarrask doesn't mind his step. You say you have three horseloads of Grefftscharr wares; any weapons?"

"Some sword blades. Some daggers, a dozen gunlocks, three good shirts of rivet-link mail, bullet molds. And brassware, and jewelry, of course."

"Well, take your loads up to Tarr-Hostigos. They have a little fair each evening in the outer bailey, you can sell anything you have. Go early. Use my name"—he gave it—"and speak to Captain Harmakros. He'll be glad of any news you have."

He re-packed his horses, when he had eaten, and led them up the road to the castle above the gap. Along the wall of the outer bailey, inside the gate, were workshops, all busy. One thing he noticed was a gun carriage for a light fieldpiece being put together, not a little cart, but two big wheels and a trail, to be hauled with a limber. The gun for it was the sort of wrought-iron four-pounder normal for this sector, but it had trunnions, which was not. The Lord Kalvan, again.

Like all the local gentry, Captain Harmakros wore a small neat beard. His armor was rich but well battered, but the long rapier on his belt was new. He asked a few questions, then listened to a detailed account of what Verkan the trader had seen and heard in Sask; the mercenary companies Sarrask had hired, the names of the captains, their strength and equipment.

"You've kept your eyes open and your wits about you," he commented. "I wish you'd come through Nostor instead. Were you ever a soldier?"

"All traders are soldiers, in their own service."

"Yes, well when you've sold your loads, you'll be welcome in ours. Not as a common trooper, as a scout. You want to sell your pack horses, too? We'll give you your own price for them."

"If I sell my loads, yes."

"You'll have no trouble doing that. Stay about, have your meals with the officers here. We'll find something for you."

He had some tools, for both wood and metal work. He peddled them among the artisans, for a good price in silver and a better one in information. Beside cannon with trunnions on regular field-carriages, Kalvan had introduced rifling in small arms. Nobody knew whence Kalvan had come, but they knew it had been a great distance.

The officers with whom he ate listened avidly to what he had to tell about his observations in Sask. Nostor first, and then Sask, seemed to be the schedule. When they talked about the Lord Kalvan, the coldest expressions were of deep respect, and shaded up to hero-worship. But they knew nothing about him before the night he had appeared at a peasant's cottage and rallied a rabble fleeing from a raided village.

He sold the mail and sword blades and gunlocks as a lot to one of the officers; the rest of the stuff he spread to offer to the inmates of the castle. He saw the Lord Kalvan strolling through the crowd, in full armor and wearing a rapier and a Colt .38 Special on his belt. He had grown a small beard since the photograph the Paratime Police had secured on Europo-American had been taken. Clinging to his arm was a beautiful blond girl in male riding dress; Prince Ptosphes' daughter Rylla, he was told. He had already heard the story of how she had shot him by mistake in a skirmish and brought him to Tarr-Hostigos to be cared for. The happy possessiveness with which she held his arm, and the tenderness with which he looked at her, made him smile. Then the smile froze on his lips and died in his eyes as he wondered what Kalvan had told her privately.

Returning to the Red Halberd, he spent some time and money in the taproom. Everybody, as far as he could learn, seemed satisfied that Kalvan had come, with or without divine guidance, to Hostigos in a perfectly normal manner. Finally he went to his room.

Pressing his thumbs to the sensitized ovals, he opened the coffer and lifted out one of the gleaming copper-mesh balls. It opened at pressure on a small stud; he drew out a wire with a mouthpiece attached, and spoke for a long time into it.

"So far," he concluded, "there seems to be no question of anything paranormal about the man in anybody's mind. I have not yet made any contacts with anybody who would confide in me to the contrary. I have been offered an opportunity to take service under him as a scout; I intend doing this. Some assistance can be given me in carrying out this work. I will find a location for a conveyer-head; this will have to be somewhere in the woods near Hostigos Town. I will send a ball through when I do. Verkan Vall, ending communication."

Then he set the timer of the transposition field generator and switched on the antigrav unit. Carrying the ball to the open window, he released it. It rose quickly into the night, and then, high above, among the many visible stars, there was an instant's flash. It could have been a meteor.

Kalvan sat on a rock under a tree, wishing that he could smoke, and knowing that he was beginning to be scared. He cursed mentally. It didn't mean anything, as soon as things got started he'd forget to be scared, but it always happened before, and he hated it. It was quiet on the mountain top, even though there were two hundred men sitting or squatting or lying around him, and another five hundred, under Chartiphon and Prince Ptosphes, five hundred yards behind. There were fifty more a hundred yards ahead, a skirmish-line of riflemen. Now there was a new word in the here-and-now military lexicon. They were the first riflemen on any battlefield in the history of here-and-now. A few of the rifles were big fifteen- to twenty-pound muskets, eight- to six-bore; mostly they were calivers, sixteen- and twenty-bore, the size and weight of a Civil War musket. They were commanded by the Grefftscharr trader, Verkan. There had been objection to giving an outland stranger so important a command; he had informed the objectors, stiffly, that he had been an outland stranger himself only recently.

Out in front of Verkan's line, in what the defenders of Tarr-Dombra thought was cleared ground, were fifteen sharp-shooters. They all had big-bore muskets, rifled and fitted with peep-sights, zeroed in for just that range. The condition of that supposedly cleared approach was the most promising thing about the whole operation. The trees had been felled and the stumps rooted out, but the Nostori thought Tarr-Dombra couldn't be taken and that nobody would try to take it, so they'd gone slack. There were bushes all over it up to a man's waist, and many of them were high enough to hide behind standing up.

His men were hard enough to see even in the open. The helmets have been carefully rusted, so had the body-armor and every gun-barrel or spear-head. Nobody wore anything but green or brown, most of them had bits of greenery fastened to their helmets and clothes. The whole operation, with over twelve hundred men, had been rehearsed a dozen times, each time some being eliminated until they were down to eight hundred of the best.

There was a noise, about what a feeding wild-turkey would make, in front of him, and then a voice said, "Lord Kalvan!" It was Verkan, the Grefftscharrer. He had a rifle in his hand, and wore a dirty green-gray hooded smock; his sword and belt were covered with green and brown rags.

"I never saw you till you spoke," he commented.

"The wagons are coming. They're around the top switch-back, now."

He nodded. "We start, then." His mouth was dry. What was that thing in "For Whom the Bell Tolls" about spitting to show you weren't afraid? He couldn't do that, now. He nodded to the boy squatting beside him; he picked up his arquebus and started back toward where Ptosphes and Chartiphon had the main force.

And Rylla! He cursed vilely, in English; there was no satisfaction in taking the name of Dralm in vain, or blaspheming Styphon. She'd announced that she was coming along. He'd told her she was doing nothing of the sort. So had her father, and so had Chartiphon. She'd thrown a tantrum; thrown other things, too. In the end, she had come along. He was going to have his hands full with that girl, when he married her.

"All right," he said softly. "Let's go earn our pay."

The men on either side of him rose, two spears or scythe-blade things to every arquebus, though some of the spearmen had pistols in their belts. He and Verkan went ahead, stopping at the edge of the woods, where the riflemen crouched behind trees, and looked across the open four hundred yards at Tarr-Dombra, the castle that couldn't be taken, its limestone walls rising beyond the chasm that had been quarried straight across the mountain top. The drawbridge was down and the portcullis was up, a few soldiers in black and orange scarves—his old college colors, he oughtn't to shoot them—loitering in the gateway. A few more kept perfunctory watch from the battlements.

Chartiphon and Ptosphes brought their men, one pike to every three calivers and arquebuses, up with a dreadful crashing and clattering that almost stood his hair on end under his helmet and padded coif, but nobody at the castle seemed to have heard it. Chartiphon wore a long sack, with neck and arm holes, over his cuirass, and what looked like a well-used dishrag wrapped around his helmet. Ptosphes was in brown, with browned armor, so was Rylla. They all looked to the left, where the road came up the side and onto the top of the mountain.

Four cavalrymen, black-and-orange scarves and lance-pennons, came into view. They were only fake Princeton men; he hoped they'd remember to tear that stuff off before some other Hostigi shot them. A long ox-wagon followed, piled high with hay and eight Hostigi infantrymen under it, then two more cavalrymen in false Nostori colors, another wagon, and six more cavalry. Two more wagons followed.

The first four cavalrymen clattered onto the drawbridge and spoke to the guards at the gate, then rode through. Two of the wagons followed. The third rumbled onto the drawbridge and stopped directly under the portcullis. That was the one with the log framework on top and the log slung underneath. The driver must have cut the strap that held that up, jamming the wagon. The fourth wagon, the one loaded to the top of the bed with rocks, stopped on the outer end of the drawbridge, weighting it down. A pistol banged inside the gate, and another; there were shouts of "Hostigos! Hostigos!" The hay seemed to explode off the two wagons in sight as men piled out of them.

He blew his Pennsylvania State Police whistle, and half a dozen big elephant-size muskets bellowed, from places he'd have sworn there had been nobody at all. Verkan's rifle platoon began firing, sharp whip-crack reports like none of the smoothbores. He hoped they were remembering to patch their bullets; that was something new to them. Then he blew his whistle twice and started running forward.

The men who had been showing themselves on the walls were all gone; a musket-shot or so showed that the snipers hadn't gotten all of them. He ran past a man with a piece of fishnet over his helmet, stuck full of oak twigs, who was ramming a musket. Gray powder-smoke hung in the gateway, and everybody who had been outside had gotten in. Yells of "Hostigo!" and "Nostor!" and shots and blade-clashing from within. He broke step and looked back; his two hundred were pouring after him, keeping properly spaced out, the arquebusiers not firing. All the shooting was coming from where Chartiphon—and Rylla, he hoped—had formed a line two hundred yards from the walls and were plastering the battlements, firing as rapidly as they could reload. A cannon went off above when he was almost at the end of the drawbridge, and then, belatedly, the portcullis came down to stop seven feet from the ground on the top of the log framework hidden under the hay on the third wagon.

All six of the oxen on the last wagon were dead; the drivers had been furnished short-handle axes for that purpose. The oxen on the portcullis-stopper had also been killed. The gate towers on both sides had already been taken. There were black-and-orange scarves lying where they had been ripped off, and more on corpses. But shots were beginning to come from the citadel, across the outer bailey, and a mob of Nostori were pouring out from its gate. This, he thought, was the time to expend some .38's.

Feet apart, left hand on hip, he aimed and emptied the Colt, killing six men with six shots, timed-fire rate. He'd done just as well at that range on silhouette targets many a time; that was all this was. They were the front six; the men behind them stopped momentarily, and then the men behind swept around him, arquebuses banging and pikemen and halberdiers running forward. He holstered the empty Colt, he only had eight rounds left, now, and drew his rapier and poignard. Another cannon on the outside wall thundered; he hoped Rylla and Chartiphon hadn't been in front of it. Then he was fighting his way through the citadel gate.

Behind, in the outer bailey, something beside "Nostor!" and "Hostigos!" was being shouted. It was:

"Mercy, comrade! Mercy; I yield!"

He heard more of that as the morning passed. Before noon, the Nostori garrison had either been given mercy or hadn't needed it. There had only been those two cannon-shots, though between them they had killed and wounded fifty men. Nobody was crazy enough to attack Tarr-Dombra, so they'd left the cannon empty, and had only been given time to load and fire two. He doubted if they'd catch Gormoth with his panzer down again.

The hardest fighting was inside the citadel. He ran into Rylla there, with Chartiphon trying to keep up with her. There was a bright scar on her browned helmet and blood on her sword; she was laughing happily. He expected that taking the keep would be even bloodier work, but as soon as they had the citadel it surrendered. By that time he had used up all his rounds for the Colt.

They hauled down Gormoth's black flag with the orange lily and ran up Ptosphes' halberd-head, blue on red. They found four huge bombards, throwing hundred-pound stone cannon balls, and handspiked them around to bear on the little town of Dyssa, at the mouth of Pine Creek, Gorge River here-and-now, and fired one round from each to announce that Tarr-Dombra was under new management. They set the castle cooks to work cutting up and roasting the oxen from the two rear wagons. Then they turned their attention to the prisoners herded in the inner bailey.

First, there were the mercenaries. They would enter the service of Ptosphes, though they could not be used against Nostor until their captain's terms of contract with Gormoth had run out. They would be sent to the Sask border. Then, there were Gormoth's own troops. They couldn't be used at all, but they could be put to work, as long as they were given soldiers' pay and soldierly treatment. Then, there was the governor of the castle, a Count Pheblon, cousin to Prince Gormoth, and his officers. They would be released, on oath to send their ransoms in silver to Hostigos. The priest of Galzar elected to go to Hostigos with his parishioners.

As for the priest of Styphon, Chartiphon wanted him questioned under torture, and Ptosphes thought he ought merely to be beheaded on the spot.

"Send him to Nostor with Pheblon," Kalvan said. "With a letter for his high priest—no, for the Supreme Priest, Styphon's Voice. Tell Styphon's Voice that we make our own fireseed, that we will teach everybody to make it, and that we will not rest until Styphon's House is utterly destroyed."

Everybody, including those who had been making suggestions for novel and interesting ways of putting the priest to death, shouted in delight.

"And send Gormoth a copy of the letter, and a letter offering him peace and friendship. Tell him we'll teach his soldiers how to make fireseed, and they can make it in Nostor when they're sent home."

"Kalvan!" Ptosphes almost howled. "What god has addled your wits? Gormoth's our enemy!"

"Anybody who can make fireseed will be our enemy, because Styphon's House will be his. If Gormoth doesn't realize that now, he will soon enough."

Verkan the Grefftscharr trader commanded the party that galloped back to Hostigos with the good news—Tarr-Dombra taken, with over two hundred prisoners, a hundred and fifty horses, four tons of fireseed, twenty cannon. And Sevenhills Valley was part of Hostigos again. Harmakros had destroyed a company of mercenary cavalry, killing twenty and capturing the rest, and he had taken Styphon's temple farm, a richly productive nitriary, freeing the slaves and butchering the priests and the guards. And the once persecuted priest of Dralm had gathered all the peasants for a thanksgiving, telling them that the Hostigi came not as conquerors but as liberators.

He seemed to recall having heard that before, on a number of paratemporal areas, including Calvin Morrison's own.

He also brought copies of the letters Prince Ptosphes had written, or, more likely, which Kalvan had written and Ptosphes had signed, to the

Supreme Priest of Styphon and to Prince Gormoth. Dropping a couple of troopers in the town to spread the good news, he rode up to the castle and reported to Xentos. It took a long time to tell the old priest-chancellor the whole story, counting interruptions while Xentos told Dralm about it. When he got away, he was immediately dragged into the officers' hall, where a wine barrel had been tapped. By the time he got back to the Red Halberd in Hostigo Town, it was after dark, and everybody was roaring drunk, and somebody had a little two-pounder in the street and was wasting fireseed that could have been better used to kill Gormoth's soldiers. The bell at the town hall, which had begun ringing while he was riding in through the castle gate, was still ringing.

Going up to his room, he opened the coffer and got out another of the copper balls, putting it under his cloak. He rode a mile out of town, tied his horse in the brush, and made his way to where a single huge tree rose above the scrub oak. Speaking into the ball, he activated and released it. Then he got out his cigarettes and sat down under the tree to wait for the half hour it would take the message-ball to reach Fifth Level Police Terminal Time-Line, and the half hour it would take a mobile antigrav conveyer to come in.

The servant brought him the things, one by one, and Lord Kalvan laid them on the white sheet spread on the table top. The whipcord breeches; he left the billfold in the hip pocket. He couldn't spend United States currency here, and his identity cards belonged to another man, who didn't exist here-and-now. The shirt, torn and bloodstained; the tunic with the battered badge that had saved his life. The black boots, one on either side; the boots they made here were softer and more comfortable. The Sam Browne belt, with the holster and the empty-looped cartridge-carrier and the handcuffs in their pouch. Anybody you needed handcuffs on, here-and-now, you just shot or knocked on the head. The Colt Official Police; he didn't want to part with that, even if there were no more cartridges for it, but the rest of this stuff would seem meaningless without it. He slipped it into the holster, and then tossed the blackjack on top of the pile.

The servant wrapped them and carried the bundle out. There goes Calvin Morrison, he thought; long live Lord Kalvan of Hostigos. Tomorrow, at the thanksgiving service before the feast, these things would be deposited as a votive offering in the temple of Dralm. That had been Xentos' idea, and he had agreed at once. Beside being a general and an ordnance engineer and an industrialist, he had to be a politician, and politicians can't slight their constituents' religion. He filled a goblet from a flagon on the smaller table and sat down, stretching his legs. Unchilled white wine was a crime against nature; have to do something about refrigeration—after the war, of course.

That mightn't be too long, either. They'd already unsealed the frontiers, and the transients who had been blockaded in would be leaving after the feast. They all knew that anybody could make fireseed, and most of them knew how. That fellow they'd gotten those Trygath horses from; he'd had a few words with him, and he was going to Nostor. So were half a dozen agents to work with Xentos' fifth column. Gormoth would begin making his own fireseed, and that would bring him under the ban of Styphon's House.

Gormoth wouldn't think of that. All he wanted was to conquer Hostigos, and without the help of Styphon's House, he couldn't. He couldn't anyhow, now that he had lost his best invasion-route. Two days after Tarr-Dombra had fallen, he'd had two thousand men at the mouth of Gorge River and lost at least three hundred by cannon fire trying to cross the Athan before his mercenary captains had balked, and the night after that Harmakros had come out of McElhattan Gap, Vrylos Gap, with two hundred cavalry and raided western Nostor, burning farms and villages and running off horses and cattle, devastating everything to the end of Listra Valley.

Maybe they'd thrown Gormoth off until winter. That would mean, till next spring. They didn't fight wars in the winter, here-and-now; against mercenary union rules. By then, he should have a real army, trained in new tactics he'd dredged from what he remembered of Sixteenth and Seventeenth Century history. Four or five batteries of little four-pounders, pieces and caissons each drawn by four horses, and as mobile as cavalry. And plenty of rifles, and men trained to use them. And get rid of all these bear spears and scythe blade things, and substitute real eighteen-foot Swiss pikes; they'd hold off cavalry.

Styphon's House was the real enemy. Beat Gormoth once, properly, and he'd stay beaten, and Sarrask of Sask was only a Mussolini to Gormoth's Hitler. But Styphon's House was big; it spread over all five Great Kingdoms, from the mouth of the St. Lawrence to the Gulf of Mexico.

Big but vulnerable, and he knew the vulnerable point. Styphon wasn't a popular god as, say, Dralm was; that was why Xentos' fifth column was building strength in Nostor. Styphon's House had ignored the people and even the minor nobility, and ruled by pressure on the Great Kings and their subject princes, and as soon as they could make their own powder, they'd turn on Styphon's House, and their people with them. This wasn't a religious war, like the ones in the Sixteenth and Seventeenth Centuries in his own former history. It was just a job of racket-busting.

He set down the goblet and rose, throwing off the light robe, and began to dress for dinner. For a moment, he wondered whether the Democrats or the Republicans would win the election this year—he was sure it was the same year, now, in a different dimension of time—and how the Cold War and the Space Race were coming along.

Verkan Vall, his story finished, relaxed in his chair. There was no direct light on this terrace, only a sky-reflection from the city lights below, so dim that the tips of their cigarettes glowed visibly. There were four of them: the Chief of Paratime Police, the Director of the Paratime Commission, the Chairman of the Paratemporal Board of Trade, and Chief's Assistant Verkan Vall, who would be chief in another hundred days.

"You took no action about him?" the director asked.

"None at all. The man's no threat to the Paratime Secret. He knows he isn't in his own past, and from things he ought to find and hasn't he knows he isn't in his own future. So he knows he's in the corresponding present in a second time dimension, and he knows that somebody else is able to travel laterally in time. I grant that. But he's keeping it to himself. On Aryan-Transpacific, in the idiom of his original time-line, he has it made. He won't take any chances on unmaking it.

"Look what he has that the Europo-American Sector could never give him. He is a great nobleman; they're out of fashion on Europo-American, where the Common Man is the ideal. He's going to marry a beautiful princess, that's even out of fashion for children's fairy tales. He's a sword-swinging soldier of fortune, and they've vanished from his own nuclear-weapons world. He's in command of a good little army, and making a better one out of it, and he has a cause worth fighting for. Any speculations about what space-time continuum he's in he'll keep inside his own skull.

"Look at the story he put out. He told Xentos that he had been thrown into the past from a time in the far future by sorcery. Sorcery, on that time-line, is a perfectly valid scientific explanation of anything. Xentos, with his permission, passed the story on, under oath of secrecy, to Ptosphes, Rylla, and Chartiphon. The story they gave out is that he's an exiled prince from a country outside local geographical knowledge. Regular defense in depth, all wrapped around the real secret, and everybody has an acceptable explanation."

"How'd you get it, then?" the Board Chairman asked.

"From Xentos, at the feast. I got him into a theological discussion, and slipped some hypno truth-drug into his wine. He doesn't remember, now, that he told me."

"Well, nobody else on that time-line'll get it that way," the Commission director agreed. "But didn't you take a chance getting those things of Morrison's out of the temple? Was that necessary?"

"No. We ran a conveyer in the night of the feast, when the temple was empty. The next morning, the priests all cried, 'A miracle! Dralm has accepted the offering!' I was there and saw it. Morrison doesn't believe that, he thinks some of these pack traders who left Hostigos the next morning stole the stuff. I know Harmakros' cavalrymen were stopping people and searching wagons and packs. Publicly, of course, he has to believe in the miracle.

"As to the necessity, yes. This stuff will be found on Morrison's original time-line, first the clothing, with the numbered badge still on the tunic, and, later, in connection with some crime we'll arrange for the purpose, the revolver. They won't explain anything, they'll make more of a mystery, but it will be a mystery in normal terms of what's locally accepted as possible."

"Well, this is all very interesting," the Trade Board chairman said, "but what have I to do with it, officially?"

"Trenth, you disappoint me," the Commission director said. "This Styphon's House racket is perfect for penetration of that subsector, and in a couple of centuries it'll be a very valuable subsector to have penetrated. We'll just move in on Styphon's House, and take it over, the way we did the Yat-Zar temples on the Hulgun Sector, and build that up to general economic and political control."

"You'll have to stay off Morrison's time-line, though," Tortha Karf said.

"You certainly will!" He was vehement about it. "We'll turn that time-line over to the University, here, for study, and quarantine it absolutely to everybody else. And about five adjoining time-lines, for control study. You know what we have here?" He was becoming excited about it. "We have the start of an entirely new subsector, and we have the divarication point absolutely identified, the first time we've been able to do that except from history. Now, here; I've already established myself with those people as Verkan the Grefftscharr trader. I'll get back, now and then, about as frequently as plausible for traveling by horse, and set up a trading depot. A building big enough to put a conveyer head into . . ."

Tortha Karf began laughing. "I knew it," he said. "You'd find some way!"

"All right. We all have hobbies; yours is fruit-growing and rabbit-hunting on Fifth Level Sicily. Well, my hobby farm is going to be the Kalvan Subsector, Fourth Level Aryan-Transpacific. I'm only a hundred and twenty years old, now. In a couple of centuries, when I'm ready to retire . . ."

SEMLEY'S NECKLACE

Ursula K. Le Guin is so universally respected as a writer these days, and so honored as one of science fiction's most profound thinkers and complex and subtle artists, that it's sometimes forgotten that when she first appeared, the writer that she was most often compared to was Leigh Brackett—indeed, she was referred to on at least one occasion as "the New Leigh Brackett." It's often also forgotten these days that her first few books—*Rocannon's World,* the strongly van Vogtian *City of Illusions,* and her best early book, the underrated and still largely overlooked (even by Le Guin fans) *Planet of Exile*—were published by Ace as pulp-adventure Space Opera of the most basic, lowest-common-denominator sort (much as Samuel R. Delany's first books were also being published as stock Space Opera, at about the same time, by the same publishing house), with garish pulp covers and lurid pulp blurbs such as "Wherever he went, his super-science made him a legendary figure!" and "Was he a human meteor or a time-bomb from the stars?"

As it turned out, Le Guin had a greater destiny to fulfill than to become merely the new Queen Of The Space-Ways—but although she became more than that, and explored literary territories far beyond the purview of Space Opera, the New Leigh Brackett lurks somewhere in her still, a vital component part of her artistic makeup. Indeed, her recent return to the star-spanning, Hainish-settled interstellar community known as the Ekumen (the fictional universe that provided the setting for those early novels) in stories such as "Forgiveness Day" and "A Woman's Liberation" and "Another Story" demonstrates that she can *still* spin a tale of Interplanetary Adventure and Intrigue as fast-paced and compelling and compulsively readable as any ever produced by anyone anywhere . . . with the additional benefit of being able to explore politics, human sexuality, competing social modes and models for civilization, and the fundamental questions of life, death, and moral responsibility, perhaps a bit more fully and more complexly than that early Le Guin of the garish Ace Doubles would have been allowed to do. But then, one thing she has in common with Brackett, and perhaps the thing that made critics compare Le Guin to her in the first place, is that Le Guin rarely if ever forgets about Story, and the fact that the deep heart of any story is provided by the *people* who live *in* it. A lesson she already knew well at the very beginning of her career, as the haunting and yet suspenseful story that follows, one of her first sales, demonstrates very well . . .

Ursula K. Le Guin is probably one of the best-known writers in the world today.

Her famous novel *The Left Hand of Darkness* may have been the most influential SF novel of its decade, and shows every sign of becoming one of the enduring classic of the genre—even ignoring the rest of Le Guin's work, the impact of this one novel alone on future SF and future SF writers would be incalculably strong. (Her 1968 fantasy novel, *A Wizard of Earthsea,* would be almost as influential on future generations of High Fantasy writers.) *The Left Hand of Darkness* won both the Hugo and Nebula Awards, as did Le Guin's monumental novel *The Dispossessed* a few years later. Her novel *Tehanu* won her another Nebula in 1990, and she has also won three other Hugo Awards and two Nebula Awards for her short fiction, as well as the National Book Award for children's literature for her novel *The Farthest Shore,* part of her acclaimed Earthsea trilogy. Her other novels include *The Lathe of Heaven, The Beginning Place, A Wizard of Earthsea, The Tombs of Atuan, Tehanu, Searoad,* and the controversial multi-media novel *Always Coming Home.* She has had six collections: *The Wind's Twelve Quarters, Orsinian Tales, The Compass Rose, Buffalo Gals and Other Animal Presences, A Fisherman of the Inland Sea,* and her most recent book, *Four Ways to Forgiveness.*

How can you tell the legend from the fact on these worlds that lie so many years away?—planets without names, called by their people simply The World, planets without history, where the past is the matter of myth, and a returning explorer finds his own doings of a few years back have become the gestures of a god. Unreason darkens that gap of time bridged by our lightspeed ships, and in the darkness uncertainty and disproportion grow like weeds.

In trying to tell the story of a man, an ordinary League scientist, who went to such a nameless half-known world not many years ago, one feels like an archaeologist amid millennial ruins, now struggling through choked tangles of leaf, flower, branch and vine to the sudden bright geometry of a wheel or a polished cornerstone, and now entering some commonplace, sunlit doorway to find inside it the darkness, the impossible flicker of a flame, the glitter of a jewel, the half-glimpsed movement of a woman's arm.

How can you tell fact from legend, truth from truth?

Through Rocannon's story the jewel, the blue glitter seen briefly, returns. With it let us begin, here:

Galactic Area 8, No. 62: FOMALHAUT II.
High-Intelligence Life Forms: Species Contacted:
Species I.

A. Gdemiar (singular Gdem): Highly intelligent, fully hominoid nocturnal troglodytes, 120–135 cm. in height, light skin, dark head-hair. When contacted these cave-dwellers possessed a rigidly stratified oligarchic urban society modified by partial colonial telepathy, and a technologically oriented Early Steel culture. Technology enhanced to Industrial, Point C, during League Mission of 252–254. In 254 an Automatic Drive ship (to-from New South Georgia) was presented to oligarchs of the Kiriensea Area community. Status C-Prime.

B. Fiia (singular Fian): Highly intelligent, fully hominoid, diurnal, av. ca. 130 cm. in height, observed individuals generally light in skin and hair. Brief contacts indicated village and nomadic communal societies, partial colonial telepathy, also some indication of short-range TK. The race appears a-technological and evasive, with minimal and fluid culture-patterns. Currently untaxable. Status E-Query.

Species II.

Liuar (singular Liu): Highly intelligent, fully hominoid, diurnal, av. height above 170 cm., this species possesses a fortress/village, clan-descent society, a blocked technology (Bronze), and feudal-heroic culture. Note horizontal social cleavage into a pseudo-races: (a) Olgyior, "midmen," light-skinned and dark-haired; (b) Angyar, "lords," very tall, dark-skinned, yellow-haired—

"That's her," said Rocannon, looking up from the *Abridged Handy Pocket Guide to Intelligent Life-forms* at the very tall, dark-skinned, yellow-haired woman who stood halfway down the long museum hall. She stood still and erect, crowned with bright hair, gazing at something in a display case. Around her fidgeted four uneasy and unattractive dwarves.

"I didn't know Fomalhaut II had all those people besides the trogs," said Ketho, the curator.

"I didn't either. There are even some 'Unconfirmed' species listed here, that they never contacted. Sounds like time for a more thorough survey mission to the place. Well, now at least we know what she is."

"I wish there were some way of knowing *who* she is. . . ."

She was of an ancient family, a descendant of the first kings of the Angyar, and for all her poverty her hair shone with the pure, steadfast gold of her inheritance. The little people, the Fiia, bowed when she passed them, even when she was a barefoot child running in the fields, the light and fiery comet of her hair brightening the troubled winds of Kirien.

She was still very young when Durhal of Hallan saw her, courted her, and carried her away from the ruined towers and windy halls of her childhood

to his own high home. In Hallan on the mountainside there was no comfort either, though splendor endured. The windows were unglassed, the
stone floors bare; in coldyear one might wake to see the night's snow in
long, low drifts beneath each window. Durhal's bride stood with narrow
bare feet on the snowy floor, braiding up the fire of her hair and laughing
at her young husband in the silver mirror that hung in their room. That
mirror, and his mother's bridal-gown sewn with a thousand tiny crystals,
were all his wealth. Some of his lesser kinfolk of Hallan still possessed
wardrobes of brocaded clothing, furniture of gilded wood, silver harness for
their steeds, armor and silver mounted swords, jewels and jewelry—and
on these last Durhal's bride looked enviously, glancing back at a gemmed
coronet or a golden brooch even when the wearer of the ornament stood
aside to let her pass, deferent to her birth and marriage-rank.

Fourth from the High Seat of Hallan Revel sat Durhal and his bride Semley, so close to Hallanlord that the old man often poured wine for Semley
with his own hand, and spoke of hunting with his nephew and heir Durhal,
looking on the young pair with a grim, unhopeful love. Hope came hard to
the Angyar of Hallan and all the Western Lands, since the Starlords had appeared with their houses that leaped about on pillars of fire and their awful
weapons that could level hills. They had interfered with all the old ways and
wars, and though the sums were small there was terrible shame to the Angyar
in having to pay a tax to them, a tribute for the Starlords' war that was to be
fought with some strange enemy, somewhere in the hollow places between
the stars, at the end of years. "It will be your war too," they said, but for a
generation now the Angyar had sat in idle shame in their revel-halls, watching their double swords rust, their sons grow up without ever striking a blow
in battle, their daughters marry poor men, even midmen, having no dowry
of heroic loot to bring a noble husband. Hallanlord's face was bleak when he
watched the fair-haired couple and heard their laughter as they drank bitter
wine and joked together in the cold, ruinous, resplendent fortress of their
race.

Semley's own face hardened when she looked down the hall and saw, in
seats far below hers, even down among the halfbreeds and the midmen,
against white skins and black hair, the gleam and flash of precious stones.
She herself had brought nothing in dowry to her husband, not even a silver
hairpin. The dress of a thousand crystals she had put away in a chest for the
wedding-day of her daughter, if daughter it was to be.

It was, and they called her Haldre, and when the fuzz on her little brown
skull grew longer it shone with steadfast gold, the inheritance of the lordly
generations, the only gold she would ever possess. . . .

Semley did not speak to her husband of her discontent. For all his gentleness to her, Durhal in his pride had only contempt for envy, for vain wishing, and she dreaded his contempt. But she spoke to Durhal's sister Durossa.

"My family had a great treasure once," she said. "It was a necklace all of gold, with the blue jewel set in the center—sapphire?"

Durossa shook her head, smiling, not sure of the name either. It was late in warmyear, as these Northern Angyar called the summer of the eight-hundred-day year, beginning the cycle of months anew at each equinox; to Semley it seemed an outlandish calendar, a mid-mannish reckoning. Her family was at an end, but it had been older and purer than the race of any of these northwestern marchlanders, who mixed too freely with the Olgyior. She sat with Durossa in the sunlight on a stone windowseat high up in the Great Tower, where the older woman's apartment was. Widowed young, childless, Durossa had been given in second marriage to Hallanlord, who was her father's brother. Since it was a kinmarriage and a second marriage on both sides she had not taken the title of Hallanlady, which Semley would some day bear; but she sat with the old lord in the High Seat and ruled with him his domains. Older than her brother Durhal, she was fond of his young wife, and delighted in the bright-haired baby Haldre.

"It was bought," Semley went on, "with all the money my forebear Ley-nen got when he conquered the Southern Fiefs—all the money from a whole kingdom, think of it, for one jewel! Oh, it would outshine anything here in Hallan, surely, even those crystals like koob-eggs your cousin Issar wears. It was so beautiful they gave it a name of its own; they called it the Eye of the Sea. My great-grandmother wore it."

"You never saw it?" the older woman asked lazily, gazing down at the green mountainslopes where long, long summer sent its hot and restless winds straying among the forests and whirling down white roads to the seacoast far away.

"It was lost before I was born."

"No, my father said it was stolen before the Starlords ever came to our realm. He wouldn't talk of it, but there was an old midwoman full of tales who always told me the Fiia would know where it was."

"Ah, the Fiia I should like to see!" said Durossa. "They're in so many songs and tales; why do they never come to the Western Lands?"

"Too high, too cold in winter, I think. They like the sunlight of the valleys of the south."

"Are they like the Clayfolk?"

"Those I've never seen; they keep away from us in the south. Aren't they white like midmen, and misformed? The Fiia are fair; they look like children, only thinner, and wiser. Oh, I wonder if they know where the necklace is, who stole it and where he hid it! Think, Durossa—if I could come into Hallan Revel and sit down by my husband with the wealth of a kingdom round my neck, and outshine the other women as he outshines all men!"

Durossa bent her head above the baby, who sat studying her own brown toes on a fur rug between her mother and aunt. "Semley is foolish," she murmured to the baby; "Semley who shines like a falling star, Semley whose husband loves no gold but the gold of her hair. . . ."

And Semley, looking out over the green slopes of summer toward the distant sea, was silent.

But when another coldyear had passed, and the Starlords had come again to collect their taxes for the war against the world's end—this time using a couple of dwarfish Clayfolk as interpreters, and so leaving all the Angyar humiliated to the point of rebellion—and another warmyear too was gone, and Haldre had grown into a lovely, chattering child, Semley brought her one morning to Durossa's sunlit room in the tower. Semley wore an old cloak of blue, and the hood covered her hair.

"Keep Haldre for me these few days, Durossa," she said, quick and calm. "I'm going south to Kirien."

"To see your father?"

"To find my inheritance. Your cousins of Harget Fief have been taunting Durhal. Even that halfbreed Parna can torment him, because Parna's wife has a satin coverlet for her bed, and a diamond earring, and three gowns, the dough-faced black-haired trollop! while Durhal's wife must patch her gown—"

"Is Durhal's pride in his wife, or what she wears?"

But Semley was not to be moved. "The Lords of Hallan are becoming poor men in their own hall. I am going to bring my dowry to my lord, as one of my lineage should."

"Semley! Does Durhal know you're going?"

"My return will be a happy one—that much let him know," said young Semley, breaking for a moment into her joyful laugh; then she bent to kiss her daughter, turned, and before Durossa could speak, was gone like a quick wind over the floors of sunlit stone.

Married women of the Angyar never rode for sport, and Semley had not been from Hallan since her marriage; so now, mounting the high saddle of a windsteed, she felt like a girl again, like the wild maiden she had been, riding half-broken steeds on the north wind over the fields of Kirien. The beast that bore her now down from the hills of Hallan was of finer breed, striped coat fitting sleek over hollow, buoyant bones, green eyes slitted against the wind, light and mighty wings sweeping up and down to either side of Semley, revealing and hiding, revealing and hiding the clouds above her and the hills below.

On the third morning she came to Kirien and stood again in the ruined courts. Her father had been drinking all night, and, just as in the old days, the morning sunlight poking through his fallen ceilings annoyed him, and the sight of his daughter only increased his annoyance. "What are you back for?" he growled, his swollen eyes glancing at her and away. The fiery hair of his youth was quenched, grey strands tangled on his skull. "Did the young Halla not marry you, and you've come sneaking home?"

"I am Durhal's wife. I came to get my dowry, father."

The drunkard growled in disgust; but she laughed at him so gently that he had to look at her again, wincing.

"Is it true, father, that the Fiia stole the necklace Eye of the Sea?"

"How do I know? Old tales. The thing was lost before I was born, I think. I wish I never had been. Ask the Fiia if you want to know. Go to them, go back to your husband. Leave me alone here. There's no room at Kirien for girls and gold and all the rest of the story. The story's over here; this is the fallen place, this is the empty hall. The sons of Leynen all are dead, their treasures are all lost. Go on your way, girl."

Grey and swollen as the web-spinner of ruined houses, he turned and went blundering toward the cellars where he hid from daylight.

Leading the striped windsteed of Hallan, Semley left her old home and walked down the steep hill, past the village of the midmen, who greeted her with sullen respect, on over fields and pastures where the great, wing-clipped, half-wild herilor grazed, to a valley that was green as a painted bowl and full to the brim with sunlight. In the deep of the valley lay the village of the Fiia, and as she descended leading her steed the little, slight people ran up toward her from their huts and gardens, laughing, calling out in faint, thin voices.

"Hail Halla's bride, Kirienlady, Windborne, Semley the Fair!"

They gave her lovely names and she liked to hear them, minding not at all their laughter; for they laughed at all they said. That was her own way, to speak and laugh. She stood tall in her long blue cloak among their swirling welcome.

"Hail Lightfolk, Sundwellers, Fiia friends of men!"

They took her down into the village and brought her into one of their airy houses, the tiny children chasing along behind. There was no telling the age of a Fian once he was grown; it was hard even to tell one from another and be sure, as they moved about quick as moths around a candle, that she spoke always to the same one. But it seemed that one of them talked with her for a while, as the others fed and petted her steed, and brought water for her to drink, and bowls of fruit from their gardens of little trees. "It was never the Fiia that stole the necklace of the Lords of Kirien!" cried the little man. "What would the Fiia do with gold, Lady? For us there is sunlight in warmyear, and in coldyear the remembrance of sunlight; the yellow fruit, the yellow leaves in endseason, the yellow hair of our lady of Kirien; no other gold."

"Then it was some midman stole the thing?"

Laughter ran long and faint about her. "How would a midman dare? O Lady of Kirien, how the great jewel was stolen no mortal knows, not man nor midman nor Fian nor any among the Seven Folk. Only dead minds know how it was lost, long ago when Kireley the Proud whose great-granddaughter is Semley walked alone by the caves of the sea. But it may be found perhaps among the Sunhaters."

"The Clayfolk?"

A louder burst of laughter, nervous.

"Sit with us, Semley, sunhaired, returned to us from the north." She sat with them to eat, and they were as pleased with her graciousness as she with theirs. But when they heard her repeat that she would go to the Clayfolk to find her inheritance, if it was there, they began not to laugh; and little by little there were fewer of them around her. She was alone at last with perhaps the one she had spoken with before the meal. "Do not go among the Clayfolk, Semley," he said, and for a moment her heart failed her. The Fian, drawing his hand down slowly over his eyes, had darkened all the air about them. Fruit lay ash-white on the plate; all the bowls of clear water were empty.

"In the mountains of the far land the Fiia and the Gdemiar parted. Long ago we parted," said the slight, still man of the Fiia. "Longer ago we were one. What we are not, they are. What we are, they are not. Think of the sunlight and the grass and the trees that bear fruit, Semley; think that not all roads that lead down lead up as well."

"Mine leads neither down nor up, kind host, but only straight on to my inheritance. I will go to it where it is, and return with it."

The Fian bowed, laughing a little.

Outside the village she mounted her striped windsteed, and, calling farewell in answer to their calling, rose up into the wind of afternoon and flew southwestward toward the caves down by the rocky shores of Kiriensea.

She feared she might have to walk far into those tunnel-caves to find the people she sought, for it was said the Clayfolk never came out of their caves into the light of the sun, and feared even the Greatstar and the moons. It was a long ride; she landed once to let her steed hunt tree-rats while she ate a little bread from her saddle-bag. The bread was hard and dry by now and tasted of leather, yet kept a faint savor of its making, so that for a moment, eating it alone in a glade of the southern forests, she heard the quiet tone of a voice and saw Durhal's face turned to her in the light of the candles of Hallan. For a while she sat daydreaming of that stern and vivid young face, and of what she would say to him when she came home with a kingdom's ransom around her neck: "I wanted a gift worthy of my husband, Lord. . . ." Then she pressed on, but when she reached the coast the sun had set, with the Greatstar sinking behind it. A mean wind had come up from the west, starting and gusting and veering, and her windsteed was weary fighting it. She let him glide down on the sand. At once he folded his wings and curled his thick, light limbs under him with a thrum of purring. Semley stood holding her cloak close at her throat, stroking the steed's neck so that he flicked his ears and purred again. The warm fur comforted her hand, but all that met her eyes was grey sky full of smears of cloud, grey sea, dark sand. And then running over the sand a low, dark creature—another—a group of them, squatting and running and stopping.

She called aloud to them. Though they had not seemed to see her, now in a moment they were all around her. They kept a distance from her windsteed; he had stopped purring, and his fur rose a little under Semley's hand. She took up the reins, glad of his protection but afraid of the nervous ferocity he might display. The strange folk stood silent, staring, their thick bare feet planted in the sand. There was no mistaking them: they were the height of the Fiia and in all else a shadow, a black image of those laughing people. Naked, squat, stiff, with lank hair and grey-white skins, dampish-looking like the skins of grubs; eyes like rocks.

"You are the Clayfolk?"

"Gdemiar are we, people of the Lords of the Realms of Night." The voice was unexpectedly loud and deep, and rang out pompous through the salt, blowing dusk; but, as with the Fiia, Semley was not sure which one had spoken.

"I greet you, Nightlords. I am Semley of Kirien, Durhal's wife of Hallan. I come to you seeking my inheritance, the necklace called Eye of the Sea, lost long ago."

"Why do you seek it here, Angya? Here is only sand and salt and night."

"Because lost things are known of in deep places," said Semley, quite ready for a play of wits, "and gold that came from earth has a way of going back to the earth. And sometimes the made, they say, returns to the maker." This last was a guess; it hit the mark.

"It is true the necklace Eye of the Sea is known to us by name. It was made in our caves long ago, and sold by us to the Angyar. And the blue stone came from the Clayfields of our kin to the east. But these are very old tales, Angya."

"May I listen to them in the places where they are told?"

The squat people were silent a while, as if in doubt. The grey wind blew by over the sand, darkening as the Greatstar set; the sound of the sea loudened and lessened. The deep voice spoke again: "Yes, lady of the

Angyar. You may enter the Deep Halls. Come with us now." There was a changed note in his voice, wheedling. Semley would not hear it. She followed the Claymen over the sand, leading on a short rein her sharp-taloned steed.

At the cave-mouth, a toothless, yawning mouth from which a stinking warmth sighed out, one of the Claymen said, "The air-beast cannot come in."

"Yes," said Semley.

"No," said the squat people.

"Yes. I will not leave him here. He is not mine to leave. He will not harm you, so long as I hold his reins."

"No," deep voices repeated; but others broke in, "As you will," and after a moment of hesitation they went on. The cave-mouth seemed to snap shut behind them, so dark was it under the stone. They went in single file, Semley last.

The darkness of the tunnel lightened, and they came under a ball of weak white fire hanging from the roof. Farther on was another, and another; between them long black worms hung in festoons from the rock. As they went on these fire-globes were set closer, so that all the tunnel was lit with a bright, cold light.

Semley's guides stopped at a parting of three tunnels, all blocked by doors that looked to be of iron. "We shall wait, Angya," they said, and eight of them stayed with her, while three others unlocked one of the doors and passed through. It fell to behind them with a clash.

Straight and still stood the daughter of the Angyar in the white, blank light of the lamps; her windsteed crouched beside her, flicking the tip of his striped tail, his great folded wings stirring again and again with the checked impulse to fly. In the tunnel behind Semley the eight Claymen squatted on their hams, muttering to one another in their deep voices, in their own tongue.

The central door swung clanging open. "Let the Angya enter the Realm of Night!" cried a new voice, booming and boastful. A Clayman who wore some clothing on his thick grey body stood in the doorway, beckoning to her. "Enter and behold the wonders of our lands, the marvels made by hands, the works of the Nightlords!"

Silent, with a tug at her steed's reins, Semley bowed her head and followed him under the low doorway made for dwarfish folk. Another glaring tunnel stretched ahead, dank walls dazzling in the white light, but, instead of a way to walk upon, its floor carried two bars of polished iron stretching off side by side as far as she could see. On the bars rested some kind of cart with metal wheels. Obeying her new guide's gestures, with no hesitation and no trace of wonder on her face, Semley stepped into the cart and made the windsteed crouch beside her. The Clayman got in and sat down in front of her, moving bars and wheels about. A loud grinding noise arose, and a screaming of metal on metal, and then the walls of the tunnel began to jerk by. Faster and faster the walls slid past, till the fireglobes overhead ran into a blur, and the stale warm air became a foul wind blowing the hood back off her hair.

The cart stopped. Semley followed the guide up basalt steps into a vast anteroom and then a still vaster hall, carved by ancient waters or by the burrowing Clayfolk out of the rock, its darkness that had never known sunlight lit with the uncanny cold brilliance of the globes. In grilles cut in the walls huge blades turned and turned, changing the stale air. The great closed space hummed and boomed with noise, the loud voices of the Clayfolk, the grinding and shrill buzzing and vibration of turning blades and wheels, the echoes and re-echoes of all this from the rock. Here all the stumpy figures of the Claymen were clothed in garments imitating those of the Starlords—divided trousers, soft boots, and hooded tunics—though the few women to be seen, hurrying servile dwarves, were naked. Of the males many were soldiers, bearing at their sides weapons shaped like the terrible light-throwers of the Starlords, though even Semley could see these were merely shaped iron clubs. What she saw, she saw without looking. She followed where she was led, turning her head neither to left nor right. When she came before a group of Claymen who wore iron circlets on their black hair her guide halted, bowed, boomed out, "The High Lords of the Gdemiar!"

There were seven of them, and all looked up at her with such arrogance on their lumpy grey faces that she wanted to laugh.

"I come among you seeking the lost treasure of my family, O Lords of the Dark Realm," she said gravely to them. "I seek Leynen's prize, the Eye of the Sea." Her voice was faint in the racket of the huge vault.

"So said our messengers, Lady Semley." This time she could pick out the one who spoke, one even shorter than the others, hardly reaching Semley's breast, with a white, fierce face. "We do not have this thing you seek."

"Once you had it, it is said."

"Much is said, up there where the sun blinks."

"And words are borne off by the winds, where there are winds to blow. I do not ask how the necklace was lost to us and returned to you, its makers of old. Those are old tales, old grudges. I only seek to find it now. You do not have it now; but it may be you know where it is."

"It is not here."

"Then it is elsewhere."

"It is where you cannot come to it. Never, unless we help you."

"Then help me. I ask this as your guest."

"It is said, *The Angyar take; the Fiia give; the Gdemiar give and take.* If we do this for you, what will you give us?"

"My thanks, Nightlord."

She stood tall and bright among them, smiling. They all stared at her with a heavy, grudging wonder, a sullen yearning.

"Listen, Angya, this is a great favor you ask of us. You do not know how great a favor. You cannot understand. You are of a race that will not understand, that cares for nothing but wind-riding and crop-raising and sword-fighting and shouting together. But who made your swords of the bright steel? We, the Gdemiar! Your lords come to us here and in the Clayfields and buy their swords and go away, not looking, not understanding. But you are here now, you will look, you can see a few of our endless marvels, the lights that burn forever, the car that pulls itself, the machines that make our clothes and cook our food and sweeten our air and serve us in all things. Know that all these things are beyond your understanding. And know this: we, the Gdemiar, are the friends of those you call the Starlords! We came with them to Hallan, to Reohan, to Hul-Orren, to all your castles, to help them speak to you. The lords to whom you, the proud Angyar, pay tribute, are our friends. They do us favors as we do them favors! Now, what do your thanks mean to us?"

"That is your question to answer," said Semley, "not mine. I have asked my question. Answer it, Lord."

For a while the seven conferred together, by word and silence. They would glance at her and look away, and mutter and be still. A crowd grew around them, drawn slowly and silently, one after another till Semley was encircled by hundreds of the matted black heads, and all the great booming cavern floor was covered with people, except a little space directly around her. Her windsteed was quivering with fear and irriation too long controlled, and his eyes had gone very wide and pale, like the eyes of a steed forced to fly at night. She stroked the warm fur of his head, whispering, "Quietly now, brave one, bright one, windlord. . . ."

"Angya, we will take you to the place where the treasure lies." The Clayman with the white face and iron crown had turned to her once more. "More than that we cannot do. You must come with us to claim the necklace where it lies, from those who keep it. The air-beast cannot come with you. You must come alone."

"How far a journey, Lord?"

His lips drew back and back. "A very far journey, Lady. Yet it will last only one long night."

"I thank you for your courtesy. Will my steed be well cared for this night? No ill must come to him."

"He will sleep till you return. A greater windsteed you will have ridden, when you see that beast again! Will you not ask where we take you?"

"Can we go soon on this journey? I would not stay long away from my home."

"Yes. Soon." Again the grey lips widened as he stared up into her face.

What was done in those next hours Semley could not have retold; it was all haste, jumble, noise, strangeness. While she held her steed's head a Clayman stuck a long needle into the golden-striped haunch. She nearly cried out at the sight, but her steed merely twitched and then, purring, fell asleep. He was carried off by a group of Clayfolk who clearly had to summon up their courage to touch his warm fur. Later on she had to see a needle driven into her own arm—perhaps to test her courage, she thought, for it did not seem to make her sleep; though she was not quite sure. There were times she had to travel in the rail-carts, passing iron doors and vaulted caverns by the hundred and hundred; once the rail-cart ran through a cavern that stretched off on either hand measureless into the dark, and all that darkness was full of great flocks of herilor. She could hear their cooing, husky calls, and glimpse the flocks in the front-lights of the cart; then she saw some more clearly in the white light, and saw that they were all wingless, and all blind. At that she shut her eyes. But there were more tunnels to go through, and always more caverns, more grey lumpy bodies and fierce faces and booming boasting voices, until at last they led her suddenly out into the open air. It was full night; she raised her eyes joyfully to the stars and the single moon shining, little Heliki brightening in the west. But the Clayfolk were all about her still, making her climb now into some new kind of cart or cave, she did not know which. It was small, full of little blinking lights like rushlights, very narrow and shining after the great dank caverns and the starlit night. Now another needle was stuck in her, and they told her she would have to be tied down in a sort of flat chair, tied down head and hand and foot.

"I will not," said Semley.

But when she saw that the four Claymen who were to be her guides let themselves be tied down first, she submitted. The others left. There was a roaring sound, and a long silence; a great weight that could not be seen pressed upon her. Then there was no weight; no sound; nothing at all.

"Am I dead?" asked Semley.

"Oh no, Lady," said a voice she did not like.

Opening her eyes, she saw the white face bent over her, the wide lips pulled back, the eyes like little stones. Her bonds had fallen away from her, and she leaped up. She was weightless, bodiless; she felt herself only a gust of terror on the wind.

"We will not hurt you," said the sullen voice or voices. "Only let us touch you, Lady. We would like to touch your hair. Let us touch your hair. . . ."

The round cart they were in trembled a little. Outside its one window lay blank night, or was it mist, or nothing at all? One long night, they had said. Very long. She sat motionless and endured the touch of their heavy grey hands on her hair. Later they would touch her hands and feet and arms, and once her throat: at that she set her teeth and stood up, and they drew back. "We have not hurt you, Lady," they said. She shook her head.

When they bade her, she lay down again in the chair that bound her down; and when light flashed golden, at the window, she would have wept at the sight, but fainted first.

"Well," said Rocannon, "now at least we know what she is."

"I wish there were some way of knowing *who* she is," the curator mumbled. "She wants something we've got here in the Museum, is that what the trogs say?"

"Now, don't call 'em trogs," Rocannon said conscientiously; as a hilfer, an ethnologist of the High Intelligence Life-forms, he was supposed to resist such words. "They're not pretty, but they're Status C Allies. . . . I wonder why the Commission picked them to develop? Before even contacting all the HILF species? I'll bet the survey was from Centaurus—Centaurans always like nocturnals and cave dwellers. I'd have backed Species II, here, I think."

"The troglodytes seem to be rather in awe of her."

"Aren't you?"

Ketho glanced at the tall woman again, then reddened and laughed. "Well, in a way. I never saw such a beautiful alien type in eighteen years here on New South Georgia. I never saw such a beautiful woman anywhere, in fact. She looks like a goddess." The red now reached the top of his bald head, for Ketho was a shy curator, not given to hyperbole. But Rocannon nodded soberly, agreeing.

"I wish we could talk to her without those tr—Gdemiar as interpreters. But there's no help for it." Rocannon went toward their visitor, and when she turned her splendid face to him he bowed down very deeply, going right down to the floor on one knee, his head bowed and his eyes shut. This was what he called his All-Purpose Intercultural Curtsey, and he performed it with some grace. When he came erect again the beautiful woman smiled and spoke.

"She say, Hail, Lord of Stars," growled one of her squat escorts in Pidgin-Galactic.

"Hail, Lady of the Angyar," Rocannon replied. "In what way can we of the Museum serve the lady?"

Across the troglodytes' growling her voice ran like a brief silver wind.

"She say, Please give her necklace which treasure her blood-kinforebears long long."

"Which necklace?" he asked, and understanding him, she pointed to the central display of the case before them, a magnificent thing, a chain of yellow gold, massive but very delicate in workmanship, set with one big hot-blue sapphire. Rocannon's eyebrows went up, and Ketho at his shoulder murmured, "She's got good taste. That's the Fomalhaut Necklace—famous bit of work."

She smiled at the two men, and again spoke to them over the heads of the troglodytes.

"She say, O Starlords, Elder and Younger Dwellers in House of Treasures, this treasure her one. Long long time. Thank you."

"How did we get the thing, Ketho?"

"Wait; let me look it up in the catalogue. I've got it here. Here. It came from these trogs—trolls—whatever they are: Gdemiar. They have a bargain-obsession, it says; we had to let 'em buy the ship they came here on, an AD-4. This was part payment. It's their own handiwork."

"And I'll bet they can't do this kind of work anymore, since they've been steered to Industrial."

"But they seem to feel the thing is hers, not theirs or ours. It must be important, Rocannon, or they wouldn't have given up this time-span to her errand. Why, the objective lapse between here and Fomalhaut must be considerable!"

"Several years, no doubt," said the hilfer, who was used to star-jumping. "Not very far. Well, neither the *Handbook* nor the *Guide* gives me enough data to base a decent guess on. These species obviously haven't been properly studied at all. The little fellows may be showing her simple courtesy. Or an interspecies war may depend on this damn sapphire. Perhaps her desire rules them, because they consider themselves totally inferior to her. Or despite appearances she may be their prisoner, their decoy. How can we tell? . . . Can you give the thing away, Ketho?"

"Oh, yes. All the Exotica are technically on loan, not our property, since these claims come up now and then. We seldom argue. Peace above all, until the War comes. . . ."

"Then I'd say give it to her."

Ketho smiled. "It's a privilege," he said. Unlocking the case, he lifted out the great golden chain; then, in his shyness, he held it out to Rocannon, saying, "You give it to her."

So the blue jewel first lay, for a moment, in Rocannon's hand.

His mind was not on it; he turned straight to the beautiful, alien woman, with his handful of blue fire and gold. She did not raise her hands to take it, but bent her head, and he slipped the necklace over her hair. It lay like a burning fuse along her golden-brown throat. She looked up from it with such pride, delight, and gratitude in her face that Rocannon stood wordless, and the little curator murmured hurriedly in his own language, "You're welcome, you're very welcome." She bowed her golden head to him and to Rocannon. Then, turning, she nodded to her squat guards—or captors?—and, drawing her worn blue cloak about her, paced down the long hall and was gone. Ketho and Rocannon stood looking after her.

"What I feel . . ." Rocannon began.

"Well?" Ketho inquired hoarsely, after a long pause.

"What I feel sometimes is that I . . . meeting these people from worlds we know so little of, you know, sometimes . . . that I have as it were blundered through the corner of a legend, or a tragic myth, maybe, which I do not understand. . . ."

"Yes," said the curator, clearing his throat. "I wonder . . . I wonder what her name is."

Semley the Fair, Semley the Golden, Semley of the Necklace. The Clayfolk had bent to her will, and so had even the Starlords in that terrible place where the Clayfolk had taken her, the city at the end of the night. They had bowed to her, and given her gladly her treasure from amongst their own.

But she could not yet shake off the feeling of those caverns about her where rock lowered overhead, where you could not tell who spoke or what they did, where voices boomed and grey hands reached out— Enough of that. She had paid for the necklace; very well. Now it was hers. The price was paid, the past was the past.

Her windsteed had crept out of some kind of box, with his eyes filmy and his fur rimed with ice, and at first when they had left the caves of the Gdemiar he would not fly. Now he seemed all right again, riding a smooth south wind through the bright sky toward Hallan. "Go quick, go quick," she told him, beginning to laugh as the wind cleared away her mind's darkness. "I want to see Durhal soon, soon. . . ."

And swiftly they flew, coming to Hallan by dusk of the second day. Now the caves of the Clayfolk seemed no more than last year's nightmare, as the steed swooped with her up the thousand steps of Hallan and across the Chasmbridge where the forests fell away for a thousand feet. In the gold light of evening in the flightcourt she dismounted and walked up the last steps between the stiff carven figures of heroes and the two gatewards, who bowed to her, staring at the beautiful, fiery thing around her neck.

In the Forehall she stopped a passing girl, a very pretty girl, by her looks one of Durhal's close kin, though Semley could not call to mind her name.

"Do you know me, maiden? I am Semley, Durhal's wife. Will you go tell the Lady Durossa that I have come back?"

For she was afraid to go on in and perhaps face Durhal at once, alone; she wanted Durossa's support.

The girl was gazing at her, her face very strange. But she murmured, "Yes, Lady," and darted off toward the Tower.

Semley stood waiting in the gilt, ruinous hall. No one came by; were they all at table in the Revel-hall? The silence was uneasy. After a minute Semley started toward the stairs to the Tower. But an old woman was coming to her across the stone floor, holding her arms out, weeping.

"O Semley, Semley!"

She had never seen the grey-haired woman, and shrank back.

"But Lady, who are you?"

"I am Durossa, Semley."

She was quiet and still, all the time that Durossa embraced her and wept, and asked if it were true the Clayfolk had captured her and kept her under a spell all these long years, or had it been the Fiia with their strange arts? Then, drawing back a little, Durossa ceased to weep.

"You're still young, Semley. Young as the day you left here. And you wear round your neck the necklace. . . ."

"I have brought my gift to my husband Durhal. Where is he?"

"Durhal is dead."

Semley stood unmoving.

"Your husband, my brother, Durhal Hallanlord was killed seven years ago in battle. Nine years you had been gone. The Starlords came no more. We fell to warring with the Eastern Halls, with the Angyar of Log and Hul-Orren. Durhal, fighting, was killed by a midman's spear, for he had little armor for his body, and none at all for his spirit. He lies buried in the fields above Orren Marsh."

Semley turned away. "I will go to him, then," she said, putting her hand on the gold chain that weighed down her neck. "I will give him my gift."

"Wait, Semley! Durhal's daughter, your daughter, see her now, Haldre the Beautiful!"

It was the girl she had first spoken to and sent to Durossa, a girl of nineteen or so, with eyes like Durhal's eyes, dark blue. She stood beside Durossa, gazing with those steady eyes at this woman Semley who was her mother and was her own age. Their age was the same, and their gold hair, and their beauty. Only Semley was a little taller, and wore the blue stone on her breast.

"Take it, take it. It was for Durhal and Haldre that I brought it from the end of the long night!" Semley cried this aloud, twisting and bowing her head to get the heavy chain off, dropping the necklace so it fell on the stones with a cold, liquid clash. "O take it, Haldre!" she cried again, and then, weeping aloud, turned and ran from Hallan, over the bridge and down the long, broad steps, and, darting off eastward into the forest of the mountainside like some wild thing escaping, was gone.

MOON DUEL

With a fifty-year career that stretched from the "Golden Age" *Astounding* of the 1940s to the beginning of the '90s, the late Fritz Leiber was an indispensable figure in the development of modern science fiction, fantasy, and horror. It is impossible to imagine what those genres would be like today without him, except to say that they would be poorer for it. Probably no other figure of his generation (with the possible exception of L. Sprague de Camp) wrote in as many different genres as Leiber, or was as important as he was to the development of each. Leiber was one of the fathers of modern "heroic fantasy," and his long sequence of stories about Fafhrd and the Gray Mouser remains one of the most complex and intelligent bodies of work in the entire subgenre of "Sword & Sorcery" (which term Leiber himself is usually credited with coining). He may also be one of the best—if not *the* best—writers of the supernatural horror tale since Lovecraft and Poe, and was writing updated "modern" or "urban" horror stories like "Smoke Ghost" and the classic *Conjure Wife* long before the work of Stephen King engendered the Big Horror Boom of the middle 1970s and brought that form to wide popular attention.

Leiber was also a towering Ancestral Figure in science fiction as well, having been one of the major writers of both Campbell's "Golden Age" *Astounding* of the '40s—with works like *Gather, Darkness*—and H.L. Gold's *Galaxy* in the '50s—with works like the classic "Coming Attraction" and the superb novel *The Big Time,* which still holds up as one of the best SF novels ever written—and *then* going on to contribute a steady stream of superior fiction to the magazines and anthologies of the '60s, the '70s, and the '80s, as well as powerful novels such as *The Wanderer* and *Our Lady of Darkness. The Big Time* won a well-deserved Hugo in 1959, and Leiber also won a slew of other awards: all told, six Hugos and four Nebulas, plus three World Fantasy Awards—one of them the prestigious Life Achievement Award—and a Grandmaster of Fantasy Award.

Leiber's relationship with Space Opera or the Space Adventure tale was complex and contradictory. His *homage* to Space Opera, the Hugo-winning novel *The Wanderer*—where attractive, seductive, (and rather dominatrix-like) alien Tiger Women in a planet-sized spaceship stop off in our solar system just long enough to demolish our moon for fuel, with disastrous consequences for the Earth—shows a genuine fondness and nostalgia for the form . . . but, at the same time, he used stock Space Opera clichés cunningly, to sharp satiric effect, in stories such as "The Secret Songs"—where a drug-dependant young husband, high on

barbiturates and paraldehyde, hallucinates that he is being put to a nightly series of pulp-adventure space-operaish "tests" by his "mentor," a Wise Old Croc-
odile From Beyond the Magnellanic Clouds—in a manner that seems to signify
that he may have grown rather tired of the Interplanetary Adventure and impatient
with its limitations (which was not an isolated opinion among the more intellectual writers of his day, just as it would not be among the radical new writers of
the generation just about to rise to prominence—most of them strongly influenced by Leiber—who would collectively produce less adventure SF, particularly
Space Opera, than any other comparable generational group of authors). At the
very least, when Leiber dabbled in Space Adventure, he insisted on doing something *new*—and often bizarre—with it, as in "A Pail of Air" or the surreal "The
Big Trek." So it will come as no surprise that the Moon that Leiber takes us to in
the sly and incisive story that follows is not quite like any *other* writer's conception of the place, or that the adventure that we have there is a quirky and surprising one, with unexpected consequences for even the simplest of actions . . .

Fritz Leiber's other books include *The Green Millennium, A Spectre Is Haunting
Texas, The Big Engine,* and *The Silver Eggheads,* the collections *The Best of Fritz
Leiber, The Book of Fritz Leiber, The Change War, Night's Dark Agents, Heroes
and Horrors, The Mind Spider,* and *The Ghost Light,* and the seven volumes of
Fafhrd-Gray Mouser stories. Much of this work is out of print, but the Fafhrd-Gray
Mouser stories are now being reissued in massive omnibus editions by White
Wolf Borealis, the first two of which are *Ill Met in Lankhmar* and *Lean Times in
Lankhmar;* the most recent such volume is *Return to Lankhmar.*

First hint I had we'd been spotted by a crusoe was a little *tick* coming to
my moonsuit from the miniradar Pete and I were gaily heaving into position near the east end of Gioja crater to scan for wrecks, trash, and nodules
of raw metal.

Then came a *whish* which cut off the instant Pete's hand lost contact
with the squat instrument. His gauntlet, silvery in the raw low polar sunlight, drew away very slowly, as if he'd grown faintly disgusted with our activity. My gaze kept on turning to see the whole shimmering back of his
helmet blown off in a gorgeous sickening brain-fog and blood-mist that was
already falling in the vacuum as fine red snow.

A loud *tock* then and glove-sting as the crusoe's second slug hit the miniradar, but my gaze had gone back to the direction Pete had been facing
when he bought it—in time to see the green needle-flash of the crusoe's gun
in a notch in Gioja's low wall, where the black of the shadowed rock met the

gem-like starfields along a jagged border. I unslung my Swift* as I dodged a long step to the side and squeezed off three shots. The first two shells must have traveled a touch too high, but the third made a beautiful fleeting violet globe at the base of the notch. It didn't show me a figure, whole or shattered, silvery or otherwise, on the wall or atop it, but then some crusoes are camouflaged like chameleons and most of them move very fast.

Pete's suit was still falling slowly and stiffly forward. Three dozen yards beyond was a wide black fissure, though exactly how wide I couldn't tell because much of the opposite lip merged into the shadow of the wall. I scooted toward it like a rat toward a hole. On my third step, I caught up Pete by his tool belt and oxy tube while his falling front was still inches away from the powdered pumice, and I heaved him along with me. Some slow or over-drilled part of my brain hadn't yet accepted he was dead.

Then I began to skim forward, inches above the ground myself, kicking back against rocky outcrops thrusting up through the dust—it was like fin-swimming. The crusoe couldn't have been expecting this nut stunt, by which I at least avoided the dreamy sitting-duck slowness of safer, higher-bounding moon-running, for there was a green flash behind me and hurtled dust faintly pittered my soles and seat. He hadn't been leading his target enough. Also, I knew now he had shells as well as slugs.

I was diving over the lip three seconds after skoot-off when Pete's boot caught solidly against a last hooky outcrop. The something in my brain was still stubborn, for I clutched him like clamps, which made me swing around with a jerk. But even that was lucky, for a bright globe two yards through winked on five yards ahead like a mammoth firefly's flash, but not quite as gentle, for the invisible rarified explosion-front hit me hard enough to *boom* my suit and make the air inside slap me. Now I knew he had metal-proximity fuses on some of his shells too—they must be very good at mini-stuff on his home planet.

The tail of the pale green flash showed me the fissure's bottom a hundred yards straight below and all dust, as ninety percent of them are—pray God the dust was deep. I had time to thumb Extreme Emergency to the ship for it to relay automatically to Circumluna. Then the lip had cut me off from the ship and I had lazily fallen out of the glare into the blessed blackness, the dial lights in my helmet already snapped off—even they might make enough glow for the crusoe to aim by. The slug had switched off Pete's.

Ten, twelve seconds to fall and the opposite lip wasn't cutting off the

---

*All-purpose vacuum rifle named for the .22 cartridge which as early as 1940 was being produced by Winchester, Remington, and Norma with factory loads giving it a muzzle velocity of 4,140 feet, almost a mile, a second.

notched crater wall. I could feel the crusoe's gun trailing me down—he'd
know moon-G, sticky old five-foot. I could feel his tentacle or finger or claw
or ameboid bump tightening on the trigger or button or what. I shoved Pete
away from me, parallel to the fissure wall, as hard as I could. Three more
seconds, four, and my suit *boomed* again and I was walloped as another green
flash showed me the smooth-sifted floor moving up and beginning to hurry
a little. This flash was a hemisphere, not a globe—it had burst against the
wall—but if there were any rock fragments they missed me. And it exactly
bisected the straight line between me and Pete's silvery coffin. The crusoe
knew his gun and his Luna—I really admired him, even if my shove had
pushed Pete and me, action and reaction, just enough out of the target
path. Then the fissure lip had cut the notch and I was readying to land like
a three-legged crab, my Swift reslung, my free hand on my belted dust-
shoes.

Eleven seconds' fall on Luna is not much more than two on earth, but
either are enough to build up a velocity of over fifty feet a second. The dust
jarred me hard, but thank God there were no reefs in it. It covered at least
all the limbs and front of me, including my helmet-front—my dial lights,
snapped on again, showed a grayness fine-grained as flour.

The stuff resisted like flour, too, as I unbelted my dust-shoes. Using
them for a purchase, I pulled my other arm and helmet-front free. The
stars looked good, even gray-dusted. With a hand on each shoe, I dragged
out my legs and, balancing gingerly on the slithery stuff, got each of my feet
snapped to a shoe. Then I raised up and switched on my headlight. I hated
that. I no more wanted to do it than a hunted animal wants to break twigs
or show itself on the skyline, but I knew I had exactly as long to find cover
as it would take the crusoe to lope from the notch to the opposite lip of the
fissure. Most of them lope very fast, they're that keen on killing.

Well, we started the killing, I reminded myself. *This time I'm the quarry.*

My searchlight made a perverse point of hitting Pete's shimmering cas-
ket, spread-eagled, seven-eighths submerged, like a man floating on his
back. I swung the beam steadily. The opposite wall was smooth except for
a few ledges and cracks and there wasn't any overhang to give a man below
cover from someone on top.

But a section of the wall on my side, not fifty yards away, was hugely
pocked with holes and half-bubbles where the primeval lava had foamed
high and big against the feeble plucking of lunar gravity. I aimed myself at
the center of that section and started out. I switched off my headlight and
guided myself by the wide band of starfields.

You walk dust-shoes with much the same vertical lift and low methodical forward swing as snowshoes. It was nostalgic, but hunted animals have no time for memory-delicatessen.

Suddenly there was more and redder brightness overhead than the stars. A narrow ribbon of rock along the top of the opposite wall was glaringly bathed in orange, while the rim peaks beyond glowed faintly, like smoldering volcanoes. Light from the orange ribbon bounced down into my fissure, caroming back and forth between the walls until I could dimly see again the holes I was headed for.

The crusoe had popped our ship—both tanks, close together, so that the sun-warmed gasses, exploding out into each other, burned like a hundred torches. The oxyaniline lasted until I reached the holes. I crawled through the biggest. The fading glow dimly and fleetingly showed a rock-bubble twelve feet across with another hole at the back of it. The stuff looked black, felt rough yet diamond-hard. I risked a look behind me.

The ribbon glow was darkest red—the skeleton of our ship still aglow. The ribbon flashed green in the middle—a tiny venomous dagger—and then a huge pale green firefly winked where Pete lay. He'd saved me a fourth time.

I had barely pushed sideways back when there was another of those winks just outside my hole, this one glaringly bright, its front walloping me. I heard through the rock faint *tings* of fragments of Pete's suit hitting the wall, but they may have been only residual ringings, from the nearer blast, in my suit or ears.

I scrambled through the back door in the bubble into a space which I made out by crawling to be a second bubble, resembling the first even to having a back door. I went through that third hole and turned around and rested my Swift's muzzle on the rough-scooped threshold. Since the crusoe lived around here, he'd know the territory better wherever I went. Why retreat farther and get lost? My dial lights showed that about a minute and a half had gone by since Pete bought it. Also, I wasn't losing pressure and I had oxy and heat for four hours—Circumluna would be able to deliver a rescue force in half that time, if my message had got through and if the crusoe didn't scupper them too. Then I got goosy again about the glow of the dial lights and snapped them off. I started to change position and was suddenly afraid the crusoe might already be trailing me by my transmitted sounds through the rock, and right away I held stock still and started to listen for *him.*

No light, no sound, a ghost-fingered gravity—it was like being tested for sanity-span in an anechoic chamber. Almost at once dizziness and the sensory mirages started to come, swimming in blue and burned and moaning from the peripheries of my senses—even waiting in ambush for a crusoe wouldn't stop them; I guess I wanted them to come. So though straining every sense against the crusoe's approach, I had at last to start thinking about him.

It's strange that men should have looked at the moon for millennia and never guessed it was exactly what it looked like: a pale marble graveyard for living dead men, a Dry Tortuga of space where the silver ships from a million worlds marooned their mutineers, their recalcitrants, their criminals, their lunatics. Not on fertile warm-blanketed earth with its quaint adolescent race, which such beings might harm, but on the great silver rock of earth's satellite, to drag out their solitary furious lives, each with his suit and gun and lonely hut or hole, living by recycling his wastes; recycling, too, the bitter angers and hates and delusions which had brought him there. As many as a thousand of them, enough to mine the moon for meals and fuel-gases and to reconquer space and perhaps become masters of earth—had they chosen to cooperate. But their refusal to cooperate was the very thing for which they'd been marooned, and besides that they were of a half thousand different galactic breeds. And so although they had some sort of electronic or psionic or what-not grapevine—at least what happened to one maroon became swiftly known to the others—each of them remained a solitary Friday-less Robinson Crusoe, hence the name.

I risked flashing my time dial. Only another thirty seconds gone. At this rate it would take an eternity for the two hours to pass before I could expect aid *if* my call had got through, while the crusoe— As my senses screwed themselves tighter to their task, my thoughts went whirling off again.

Earthmen shot down the first crusoe they met—in a moment of fumbling panic and against all their training. Ever since then the crusoes have shot first, or tried to, ignoring our belated efforts to communicate.

I brooded for what I thought was a very short while about the age-old problem of a universal galactic code, yet when I flashed my time dial again, seventy minutes had gone somewhere.

That really froze me. He'd had time to stalk and kill me a dozen times—he'd had time to go home and fetch his dogs!—my senses couldn't be *that* good protection with my mind away. Why even now, straining them in my fear, all I got was my own personal static: I heard my heart pounding, my blood roaring, I think for a bit I heard the Brownian movement of the air molecules against my eardrums.

What I hadn't been doing, I told myself, was thinking about the crusoe in a systematic way.

He had a gun like mine and at least three sorts of ammo.

He'd made it from notch to fissure-lip in forty seconds or less—he must be a fast loper, whatever number feet; he might well have a jet unit.

And he'd shot at the miniradar ahead of me. Had he thought it a communicator?—a weapon?—*or some sort of robot as dangerous as a man . . . ?*

My heart had quieted, my ears had stopped roaring, and in that instant I heard through the rock the faintest *scratching.*

Scratch-scratch, scratch-scratch, scratch, scratch, scratch it went, each time a little louder.

I flipped on my searchlight and there coming toward me across the floor of the bubble outside mine was a silver spider as wide as a platter with four opalescent eyes and a green-banded body. Its hanging jaws were like inward-curving notched scissor blades.

I fired by automatism as I fell back. The spider's bubble was filled with violet glare instantly followed by green. I was twice walloped by explosion-fronts and knocked down.

That hardly slowed me a second. The same flashes had shown me a hole in the top of my bubble and as soon as I'd scrambled to my feet I leaped toward it.

I did remember to leap gently. My right hand caught the black rim of the hole and it didn't break off and I drew myself up into the black bubble above. It had no hole in the top, but two high ones in the sides, and I went through the higher one.

I kept on that way. The great igneous bubbles were almost uniform. I always took the highest exit. Once I got inside a bubble with no exit and had to backtrack. After that I scanned first. I kept my searchlight on.

I'd gone through seven or seventeen bubbles before I could start to think about what had happened.

That spider had almost certainly not been my crusoe—or else there was a troop of them dragging a rifle like an artillery piece. And it hadn't likely been an hitherto-unknown, theoretically impossible, live vacuum-arthropod—or else the exotic biologists were in for a great surprise and I'd been right to wet my pants. No, it had most likely been a tracking or tracking-and-attack robot of some sort. Eight legs are a useful number, likewise eight hands. Were the jaws for cutting through suit armor? Maybe it was a robot pet for alonely being. Here, Spid!

The second explosion? Either the crusoe had fired into the chamber from the other side, or else the spider had carried a bomb to explode when it touched me. Fine use to make of a pet! I giggled. I was relieved, I guess, to think it likely that the spider had been "only" a robot.

Just then—I was in the ninth or nineteenth bubble—the inside of my helmet misted over everywhere. I was panting and sweating and my dehumidifier had overloaded. It was as if I were in a real peasouper of a fog. I could barely make out the black loom of the wall behind me. I switched out my headlight. My time dial showed seventy-two minutes gone. I switched it off and then I did a queer thing.

I leaned back very carefully until as much of my suit as possible touched rock. Then I measuredly thumped the rock ten times with the butt of my Swift and held very still.

Starting with ten would mean we were using the decimal system. Of course there were other possibilities, but . . .

Very faintly, coming at the same rate as mine, I heard six thuds.

What constant started with six? If he'd started with three, I'd have given him one, and so on through a few more places of pi. Or if with one, I'd have given him four—and then started to worry about the third and fourth places in the square root of two. I might take his signal for the beginning of a series with the interval of minus four and rap him back two, but then how could he rap me minus two? Oh why hadn't I simply started rapping out primes? Of course all the integers, in fact all the real numbers, from thirty-seven through forty-one had square roots beginning with six, but which one . . . ?

Suddenly I heard a scratching . . .

My searchbeam was on again, my helmet had unmisted, my present bubble was empty.

Just the same I scuttled out of it, still trending upward where I could. But now the holes wouldn't trend that way. They kept going two down for one up and the lines of bubbles zigzagged. I wanted to go back, but then I might hear the scratching. Once the bubbles started getting smaller. It was like being in solid black suds. I lost any sense of direction. I began to lose the sense of up-down. What's moon-gravity to the numbness of psychosis? I kept my searchlight on although I was sure the glow it made must reach ten bubbles away. I looked all around every bubble before I entered it, especially the overhang just above the entry hole.

Every once in a while I would hear somebody saying Six! Six? Six! like that and then very rapidly seven-eight-nine-five-four-three-two-one-naught. How would you rap naught in the decimal system? That one I finally solved: you'd rap ten.

Finally I came into a bubble that had a side-hole four feet across and edged at the top with diamonds. Very fancy. Was this the Spider Princess' boudoir? There was also a top hole but I didn't bother with that—it had no decor. I switched off my searchlight and looked out the window without exposing my head. The diamonds were stars. After a bit I made out what I took to be the opposite lip of the fissure I'd first dove in, only about one hundred feet above me. The rim-wall beyond looked vaguely familiar, though I wasn't sure about the notch. My time dial said one hundred eighteen minutes gone as I switched it off. Almost time to start hoping for rescue. Oh great!—with their ship a sitting duck for the crusoe they wouldn't be expecting. I hadn't signaled a word besides Extreme Emergency.

I moved forward and sat in the window, one leg outside, my Swift under my left arm. I plucked a flash grenade set for five seconds from my belt, pulled the fuse and tossed it across the fissure, almost hard enough to reach the opposite wall.

I looked down, my Swift swinging like my gaze.

The fissure lit up like a boulevard. Across from me I knew the flare was dropping dreamily, but I wasn't looking that way. Right below me, two hundred feet down, I saw a transparent helmet with something green and round and crested inside and with shoulders under it.

Just then I heard the *scratching* again, quite close.

I fired at once. My shell made a violet burst and raised a fountain of dust twenty feet from the crusoe. I scrambled back into my bubble, switching on my searchlight. Another spider was coming in on the opposite side, its legs moving fast. I jumped for the top-hole and grabbed its rim with my free hand. I'd have dropped my Swift if I'd needed my other hand, but I didn't. As I pulled myself up and through, I looked down and saw the spider straight below me eyeing me with its uptilted opalescent eyes and doubling its silver legs. Then it straightened its legs and sprang up toward me, not very fast but enough against Luna's feeble gravitational tug to put it into this upper room with me. I knew it mustn't touch me and I mustn't touch it by batting at it. I had started to shift the explosive shell in my gun for a slug, and its green-banded body was growing larger, when there was a green blast in the window below and its explosion-front, *booming* my suit a little, knocked the spider aside and out of sight before it made it through the trap door of my new bubble. Yet the spider didn't explode, if that was what had happened to the first one; at any rate there was no second green flash.

My new bubble had a top hole too and I went through it the same way I had the last. The next five bubbles were just the same too. I told myself that my routine was getting to be like that of a circus acrobat—except who stages shows inside black solidity?—except the gods maybe with the dreams they send us. The lava should be transparent, so the rim-wall peaks could admire.

At the same time I was thinking how if the biped humanoid shape is a good one for medium-size creatures on any planet, why so the spider shape is a good one for tiny creatures and apt to turn up anywhere and be copied in robots too.

The top hole in the sixth bubble showed me the stars, while one half of its rim shone white with sunlight.

Panting, I lay back against the rock. I switched off my searchlight. I didn't hear any scratching.

The stars. The stars were energy. They filled the universe with light, except for hidey holes and shadows here and there.

Then the number came to me. With the butt of my Swift I rapped out five. No answer. No scratching either. I rapped out five again.

Then the answer came, ever so faintly. Five knocked back at me.

Six five five—Planck's Constant, the invariant quantum of energy. Oh, it should be to the minus 29th power, of course, but I couldn't think how to rap that and, besides, the basic integers were all that mattered.

I heard the *scratching* . . .

I sprang and caught the rim and lifted myself into the glaring sunlight . . . and stopped with my body midway.

Facing me a hundred feet away, midway through another top-hole—he must have come very swiftly by another branch of the bubble ladder—he'd know the swiftest ones—was my green-crested crusoe. His face had a third eye where a man's nose would be, which with his crest made him look like a creature of mythology. We were holding our guns vertically.

We looked like two of the damned, half out of their holes in the floor of Dante's hell.

I climbed very slowly out of my hole, still pointing my gun toward the zenith. So did he.

We held very still for a moment. Then with his gun butt he rapped out ten. I could both see and also hear it through the rock.

I rapped out three. Then, as if the black bubble-world were one level of existence and this another, I wondered why we were going through this rigamarole. We each knew the other had a suit and a gun (and a lonely hole?) and so we knew we were both intelligent and knew math. So why was our rapping so precious?

He raised his gun—I think to rap out one, to start off pi.

But I'll never be sure, for just then there were two violet bursts, close together, against the fissure wall, quite close to him.

He started to swing the muzzle of his gun toward me. At least I think he did. He must know violet was the color of my explosions. I know I thought someone on my side was shooting. And I must have thought he was going to shoot me—because a violet dagger leaped from my Swift's muzzle and I felt its sharp recoil and then there was a violet globe where he was standing and moments later some fragment *twinged* lightly against my chest—a playful ironic tap.

He was blown apart pretty thoroughly, all his constants scattered, including—I'm sure—Planck's.

• • •

It was another half hour before the rescue ship from Circumluna landed. I spent it looking at earth low on the horizon and watching around for the spider, but I never saw it. The rescue party never found it either, though they made quite a hunt—with me helping after I'd rested a bit and had my batteries and oxy replenished. Either its power went off when its master died, or it was set to "freeze" then, or most likely go into a "hide" behavior pattern. Likely it's still out there waiting for an incautious earthman, like a rattlesnake in the desert or an old, forgotten land mine.

I also figured out, while waiting in Gioja crater, there near the north pole on the edge of Shackleton crater, the only explanation I've ever been able to make, though it's something of a whopper, of the two violet flashes which ended my little mathematical friendship-chant with the crusoe. They were the first two shells I squeezed off at him—the ones that skimmed the notch. They had the velocity to orbit Luna, and the time they took—two hours and five minutes—was right enough.

Oh, the consequences of our past actions!

Roger Zelazny

THE DOORS OF HIS FACE, THE LAMPS OF HIS MOUTH

Like a number of other writers, the late Roger Zelazny began publishing in 1962 in the pages of Cele Goldsmith's *Amazing.* This was the so-called "Class of '62," whose membership also included Thomas M. Disch, Keith Laumer, and Ursula K. Le Guin. Everyone in that "class" would eventually achieve prominence, but some of them would achieve it faster than others, and Zelazny's subsequent career would be one of the most meteoric in the history of SF. The first Zelazny story to attract wide notice was "A Rose for Ecclesiastes," published in 1963 (it was later selected by vote of the SFWA membership to have been one of the best SF stories of all time). By the end of that decade, he had won two Nebula Awards and two Hugo Awards and was widely regarded as one of the two most important American SF writers of the '60s (the other was Samuel R. Delany). His famous novel *Lord of Light* may have been one of the most popular, widely acclaimed, and hugely influential novels of that whole era. By the end of the '70s, although his critical acceptance as an important science fiction writer had dimmed, his long series of novels about the enchanted land of Amber—beginning with *Nine Princes in Amber*—had made him one of the most popular and best-selling fantasy writers of our time, and inspired the founding of worldwide fan clubs and fanzines.

Zelazny's early novels, such as *This Immortal* and *The Dream Masters,* were, on the whole, well-received, but it was the strong and stylish short work he published in magazines like *F&SF* and *Amazing* and *Worlds of If* throughout the middle years of the decade of the 1960s that electrified the genre, and it was these early stories—stories like "This Moment of the Storm," "The Graveyard Heart," "He Who Shapes," "The Keys to December," "For a Breath I Tarry," and "This Mortal Mountain,"—that established Zelazny as a giant of the field, and that many consider to be his best work. These stories are still amazing for their invention and elegance and verve, for their good-natured effrontery and easy ostentation, for the risks Zelazny took in pursuit of eloquence without ruffling a hair, the grace and nerve he displayed as he switched from high-flown pseudo-Spenserian to wisecracking Chandlerian slang to vivid prose-poetry to Hemingwayesque starkness in the course of only a few lines—and for the way he made it all look easy and effortless, the same kind of illusion Fred Astaire used to generate when he danced.

Unlike some of his peers, Zelazny's fondness for fast-paced adventure writing never faded, which may be one reason for the dimming of his critical reputation in the '70s, as he continued to turn out what were dismissed as "routine Space Adventures" by hostile critics during a period that demanded more "serious" and "ambitious" work by its writers. Zelazny's work was *never* "routine," however—some of his books of this period *were* rather weak by his own standards, but in even the weakest of them, you could count on inventiveness, vivid color, scope, intricate plotting, quirky characters . . . and, of course, plenty of action.

One of the inspirations for the famous story that follows, as well as for the even-more famous "A Rose for Ecclesiastes," is clearly a loving nostalgia for the era of the pulp adventure story that was then widely supposed to be ending. By the time Zelazny wrote this story, he knew perfectly well that Venus was probably *not* an Earth-like planet girded by vast seas full of immense swimming dinosaur-like creatures, just as he knew that in all likelihood there were no canals and decadent, dying, ancient races of intelligent beings on Mars—so that these stories, which still feature the lushly romantic pulp version of those planets that had been popularized in tales from *Planet Stories* and *Thrilling Wonder Stories* decades before, can be seen as an homage, a deliberate act of retro nostalgia for those beloved worlds, written in the last possible tick of time before the hardest of hard proof—the actual *visitation* of those planets by exploring space probes, only a few years later—would come along to make those garish, melodramatic, and gorgeously colored pulp visions of what Venus and Mars were like totally untenable. For a long time after this, it was considered to be no longer possible to write an adventure story or a Planetary Romance set on any of the planets of the solar system—which were now considered to be just sterile, lifeless balls of rock (especially after the first Viking lander mission in 1976 had found no trace of life in the soil of Mars), as unromantic and uninteresting and drab as a parking lot, settings that offered few opportunities for stories at all, let alone for John Carter-like swashbuckling—and indeed, few stories set on any planet of the solar system except for the Earth were written for the next decade. It wasn't until late in the '70s and the early '80s that new generations of writers would come along who began to find the solar system romantic and evocative *just as it was,* and began to write stories, even lush adventure stories, once again set on planets such as Venus and Mars. So even though Zelazny almost certainly intended "The Doors of His Face, the Lamps of His Mouth" to be a Farewell to Fantastic Venus (to paraphrase an Aldiss anthology title), he was being premature—within another decade or so, writers would be back exploring Venus again; thanks to the notion of terraforming, even the *seas* of Venus would be back in some stories—although the monstrous, mountain-like Inky remains, so far, unique to the vivid story that follows.

Zelazny won another Nebula and Hugo Award in 1976 for his novella "Home Is the Hangman," another Hugo in 1986 for his novella "24 Views of Mt. Fuji, by Hokusai," and a final Hugo in 1987 for his story "Permafrost." His other books include, in addition to the multi-volume *Amber* series, the novels *This Immortal, The Dream Master, Isle of the Dead, Jack of Shadows, Eye of Cat, Doorways in the Sand, Today We Choose Faces, Bridge of Ashes, To Die in Italbar,* and *Roadmarks,* and the collections *Four For Tomorrow, The Doors of His Face, the Lamps of His Mouth and Other Stories, The Last Defender of Camelot,* and *Frost and Fire.* Among his last books are two collaborative novels, *A Farce to Be Reckoned With,* with Robert Sheckley, and *Wilderness,* with Gerald Hausman, and, as editor, two anthologies, *Wheel of Fortune* and *Warriors of Blood and Dream.* Zelazny died—a tragically untimely death—in 1995.

A collaborative novel with Jane Lindskold, *Donnerjack,* was published recently, and another posthumous collaboration. Zelazny's completion of an unfinished Alfred Bester novel entitled *Psychoshop,* has just been published.

I'm a baitman. No one is born a baitman, except in a French novel where everyone is. (In fact, I think that's the title, *We Are All Bait,* Pfft!) How I got that way is barely worth telling and has nothing to do with neo-exes, but the days of the beast deserve a few words, so here they are.

The Lowlands of Venus lie between the thumb and forefinger of the continent known as Hand. When you break into Cloud Alley it swings its silverblack bowling ball toward you without a warning. You jump then, inside that firetailed tenpin they ride you down in, but the straps keep you from making a fool of yourself. You generally chuckle afterwards, but you always jump first.

Next, you study Hand to lay its illusion and the two middle fingers become dozen-ringed archipelagoes as the outers resolve into greengray peninsulas; the thumb is too short, and curls like the embryo tail of Cape Horn.

You suck pure oxygen, sigh possibly, and begin the long topple to the Lowlands.

There, you are caught like an infield fly at the Lifeline landing area—so named because of its nearness to the great delta in the Eastern Bay—located between the first peninsula and "thumb." For a minute it seems as if you're going to miss Lifeline and wind up as canned seafood, but afterwards—shaking off the metaphors—you descend to scorched concrete and present your middle-sized telephone directory of authorizations to the short, fat man in the gray cap. The papers show that you are not subject to mysterious inner rottings and etcetera. He then smiles you a short, fat, gray smile and motions you toward the bus which hauls you to the Reception Area. At the R.A. you spend three days proving that, indeed, you are not subject to mysterious inner rottings and etcetera.

Boredom, however, is another rot. When your three days are up, you generally hit Lifeline hard, and it returns the compliment as a matter of reflex. The effects of alcohol in variant atmospheres is a subject on which the connoisseurs have written numerous volumes, so I will confine my remarks to noting that a good binge is worthy of at least a week's time and often warrants a lifetime study.

I had been a student of exceptional promise (strictly undergraduate) for going on two years when the *Bright Water* fell through our marble ceiling and poured its people like targets into the city.

Pause. The Worlds Almanac re Lifeline: ". . . Port city on the eastern coast of Hand. Employees of the Agency for Non-terrestrial Research compromise approximately 85% of its 100,000 population (2010 Census). Its other residents are primarily personnel maintained by several industrial corporations engaged in basic research. Independent marine biologists, wealthy fishing enthusiasts, and waterfront entrepreneurs make up the remainder of its inhabitants."

I turned to Mike Dabis, a fellow entrepreneur, and commented on the lousy state of basic research.

"Not if the mumbled truth be known."

He paused behind his glass before continuing the slow swallowing process calculated to obtain my interest and a few oaths, before he continued.

"Carl," he finally observed, poker playing, "they're shaping Ten-square."

I could have hit him. I might have refilled his glass with sulfuric acid and looked on with glee as his lips blackened and cracked. Instead, I grunted a noncommittal.

"Who's fool enough to shell out fifty grand a day? ANR?"

He shook his head.

"Jean Luharich," he said, "the girl with the violet contacts and fifty or sixty perfect teeth. I understand her eyes are really brown."

"Isn't she selling enough face cream these days?"

He shrugged.

"Publicity makes the wheels go 'round. Luharich Enterprises jumped sixteen points when she picked up the Sun Trophy. You ever play golf on Mercury?"

I had, but I overlooked it and continued to press.

"So she's coming here with a blank check and a fishhook?"

"*Bright Water*, today," he nodded. "Should be down by now. Lots of cameras. She wants an Ikky, bad."

"Hmm," I hmmed. "How bad?"

"Sixty day contract, Tensquare. Indefinite extension clause. Million and a half deposit," he recited.

"You seem to know a lot about it."

"I'm Personal Recruitment. Luharich Enterprises approached me last month. It helps to drink in the right places.

"Or own them." He smirked, after a moment.

I looked away, sipping my bitter brew. After awhile I swallowed several things and asked Mike what he expected to be asked, leaving myself open for his monthly temperance lecture.

"They told me to try getting you," he mentioned. "When's the last time you sailed?"

"Month and a half ago. The *Corning*."

"Small stuff," he snorted. "When have you been under, yourself?"

"It's been awhile."

"It's been over a year, hasn't it? That time you got cut by the screw, under the *Dolphin?*"

I turned to him.

"I was in the river last week, up at Angleford where the currents are strong. I can still get around."

"Sober," he added.

"I'd stay that way," I said, "on a job like this."

A doubting nod.

"Straight union rates. Triple time for extraordinary circumstances," he narrated. "Be at Hangar Sixteen with your gear, Friday morning, five hundred hours. We push off Saturday, daybreak."

"You're sailing?"

"I'm sailing."

"How come?"

"Money."

"Ikky guano."

"The bar isn't doing so well and baby needs new minks."

"I repeat—"

". . . And I want to get away from baby, renew my contact with basics— fresh air, exercise, make cash. . . ."

"All right, sorry I asked."

I poured him a drink, concentrating on H_2SO_4, but it didn't transmute. Finally I got him soused and went out into the night to walk and think things over.

Around a dozen serious attempts to land *Ichthyform Leviosaurus Levianthus*, generally known as "Ikky," had been made over the past five years. When Ikky was first sighted, whaling techniques were employed. These proved either fruitless or disastrous, and a new procedure was inaugurated. Tensquare was constructed by a wealthy sportsman named Michael Jandt, who blew his entire roll on the project.

After a year on the Eastern Ocean, he returned to file bankruptcy. Carlton Davits, a playboy fishing enthusiast, then purchased the huge raft and laid a wake for Ikky's spawning grounds. On the nineteenth day out he had a strike and lost one hundred and fifty bills' worth of untested gear, along with one *Ichthyform Levianthus*. Twelve days later, using tripled lines, he hooked, narcotized, and began to hoist the huge beast. It awakened then, destroyed a control tower, killed six men, and worked general hell over five square blocks of Tensquare. Carlton was left with partial hemiplegia and a bankruptcy suit of his own. He faded into waterfront atmosphere and Tensquare changed hands four more times, with less spectacular but equally expensive results.

Finally, the big raft, built only for one purpose, was purchased at auction by ANR for "marine research." Lloyd's still won't insure it, and the only marine research it has ever seen is an occasional rental at fifty bills a day—to people anxious to tell Leviathan fish stories. I've been baitman on three of the voyages, and I've been close enough to count Ikky's fangs on two occasions. I want one of them to show my grandchildren, for personal reasons.

I faced the direction of the landing area and resolved a resolve.

"You want me for local coloring, gal. It'll look nice on the feature page and all that. But clear this—If anyone gets you an Ikky, it'll be me. I promise."

I stood in the empty Square. The foggy towers of Lifeline shared their mists.

Shoreline a couple eras ago, the western slope above Lifeline stretches as far as forty miles inland in some places. Its angle of rising is not a great one, but it achieves an elevation of several thousand feet before it meets the mountain range which separates us from the Highlands. About four miles inland and five hundred feet higher than Lifeline are set most of the surface airstrips and privately owned hangars. Hangar Sixteen houses Cal's Contract Cab, hop service, shore to ship. I do not like Cal, but he wasn't around when I climbed from the bus and waved to a mechanic.

Two of the hoppers tugged at the concrete, impatient beneath flywing haloes. The one on which Steve was working belched deep within its barrel carburetor and shuddered spasmodically.

"Bellyache?" I inquired.

"Yeah, gas pains and heartburn."

He twisted setscrews until it settled into an even keening, and turned to me.

"You're for out?"

I nodded.

"Tensquare. Cosmetics. Monsters. Stuff like that."

He blinked into the beacons and wiped his freckles. The temperature was about twenty, but the big overhead spots served a double purpose.

"Luharich," he muttered. "Then you *are* the one. There's some people want to see you."

"What about?"

"Cameras. Microphones. Stuff like that."

"I'd better stow my gear. Which one am I riding?"

He poked the screwdriver at the other hopper.

"That one. You're on video tape now, by the way. They wanted to get you arriving."

He turned to the hangar, turned back.

"Say 'cheese.' They'll shoot the close-ups later."

I said something other than "cheese." They must have been using tele-lens and been able to read my lips, because that part of the tape was never shown.

I threw my junk in the back, climbed into a passenger seat, and lit a cigarette. Five minutes later, Cal himself emerged from the office Quonset, looking cold. He came over and pounded on the side of the hopper. He jerked a thumb back at the hangar.

"They want you in there!" he called through cupped hands. "Interview!"

"The show's over!" I yelled back. "Either that, or they can get themselves another baitman!"

His rustbrown eyes became nailheads under blond brows and his glare a spike before he jerked about and stalked off. I wondered how much they had paid him to be able to squat in his hangar and suck juice from his generator.

Enough, I guess, knowing Cal. I never liked the guy, anyway.

Venus at night is a field of sable waters. On the coasts, you can never tell where the sea ends and the sky begins. Dawn is like dumping milk into an inkwell. First, there are erratic curdles of white, then streamers. Shade the bottle for a gray colloid, then watch it whiten a little more. All of a sudden you've got day. Then start heating the mixture.

I had to shed my jacket as we flashed out over the bay. To our rear, the skyline could have been under water for the way it waved and rippled in the heatfall. A hopper can accommodate four people (five, if you want to bend

Regs and underestimate weight), or three passengers with the sort of gear a baitman uses. I was the only fare, though, and the pilot was like his machine. He hummed and made no unnecessary noises. Lifeline turned a somersault and evaporated in the rear mirror at about the same time Tensquare broke the fore-horizon. The pilot stopped humming and shook his head.

I leaned forward. Feelings played flopdoodle in my guts. I knew every bloody inch of the big raft, but the feelings you once took for granted change when their source is out of reach. Truthfully, I'd had my doubts I'd ever board the hulk again. But now, now I could almost believe in predestination. There it was!

A tensquare football field of a ship. A-powered. Flat as a pancake, except for the plastic blisters in the middle and the "Rooks" fore and aft, port and starboard.

The Rook towers were named for their corner positions—and any two can work together to hoist, co-powering the graffles between them. The graffles—half gaff, half grapple—can raise enormous weights to near water level; their designer had only one thing in mind, though, which accounts for the gaff half. At water level, the Slider has to implement elevation for six to eight feet before the graffles are in a position to push upward, rather than pulling.

The Slider, essentially, is a mobile room—a big box capable of moving in any of Tensquare's crisscross groovings and "anchoring" on the strike side by means of a powerful electromagnetic bond. Its winches could hoist a battleship the necessary distance, and the whole craft would tilt, rather than the Slider come loose, if you want any idea of the strength of that bond.

The Slider houses a section operated control indicator which is the most sophisticated "reel" ever designed. Drawing broadcast power from the generator beside the center blister, it is connected by shortwave with the sonar room, where the movements of the quarry are recorded and repeated to the angler seated before the section control.

The fisherman might play his "lines" for hours, days even, without seeing any more than metal and an outline on the screen. Only when the beast is graffled and the extensor shelf, located twelve feet below waterline, slides out for support and begins to aid the winches, only then does the fisherman see his catch rising before him like a fallen Seraph. Then, as Davits learned, one looks into the Abyss itself and is required to act. He didn't, and a hundred meters of unimaginable tonnage, undernarcotized and hurting, broke the cables of the winch, snapped a graffle, and took a half-minute walk across Tensquare.

We circled till the mechanical flag took notice and waved us on down. We touched beside the personnel hatch and I jettisoned my gear and jumped to the deck.

"Luck," called the pilot as the door was sliding shut. Then he danced into the air and the flag clicked blank.

I shouldered my stuff and went below.

Signing in with Malvern, the de facto captain, I learned that most of the others wouldn't arrive for a good eight hours. They had wanted me alone at Cal's so they could pattern the pub footage along twentieth-century cinema lines.

Open: landing strip, dark. One mechanic prodding a contrary hopper. Stark-o-vision shot of slow bus pulling in. Heavily dressed baitman descends, looks about, limps across field. Close-up: he grins. Move in for words: "Do you think this is the time? The time he *will* be landed?" Embarrassment, taciturnity, a shrug. Dub something—"I see. And why do you think Miss Luharich has a better chance than any of the others? It is because she's better equipped? [Grin.] Because more is known now about the creature's habits than when you were out before? Or is it because of her will to win, to be a champion? Is it any one of these things, or is it all of them?" Reply: "Yeah, all of them." "—Is that why you signed on with her? Because your instincts say, 'This one will be it'?" Answer: "She pays union rates. I couldn't rent that damned thing myself. And I want in." Erase. Dub something else. Fadeout as he moves toward hopper, etcetera.

"Cheese," I said, or something like that, and took a walk around Tensquare, by myself.

I mounted each Rook, checking out the controls and the underwater video eyes. Then I raised the main lift.

Malvern had no objections to my testing things this way. In fact, he encouraged it. We had sailed together before and our positions had even been reversed upon a time. So I wasn't surprised when I stepped off the lift into the Hopkins Locker and found him waiting. For the next ten minutes we inspected the big room in silence, walking through its copper coil chambers soon to be Arctic.

Finally, he slapped a wall.

"Well, will we fill it?"

I shook my head.

"I'd like to, but I doubt it. I don't give two hoots and a damn who gets credit for the catch, so long as I have a part in it. But it won't happen. That gal's an egomaniac. She'll want to operate the Slider, and she can't."

"You ever meet her?"

"Yeah."

"How long ago?"

"Four, five years."

"She was a kid then. How do you know what she can do now?"

"I know. She'll have learned every switch and reading by this time. She'll be up on all theory. But do you remember one time we were together in the starboard Rook, forward, when Ikky broke water like a porpoise?"

"How could I forget?"

"Well?"

He rubbed his emery chin.

"Maybe she can do it, Carl. She's raced torch ships and she's scubaed in bad waters back home." He glanced in the direction of invisible Hand. "And she's hunted in the Highlands. She might be wild enough to pull that horror into her lap without flinching.

". . . For John Hopkins to foot the bill and shell out seven figures for the corpus," he added. "That's money, even to a Luharich."

I ducked through a hatchway.

"Maybe you're right, but she was a rich witch when I knew her."

"And she wasn't blonde," I added, meanly.

He yawned.

"Let's find breakfast."

We did that.

When I was young I thought that being born a sea creature was the finest choice Nature could make for anyone. I grew up on the Pacific coast and spent my summers on the Gulf or the Mediterranean. I lived months of my life negotiating coral, photographing trench dwellers, and playing tag with dolphins. I fished everywhere there are fish, resenting the fact that they can go places I can't. When I grew older I wanted bigger fish, and there was nothing living that I knew of, excepting a Sequoia, that came any bigger than Ikky. That's part of it. . . .

I jammed a couple of extra rolls into a paper bag and filled a thermos with coffee. Excusing myself, I left the galley and made my way to the Slider berth. It was just the way I remembered it. I threw a few switches and the shortwave hummed.

"That you, Carl?"

"That's right, Mike. Let me have some juice down here, you double-crossing rat."

He thought it over, then I felt the hull vibrate as the generators cut in. I poured my third cup of coffee and found a cigarette.

"So why am I a double-crossing rat this time?" came his voice again.

"You knew about the cameramen at Hangar Sixteen?"

"Yes."

"Then you're a double-crossing rat. The last thing I want is publicity. 'He who fouled up so often before is ready to try it, nobly once more.' I can read it now."

"You're wrong. The spotlight's only big enough for one, and she's prettier than you."

My next comment was cut off as I threw the elevator switch and the elephant ears flapped above me. I rose, settling flush with the deck. Retracting the lateral rail, I cut forward into the groove. Amidships, I stopped at a juncture, dropped the lateral, and retracted the longitudinal rail.

I slid starboard, midway between the Rooks, halted, and threw on the coupler.

I hadn't spilled a drop of coffee.

"Show me pictures."

The screen glowed. I adjusted and got outlines of the bottom.

"Okay."

I threw a Status Blue switch and he matched it. The light went on. The winch unlocked. I aimed out over the waters, extended the arm, and fired a cast.

"Clean one," he commented.

"Status Red. Call strike." I threw a switch.

"Status Red."

The baitman would be on his way with this, to make the barbs tempting.

It's not exactly a fishhook. The cables bear hollow tubes; the tubes convey enough dope for any army of hopheads; Ikky takes the bait, dangled before him by remote control, and the fisherman rams the barbs home.

My hands moved over the console, making the necessary adjustments. I checked the narco-tank reading. Empty. Good, they hadn't been filled yet. I thumbed the Inject button.

"In the gullet," Mike murmured.

I released the cables. I played the beast imagined. I let him run, swinging the winch to stimulate his sweep.

I had an air conditioner on and my shirt off and it was still uncomfortably hot, which is how I knew that morning had gone over into noon. I was dimly aware of the arrivals and departures of the hoppers. Some of the crew sat in the "shade" of the doors I had left open, watching the operation. I didn't see Jean arrive or I would have ended the session and gotten below.

She broke my concentration by slamming the door hard enough to shake the bond.

"Mind telling me who authorized you to bring up the Slider?" she asked.

"No one," I replied. I'll take it below now."

"Just move aside."

I did, and she took my seat. She was wearing brown slacks and a baggy shirt and she had her hair pulled back in a practical manner. Her cheeks were flushed, but not necessarily from the heat. She attacked the panel with a nearly amusing intensity that I found disquieting.

"Status Blue," she snapped, breaking a violet fingernail on the toggle.

I forced a yawn and buttoned my shirt slowly. She threw a side glance my way, checked the registers, and fired a cast.

I monitored the lead on the screen. She turned to me for a second.

"Status Red," she said levelly.

I nodded my agreement.

She worked the winch sideways to show she knew how. I didn't doubt she knew how and she didn't doubt that I didn't doubt, but then—

"In case you're wondering," she said, "you're not going to be anywhere near this thing. You were hired as a baitman, remember? Not a Slider operator! A baitman! Your duties consist of swimming out and setting the table for our friend the monster. It's dangerous, but you're getting well paid for it. Any questions?"

She squashed the Inject button and I rubbed my throat.

"Nope," I smiled, "but I am qualified to run that thingamajigger—and if you need me I'll be available, at union rates."

"Mister Davits," she said, "I don't want a loser operating this panel."

"Miss Luharich, there has never been a winner at this game."

She started reeling in the cable and broke the bond at the same time, so that the whole Slider shook as the big yo-yo returned. We skidded a couple of feet backward. She raised the laterals and we shot back along the groove. Slowing, she transferred rails and we jolted to a clanging halt, then shot off at a right angle. The crew scrambled away from the hatch as we skidded onto the elevator.

"In the future, Mister Davits, do not enter the Slider without being ordered," she told me.

"Don't worry. I won't even step inside if I am ordered," I answered. "I signed on as a baitman. Remember? If you want me in here, you'll have to *ask* me."

"That'll be the day," she smiled.

I agreed, as the doors closed above us. We dropped the subject and headed in our different directions after the Slider came to a halt in its berth. She did say "good day," though, which I thought showed breeding as well as determination, in reply to my chuckle.

Later that night Mike and I stoked our pipes in Malvern's cabin. The winds were shuffling waves, and a steady spattering of rain and hail overhead turned the deck into a tin roof.

"Nasty," suggested Malvern.

I nodded. After two bourbons the room had become a familiar woodcut, with its mahogany furnishings (which I had transported from Earth long ago on a whim) and the dark walls, the seasoned face of Malvern, and the perpetually puzzled expression of Dabis set between the big pools of shadow that lay behind chairs and splashed in cornets, all cast by the tiny table light and seen through a glass, brownly.

"Glad I'm in here."

"What's it like underneath on a night like this?"

I puffed, thinking of my light cutting through insides of a black diamond, shaken slightly. The meteor-dart of a suddenly illuminated fish, the swaying of grotesque ferns, like nebulae—shadow, then green, then gone—swam in a moment through my mind. I guess it's like a spaceship would feel, if a spaceship could feel, crossing between worlds—and quiet, uncannily, preternaturally quiet; and peaceful as sleep.

"Dark," I said, "and not real choppy below a few fathoms."

"Another eight hours and we shove off," commented Mike.

"Ten, twelve days, we should be there," noted Malvern.

"What do you think Ikky's doing?"

"Sleeping on the bottom with Mrs. Ikky if he has any brains."

"He hasn't. I've seen ANR's skeletal extrapolation from the bones that have washed up—"

"Hasn't everyone?"

". . . Fully fleshed, he'd be over a hundred meters long. That right, Carl?"

I agreed.

". . . Not much of a brain box, though, for his bulk."

"Smart enough to stay out of our locker."

Chuckles, because nothing exists but this room, really. The world outside is an empty, sleet drummed deck. We lean back and make clouds.

"Boss lady does not approve of unauthorized fly fishing."

"Boss lady can walk north till her hat floats."

"What did she say in there?"

"She told me that my place, with fish manure, is on the bottom."

"You don't Slide?"

"I bait."

"We'll see."

"That's all I do. If she wants a Slideman she's going to have to ask nicely."

"You think she'll have to?"

"I think she'll have to."

"And if she does, can you do it?"

"A fair question," I puffed. "I don't know the answer, though."

I'd incorporate my soul and trade forty percent of the stock for the answer. I'd give a couple years off my life for the answer. But there doesn't seem to be a lineup of supernatural takers, because no one knows. Supposing when we get out there, luck being with us, we find ourselves an Ikky?

Supposing we succeed in baiting him and get lines on him. What then? If we get him shipside, will she hold on or crack up? What if she's made of sterner stuff than Davits, who used to hunt sharks with poison-darted air pistols? Supposing she lands him and Davits has to stand there like a video extra.

Worse yet, supposing she asks for Davits and he still stands there like a video extra or something else—say, some yellowbellied embodiment named Cringe?

It was when I got him up above the eight-foot horizon of steel and looked out at all that body, sloping on and on till it dropped out of sight like a green mountain range . . . And that head. Small for the body, but still immense. Fat, craggy, with lidless roulettes that had spun black and red since before my forefathers decided to try the New Continent. And swaying.

Fresh narco-tanks had been connected. It needed another shot, fast. But I was paralyzed.

It had made a noise like God playing a Hammond organ. . . .

And looked at me!

I don't know if seeing is even the same process in eyes like those. I doubt it. Maybe I was just a gray blur behind a black rock, with the plexi-reflected sky hurting its pupils. But it fixed on me. Perhaps the snake doesn't really paralyze the rabbit, perhaps it's just that rabbits are cowards by constitution. But it began to struggle and I still couldn't move, fascinated.

Fascinated by all that power, by those eyes, they found me there fifteen minutes later, a little broken about the head and shoulders, the Inject still unpushed.

And I dream about those eyes. I want to face them once more, even if their finding takes forever. I've got to know if there's something inside me that sets me apart from a rabbit, from notched plates of reflexes and instincts that always fall apart in exactly the same way whenever the proper combination is spun.

Looking down, I noticed that my hand was shaking. Glancing up, I noticed that no one else was noticing.

I finished my drink and emptied my pipe. It was late and no songbirds were singing.

I sat whittling, my legs hanging over the aft edge, the chips spinning down into the furrow of our wake. Three days out. No action.

"You!"

"Me?"

"You."

Hair like the end of the rainbow, eyes like nothing in nature, fine teeth.

"Hello."

"There's a safety rule against what you're doing, you know."

"I know. I've been worrying about it all morning."

A delicate curl climbed my knife then drifted out behind us. It settled into the foam and was plowed under. I watched her reflection in my blade, taking a secret pleasure in its distortion.

"Are you baiting me?" she finally asked.

I heard her laugh then, and turned, knowing it had been intentional.

"What, me?"

"I could push you off from here, very easily."

"I'd make it back."

"Would you push me off, then—some dark night, perhaps?"

"They're all dark, Miss Luharich. No, I'd rather make you a gift of my carving."

She seated herself beside me then, and I couldn't help but notice the dimples in her knees. She wore white shorts and a halter and still had an off-world tan to her which was awfully appealing. I almost felt a twinge of guilt at having planned the whole scene, but my right hand still blocked her view of the wooden animal.

"Okay, I'll bite. What have you got for me?"

"Just a second. It's almost finished."

Solemnly, I passed her the wooden jackass I had been carving. I felt a little sorry and slightly jackass-ish myself, but I had to follow through. I always do. The mouth was split into a braying grin. The ears were upright.

She didn't smile and she didn't frown. She just studied it.

"It's very good," she finally said, "like most things you do—and appropriate, perhaps."

"Give it to me." I extended a palm.

She handed it back and I tossed it out over the water. It missed the white water and bobbed for awhile like a pigmy seahorse.

"Why did you do that?"

"It was a poor joke. I'm sorry."

"Maybe you are right, though. Perhaps this time I've bitten off a little too much."

I snorted.

"Then why not do something safer, like another race?"

She shook her end of the rainbow.

"No. It has to be an Ikky."

"Why?"

"Why did you want one so badly that you threw away a fortune?"

"Many reasons," I said. "An unfrocked analyst who held black therapy sessions in his basement once told me, 'Mister Davits, you need to reinforce the image of your masculinity by catching one of every kind of fish in existence.' Fish are a very ancient masculinity symbol, you know. So I set out to do it. I have one more to go. Why do you want to reinforce *your* masculinity?"

"I don't," she said. "I don't want to reinforce anything but Luharich Enterprises. My chief statistician once said, 'Miss Luharich, sell all the cold cream and face powder in the System and you'll be a happy girl. Rich, too.' And he was right. I am the proof. I can look the way I do and do anything, and I sell most of the lipstick and face powder in the System—but I have to be *able* to do anything."

"You do look cool and efficient," I observed.

"I don't feel cool," she said, rising. "Let's go for a swim."

"May I point out that we are making pretty good time?"

"If you want to indicate the obvious, you may. You said you could make it back to the ship, unassisted. Change your mind?"

"No."

"Then get us two scuba outfits and I'll race you under Tensquare."

"I'll win, too," she added.

I stood and looked down at her, because that usually makes me feel superior to women.

"Daughter of Lir, eyes of Picasso," I said, "you've got yourself a race. Meet me at the forward Rook, starboard, in ten minutes."

"Ten minutes," she agreed.

And ten minutes it was. From the center blister to the Rook took maybe two of them, with the load I was carrying. My sandals grew very hot and I was glad to shuck them for flippers when I reached the comparative cool of the corner.

We slid into harnesses and adjusted our gear. She had changed into a trim one-piece green job that made me shade my eyes and look away, then look back again.

I fastened a rope ladder and kicked it over the side. Then I pounded on the wall of the Rook.

"Yeah?"

"You talk to the port Rook, aft?" I called.

"They're all set up," came the answer. "There's ladders and drag-lines all over that end."

"You sure you want to do this?" asked the sunburnt little gink who was her publicity man, Anderson yclept.

He sat beside the Rook in a deckchair, sipping lemonade through a straw.

"It might be dangerous," he observed, sunken-mouthed. (His teeth were beside him, in another glass.)

"That's right," she smiled. "It *will* be dangerous. Not overly, though."

"Then why don't you let me get some pictures? We'd have them back to Lifeline in an hour. They'd be in New York by tonight. Good copy."

"No," she said, and turned away from both of us.

She raised her hands to her eyes.

"Here, keep these for me."

She passed him a box full of her unseeing, and when she turned back to me they were the same brown that I remembered.

"Ready?"

"No," I said, tautly. "Listen carefully, Jean. If you're going to play this game there are a few rules. First," I counted, "we're going to be directly beneath the hull, so we have to start low and keep moving. If we bump the bottom, we could rupture an air tank. . . ."

She began to protest that any moron knew that and I cut her down.

"Second," I went on, "there won't be much light, so we'll stay close together, and we will *both* carry torches."

Her wet eyes flashed.

"I dragged you out of Govino without—"

Then she stopped and turned away. She picked up a lamp.

"Okay. Torches. Sorry."

". . . And watch out for the drive-screws," I finished. "There'll be strong currents for at least fifty meters behind them."

She wiped her eyes again and adjusted the mask.

"All right, let's go."

We went.

She led the way, at my insistence. The surface layer was pleasantly warm. At two fathoms the water was bracing; at five it was nice and cold. At eight we let go the swinging stairway and struck out. Tensquare sped forward and we raced in the opposite direction, tattooing the hull yellow at ten-second intervals.

The hull stayed where it belonged, but we raced on like two darkside satellites. Periodically, I tickled her frog feet with my light and traced her antennae of bubbles. About a five meter lead was fine; I'd beat her in the home stretch, but I couldn't let her drop behind yet.

Beneath us, black. Immense. Deep. The Mindanao of Venus, where eternity might eventually pass the dead to a rest in cities of unnamed fishes. I twisted my head away and touched the hull with a feeler of light; it told me we were about a quarter of the way along.

I increased my beat to match her stepped-up stroke, and narrowed the distance which she had suddenly opened by a couple meters. She sped up again and I did, too. I spotted her with my beam.

She turned and it caught on her mask. I never knew whether she'd been smiling. Probably. She raised two fingers in a V-for-Victory and then cut ahead at full speed.

I should have known. I should have felt it coming. It was just a race to her, something else to win. Damn the torpedoes!

So I leaned into it, hard. I don't shake in the water. Or, if I do it doesn't matter and I don't notice it. I began to close the gap again.

She looked back, sped on, looked back. Each time she looked it was nearer, until I'd narrowed it down to the original five meters.

Then she hit the jatoes.

That's what I had been fearing. We were about half-way under and she shouldn't have done it. The powerful jets of compressed air could easily rocket her upward into the hull, or tear something loose if she allowed her body to twist. Their main use is in tearing free from marine plants or fighting bad currents. I had wanted them along as a safety measure, because of the big suck-and-pull windmills behind.

She shot ahead like a meteorite, and I could feel a sudden tingle of perspiration leaping to meet and mix with the churning waters.

I swept ahead, not wanting to use my own guns, and she tripled, quadrupled the margin.

The jets died and she was still on course. Okay, I was an old fuddyduddy. She *could* have messed up and headed toward the top.

I plowed the sea and began to gather back my yardage, a foot at a time. I wouldn't be able to catch her or beat her now, but I'd be on the ropes before she hit deck.

Then the spinning magnets began their insistence and she wavered. It was an awfully powerful drag, even at this distance. The call of the meat grinder.

I'd been scratched up by one once, under the *Dolphin*, a fishing boat of the middle-class. I *had* been drinking, but it was also a rough day, and the thing had been turned on prematurely. Fortunately, it was turned off in time, also, and a tendon-stapler made everything good as new, except in the log, where it only mentioned that I'd been drinking. Nothing about it being off-hours when I had a right to do as I damn well pleased.

She had slowed to half her speed, but she was still moving crosswise, toward the port, aft corner. I began to feel the pull myself and had to slow down. She'd made it past the main one, but she seemed too far back. It's hard to gauge distances under water, but each red beat of time told me I was right. She was out of danger from the main one, but the smaller port screw, located about eighty meters in, was no longer a threat but a certainty.

She had turned and was pulling away from it now. Twenty meters separated us. She was standing still. Fifteen.

Slowly, she began a backward drifting. I hit my jatoes, aiming two meters behind her and about twenty back of the blades.

Straightline! Thankgod! Catching, softbelly, leadpipe on shoulder SWIMLIKEHELL! maskcracked, not broke though AND UP!

We caught a line and I remember brandy.

Into the cradle endlessly rocking I spit, pacing. Insomnia tonight and left shoulder sore again, so let it rain on me—they can cure rheumatism. Stupid as hell. What I said. In blankets and shivering. She: "Carl, I can't say it." Me: "Then call it square for that night in Govino, Miss Luharich. Huh?" She: nothing. Me: "Any more of that brandy?" She: "Give me another, too." Me: sounds of sipping. It had only lasted three months. No alimony. Many $ on both sides. Not sure whether they were happy or not. Wine-dark Aegean. Good fishing. Maybe he should have spent more time on shore. Or perhaps she shouldn't have. Good swimmer, though. Dragged him all the way to Vido to wring out his lungs. Young. Both. Strong. Both. Rich and spoiled as hell. Ditto. Corfu should have brought them closer. Didn't. I think that mental cruelty was a trout. He wanted to go to Canada. She: "Go to hell if you want!" He: "Will you go along?" She: "No." But she did, anyhow. Many hells. Expensive. He lost a monster or two. She inherited a couple. Lot of lightning tonight. Stupid as hell. Civility's the coffin of a conned soul. By whom?—Sounds like a bloody neo-ex. . . . But I hate you, Anderson, with your glass full of teeth and her new eyes. . . . Can't keep this pipe lit, keep sucking tobacco. Spit again!

Seven days out and the scope showed Ikky.

Bells jangled, feet pounded, and some optimist set the thermostat in the Hopkins. Malvern wanted me to sit out, but I slipped into my harness and waited for whatever came. The bruise looked worse than it felt. I had exercised every day and the shoulder hadn't stiffened on me.

A thousand meters ahead and thirty fathoms deep, it tunneled our path. Nothing showed on the surface.

"Will we chase him?" asked an excited crewman.

"Not unless she feels like using money for fuel." I shrugged.

Soon the scope was clear, and it stayed that way. We remained on alert and held our course.

I hadn't said over a dozen words to my boss since the last time we went drowning together, so I decided to raise the score.

"Good afternoon," I approached. "What's new?"

"He's going north-northeast. We'll have to let this one go. A few more days and we can afford some chasing. Not yet."

Sleek head . . .

I nodded. "No telling where this one's headed."

"How's your shoulder?"

"All right. How about you?"

Daughter of Lir . . .

"Fine. By the way, you're down for a nice bonus."

Eyes of perdition!

"Don't mention it," I told her back.

Later that afternoon, and appropriately, a storm shattered. (I prefer "shattered" to "broke." It gives a more accurate idea of the behavior of tropical storms on Venus and saves lots of words.) Remember that inkwell I mentioned earlier? Now take it between thumb and forefinger and hit its side with a hammer. Watch your self! Don't get splashed or cut—

Dry, then drenched. The sky one million bright fractures as the hammer falls. And sounds of breaking.

"Everyone below?" suggested loudspeakers to the already scurrying crew. Where was I? Who do you think was doing the loudspeaking?

Everything loose went overboard when the water got to walking, but by then no people were loose. The Slider was the first thing below decks. Then the big lifts lowered their shacks.

I had hit it for the nearest Rook with a yell the moment I recognized the pre-brightening of the holocaust. From there I cut in the speakers and spent half a minute coaching the track team.

Minor injuries had occurred, Mike told me over the radio, but nothing serious. I, however, was marooned for the duration. The Rooks do not lead anywhere; they're set too far out over the hull to provide entry downwards, what with the extensor shelves below.

So I undressed myself of the tanks which I had worn for the past several hours, crossed my flippers on the table, and leaned back to watch the hurricane. The top was black as the bottom and we were in between, and somewhat illuminated because of all that flat, shiny space. The waters above didn't rain down—they just sort of got together and dropped.

The Rooks were secure enough—they'd weathered any number of these onslaughts—it's just that their positions gave them a greater arc of rise and descent when Tensquare makes like the rocker of a very nervous grandma. I had used the belts from my rig to strap myself into the bolted-down chair, and I removed several years in purgatory from the soul of whoever left a pack of cigarettes in the table drawer.

I watched the water make teepees and mountains and hands and trees until I started seeing faces and people. So I called Mike.

"What are you doing down there?"

"Wondering what you're doing up there," he replied. "What's it like?"

"You're from the Midwest, aren't you?"

"Yeah."

"Get bad storms out there?"

"Sometimes."

"Try to think of the worst one you were ever in. Got a slide rule handy?"

"Right here."

"Then put a one under it, imagine a zero or two following after, and multiply the thing out."

"I can't imagine the zeros."

"Then retain the multiplicand—that's all you can do."

"So what are you doing up there?"

"I've strapped myself in the chair. I'm watching things roll around the floor right now."

I looked up and out again. I saw one darker shadow in the forest.

"Are you praying or swearing?"

"Damned if I know. But if this were the Slider—if only this were the Slider!"

"He's out there?"

I nodded, forgetting that he couldn't see me.

Big, as I remembered him. He'd only broken surface for a few moments, to look around. *There is no power on Earth that can be compared with him who was made to fear no one.* I dropped my cigarette. It was the same as before. Paralysis and an unborn scream.

"You all right, Carl?"

He had looked at me again. Or seemed to. Perhaps that mindless brute had been waiting half a millenium to ruin the life of a member of the most highly developed species in business. . . .

"You okay?"

. . . Or perhaps it had been ruined already, long before their encounter, and theirs was just a meeting of beasts, the stronger bumping the weaker aside, body to psyche. . . .

"Carl, dammit! Say something!"

He broke again, this time nearer. Did you ever see the trunk of a tornado? It seems like something alive, moving around in all that dark. Nothing has a right to be so big, so strong, and moving. It's a sickening sensation.

"Please answer me."

He was gone and did not come back that day. I finally made a couple of wisecracks at Mike, but I held my next cigarette in my right hand.

The next seventy or eighty thousand waves broke by with a monotonous similarity. The five days that held them were also without distinction. The morning of the thirteenth day out, though, our luck began to rise. The bells broke our coffee-drenched lethargy into small pieces, and we dashed from the galley without hearing what might have been Mike's finest punchline.

"Aft!" cried someone. "Five hundred meters!"

I stripped to my trunks and started buckling. My stuff is always within grabbing distance.

I flipflopped across the deck, girding myself with a deflated squiggler.

"Five hundred meters, twenty fathoms!" boomed the speakers.

The big traps banged upward and the Slider grew to its full height, m'lady at the console. It rattled past me and took root ahead. Its one arm rose and lengthened.

I breasted the Slider as the speakers called, "Four-eighty, twenty!"

"Status Red!"

A belch like an emerging champagne cork and the line arced high over the waters.

"Four-eighty, twenty!" it repeated, all Malvern and static. "Baitman, attend!"

I adjusted my mask and hand-over-handed it down the side. Then warm, then cool, then away.

Green, vast, down. Fast. This is the place where I am equal to a squiggler. If something big decides a baitman looks tastier than what he's carrying, then irony colors his title as well as the water about it.

I caught sight of the drifting cables and followed them down. Green to dark green to black. It had been a long cast, too long. I'd never had to follow one this far down before. I didn't want to switch on my torch.

But I had to.

Bad! I still had a long way to go. I clenched my teeth and stuffed my imagination into a straightjacket.

Finally the line came to an end.

I wrapped one arm about it and unfastened the squiggler. I attached it, working as fast as I could, and plugged in the little insulated connections which are the reason it can't be fired with the line. Ikky could break them, but by then it wouldn't matter.

My mechanical eel hooked up, I pulled its section plugs and watched it grow. I had been dragged deeper during this operation, which took about a minute and a half. I was near—too near—to where I never wanted to be.

Loathe as I had been to turn on my light, I was suddenly afraid to turn it off. Panic gripped me and I seized the cable with both hands. The squiggler began to glow, pinkly. It started to twist. It was twice as big as I am and doubtless twice as attractive to pink squiggler-eaters. I told myself this until I believed it, then I switched off my light and started up.

If I bumped into something enormous and steel-hided my heart had orders to stop beating immediately and release me—to dart fitfully forever along Acheron, and gibbering.

Ungibbering, I made it to green water and fled back to the nest.

As soon as they hauled me aboard I made my mask a necklace, shaded my eyes, and monitored for surface turbulence. My first question, of course, was: "Where is he?"

"Nowhere," said a crewman; "we lost him right after you went over. Can't pick him up on the scope now. Musta dived."

"Too bad."

The squiggler stayed down, enjoying its bath. My job ended for the time being, I headed back to warm my coffee with rum.

From behind me, a whisper: "Could you laugh like that afterwards?"

Perceptive Answer: "Depends on what he's laughing at."

Still chuckling, I made my way into the center blister with two cupfuls.

"Still hell and gone?"

Mike nodded. His big hands were shaking, and mine were steady as a surgeon's when I set down the cups.

He jumped as I shrugged off the tanks and looked for a bench.

"Don't drip on that panel! You want to kill yourself and blow expensive fuses?"

I toweled down, then settled down to watching the unfilled eye on the wall. I yawned happily; my shoulder seemed good as new.

The little box that people talk through wanted to say something, so Mike lifted the switch and told it to go ahead.

"Is Carl there, Mister Dabis?"

"Yes, ma'am."

"Then let me talk to him."

Mike motioned and I moved.

"Talk," I said.

"Are you all right?"

"Yes, thanks. Shouldn't I be?"

"That was a long swim. I—I guess I overshot my cast."

"I'm happy," I said. "More triple-time for me. I really clean up on that hazardous duty clause."

"I'll be more careful next time," she apologized. "I guess I was too eager. Sorry—" Something happened to the sentence, so she ended it there, leaving me with half a bagful of replies I'd been saving.

I lifted the cigarette from behind Mike's ear and got a light from the one in the ashtray.

"Carl, she was being nice," he said, after turning to study the panels.

"I know," I told him. "I wasn't."

"I mean, she's an awfully pretty kid, pleasant. Head-strong and all that. But what's she done to you?"

"Lately?" I asked.

He looked at me, then dropped his eyes to his cup.

"I know it's none of my bus—" he began.

"Cream and sugar?"

Ikky didn't return that day, or that night. We picked up some Dixieland out of Lifeline and let the muskrat ramble while Jean had her supper sent to the Slider. Later she had a bunk assembled inside. I piped in "Deep Water Blues" when it came over the air and waited for her to call up and cuss us out. She didn't, though, so I decided she was sleeping.

Then I got Mike interested in a game of chess that went on until daylight. It limited conversation to several "checks," one "checkmate," and a "damn!" Since he's a poor loser it also effectively sabotaged subsequent talk, which was fine with me. I had a steak and fried potatoes for breakfast and went to bed.

Ten hours later someone shook me awake and I propped myself on one elbow, refusing to open my eyes.

"Whassamadder?"

"I'm sorry to get you up," said one of the younger crewmen, "but Miss Luharich wants you to disconnect the squiggler so we can move on."

I knuckled open one eye, still deciding whether I should be amused.

"Have it hauled to the side. Anyone can disconnect it."

"It's at the side now, sir. But she said it's in your contract and we'd better do things right."

"That's very considerate of her. I'm sure my Local appreciates her re-membering."

"Uh, she also said to tell you to change your trunks and comb your hair, and shave, too. Mister Anderson's going to film it."

"Okay. Run along; tell her I'm on my way—and ask if she has some toe-nail polish I can borrow."

I'll save on details. It took three minutes in all, and I played it properly, even pardoning myself when I slipped and bumped into Anderson's white tropicals with the wet squiggler. He smiled, brushed it off; she smiled, even though Luharich Complectacolor couldn't completely mask the dark circles under her eyes; and I smiled, waving to all our fans out there in videoland. —Remember, Mrs. Universe, you, too, can look like a monster-catcher. Just use Luharich face cream.

I went below and made myself a tuna sandwich, with mayonnaise.

• • •

Two days like icebergs—bleak, blank, half-melting, all frigid, mainly out of sight, and definitely a threat to peace of mind—drifted by and were good to put behind. I experienced some old guilt feelings and had a few disturbing dreams. Then I called Lifeline and checked my bank balance.

"Going shopping?" asked Mike, who had put the call through for me.

"Going home," I answered.

"Huh?"

"I'm out of the baiting business after this one, Mike. The Devil with Ikky! The Devil with Venus and Luharich Enterprises! And the Devil with you!"

Up eyebrows.

"What brought that on?"

"I waited over a year for this job. Now that I'm here, I've decided the whole thing stinks."

"You knew what it was when you signed on. No matter what else you're doing, you're selling face cream when you work for face cream sellers."

"Oh, that's not what's biting me. I admit the commercial angle irritates me, but Tensquare has always been a publicity spot, ever since the first time it sailed."

"What, then?"

"Five or six things, all added up. The main one being that I don't care any more. Once it meant more to me than anything else to hook that critter, and now it doesn't. I went broke on what started out as a lark and I wanted blood for what it cost me. Now I realize that maybe I had it coming. I'm beginning to feel sorry for Ikky."

"And you don't want him now?"

"I'll take him if he comes peacefully, but I don't feel like sticking out my neck to make him crawl into the Hopkins."

"I'm inclined to think it's one of the four or five other things you said you added."

"Such as?"

He scrutinized the ceiling.

I growled.

"Okay, but I won't say it, not just to make you happy you guessed right."

He, smirking: "That look she wears isn't just for Ikky."

"No good, no good." I shook my head. "We're both fission chambers by nature. You can't have jets on both ends of the rocket and expect to go anywhere—what's in the middle just gets smashed."

"That's how it *was*. None of my business, of course—"

"Say that again and you'll say it without teeth."

"Any day, big man"—he looked up—"any place . . ."

"So go ahead. Get it said!"

"She doesn't care about that bloody reptile, she came here to drag you back where you belong. You're not the baitman this trip."

"Five years is too long."

"There must be something under that cruddy hide of yours that people like," he muttered, "or I wouldn't be talking like this. Maybe you remind us humans of some really ugly dog we felt sorry for when we were kids. Anyhow, someone wants to take you home and raise you—also, something about beggars not getting menus."

"Buddy," I chuckled, "do you know what I'm going to do when I hit Lifeline?"

"I can guess."

"You're wrong. I'm torching it to Mars, and then I'll cruise back home, first class. Venus bankruptcy provisions do not apply to Martian trust funds, and I've still got a wad tucked away where moth and corruption enter not. I'm going to pick up a big old mansion on the Gulf and if you're ever looking for a job you can stop around and open bottles for me."

"You are a yellowbellied fink," he commented.

"Okay," I admitted, "but it's her I'm thinking of, too."

"I've heard the stories about you both," he said. "So you're a heel and a goofoff and she's a bitch. That's called compatibility these days. I dare you, baitman, try keeping something you catch."

I turned.

"If you ever want that job, look me up."

I closed the door quietly behind me and left him sitting there waiting for it to slam.

The day of the beast dawned like any other. Two days after my gutless flight from empty waters I went down to rebait. Nothing on the scope. I was just making things ready for the routine attempt.

I hollered a "good morning" from outside the Slider and received an answer from inside before I pushed off. I had reappraised Mike's words, sans sound, sans fury, and while I did not approve of their sentiment or significance, I had opted for civility anyhow.

So down, under, and away. I followed a decent cast about two hundred-ninety meters out. The snaking cables burned black to my left and I paced their undulations from the yellowgreen down into the darkness. Soundless lay the wet night, and I bent my way through it like a cock-eyed comet, bright tail before.

I caught the line, slick and smooth, and began baiting. An icy world swept by me then, ankles to head. It was a draft, as if some one had opened a big door beneath me. I wasn't drifting downwards that fast either.

Which meant that something might be moving up, something big enough to displace a lot of water. I still didn't think it was Ikky. A freak current of some sort, but not Ikky. Ha!

I had finished attaching the leads and pulled the first plug when a big, rugged, black island grew beneath me. . . .

I flicked the beam downward. His mouth was opened.

I was rabbit.

Waves of the death-fear passed downward. My stomach imploded. I grew dizzy.

Only one thing, and one thing only. Left to do. I managed it, finally. I pulled the rest of the plugs.

I could count the scaly articulations ridging his eyes by then.

The squiggler grew, pinked into phosphorescence . . . squiggled!

Then my lamp. I had to kill it, leaving just the bait before him.

One glance back as I jammed the jatoes to life.

He was so near that the squiggler reflected on his teeth, in his eyes. Four meters, and I kissed his lambent jowls with two jets of backwash as I soared. Then I didn't know whether he was following or halted. I began to black out as I waited to be eaten.

The jatoes died and I kicked weakly.

Too fast, I felt a cramp coming on. One flick of the beam, cried rabbit. One second, to know . . .

Or end things up, I answered. No, rabbit, we don't dart before hunters. Stay dark.

Green waters finally, to yellowgreen, then top.

Doubling, I beat off toward Tensquare. The waves from the explosion behind pushed me on ahead. The world closed in, and a screamed, "He's alive!" in the distance.

A giant shadow and a shock wave. The line was alive, too. Happy Fishing Grounds. Maybe I did something wrong. . . .

Somewhere Hand was clenched. What's bait?

A few million years. I remember starting out as a one-celled organism and painfully becoming an amphibian, then an air-breather. From somewhere high in the treetops I heard a voice.

"He's coming around."

I evolved back into homosapience, then a step further into a hangover.

"Don't try to get up yet."

"Have we got him?" I slurred.

"Still fighting, but he's hooked. We thought he took you for an appetizer."

"So did I."

"Breathe some of this and shut up."

A funnel over my face. Good. Lift your cups and drink. . . .

"He was awfully deep. Below scope range. We didn't catch him till he started up. Too late, then."

I began to yawn.

"We'll get you inside now."

I managed to uncase my ankle knife.

"Try it and you'll be minus a thumb."

"You need rest."

"Then bring me a couple more blankets. I'm staying."

I fell back and closed my eyes.

Someone was shaking me. Gloom and cold. Spotlights bled yellow on the deck. I was in a jury-rigged bunk, bulked against the center blister. Swaddled in wool, I still shivered.

"It's been eleven hours. You're not going to see anything now."

I tasted blood.

"Drink this."

Water. I had a remark but I couldn't mouth it.

"Don't ask how I feel," I croaked. "I know that comes next, but don't ask me. Okay?"

"Okay. Want to go below now?"

"No. Just get me my jacket."

"Right here."

"What's he doing?"

"Nothing. He's deep, he's doped but he's staying down."

"How long since last time he showed?"

"Two hours, about."

"Jean?"

"She won't let anyone in the Slider. Listen, Mike says come on in. He's right behind you in the blister."

I sat up and turned. Mike was watching. He gestured; I gestured back.

I swung my feet over the edge and took a couple of deep breaths. Pains in my stomach. I got to my feet and made it into the blister.

"Howza gut?" queried Mike.

I checked the scope. No Ikky. Too deep.

"You buying?"

"Yeah, coffee."

"Not coffee."

"You're ill. Also, coffee is all that's allowed in here."

"Coffee is a brownish liquid that burns your stomach. You have some in the bottom drawer."

"No cups. You'll have to use a glass."

"Tough."

He poured.

"You do that well. Been practicing for that job?"

"What job?"

"The one I offered you—"

A bolt on the scope!

"Rising, ma'am! Rising!" he yelled into the box.

"Thanks, Mike. I've got it in here," she crackled.

"Jean!"

"Shut up! She's busy!"

"Was that Carl?"

"Yeah," I called. "Talk later," and I cut it.

Why did I do that?

"Why did you do that?"

I didn't know.

"I don't know."

Damned echoes! I got up and walked outside.

Nothing. Nothing.

Something?

Tensquare actually rocked! He must have turned when he saw the hull and started downward again. White water to my left, and boiling. An endless spaghetti of cable roared hotly into the belly of the deep.

I stood awhile, then turned and went back inside.

Two hours sick. Four, and better.

"The dope's getting to him."

"Yeah."

"What about Miss Luharich?"

"What about her?"

"She must be half dead."

"Probably."

"What are you going to do about it?"

"She signed the contract for this. She knew what might happen. It did."

"I think you could land him."

"So do I."

"So does she."

"Then let her ask me."

Ikky was drifting lethargically, at thirty fathoms.

I took another walk and happened to pass behind the Slider. She wasn't looking my way.

"Carl, come in here!"

Eyes of Picasso, that's what, and a conspiracy to make me Slide . . .

"It that an order?"

"Yes—No! Please."

I dashed inside and monitored. He was rising.

"Push or pull?"

I slammed the "wind" and he came like a kitten.

"Make up your own mind now."

He balked at ten fathoms.

"Play him?"

"No!"

She wound him upwards—five fathoms, four . . .

She hit the extensors at two, and they caught him. Then the graffles.

Cries without and a heat lightning of flashbulbs.

The crew saw Ikky.

He began to struggle. She kept the cables tight, raised the graffles . . .

Up.

Another two feet and the graffles began pushing.

Screams and fast footfalls.

Giant beanstalk in the wind, his neck, waving. The green hills of his shoulders grew.

"He's big, Carl!" she cried.

And he grew, and grew, and grew uneasy . . .

"*Now!*"

He looked down.

He looked down, as the god of our most ancient ancestors might have looked down. Fear, shame, and mocking laughter rang in my head. Her head, too?

"Now!"

She looked up at the nascent earthquake.

"I can't!"

It was going to be so damnably simple this time, now the rabbit had died. I reached out.

I stopped.

"Push it yourself."

"I can't. You do it. Land him, Carl!"

"No. If I do, you'll wonder for the rest of your life whether you could have. You'll throw away your soul finding out. I know you will, because we're alike, and I did it that way. Find out now!"

She stared.

I gripped her shoulders.

"Could be that's me out there," I offered. "I am a green sea serpent, a hateful, monstrous beast, and out to destroy you. I am answerable to no one. Push the Inject."

Her hand moved to the button, jerked back.

"Now!"

She pushed it.

I lowered her still form to the floor and finished things up with Ikky.

It was a good seven hours before I awakened to the steady, sea-chewing grind of Tensquare's blades.

"You're sick," commented Mike.

"How's Jean?"

"The same."

"Where's the best?"

"Here."

"Good." I rolled over. ". . . Didn't get away this time."

So that's the way it was. No one is born a baitman, I don't think, but the rings of Saturn sing epithalamium the sea-beast's dower.

James Tiptree, Jr.

MOTHER IN THE SKY WITH DIAMONDS

As most of you probably know by now, multiple Hugo- and Nebula- winning author James Tiptree, Jr.—at one time a figure reclusive and mysterious enough to be regarded as the B. Traven of science fiction—was actually the pseudonym of the late Dr. Alice Bradley Sheldon, a semi-retired experimental psychologist who also wrote occasionally under the name of Raccoona Sheldon. Dr. Sheldon's tragic death in 1987 put an end to "both" authors' careers, but, before that, she had won two Nebula and two Hugo Awards as Tiptree, won another Nebula Award as Raccoona Sheldon, and established herself, under whatever name, as one of the best writers in SF.

Although "Tiptree" published two reasonably well-received novels—*Up the Walls of the World* and *Brightness Falls From the Air*—she was, like Damon Knight and Theodore Sturgeon (two writers she aesthetically resembled, and by whom she was strongly influenced) more comfortable with the short story, and more effective with it. She wrote some of the very best short stories of the '70s: "The Screwfly Solution," "The Girl Who Was Plugged In," "The Women Men Don't See," "Beam Us Home," "And I Awoke and Found Me Here on the Cold Hill's Side," "I'm Too Big But I Love to Play," "The Man Who Walked Home," "Slow Music," "Her Smoke Rose Up Forever." Already it's clear that these are stories that will last. They—and a dozen others almost as good—show that Alice Sheldon was simply one of the best short-story writers to work in the genre in our times. In fact, with her desire for a high bit-rate, her concern for societal goals, her passion for the novel and the unexpected, her taste for extrapolation, her experimenter's interest in the reactions of people to supernormal stimuli and bizarre situations, her fondness for the apocalyptic, her love of color and sweep and dramatic action, and her preoccupation with the mutability of time and the vastness of space, Alice Sheldon was a natural SF writer. I doubt that she would have been able to realize her particular talents as fully in any other genre, and she didn't even seem particularly interested in trying. At a time when many other SF writers would be just as happy—or happier—writing "mainstream" fiction, and chaffed at the artistic and financial restrictions of the genre, what *she* wanted to be was a *science fiction writer;* that was *her* dream, and her passion.

Sheldon clearly loved space adventure and Space Opera, even of the most basic, junk-food, lowest-common-denominator sort—the kind of stuff you consume with guilty pleasure although you know it is Bad for you, and is probably clogging your arteries—and worked variations on slambang space adventure motifs into many of her stories and both of her novels, although often they were played in a discordant, somber—sometimes unrelievedly bleak—minor key, with lots of curious fluting and eccentric fingerings. (In the '80s, toward the end of her life, she would make a deliberately "retro" attempt to write Nostalgic Space Opera with tales like "The Only Neat Thing To Do" and "Collision," later collected in *The Starry Rift*. Although they contain much excellent material, the tone of these stories is perhaps too self-conscious to match the power of her earlier, less mannered, more naive and genuine—if sometimes considerably rawer and clumsier—explorations of the form.) Tiptree's considerable impact on future generations of science fiction writers was especially pronounced on the cyberpunks—with stories like "The Girl Who Was Plugged In" directly ancestral to that form—but I think that she had a good deal of impact on the future evolution of the space adventure tale as well. For instance, although it's not one of her better-known stories, rarely if ever remarked on by critics, I think that I can see the footprints of "Mother in the Sky with Diamonds" on a lot of subsequent work, from John Varley's stuff a few years later, to Bruce Sterling's early Shaper/Mechanist stories such as "Swarm," and on to the Modern Baroque Space Opera of the '90s.

It's an inelegant story in some ways, so jammed with new ideas and packed with plot that it's almost claustrophobic, a sweaty, dense, exhausting read, brutally and ruthlessly paced, with no changes of mood or breathing spaces, that might have worked better as a novella (John W. Campbell reportedly referred to this story as a "condensed novel" in his rejection letter—and he was probably right about that, anyway). But look at the *thinking* that's going on in the background, as Sheldon reinvents the familiar Asteroid Belt civilization of past science fiction from top to bottom, replacing it with a bizarre and fascinating society of her own, featuring remote-controlled cyborg slaves, biologically-altered people adapted for living in space, spaceships made of monomolecular bubbles of "quasi-living cytoplasm," degenerate drug-runners, and, most importantly, an entire psychological set radically different both from our own and from that of the Asteroid Belt-dwellers of earlier science fiction stories. You're going to see these tropes show up again and again in the science fiction of the '80s and '90s, as will, increasingly, the idea that the people who live in the future will be *different* from you and me, with different perspectives, goals, and ethics, shaped by technology and the social changes driven by that technology, and by new environments. In a brutally compressed context of less than 10,000 words, this little story contains within it many of the seeds that will blossom and cross-fertilize and mutate into a rich crop of Story in the years to come . . .

As James Tiptree, Jr., Alice Sheldon also published nine short-story collections: *Ten-Thousand Light Years from Home, Warm Worlds and Otherwise, Star Songs of an Old Primate, Out of the Everywhere, Tales of the Quintana Roo, Byte*

Beautiful, The Starry Rift, the posthumously published *Crown of Stars,* and the recent retrospective collection *Her Smoke Rose Up Forever.*

"Signal coming in now, 'Spector."

The Coronis operator showed the pink of her tongue to the ugly man waiting in the Belt patrolboat, half a mega-mile downstream. *All that feky old hair, too,* she thought. *Yick.* She pulled in her tongue and said sweetly, "It's from—oh—Franchise Twelve."

The man in the patrolboat looked uglier. His name was Space Safety Inspector Gollem and his stomach hurt.

The news that a Company inspector was in pain would have delighted every mollysquatter from Deimos to the Rings. The only surprise would be the notion that Inspector Gollem had a stomach instead of a Company contract tape. Gollem? All the friends Gollem had could colonize a meson and he knew it.

His stomach was used to that, though. His stomach was even getting used to working for Coronis Mutual, and he still hoped it might manage to survive his boss, Quine.

What was murdering him by inches was the thing he had hidden out beyond Franchise Fourteen on the edge of Coronis sector.

He scowled at the screen where Quine's girl was logging in the grief for his next patrol. Having a live girl-girl for commo was supposed to be good for morale. It wasn't doing one thing for Gollem. He knew what he looked like and his stomach knew what the flash from Twelve could be.

When she threw it on the screen he saw it was a bogy complaint, all right. Ghost signals on their lines.

Oh, no. Not again.

Not when he had it all fixed.

Franchise Twelve was West Hem Chemicals, an itchy outfit with a jill-abuck of cyborgs. They would send out a tracker if he didn't get over there soon. But how? He had just come that way, he was due upstream at Franchise One.

"Reverse patrol," he grunted. "Starting Franchise Fourteen. Purpose, uh, unscheduled recheck of aggregation shots in Eleven plus expedited service to West Hem. Allocate two units additional power."

She logged it in; it was all right with her if Gollem started with spacerot.

He cut channel and coded in the new course, trying not to think about the extra power he would have to justify to Quine. If anyone ever got into his console and found the bugger bypass on his log he would be loading ore with electrodes in his ears.

He keyed his stomach a shot of Vageez and caught an error in his code which he corrected with no joy. Most Belters took naturally to the new cheap gee-cumulator drive. Gollem loathed it. Sidling around arsy-versy instead of *driving* the can where you wanted to go. The old way, the real way.

I'm the last machine freak, he thought. A godlost dinosaur in space . . .

But a dinosaur would have had more sense than to get messed up with a dead girl.

And *Ragnarok*.

His gee-sum index was wobbling up the scale, squeezing him retrograde in a field stress-node—he hoped. He slapped away a pod of the new biomonitor they had put in his boat and took a scan outside before his screens mushed. Always something to see in the Belts. This time it was a storm of little crescents trailing him, winking as the gravel tumbled.

In the sky with diamonds . . .

From *Ragnarok's* big ports you could see into naked space. That was the way they liked it, once. His Iron Butterfly. He rubbed his beard, figuring: five hours to *Ragnarok*, after he checked the squatternest in Fourteen.

The weathersignal showed new data since he'd coded in the current field vortices and fronts. He tuned up, wondering what it must be like to live under weather made of gales of gas and liquid water. He had been raised on Luna.

The flash turned out to be a couple of rogue males coming in from Big J's orbit. Jup stirred up a rock now and then. This pair read like escaped Trojans, estimated to node downstream in Sector Themis. Nothing in that volume except some new medbase. His opposite number there was a gigglehead named Hara who was probably too busy peddling mutant phage to notice them go by. A pity, Trojans were gas-rich.

Feeding time. He opened a pack of Ovipuff and tuned up his music. *His* music. Old human power music from the frontier time. Not for Gollem, the new subliminal biomoans. He dug it hard, the righteous electronic decibels. Chomping the paste with big useless teeth, the cabin pounding.

I can't get no—satisFACTION!

The biomonitor was shrinking in its pods. Good. Nobody asked you into Gollem's ship, you sucking symbiote.

The beat helped. He started through his exercises. Not to let himself go null-gee like Hara. Like them all now. Spacegrace? Shit. His unfashionable body bucked and strained.

A gorilla, no wonder his own mother had taken one look and split. *Two thousand light-years from home* . . . what home for Gollem? Ask Quine, ask the Company. The Companies owned space now.

It was time to brake into Fourteen.

Fourteen was its usual disorderly self, a giant spawn of molly-bubbles hiding an aggregate of rock that had been warped into synch long before his time. The first colonists had done it with reaction engines. Tough. Now a kid with a gee-cumulator could true an orbit.

Fourteen had more bubbles every time he passed—and more kids. The tissue tanks that paid the franchise were still clear but elsewhere the bubbles were layers deep, the last ones tethered loose. Running out of rock for their metabolite to work on. Gollem hassled them about that every time he passed.

"Where are your rock nudgers?" he asked now when the squatterchief came on his screen.

"Soon, soon, 'Spector Gollem." The squatterchief was a slender skinhead with a biotuner glued to one ear.

"The Company will cancel, Juki. Coronis Mutual won't carry you on policyholder status if you don't maintain insurable life-support."

Juki smiled, manipulated the green blob. They were abandoning the rocks all right, drifting off into symbiotic spacelife. Behind Juki he saw a couple of the older chiefs.

"You can't afford to cut the services the Company provides," he told them angrily. Nobody knew better than Gollem how minimal those services were, but without them, what? "Get some rock."

He couldn't use any more time here.

As he pulled away he noticed one of the loose bubbles was a sick purple. Not his concern and not enough time.

Cursing, he eased alongside and cautiously slid his lock probes into the monomolecular bubbleskin. When the lock opened a stink came in. He grabbed his breather and kicked into the foul bubble. Six or seven bodies were floating together in the middle like a tangle of yellow wires.

He jerked one out, squirted oxy at its face. It was a gutbag kid, a born null-gee. When his eyes fanned open Gollem pushed him at the rotting metabolite core.

"You were feeding it phage." He slapped the boy. "Thought it would replicate, didn't you? You poisoned it."

The boy's eyes crossed, then straightened. Probably didn't get a word, the dialect of Fourteen was drifting fast. Maybe some of them truly were starting to communicate symbiotically. Vegetable ESP.

He pushed the boy back into the raft and knocked the dead metabolite through the waster. The starved molly-bubble wall was pitted with necrosis, barely holding. He flushed his CO_2 tank over it and crawled back to his boat for a spare metabolite core. When he got back the quasi-living cytoplasm of the bubbleskin was already starting to clear. It would regenerate itself if they didn't poison it again with a CO_2-binding mutant. That was the way men built their spacehomes now, soft heterocatalytic films that ran on starlight, breathed human wastes.

Gollem rummaged through the stirring bodies until he found a bag of phage between a woman and her baby. She whimpered when he jerked it loose. He carried it back to his boat and pulled carefully away, releasing a flow of nutrient gel to seal his probe-hole. The mollybubble would heal itself.

At last he was clear for *Ragnarok*.

He punched course for Twelve and then deftly patched in the log bypass and set his true trajectory. The log would feed from his cache of duplicates, another item nobody had better find. Then he logged in the expendables he'd just used, padding it a piece as always. Embezzlement. His stomach groaned.

He tuned up a rock storm to soothe it. There was an old poem about a man with a dead bird tied around his neck. Truly he had his dead bird. All the good things were dead, the free wild human things. He felt like a specter, believe it. A dead one hanging in from the days when men rode machines to the stars and the algae stayed in pans. Before they cooked up all the metabolizing Martian macromolecules that quote, tamed space, unquote. Tame men, women and kids breathing through 'em, feeding off 'em, navigating and computing and making music with 'em—mating with them, maybe!

Steppenwolf growled, worried the biomonitor. His metal-finder squealed.

Ragnarok!

Time shivered and the past blazed on his screens. He let himself have one quick look.

The great gold-skinned hull floated in the starlight, edged with diamonds against the tiny sun. The last Argo, the lonesomest Conestoga of them all. *Ragnarok.* Huge, proud, ungainly star machine, blazoned with the symbols of the crude technology that had blasted man to space. *Ragnarok* that opened the way to Saturn and beyond. A human fist to the gods. Drifting now a dead hulk, lost in the sea she'd conquered. Lost and forgotten to all but Gollem the specter.

No time now to suit up and prowl over and around her, to pry and tinker with her archaic fitments. The pile inside her was long dead and cold. He dared not even try to start it, a thing like that would set off every field-sounder in the zone. Quine's stolen power in her batteries was all that warmed her now.

Inside her also was his dead bird.

He coasted into the main lock, which he had adapted to his probe. Just as he hit he thought he glimpsed a new bubble firming up in the storage cluster he had hung on *Ragnarok's* freightlock. What had Topanga been up to?

The locks meshed with a soul-satisfying clang of metal and he cycled through, eye to eye with the two old monster suits that hung in *Ragnarok's* lock. Unbelievable, so cumbersome. How ever had they done it? He kicked up through dimness to the bridge.

For one moment his girl was there.

The wide ports were a wheeling maze of starlight and fire-studded shadows. She sat in the command couch, gazing out. He saw her pure, fierce profile, the hint of girl-body in the shadows. Star-hungry eyes.

Then the eyes slid around and the lights came up. His star girl vanished into the thing that had killed her.

Time.

Topanga was an old, sick, silly woman in a derelict driveship.

She smiled at him from the wreckage of her face.

"Golly? I was remembering—" What an instrument it was still, that husky voice in the star haze. The tales it had spun for him over the years. She had not always been like this. When he had first found her, adrift and ill—she had still been Topanga then. The last one left.

"You were using the caller. Topanga, I warned you they were too close. Now they've picked you up."

"I wasn't sending, Golly." Eerie blue, the wide old eyes reminded him of a place he had never seen.

He began to check the telltales he had hung on her console leads. Hard to believe those antiques were still operational. Completely inorganic, a ton of solid-state circuitry. Topanga claimed she couldn't activate it, but when she had had her first crazy fit he had found out otherwise. He'd had her parked in Four then, in a clutch of spacejunk. She started blasting the bands with docking signals to men twenty years dead. Company salvage had nearly blown her out of space before he got there—he'd had to fake a collision to satisfy Quine.

A telltale was hot.

"Topanga. Listen to me. West Hem Chemicals are sending a hunter out to find you. You were jamming their miners. Don't you know what they'll do to you? The best—the very best you'll get is a geriatric ward. Needles. Tubes. Doctors ordering you around, treating you like a thing. They'll grab *Ragnarok* for a space trophy. Unless they blast you first."

Her face crumpled crazily.

"I can take care of myself. I'll turn the lasers on 'em."

"You'd never see them." He glared at the defiant ghost. He could do anything he wanted here, what was stopping him? "Topanga, I'm going to kill that caller. It's for your own good."

She stuck up her ruined chin, the wattles waving.

"I'm not afraid of them."

"You have to be afraid of a jerry ward. You want to end as a mess of tubing, under the gees? I'm going to dismantle it."

"No, Golly, no!" Her stick arms drummed in panic, trailing skin. "I won't touch it, I'll remember. Don't leave me helpless. Oh, please don't."

Her voice broke and so did his stomach. He couldn't look at it, this creature that had eaten his girl. Topanga inside there somewhere, begging for freedom, for danger. Safe, helpless, gagged? No.

"If I nudge you out of West Hem's range you'll be in three others. Topanga, baby, I can't save you one more time."

She had gone limp now, shrouded in the Martian oxy-blanket he had brought her. He caught a blue gleam under the shadows and his stomach squirted bile. Let go, witch. Die before you kill me too.

He began to code in the gee-sum unit he had set up here. It was totally inadequate for *Ragnarok's* mass but he could overload it for a nudge. He would stabilize her on his next pass-by, if only he could find her without wasting too much power.

From behind him came a husky whisper. "Strange to be old—" Ghost of a rich girl's laugh. "Did I ever tell you about the time the field shifted, on Tethys?"

"You told me."

Ragnarok was stirring.

"Stars," she said dreamily. "Hart Crane was the first space poet. Listen. *Stars scribble on our eyes the frosty sagas, the gleaming cantos of unvanquished space. O silver sinewy—*"

Gollem heard the hull clang.

Someone was trying to sneak out of *Ragnarok*.

He launched himself down-shaft to the freightlock, found it cycling and jacknifed back to get out through his boat at the main lock. Too late. As he sprang into his cabin the screens showed a strange pod taking off from behind that new bubble.

Dummy, dummy—

He suited up and scrambled out across *Ragnarok's* hull. The new bubble was still soft, mostly nutri-gel. Pushing his face into it he cracked his breather.

He came back to Topanga in a blue rage.

"You are letting a phage-runner park on *Ragnarok*."

"Oh, was that Leo?" She laughed vaguely. "He's a courier from the next zone—Themis, isn't it? He calls by sometimes. He's been beautiful to me, Golly."

"He is a stinking phage-runner and you know it. You were covering for him." Gollem was sick. The old Topanga would have put "Leo" out the trash hole. "Not phage. Not phage on top of everything, Topanga."

Her ancient eyelids fell. "Let it be, Golly. I'm alone so long," she whispered. "You leave me for so long."

Her withered paw groped out, seeking him. Brown-spotted, criss-crossed with reedy pulses. Knobs, strings. Where were the hands of the girl who had held the camp on Tethys?

He looked up at the array of holographs over the port and saw her. The camera had caught her grinning up at black immensity, the wild light of Saturn's rings reflected in her red-gold hair. . . .

"Topanga, old mother," he said painfully.

"Don't call me mother, you plastic spacepig!" she blazed. Her carcass jerked out of the pilot couch and he had to web her back, hating to touch her. A quarter-gee would break these sticks. "I should be dead," she mumbled. "It won't be long, you'll be rid of me."

Ragnarok was set now, he could go.

"Maintain, spacer, maintain," he told her heartily. His stomach knew what lay ahead. None of it was any good.

As he left he heard her saying brightly, "Gimbals, check," to her dead computer.

He took off high-gain for Franchise Twelve and West Hem. Just as he had the log tied back into real time his caller bleeped. The screen stayed blank.

"Identify."

"Been waitin' on you, Gollem." A slurred tenor; Gollem's beard twitched.

"One freakin' fine ship." The voice chuckled. "Main-mouth by Co'onis truly flash that ship."

"Stay off *Ragnarok* if you want to keep your air," Gollem told the phage-runner.

The voice giggled again. "My pa'tners truly grieve on that, 'Spector." There was a click and he heard his own voice saying, "Topanga, baby, I can't save you one more time."

"Deal, 'Spector, deal. Why we flash on war?"

"Blow your clobbing tapes," Gollem said tiredly. "You can't run me like you run Hara."

" 'Panga," the invisible Leo said reflectively. "Freakin' fine old fox. She tell I fix her wire fire?"

Gollem cut channel.

The phager must have made a circuit smoke to win her trust. Gollem's stomach wept acid. So vulnerable. An old sick eagle dead in space and the rats have found her. . . .

They wouldn't quit, either. *Ragnarok* had air, water, power. Transmitters. Maybe they were using her caller, maybe she'd been telling the truth. They could take over. Shove her out through the lock. . . .

Gollem's hand hovered over his console.

If he turned back now his log would blow it all. And for what? No, he decided. They'll wait, they'll sniff around first. They want to take me too. They want to see how much squeeze they have. Pray they don't find out.

He had to get some power somewhere and jump *Ragnarok* out. How, how? Like trying to hide Big Jup.

He noticed that he had punched the biomonitor into a sick yellow blob and hurled it across the cabin. . . . How much longer could he cool Coronis?

Right on cue, his company hotline blatted.

"Why aren't you at Franchise Two, Gollem?"

It was mainmouth Quine himself. Gollem took a deep breath and repeated his course reversal plan, watching Quine's little snout purse up.

"After this clear with me. Now hear this, Gollem," Quine leaned back in his bioflex, pink and plump. Coronis was no hardship station. "I don't know what you think you're into with Franchise Three but I want it stopped. The miners are yelling and our Company won't tolerate it."

Gollem shook his shaggy head like a dazed bull. Franchise Three? Oh yeah, the heavy metal-mining outfit.

"They're overloading their tractor beams for hot extraction," he told Quine. "It's in my report. If they keep it up they'll have one bloody hashup. And they won't be covered because their contract annex specifies the load limits."

Quine's jowls twitched ominously. "Gollem. Again I warn you. It is not your role to interpret the contract to the policyholder. If the miners choose to get their ore out faster by abrogating their contract that's their decision. Your job is to report the violation, not to annoy them with technicalities. Right now they are very angry with *you*. And I trust you don't imagine that our Company"—reverent pause—"appreciates your initiative?"

Gollem made an inarticulate noise in his throat. He should be used to this. Coronis wanted its piece quickly *and* it wanted to avoid paying compensation when the thing blew. The miners got paid by the shuttle load and most of them couldn't tell a contract annex from a flush valve. By the time they found out they'd be dead.

"Another item." Quine was watching him. "You may be getting some noise from Themis sector. They seemed to be all sweated up about a bit of rock."

"You mean those Trojans?" Gollem was puzzled. "What's there?"

"Have you been talking to Themis?"

"No."

"Very well. You will not, repeat not, deviate from your patrol. You are on a very thin line with us, Gollem. If your log shows anything *whatever* in connection with Themis you're out of the Company and there will be a lien against you for your overdrawn pension. *And* there will be no transport rights. Do I make myself clear?"

Gollem cut channel. When he could control his hands he punched Weather for the updated rogue orbits. Both rocks were now computed to node in sector Themis, but well clear of Themis main. He frowned. Who was hurting? His ephemeris showed only the new medbase in the general volume, listed as Nonaffiliated, no details. It seemed to be clear, too. If that polluted Hara . . .

Gollem grunted. He understood now. Quine was hoping for some hassle in Themis which might persuade Ceres Control to reassign part of that sector to him. And the medbase wasn't Company, it was expendable for publicity purposes. Truly fine, he thought. Much gees for Quine if it works.

He was coming into West Hem Chemicals. Before he could signal, his audio cut loose with curses from the cyborg chief. Gollem swerved to minimize his intrusion on their body lines and the chief cooled down enough to let him report that he had killed their bogy.

"It was an old field-sounder," Gollem lied. Had they identified *Ragnarok?*

"Slope out. Go." The old cyborg op couldn't care less. He had electrode jacks all over his skull and his knuckles sprouted wires. Much as Gollem loved metal, this was too much. He backed out as gingerly as he could. The men—or maybe the creatures—in there were wired into the controls of robot refining plants on all the nearby rocks, and he was hashing across their neural circuit. Wouldn't be surprising if they fired on him one day.

His next stop was the new aggregation franchise in Eleven. It was a slow-orbit complex on the rim of the Kirkwood Gap, a touchy location to work. If they started losing rocks they could spread chaos in the zone.

Aggregation meant power units, lots of them. Gollem began figuring *Ragnarok's* parameters. His stomach also began to gripe him; the outfit that had leased Eleven had big plans for a self-sustaining colony on a slim budget. They needed those units to bring in gas-rich rocks.

When he got inside Gollem saw they had other problems too.

"We've computed for two-sigma contingency," the Eleven chief repeated tiredly. They were standing beside a display tank showing the projected paths of the rocks they intended to blast.

"Not enough," Gollem told him. "Your convergence-point is smeared the hell all over. You lose a big one and it'll plow right into Ten."

"But Franchise Ten isn't occupied," the chief protested.

"Makes no difference. Why do you think you got this franchise cheap? The Company's delighted to have you aggregating this lode, they're just waiting for you to lose one rock so they can cancel and resell your franchise. I can't certify your operation unless you recompute."

"But that means buying computer input from Ceres Main!" he yelped. "We can't afford it."

"You should have looked at the instability factors before you signed," Gollem said woodenly. He was wishing the chief didn't have all his hair; it would be easier to do this to a skinhead.

"At least let me bring in the rocks we have armed," the chief was pleading.

"How many one-gee units have you got out there?" Gollem pointed.

"Twenty-one."

"I'll take six of them and certify you. That's cheaper than recomputing." The chief's jaw sagged, clenched in a snarl.

"You polluted bastard!"

Suddenly there was a squeal behind them and the commo op tore off her earphones. The chief reached over and flicked on the speaker, filling the bubble with an all-band blare. For a minute Gollem thought it was a flare-front, and then he caught the human scream.

"MAYDAY! MA-A-Y-DAY-AAY! GO-OLLEE—"

Oh no! Oh Jesus, no. He slammed down the speaker, the sweat starting out all over him.

"What in space—" the chief began.

"Old beacon in the Gap." Gollem bunted through them. "I have to go kill it."

He piled into his boat and threw in the booster. No time for power units now. That yell meant Topanga was in real trouble, she wasn't calling dead men.

If he tied in the spare booster he could override the field-forms for a straighter course. Strictly *verboten*. He did so and then opened his commo channels. Topanga wasn't there.

Fire? Collision? More like, Leo and friends had made their move.

He hurtled downstream in a warp of wasted power, his hands mechanically tuning the board in hopes of pulling in some phagers' signals, something. He picked up only far-off mining chatter and a couple of depot ops asking each other what the Mayday was. Someone in Sector Themis was monotonously calling Inspector Hara. As usual Hara wasn't answering, there was only the automatic standby from Themis main. Gollem cursed them all impartially, trying to make his brain yield a plan.

Why would the phagers move in on *Ragnarok* so fast? Not their style, confrontation. If he blew they'd lose the ship, they'd have to cope with a new inspector. Why risk it when they had him by the handle already?

Maybe they figured it was no risk. Gollem's fist pounded on the tuner in a heavy rhythm. *Paint it black. . . .* But they have to keep her alive till I get there. They want me.

What to do? Would they believe a threat to call Ceres Control? Don't bother to answer. They know as well as I do that a Company bust would end with Topanga in a gerry ward, *Ragnarok* in Quine's trophy park and Gollem in a skull-cage. . . . How to break Topanga loose from them? If I try to jive along the first thing they'll do will be to shoot us both up on phage. Addiction dose. *Why, why did I leave her there alone?*

He was going around this misery orbit for the nth time when he noticed the Themis voice had boosted gain and was now trying to reach Coronis, his home base. Correction, Quine's home base. No answer.

Against his stomach's advice he tuned it up.

"Medbase Themis to Coronis main, emergency. Please answer, Coronis. Medbase Themis calling Coronis, emergency, please—"

The woman was clearly no commo op.

Finally Quine's girl chirped: "Medbase Themis, you are disturbing our traffic. Please damp your signal."

"Coronis, this is an emergency. We need help—we're going to get hit!"

"Medbase Themis, contact your sector safety patrol officer, we have no out-of-sector authorization. You are disturbing our traffic."

"Our base won't answer! We have to have help, we have casualties—"

A male voice cut in. "Coronis, put me through to your chief at once. This is a medical priority."

"Medbase Themis, Sector Chief Quine is outstation at present. We are in freight shuttle assembly for the trans-Mars window, please stand by until after launch."

"But—"

"Coronis out."

Gollem grimaced, trying to picture Quine going outstation.

He went back to pounding on his brain. The Themis woman went on calling. "We are in an impact path, we need power to move. If anyone can help us please come in. Medbase Themis—"

He cut her off. One *Ragnarok* was enough and his was just ahead now.

There was a faint chance they weren't expecting him so soon. He powered down and drifted. As his screens cleared he saw a light move in the bubbles behind the freightlock.

His one possible break, if they hadn't yet moved that phage inboard.

He grabbed the wrecking laser controls and kicked the patrolboat straight at *Ragnarok's* main lock. The laser beam fanned over the bubbles, two good slices before he had to brake. The crash sent him into his boards. The docking probes meshed and he sprang headfirst into *Ragnarok's* lock. As it started to cycle he burned the override, setting off alarms all over the ship. Then he was through and caroming up the shaft. Among the hoots he could hear more clanging. Phagers were piling out through the freight-lock to save their bubbles. If he could get to the bridge first he could lock them out.

He twisted, kicked piping and shot into the bridge, his arm aimed at the emergency hatch-lock lever. It hadn't been used for decades—he nearly broke his wrist, yanking the lever against his own inertia and was rewarded by the sweet grind of lock toggles far below.

Then he turned to the command couch where Topanga should be and saw he was too late.

She was there all right, both hands to her neck and her eyes rolling. Behind her a lank hairless figure was holding a relaxed pose, in his fist a wirenoose leading around Topanga's throat.

"Truly fine, 'Spector." The phager grinned.

For a second Gollem wondered if Leo hadn't noticed the hand-laser Gollem pointed. Then he saw that the phagehead was holding a welder against Topanga's side. Its safety sleeve was off.

"Deal, Gollyboy. Deal the fire down."

No way. After a minute Gollem sent his weapon drifting by Leo's arm. Leo didn't take the bait.

"Open up." The phager jerked his chin at the hatch lever and Topanga gave a bubbling whine.

When Gollem opened the hatch the game would be over all the way. He hung frozen, his coiled body sensing for solidity behind him, measuring the spring.

The phager jerked the wire. Topanga's arms flailed. One horrible eye rolled at Gollem. A spark in there, trying to say no.

"You're killing her. Then I tear your head off and throw you out the waster."

The phager giggled. "Why you flash on killin'?" Suddenly he twisted Topanga upside down, feet trailing out toward Gollem. She kicked feebly. Weird, her bare feet were like a girl's.

"Open up."

When Gollem didn't move the phager's arm came out in a graceful swing, his fingers flaring. The welding arc sliced, retraced, sliced again as Topanga convulsed. One girlish foot floated free, trailing droplets. Gollem saw a white stick pointing at him out of the blackened stump. Topanga was quiet now.

"Way to go." The phager grinned. "Truly tough old bird. Open up."

"Turn her loose. Turn her loose. I'll open."

"Open now." The welder moved again.

Suddenly Topanga made a weak twist, scrabbling at Leo's groin. The phager's head dipped.

Gollem drove inside his arm, twisted it against momentum. The welder rocketed out around the cabin while he and the phager thrashed around each other, blinded by Topanga's robe. The phager had a knife now but he couldn't get braced. Gollem felt legs lock his waist and took advantage of it to push Topanga away. When the scene cleared he clamped the phager to him and began savagely to collect on his investment in muscle-building.

Just as he was groping for the wire to tie up the body something walloped him back of the ear and the lights went out.

He came to with Topanga yelling, "Val, Val! I've got em!"

She was hanging on the console in her hair using both hands to point an ancient Thunderbolt straight at him. The muzzle yawned smoke a foot from his beard.

"Topanga, it's me—Golly. Wake up, spacer, let me tie him up."

"Val?" A girl laughing, screaming. "I'm going to finish the murdering mothers, Val!"

Valentine Orlov, her husband, had been in the snows of Ganymede for thirty years.

"Val is busy, Topanga," Gollem said gently. He was hearing hull noises he didn't like. "Val sent me to help you. Put the jolter down spacegirl. Help me tie up this creep. They're trying to steal my boat."

He hadn't had time to lock it, he remembered now.

Topanga stared at him.

"And why do I often meet your visage here?" she croaked. *"Your eyes like unwashed platters—"*

Then she fainted and he flung himself downshaft to the lock.

His patrolboat was swinging away. Tethered to it was the phage-runners' pod.

He was stranded on *Ragnarok*.

Rage exploded him back to the bridge consoles. He managed to send one weak spit from *Ragnarok's* lasers after them as they picked up gees. Futile. Then he pulled the phager's head over his knee and clouted it and turned to setting up Topanga with an i.v. in her old cobweb veins. How in hell had those claws held a jolter? He wrapped a gel sheath over her burns, grinding his jaw to still the uproar in his stomach. He completed his cleaning by towing the phager and the foot to the waste lock.

With one hand on the cycle button he checked frowning. He could use some information from Leo—what were they into in his patrol sector?

Then his head came together and his fist crunched the eject. *His* patrol sector?

If the Companies ever got their hands on him he'd spend the rest of his life with his brains wired up, paying for that patrolboat. If he were lucky. No way, no where to go. The Companies owned space. Truly he was two thousand light-years from home now—on a dead driveship.

Dead?

Gollem threw back his lank hair and grinned. *Ragnarok* had a rich ecosystem, he'd seen to that. Nobody but the phagers knew she was here and he could hold them out for a while. Long enough, maybe, to see if he could coax some power out of that monster-house without waking up the sector. Suddenly he laughed out loud. Rusty shutter sliding in his mind, letting in glory.

"Man, man!" he muttered and stuck his head into the regeneration chamber to check the long trays of culture stretching away under the lights.

It took him a minute to understand what was wrong.

No wonder the phagers came back so fast, no wonder he was laughing like a dummy. They'd seeded the whole works with phage culture. A factory. The first trays were near sporing, the air was ropy. He hauled them out, inhaled a clean lungful and jettisoned the ripe trays.

Then he crawled back in to search. On every staging the photosynthetic algae were starting to clump, coagulating to the lichen-like symbiote that was phage. Not one clean tray.

In hours *Ragnarok* would have no more air.

But he and Topanga wouldn't care. They'd be through the walls in phagefreak long before.

He was well and truly shafted now.

He flushed some oxy into the ventilators and kicked back to the bridge. Get some clean metabolite or die.

Who would give him air? Even if he could move *Ragnarok*, the company depots and franchises would be alerted. He might just as well signal Coronis and give himself up. Maybe Quine wouldn't bother to reach him and Topanga in time. Maybe better so. Wards. Wires.

Topanga groaned. Gollem felt her temples. Hot as plasma, old ladies with a leg shortened shouldn't play war. He rummaged out biogens, marveling at the vials, ampoules, tabs, hyposprays. Popping who knew what to keep alive. Contraband she and Val had picked up in the old free days, her hoard would stock a . . .

Wait a minute.

Medbase Themis.

He tuned up *Ragnarok's* board. The Themis woman was still calling, low and hoarse. He cranked the antennae for the narrowest beam he could get.

"Medbase Themis, do you read?"

"Who are you? Who's there?" She was startled out of her code book.

"This is a spacesweep mission. I have a casualty."

"Where—" The male voice took over.

"This is Chief Medic Kranz, spacer. You can bring in your casualty but we have a rogue headed through our space with a gravel cloud. If we can't get power to move the station in about thirty hours we'll be holed out. Can you help us?"

"You can have what I've got. Check coordinates."

The woman choked up on the decimals. No use telling them he couldn't do them any good. The gee-sum unit he had in *Ragnarok* wouldn't nudge that base in time for Halley's comet. And *Ragnarok's* drive—if it worked it would be like trying to wipe your eye with a blowtorch.

But their air could help *him.*

The drive. He bounced down the engineway, knowing the spring in his muscles was partly phage. Only partly. A thousand times he had come this way, a thousand times torn himself away from temptation. Gleefully now he began to check out the circuits he had traced, restored the long-pulled fuses. There was a sealed hypergolic reserve for ignition. A stupefying conversion process, a plumber's nightmare of heat-exchangers and back-cycling. Crazy, wasteful, dangerous. Enough circuitry to wire the Belt. Unbelievable it had carried man to Saturn, more unbelievable it would work today.

He clanked the rod controls. No telling what had crystallized. The converter fuel chutes jarred out thirty years' accumulated dust. The ignition reserve was probably only designed for one emergency firing. Would he be able to ignite again to brake? Learn as you go. One thing sure, when that venerable metal volcano burst to life every board from here to Coronis would be lit.

When he got back to the bridge Topanga was whispering.

"We left the haven hanging in the night— O thou steel cognizance whose leap commits—"

"Pray it leaps," he told her and began setting course, double-checking everything because of the phagemice running in the shadows. He wrapped Topanga's webs.

He started the ignition train.

The subsonic rumble that grew through *Ragnarok* filled him with terror and delight. He threw himself into the webs, wishing he had said something, counted down maybe. Blastoff. *Go.* The rumble bloomed into an oremill roar. Gees smashed down on him. Everything in the cabin started raining on the deck. The web gave sideways and the roar wound up in a scream that parted his brain and then dwindled into silence.

When he struggled back to the board he found the burn had cut right. *Ragnarok* was barreling toward Themis. He saw Topanga's eyes open.

"Where are we headed?" She sounded sane as soap.

"I'm taking you over to the next sector, Themis. We need metabolite, oxygen. The phagers ruined your regenerators."

"Themis?"

"There's a medbase there. They'll give us some."

Mistake.

"Oh, no—no!" She struggled up. "No, Golly! I won't go to a hospital—don't let them take me!"

"You're not going to a hospital, Topanga. You're going to stay right here in the ship while I go in for the cores. They'll never know about you. We'll be out of there in minutes."

No use.

"God hate you, Gollem." She made an effort to spit. "You're trying to trap me. I know you! Never let me free. You won't bury me here, Gollem. Rot in Moondome with your ugly cub—I'm going to Val!"

"Cool, spacer, you're yawning." He got some tranks into her finally and went back to learning *Ragnarok*. The phage was getting strong now. When he looked up the holographs were watching him drive their ship. The old star heroes. Val Orlov, Fitz, Hannes, Mura, all the great ones. Sometimes only a grin behind a gold-washed headplate, a name on a suit beside some mad hunk of machine. Behind them, spacelost wildernesses lit by unknown moons. All alive, all so young. There was Topanga with her arm around that other spacegirl, the dark Russian one who was still orbiting Io. They grinned past him, bright and living.

When they start talking, we've had it. . . .

He set the gyros to crank *Ragnarok* into what he hoped was attitude for the retro burn. If he could trust the dials, there was enough ignition for braking and for one last burn to get out of there. But where would he go from Medbase? Into the sky with diamonds . . .

He heard himself humming and decided to lock the whole thing into autopilot. No matter what shape that computer was in it would be saner than he was.

Have you seen your mother, baby, standing in the shadows? . . .

When he began hearing the Stones he went down and threw out half the trays. The three remaining oxy tanks struck him as hilarious. He cracked one.

The oxy sobered him enough to check the weather signal. The Medbase woman was still trying to raise Themis Main. He resisted the impulse to enlighten her about the Companies and concentrated on the updated orbits of the Trojan rogues. He saw now what had Medbase sweating. The lead rogue would miss them by megamiles but it was massive enough to have stirred up a lot of gravel. The small rogue behind was sweeping up a tail. The rock itself would go by far off—but that gravel cloud would rip their bubbles to shreds.

He had to get in there and out again fast.

He sniffed some more oxy and computed the rogue orbits on a worst-contingency basis. It looked O.K.—for him. His stomach flinched; even under phage it had an idea what it was going to be like when those medics found out they were wasted.

He saw Topanga grinning. The phage was doing her more good than the tranks.

"Not to worry, star girl. Golly won't let 'em get you."

"Air." She was trying to point to life-support, which had long since gone red.

"I know, spacer. We're getting air at Medbase."

She gave him a strange un-Topanga smile. "Whatever you say, little Golly." Whispering hoarsely, "I know—you've been beautiful—"

Her hand reached, burning. This he positively could not take. Too bad his music was gone.

"Give us verses as we go, star girl."

But she was too weak.

"Read me—"

Her scanner was full of it.

"*In oil-rinsed circles of blind ecstasy.*" Hard to dig, until the strobing letters suddenly turned to music in his throat. "*Man hears himself an engine in a cloud!*" he chanted, convoyed by ghosts.

"*—What marathons new-set among the stars! . . . The soul, by naphtha fledged into new reaches, already knows the closer clasp of Mars—*"

. . . It was indeed fortunate, he discovered, that he had set the autopilot and stayed suited up.

His first clear impression of Medbase was a chimpanzee's big brown eyes staring into his under a flashprobe. He jerked away, found himself peeled and tied on a table. The funny feeling was the luxury of simulated gravity. The chimpanzee turned out to be a squat little type in med-whites, who presently freed him.

"I told you he wasn't a phager." It was the woman's voice.

Craning, Gollem saw she was no girl-girl and had a remarkable absence of chin. The chimpanzee eventually introduced himself as Chief Medic Kranz.

"What kind of ship *is* that?" the woman asked as he struggled into his suit.

"A derelict," he told them. "Phagerunners were using it. My teammate's stoned. All he needs is air."

"The power units," said Kranz. "I'll help you bring them over."

"No need for you to go in—I've got them ready to go. Just give me a couple of metabolite cores to take back to start the air cleaning."

Unsuspicious, Kranz motioned the woman to show the way to their stores. Gollem saw that their base was one big cheap bubble behind a hard-walled control module. The molly hadn't even seamed together under the film; a couple of pebbles would finish them. The ward had twenty-odd burn cases in cocoons. Themis didn't bother much with burns.

An old spacerat minus a lot of his original equipment came wambling over to open up. Gollem loaded as much metabolite as he could carry and headed for the lock. At the port the woman grabbed his arm.

"You *will* help us?" Her eyes were deep green. Gollem concentrated on her chin.

"Be right back." He cycled out.

Ragnarok was on a tether he didn't recall securing. He scrambled over, found the end fouled in the lock toggles. If there had been tumble—bye-bye.

When he got inside he heard Topanga's voice. He hustled up the shaft. Once again he was too late.

While he'd been in the stores unsuspicious Chief Medic Kranz had suited up and beat him into *Ragnarok*.

"This is a very sick woman, spacer," he informed Gollem.

"The legal owner of this derelict, doctor. I'm taking her to Coronis Base."

"I'm taking her into my ward right now. We have the facilities. Get those power units."

He could see Topanga's eyes close.

"She doesn't wish to be hospitalized."

"She's in no condition to decide that," Kranz snapped.

The metabolite was on board. Doctor Chimpanzee Kranz appeared to have elected himself a driveship ride to nowhere. Gollem began drifting toward the ignition panel, beside Topanga's web.

"I guess you're right, sir. I'll help you prepare her and we'll take her in."

But Kranz's little hand had a little stungun in it.

"The power units, spacer." He waved Gollem toward the shaft.

There weren't any power units.

Gollem backed into the metabolite, watching for the stunner to waver. It didn't. There was only one chance left, if you could call it a chance.

"Topanga, this good doctor is going to take you into his hospital," he said loudly. "He wants you where he can take good care of you."

One of Topanga's eyelids wrinkled, sagged down again. An old, battered woman. No chance.

"Can you handle her, doctor?"

"Get that power *now*." Kranz snapped the safety off.

Gollem nodded sourly and started downshaft as slowly as he could. Kranz came over to watch him, efficiently out of reach. What now? Gollem couldn't reach the ignition circuits from here even if he knew how to short them.

Just as he turned around to look for something to fake a power cell it happened.

A whomp like an imploding mollybubble smacked into the shaft. Chief Medic Kranz sailed down in a slow cartwheel.

"Good girl!" Gollem yelled. "You got him!" He batted the stunner out of Kranz' limp glove and kicked upward. When his head cleared the shaft he found he was looking into the snout of Topanga's jolter.

"Get out of my ship," she rasped. "You lying suitlouse. And take your four-eyed, needle-sucking friend with you!"

"Topanga, it's me—it's Golly—"

"I know who you are," she said coldly. "You'll never trap me."

"Topanga!" he cried. A bolt went by his ear, rocking him.

"Out!" She was leaning down the shaft, squeezing on the jolter.

Gollem backed slowly down, collecting Kranz. The witch figure above him streamed biotape and bandages, the hair that once shone red standing up like white fire. She must be breathing pure phage, he thought.

Can't last long. All I have to do is go slow.

"Out!" She screamed. Then he saw she had Kranz's oxy tube clamped under one arm. This seemed to be his day for underestimating people.

"Topanga," he began to plead and had to dodge another jolt-bolt. She couldn't go on missing forever. He decided to haul Kranz out and cut back into the ship through the emergency port. He recalled seeing a welding torch in the medbase port rack.

He boosted Kranz along the tether and into the med-base lock. The woman was waiting on the other side. As the port opened he pushed Kranz at her and grabbed the welder. The chinless wonder learned fast—she flung herself on the welder and started to wrestle. There was solid woman-muscle under her whites, but he got a fist where her jaw should have been and threw himself back into the lock.

As it started to cycle he realized she had probably saved his life.

The outer lock had a viewport through which he could see *Ragnarok's* vents. The starfield behind them was dissolving.

He let out an inarticulate groan and slammed the reverse cycle to let himself back into Medbase. As soon as it cracked he bolted through, carrying the medics to the deck. The port behind him lit up like a solar flare.

They all stared at the silent torrent of flame pouring out of *Ragnarok*. Then she was moving, faster, faster yet. The jetstream swung and the port went black.

"It's burning! Get the foam!"

Kranz grabbed a sealant cannister and they raced to the edge of the hard-wall area, where *Ragnarok's* exhaust had seared the bubble. When the burns were sealed the ship was a dwindling firetail among the stars.

"Topanga doesn't like hospitals," Gollem told them.

"The power units!" Kranz said urgently. "Call her back!"

They were pushing Gollem toward the commo board.

"No way. She just blew the last ignition charge. Where she's headed now she goes."

"What do you mean? To Coronis?"

"Never." He rubbed his shaggy head. "I—I don't recall exactly. Mars, maybe the sun."

"With the power units that would have saved these people." Kranz's face had the expression he probably used on gangrene. "Thanks to you. I suggest that you remove yourself from my sight for the remainder of our joint existence."

"There never were any power units," Gollem said, starting to go out. "The phagers got my boat and you saw for yourself what the drive was like. Her acceleration would have broken you apart."

The woman followed him out.

"Who was she, spacer?"

"Topanga Orlov," Gollem said painfully. "Val Orlov's wife. They were the first Saturn mission. That was their ship, *Ragnarok*. She was holed up in my sector."

"You just wanted air."

Gollem nodded.

They were by the base display tank. The computer was running a real-time display of the uncoming Trojans. The green blip was Medbase and the red blip with the smear was the smaller Trojan and attendant gravel tail. He studied the vectors. No doubt.

It was now dark-period. Sleep time coming up. The people here might eat breakfast, but for true they wouldn't eat lunch. By noon or thereabouts Medbase ould be organic enrichment on a swarm of space ice.

So would ex-Inspector Gollem.

The two medics went out on the wards and Kranz unbent enough to accept Gollem's offer to man the commo board. The spacer wobbled in to watch him. The sight of *Ragnarok's* blast-out had lit his fires.

Gollem taped a routine red-call and began to hunt across the bands. The old man mumbled about ships. Nobody was answering, nobody would. Once Gollem thought he heard an echo from Topanga, but it was nothing. Her oxy must be long gone by now, he thought. A mad old phage-ghost on her last trip. Where had he computed her to? He seemed to recall something about Mars. At least they wouldn't end in some trophy-hunter's plastic park.

"You know what they got in them cocoons? Squatters!" The old man squinted out of his good side to see how Gollem took this. "Skinheads. Freaks 'n' crotties. Phagers, even. Medics, they don't care." He sighed, scratched his burned skin with his stump. "Grounders. They won't last out here."

"Too right," Gollem agreed. "Like maybe tomorrow." That tickled the old man.

Toward midnight Kranz took over. The woman brought in some hot redeye. Gollem started to refuse and then realized his stomach wasn't hurting any more. Nothing to worry about now. He sipped the stimulant. The woman was looking at a scanner.

"She was beautiful," she murmured.

"Knock it off, Anna," Kranz snapped.

She went on scanning and suddenly caught her breath.

"Your name. It's Gollem, isn't it?"

Gollem nodded and got up to go look at the tank.

Presently the woman Anna came out after him and looked at the tank, too. The old spacer was asleep in the corner.

"Topanga was married to a George Gollem once," Anna said quietly. "They had a son. On Luna."

Gollem took the scanner cartridge out of her hand and flipped it into the wastechute. She said nothing more. They both watched the tank for a while. Gollem noticed that her eyes were almost good enough to make up for her chin. She didn't look at him. The tank didn't change.

Around four she went in and took over from Kranz and the men settled down to wait.

"Medbase Themis calling, please come in. Medbase Themis calling anyone," the woman whispered monotonously.

Kranz went out. It seemed a lot of work to breathe.

Suddenly Kranz snapped his fingers from the next room. Gollem went to him.

"Look."

They hung over the tank. The red smear was closer to the green blip. Between them was a yellow spark.

"What is that?"

Gollem shrugged. "A rock."

"Impossible, we scan-swept that area a dozen times."

"No mass," Gollem frowned. "It's a tank ghost."

Kranz began systematically flushing the computer input checks. The woman left the board and came to lean over the tank. Gollem watched absently, his brain picking at phage-warped memories. Something about the computer.

On impulse he went to the commo board and ran the receiver through its limits. All he got was a blast of squeals and whistles, the stress-front of the incoming rocks.

"What is it?" Anna's eyes were phosphorescent.

"Nothing."

Kranz finished his checks. The yellow ghost stayed in, sidling toward the red smear. If that were a rock, and it had about a hundred times more mass than it could have, it just might deflect the Trojan's gravel swarm. But it didn't.

Gollem played monotonously with the board. The old spacer snored. The minutes congealed. Kranz shook himself, took Anna out to tour the wards. When they came back they stopped at the tank.

The whatever-it-was stayed in, closing on the Trojan.

Sometime in the unreal dimlight hours Gollem caught it, wavering on a gale of space noise:

"I have contact! Val! I'm coming—"

They crowded around him as he coaxed the tuners but there was nothing there. Presently a ripple of relays tripped off in the next room and they all ran to the tank. It was dead; the computer had protected itself against an induction overload.

They never knew exactly what happened.

"It's possible," Gollem admitted to them. It was long after noon when they decided to eat.

"While we were on the way here I know I computed that Trojan all the way to Medbase, before that I got really bombed. Maybe I threw a bridge into the course computer, maybe it was already in. Say she took off with no course setting. Those old mechs are set to hunt. It's possible it inverted and boosted straight back out that trajectory to the rock."

"But your ship had no mass," Kranz objected.

"That thing was a space-scoop feeding a monster drive. The pile dampers were cheese. *Ragnarok* could have scooped herself solid right through the gravel cloud and blown as she hit the Trojan. You could get a pocket sun."

• • •

They went over it again at dark-period. And again later while he and Anna looked at nothing in particular out the ports. A long time after that he showed her a script he'd fixed for the wall of Medbase Free Enclave:

Launched in abyssal cupolas of space
Toward endless terminas, Easters of speeding light—
Vast engines outward veering with seraphic grace
On clarion cylinders pass out of sight.

Recommended Reading

There has been so much adventure SF of one sort or another published over the years that making a definitive list of novels and collections is almost impossible; I'm not even going to try—for suggestions, read the Preface, and the storynotes for the individual authors. Making a list of anthologies is almost as difficult, since a great many anthologies will contain one or two such stories even when that sort of material isn't the major emphasis of the book.

Here's a quick and inadequate list, though, of some of the major anthologies that emphasize adventure work from the '30s, '40s, '50s, and '60s. Most of the SF magazines, *Astounding/Analog*, *Galaxy*, *Worlds of If*, *The Magazine of Fantasy & Science Fiction*, have a number of "Best of" collections, too many to list individually, though I have listed a few of them below that arbitrarily strike me as functioning as more generally retrospective overviews. Anthologies are listed alphabetically by the name of the editor:

Ackermanthology, Forrest J. Ackerman
All About Venus, Brian W. Aldiss
Evil Earths, Brian W. Aldiss
Galactic Empires, Volumes 1–2, Brian W. Aldiss
Space Oddessys, Brian W. Aldiss
Space Opera, Brian W. Aldiss
Spectrum, volumes 1–4, Kingsley Amis and Robert Conquest
Before the Golden Age, Isaac Asimov
The Hugo Winners, volumes 1 & 2, Isaac Asimov (the other volumes of Hugo-winners are valuable as well, but the first two are the best for older work)
The Mammoth Book of Classic Science Fiction: Short Novels of the 1930s (in the U.S. as *Great Tales of Classic Science Fiction*), Isaac Asimov, Martin H. Greenberg, and Charles G. Waugh
The Mammoth Book of Golden Age Science Fiction: Short Novels of the 1940s, Isaac Asimov, Martin H. Greenberg, and Charles G. Waugh
The Mammoth Book of Vintage Science Fiction: Short Novels of the 1950s, Isaac Asimov, Martin H. Greenberg, and Charles G. Waugh
The Mammoth Book of New World Science Fiction: Great Short Novels of the 1960s, Isaac Asimov, Martin H. Greenberg, and Charles G. Waugh

Wonderful Worlds of Science Fiction 1: Intergalactic Empires, Isaac Asimov, Martin H. Greenberg, and Charles G. Waugh
(Asimov and Greenberg also edited a long-running series—24 volumes, too many to individually list here—called *Isaac Asimov Presents the Great SF Stories*, which gives a year-by-year overview, starting with 1939 and ending with 1962)
The Best Science Fiction Stories, 1949–1954, Everett F. Bleiler & T. E. Dikty
Year's Best Science Fiction Novels, 1952–1954
The Best from Planet Stories No. 1, Leigh Brackett
A Treasury of Great Science Fiction, volumes 1 & 2, Anthony Boucher
The Science Fiction Hall of Fame, volume 2, Ben Bova
The Astounding Science Fiction Anthology, John W. Campbell
The Big Book of Science Fiction, Groff Conklin
The Omnibus of Science Fiction, Groff Conklin
Seven Trips Through Time and Space, Groff Conklin
A Treasury of Science Fiction, Groff Conklin
Modern Classics of Science Fiction, Gardner Dozois
Modern Classic Short Novels of Science Fiction, Gardner Dozois
The Magazine of Fantasy & Science Fiction, a 30 Year Retrospective, Edward L. Ferman
The Best from the Magazine of Fantasy & Science Fiction: A 45th Anniversary Anthology, Edward L. Ferman and Kristine Kathryn Rusch
Science Fiction of the '50s, Martin H. Greenberg and Joseph Olander
The Road to Science Fiction, volumes 1–4, James Gunn
Astounding, Harry Harrison
Ascent of Wonder, David G. Hartwell
A Science Fiction Century, David G. Hartwell
Visions of Wonder, David G. Hartwell
A World Treasury of Science Fiction, David G. Hartwell
Adventures in Time and Space, Raymond J. Healy and J. Francis McComas
Mars, We Love You, Jane Hipolito and Willis E. McNelly
First Step Outward, Robert Hoskins
The Stars Around Us, Robert Hoskins
One Hundred Years of Science Fiction, Damon Knight
A Science Fiction Argosy, Damon Knight
Science Fiction of the Thirties, Damon Knight
Worlds To Come, Damon Knight
The End of Summer: Science Fiction of the Fifties, Barry N. Malzberg and Bill Pronzini
SF: The Best of the Best, Judith Merril
The Year's Best S-F, volumes 1–12, Judith Merril

Galaxy: Thirty Years of Innovative Science Fiction, Frederik Pohl, Martin H. Greenberg, and Joseph Olander

The Great Science Fiction Series, Frederik Pohl, Martin H. Greenberg, and Joseph Olander

Worlds of If: A Retrospective Anthology, Frederik Pohl, Martin H. Greenberg, and Joseph Olander

Yesterday's Tomorrows, Frederik Pohl

Alpha, volumes 1–9, Robert Silverberg

The Arbor House Treasury of Great Science Fiction Short Novels, Robert Silverberg and Martin H. Greenberg

The Arbor House Treasury of Modern Science Fiction, Robert Silverberg and Martin H. Greenberg

The Arbor House Treasury of Science Fiction Masterpieces, Robert Silverberg and Martin H. Greenberg

Deep Space, Robert Silverberg

The Ends of Time, Robert Silverberg

Explorers of Space, Robert Silverberg

Great Short Novels of Science Fiction, Robert Silverberg

Invaders from Space, Robert Silverberg

The Mirror of Infinity, Robert Silverberg

A Century of Science Fiction 1950–1959, Robert Silverberg

Robert Silverberg's Worlds of Wonder, Robert Silverberg

The Science Fiction Hall of Fame, Volume 1, Robert Silverberg

Adventures on Other Planets, Donald A. Wollheim

More Adventures on Other Planets, Donald A. Wollheim

Swordsmen in the Sky, Donald A. Wollheim

Libraries may still be your best bet for finding many of these titles, although, alas, libraries don't carry as many old titles as they did twenty years ago (try a university library, if you have one near you, preferably one with a science fiction collection). If libraries and regular used-book stores fail you, try science fiction specialty stores and the dealer's rooms at science fiction coventions. If they fail you as well, as they may, then you have no choice but to mail-order. We've mentioned the addresses of NESFA Press and Charles L. Miller in the storynotes. Some of the biggest mail-order services are Barry R. Levin, 720 Santa Monica Blvd., Santa Monica CA, 90401-2602; Robert A. Madle, 44606 Bestor Drive, Rockville MD 20853; Greg Ketter, DreamHaven Books, 912 West Lake Street, Minneapolis, MN 55408; Lloyd Currey, Box 187, Elizabethtown, NY 12932; and Mark V. Ziesing, P.O. Box 97, Shingletown CA 96088, all of whom publish catalogs periodically. Listings for other mail-order dealers can usually be found in the classified ads of the news magazine *Locus* (Locus Publications, P.O. Box 13305, Oakland CA 94661—$43 for a 12-issue subscription in the U.S. via periodical mail; $53 for a first-class subscription in the U.S.)

On the Internet, try Amazon.com or abebooks.com, among other services.

About the Editor

Gardner Dozois has been the editor of *Asimov's Science Fiction* magazine for more than a decade, during which time he has won many Hugo Awards for Best Editor. He is the author of the novels *Nightmare Blue* (with George Alec Effinger) and *Strangers*, and his short fiction (which has earned him two Nebula Awards) has been collected in *Geodesic Dreams*. Another collection, *Slow Dancing Through Time*, contains his collaborative work with such writers as Jack Dann, Michael Swanwick, and Susan Casper. Born in Salem, Massachusetts, he resides in Philadelphia, Pennsylvania.

Also available from St. Martin's Press

		Quantity	Price
The Year's Best Science Fiction: *Fifteenth Annual Collection* ISBN: 0-312-19033-6 (trade paperback)	($17.95)	_____	_____
The Year's Best Science Fiction: *Fourteenth Annual Collection* ISBN: 0-312-15703-7 (trade paperback)	($17.95)	_____	_____
Modern Classics of Science Fiction edited by Gardner Dozois ISBN: 0-312-08847-7 (trade paperback)	($16.95)	_____	_____
Modern Classic Short Novels *of Science Fiction* edited by Gardner Dozois ISBN: 0-312-11317-X (trade paperback)	($15.95)	_____	_____
Modern Classics of Fantasy edited by Gardner Dozois ISBN: 0-312-16931-0 (trade paperback)	($15.95)	_____	_____
Writing Science Fiction & Fantasy: edited by the editors of *Asimov's* and *Analog* ISBN: 0-313-08926-0 (trade paperback)	($9.95)	_____	_____
The Encyclopedia of Science Fiction by John Clute and Peter Nicholls BN: 0-312-13486-X (trade paperback)	($29.95)	_____	_____

Postage & Handling

(Books up to $12.00 - add $3.00; books up to $15.00 - add $3.50; books above $15.00 - add $4.00— plus $1.00 for each additional book) _____

8% Sales Tax (New York State residents only) _____

Amount enclosed _____

Name _____

Address _____

City _____ State _____ Zip _____

Send this form with payment to:
Publishers Book & Audio, P.O. Box 070059, 5448 Arthur Kill Road, Staten Island, NY 10307. Telephone (800) 288-2131. Please alow three weeks for delivery.

For bulk orders (10 copies or more) please contact the St. Martin's Press Special Sales Department toll free at 800-221-7945 ext. 645 for information. In New York State call 212-674-5151.